Candlelight Romances

FIVE COMPLETE NOVELS

Candlelight Romances

FIVE COMPLETE NOVELS

A Love to Remember
Ida Hills

The Wedding Journey
Marjorie Eatock

No Time for Love
Lori Herter

Morning Rose, Evening Savage
Amii Lorin

Too Close for Comfort
Lori Herter

AVENEL BOOKS · NEW YORK

This 1982 edition is published by Avenel Books
distributed by Crown Publishers, Inc. by arrangement with
Dell Publishing Company, Inc.

Manufactured in the United States of America

Library of Congress Cataloging in Publication Data
Main entry under title:
Candelight romances.
Contents: Too close for comfort/Lori Herter—
The wedding journey/Marjorie Eatock—
No time for love/Lori Herter—[etc.]
1. Love stories, American.
PS648.L6C36   813′.085′08   82-6828
AACR2

ISBN: 0-517-385600

h g f e d c b a

CONTENTS

A Love to Remember......................*1*

The Wedding Journey...................*81*

No Time for Love.......................*209*

Morning Rose, Evening Savage.......*315*

Too Close for Comfort..................*405*

A Love to Remember

by Ida Hills

1

The fog that held San Francisco Airport in silent isolation began to lift, and Wendy Devin watched the runway lights reappear like sparkling jewels against a background of white chiffon. She breathed a sigh of relief; she couldn't bear more cancelled plans, more waiting. "Flight 205 for Tahiti is now ready for boarding," announced the intercom.

Wendy ran her fingers through the tumble of soft, brown curls framing her pixie face, slung the flight bag crammed with travel folders over her slender shoulder, and walked quickly to the check-in counter. She examined her papers again—passport, inoculation record, ticket, and the cards that identified her as the representative of Personal World Travel. She was proud of Mr. Vance's confidence in her ability to organize their new Pacific tours. It did much to restore her self-confidence that had been so badly shaken by events of the past week.

"Welcome aboard," greeted a smiling blonde stewardess.

It was the first time Wendy had been inside a 747. She was surprised to find a broad center section of seats in addition to the usual three down each side. It was hard to believe something so huge could fly. She had been assigned a window seat ahead of the wing, which allowed a clear view on takeoff and landing, though there would be only the ocean in between. The massive plane filled with surprising speed, and in a few minutes it was roaring down the runway. Wendy watched the twinkling lights of her beloved San Francisco disappear.

She settled back in her seat, glad the seat beside her was vacant. She usually enjoyed meeting and talking to new people, but tonight she just wanted to relax, to sort things out. She hadn't realized how tired she was. It must have been a week since she had had a good night's sleep—all the plans for the wedding had kept her occupied day and night. Wendy's thoughts shied gingerly around the word, but she was determined to think it through—the wedding, or should she say the non-wedding?

She stared out the window. A full moon touched the ocean with a ladder of moonbeams. A similar path of silver light had seemed an omen holding special promise that night she and Marvin had stood on the cliff beside the little Star of the Sea Chapel.

"I think this is where we should be married," he had said, squeezing her hand.

Wendy waited for him to go on. Though he often implied that he expected them to marry, Marvin had never directly asked her. When he said no more, Wendy answered, "I'd like that. It's such a beautiful chapel."

3

"What about May 25th? That would give us a three-day weekend."

Wendy started to protest that it was too sudden, but decided she was being silly. They had been going together since her last year in college, almost three years. This wasn't the proposal she had dreamed of, but she couldn't expect a scientist to be a dashing romantic. She did love Marvin—his idealism, his intense dedication to his work, the way he relied on her to handle outside distractions when he was busy with his research.

"That's only two weeks away," Wendy demurred.

"I know," Marvin replied apologetically. "But you know how I dislike long-range plans." His eyes searched her face. "Do you think it's too short a time to arrange a simple wedding?"

"No, I guess not," she said, feeling as if, while wading along the shore, a high wave had caught her before she was really ready to plunge in.

Marvin pulled her to him and kissed her, lightly at first, then more fervently. Slowly Wendy relaxed in his arms, the tension and doubt draining from her. If the words hadn't been romantic, certainly the setting was—the waves lapping rhythmically against the sand below them, the chapel silhouetted in the moonlight. Yes, she could picture herself walking down the aisle of this dollhouse church to marry the man beside her. Wendy smiled to herself, thinking that he even looked like the man on top of a wedding cake—precise, even features; neatly trimmed dark hair; and a perfectly proportioned height, several inches taller than the bride.

The next two weeks disappeared in a blur of activity. Wendy had acquired her ability to handle details smoothly from her mother. Together they worked out the arrangements for her wedding. As her childhood dreams of scores of bridesmaids, a flowing train, and a full stage production were pared to fit the simple chapel by the sea, she began to feel how comfortable and right her new plans were. The family reception at her parents' home in nearby Monterey would be equally simple.

"Looks like we did it," Wendy declared as she placed the bouquet of pale pink dogwood on the mantel of her parents' rambling ranch-style house. She paused to watch her mother put the last sprig of lily of the valley in the old-fashioned nosegay of sweetheart roses.

"I was betting on us," her mother teased. "It's going to be a lovely wedding, dear, and a very lovely bride." Kathleen Devin smiled fondly at her daughter. A fair Irish lass she was, Kathleen thought, with merry green eyes in a small face enhanced by light-brown hair. "I do wish Marvin had come to Monterey with you tonight as he planned, instead of coming down in the morning."

Wendy's green eyes clouded. "There was an important development in one of the rice cultures he is working on and he felt it had to be transplanted tonight. He said he would be here early in the morning. The wedding isn't until noon."

Kathleen Devin shrugged in her expressive Irish way and went to put the finished bridal bouquet in the refrigerator for the night.

The next morning the first rays of sunlight filtering through the redwood trees awakened Wendy. She could hear her mother already making muffled noises in the kitchen as she attended to last-minute details and tried not to awaken the rest of the family. The ringing of the telephone cut sharply into the subdued sounds. It's Marvin, Wendy's panicked thoughts told her as she jumped out of bed and raced for the telephone.

"Wendy, my car won't start, and my best man can't leave the laboratory. What'll I do?" Marvin's voice rasped with tension.

Marvin's Volkswagen was one of the practical details of life he often neglected. "You could call a service station to start the car, but you sound upset. It might be better to have a friend bring you down, or take the bus," Wendy soothed.

"What if I can't make it in time?"

"Fortunately everyone is coming here first. We'll make whatever changes are necessary when you arrive. Just come as soon as possible." Wendy forced her voice to sound as light and encouraging as she could.

"All right, I'll do what I can. I sure wish you were here. You handle these things so much better than I do." Sounding more cheerful, he said, "Good-bye, sweet, see you soon."

Wendy painfully remembered the long wait that had followed his promise to see her soon. She recalled her mother's tactful phone calls to the minister, organist, photographer, and the reassurance of each that the wedding could be rescheduled when the groom arrived. She thought of the awkward moment when the guests began to arrive—how each acted as if it were perfectly normal, and joined in the exchange of news, small talk, and banter that marked any gathering of the family.

As the big grandfather's clock struck twelve, the tension began to spark like static electricity. Wendy's mother passed the large trays of canapes while her father served chilled glasses of his homemade plum wine. Wendy tried to convince herself that Marvin would be on the one o'clock bus from San Francisco.

"What'll you do if he doesn't show up?" Her brother Kevin whispered the question in her ear.

"I—I don't know—I wish I had taken that trip to the South Pacific Mr. Vance offered me."

"Great place. You'd like it, especially Tahiti—warm sandy beaches, coconut palms. Do you still have the little gold palm tree I sent you?" he reminisced.

The gold charms for her bracelet and the enthusiastic letters Kevin had sent when he was flying in the Pacific had first aroused Wendy's interest in travel. She extended her arm and jangled her bracelet for his inspection. The phone rang and she raced for the privacy of the extension in her bedroom.

"Wendy, I'm afraid I can't make it today," said Marvin in the apologetic, absentminded way she had heard so often when he cancelled their plans in order to work. "Dr. Pridi of the World Food Institute arrived from Thailand unexpectedly, and I'm showing him our work. Their sponsorship could mean a big step forward for the project. We can be married next Saturday, can't we?"

Too hurt and angry to trust her voice, Wendy replaced the phone on the stand, blinked back the tears, firmed her small pointed chin, and went to face the guests. She was intercepted by her mother, who took in the situation with one shrewd glance. "Why don't you cut the cake, dear?" she asked in her most matter-of-fact way.

"Have to take the groom off first," Kevin said in the half-taunting, half-encouraging way he always used to challenge her to new adventures.

All the Irish temper that had been building up in her since morning exploded at that moment. Wendy made one quick swipe with the knife and the bride stood alone on the wedding cake.

The stunned silence which followed her action was broken by the piping voice of her nephew Mark demanding, "Can I have the first piece?" Suddenly it was just another cake. She cut a very large piece for the very small boy.

"Let's break out the champagne," Kevin called, already on his way to the refrigerator. He popped the cork and began filling glasses. There was an awkward moment as the guests looked at their champagne glasses, wondering if someone should say something.

"To Tahiti," Kevin had toasted.

"To Tahiti," Wendy had acknowledged.

I'm sure I shall like Tahiti best of all, Wendy now thought in silent gratitude to her brother. The charms jangled on her bracelet as she folded back the arm between her seat and the vacant one next to her and stretched out for the long night flight.

2

The sky was awash with red and gold, announcing the imminent sunrise, when Wendy awoke. Her watch indicated it was nine-thirty, but they had crossed four time zones and Wendy wasn't sure what time it really was. A tall blonde stewardess brought her breakfast. As she savored fresh pineapple, Wendy realized she hadn't eaten much in the past few days. Dollar pancakes, sweet and crunchy with coconut syrup and spicy crisp link sausages, were far from her usual working girl's breakfast.

When she finished, Wendy turned her attention to the window to catch the first glimpse of the islands. The towering peaks of Mooréa suddenly loomed into view as if they had just emerged from the sea. Beyond them lay the emerald geen coastline of Tahiti. The coral right around the island gave it startling beauty, the sapphire blue of the sea encircling a band of turquoise where the water flowed over the coral. The two were joined by a ribbon of white water. As the plane banked for its descent, Tahiti took form before her eyes. Lush green foliage descended from jagged mountain peaks to frame narrow, white beaches.

The plane rolled to a halt before a low compound of buildings connected by open lanai sheltered by palm trees. As Wendy disembarked, the breeze felt soft and warm in spite of the early-morning hour.

"You're Wendy Devin, aren't you?" the tall blonde stewardess asked as Wendy collected her luggage from customs.

"Yes, I'm surprised you remembered."

"I'm Sue Pritchard. I had a note on my passenger list that you are with Personal World Tours. We try to take good care of our travel agents. Are you staying at the Taharaa?"

Wendy checked her reservation card. "That's what it says. The reservation was made for me at the last minute."

"Our crew bus will be picking us up to go to the Taharaa," explained the stewardess. "It's about ten miles. Would you care to join us?"

"Thanks, I'd love to."

The jitney bus followed Tahiti's main circle-island road between the palm trees flanking the beaches. The lush green was broken at intervals by brilliant red poinciana flame trees and white-flowering frangipani from which leis are made. Abruptly the bus left the beach road and turned up a steep valley. Sprawling, open-sided thatched buildings clung to a green mountainside. Behind them, a crystal stream tumbled over gurgling waterfalls into placid pools. Small cottages, secluded from each other by lush tropical growth, peeped from under towering palm trees. What a romantic setting—what a perfect place for a honeymoon, thought Wendy ruefully.

She spent the remainder of the morning wandering along the enchanted paths of the Taharaa, pausing to rest beside a gurgling waterfall, watching fish in a sparkling clear pool. She was dazzled by bright bursts of tropical flowers. In the afternoon she took the circle-island tour. Though she was anxious to become familiar with the landmarks of Tahiti and its history, Wendy found herself paying more attention to the handsome, smiling people swimming, canoeing, and fishing in the surf, or strolling barefoot along the sand in their colorful, wraparound pareu skirts.

At dinner Sue Pritchard invited Wendy to join their group. A colorful floor show followed the traditional feast of roast pig and native fruits. The long dining room vibrated to the fast rhythmic pace of the Tahitian hula, and a fire dance with flaming torches added to the drama. The native music and chants were melodious and romantic.

Wendy enjoyed the entertainment and the attentions of a young co-pilot. "Call me when you get back to San Francisco," he urged at the conclusion of the evening. But Wendy knew that their relationship was what the Polynesians call a hibiscus friendship, blooming bright and exciting for a day and folding when the day ended.

Wendy slept late the next morning. She was just finishing a leisurely breakfast at the open-air poolside café when a tall, sandy-haired American in his early thirties approached her table. He was followed by a striking brunette with a continental flair. "You're Wendy Devin?"

"Yes."

"I'm Tom Bradley," he said with a definite Texan accent, "and this is my wife, Mignette. We own the *Haape* on Mooréa. I saw your name listed representing Personal World. Some of your tours have stayed with us. We'd like to have you visit us if you have the time."

"I'd like that. I've heard nice things about the *Haape*. Won't you join me?"

"Migin and I have eaten, but I could use another cup of coffee," Tom answered.

"Your hotel is quite new, isn't it?"

"Yes, though I'm not sure hotel is the right word. We have tried to make it more a copy of a native village in natural surroundings. Club Mediterranée complains I stole the idea from them, as well as their best director," he added, indicating his wife.

"You were part of the Club Med staff?" Wendy asked.

"Yes, I came out five years ago to coordinate their entertainment and sports program," she replied.

"My wife is too modest to say she is one of the world's best woman scuba divers,'' Tom added proudly. "Water skiing and diving are mainstays of our program."

"I'd hardly expect anyone as chic and feminine as Mignette to be so athletic."

"Thanks for the compliment, and please call me Migin, everyone does. We brought the boat over for its annual inspection and will be going back in the morning. Would you like to join us if you don't have commitments here?"

"I can see more of Tahiti when I get back. I think a few days' relaxation on *Haape* sounds like just what I need."

"Have you been down to the beach yet?" Tom asked.

"No, I thought I would go this morning."

"It's a beautiful coral beach, but the water is quite shallow on top of the reef. You have to go out a ways for it to be deep enough to swim. We are on our way to take the boat out to the floating dock this morning. Would you like to come?"

"Sounds great. I'll put on my bathing suit."

"Just bring it along. You can change in the cabin," Migin suggested.

"What a beautiful boat," Wendy exclaimed admiring the trim twenty-eight-foot cabin cruiser with HAAPE emblazoned on the rosewood hull.

"It's our one luxury. The rest of our living is very simple. But it's a workhorse too, for our guests' fishing, diving, and excursions to coral reefs and outer islands," Tom answered.

"If you will excuse me, I'll go below and get us some cold pineapple juice," said Migin as she disappeared into the cabin.

"Just make yourself at home, Wendy, while I get ready to cast off," directed Tom.

"If she's Wendy, can I play Peter Pan?" asked a rich masculine voice as its owner made a flying leap from the dock to the deck of the *Haape*.

He looks more like a Viking prince than Peter Pan, thought Wendy, assessing the tall, lean, broad-shouldered young man with wind-blown blond hair and startling blue eyes. "You're a little big for the part, but you fly very well," Wendy responded, picking up the storybook reference to her name.

"You're quite right, but not the way you meant," Tom broke in. "This is Captain Erick Randall, and he flies helicopters."

"Erick!" cried Migin with delight as she bounded up the stairs from the galley and threw her arms around the newcomer. Her hug and kiss seemed to hold more warmth than a routine French greeting.

"I thought you were in the Pentagon helping General Phillerie behind a desk," Tom broke in.

"I was, but he hated it as much as I did. The other morning we were both standing at the window watching a chopper land, and he must have read my mind. 'I can't get out of this cage, but at least I can spring you,' he told me.

"I told him I'd feel like I was deserting the ship," Erick continued, "but he said, 'Nonsense, that bright young lieutenant from the Academy can help me shuffle these papers without making them into paper airplanes behind my back, like a kid I know who dreams of flying.' So here I am."

"Where are you assigned?"

"Back to Bangkok, but I have two weeks' leave coming, so I thought I would check on some of my old buddies before I report in."

"We're delighted you came," said Migin warmly. "We are taking Wendy out to the floating dock for a swim. Can you join us?"

"That's what I said. It looks like the script calls for a Peter Pan to go with Wendy, and I'm applying for the job."

"If the play calls for a pretty girl and flying, you're sure to be there," teased Tom. "I'll start the engine. Stand by to cast off the rope."

Tom expertly maneuvered the sleek craft between the floating buoys marking the channel through the coral. "Shall we go change?" Migin asked Wendy.

Wendy slipped into her butter-yellow bikini, regretting that she had not yet had time to acquire the tan which the color was designed to accentuate. Migin put on a French-cut, red, pareu print bikini that made Wendy feel like a little girl in her American-designed suit. Bet she doesn't wear that diving, Wendy thought, and immediately felt guilty for such a jealous impulse toward her charming hostess.

"Ah, the best of two worlds," quipped Erick as he slipped one arm around the sophisticated, bronzed French girl, and the other around Wendy, who did look like a pixie out of a fairy tale, except for her flashing green eyes, which left no doubt that she was a very real woman.

Wendy would have ducked the move had she been singled out for this attention on such slight acquaintance, but since the motion was all-encompassing, she didn't resist. The strong but gentle arm that encircled her waist seemed more playful than personal.

Two outrigger canoes were tied to the floating dock when the *Haape* anchored a few yards away. "Race you to the dock," Tom challenged Erick. The two men poised on the stern of the boat as Migin gave the signal to go. Their dives would have qualified them for a swimming meet, but during the race they looked more like two schoolboys as they splashed, cavorted, and passed each other. Tom beat Erick by half a length. "You got soft in the big city," he chided.

"Let's join them," said Migin, cutting the water with a graceful dive.

Wendy followed with a sharp, clean dive. She was an excellent swimmer, but she felt out of her class with such experts. After their swim—an odd combination of professional competence and clowning—the four climbed up on the dock to sun themselves. "Better get our fairy princess back to the boat before she becomes the Red Queen," suggested Erick, noting the pink glow on Wendy's shoulders.

"It's time we got the boat back for the inspector anyway," Tom answered.

Reluctantly Wendy swam back to the boat. It was such a beautiful place to swim—clear blue water above a mosaic of blue, pink, and turquoise coral.

Wendy stood on the deck of the *Haape* enjoying the view of Tahiti as they approached it from the sea. The great, high mass of green island with its uppermost tip shrouded in mist seemed more like a vision than a reality.

"Breathtaking isn't it?' asked Erick standing close beside her.

"Just like I always dreamed it would be," Wendy answered. "Those little thatched huts along the beach look like toys in a sandbox."

"Are you staying on the beach?"

"No, I'm at the Taharaa."

"Fraternizing with the wealthy tourists?" he jibed.

"Afraid so. It was the company's choice. They made the reservation."

"The company?"

"Wendy is a representative of Personal World Tours," Tom explained as he joined them.

"Don't tell me the *Haape* is out courting tour groups?" Erick mocked.

"Definitely not," Tom snapped. "We did contact Wendy because she was Personal World's representative. I like the atmosphere of their tours. But if she had been starchy and strictly business, we would have given her the resort brochure and gone on." Tom's tone left no doubt that it was Wendy Devin herself, not the representative of Personal World, who was their guest.

"Just checking to see if Tahitian hospitality had gone commercial since I left," said Erick.

"If it ever happens on Mooréa, I'm afraid the *Haape* will be out of business," said Migin, who had been listening to the exchange between the two men. "Would you like to go shopping while the men deliver the boat?" she asked turning to Wendy.

"Why don't you meet us for lunch at the Vaima?" invited Erick.

As the boat neared the dock at Papeete, Wendy saw an exotic jumble of wooden store buildings with Chinese signs, contemporary hotels, and French boutiques all facing the flower- and palm-lined harbor park. Shouts from the waterfront began to drift out to them in an odd blend of Tahitian and French, the two official languages. The result was a colorful explosion of people, traffic, and sea craft competing with the idyllic surroundings for attention.

"I need some material," said Migin as the two girls paused before a Chinese shop stuffed to the rafters with bright bolts of fabric in wild Tahitian pareu prints. She selected fifteen yards of bright red with white hibiscus and other tropical flowers printed on it. Wendy wondered what she planned to make with so much fabric.

Neighboring shops offered colorful Polynesian beach wear, sophisticated French imports, and exotic Chinese items of every description.

"That's what I need, a sunshade on the beach," said Wendy, indicating a woven coconut palm hat in a Tahitian handicraft store. Inside, the shelves were lined with exquisite wood carvings, polished shells, woven hats, baskets, purses, and mats. Wendy settled for the hat, knowing she would be back later for a closer look at the wood carvings.

"Are those perfumes genuine?" Wendy asked examining a display of the world's most renowned fragrances.

"Yes, I get my favorite here for the same price I would pay in Paris, since Tahiti is a French territory," answered Migin.

It was eleven-thirty and the shops began to close for their two-hour lunch break. Wendy and Migin walked through Bougainville Park ablaze with red and yellow hibiscus, white tiari, and purple bougainvillea. The brilliant shrubs were overhung by palm, feathery acacia, and flaming royal poinciana.

Tom and Erick were already seated at one of the Vaima's sidewalk tables when the girls arrived. The extensive menu Wendy received was in French. "Need any help?" Migin inquired tactfully.

"My French is pretty shaky, but I think I can manage," Wendy replied. In spite of the temptations of French cuisine, she selected a native Tahitian fruit plate. It soon arrived, looking like an offering to the sun goddess with creamy bananas, pale yellow pineapple, and deep orange papaya, mango, and tangerines.

Wendy noted that Erick's French was almost as fluent as Migin's, while Tom's somehow managed to incorporate a Texas twang. "Migin and I have to get supplies this afternoon," said Tom when lunch was finished. "Will you take Wendy back to her hotel, Erick?"

"I can take the hotel jitney," Wendy protested.

"After all I said about Tahitian hospitality?" Erick demanded with mock injury.

"We'll pick you up in the morning at seven," Tom told Wendy as she and Erick rose to leave.

"Any commitments this afternoon?" Erick asked as he and Wendy strolled down the quay.

She shook her head.

"Fine. Then I'll rent a car, and show you what a good tour guide I could be if the army gets tired of putting up with me."

Erick insisted on a convertible, even though the only one available was old and battered. He maneuvered it expertly through the jumble of traffic and turned north on the shore road to Captain Cook's monument. There on the headland above Matavi Bay, Wendy looked down at the crescent of black coral beach and the lagoon where each of Tahiti's three discoverers had landed. "Captain Samuel Wallis came here in 1767, followed by de Bougainville and Captain Cook, each of whom thought they were the first," recited Erick like a tour guide.

Wendy's circle-island tour had visited here the day before, but standing now with Erick, it was somehow more breathtakingly beautiful, as if she too were discovering Tahiti for the first time.

The "tour de Erick," as he laughingly called it, left the shore road after that to follow a winding trail through a lush tropical valley. A small stream plunged down the volcanic rock from one pool to the next, often completely disappearing from sight in a fern grotto whose delicate greenery contrasted with the huge leaves of elephant ear.

Erick parked the rented convertible at the end of the road, where a gushing waterfall splashed into a placid pool. "Come fly with me," he invited as he helped Wendy from the car and continued to hold her hand as they climbed over the rocks marking the path to the top of the falls.

It was a steep climb. At the top Erick dropped down on the grass and pulled Wendy down beside him. They sat in silence, listening to the splashing of the falls and the cries of tropical birds. "I can't say that I blame Tom for giving up his career in the army for a paradise like this," Erick said, breaking the long silence.

"You've known each other a long time?"

"We took our pilot training together, then went on to helicopter school, and were assigned to the same squad in Bangkok for three years. Then he came here and I was sent back to Washington."

"Did he meet Migin here?"

'Yes, she was the scuba diving instructor for Club Med. Her father is one of the divers with Jacques Cousteau. She says their family used to go diving like other families go camping or picnicking. She's fantastic underwater. That's why their place is so popular with divers.''

"Does Tom dive too?''

"Yes, he and I spent every spare minute diving at Pattaya when we were in Bangkok. He's very good. I told them they should be married underwater. I was their best man. Migin said she would settle for the fern grotto on Mooréa. It was a very moving ceremony.''

At the mention of a wedding, Wendy felt the tropical day become a little cooler, the idyllic setting became just trees beside a waterfall. She carefully withdrew her hand from Erick's.

The mood shattered, they scrambled back down the path, each trying to make bright conversation. On the drive back down the valley Erick pointed out various tropical plants with a knowledge that surprised Wendy.

As they entered the outskirts of Papeete, Wendy assumed the tour was over, but Erick turned inland again. This time a paved road wound up the steep incline of Signal Hill. At the crest of the hill a complicated-looking camera mounted on a tripod pointed out at the ocean as if expecting some dramatic event. As Wendy and Erick walked out to join the photographer on the point looking west toward Mooréa, the sun sank rapidly in an explosion of color that marks a Mooréan sunset. Wendy caught her breath sharply at the magic splendor of the scene. Then, almost as suddenly as it had begun, the flaming reds and burnished yellows drained from the sky behind the purple silhouette of Mooréa.

"Until now I never really believed the pictures I saw of tropical sunsets,'' Wendy said quietly.

"A specialty of the tour,'' Erick answered lightly.

"I really should be getting back to the hotel,'' Wendy said as they returned to the car.

In spite of Erick's teasing about it, Wendy was once again delighted by the perfection of the Taharaa's setting as they drove along its palm-studded drive. "It's been a wonderful day, Erick,'' she told him, laying her hand lightly on his arm.

"We have a fascinating night life tour—half price, lady,'' responded Erick mimicking a tourist hustler.

Wendy giggled in spite of herself.

"Pick you up at seven-thirty?'' Erick urged.

Wendy hesitated, reluctant to spend so much time with a comparative stranger— although a charming one. Her own impulse, plus the whimsy of his invitation, won over caution, however. "Okay, seven-thirty,'' she said.

It had been a long day, but a leisurely bath and the excitement of anticipation thoroughly revived Wendy. She put on a white linen sheath, glad that the morning swim had only left a slight glow on her skin and not the flaming red she had at first feared. She had just finished brushing her hair in place when a knock sounded on her door.

"Welcome to my special island,'' Erick greeted her, placing a white ginger lei around her neck. He kissed her playfully, tentatively, in a way that seemed to say, "Come have fun with me—come love me, the choice is yours.''

Wendy's response indicated her acceptance of the invitation to have fun, but left unanswered the question of love.

In the soft light the trees seemed more green, the sea a deeper blue. Wendy and Erick shared a feeling of relaxed harmony as they drove south along the coast road.

Erick parked at the entrance to the botanical garden. The attendant glanced at his watch, then at the smiling couple in front of him, and shrugged. Evidently closing time isn't closely observed in Tahiti, Wendy thought.

"What a gardener's dream come true!" Wendy exclaimed as the brilliant colors of hibiscus and bird of paradise dazzled her eyes and the scent of gardenia, ginger, and frangipani blended their perfumed delights; orchids and night-blooming cereus added their exotic sorcery.

"A triumph for your garden club tours," teased Erick.

"Do you promise a white ginger lei to everyone?" she countered.

"Only the ones who look like pixies with green eyes."

Leaving the garden, they followed the path to the Musée Gauguin, an open building in the Tahitian manner, similar to the natural settings the artist so often painted.

"There are only a couple of Gauguin's oils here," Erick explained. "The others are in museums and private collections around the world. But there are water colors, and the initial sketches of some of his most famous works. Mostly you get the feel of the man himself and the Tahiti he loved."

"You like his work, don't you?" Wendy asked.

"Yes, I think his 'Day of the God' and some of his other paintings really capture the spirit of the Polynesian people and the color of the islands."

"I'll have to hire you for the art tour as well as the garden tour," Wendy replied.

As they entered the large pandanus and bamboo hut of the Gauguin Restaurant, the headwaiter hurried over to greet Erick with a broad smile. "Captain Randall, it's good to see you again. I have your favorite table." He led them out on the deck which extended on pilings over the ocean.

"Thank you, Timi—it's good to be back," said Erick as they were seated at a table by the low half-wall open to the panorama of the lagoon below. The flow of Erick's French as he gave their order was more rapid than Wendy could follow. She wasn't sure what to expect but was sure it would be delicious. She enjoyed being with her handsome escort who was an accepted regular, yet she also realized that he had been here many times with other girls.

"It's just perfect, Erick," said Wendy as soft twilight reflected on the water lapping over the multicolored coral below. He slid his hand gently over hers as the first star of evening began to twinkle in the sky.

The dinner exceeded Wendy's expectations—delicate fresh water shrimp, crisp salad with buttery avocados, and Tahitian lobster. Timi brought a frosty bottle of sparkling white wine which he poured with a flourish. The wine was cool and delicate with just a hint of sweetness that reminded Wendy of her father's homemade plum wine. The last occasion when her father had served his wine returned to her thoughts, but Wendy told herself resolutely, I will not let Marvin spoil this beautiful evening. She turned to Erick with a smile.

"You left me for a while there," he said gently, watching her closely.

"I'm back now," she answered gaily, and meant it.

By the time they had finished dinner, the sky was a picture book display of twinkling stars. In the light of the bright tropical moon they saw three girls with baskets on their heads walking along the beach below.

"Those are the flowers they didn't need to decorate the tables with tonight," Erick explained. "Watch the girls toss them into the ocean to appease the Gods for having picked them."

"Let's go down with them and walk on the beach," Wendy said impulsively. In seconds the two Americans, who had been dining elegantly on French cuisine, became truant schoolchildren wading along the water's edge, shoes in hand. The kisses they exchanged were light and gay, avoiding deep emotion.

When Wendy returned to her hotel that night, she scarcely felt her feet touch the floor and was oblivious to the sand she was trailing behind her. "Letter for you, miss," said the clerk handing her a small, heavy envelope along with her key.

Wendy was surprised to see the address in Marvin's hasty scrawl. Dropping the letter in her purse, she hurried to her room, her heels sharply ringing along the stones of the path.

With the door firmly closed behind her, Wendy took the letter from her purse and stared at it for a long moment. She was tempted to drop it unopened into the wastebasket, but as she tapped it against her fingers in indecision, she felt a heavy metal object in the envelope. Curiosity triumphed, and she ripped the envelope open impatiently; out slid a small gold object—a forget-me-not for a charm bracelet.

Wendy examined the exquisite detail of the small gold flower she held in her hand. It must have taken a determined search to find such a fine piece of work. Wendy could imagine the effort it cost Marvin, who hated shopping. In spite of herself, an understanding smile crept across her face as she pictured him on such a quest. She removed a small, neatly printed card from the envelope and read:

> "Joy to forgive and joy to be forgiven
> Hang level in the balance of Love."
>
> Marvin

3

Wendy was waiting in the lobby the following morning when Tom and Migin arrived. What a handsome couple, she thought as she watched the tall, ruggedly masculine Texan and his vivacious French wife.

"How's our favorite travel agent?" Tom greeted her. He hesitated, as if remembering Erick's barbs about promoting their resort.

"Wendy, we're so glad you can come," Migin tactfully added.

"I'm looking forward to it," Wendy replied warmly as Tom loaded her suitcase into the back of the taxi.

With the morning sun striking its gleaming bow, the *Haape* seemed even more inviting. "Ready to go battle Captain Hook and the pirates?" asked Erick as his head emerged from the galley.

Wendy laughed at this reference to Peter Pan and Wendy, although the joke had always annoyed her when she was younger. With Mooréa looming before them, a purple shape on a background of azure sea and sky, the world of fairy tales did not seem so farfetched.

As the *Haape* approached Mooréa, the purple turned deep green, the landscape more lush than Tahiti with sharper, more jagged mountains. With an ease which belied the difficulty of the task, Tom maneuvered the *Haape* through the pass in the barrier reef, across the colorful coral, and into the blue lagoon.

"That's the Bali Hai," said Erick pointing to a collection of huts set on pilings constructed out over the water. Bronzed figures swam in the lagoon or lazed on the white sand beach.

"Watch the tallest mountain on the left, and see if the Gods of Mooréa welcome you," Erick instructed.

As Wendy watched, the clouds covering the peak he had indicated began to lift. In the top of the mountain was a round hole as if a cannon had been shot through it. "That's the Eye of the Gods that watch over Mooréa come out to take a look and bid you welcome," he told her.

Adding their own welcome, two native boys in an outrigger canoe, a small copy of the war canoes which originally brought their ancestors to the islands, paddled alongside and shouted greetings. At the end of the bay Tom docked the boat beside a number of outrigger canoes. When Wendy stepped onto the dock she noticed the open-sided, native style huts hidden among the palms. "*Haape* landing," quipped Erick.

Migin led Wendy to a pandanus and bamboo hut raised off the ground on coconut-trunk stilts. Split log steps led up to a small open-faced porch, with bamboo shutters swung upward to the eaves in place of windows. A woven straw mat on the floor blended with the natural materials of the walls and thatched roof. A red-and-white pareu print covered the bed and divided the tiny bath from the rest of the room. Now Wendy knew why Migin had bought all the pareu print when they were shopping in Papeete.

"It's just perfect, Migin," said Wendy.

"We think people want to experience Mooréa as it really is," answered Migin. "Tom will bring up your suitcase when he gets the supplies unloaded. I'll be down in the main compound."

Erick came bounding up the path a few minutes later, swinging her suitcase like a small boy's book satchel. Wendy hoped that a suitcase which had come as far as hers had could be trusted not to fly open.

"What do you think of it?" he asked.

"It's like a travel poster of the South Pacific come to life."

"We aim to please," he answered as if he had conjured up the entire setting himself. "Shall we explore?"

He led her along the beach, past several similar huts hidden in the trees. "Need any help?" he called to Migin as they passed the open-sided dining hall. Long tables and benches set around a square platform looked like a combination scout camp mess hall and a makeshift nightclub.

"No thanks, the boys have things so well organized they could really run the place without us," Migin answered, nodding to the Polynesian boys preparing the room for lunch.

The beach was a narrow ribbon of white sand between the coral-patterned blue lagoon and the lush tropical foliage. The warm sun on the sand had enticed small, brown land crabs out of their hiding places. Wendy and Erick passed hundreds of their holes. When Erick came close to one, he scampered after it, trying to outrace it before the small creature could vanish into its hole. Finally, running full speed, he cornered one between two rocks. The crab put up both claws like a fighter in the ring and snapped at anything within reach.

"I told you we would battle Captain Hook and his men," Erick said as the small crab cut cleanly through the twigs he offered.

"I got heem," shouted a young voice as a small brown hand shot out between the rocks, grasping the crab just behind the claws.

Wendy and Erick had been so engrossed with the crab that they had not noticed the small native boy slip out through the trees. He held a long bamboo pole with palm leaves tied to one end with a string. He took the crab to a reed basket up the beach. "I'm Tautu," the boy introduced himself, holding out a bronzed hand after first wiping it on his ragged shorts.

"What do you have there?" Erick asked indicating the bamboo pole.

"That's a crab pole," Tautu said, casting the bunch of leaves into one of the crab holes. He jiggled the bait slightly until the pole began to bend like a fishing rod with a catch. He whipped the pole into the air with a crab dangling from it by one claw entangled in the palm leaves. The crab let go and plopped at the boy's feet, another addition for the bamboo basket.

"You want to try?" he asked passing the pole to Erick. Erick made three attempts but failed to bring a crab out of its hole. "You gotta wait until he has a tight hold," the boy instructed. Erick's next attempt was successful.

Wendy watched as Erick and Tautu passed the pole back and forth, alternating catches like Tom Sawyer and Huckleberry Finn or Peter Pan and the Lost Boys.

"I got enough for bait, and Dad's waiting to go fishing," Tautu told them when he and Erick had landed about a dozen. He picked up the basket and jogged up the beach, pausing to wave before he disappeared into the palm trees.

Erick returned the boy's signal. "I guess it's time we got back to our *Haape* home for lunch."

She wrinkled a lightly freckled nose at his play on words, and hand-in-hand they turned back down the beach. As they came within sight of the first hut, a blast sounded on the conch horn. By the time they reached the open-air dining hall, the other guests were already seated. There were two dozen people, mostly young, an equal number of men and women. The snatches of conversation which reached Wendy as they entered were mostly in French with a sprinkling of English and German.

From one end of a long table Migin beckoned them to join her. As she stepped lightly over the bench and sat down, Wendy realized how hungry she was. The table had a hibiscus in the center, flanked by pineapple boats filled with tropical fruit. Polynesian boys served steaming plates of rice and small freshwater shrimp in a rich sauce.

"A perfect blend," Wendy told Migin, enjoying the mixture of French cuisine and native delicacies.

"Tonight will be the real feast," Migin replied. "We have been invited to Club Med for a *tamaaraa*, a native feast. Each resort on Mooréa takes a turn at hosting the feast and invites all the guests on the island. Actually the feast is prepared by the Mooréans; we just furnish the food.''

''Sounds like fun.''

Wendy was glad she had taken the time to buy a pareu in Tahiti. The salesgirl had called the native wraparound of white with red flowers instead of the usual red with white flowers a reverse print. The white made a glowing bronze of Wendy's newly acquired tan.

Tom drove the microbus, since the boy who usually drove had gone ahead to help prepare the feast. The bus followed the graveled circle-island road along the white sandy beach. Lush tropical growth reached down to the road and sometimes arched over it. As the sun sank in the sky, the bright coral of the ocean bottom began to develop colorful shadow patterns. The road was deserted.

The thatched huts of Club Mediterranée were A-frame rather than the open-sided Tahitian design. There were nearly a hundred of them scattered in the trees around the central compound. Marked whiterock trails led from one area to another.

Erick and Wendy followed one that led to the beach, where the setting sun made a blazing path across the water.

''I crown you Sunset Island Princess,'' said Erick, placing a flower *couronnes* he had coaxed from one of the native girls on Wendy's head. He kissed her on each cheek, his arms slipping from her shoulders to her waist, pulling her to him. As he kissed her tenderly, Wendy did indeed feel like the princess of an enchanted isle.

Erick released her reluctantly. The agelessness of sea and sand imparted a timeless quality to their short friendship, and the magic of the tropical twilight needed no words. . . .

''Eeerek!'' cried a tall blonde girl dashing up behind him. As he turned, she flung her arms around him and smothered him with a kiss. ''Migin didn't tell me you were coming.''

''They didn't know I was. I didn't know myself until the last minute.''

''With you things are always quite sudden,'' she said accusingly.

''Dominique Maraux, this is Wendy Devin,'' Erick replied with belated introductions.

''Bonjour,'' the French girl nodded, eyeing Wendy appraisingly.

''Wendy is with Personal World Travel,'' Erick added.

Wendy felt vaguely insulted by his apparent need to explain her presence, and found it difficult to keep the chill out of her voice as she acknowledged the introduction.

''You're looking well, Niki,'' Erick said, regarding the shapely girl in her halter-topped native costume.

''And you are dashing as usual,'' she returned. ''Are you staying long?''

''Only a few days. I have to be back in Bangkok in a week.''

At the mention of Bangkok a shadow crossed the girl's smiling face, but it was gone so quickly that Wendy wondered if she had just imagined it.

''It looks as if our painted South Seas sunset has vanished. Shall we join the others?'' Erick asked as he slipped an arm around each girl and started back up the beach.

There was a long blast on the conch shell and everyone gathered around the *ahimaa,* the earth oven. A Mooréan boy scraped the steaming lava rocks from the top with a shovel. When the oven was open, four men lifted out a leaf-wrapped pig which had been roasting on a spit inside. Two boys dipped their hands into a bucket of cold water and, reaching inside the roast pig, tossed out smoldering lava rocks. The pig was carved with ceremony and generous slices were placed on the guests' plates, which were then piled high with baked yams, taro, baked wild banana, breadfruit, and coconut.

Wendy, Niki, and Erick joined Migin and Tom at one of the long tables in the dining hall—a building several times larger than the *Haape*'s but of the same open-sided design. While the others reminisced about their past times together, Wendy wished she felt less of an intruder. Any attempt to leave would be more embarrassing than just sitting, smiling, and commenting politely whenever Erick turned to include her in the conversation.

"Did Migin tell you Dad and Uncle Maurice are coming out Saturday? They want to do some diving off Bora Bora. A postman's holiday they call it. We will be diving with them. Won't you join us?" Niki asked Erick.

He hesitated, and she added, "You met Uncle Maurice, Migin's father, at the wedding. He's fun to dive with."

"I'm afraid I would be way out of my class," Erick answered.

"Nonsense. We'll just be diving for fun and to look for new species of fish. It takes more luck than anything else for that. We'd love to have you," she pleaded.

"Dad always says the more eyes looking the better chance of spotting something," Migin added.

"It's not often an amateur has the opportunity to dive with the Cousteau divers, even when they are on vacation," Erick acknowledged.

The soft strum of guitars brought an end to conversation. The tempo became faster, more insistent, and three girls in grass skirts and flower leis began gyrating in the vigorous, sensuous Tahitian hula. Their exuberance was matched by men with flaming torches in the fire dance, and by a sword dance of combat with bamboo poles, all done to the ritual of ancient chants. The performances were less polished than those in Tahiti, but more spontaneous and enthusiastic. The dances became group affairs with most of the natives and some of the guests joining in.

"Come on, Erick. I'm sure you still remember how," urged Niki, taking him by the hand.

They were quite a striking contrast, the tall blond couple almost a head taller than the native dancers. Niki moved with natural grace and rhythm, and after a few tentative steps, Erick picked up the beat.

"Aren't they beautiful?" Wendy said turning to Migin, who had moved beside her when Niki and Erick left. "Did she say she's your cousin?"

"Not really. We grew up in the same town. Our fathers both dive for Jacques Cousteau. That's why she calls my father Uncle Maurice. We came out to Mooréa together to direct Club Med's diving program. She was maid of honor at my wedding."

"And is that where she met Erick?"

"Yes, and she fell madly in love with him. Of course Niki is always falling madly in love, but Erick was different."

"What happened?"

"There was a girl back in Bangkok. Neither Tom nor Erick ever talk much about it."

The throbbing drums stopped abruptly. Niki and Erick returned to the table breathless and laughing. "What's the matter, you getting too old for native dancing?" Erick asked Tom.

"I always figured dying and dancing should be done with your boots on," answered Tom in an exaggerated drawl.

"Do you ever call him Tex instead of Tom?" Wendy asked Migin.

"It's a temptation I fight with great willpower," confessed Migin affectionately.

The guitars began to strum the haunting strains of "Aloha" and the guests started to leave. The regular driver was already in the microbus when they arrived. Tom and Migin took the seat behind him, and Wendy the one by the window across from them. She saw Erick brush Niki's cheek lightly with a kiss, then come bounding up the steps as she called after him, "Don't forget Saturday."

It was a quiet ride back to the *Haape* through the starlit tropical night. Soon the hum of the motor began to blend with the lapping of the waves, and Wendy's head dropped lightly onto Erick's shoulder.

She awoke with a start, somewhat embarrassed as the bus rocked to a stop in the *Haape*'s main compound. Erick took her hand to help her down the steps of the bus and held it as they walked along the beach to her cabin. When they reached her porch, he raised her hand to his lips and kissed it in the continental manner. Then he turned abruptly and vaulted down the steps. "Tomorrow we go native," he called back over his shoulder as he disappeared into the shadows.

Wendy stood a moment, thoroughly confused and shaken by the evening and its abrupt ending. Shrugging, she went into her hut to get ready for bed.

The cries of myna birds awakened Wendy to the crisp freshness of the tropical morning. She lay still for several minutes, listening to the exotic sounds of the birds greeting the day. What do you wear to go native, she wondered. In these islands going native must involve the water, she decided, so she put on her butter-yellow bikini. This time the contrast with her bronzed skin gave the effect she had hoped for when buying it. She slipped on the matching painter's smock over the top, wishing the smock didn't make her look so much like a little girl.

As Wendy stepped quietly out her door she saw Erick sitting on the beach a few yards away, completely absorbed in the sea and sky. He did not hear her approach until she sat down beside him. "I was hoping you would be up early," he said, smiling his approval. "Let's get a bite to eat in the kitchen and we can get started."

"Want me to fix some sandwiches?" the cook offered when they had finished breakfast.

"No thanks, we're going native," Erick answered.

Erick led her to one of the small outrigger canoes, helped her into the bow, and handed her a paddle. "Even an island princess has to paddle her own canoe," he told Wendy as he picked up the other paddle and shoved the canoe away from the dock.

It had been several years since she had gone canoeing, but Wendy was grateful she had learned to paddle at scout camp. She bit the blade of the paddle into the water in a long sweeping motion.

"You *are* a native princess," said Erick approvingly.

"Just a well-trained Girl Scout," she answered honestly, hoping she didn't look too much like one.

Erick guided the canoe out of the bay and into the Opunohu River. The stream was so overhung with branches and trailing vines that they might have been in an African jungle. Paddling slowly, they passed a continual parade of floating red and yellow pareu blossoms—a giant lei on a broken string.

"It is so beautiful, I think you conjured it up," said Wendy as they paused to enjoy the solitude and splendor of the river.

"A fairy tale needs a wonderland setting," Erick replied. With wordless accord they began paddling again. After a while, the sound of birds in the trees was replaced by an increasing roar. The canoe broke into a clearing where the river tumbled over a lava cliff into a deep pool. They beached the canoe on the black lava sand.

"Last one in is a sissy," Erick called as he began peeling off his shirt and dashing into the clear blue water. With a quick zip Wendy was out of her smock and into the water ahead of him.

"That's not fair—shirts don't have zippers," he complained in mock indignation.

After the salt water of the lagoon, the pool felt clean and refreshing. They splashed and dived like dolphins at play. When they had finished their swim and lay in the sun to dry, Wendy was surprised to find the black sand was as smooth and comfortable as the best white sand beach. She was almost asleep when Erick announced. "Time to start lunch."

He took a coil of fish line and a hook from his shirt pocket. A few minutes' search produced a large caterpillar for bait. Climbing onto a large boulder beside the falls, he dropped the line over the edge. He didn't have to wait long before there was a tug on the line; a deft flip landed his catch. The second bite flipped off the hook halfway out of the water, but a third try was again successful.

They quickly gathered enough dry wood for a small fire on the beach and Erick surprised Wendy by expertly gutting and scaling the fish. "But I failed the course in stick rubbing," he quipped, producing matches from his shirt pocket to light the fire. "While that burns down to coals, we'll get the rest of our dinner," he said, starting along a dim path through the underbrush. The path led to breadfruit and mango trees.

"Nature's delicatessen," said Wendy as they filled their arms.

"Now for the final touch," Erick announced as they deposited their treasures beside the small beach fire. He went to a spot where the stream entering the clearing had undercut the bank. A coconut palm leaned out over the water at a sharp angle. Walking up the trunk monkey fashion, he tossed down drinking nuts.

"Just right," was Erick's verdict on the coals when they returned to the fire. He skewered the flattened fish on sharpened sticks which they held over the glowing coals. "Survival training was never like this," he mumbled between bites of broiled fish and breadfruit.

"Neither was scout camp," agreed Wendy, wiping the mango which dripped down her chin.

"Now you get your nap," Erick told her as he finished burying the last telltale signs of their meal and sprawled lazily on the sand. Wendy stretched luxuriously in the sun, determined not to doze off as she had on the bus the night before but the early start, the morning's activity, and the rich lunch made sleep irresistible. . . .

Wendy awakened to the light touch of Erick's lips brushing hers. "Only way to wake a sleeping beauty," he said, kissing her again more fervently.

Wendy longed to return Erick's kiss with equal ardor, but her feelings were complicated by thoughts of the glamorous Niki and a mysterious girl in Bangkok. Erick moved abruptly away from her, and she realized that her sudden chill came from a menacing dark cloud blotting out the clearing overhead.

"Have to make a dash for it," Erick said, pulling her toward the canoe so fast that her feet scarcely touched the ground. Just as they reached the canoe, the rain hit, driven by such fierce wind that it struck their faces like hail. Erick turned abruptly and pulled Wendy back along the beach as the rain now pelted down against their backs.

At the edge of the falls behind the rock from which Erick had fished there was a deep crevass slightly taller than Wendy. Crouching, Erick ducked through the opening with Wendy close at his heels. Behind the rock was a wind-hollowed cave the size of a child's playhouse, protected from the driving rain by the large rock which almost blocked the entrance. As they peered out of the narrow opening, the rain began to come down in almost solid sheets. Instinctively they huddled close together as Erick slipped a protective arm around her, his playful manner of a few minutes ago gone now. It was an oddly satisfying experience to huddle in that small, private world while the storm raged about them. The roar of wind and water made conversation impossible, but the communication between them was complete. Wendy had never known such a sense of peace and contentment.

The storm and the enchanted moments that accompanied it ended as abruptly as they had begun. The violent tropical storm turned to a slow drizzle.

"A *marazmu,* the cold wind and rain that sweeps down from the north several times each year," Erick explained. "It will probably rain all day. Tom and Migin may be concerned about us, so I think we should start back."

They walked hand-in-hand down the beach. Already soaked through, they did not hurry. "Since we'll be going downstream, just use your paddle to steer and hold the front as straight as possible," Erick instructed, as he helped Wendy into the canoe and shoved it away from shore. It glided rapidly over the churning red-brown water. At several points, small tumbling streams rushed to join the river. At such places, Wendy was able to keep the bow of the canoe pointed downriver by a series of short, sharp strokes against the current. With each additional stream, the river rushed faster and roared louder.

Suddenly Wendy heard Erick's voice above the rumbling water, but she was unable to distinguish his words. Looking back quickly, she saw him signal toward the shore. At the same moment, the surging water twisted the canoe with a rough jolt. Wendy worked furiously to hold the bow of the canoe against the spiraling current, but it was too strong for her. She felt the struggle being waged between the whirling water and the man seeking to control the fragile craft. Finally the man won, and the canoe swung toward shore. Wendy paddled rapidly with short, biting motions, feeling the thrust of Erick's powerful strokes. As the bow of the canoe touched the bank, Erick leapt out and pushed the front onto shore. Wendy jumped out lightly after him and helped him drag the canoe out of the water.

Erick stood motionless, staring at the tremendous rush of water and the small, shivering girl beside the fragile boat. As if determined to protect Wendy from the water, the rain, or any other force, he gathered her in his arms and kissed her possessively, then slowly released her.

"We'll walk from here. The boys will come for the canoe when the storm is over."

The thick growth formed an umbrella over them, but whenever they had to push the undergrowth aside, it released a shower of trapped water. When they finally emerged onto the beach where they had chased land crabs the first day, the sea was running so high that the spray dashed against their legs. It would have made short work of a canoe.

"Alo!" shouted Ruanu the cook as they came in sight of the cabins.

Migin came racing down the beach and threw her arms around Erick and then Wendy. "We were afraid you were marooned on one of the little coconut islands. Tom and some of the boys are out in the boat looking for you."

"We went up the river, but the current was too strong to bring the canoe out into the lagoon, so we beached it and walked across above the delta," Erick told her.

"Go radio Tom," Migin directed Ruanu. "Wendy, you're drenched and shivering. Go get a hot bath and hop into bed and Ruanu will bring you up something warm," Migin ordered.

As she headed for her cabin, Wendy giggled at the thought of Migin's chicken-soup-mothering on a Pacific hideaway. She had scarcely finished the prescribed shower and settled into bed with a blanket around her Indian fashion when there was a knock at the door. Migin entered, followed by Erick, who was carrying a covered bowl from which spiraled wisps of steam. He set the bowl on the table beside her bed. Wendy lifted the cover—it was fish chowder, not chicken soup.

"Bouillabaisse we called it at home," said Migin. "Ruanu starts a big pot whenever a norther blows up."

"It looks marvelous—shrimp, crab, mahi mahi, and some things I'm sure I've never seen before."

"Probably not," said Erick. "There are some very unusual and beautiful fish here. You'll have to get acquainted with them on the first sunny day." He gazed at her fondly.

A bit chagrined at the bedraggled ending to her romantic escapade, Wendy nevertheless smiled up at her two friends.

"Thanks so much for everything," she said. "I feel fine now."

Erick bent over to kiss her on the forehead and, despite her exotic adventures, she felt like a little girl again.

The next morning Wendy was again awakened by the myna bird greeting the sun. The rain had stopped in the night, but water still dripped from the trees. As she raised the shutter to the warm sunlight, Wendy saw Erick sitting on the beach where he had been the previous morning. It would be perfect to spend endless days playing in the sun, sand, and sea, but Wendy knew this must be the last day for her. She reminded herself sternly that this was a business trip, not a vacation.

"Hi, ready to go meet the fish?" Erick greeted as she sat down on the sand beside him.

"I'm afraid I'm going to have to snub the fish and go back to work."

"Have you told Migin?"

"No. They're so busy with their other guests that I hate for them to have to take me back. Is there a public boat or plane I can take?"

"Yes, you can get either one from Temae in the afternoon. Where will you go next?"

"Bali."

"I like Bali. Where will you be staying?"

"Tandjung Sari. It's Balinese style."

Later, Migin, joined them for breakfast. "Do you really have to go?" she protested.

"Business before pleasure, I'm afraid, though I have already made up my mind which area I want to represent," answered Wendy. "Your beautiful Pacific Islands have completely captivated me."

"It's our super-salesman who does it," said Tom, turning to Erick with a mischievous grin.

"I'll take the afternoon plane," said Wendy, cutting short Tom's offer to take her back to Tahiti.

"Then you'll still have time to meet my friends the fish," interposed Erick.

When breakfast was finished, the four friends took the cruiser down the now glassy-calm bay and anchored just beyond the coral reef. Erick helped Wendy put on fins. She flapped across the deck feeling like a circus clown in great floppy shoes. He adjusted a face mask over her eyes and nose, pulling it tight enough to prevent seepage, and showed her how to breathe through the snorkel. At first Wendy felt a brief moment of panic with her eyes and nose confined in the glass enclosure, but she adjusted quickly.

Wendy and Erick slipped over the side of the boat and clung to it for a moment. Then Erick floated face-down on top of the water. Wendy pushed off from the side of the boat in a long smooth glide, but became confused about breathing through her mouth and surfaced, spluttering and coughing.

"Breathe only through the mouthpiece," Erick told her, flipping her mask up on top of her head.

Tom and Migin were gliding smoothly over the surface of the water, intent on the underwater view. Wendy replaced her mask, determined to try again. This time she started more slowly with a few gentle flutters of her feet as she led with her hands to keep from running into anything. The view was breathtaking. The coral beneath them was clearly visible in colors of blue, pink, yellow, white, and red. Fish looking like creations of a modern artist began to swim past— black, white, and yellow striped ones, and red, green, blue, and pink ones. Erick took Wendy's hand and they floated side by side as he pointed out some of the shyer creatures peering from holes or flattening themselves against the rocks like colorful flowers.

Wendy had originally thought that going snorkeling would be an odd way to spend their last day together, but floating through this undersea wonderland now seemed a fitting conclusion to her brief but joyous interlude with Erick.

4

The sun was just tinging the blue waters of the Pacific with a rosy glow as the plane circled for its landing on Bali. Wendy wondered whether flights to South Sea islands were scheduled to arrive at sunrise because it made the flight routine easier or because it was such a beautiful time of day for visitors to get their first look at these lovely islands.

As they approached, Bali did not appear very different from Tahiti—a lush tropical island rising to jagged mountain peaks out of the blue water. The multicolored coral was not as brightly noticeable around Bali as it had been around Tahiti.

In spite of a day's layover in Sydney, it had been a longer trip than Wendy had expected. Familiar as she was with the map of the area that hung on her office wall, she hadn't fully visualized the vast distances of the Pacific and the International Date Line. The confusion of time and distance vanished as she stepped from the plane into the soft tropical morning and heard the familiar cry of the myna bird greeting the day.

Customs clearance was smooth and orderly with a touch of Oriental courtesy. A microbus waited at the exit to take guests to the Sanur beach hotels. All roads in Bali lead to Denpasar, the capital, so the bus turned in that direction. As they passed rice fields and pagoda-shaped temples, it was apparent that Bali is a part of the Orient, geographically and culturally.

In Denpasar Wendy tried to concentrate on the interesting contrasts of architecture—Balinese, Dutch colonial, and modern. But an even more fascinating pageant was passing in the streets with buses, taxis, horse-drawn carts, motorcycles, bicycles, and even bicycle-powered rickshaws all traveling on the left side of the road.

"Pemetjutan Palace," the driver announced, pointing to a series of shaded pavilions. Wendy caught a glimpse of beautiful wood carvings decorating pillars and doorways.

As the bus turned toward Sanur, it passed an open market where women in colorful costumes and turbans offered a wide variety of goods, both common and exotic. Flat reed baskets were piled high with strange fruit and foods. Colorful materials hung above the heads of seated vendors. A blend of unidentifiable spices drifted through the open window of the bus. The market offered the promise of an intriguing morning of browsing and shopping.

At Sanur beach the microbus passed the gleaming ten-story Bali Beach Hotel, a bit of transplanted America. A few miles farther down the beach, the bus turned in to the lovely garden of Tandjung Sari with its individual thatched bungalows and exotic tropical plants nestled among palm trees. As Wendy signed the guest register, she noticed that a group arranged by Personal World Tours was staying there.

Wendy's cottage was a modified A-frame with a thatched roof and large windows. A ceiling fan turned lazily above beautiful teakwood furniture. The floor was mat-covered, and there were rattan chairs on the lanai. Like the island itself, the room was a charming blend of South Seas and Oriental influences.

Wendy changed into shorts and a sleeveless, knotted midriff shirt and went out to explore her new surroundings. Neatly marked paths meandered among ponds, streams, and waterfalls. She stopped to watch giant goldfish swimming in the pools. Brilliant tropical birds hopped along the path and flashed from tree to tree—baby-pink cockatoos and bright, turquoise blue birds. They were so unafraid of humans that one of the cockatoos hopped up on her basket-purse and began pulling out a tissue.

One path led down to the beach. The sand had very little coral and was soft beneath Wendy's feet. Farther out the coral created a white breakwater where the deep blue of the ocean met the pale blue water of the lagoon. As Wendy watched the water, two Balinese boys approached, selling postcards and fine wood carvings of dancers, temples, and animals. Wendy bought several cards showing colorful Balinese dancers, but decided to buy her mother a carving from a store that would pack and ship it.

Back at her cabin Wendy had just settled down to the task of writing postcards when there was a knock on her door. "Miss Devin?"

"Yes."

"I am Muda Tamjong. I am the Balinese guide for Personal World Tours. The clerk told me you were staying here. I want to welcome you to Bali and offer you my services if there is anything I can do to help you." He handed her his card.

"Thank you," Wendy answered the handsome young man. "I haven't made any plans yet, but if I need anything I'll call you."

"I am taking one of your tours to a Barong play and Kris dances tonight, and I would be happy to have you join us."

"That sounds very interesting. I have heard a good deal about Balinese dancers."

"We'll meet in the lounge at eight."

Wendy went back to her postcards. She sent one to her mother, filled with as much detail of beautiful Bali as she could cram in. She would postpone writing to Mr. Vance, her boss, until after the dances when she would have a firsthand report on one of their tours in Bali.

That left Marvin. Wendy couldn't remember ever delaying so long acknowledging a gift. She addressed one of the cards and then paused, chewing thoughtfully on the end of her pen. Once she had said, "Thank you for the lovely charm," there seemed to be nothing more to say. Even "Having a wonderful time," or "Wish you were here," seemed inappropriate to the groom who had failed to show up for their wedding. She searched through her thoughts for something she might say about Bali. The rice fields—she had passed workers planting rice and hadn't even thought of Marvin. It had once seemed so important, helping him in his work to find a superior rice hybrid. Was she letting wounded pride stand in the way of her dedication to making a worthwhile commitment? She thought of the contrast between the serious scientist in San Francisco and charming, carefree Erick and remembered her disappointment that Erick hadn't asked about seeing her in Bangkok. It was hardly a city where two people could expect to meet by chance, and calling all the hotels would be quite a project. Then too, there was the mysterious girl in Bangkok whom Migin had mentioned.

With an effort, Wendy returned her attention to the postcard to Marvin, managing to fill it with general comments from her casual observations.

As Wendy entered the lounge a few minutes before eight, Muda came forward to greet her. "We are so glad you could join us."

Wendy was grateful that he did not make a special point of introducing her to the group. She wanted their reactions to the tour to be as natural as possible. A plump middle-aged lady came puffing into the lounge. Muda nodded to her, took a quick head count, and announced, "Our bus is here. Shall we go?"

A microbus similar to the one which had brought her from the airport took them along the coast to a large white building on the grounds of the temple. They entered the dance pavilion through intricately carved doors depicting a jungle world of animals, giving favored position to the monkeys.

Their group was seated on brocaded cushions as girls in colorful embroidered silk sarongs served them Chinese tea and delicious cakes made of raw sugar and nuts. Balinese women must be among the most beautiful in the world, Wendy thought, with their flawless ginger-colored complexions, large almond eyes, and jet-black hair coiled on top of shapely heads. Even the serving girls moved with the grace of trained dancers.

The *gamelan,* an orchestra composed of gongs of many sizes and shapes, as well as flutes, drums, cymbals, and bamboo clicking instruments, began its vibrant beat. Through the split temple gate that formed a backdrop for the play appeared the Barong, the mystical creature with a long swayback and curved tail, which represents the forces of good. The two men inside the fantastic costume sidestepped and whirled, snapped at the *gamelan* and swished flies with its tail. The Barong was joined by a dancer in monkey costume and three men wearing masks who danced a comedy number as prelude to the play.

The play was an involved, ritualistic story of the struggle between the good Barong and the bad Rangda, who practices black magic and takes many forms, both animal and human.

During intermission two beautiful Legong dancers became divine nymphs wrapped in gold brocade and wearing crowns of gold and flowers. Their dance combined graceful, dynamic gestures and subtle movements of eyes and fingers.

The play concluded with a frenzied battle between the disciples of evil and the Kris dancers, the army of the good Barong, holding carved and jeweled ritual swords of great beauty. The fight had no victors to show that the war against evil is eternal. At the conclusion of the performance, the temple priest sprinkled the Kris dancers with holy water and then killed a chicken, spilling its blood on the ground to ward off evil spirits. The gesture made Wendy shudder.

In spite of the rather gruesome ending, the play and dancing made for a delightful evening. A young architect from Los Angeles had been particularly attentive to Wendy in the noncommitted manner of travelers who expect to go their separate ways when the encounter ends. Had that also been true of her romance with Erick? Wendy wondered.

Wendy had been so favorably impressed with Muda and the tour that her intended postcard to Mr. Vance became a letter. Muda had been charming and knowledgeable, speaking excellent English, and remaining particularly tactful when the plump matron showed signs of becoming ill at the sight of the chicken blood.

Wendy was already awake the next morning when the myna birds began their dawn symphony. She slipped quickly into her bikini and matching smock cover and ran down to the shore to await the glorious burst of the tropical sunrise. As the flaming rim spread molten bronze over the Indian Ocean, a cockatoo began to scold raucously. Looking up the beach, Wendy saw a tall blond American come striding toward her. He moved with a swift boyish gait just like Erick's—it was Erick!

Wendy ran to meet him. He swept her off her feet in a dizzying whirl and smothered her with a lingering kiss.

"You fly very well," he told her, recalling her words at their first meeting as he set her back on her feet.

"You must have done some flying yourself to be here," she countered, breaking off in midsentence as she remembered the other girls who had run to greet his arrival—first Migin, then Niki. What was there about this dashing adventurer that caused girls to fly into his arms? "With you, things are always so sudden," Niki had said. Was it just the delight of his sudden appearance? Wendy wondered. "How was the dive?" she asked in a more restrained tone.

"Marvelous. Migin thinks they found a new species. Her father will have it checked by the Cousteau researchers. If it is, he wants to name it 'Mignette,' but she wants to call it 'Haape.' ''

"I like that, a 'Haape fish.' What's it like?"

"It's a small fish, electric-blue with bronze overtones—rather like that sunrise," he said.

"That was beautiful, wasn't it?" she agreed as they settled on the sand, enjoying the morning newness of the beach marked only by their own footprints.

"I thought you would be on your way to Bangkok," Wendy said.

"I am. Bali is on the way. Just stopped off to see an old friend."

Wendy eyed him suspiciously. "Does he own a resort?"

"No, just a boat—or several of them: a cruiser for diving and the local version of the outrigger."

"Your friends seem to have a monopoly on boating and diving in the Far East."

Erick laughed. "I guess our group in Bangkok was a little boat happy. Both Tom and Mike have built their business around them. You'll have to meet Mike."

"Is he married?"

"No. On second thought, maybe you shouldn't meet him. He's a real charmer."

"That seems to be a characteristic of the group too," Wendy teased.

"I hope you don't have plans for the day," Erick said with a sudden hesitation.

"No, just enjoying things as they come in the South Seas spirit."

"Good. Do you mind riding a motorcycle?"

"No, though I have never tried it," she replied honestly, remembering her mother's dictum against motorcycles at home.

"It's the best way to get where we're going. I have one rented for the day."

"Pretty sure of yourself, weren't you?" she bantered.

He pulled her to her feet and settled the matter with a quick kiss. "Go change, and I'll meet you in front of the office."

A few minutes later Erick helped Wendy onto a saddlelike seat fastened to the frame of the bike, and instructed her to put her feet on the pegs protruding from the rear wheel. "Just put your arms around my waist and hang on," he told her.

Wendy took a secure hold of Erick and balanced herself for the roaring start she had observed of cyclists at home. But Erick started the sputtering machine smoothly and they breezed along at a moderate speed to enjoy the passing scenery.

At Denpasar they slowed to enjoy the beauty of Pura Djagatnata, the temple newly built of white coral. The split gate framed its graceful carved tower gleaming in the morning sun.

At the main intersection, Erick waved a greeting to its demon guardian. "So no evil will come to the spot," he explained.

In the swirl of converging traffic, Wendy hoped he was right about claiming there were rarely any accidents. At the corner of the market they turned north through a residential area where chickens, children, and housewives mingled in the confusion of the morning's activities.

As they reached the outskirts of the city, most of the traffic consisted of bicycles carrying an amazing assortment of items, some of them very large and unwieldy. They passed one man with a live pig stretched out on a rack on the back of his bike.

"He's passed out from distillery mash," Erick explained. "The farmer has to deliver him before he comes to."

The road climbed steadily and the size and age of the trees increased. Erick stopped before a temple gate in a heavily forested area. "Bukit Sari, the Monkey Forest. It was established by one of the rajas as a refuge for the monkeys. The forest is considered sacred and no one is allowed to chop wood here. Legend says that these monkeys were part of the army of the monkey general Hanuman who killed the giant Rawana in the Ramayana epic Hindu poem."

"You know so much about the customs and religions of Asia," said Wendy. "Are you interested in religions?"

"I'm interested in people, and their customs and beliefs are a part of them. But we're getting very serious about a fun place. Come on, you'll see."

At the gate they bought bags of peanuts. The attendant placed the small paper envelopes of nuts in a larger plastic bag with a handle. "That's to keep the monkeys from snatching the peanuts away from you and running off with them," Erick explained.

Small, sprite monkeys seemed to be everywhere. As they walked along the path to the temple, both Wendy and Erick handed out peanuts to the monkeys gathered around them. "Hey, stop that," Erick scolded a particularly large monkey, who was walking along behind them collecting the nuts from the smaller monkeys. "He's king of this region, and it looks like he's a real dictator."

Erick picked up a small monkey who had been forced to surrender his nut, and set him on his shoulder. The monkey ran his fingers through Erick's hair, examined his ear, and gobbled down the peanuts Erick handed him. Safe beyond the reach of the king, he was lord of all he surveyed.

Another small victim of the king's greed studied the situation a moment and jumped up onto Wendy's shoulder. He ate a peanut sitting on her shoulder and then ran around her neck to the other shoulder. The empty shoulder was filled immediately by another monkey. A third one decided that her purse looked like a good refuge from the big monkey.

Eventually they came to a moss-covered temple, it too filled with monkeys. A beautiful raised teakwood platform stood in the temple area. "Is it for dances?" Wendy asked.

"Yes, once a year a festival is held here to honor the gods who look after the forest and the forest creatures, particularly the monkeys." Erick answered.

Their walk back to the main gate became a regular parade with at least thirty monkeys following Wendy and Erick. Occasionally a bolder one would run in front of them, hold out his hand and with a "chi-chi-chi" demand more peanuts. They took shells or anything else that was offered.

"That one reminds me of a major I know," said Erick of a large monkey commanding the smaller ones to make way for him.

"I think I see some familiar faces here too," Wendy added as they waved good-bye to the monkeys. One bright monkey copied their waving motion.

Laughing, Erick helped Wendy back on the motorcycle. "Wendy Devin, you are my kind of girl," he said, brushing her cheek lightly with a kiss.

But are you my kind of man? Wendy wondered as she clasped her arms around his waist. Could I spend my life frolicking with this Peter Pan, this boy who never grew up?

"I think we better call it a day," Erick said when they got back to Wendy's bungalow. "I hope the motorcycle won't make you stiff."

"I feel fine. It's been fun," Wendy answered.

"Try to sleep in. Tomorrow is the night of the full moon, and you won't want to miss it."

"Sounds spooky, like Halloween."

"It is. How about my picking you up around noon for a sail in one of Mike's outriggers? That should leave us fresh for the evening."

"Providing I get to meet the charming Mike," she teased.

"Ah, the price of friendship," Erick mourned as he mounted the motorcycle and took off in one smooth motion.

When Wendy's feathered alarm, the myna, sounded the next morning, she realized she really was tired from the previous day's motorcycling. It was sheer luxury to turn over and go back to sleep. She was just finishing a late-morning bunch of tropical fruit with crisp rolls and cheese, a legacy of Bali's former Dutch occupants, when Erick arrived. They walked the short distance to the dock.

"Where did you find that Colleen out here?" a big red-haired Irishman asked in a brogue deliberately thickened, as he stared approvingly into Wendy's green eyes.

"Wendy Devin, this is Mike O'Connor, and you've been warned about his blarney."

"Now would you look who's talkin'," Mike responded. Turning to Wendy, he said, "I know the night of the full moon is supposed to bring out the good spirits, but I didn't expect leprechauns and an Irish lass to celebrate it with. You are going to Turtle Island with me tonight, aren't you?''

"We'll go wherever you say, as long as Wendy gets to see one of the temple festivals of the full moon," Erick answered.

"I'd like to sail in my prao across the harbor to Serangan, the sea temple. It's one of the few dedicated to Dewi Danu, goddess of the waters. The Balinese are not seafaring people. They believe demons and ghosts hide in the ocean. Very few of them can even swim. The Polynesians brought the praos to Bali, and there should be a lot of them there tonight," said Mike.

"I'm anxious to try one," said Erick.

"There isn't a finer outrigger in all the South Seas. That triangular sail, shot like an arrowhead into the bow of the boat, gives it the speed and grace of a bird. If you're ready, we can get started."

Under Mike's expert guidance, the prao skimmed the still waters of Badung Strait. "It seems as if we are flying or gliding over the water," said Wendy. Mike beamed with delight at his guest as the breeze swept her tumble of light-brown hair back from her pixie face, making her green eyes sparkle.

"What in the world is that?" Wendy asked, pointing to a brilliantly colored fishlike form in the sky.

"That is a giant kite. Some of them are as much as twenty-five feet long," answered Mike.

"How do people get them up in the air?"

"You'll see when we get closer to the island."

The next kite they spotted looked like a sea gull, another like a box in rainbow hues. "There's one of our friends," said Erick, pointing to a giant replica of a monkey. This time they were close enough so that Wendy could see that the kite was being towed by a prao.

"That's how they get enough speed to launch them," Mike explained.

"Are they just for the celebration tonight?" Wendy asked.

"No. Children like to fly the giant kites anytime. In fact, they are so popular the government has asked people to shorten the strings so they won't distract pilots on their descent for the airport across the harbor."

Though they were early, Mike had as much trouble finding a place to anchor the prao as a motorist trying to park for a parade. Finally, two smiling Balinese eased their boats over and made room for him to nose the slender craft onto the sandy beach.

The trio walked up the beach to the turtle pens, from which Turtle Island received its nickname. "I never dreamed a turtle could get so big," said Wendy watching a giant sea turtle paddle lazily through the shallow water of the pen. "Why are they penned up?"

"They are being fattened on sea grass for special banquets. Sea turtle is considered a great delicacy."

Excited shouting came from a circle of men partly hidden in a grove of palm trees. Wendy started in the direction of the noise. "That's a cock fight," said Erick. "They get a little bloody—I don't think you would care for it."

Wrinkling her nose in distate, Wendy turned in the opposite direction and followed a winding path leading to gaily decorated stands. There were cakes of ground nuts and raw sugar like those Wendy had sampled the first evening.

Children eagerly bought coconut candies and other bright-colored sweets. The shy, smiling children stole furtive glances at the big red-haired man and the equally tall blond one towering over the crowd, but they did not seem to be frightened by them.

The *gamelan* orchestra had begun to play by the time they arrived at the temple. There were a number of solo dances as the crowd gathered; then the play began. Like the one Wendy had seen earlier, it was a dance-drama based on the Hindu epic, the *Ramayana,* depicting the battle between good and evil in many guises. Here, however, the audience became a part of the play as the familiar story unfolded. Children in the front scampered back when the demons came too close. The audience hissed at the villain and applauded the hero as for a melodrama, but with more serious support for good over evil.

The moon shone high in the sky when Mike eased the prao away from Turtle Island. Wendy leaned her head on Erick's shoulder, convinced that the Balinese were right in believing there is magic on the night of the full moon.

The sand and sea were patterned with shimmering white and even the ancient wood of the dock gleamed with a silvery sheen when Wendy and Erick bade Mike good-bye with repeated thanks for a delightful evening. Still carrying their shoes, which they had removed in the boat, they walked hand-in-hand along the edge of the water where the moonstruck current made eddying pools of light around their ankles. No one intruded on their ethereal domain.

"Did you say you learned about canoes at summer camp?" Erick asked.

"Yes," she answered, puzzled and a little annoyed by his unusual question.

"Then I'll bet you have your bikini on under your slacks and shirt."

Wendy nodded, flushed with embarrassment, and wished the night was not so light that he could see her rising color.

"Good! I'll beat you into the water," he called, rapidly shedding shirt and trousers to reveal that he too had worn a swimsuit.

Caught by surprise, she was still struggling with a balky shirt button when he raced into the surf and dived into a cresting wave in a graceful arc. Sprinting through the gently curling surf behind him, she stopped to watch as his powerful strokes carried him smoothly through the water while shimmering spray reflecting the moonlight outlined his athletic body in luminescence.

Erick circled back in her direction and she swam to meet him. The indigo water was warm and silky, more conducive to languid play than a vigorous swim. Like dolphins they dived and splashed, tumbled and frolicked. She lost sight of him beyond a rolling wave and stopped to tread water and look about her in confusion. Suddenly he emerged beside her, the brilliant moonlight gleaming off the wetness of his blond hair, handsome face, and broad shoulders. He was a Viking prince rising from the sea. Laughing, he caught her in the circle of one powerful arm while easy strokes with his other arm kept them both afloat. Without effort he carried her along with him until his feet touched bottom, then his other arm came around her. The ebbing tide brought her floating form against the shiny, wet muscles of his broad chest. His hands slid sensuously down her water-slick body; then suddenly he let her go. Instinctively, she flung her arms around his neck for support. Laughing, he closed his arms around her and kissed her, at first casually as they had before, then persuasively leading her passion to respond to his.

Her whole being seemed suspended in the warm, caressing water, the tropic air, the moonlight. There was a threat of breathless madness in the lustrous radiance of the full moon. She wasn't sure she could retreat from that madness if he did not.

With a deeper, huskier, more emotion-filled laugh, he caught her in his arms and lifted her from the water as though she were a child. He carried her to the beach and stood her unsteadily on her feet. Throwing back his head he gave a long, low howl like a wolf baying at the moon. Wendy laughed in spite of herself and the enchantment was broken. The moon slid discreetly behind a cloud.

"Playtime is over," Erick said as they walked to her cottage. "I have to report for duty tomorrow, so I'll be leaving on the early-morning plane."

"Can I see you off?" she asked.

"Airports are for takeoff and landing, not for greetings or good-byes," he said firmly. He held her close and kissed her tenderly, then turned and walked resolutely away without looking back.

5

Have I left the magic behind, Wendy wondered. She looked out the airplane window at the rice paddies of Thailand stretching smooth and green as the turf of a football field, with the *klongs*—canals of brown water—looking like yardage markers. In a few minutes her plane landed in Bangkok in the shimmering brightness of midday, far different from her misty morning arrivals in Tahiti and Bali.

He didn't ask where I would be in Bangkok, Wendy mused as she collected her overnight case and the flight bag of travel information. Maybe that was the way it had been with Niki, when Erick went back to the mysterious girl in Bangkok.

The terminal building was simple and functional without distinctive features. "Miss Wendy?" asked a teen-age Thai boy as she emerged from customs.

"Yes," she answered, trying to gather a clue as to the boy's identity from the bright red baseball cap he wore at a rakish angle.

"I'm Tahn," he said, wiping his hand on his short pants before extending it in greeting. "Captain Erick said I should be your guide in Bangkok."

"How did you know who I was?" she asked as Tahn pumped her hand enthusiastically.

"He showed me a picture—very pretty with flowers on your head."

The one taken at Club Mediterranée, Wendy thought, remembering the enchanted moments before Niki had appeared.

Tahn picked up her suitcase and led her out of the terminal to the line of waiting taxis. Tahn and the driver engaged in a lively dialogue in Thai. Wendy caught frequent mention of *baht*, the money of Thailand. Finally an agreement was reached and Tahn helped Wendy into the cab, put her suitcase in the trunk, and climbed in beside her.

"How did Erick know when I would arrive?" Wendy asked as the taxi turned into the main highway from Don Muang Airport.

"There is just one plane a day from Bali, so I come yesterday and today. If you do not come today, tomorrow."

"I'm sorry you came and waited yesterday," Wendy told him.

"Waiting very good," Tahn replied. "Three men like my red cap and motion for me to be their guide to the taxi. I carry their suitcases. I tell them about Thailand and our customs. I tell them that in Thailand you must bargain with the taxi driver for the price to go to Bangkok. When we go out to the taxi the man bargains with the driver. He does not bargain very good, but when the price is less than the driver say first, he is very pleased. He give me a big tip. Now I can hire boat for me to water-ski."

"Do you like to ski?"

"Yes. Captain Erick teach me when I am a small boy before he go back to America."

"Where do you ski?"

"Pattaya. My village is near Pattaya."

"If I go to Pattaya, will you teach me to ski?" Wendy asked, hoping to avoid the awkward moments when Erick had to teach her to snorkel or ride a motorcycle.

"I would teach you good," Tahn answered. "Erick teach me good."

"He is a good teacher," Wendy said knowingly.

They had reached the noisy, bustling outskirts of Bangkok where small shops heaped to the ceiling with their wares competed for space with shabby apartment buildings.

"Where did you tell the driver to take us?" Wendy asked as the taxi turned from the crowded highway onto a broad avenue lined with handsome, modern buildings.

"The Siam Hotel. Captain Erick said you would like the garden. It has monkeys."

The taxi skirted a clear, lotus-filled reflecting pool and stopped before a replica of an old Siamese palace. The sharply peaked red roof swept heavenward at the tips of the eaves. Carved monkeys, guardians against evil spirits, adorned the ridge pole and the corners. The magic of fairy tales might well be lurking here, Wendy decided.

"I must go back to Pattaya," Tahn told her as he deposited her suitcase beside the desk. "Tomorrow I ski."

"Do I bargain with my guide for his fee too?" Wendy asked lightly, seeking some clue as to what was expected.

"One does not accept pay from friends. You are my friend because you are a friend of Erick," Tahn replied, suddenly very serious. He placed his fingertips together, prayerlike, and bowed deeply in a gesture called a *wai*, then turned and walked away.

Wendy was concerned that she had offended her new friend, but as he reached the door he doffed his red cap and waved it in a wide sweeping arc, then bounded down the steps with schoolboy abandon.

A friend of Erick, that seemed to be the magic word, Wendy thought—Tom and Migin in Mooréa, Mike in Bali, and Tahn waiting to meet her when she arrived in Bangkok.

Wendy's room was very modern with touches of Thailand in its decor—a woven cotton bedspread and drapes dyed in the subtle blends of Thai silk, a low teak table surrounded by cushions. She spent the afternoon relaxing in its air-conditioned comfort while the realities of time and place caught up with her.

The heat of the day was giving way to an evening breeze from distant mountains when Wendy crossed the *klong* which divided the broad lawn from the garden. It was a cool, inviting haven under a canopy of tropical trees. A small stream gurgled under arching oriental bridges into lotus-filled pools. A pair of honey-colored monkeys frolicked across her path and sat scolding her from an orchid-draped tree. Brilliant birds of many exotic species turned in their cages to watch a dispute among a group of small monkeys. A large black monkey with a white ruff around his neck grunted commands which seemed to settle the matter.

"I see you've met The General," said Erick close behind her.

Wendy turned in surprise and had to restrain the urge to rush toward him. Erick showed no hesitation as he bridged the distance between them in two long strides, took her in his arms, and kissed her tenderly. "Welcome to Bangkok," he said, releasing her reluctantly.

"It has been a nice welcome, starting with Tahn to greet me and now you," Wendy answered.

"He's quite a boy," said Erick fondly. "He was such a shy, skinny kid when he first began to hang around the docks in Pattaya."

"He says you taught him to ski."

"Yes, he was my lookout boy."

"Lookout boy?"

"When a lone skier rents a Thai motorboat, he has to take a boy along to watch out for swimmers and other boats while he skis. 'Look out' was the first English Tahn learned. We'll have to try some skiing this weekend."

They crossed one of the gracefully arching bridges leading to the street, and strolled along a broad boulevard crowded with people enjoying the early twilight hours.

"Does that little shrine mark something special?" Wendy asked, noting people bringing flowers and candles to a white-and-gold shrine the size of a large birdhouse on a pedestal.

"That's a spirit house for the guardian spirit which controls good and bad fortune on the property. That one is in front of the visitor's bureau. People who make a living from the tourist business bring offerings."

The smell of tropical flowers and the shouts of children at play filled the deepening twilight as they crossed the edge of Lumpini Park. "I want you to see the city spread out at your feet," said Erick when they had dodged through the busy traffic circle to the tall imposing Dusit Thani Hotel.

They climbed the steps to the main entrance where a small crowd was gathered. Suddenly the automatic door swung open and a colorfully dressed attendant appeared, pulling and prodding a baby elephant. Several bellboys shoved and urged him along from behind.

"Is that the way they treat their guests?" Wendy quipped.

"Only that one," Erick answered. "He's the hotel's mascot, and sometimes on a hot afternoon he feels the cool air inside when the doors open, steps on the automatic door pad, and goes in. I don't know what would cause him to go in this time of day—perhaps a child with some peanuts. Even though he is just a baby, it's quite a job to get him out. An older elephant would be trained, but that one is popular because he's small.''

An express elevator carried them quickly to the glass-enclosed tower lounge. ''It's breathtaking,'' said Wendy, looking out at the skyline pierced at intervals by the graceful spires of temples and palaces. The Chao Phya River bounding the city was a busy thoroughfare of boats which looked like toys from their high vantage point.

''I wish I could show you the city tomorrow,'' said Erick, ''but the squadron is shorthanded and I have to fly an Air-Evac to Chiengmai. It will be three-day duty.''

''An Air-Evac?'' Wendy asked.

''Our helicopter squadron is assigned to the hospital here and we're sort of an airborne ambulance when anyone at an outlying base needs to come in to Bangkok for special medical care.''

It was hard for Wendy to imagine Erick, her modern Viking, flying a slow, awkward helicopter. A sleek, swept-wing supersonic jet would have seemed more his style, she thought as she watched the lights of a modern airliner illuminate the ancient spires. Reluctantly she turned from the observation window, where all of picturesque Bangkok lay spread at her feet—just as he had promised.

Back on street level Erick waved away the doorman and the waiting taxis and paused to give the independent little elephant a pat. Casually he hailed an oddlooking, three-wheeled vehicle with open sides and a canvas top. The driver pulled to the curb and they climbed up on the small carriage seat. ''A *samlor*,'' explained Erick. ''Out in the country they are pedicabs powered by a bicycle, but for safety in Bangkok traffic they have to be motorized.''

''Around the park,'' he instructed as the driver deftly maneuvered the small vehicle into traffic. It was a soft and starlit night filled with the musical sounds of the Thai language and the laughter of children. Couples paddled small boats on the lake while others spread picnics beneath the palm trees. Wendy nestled contentedly against Erick's shoulder. It was the perfect carriage to take the princess back to her palace, even if the palace was only a replica.

Apparently playtime is not over, Wendy mused as she leaned against her door and brushed the back of her hand across her lips, still tingling from Erick's goodnight kiss. Had the mystery girl in Bangkok Migin had mentioned stopped waiting for Erick's return? Even if she had not, Wendy wondered if she really wanted to continue this playtime romance. As a travel agent, she knew that summer romance was part of a working girl's dream vacation. Though hers was a business trip, Erick had certainly made it a dream come true. But where would it end? Was she building up to another letdown? If she let herself love Erick in the way she knew she could, the hurt could go far deeper than the burst of Irish temper and humiliation she had known with Marvin. At least with Erick away for the next three days she would have time to think things out. . . .

The next morning Wendy was awakened by sounds of traffic and people going about their business, and recalled the peaceful calm of the Pacific islands. But there was one place she particularly wanted to see. She dressed quickly, and the doorman finally got her a taxi, in spite of the rush of early-morning traffic.

Wendy walked through the gates of the Grand Palace and paused before the real-life setting of her favorite musical, "The King and I." She stood in a wonderland created by succeeding rulers of Siam who had each sought to outdo his predecessors in splendor. A pink-pillared palace in the center was flanked by gleaming white ones on either side, while a carved and gilded gazebo united them in an architectural whole. She mounted the steps of the gleaming central building, half-expecting to find the legendary King of Siam holding court inside. The intricate carving, rich silks, brocades, and gold leaf of the ceremonial room in which she found herself made her feel as if Anna and the King might have just left. The nine-tiered white canopy, like a giant wedding cake above the royal throne, reminded her that this palace was still used for state functions by Thailand's present royalty. Her guide led her from one dazzling room to another, and finally through a gate to the most beautiful building in Siam, the Temple of the Emerald Buddha. The five-hundred-year-old image inside was carved from a single piece of jade. The exquisitely rendered figure appeared quite small atop the high, elaborate gold altar designed to represent an aerial chariot.

Though it was a busy weekday morning, an unending succession of Thais came to pay their respects. Here the past and the present flowed smoothly together.

Before returning to her hotel, Wendy stopped at the office of her company's tour representative to see if any mail had preceded her to Bangkok. There were two letters: one bore the distinctive seal of Personal World Tours, the other Marvin's hasty scrawl. Wendy turned Marvin's letter over in her hand with a troubled feeling, then put both letters in her purse to read at leisure when she got back to her room.

She walked down the street, pausing before a window of beautifully draped and displayed Thai silk. The colors were soft and subtly blended. Though she wanted to send some to her mother, Wendy was experienced enough at travel shopping to wait until she became more familiar with values and prices. The next window displayed blue star sapphires winking invitingly in beautifully crafted rings and pendants. This was an indulgence Wendy had promised herself, but again the words were wait and compare. At the corner she hailed a taxi. Settling back to watch the colorful passing panorama, she realized how tired she was.

Once propped up on her bed in the air-conditioned comfort of her room, Wendy turned her attention to her mail. The letter from Mr. Vance was short, wishing her a good trip. Apparently their letters had crossed in the mail.

Wendy was surprised by the length of Marvin's letter—several neatly folded pages of lined note paper—because he was usually so preoccupied. She started to read with as little enthusiasm as she would have had for an overdue bill:

> "Dear Wendy, I hope by now you realize how important
> it was that I should confer with Dr. Pridi when he
> was here—even though it was (or should have been)
> our wedding day—and have forgiven me."

She paused, trying to sort out her tangled feelings about Marvin. She did not feel anger; that had passed in the first flash of her Irish temper. Wounded pride? Perhaps, but mostly confusion about the place of Marvin's work in their relationship, and its importance to him—to her. What role, if any, did Erick play in her jumbled emotions? Finding no answers, Wendy continued Marvin's letter:

> "The analysis of the rice cultures has exceeded our expectations."

Wendy felt again the old glow of pride in Marvin's dedication to the needs of hungry people.

> "I walked down to the marina yesterday evening to watch the sailboats coming in—the way we did so often. The fog was beginning to roll through the Golden Gate so that the bridge seemed to be floating on the clouds."

Wendy could almost feel the tingling coolness of the fog on her face. Marvin seemed to have anticipated her feelings far from home, leading her memory on a wave of nostalgia. The same cautious voice that had warned her of being swept off her feet by the dashing, romantic Erick, now warned that Marvin seemed to be devoting the full resources of his brilliant mind to regaining her love and loyalty. It was a thought both flattering and frightening.

6

"Miss Wendy!" shouted Tahn as she stepped from the bus in Pattaya Saturday morning.

"How did you know this time when I would be coming?" Wendy asked.

"I do not know. Every Saturday I come to the morning bus. If someone ask where is boat harbor, I show them. Sometimes I get to be lookout boy."

"Do you get to ski when you are lookout?"

"No, only Mr. Erick let me ski when he rents boat; and Miss Jane."

"Miss Jane?"

"She is friend of Mr. Erick long time ago."

"Is she still here?"

"No, she lives in Bangkok at the hospital."

Feeling as if she had been prying without intending to, Wendy did not pursue the subject further.

"You want I take your suitcase in the hotel?" asked Tahn, indicating the sprawling lodge before which the bus had stopped.

"Please do," Wendy answered. She didn't need help with the small overnight case, but she could see it pleased Tahn to help. They crossed the beautifully landscaped garden, skirted the crowded pool, and entered the lodge, which was open across the front to the cool morning breeze off the Gulf of Siam.

The bellboy seemed confused when Tahn clung tenaciously to Wendy's suitcase, but bowed politely and showed her to her room.

"You go ski and I be your lookout?" Tahn asked hopefully.

"No, I want to learn to ski, and you be my teacher so I won't be so dumb when Erick comes this afternoon."

"Mr. Erick is coming today?" Tahn asked eagerly.

Wendy nodded. "Go wait for me by the pool until I get my suit on, and we'll get started with that lesson."

"Do we rent a boat here?" Wendy asked as she joined Tahn.

"No, we go see my boat man at the harbor."

"Let's take a *samlor*," Wendy suggested. She was surprised when Tahn climbed into the little pedicab without preliminary bargaining. "Don't you bargain with the *samlor* driver?" she asked.

"No, only with taxi driver. *Samlor* driver charge everyone five baht to boat harbor."

Wendy arranged to rent a motorboat and skis for an hour. "You go first, and I'll watch you," she told the delighted Tahn. She took the seat in the rear of the boat while Tahn sat on the edge of the dock and put on the skis. The driver tossed him the tow rope and accelerated rapidly away from the dock so that Tahn took off in a jet of motion. When the boat reached deep water, the driver cut into a series of sharp turns, leaving Tahn to jump the wake of the boat as they crossed and recrossed it. On a straight run down the harbor Tahn did a series of tricks, some on only one ski. It was a showy performance reminding Wendy of a small boy hanging by his knees in a tree to impress the new girl on the block.

"You try it?" Tahn asked Wendy.

"Might as well," she replied, hoping her experience skiing in the snow of the Sierras would be of some help. The skis did not feel too awkward on her feet. Though Tahn had used only one hand, Wendy grasped the tow rope firmly in both hands. Feeling the rope begin to take up, Wendy flexed her knees as she had done on the snow. The skis leveled and for a brief moment she was up on the water. But she was too far up and over she went.

"You all right?" Tahn asked with concern as Wendy emerged sputtering and gasping.

"No worse than when I make a bad dive, just swallowed a lot of water."

Tahn burst out with the laugh he had been suppressing. "Want to try it again?"

"Only way to learn," she answered, collecting the skis as they floated nearby.

"Hold back till the boat pull you up," Tahn directed.

Following his instructions, Wendy was able to glide smoothly off the dock and balance herself above the skis, but she was unable to rise from a sitting position as she dragged the bottom of her bikini through the water. She followed behind the boat several hundred yards, struggling to get up on her feet, but finally had to drop the rope. Water-skiing was definitely not a skill to learn in one easy lesson.

"That's enough, You can finish out the hour," said Wendy after three more attempts, each only slightly more successful than the last.

"Can I take my brothers?" Tahn asked.

"Sure," Wendy answered, and Tahn made a great sweeping wave to two smaller boys on the dock. As Wendy climbed out onto the dock, the smaller of the two scrambled into the boat while the older one hurriedly donned the skis. He was a small copy of Tahn. As the boat sped down the harbor, he tried valiantly to duplicate Tahn's earlier performance.

Wendy took a *samlor* back to the lodge for some sunning—the reason she had given Erick for coming down to the beach in the morning rather than waiting until he got off work.

"Done just the way I like it," said Erick's familiar voice as he pressed a finger on Wendy's shoulder as if testing a cake.

"I must have dozed off. Feels like you found me just in time," she answered, a warm inner glow matching the warmth of her sun-drenched shoulders.

"I think you need a swim—last one in is a lobster," called Erick, racing for the gently breaking surf.

The water was cool and refreshing as the two of them splashed and bobbed in the surf, which broke too sharply for serious swimming. Fun and a zest for living seemed to be part of everything Erick did.

As they ran back up the beach, Wendy was surprised to meet a boy leading a small elephant.

"I'll bet you haven't ridden an elephant," said Erick.

"Nooo," answered Wendy dubiously.

"That one looks about your size," he said indicating the approaching animal, whose head was not much higher than Wendy's. After negotiating with the elephant boy, Erick held his hands together to help Wendy mount. The elephant's hair was extremely coarse as it rubbed against her wet skin. The boy led the elephant by its trunk in slow, lumbering stomps around the swimming pool. He cut around one of the corners so close that Wendy thought they might fall in. Erick took her camera from her beach bag and they posed for pictures. The boy handed Wendy peanuts so that the elephant would reach his trunk up to her in a trumpeting pose. When Erick finished taking pictures, the elephant knelt on its front knees to let her know the ride was over. As he started down, Wendy thought she might pitch off over his head, but his motion was slow and deliberate and she was able to balance herself and slide off easily.

"The elephant follows the boy around just like a big dog," said Wendy as she and Erick continued down the beach.

"That just about describes it. Much of the heavy work in northern Thailand is done by elephants—particularly in the teak forests. If a family can give their son a baby elephant when he is a small child, he has an assured source of income. Boy and elephant will grow up together, and the elephant will obey and work only for his boy."

"Northern Thailand was where you went this week, wasn't it?"

"Yes."

"I hope your patient wasn't serious."

"Just an appendectomy. He was with an advisory mission in a remote area where there wasn't a hospital, so we picked him up and brought him to Bangkok. But enough of this shop talk, we came down here to ski, and I see our boat coming."

"When did you arrange for it?" Wendy asked, recognizing the boat and driver who had taken her skiing that morning, followed by the exuberant Tahn shouting and waving from the end of the tow line.

"Before I came down to the beach. A half hour skiing is enough for me, so I always let the boys have the other half hour," answered Erick returning Tahn's sweeping wave.

The boat pulled in to the hotel landing and Wendy climbed in as Tahn turned the skis over to Erick and climbed in beside her. The driver eased the boat smoothly away from the dock, and as the tow rope tightened, Erick rose gracefully on the skis in one fluid motion. The driver moved out into the harbor in a series of sweeping turns, Erick following behind as if man, skis, and rope were one— a piece of modern bronze sculpture.

Then it was Wendy's turn. She mentally reviewed Tahn's instructions: hold back and let the boat bring you up—balance with your knees and ankles. She managed to stay up for about ten seconds before losing her balance and toppling into the water. She hadn't learned to ski, but she had been spared having Erick watch her first awkward attempts.

Erick looked suspiciously from Wendy to Tahn, as if her performance had been better than might be expected for a first trial on water skis. "You learn fast," he commented.

Tahn grinned and ducked his head.

After another beautiful performance by Erick and another faltering one by Wendy, Erick once more donned the skis and told the driver, "Give us a circle tour of the harbor and then head back to the boat dock."

There were beautiful yachts and colorful junks tied up in the harbor, but Wendy only had eyes for Erick as he skimmed the water with effortless grace. She came back from her preoccupation with a start as they coasted in to the boat dock.

Tahn's brothers were waiting on the dock, balancing a bicycle between them. Tahn climbed on the seat, the youngest brother mounted the handlebars, and the third stood behind Tahn on two pegs which extended from the socket of the rear wheel. "Their family can only afford one bicycle," Erick explained as the three boys rode off waving, undaunted by their precarious balance.

"Would you like to change for dinner?" Erick asked.

"Sounds good after that workout," Wendy agreed.

Erick had not yet returned when Wendy strolled out into the garden wearing the pareu print she had bought in Tahiti. She wasn't sure why she had selected that dress. Perhaps she was trying to recapture the magic of those earlier evenings.

Wendy sat on a bench by the children's playground, her position partly screened by a softly scented jasmine so that she could watch the games without making the children self-conscious. Wendy thought she had never seen such beautiful children. One little girl—a child of about three or four—seemed a doll come to life.

As if drawn by Wendy's concentration, the child came skipping over to the bench. "Hello, what's your name?" Wendy asked, regretting that she had not yet learned the language well enough to ask in Thai.

"Urai," the child answered, pressing her chubby fingers together and bowing in greeting.

"My name is Wendy. How old are you?" Wendy continued, testing whether the child understood English or always started a new encounter with her name.

"Free."

As Wendy tried to think of suitable words to continue the conversation, the child emitted a joyful shriek, "Daaady," and went flying across the lawn.

Wendy was stunned to see that the man who swooped Urai up and tossed her in the air was Erick. She had been prepared for a mysterious woman in Erick's life in Bangkok, but not a child.

The next few seconds seemed like an eternity to Wendy. Finally, her pulse began to beat again as a soft, musical voice called "Urai."

The beautiful Thai woman who came down the path had the same doll-like quality as Urai. "Erick!" she cried in surprise when she saw the two of them. She did not rush to him as Migin, Niki, and Wendy herself had done; instead she held out her hands in greeting.

Erick took her two small hands in his and kissed them gently. "You're looking lovely as ever, Sumnieng. How are things with you?"

"Things go well. I dance again at the restaurant—and then there is Urai."

The tenderness and pain evident between them made Wendy feel as if she had opened the wrong door, intruded on two people at a very private moment.

Sumnieng and Erick turned and went back up the path to the garden, Urai skipping and dancing between them as she clung tightly to Erick's hand. Wendy sat motionless until they were out of sight, lest any movement attract their attention. When she was sure she would not be seen, she ran blindly up the walk to the hotel narrowly missing a waiter with a tray of drinks at the corner of the swimmming pool.

When she reached the solitude of her room, Wendy looked down at her trembling hands, waiting for the burst of temper with which she usually met such frustration, but it did not come. Instead, she felt drained and empty. She slumped into a chair and sat motionless, searching her memory for some chance word anyone might have said which would provide a clue to the scene she had just witnessed. She could not say how long she sat there when her phone rang.

"Hi, I was afraid I might have missed you," said Erick, an odd defensive note in his voice. "I'm afraid I have bad news. There is an emergency at Nongkai, and the other pilots are all out on missions, so I've been called back. Sorry to desert you like this—I warned you pilots are a bad risk. We have to leave now. I'll call you when I get back."

Wendy was glad he hadn't waited for an answer; at the moment she was completely out of them. Erick's call had only added more questions: how had he been called back to Bangkok when she had seen him only minutes before walking in the garden with Sumnieng? Was it a slip when he said, "we have to leave now"? Or had he been trying to tell her that he was leaving with Sumnieng and Urai? She felt more abandoned than she had when Marvin failed to arrive for their wedding. The delightful resort of a few hours before had become a strange land where she was completely alone. Utterly desolated, she threw herself on the bed and cried. . . .

When it was over she felt better. She got up and washed her face in cold water. After all, Pattaya was one of Thailand's most popular tourist resorts, a place to be included by Personal World Tours, which meant there was work here for her to do. She put her notebook in her purse, brushed back a tumble of wayward curls, and headed resolutely down the path past the swimming pool.

7

Wendy spent the days following her return from Pattaya familiarizing herself with Bangkok and the places Personal World would want to include in their tours—the Royal Palace, beautiful and varied Buddhist temples, the floating markets, the silk factory, and gem shops. She was too busy by day and too tired at night to dwell on her personal problems; but without Erick people and places just didn't come alive as they had before.

When the phone rang Wednesday evening, Wendy restrained herself from racing to it like a teen-age girl.

"I hear you need tour guide," said Erick in a rich, playful Thai accent which sent a tingle through her.

"Do you have references?" she asked, joining in the game.

"Very fine references. I show you Thai restaurant with dancing. The star is friend of mine," said Erick, continuing the imitation.

Remembering Erick's meeting with Sumnieng and her reference to dancing, Wendy had to concentrate on keeping her tone light as she replied, "What time does the tour start?"

"Tour bus arrive at seven o'clock," he answered and hung up. If he was going to offer any further explanation of his sudden departure from Pattaya, he obviously did not want to do it over the phone.

In spite of her stern admonitions, Wendy found it difficult to suppress her excitement as she dressed for their dinner date in the soft green silk dress the seamstress had finished for her just that afternoon. She told herself that the sparkle in her green eyes was just a complement of the color of the dress.

"I have a surprise for you." Erick greeted her with the enthusiasm of a child with a new toy and led her to the parking lot. "The new tour bus," he said, waving his hand grandly to indicate a small, battered green Toyota. "After Pattaya, I realized I had to have a car, and when one of the mechanics returning to the States offered to sell me this one, I jumped at the chance."

Wendy waited for a further explanation of what had happened at Pattaya, and what the incident had to do with owning a car, but Erick was engrossed with his new toy.

"At least it's the right color," he said, turning to look for a long moment into the depth of her eyes. "I call it shamrock because finding it was a piece of good luck."

"A Japanese shamrock?" Wendy giggled in spite of herself.

"You can find shamrocks in lots of odd corners of the world," he said, and abruptly turned his attention back to the car. When he started the engine, the purr of the motor belied its age. It had obviously been an object of loving care from a man who knew motors. As he skillfully maneuvered the little car through the confusion of Bangkok traffic, Erick drove with an ease Wendy had often observed in pilots.

They crossed the arching bridge of the Baan Thong Restaurant, and Wendy felt the change from bustling, modern Bangkok to ancient Siam. In the entry of the converted teak mansion they removed their shoes and received slippers from the attendant. A smiling hostess in a sarong led them up the broad, curving stairway covered with thick red carpeting. The dining room was filled with low, carved teak tables surrounded by wedge-shaped cushions for reclining. Three Americans were already seated at the table. Erick introduced the attractive girl with short honey-colored hair as Captain Jane Adams; a distinguished man with gray at the temples as Major Warren Sims; and a scholarly looking man with glasses as Captain Paul Hess.

When the introductions were completed, the Major indicated the places beside him for Wendy and Erick. "No wonder you've been hiding her," he said with approval. "How was the flight to Nongkai?"

"No problem with the flight. The boy was near shock and weakening when we got him in," Erick answered. "How is he?" he asked, turning to Jane.

"He responded to the serum, and should be all right in a few days," she answered.

"A boy from one of the hill tribes was bitten by a cobra," Erick explained to Wendy. "They used a primitive treatment instead of antitoxen, and when it didn't work a ranger asked us to go up and bring him in."

"We try to keep all areas supplied with anti-venom from the Pasteur Institute here in Bangkok, but there are some of the more remote hill tribes that still don't use it," Jane added.

"I hope you like Thai food," the Major said. "Here everything is served as if we were guests at a Thai banquet."

The waitress, carrying a teak tray filled with small, artistically arranged dishes, dropped gracefully to her knees beside the low table and began serving the colorful foods.

Crisp cubes of pork garnished with pineapple and green peppers, succulent baby shrimp with snow peas, and other combinations of tasty morsels of meat with crunchy vegetables reminded Wendy of San Francisco's Chinatown. Yet the subtle spices and the frequent use of ground peanuts made the colorfully arranged dishes distinctly Thai. There were so many different dishes, Wendy was hard-pressed to sample each of the inviting offerings. A pot of green tea kept hot by a brightly decorated caddy, and a plate of chilled fruit and melon completed the meal.

The waitress was just removing the fruit plate when the orchestra, which had played soft, hauntingly elusive music throughout dinner, began a more insistent beat, and the first group of elaborately costumed dancers appeared on stage. The dance depicted a mass battle scene from the epic Ramayana; not the entire story as the Balinese dancers had told it, but only the dramatic concluding scene. Monkeys and other animal characters wore fierce stylized masks beneath their towering headdresses. The dancers representing human characters did not wear masks, but kept their faces immobile except for their expressive eyes.

The polite applause which followed the number gave way to an enthusiastic reception as the next dancer, a soloist, appeared. Wendy immediately recognized Sumnieng, her lovely face framed by a towering gold and jeweled headdress. The heavy, jeweled brocade of her Siamese costume did not conceal the remarkable grace of her slender body as she began the ancient ceremonial dance.

Erick and his friends followed every subtle motion of her delicate hands and flashing eyes with rapt attention. The applause which followed Sumnieng's dance left no doubt that she had brought something special to the familiar ritual.

"She's marvelous," enthused Erick. "More polished and confident than when I saw her last."

"She has become one of Thailand's most talented dancers," replied the Major. "You will notice that most of the customers are not tourists but Thai. Many have come particularly to see Sumnieng dance. When Dhamak, the owner, gloats over his find, I am tempted to remind him of his reluctance to rehire a widow— it took a bit of arm twisting."

"An old specialty of yours, arm twisting, as I remember," prodded Erick.

"She makes me feel as ancient and graceless as a helicopter," complained Jane, whose trim figure, dynamic appeal, and quick, efficient movements belied both statements.

"Don't knock our trusted beast of burden," admonished Paul.

A comic monkey dance and a romantic duet preceded Sumnieng's next appearance. She performed the fingernail dance with long, curved, golden fingernails accenting the delicate expressive movements of her hands. Though the dance was sheer poetry in motion, it was Sumnieng's serene, beautiful eyes which riveted Wendy's attention. The applause was even more enthusiastic when the dance ended.

"I wish I could go backstage and tell her how much I enjoyed it," said Erick.

"Afraid not," answered the Major. To Wendy he explained, "Though classic Thai dances are no longer restricted to the temples and palaces, contact between dancers and spectators is not encouraged."

"I'm taking Urai to the zoo tomorrow," said Paul. "I'll give Sumnieng your compliments."

"With a whole squadron of American daddies, you'll spoil that child rotten in spite of Sumnieng's careful training," chided Jane.

"I've offered to cut the number to one," said Paul.

Erick too? Wendy wondered, recalling his meeting with Sumnieng in Pattaya.

"She's come a long way since Jimmy's death, but until she really finds herself again, I'm afraid those decisions will have to wait," said the Major.

"Did the Thompsons ever come to their senses and accept her and Urai?" asked Erick so quietly only the Major and Wendy could hear.

"She has heard nothing more from them. They still refuse to acknowledge that Jimmy was married, that she even exists."

A clash of cymbals brought the final victory dance to a close and the house lights came on. Wendy and Erick said good night to the others. The streets were almost deserted as Erick turned the small car out of the Baan Thong parking lot.

The Bangkok which Wendy knew as a modern, bustling city by day had become a starlit Oriental wonderland by night; roofs curling upward with carved monkeys on the tips; slender, spired temples gleaming white and gold in the moonlight. Even the neon signs winked back an exotic alphabet that looked more like music than words. Or was it the companion beside her who produced the magic?

"I'm afraid I'll have to renege again on that tour," said Erick as they approached Wendy's hotel. "I have to fly Jane and some antitoxin up to Nongkai tomorrow. The Major feels we should press our advantage while the people are still excited about the boy and the helicopter. Jane will spend the day teaching their medicine men how to adminster the serum.''

"You mean medicine men like those with American Indian tribes?''

"These men are trained in ancient Chinese herbal medicine, but there is a good deal of superstition and ritual mixed in.''

"Does Jane speak Thai?'' Wendy asked.

"Well enough to give her demonstration in it,'' answered Erick, his voice reflecting respect for Jane's abilities. "But the hill tribes speak their own language. The Thai government will send an interpreter along. It's a joint project. I think she could do it in pantomime if she had to. It's a pretty sound international language if you are really trying to communicate.''

"Pantomime is a language I'm getting pretty good at,'' laughed Wendy.

As Erick kissed her good night, Wendy forced herself to keep her response light and casual. There were so many questions left unanswered. Who was the girl in Bangkok Migin had spoken of? Was it pert, efficient Jane who was a part of his work—who shared so much of Erick's life? Or was it the beautiful, talented Sumnieng, cherished by all of them? Wendy felt as if she had come in during the second act of a play without knowing what had gone before, or quite what was going on now. At least the emergency at Nongkai had been real enough. She hated to admit to herself that she had questioned it.

8

Wendy slept restlessly, then lingered over breakfast, finding it hard to concentrate on completing her Bangkok program for Personal World Tours. The morning mail had arrived by the time she finished. The clerk handed her a thin envelope bearing Marvin's return address. The short note read:

> Dear Wendy,
> Dr. Pridi has asked me to present our findings at the International Rice Research Conference at their head-quarters in Bangkok on the 15th. It is more good fortune than I had hoped for to have my two favorite projects in the same place. You will still be in Bangkok, won't you? I do want to make you understand how I feel about you.
>
> Love,
> Marvin

It seemed ironic that the man who couldn't manage to travel a hundred miles to marry her should follow her halfway around the world. But that wasn't really true; he was in fact coming to see Dr. Pridi, the same man whose visit had taken precedence over their wedding. And Marvin didn't have to take much trouble to get himself here; the laboratory's efficient secretary, Mrs. Jenkins, would have arranged for his passport, typed his notes, made his reservations—done everything but pack his clothes. That was where Wendy would have come in if they had been married. She wrinkled her upturned nose, but her anger and frustration were gone. She wasn't sure what feelings remained. You really should feel something about a man you were within hours of marrying, Wendy told herself.

She took her appointment calendar from her purse. She was forced to face the question she had been avoiding: when was she going on to Hong Kong? Was she staying in Bangkok for the snatches of time she could be with Erick? Was her work here really finished?

Avoiding an answer, she began drawing up charts of the itineraries for the various tours. They seemed quite complete. She could of course check on side trips to Chiengmai and the hill country. They sounded so fascinating when Erick and his friends talked about them. She could fly up for two days and still be back to ski on the weekend—and maybe go to Hong Kong Monday. She wasn't planning to leave Bangkok soon to avoid Marvin, she told herself.

There was a light tap on the door. It was Tahn. He raised his familiar red cap in greeting.

"Tahn, come in," she invited.

"I must make big hurry, or I will be late at the temple. I would like for you to come to my house on the night of the new moon—that is in five days, for party when I become Buddhist monk."

"I thought you were going to be a boatman," Wendy answered, surprised by the announcement.

"In three months I will be a boatman, but first I will be a monk. I am the oldest son, and to be a monk will gain much merit for my family."

"I'd love to come," said Wendy, not quite understanding, but eager to meet Tahn's family and friends and share such an occasion. "Is Erick coming?"

"Of course, he is my special friend."

"And Miss Jane?"

"Yes, she is good friend too." A quizzical look crossed Tahn's face. He turned abruptly and left, pausing for a familiar wave of the cap as he bounded out into the courtyard. Wendy felt an odd mixture of pleasure at having been invited by Tahn to such an important occasion, and doubt because she could not reconcile her view of him with this new role. However, the invitation did provide the answer to her immediate problem. She would stay in Bangkok another week and check on potential side trips.

The silvery crescent of the new moon rose slowly above the horizon as Wendy and Erick turned off the main highway onto the wagon road which led to Tahn's village. Wendy read the ancient promise of new beginnings in such a heavenly sign. As they approached the village, it was easy to identify Tahn's house. Colored lights were strung in the trees in front of the small house set on stilts. Sounds of music and laughter came from inside.

As Erick and Wendy climbed the stairs, Tahn greeted them with a deep *wai* in place of his usual wave and "hi!" "Miss Jane does not come?" he asked, disappointment in his voice.

"There was an emergency at the hospital," answered Erick. "She had to work late. She'll be here when she finishes."

Wendy and Erick were presented to Tahn's parents, grandparents, aunts, uncles, brothers, sisters, and other relatives and friends. Three large silk cushions had obviously been saved for the American guests. As soon as they were seated, beautiful girls in *pasin*, the colorful batik sarongs, served Wendy and Erick nuts and fruits, arranged on lacquer trays in a colorful mosaic of tempting delicacies.

"I am Tawee," said a schoolboy settling himself on the cushion beside Erick, which had been left vacant by Jane's absence. Wendy recognized the boy as the brother who had ridden on the handlebars of the group bicycle when Tahn went to Pattaya. The boy asked the English textbook questions he had learned in school about Erick's family and where he was from. Erick answered with as near textbook answers as possible. Only the reply that he was from Wisconsin seemed to bother the boy, who apparently believed from the tourists he had met that all Americans were from California, New York, or Texas. With the formalities completed, Tawee came to the most important matter. "While Tahn is a monk, can I be your lookout boy?" he asked.

"Can you shout 'lookout' very loud?" teased Erick.

"Lookout," the boy shouted so loud that the startled guests turned toward him, and then began to roar with laughter at his embarrassment.

"I'm sure that will do just fine," said Erick. "Can you meet me in Pattaya Saturday morning?"

"Yes, I can pedal a long way," said Tawee, now promoted to the seat of the bicycle as well as the job of lookout.

Tawee was replaced on the cushion beside Erick by three progressively younger boys testing their mastery of the required school English. Wendy was amazed at Erick's patience and good humor as he carefully repeated the answers.

The music they had heard when arriving began again, provided by gongs suspended in a round frame and a drum. The guests sang along with the music. Two very old ladies wearing bright *pasin* sat in a corner pounding betel nuts. Occasionally they puckered their scarlet, betel-stained lips and joined in an ancient chant.

Then it was time for a solo. The drummer passed the drum to the guest sitting next to him. The man sang a simple tune while he beat out the rhythm on the drum. The next man to receive the drum collaborated with his neighbor by playing a rapid beat resembling a jig, while the other man performed a monkey dance. The round of singing and dancing continued until the drum was passed to Erick. "Would you care to join me, or do you want to solo?" he asked Wendy with a touch of mischief.

"Wherever thou leadest," she responded.

Erick began a familiar rhythm and his rich baritone filled the room with "I Left My Heart in San Francisco." As Wendy joined in, she wondered if he sang of the lonely servicemen in the Orient whose last glimpse of the United States had been the Golden Gate, or whether he was expressing a more personal message.

"Bravo!" applauded Jane, who had entered as they were finishing.

The entertainment paused for a new round of introductions before Jane was seated beside Erick. While the traditional refreshments were still being served, a lovely, shy girl Wendy had noticed hovering in the background all evening moved quietly beside Jane and sat at her feet. "You are a nurse?" she asked with awe.

During the singing and dancing the young girls stayed on one side of the room making delicate paper flowers that would be presented at the temple the next day. Now several of them sat beside Jane to work and listen to her conversation with Tahn's sister, Kokay.

The entertainment resumed, first with community singing and then with more solos. When the drum completed the circle and came to Jane, she handed it to Erick. As he began the familiar beat of "When the Saints Come Marching In," Jane took a folded paper nurse's cap from her purse and pinned it on her head at a rakish angle, then slowly pulled out a long honeycomb tissue paper vaccination needle. She charged and pranced about the room feinting and jabbing her oversized needle at the guests, who clapped in time to the drum beat and shouted their approval. It was a routine she and Erick had obviously used before. Wendy could not deny feeling envious of the esteem with which the guests regarded the American nurse, and of the unspoken communication between Jane and Erick.

Group singing and dancing continued. "We have to drive back to Pattaya so we must go," Erick told Tahn. "Good luck."

"You will be back tomorrow?" Tahn asked anxiously.

"Oh, yes, I wouldn't miss the chance to see you speechless all that time," Erick teased his young friend.

"The silence before being presented at the temple gives the novice a chance to appear more wise than he really is, and not half so scared," answered Tahn in the stage whisper of a conspirator.

When they returned to Tahn's village the following morning, Wendy could scarcely believe that the serious young man with the shaved head and wearing white robes was the lively, fun-loving Tahn who had taught her to water-ski. Nine monks in traditional saffron robes chanted from a scroll of Buddhist writings. The ordination was scheduled for noon, when the monks at the *wat* would have finished their last meal of the day.

"Tahn would be pleased to ride in your car—our family does not have a car, or horse, or elephant," Tawee told Erick.

Erick ceremoniously opened the door and Tahn, holding a candle and a flower between his hands, slid into the front seat. Tawee seated himself beside Tahn to give directions, since Tahn was not allowed to speak. An awkward pause followed, which Jane broke by asking so all could hear, "Wendy, would you like to ride with me?"

With the protocol problem solved, Tahn's father, grandfather, and eldest uncle seated themselves in the back of Erick's car. In the meantime, Jane bowed to Tahn's mother, who did not speak English, and gestured toward her car. Tahn's grandmother was invited in a similar manner. Then, while Tahn's eldest aunt and the wife of his eldest uncle each smiled shyly in anticipation, Jane turned to Tahn's sister Kokay and said, "Why don't you ride with me, and we can talk more about being a nurse?"

Kokay lowered her eyes and nodded acceptance, the trace of a smile on her lips.

Wendy suspected that Jane had planned this gesture of equality from the time she had declined Erick's offer to ride with them from Pattaya to the village and instead drove her own car. It turned out to be a two-edged gesture—it had given the women of the family equal transportation with the men riding in Erick's car ahead of them; it had also given Jane's new-found protegée, Kokay, the prestige of the mature women of the family.

The cars were followed by *samlors* for the aunts—not the motorized *samlors* of Bangkok, but rickshaws pulled by a bicycle. The younger members of the family and some of the older ones rode bicycles, the boys piling up in every available combination. Tahn's younger brother had advanced from the spokes of the rear wheel of the family bicycle to the seat, since the older boys were riding in Erick's car. The rest of the family and friends walked behind the bicycles. The marching group was preceded by the drummer from the evening's festivities. He kept up a lively beat and the guests sang as the procession wound through the streets to the temple.

When they arrived at the temple, the procession was reversed. The drummer and a guest playing a flute led, followed by the marchers, the bicyclists, Tahn's immediate family, and finally Tahn himself, carried on Tawee's shoulders, while a younger brother held an umbrella over his head to shield him from the sun. They marched around the *wat* three times and entered.

Two rows of monks, seated facing each other, formed an aisle on the platform in front of the image of Buddha. As the procession entered, the men seated themselves on the floor on the right side of the temple, the women on the left. Tawee motioned for Erick, Jane, and Wendy to join him in the center of the room, seated so that he and Erick were on the right side of Wendy and Jane.

Tahn approached the abbot, who was sitting in front of the huge statue, and repeated a chant three times.

"He's speaking Pali, the ancient language, asking to be admitted to the brotherhood," Tawee whispered.

Wendy was embarrassed by the distraction, but other spectators also talked among themselves, perhaps because few of them understood Pali.

The abbot answered in a long chant. "He is being told the rules against killing, stealing, adultery, lying, and drinking alcohol," their self-appointed interpreter told them. "He is also told that monks may not eat after midday or wear any type of ornament."

Two monks gave Tahn his saffron robes and a large rice bowl, and went to help him change. When Tahn returned in his yellow robes, he was asked a set of ritual questions by his teacher, the abbot, and each monk in the room. To each question he gave the same ritual answers.

"They ask if he is human, and if he is an adult male," Tawee explained.

After more questions, answers, and instructions, Tahn announced the name in Pali by which he would be known, and the ordination was concluded. The paper flowers and other decorations were presented to the abbot for the temple. Tahn's friends gave him gifts of the few items a monk is allowed to possess: books of the Buddha's teachings, candles, soap, an umbrella. A slim, leather-bound volume of the *Jataka Tales* lay beside Tahn's rice bowl. When he spied it, Tahn picked it up, ran his fingers appreciatively over the embossed leather, and turned a broad smile toward Erick, who made a slight *wai* in return. Taking Wendy's hand, Erick led her out of the temple.

"Well, what do you think of our boy?" he asked.

"He seemed so serious, so capable. It was a side I wouldn't have suspected," she answered. "But I shudder at the thought of him having to beg for food in the streets, even if it is only for three months."

"The monks don't really beg. They collect the donations from the faithful each morning. These gifts of food are the lay person's opportunity to earn merit. The monk isn't allowed to thank the giver because that would reduce the merit. Instead, the donor thanks the monk for accepting the offering."

Resuming her place beside Erick in his car, Wendy thought that Tahn wasn't the only one who had shown a surprising new depth.

Leaving their hosts to finish the traditional celebration, Wendy and Erick drove back to Pattaya. The inviting cool of the breaking surf was the perfect answer to the heat of the afternoon. They romped and frolicked in the waves as if to wash away memories of their last visit to Pattaya, which had ended so abruptly.

The new moon was just rising over the horizon like a small silver sail when they headed back to Bangkok. An almost mystical serenity hung over the ancient land. The highway, so jammed with pedestrians, bicycles, carts, and buses during the day, was nearly deserted. Crickets competed with the sound of distant temple bells to provide evening vespers. With Erick's hand gently covering hers, Wendy felt completely at peace.

At a lookout point on the crest of a hill Erick stopped the car. Joining the sliver of a moon, the stars twinkled so brightly in the velvet sky that it seemed to Wendy they could reach up and touch them. In the broad valley below them, the twinkling lights were repeated. Those gliding down the inky outline of the river were the torches of night fishermen. Flickering lights outlining the river were lanterns in houses which rose on stilts along its banks. The scene seemed untouched by time.

Erick and Wendy watched it in silence, and then his arm around her shoulders gently turned her toward him and he kissed her. It was not the flaming, passionate kiss of the night of the full moon in Bali; it was a lingering kiss of tenderness and promise.

He raised his head and looked at her for a long moment, then he ran his fingers gently through the tumble of soft curls which framed her face. He kissed the tip of her perky nose and again, gently, her trembling lips. Desperately she longed to share her life with this man whose many changing moods captured her own.

9

Wendy closed her eyes and leaned back from the writing table. It had been a busy day—she always seemed to try to cram the days too full when Erick was flying. It can't be Erick, she told herself as the phone jolted her back into action, but the tingle in her fingers as she reached for it contradicted the logic of her thought.

"Hello?"

"Hello, Wendy, this is Marvin. I came a couple of days early so I could see you before the conference." His voice sounded a long way off although the connection was perfectly clear.

"Marvin, where are you?" Wendy answered, feeling like a schoolgirl who, after having failed to work out an assigned problem, was being called on to recite.

"At the Dusit Thani—our conference will be held here. Will you have dinner with me?"

Wendy was tempted to say that she had already eaten, but the hour was too early, and it was her habit to tackle a problem head-on. "Fine," she answered, hoping he hadn't heard the deep breath that preceded her decision to accept.

"Pick you up in half an hour," Marvin said, and hung up before she could change her mind.

As she replaced the receiver and stood staring down at it, reluctant to get ready for her date, Wendy smiled at the thought of Marvin ever being two days early for anything.

She glanced at herself in the mirror. The well-designed, beige linen dress she had just put on suited a quiet dinner alone but was hardly appropriate for a dinner date. She shrugged, and added a pale green Thai silk scarf at the V neckline. Did Marvin like for her to wear green to bring out the color of her eyes? She couldn't seem to remember.

"You're looking well," Marvin greeted her as she walked across the lobby to meet him.

"So are you," she answered. That was certainly an understatement, she thought. His shirt and tie were carefully coordinated with his expensively tailored suit. His dark hair was longer than when she had seen him last, styled in a continental manner. Gone was the scholarly look she used to tease him about; only the tip of his dark-rimmed glasses peaked from his breast pocket. His choices had obviously been made to impress a young lady, not a gathering of scientists. Must mean that I am the top priority project, at least for the moment, she concluded, smiling at the thought.

Encouraged by her smile, he continued. "I've made reservations at the Starlight Room; is that all right?"

Wendy would have preferred any other place to the one where she and Erick had gone on her first night in Bangkok, but she answered, "It's very nice."

Marvin asked the doorman to hail a taxi and directed the driver to the Dusit Thani. "You should hail the cab yourself and agree on the price with the driver before you get in," Wendy told him.

"I know, I've read that in the guide book, but I just can't," Marvin answered.

The cab took them to the porticoed carriage entrance below which the baby elephant stood in the center of a small group of children. Wendy ridiculously felt as if she had passed an old friend without saying hello.

They took the express elevator to the tower. Wendy was relieved when Marvin did not stop at the panorama window from which she had first become fascinated by Bangkok, but turned instead toward the dining room.

"I haven't congratulated you on your selection for the conference," Wendy said when they were seated.

"I was pleased to be asked," Marvin admitted. "We are making important progress in the Green Revolution, as they call it over here. Our new high-yield hybrid and those of some of the other researchers should increase the world's rice supply fifty percent in the next three years.''

Wendy again felt pride in the importance of Marvin's work and his dedication to it.

The waiter interrupted then, and Marvin ordered his usual steak well-done. At least that hasn't changed, Wendy thought. She compromised on the herbed roast chicken rather than the more exotic Thai dishes she and Erick would have ordered. She imagined that Erick and Jane would be guests tonight at a dinner in their honor somewhere in the hills near Nongkai.

"Have you visited any of the rice fields near Bangkok?" Marvin's voice brought her wandering thoughts back to their dinner.

"No, I've only seen them from the road. They do look good, though."

"Some of the best in the Orient. Would you like to visit them tomorrow, then we could do some sightseeing?"

Wendy hesitated, searching for an excuse.

"It's the only free time I'll have before the conference starts." His eyes pleaded for her to accept.

"I guess there's nothing I can't postpone," she admitted.

Encouraged by her acceptance, Marvin spent the rest of dinner giving her a detailed report on the progress of his work. On the way back to her hotel, his hand covered hers and pressed it gently. She started to withdraw it, but decided that would be childish when he was trying so hard to please her.

"See you at eight," he said at her door. "Good night." He pressed her hand again, turned, and left. Wendy was grateful that he had not tried to kiss her. Anger and the hurt had left her long ago, but so had whatever feelings she had mistaken for love.

Marvin was waiting for her when Wendy crossed the lobby a few minutes before eight the next morning. This is new, she thought, remembering all the times she had waited for him—including that last embarrassing wait.

"I'm so glad you decided to come," he greeted her.

They took a taxi to the International Rice Institute. A tour bus was parked in front of the building, and small groups of men and women of different nationalities gathered on the sidewalk. If Wendy had realized the visit to the rice fields was a tour of the delegates, she would not have accepted. Still, it was an opportunity to study the organization of professional interest tours. She sighed quietly and followed Marvin toward the others. The guide was just announcing the loading of the bus.

They visited three rice fields. At each one, a member of the Thai delegation explained the planting and cultivating techniques, varieties, and yield, and answered questions posed in several languages. Marvin and the other delegates diligently took notes. Wendy had to keep reminding herself how important increased rice yields were to the people of Asia, as she smiled politely and nodded to wives of other delegates. It was almost noon when they returned to Bangkok.

"Would you like to take a boat trip on the *klongs* to see the floating market?" Wendy asked Marvin as they finished their lunch at the cafeteria of the Rice Institute.

"You know what I like. Whatever you think would be interesting," answered

Marvin. In the old, familiar pattern Wendy found herself making arrangements which she hoped would suit him.

"After being with all those people this morning, let's take a boat by ourselves rather than join a tour," she suggested.

The beaming smile Marvin gave her at this suggestion made Wendy hope he hadn't misunderstood her reasons for selecting a boat by themselves. It was part of her personalized tour planning to always balance independent shopping and sightseeing against group tours.

The boatman took them across the swirling, muddy Chao Phya River to the Wat Arun, Temple of the Dawn. Wendy was as enchanted as she had been the first time she saw its towers glimmering like jewels, as the sunlight reflected off the walls made of broken table pottery set in flower patterns. The boatman tied the canopied motor launch to the temple dock, and the three of them climbed the gentle incline to the temple. The boatman lit a prayer stick before the huge, gilded image of Buddha, and pressed his palms together in silent prayer.

The smell of incense hung in the air, and Wendy found the atmosphere both peaceful and exotic. She glanced at Marvin, who was carefully examining the imposing figure, the offerings of food and flowers, the massive teakwood beams and supports against the whitewashed walls. Wendy thought Erick would have been fascinated by the people in the temple; Marvin found the temple itself more interesting. Marvin began to move toward the door, and the others followed him.

They paused on the dock to watch the colorful panorama passing on the river, one of Thailand's main avenues of commerce. A constant stream of small, flat-bottomed boats passed them, carrying fruits and vegetables to Bangkok—peanuts, coconuts, oranges, papayas, mangos, and bananas. Wendy had never seen so many bananas. Some of the boats had umbrellas or low, curved covers to shade the passengers from the tropical sun. The boats were steered from the rear with a long pole.

"Seems like another world, doesn't it?" said Wendy. The driver carefully steered the boat through the main channel so as not to disturb mothers bathing their children in the muddy water in front of their houses perched on stilts out over the water.

Marvin only nodded as he reached out and covered her hand with his. He seemed to be searching for something to say, or perhaps the right words to say it, when a small, flat-bottomed canoe pulled alongside their motor launch and a boy held out a tray of carved teakwood figures. Marvin waved him away impatiently.

"This isn't exactly the way I pictured a river cruise," complained Marvin.

"Does the way these people live bother you?" Wendy asked.

"It seems so unsanitary," he answered, and Wendy remembered the antiseptic sterility of the laboratory where Marvin worked. Yet the whole purpose of his experiments was to provide more food for people like these.

"You've been here more than two weeks," Marvin continued. "Do you really like it here?"

There seemed no way that Wendy could make Marvin understand about Sumnieng, Urai, Tahn and his family; or about wanting to communicate to the people on the tours she planned the feeling she had for Thailand and its people. At that moment she realized that she wanted to specialize in Thailand. Because of Erick? the little pixie voice inside her asked. She staunchly denied it to herself. There was something about these serene, smiling people and their ancient culture that struck a responsive chord in her. She only regretted that the country was no longer called Siam, a name which for her tied the present to the past.

"When are you coming home?" Marvin's impatient voice interrupted her thoughts.

He sounds like a father talking to a college student spending a summer vacation abroad, she thought. Marvin had never taken her work very seriously.

Apparently noting the flash of annoyance in her green eyes, he became contrite. "I guess I had no right to ask that. What I've really been trying to ask since the night I arrived is . . . can you forgive me?"

"That happened a long time ago."

"I think I sensed that when I saw you coming across the lobby to meet me, your eyes as soft as the silk scarf you were wearing."

Wendy remembered how precise and observant Marvin could be when he really devoted his attention to a project—or a girl.

"Then perhaps we can go back and start again, just as I do when I make a mistake or grow careless about my research projects?" he asked hopefully.

Wendy was startled that he had picked up her thoughts, comparing his approach to her with his approach to one of his scientific projects.

"I'm not sure it would be that easy," she answered.

"But I can try, starting as soon as the conference ends."

As if on signal, a small boat loaded with flowers pulled beside the launch, and Marvin turned to examine them.

"I'll take the best white orchid," he said, indicating a clump of small white dendrobiums.

For her wedding gown . . . Wendy's mind completed the familiar line from the song. She turned away as the memory of her wedding day caused a shiver to run through her, in spite of the heat of the summer day.

When the launch returned to the main Chao Phya River dock, she declined Marvin's invitation to dinner, saying, "It's been a long day." She had just begun to realize how long.

A cool evening breeze had sprung up by the time she reached her hotel. Her decision to choose Thailand as her special interest in the new tour program gave direction to her plans, which she felt had been drifting, and lifted her spirits as much as the change in the weather. After a light supper of colorful Thai dishes of native fruits and nuts, she returned to her room to review the information she had collected for tours in Thailand. She searched for ways to include more person-to-person contact with the Thai people.

The next day she went back to Timland, the park on the outskirts of Bangkok where Erick had taken her when she first arrived. She took more detailed notes about the representative work and culture of Thailand that was assembled there. The dancers were students from the Royal Dance Academy—young, graceful, and well-practiced in their roles, but lacking the polish of Sumnieng and her group. The Thai boxers were also young, and engaged each other with flying feet, fists, heads, their whole bodies. They fought with great gusto and good humor, but an occasional jolting blow would produce a burst of temper. Both boys and girls showed the same exuberance fighting with swords and bamboo poles. She was fascinated by women who wove delicate fabrics of Thai silk, and by men who painstakingly carved exquisite teakwood figures.

Best of all, she liked watching the elephants work, a throwback to her childhood enchantment with circus elephants, she told herself. These were not like the baby elephants of the Dusit Thani or the one on which she had ridden at Pattaya. They were huge working animals who felled, hauled, and floated teak logs in unquestioning obedience to the elephant boys who tended them.

The snakes in the serpentarium made her think of the work Jane and Erick were doing. The memory of swaying cobras remained with Wendy that evening as she waited for Erick's return from Nongkai. Her work, which had been going so well, bogged down. She tried to read some of the tales of the Ramayana to better understand Thai dancing and drama, but found herself unable to concentrate.

It was almost eleven o'clock when she gave up waiting for Erick's phone call and started preparing for bed. She heard the soft plop of the late edition of the English language newspaper outside her door—a courtesy which the hotel supplied its English-speaking guests.

Collecting the paper, she dropped it on her dressing table and picked up her hairbrush. As she vigorously brushed her thick tumble of soft brown curls, a routine for which she had found little time recently, she glanced at the headlines. Near the bottom of the front page she read:

PLANE WITH INJURED BOY MISSING

Chiengmai—A fourteen-year-old boy working in the teak forest . . . leg crushed by a falling tree . . . picked up by an American medical-evac helicopter from Bangkok . . .

The hairbrush stopped in mid-stroke, slipped from her limp fingers, and fell unnoticed to the floor as her mind screamed in stunned protest: Erick is missing!

10

Too numb to cry, Wendy stared back at her reflection in the dressing-table mirror with unseeing eyes. Her senses had ceased to function. She was roused from her stupor by a gentle tapping on her door. Like a person coming out of a trance, she went to answer it.

Dressed in the simple black skirt and white blouse of the peasants, Sumnieng stood with her eyes lowered in the manner of Oriental women. Her gleaming black hair was pulled into a coil at the nape of her slender neck. Simple and artless in dress and manner, she appeared to Wendy even more beautiful than she was in her glamorous dance costumes.

"Sumnieng! Come in. I'm sorry, I mean Mrs. Thompson."

"It's been a long time since anyone called me Mrs. Thompson. It is good to remember, but please call me Sumnieng. I have grown used to having just one

name professionally. It is an ancient custom in our country.'' Looking from
Wendy's drawn face to the newspaper on the dresser, she continued more slowly.
''I see you already have the bad news. I hoped to be here when you heard.''
She held out her hand to Wendy.

Sumnieng declined the chair Wendy offered in favor of the large floor cushion
on which she sat in the modest native fashion with her feet tucked under her.
Wendy plopped cross-legged on the other fat silk cushion. The vision of a
helicopter caught in her mind and caused a choking in her throat, which she
attempted to hide behind the routines of hospitality. ''Can I order you some tea
or a cool drink?'' she asked.

''Tea would only taste salty from our unshed tears as we wait,'' Sumnieng
answered. ''I have learned much about waiting and about being alone. That is
why I have come to share with you the wait for word of Erick.''

''How did you know about me?''

''In Pattaya I heard Erick telephone you from Paul's cottage after the Major
called them back to Bangkok. I should have had the courage to go see you
because I knew you were all alone in a strange place. But I did not know you
were in love with Erick until the night you came with him to see me dance.''

''You are very perceptive. When you are dancing you don't look like you are
aware of anything else in the world.''

''It is because I remember the joy of a woman's first love that I can read the
look in your eyes.''

Wendy started to protest, but she realized that Sumnieng was right. Erick was
the first man, the only man she had ever truly loved.

Following her memory, Sumnieng continued. ''My parents died when I was
a child, and Jimmy was my whole life, my whole family. When he was killed,
his parents in America would not accept his Thai wife, his unborn child. He
was afraid there would be problems, that was why he did not tell them about
me, about our marriage. He said when they met me everything would be all
right. He was going to take me to America to meet his parents when my papers
were ready. I was so alone, so lost when he died.'' Sumnieng's voice faltered.

Wendy could not look at the other girl lest she lose control of the tears she
was so desperately blinking back.

''Jimmy's friends became my family,'' Sumnieng began again more slowly.
''Tom and Mike, the Major, Jane, but most of all Erick, who had been Jimmy's
best friend. He did all of the things that the oldest brother does in a Thai family—
took care of the necessary arrangements, filled out all the papers. For the army
there are so many. And he talked to me about my baby, and about her being
very special because Jimmy and I had been so much in love. When Urai was
born, Erick and Jane took me to the hospital, stayed with me all the time.''

Engrossed as she was in Sumnieng's story, Wendy could not help note that,
as always, it had been Erick and Jane together.

After a pause, Sumnieng continued. ''The other women in the hospital room
could not understand. Each of these American officers would come to see me,
and make funny noises for Urai and talk about what a beautiful baby she was,
as if each one was her father. The sadness about Jimmy was always there, but
Urai would not be without family as I was when my parents died. I would be

able to keep her and raise her, and she would have her American daddies to spoil her. Jane was like an older sister to me.''

Wendy recalled Jane complaining about how the American daddies were spoiling Urai.

''Sometimes when they came, Jimmy's friends joked too much, and laughed too much, and tried too hard to make me smile. I knew they were troubled. First it was Tom when he and Migin were to be married. I knew he was thinking how it would be for her if something happened to him like it did to Jimmy. Finally he decided to leave the army, but I think he is happy with the resort and diving and his boats. He always loved boats and they were part of Migin's life as they were of his.''

''Did you meet Migin?'' Wendy asked.

''No. Tom showed me pictures of her, and talked so much about her I feel I know her.''

''I met Migin and Tom in Tahiti,'' said Wendy. ''They're wonderful people, and seemed very happy.''

''I'm glad,'' said Sumnieng. ''Was that where you met Erick?''

''Yes, at their resort,'' answered Wendy, remembering with longing the happy, carefree days she and Erick had spent at their island retreat.

''When Tom and Migin were married, Erick went to their wedding. Tom wanted him to leave the army and go into business with them, but Erick came back. Like Jimmy, Erick felt the work here was very important, helping the Thai government bring medical care and health programs to the remote villages.''

''Are you in love with Erick?'' Wendy finally blurted the question which had been nagging at her since the day she had been an unseen witness to their reunion in Pattaya.

''I have spoken English since I was a child in a mission school, but sometimes there are things which I find difficult to explain,'' answered Sumnieng. ''You say you love your parents, your family, but that you are in love with your husband, your lover. In Thai the words are different, it is not so confusing. I love Erick like the older brother whose place he has taken for me. I love the Major as the father he has tried to be, but I am not in love with them like Jimmy.''

''What about Paul?'' Wendy asked, recalling his avowed interest in marrying Sumnieng.

Sumnieng lowered her eyes and hesitated several minutes before answering. ''Paul is different. He was not a friend of Jimmy's. He did not come to Thailand when they did; he was Jimmy's replacement. But he says he does not want to take Jimmy's place with me. He says Jimmy and I were young lovers like the song in the play about the English woman Anna and our King when our country was still called Siam. Paul says that after so much sorrow and so much hard work and being alone, I have matured—that we would share a different kind of love.''

Wendy knew that for Sumnieng no one could ever replace her first love, and that for her too, no one could ever replace her love for Erick.

Like a person weighing both sides of a problem, Sumnieng continued, ''I do not know. Paul knows I could never marry anyone whose family would not accept me and Urai. His mother wrote me a beautiful letter. She said they have no daughter, and would be very happy to have me for one, and to have Urai for their grandchild. Her letter made me very happy. I carry it with me.'' Her hand went to her waistband where a small silk purse was fastened in Thai custom.

''I did not mean to ask personal questions about you and Paul,'' said Wendy.

''It is to share with you as a friend that I have come,'' answered Sumnieng, ''but it is you who have helped me see things more clearly. Perhaps you have helped me more than I have helped you.''

''You have given me what I needed,'' said Wendy. ''You have helped me understand what Erick and his friends are doing, how they feel about their work and about each other. Most of all, when I needed someone, I was not alone, even though speaking of these things brings back painful memories for you.''

''For a few bad minutes, this is true. Then I know it is different. Greedy, angry men with hate in their hearts shot down Jimmy's helicopter as he tried to rescue wounded men, and he was lost for nothing. Erick flew his helicopter into dangerous mountains to help an injured boy. It was something he chose to do because it was important to him. But we must not think that Erick is dead. Finding people lost at sea or in remote mountains is part of the American squadron's work here. When it is light, all the American planes and helicopters in Thailand will be looking for Erick, and all the villagers they have helped will be looking too.''

The mention of daylight made Wendy realize with a start how late it was. Time had begun to have signficance again. She turned to the other girl with concern.

''Sumnieng, it is late and you have been working. You must be very tired.''

''That is of no matter, but for Urai I must return. Even though she cannot tell time, if she awakens very late at night and I am not there, she becomes frightened. Perhaps it is because she senses that the housekeeper is worried. My house is very small, but will you come home with me so you will not be alone?''

''Thank you, no. This is where Erick expects me to be. If there is word of him, I should be here. I'll be all right now.''

''I think American women are very brave,'' said Sumnieng as she rose to leave.

Wendy put her arms around the tiny dancer in a warm embrace that seemed to both startle and please her. She was reminded again of the great inner strength of Thai women beneath their doll-like beauty.

As the door closed softly behind Sumnieng, Wendy crumpled onto the bed and the long pent-up tears came in a great flood—for Sumnieng, for herself, for all women whose men lead lives of constant danger.

11

Slowly the tears subsided, leaving Wendy feeling empty, emotionally exhausted. She sank into a deep, troubled sleep. Some time later she was jarred awake by the ringing of the phone. She catapulted out of bed, her whole being keyed to that sound. She snatched up the phone, saying ''hello!'' before the receiver had reached her ear.

''Good morning, this is Marvin,'' said the overly cheery voice.

Wendy steadied herself against the edge of the bed as a wave of disappointment swept over her. If there was a prize for bad timing, Marvin would certainly win it.

"Can you have breakfast with me? I have to see you." When she didn't answer, he continued, "It's awfully important."

If she was home, she would probably have cleaned her apartment or done some other routine job to keep busy, but with no such occupation, perhaps listening to Marvin would be some distraction from the endless waiting which stretched ahead of her.

"All right. Here in the hotel coffee shop in half an hour. I'm expecting an important phone call, and they can page me there."

As she hung up the phone, Wendy wondered if there was really any chance of her receiving a call.

A brisk shower washed away most of the external evidence of the painful hours she had spent. As she crossed to her dressing table, the newspaper headlines about the missing helicopter leaped out at her, receded, then blurred like a vision under water. She opened a drawer and dropped the paper into it, not wanting the maid to throw away even this painful reminder of Erick. She retrieved her hairbrush from the floor where it had fallen the night before, but unwilling to resume the interrupted brushing, ran a comb brikly through her hair. She dusted a light film of powder over her shiny nose and tear-puffed eyes, and reluctantly left to keep her appointment with Marvin.

He was already seated at a table sipping coffee when Wendy arrived. She ordered orange juice, toast, and coffee, wondering if she would be able to eat. She recalled Sumnieng's words about tea tasting salty with unshed tears.

"I have the most wonderful news," Marvin began excitedly as soon as the waitress left the table. "The laboratory cabled me that the directors were very pleased with the progress I am making here, and have voted to name our new hybrid rice 'Mortimer's variety' in my honor."

"That's marvelous," said Wendy, trying to sound enthusiastic. She knew it really was an honor to have the new rice named after him, particularly since the new variety could make an important addition to the food supply in Asia.

Marvin outlined in detail all the contacts he had made and the promotions he had planned for Mortimer rice. Wendy sipped her coffee and nibbled her toast in a dispirited, preoccupied way.

"I don't think you've heard a word I've said," he accused when, during a pause, she failed to give the approving response he expected.

On the contrary, he hasn't given a single thought to me, hasn't really looked at me or sensed that something is wrong, she realized. How could he be so insensitive, so unaware of her distress, so oblivious to anyone's needs and feelings but his own? How unlike Erick, who had been so sensitive, so completely in tune with her moods and feelings.

She could see now that it had been the same with their non-wedding. Marvin had not given any thought to the feelings, cost, or embarrassment of her family or her when he saw an opportunity for his own advancement. In the same self-centered way, his attitude toward the Thai people, who would grow his rice, was one of condescension and insensitivity.

"Oh, yes, I've heard every word you said about Mortimer rice. I'm sure you'll do great things with it," she replied dutifully.

Mollified, Marvin started to launch into more detail, when he was interrupted by the arrival of a bellboy.

"Telephone for you, Miss Devin. You can take it in the lobby," he told her in a low voice.

She jumped up so suddenly that her purse clattered to the floor, but fortunately the contents did not spill. She scooped it up, and, restraining the urge to run, walked rapidly across the dining room and lobby to the indicated phone.

"Hello, this is Wendy," she identified herself anxiously.

"Wendy, this is Jane Adams," said a hesitant, throaty voice. "Have you seen the paper about Erick and the boy?"

"Yes," answered Wendy so low it was hardly audible.

"The planes went out last night as soon as he failed to report, and the helicopters went out as soon as it was light this morning. I thought the waiting might be easier for you out here where the search is being directed and where the first reports will come in. I'll be in the Hospital Staff lounge behind the main desk. Would you like to join me?"

Wendy murmured her thanks, and dashed across the lobby and out the main entrance where a line of taxis waited. She climbed into the first one and directed the driver, "Baansum Long Service Hospital, and please hurry."

Wendy was grateful that she had found a driver who spoke English. The taxi crept through Bangkok's morning traffic with agonizing slowness—beyond the modern buildings to the colorful, cluttered shops and crowded apartment houses, across *klongs* with their boats and stilt-supported shanties, and finally through lush fields of rice.

Rice! Marvin! She had dashed out after the phone call, leaving him sitting in the dining room, awaiting her return. She laughed helplessly and felt a little better. Waiting in a coffee shop wasn't like waiting at the altar, but it helped to balance the scales a little bit.

As the taxi turned into the curving drive of Baansum Hospital, Wendy realized that in her mad dash to get here nothing had been said about price.

"How much do I owe you?" she asked, forcing a smile.

The driver looked at the worried, drawn face of his passenger, shrugged, and replied, "Twenty baht."

Knowing that this was considerably less than the best price she could have bargained for, Wendy ignored the non-tipping tradition of the Thais and added ten baht to the price named. She walked rapidly through the coldly antiseptic reception room of the American service hospital, hesitating at the reception desk. Several people were waiting for the attention of the busy corpsman, so she turned down the hall. The second door on the right bore the inscription "Staff Lounge No Admittance." She knocked and was relieved when Jane, looking tense and tired, opened the door.

Wendy's apprehension rose when she entered the room and found Paul huddled at the table, listlessly sipping a cup of coffee. He was wearing flight gear.

"Can I get you a cup of coffee?" he greeted.

"Yes, please," she answered knowing they were both postponing facing an unpleasant reality. "Have they learned anything about Erick?" she asked when he returned with a steaming mug of coffee.

"We lost radio contact last night right after he reported he was taking off with the boy," said Paul as if reciting an official report. "When he didn't arrive in the normal flying time and our radar monitor couldn't pick him up, it was too near dark for our choppers to fly to Chiengmai. Search and Rescue sent out jets, but they fly rather high and fast to spot anything on the ground. Our men have been searching the area since dawn."

Just then the Major came in.

"Any word?" asked Jane anxiously.

"Nothing yet. That's awfully rugged country. The helicopters are coming in to refuel." Turning to Paul he asked, "You going out this time?"

"I sure am."

"Search the bottoms of those valleys, but if you happen across any poppy fields, watch out for sniper fire."

"I know. If we happen to fly over a hidden opium field, they think we were sent to spy on them, and you never know what kind of arms those growers have."

Wendy drew in her breath sharply and the Major turned to look at her, as if he had been unaware there was an outsider present.

"Did they learn anything at all?" asked Jane doggedly.

She's in love with Erick too, thought Wendy, anguish and fear forcing her to face the depth of her own love for him.

"One of the copters carrying an interpreter landed on the logging camp air strip. They said Erick didn't seem to be having any trouble when he picked up the boy and took off, but we knew that from his radio contact. They're working on the north slope of the mountain so the helicopter would be out of sight as soon as it broke over the ridge. They have ground teams out searching. The boy belongs to an important family, so they're doing all they can, but there's heavy underbrush and it's hard going."

"I'll let you know if I spot anything," said Paul, moving rapidly to the door as a helicopter whirred overhead. The Major followed close behind, leaving the two girls staring anxiously after them.

Wendy looked at the trim, efficient nurse beside her and wondered how many people she had waited with while matters of life and death were decided. This time Wendy knew she shared the anxiety. Finally she voiced the thought that had haunted her since she had received Jane's call. "Was it like this when Jimmy Thompson went down?"

"We knew he'd been hit. He had radio contact and was able to give his position before he crashed. Erick and Tom were at the wreck within an hour," Jane answered, as if Wendy had almost read her thoughts.

"It must have been awful for them."

"Yes, I think that's when Tom decided to quit the squadron. He and Migin were engaged. You've met them?"

"I met them in Tahiti," Wendy answered. "They're delightful, and I loved their resort."

"I thought for a while Erick might join them. They wanted him to, but something brought him back to Bangkok."

Was Jane that something? Wendy wondered.

A helicopter sounded above them and the two girls moved to the window with one accord. As the helicopter reached the horizon, it was followed by five others across the sky like a string of awkward toys trailed by a child.

Time dragged slowly. "Have you been in Bangkok long?" Wendy asked when the waiting became unbearable.

"Almost five years. I was with the squadron when we first opened this Air-Evac operation. So were Erick, Tom, Jimmy Thompson, the Major, and Mike O'Connor."

"I met Mike in Bali. He's a real charmer," said Wendy.

"Yes, I almost married him three years ago," answered Jane matter-of-factly.

"What happened?" Wendy asked, regretting the words the moment they were out.

"When Jimmy was killed, Mike decided he couldn't ask a woman to share the hazards and uncertainties of this life. When his commitment was up, he went to Bali to start his own business. He said he would come back for me when he got it going. I didn't agree. When I marry I expect to share whatever risks my man's way of life involves him in, whether they are financial or personal."

Wendy thought with a pang how closely Jane and Erick worked together, sharing whatever danger or hardships their trips involved. Now she and Jane were sharing the endless waiting.

The Major came striding back into the room. "I think waiting is the hardest part," he said giving words to their thoughts. He was just finishing the cup of coffee Jane brought him when the phone rang. "Major Sims here," he answered. "Still nothing . . . an elephant you say—strange, but I guess there are lots of them up there. Tell the crews to keep looking."

His voice was strained as he turned to Jane. "They haven't found a thing—no sign of the helicopter or wreckage. Paul says there isn't a farm or a poppy field or anything else growing there except trees."

"What was that about an elephant?" Jane asked.

"Paul said the only living thing he saw was an elephant tramping around in a circle on a virtual rampage."

"There aren't any wild elephants up there," said Jane frowning. "Only those which have been brought in or raised there to help work the teak."

"That's right. One must have escaped from the logging camp."

"I didn't think the ones raised to work ever run away," said Wendy.

"They don't usually unless something happens to their mahout," replied the Major.

"Was the boy who was hurt an elephant boy?" asked Wendy.

"I don't know. Who handled the call, Jane?"

"The Emergency Room, I think. I'll get the record."

Jane returned in minutes and thrust the message in the Major's hands:

ELEPHANT PULLED TREE ON BOY—
CRUSHED LEG—REQUEST ASSISTANCE

"Sounds like an inexperienced elephant and an inexperienced boy. They might go together, but I'm not sure I see the connection," said the Major.

"Erick tells me that when a boy is given an elephant to raise, the elephant will follow the boy around like a big dog," Wendy said. "But you're right, I don't see how that could have anything to do with a helicopter. Guess I'm grasping at straws."

"We don't seem to have anything else to grasp at. Let's go over to the control room."

A young airman looked up from the radar scope on which he was concentrating and smiled appreciatively at his unexpected, attractive guests.

"Get me Captain Hess in the lead helicopter," barked the Major. In seconds Paul's voice was responding to the call. "Get back to where you saw the elephant. Go in as low as possible. Let me know if you see anything unusual at all," ordered the Major.

The airman indicated a bright blip on the radar screen, which suddenly reversed its direction and moved back along the path of the sweep. It stopped moving and Paul's voice came crackling back, tinged with excitement. "There's something there! It's back in the trees so I can't see what—might be another elephant—but something broke through the trees recently. There's no place to land, and I'm not sure I could get in anyway. That's one mad elephant."

"Just hover. I'll be right up with a pocketful of peanuts," answered the Major, the bounce returning to his voice. He turned to the excited spectators. "Anyone know where there's an experienced elephant handler?"

"There are some mahouts working their elephants at Timland. I saw them yesterday," answered Wendy.

The Major picked up the phone and dialed rapidly. "Get me an elephant trainer, one from the Chiengmai area . . . call Timland . . . call the Minister of Health if you have to, he owes me a favor . . . I don't care what it takes, just get one! Promise the trainer a ride in a helicopter. I'll pick him up on the parking lot at Timland with the admin chopper in fifteen minutes."

Wendy remembered Erick's remark about the Major being good at twisting arms.

Turning to Jane he said, "If anyone asks what you're doing up here, tell them you're monitoring my flight; I asked for a nurse and an assistant."

Wendy was grateful that the Major had included her in the anxious vigil.

Obviously a man more accustomed to action than to waiting, the Major strode out of the room, firing instructions to the sergeant who had fallen in step beside him.

"Does the Major fly his own helicopter?" Wendy asked.

"Not much anymore, but he's one of the best," said Jane, pride in her voice.

Wendy and Jane watched the small helicopter, the type used in police and traffic patrol, rise rapidly from the runway and head north. As it disappeared from sight, the airman monitoring the radar screen indicated a small, bright blip. It was visible only briefly and then disappeared.

"He's landing at Timland," explained the young man.

In a few minutes, the blip reappeared in the spot from which it had vanished. "It'll take him over an hour to get up there. You girls might as well relax."

Wendy watched the bright spots at the top of the radar screen, crossing and recrossing like bright shuttlecocks weaving an intricate pattern. Only one remained stationary. From the bottom of the screen a brighter image headed toward the others at a seeming snail's pace. Wendy finally walked away from the screen to a tower window facing north. Erick is up there somewhere, she thought. But will they find him? Is he alive—is he injured?

"Remember, they're trained to locate downed pilots. Rescue is part of what they're here for," said Jane, joining Wendy at the window.

"Suppose I started the Major off on a wild goose chase. Suppose there's no connection between the elephant and Erick's helicopter?" Wendy asked.

"Don't worry about that," answered Jane. "When they're on a search mission, they follow every lead, no matter how unlikely. They expect most of them to be blanks. A search party may follow dozens of useless leads before getting the one that pays off."

With agonizing slowness the small, bright spot from the bottom of the screen approached the stationary one at the top.

"Admin calling Search Leader . . . What's going on now?" The Major's voice crackling on the intercom broke the silence of the control tower.

"Search Leader . . . Craziest thing I ever saw," Paul replied. "The elephant looks like a rookie on patrol. He comes crashing out of the timber, walks to a corner of the clearing, raises his trunk as if trumpeting at me, then he turns and goes to the other corner and does the same thing, and finally goes back into the trees a couple of hundred feet from where he came out."

"I'm coming in range," said the Major. "Next time the elephant comes out, hover over him all along his path to keep him distracted. I'll drop in behind him and lower my passenger. It'll be a ladder descent, not a jump, so keep the elephant too occupied to turn around," directed the Major.

The girls watched as the smaller spot approached the larger one on the radar screen until they were barely discernible as two distinct objects.

"He's coming out," warned Paul.

"Wait until he raises his trunk, then lead him along his usual path at fairly close range . . . that's it. The mahout says he can handle him. When he gets the elephant under control, lower your evacuation team at the opposite end of the clearing. The trainer doesn't seem to be having any trouble with the elephant, but slip your people in as carefully as possible—don't rock the boat," directed the Major.

A maddening silence followed while Wendy and Jane could only watch the two bright specks on the radar as the other bright dots on the screen rapidly joined them like a convention of fireflies. Wendy's heart was pounding in her ears so loudly she wondered if Jane could hear it, but Jane's face remained immobile.

"Evac team reports it's the chopper!" shouted Paul. "Wings and rotor chewed up, but the fuselage appears to be intact."

"They're alive!" The crackling and static that punctuated that joyous shout indicated it came directly from the walkie-talkie carried by the evacuation team on the ground.

Jane and Wendy dissolved into tears simultaneously. The puzzled airman looked at them and shook his head dubiously.

"The corpsman has a splint on the boy's leg, and he's sedated. Erick's injured—jammed a leg on the rudder when they crashed." Paul resumed relaying details supplied from the ground.

"Bring them in," said the Major. "I'm going home. I'm almost out of gas in this baby buggy, and I see you have plenty of help—in fact, it looks like the squadron is holding an airborne convention."

"Let's go back to the hospital," said Jane. "It'll take them over an hour to get in. All you ever do in this outfit is wait." The relief in her voice denied the complaint in her words.

Wendy knew there would be a great deal this efficient nurse would do to prepare for the arrival of the two patients, not just wait. Wendy envied her having some activity to fill the remaining eternity of waiting.

Finally Wendy heard the whir of a helicopter and followed Jane out the emergency entrance to the landing pad. She expected to see the small administration helicopter the Major was flying, but instead it was a large army "flying banana" painted white with a red cross on its side. Portable steps were rolled in place almost before the giant blade ceased turning. Corpsmen with stretchers bounded up them. Wendy clenched her fists, fighting back the urge to go dashing up the stairs in search of Erick.

A few minutes later the corpsmen reappeared, carrying a boy who looked pathetically small on the big army stretcher. His right leg was strapped to a retaining board. As the sun struck his eyes, he raised a thin hand to shade them, and smiled broadly. Jane, who had been standing beside Wendy, moved quickly to the boy's side, took his hand, and began talking to him in Thai. For the second time that day, Wendy could feel the tears welling up in her eyes.

As she turned her face away, she saw Erick's blond head appear in the copter door. Wendy dashed to the stairs, but Erick was already swinging himself down them, supporting his weight on the handrails as he balanced on his right leg. Wendy stopped, holding her breath as she watched him, so ruggedly handsome in his flying gear.

When he reached the runway, he scooped her up with one arm while maintaining his balance with the other. He leaned his weight against her in the rush of their eager embrace. His lips crushed hers, releasing a flood of joy to replace the agony of fear-filled waiting. Her hands caressed his beloved face, clung convulsively around his neck, aware of nothing except the ecstasy of his return to her.

Slowly, reluctantly, he raised his head. As she opened her eyes, Wendy flushed with embarrassment to see Paul and the crew standing on the steps they were blocking. A corpsman had arrived with a wheelchair and was waiting to help Erick. The Major came striding around the tail of the copter. She had been so oblivious to everything but the sensation of Erick's nearness, that she hadn't even heard the other helicopter land.

"I know you have a thing about animals, but what's with you and that elephant?" the Major demanded of Erick with a twinkle in his eye.

"Sorry, I can't claim him," Erick said. "He belongs to Kau, the boy we brought in. Came crashing through the timber about daybreak. I was afraid he would tear apart what was left of the helicopter after that downdraft slammed us into the timber. Kau had the Thai corpsman carry him to the door, and shouted commands. The elephant began marching around like he was in a circus ring. The corpsman said he ordered the elephant to stand guard."

"Wendy figured it might be something like that from what you told her about those boys and their elephants,'' said the Major, giving her an approving look. ''How do you suppose the elephant ever found you?''

''I don't know. Kau told the elephant to stay when we first boarded the helicopter. Last I saw of him, he was standing by the runway in the logging camp with his trunk raised. You never know about an elephant—whether he heard or sensed something when we went down, or was just trying to follow us, crossing the ridge where the helicopter disappeared from his sight.'' Erick turned from the Major to Wendy, whose hand he was still holding. ''But it's good to know a woman who listens to what you say about elephants and other things, and remembers it,'' he finished by pressing her hand gently to his lips.

Jane came briskly out of the emergency door and crossed quickly to Erick. ''Welcome home, oh Lord of the Jungle,'' she teased. She threw her arms around his neck and gave him a big kiss which Erick returned with marked enthusiasm.

It was not the kiss, but the look of complete understanding which passed between them which sent Wendy's spirits crashing back to earth. It struck her with a pang that she was the one to meet Erick on his return because Jane had gone to tend the wounded boy—that it was Jane who had sensed her need to be there in the first place. How could she compete with someone like that, she thought, remembering the love she had sensed in Jane when Erick was missing.

''There's a man in X-ray who insists on seeing you,'' said Jane, taking command of the wheelchair.

12

It was almost eleven o'clock when Wendy awoke. She glanced at her travel alarm and stretched luxuriously. She hadn't slept that late since she left San Francisco. It felt great to be alive, to know that Erick was alive. She dressed carefully in the blue dress that was Erick's favorite.

Seated in the coffee shop, Wendy remembered how little she had eaten the previous day, and ordered the special brunch. The papaya was rich, mellow, and golden ripe; small hotcakes floated in coconut syrup; the jasmine tea was sweet and fragrant—today there were no salty unshed tears.

Even her timing was perfect. By the time she arrived at the hospital they would have finished serving lunch.

Waiting at the taxi stand was the cab that had taken her to the hospital the previous day.

''Baansum Hospital,'' she directed.

''You should bargain for the fare,'' chided the driver. ''When a passenger looks as happy as you do, sometimes I charge them double.''

Sensing the game the driver wished to play to relieve the boredom of his job, Wendy climbed out of the taxi and asked, ''How much to Baansum Hospital?''

''Forty baht,'' he replied.

''What do you think I am, a tourist who does not know Bangkok? Yesterday a driver took me there for twenty baht,'' she said with mock indignation.

''We have a fuel crisis, too,'' responded the driver. ''Yesterday an American lady paid me thirty baht.''

"Fair enough," answered Wendy climbing back into the cab. They both laughed.

"Your friend in the hospital is better?" the driver asked when the traffic had thinned and no longer required his complete attention.

"Much better, thank you."

"Did you read in the newspaper about the elephant boy in the American helicopter?" he asked.

"Yes, it is Captain Randall I am going to visit," she admitted, feeling herself flush with excitement.

"Then it is truly a day to be happy," said the driver, pulling up in front of the hospital.

Pardon me if I don't stand," quipped Erick as he lay with his left leg in massive bandages and firmly immobilized.

Wendy ran to the bed and threw her arms around him. He pulled her to him and pressed his lips hungrily to hers. She clung to him as if the fates that had brought him back might snatch him away again. Her happiness, the tingling excitement which flooded through her, left no doubt that he was the man for her. She shuddered to think that she might have lost him. Tears began to squeeze out of the corners of her tightly closed eyes and form beads under her long lashes.

"Hey, I'm back. I'm all right," he said, lightly kissing her eyelids, her cheeks, her lips.

Wendy opened her eyes, feeling the tips of her long lashes brush against his cheek. She looked at him, hoarding every detail of his face and voice in her memory, knowing that whatever happened she would always love this man.

Even as she watched, his eyes changed, clouded as if a curtain had been dropped over them. There would be no further communication between them, no loving message like the one he had flashed to Jane yesterday when she came to meet him. This memory, which she had been blocking out all day, rose to taunt her. Slowly Wendy pulled back from the man whose lips promised love to one girl, while his eyes promised love to another.

"I hear you're quite the hero now," she said, imitating Erick's usual light and playful mood.

"The way I hear it, I'm getting second billing to an elephant," he replied, matching her teasing. "But the unsung heroine is you—the one who listened, remembered, and used that smart little head to figure out what was going on," he said, entwining his fingers in hers and looking at her with admiration.

"I'm afraid one good idea wouldn't have been worth much without the Major and Jane to put it into action," she answered blushing.

"The Major is quite a character," agreed Erick. "Yesterday he was doing what he does best, getting everyone's cooperation, organizing and leading an emergency mission. And our girl Jane seems to always be on hand when we need her."

She even understood how I needed to feel a part of the search and brought me into it, thought Wendy miserably.

"You should have seen the squadron when we first came to Thailand," he continued, warming to his subject. "All of us competing for Jane's attention."

"I can imagine," said Wendy, letting bitterness at the thought of losing him again triumph over hèr feeling of gratitude to Jane.

"I believe you're jealous of Jane," he said in a tone that suggested a deeper meaning to the teasing. This annoyed Wendy even more. The conceit of him, she thought, so sure I'm one of his conquests that he can taunt me about being jealous. But she was honest enough to admit to herself that he was right.

A light tapping on the door cut short any reply. It took Wendy a moment to recognize the saffron-robed monk standing in the doorway as Tahn. He raised a hand to his shaved head as if removing the familiar red cap and waving it in the air. Erick pressed his hands together and made as much of a *wai* as was possible lying flat on his back with one foot raised in the air.

This is truly Peter Pan and one of the boys who never grew up, thought Wendy, the anger of a moment before dissolving in their contagious good humor.

"I told my teacher that my uncle was in the hospital in Bangkok, and I must go and see him," said Tahn. "He said: 'The American uncle who gave you the beautiful book of *Jataka Tales*?' He says it is the most beautiful book he ever saw. He arranged for my leave to come visit you."

"You bring sunshine to match the color of your robes," said Erick in a tone Wendy had never heard before. The fleeting glimpses of unsuspected depths in him never ceased to amaze her.

The moment passed as suddenly as it had come.

"The monks of your monastery should have grown fat with such a pirate as you to collect the food," teased Erick.

"I thought yesterday you were going to bring us an elephant," replied Tahn, giving as good as he received. "Your leg, is it broken?" he asked, shifting to a tone of concern.

"No, just the . . . muscles," replied Erick searching for a word Tahn would understand. "I'll be back skiing by the time you are. How is your family?"

"They are well. There is very good news for my sister Kokay. After you and Miss Jane came to our house for my party, my family agreed to let Kokay come to school in Bangkok to study to be a nurse. Miss Jane arranged that she does not have to pay the school because she is a very good student."

"Oh, a scholarship," Erick added.

More of Jane's quiet, efficient caring, Wendy thought. She was also aware of the manner in which Tahn had linked Jane and Erick together in speaking of their visit. Everyone seemed to feel that they belonged together. She was happy for the shy, lovely Kokay, whom she had first noticed sitting in the corner making paper flowers for the temple. She hardly seemed the equal of emergency rooms and sickbeds, but there was an unsuspected strength behind the delicate beauty of Thai women. Wendy remembered how Kokay had come shyly forward to speak English with her, and to examine in fascination the tiny charms on her bracelet. When Wendy complimented her on the lovely flowers she was making, Kokay had replied, "They are not so beautiful as the tiny gold flower on your arm."

As Tahn and Erick resumed their playful banter, Wendy removed the small golden forget-me-not from her bracelet. In spite of Marvin's poetic note, Wendy knew now that the only way the scales of love could be balanced was to put an equal amount on both sides. Neither forgiveness alone nor a lovely gold forget-me-not could make up for a lack of love. She handed the little charm to Tahn and said, "Please give this to Kokay and wish her success for me."

Tahn examined the workmanship appreciatively, wrapped the charm in a tissue from Erick's bedside, and tucked it carefully in a leather pouch hanging on his belt. "I fear I must start back now. It is a long walk to the place where I catch the bus for my village, and I must not be late for evening prayers."

"If you will hail a cab and bargain with the driver for me, we can ride downtown together," said Wendy, remembering how Tahn had been waiting for her at the airport when she arrived in Bangkok.

"It is proper that I should walk," replied Tahn, "but it is also proper that I should help a stranger in our land, so I will help you find your way with the taxi."

"I'm so glad you're all right," Wendy told Erick, squeezing his hand. Was she using Tahn's presence as an excuse not to betray her feelings by kissing Erick again? she wondered.

He lifted her hand lightly to his lips, and let her go. To Tahn he said, "Please give my best wishes to your family, and my thanks to your teacher for allowing you to visit your American uncle."

"Will you take more ski lessons when I return from the monastery?" asked Tahn in the taxi.

"I'm afraid not. I have to go to Hong Kong, then back to San Francisco," Wendy answered.

"You don't like Bangkok?"

"Oh, yes, I like Bangkok very much, but it is my job to find places other people would like to visit and arrange tours for them. I must get back to my job."

"I'll bet Erick could find a job for you in Bangkok," said Tahn.

Wendy wished that were true, but the fact that she had no part in the job Erick and Jane shared seemed to be one of the problems keeping them apart.

"There is a temple near the place where I catch my bus that I will show you. I think your tourists would like to see Wat Trimitr, temple of the gold Buddha," said Tahn.

"I thought most images of Buddha were gold."

"No, most Buddhas are other material covered with thin gold. The Buddha at Wat Trimitr is gold all the way through. He is only ten feet tall, but weighs more than five tons. He is in a small, new temple downtown. This Buddha is special to me because he came out of hiding the year I was born. The crane putting the Buddha in the new temple dropped him and chipped the plaster which was used to hide the gold from raiders long ago. With my people it is not a great temple because it is not old and known to their ancestors, but Americans like to go there. They like to think about all that gold."

Wendy laughed in spite of herself at Tahn's shrewd typecasting of both Thais and Americans.

She could not see the temple from the main street where the taxi stopped, but Tahn led her to an entrance down a narrow sidestreet. He had been right about an American's reaction to the statue, Wendy thought as she caught her breath at the deep glowing beauty of the figure, smaller than most, sitting in the modest temple whose principal decorations were light, airy woodcarvings.

When she had fully enjoyed the lovely jewel of a temple and its priceless treasures, Wendy returned her attention to the slightly built monk in saffron robes standing beside her. Completely absorbed in his prayers, he too revealed another, deeper part of himself.

Wendy's farewell to Tahn left her depressed. His alternating happy and serious moods had caused her to relax, to forget for a while the pain of the realization that Jane was the woman with whom Erick would share his life.

Reluctant to return to the loneliness of her room, she found a seat in a secluded corner of the lobby where she could observe and listen to the comments of tourists beginning to return from afternoon tours. In the past their reactions had been helpful in organizing her own plans.

Since the publicity given the rescue of Erick and the boy as well as the part played in it by the elephant and the mahout, Timland had become a popular destination. The remarks Wendy heard were enthusiastic about the Thai crafts, dance and martial arts performances, and particularly about the elephants at work.

When most of the tourists had gone on to their rooms, Wendy noticed a middle-aged couple waiting nervously on the other side of the lobby. There was something vaguely familiar about the tall, gray-haired, scholarly looking man who stood watching the entrance expectantly. She must have seen him in a tour group somewhere, Wendy decided, although she did not have the same feeling of recognition for the slightly plump, matronly woman standing beside him.

From somewhere behind her came the cry, "Daaaddy!" and like an animated doll Urai came flying across the lobby.

The man Wendy had been watching scooped Urai up and tossed her in the air as Erick had done. As he lowered the giggling, shrieking child, he turned to the woman beside him who was shyly holding out her arms. He gently handed Urai to his wife, who lovingly gathered the little girl to her.

Turning her head, Wendy saw Paul and Sumnieng going toward the older couple. Suddenly Wendy realized that the man she had been watching seemed familiar because he looked like an older version of Paul. Already the big man was closing the distance between himself and Sumnieng—holding out his arms to her. Sumnieng's apprehensive expression turned to mixed embarrassment and pleasure as he gave her a big bear hug.

As the trio turned to Paul's mother, she continued to cuddle Urai as if defying anyone to take the child from her. Sumnieng's graceful *wai* caused a startled, confused look to cross the older woman's face. She solved the dilemma by freeing one arm from around Urai and slipping it around Sumnieng's shoulders while she kissed her cheek.

A feeling of shared happiness surged through Wendy, who for the second time had been an unintentional spectator at a very emotional meeting in Sumnieng's life. As before, she sat very still, lest her presence become an intrusion on the happiness of the small group across the room.

13

Again Wendy slept fitfully, but this time it was Jane who cavorted through her dreams, prancing and jabbing with the giant paper vaccination needle as she had at Tahn's party. Waking slowly, Wendy giggled at the image which her dreams had produced. At least laughing at herself was a good sign, she thought as she slipped reluctantly out of bed, determined to do what she knew had to be done.

After breakfast she stopped at the Thai Airways reservation desk in the lobby and made her reservation for Hong Kong on the following morning's flight. She began making a list of the things she wanted to do on this, her last day in Bangkok. First she would go to the hospital and say good-bye to Erick. This time she would take a note from the comedians—or was it Erick himself whose philosophy was always leave them laughing. She would not let anyone worry about breaking her heart.

Wendy waited until almost ten o'clock, when Bangkok's morning traffic had thinned, before taking a cab to Baansum Long Service Hospital for the third consecutive day. When she paused to knock on Erick's partially open door, she was startled to see that he was gone.

"Has Captain Randall been moved?" Wendy asked the young Thai nurse busily filling out records behind the desk.

"Captain Randall left about an hour ago with Miss Jane."

"I didn't expect him to be released so soon."

"He was not released, just signed out on leave. When Miss Jane came in so happy and excited, they talk. Then she gets crutches for him and they go out."

"You said he signed out. When is he due back?" Wendy asked.

"Tonight at ten o'clock when the hospital closes."

Gone for the whole day! Wendy was stunned by this unexpected turn of events. She couldn't leave Bangkok without telling Erick good-bye. Never to see Erick again—the thought was unbearable. Slowly she realized that never seeing him again was exactly what she faced, with or without the brief parting she had planned. She could, of course, change her reservations for Hong Kong to the following day, but she wasn't sure she could bear to come back to the hospital again. She never had liked hospitals and was beginning to hate the place. Perhaps he wouldn't even be here tomorrow. She could hardly call and make an appointment. Wendy pictured Jane and Erick leaving together, laughing and joking in spite of his crutches.

As she thought of Jane, so poised, so in command of any situation, Wendy wondered what had happened to excite her so much that even the Thai nurse was aware of it. Had she and Erick resolved whatever differences had kept them apart? The relationship and the problem obviously went back long before Wendy had met Erick. She couldn't even claim the role of other woman in their triangle. Certainly there had been no animosity between them that fateful day when Erick was missing. Had the crisis resolved their problem? Had Erick asked Jane to marry him? Perhaps by not seeing Erick, she had been spared the role of cheerful loser—it was not a role she played very well.

The ride back to town was hot and oppressive. Only the long list of things which must be done on her last day in Bangkok kept her from retreating to the air-conditioned comfort of her room. First she must buy the deep-blue star sapphire pendant she had promised herself—that should raise her spirits if anything could.

The pendant was lovely. A perfect star twinkled brightly from the center of the brilliant blue stone—the color of Erick's eyes, she had told herself when she first saw it. Now she amended the comparison to the color of the lagoon in Mooréa—but that was no better. Would the stone forever remind her of Erick, she wondered as she hesitated over buying it. Did she want a reminder of the happy days they had spent together, or was it best just to try to forget? It was too soon to know; the hurt was too fresh.

Seeing her hesitation, the owner draped the pendant over his hand and held it closer for her to admire. "Notice how perfectly the star is centered," he said. "There is a legend that if one wears the stone of the magic star which is perfect and true, his love will also be true."

Wendy had heard of star-crossed lovers, but this was a new approach, a star to ward off such tragedy. The star in the jewel winked invitingly. It was as perfect a stone as she had seen, so, after proper negotiations over price, she bought it. She started to put the small box in her purse.

"Oh, no, miss, you must wear it so the star can reply to the pulse which beats in your throat." Apparently he believed his own legend, Wendy thought. She took the pendant out of the box and put it around her neck, carefully fastening the safety clasp. The merchant held up a mirror for her inspection. The sparkling blue sapphire looked lovely against her bronzed skin, and the star hung perfectly true. It would take more than a small silver star to bring back her true love, but she did feel better.

Next she must buy the piece of carved teakwood for her mother. She wanted to buy this directly from the artist who made it, so she took a taxi to Phra Mane Park. This was the first Saturday she had been free to attend the weekend market held there. She found herself among a noisy confusion of portable stalls covered by cloth awnings, which were erected each market day by farmers, craftsmen, and small merchants. The same array of fruit and vegetables she had seen at the floating market was offered here. She skirted gingerly around the most odorous of the fish stalls, and did not find the hanging poultry inviting either. The standard items of Thai dress—white shirts and blouses, dark trousers and long wrap skirts such as Sumnieng wore on her visit—were amply offered, as were underwear and shoes. Bolts of material were artfully draped to suggest their appearance in the finished product. She wished she could bring her mother some of the beautiful native plants. A wide variety of small, delicate orchids, some of which she had never seen before, were displayed against plants with bold, vivid tropical foliage. She knew that these plants were strictly forbidden by the plant quarantine, so she turned her attention to the cluster of stalls offering carved teakwood. She examined one beautifully carved piece after another, pausing to watch artists whose skilled hands were busy with new creations. Finally she found the figure of a Thai dancer for whose classically beautiful face Sumnieng might have been the model. It was a gift for her mother, but Wendy knew it would give her pleasure whenever she saw it.

She left the park on the side adjoining the Grand Palace, and paused for a moment to enjoy the panoramic view of brilliant, multi-tiered, red-and-gold roofs spiked with graceful spires above gleaming white walls. She would have liked to enjoy a last look at the exquisite Emerald Buddha, but time was growing short and the business part of her last day in Bangkok was not complete.

She took a taxi back to the modern, bustling, downtown section of the city and spent the balance of the afternoon at the office of Personal World Tour's Bangkok representative. She checked carefully the details of the tours she had been working on. There was so much to be worked out for the "People to People" program she planned to present to Mr. Vance. She hoped to arrange invitations for small groups to visit private homes, hobby and special interest groups, and small village functions. There would have to be cars instead of buses for transportation, and interpreters available where needed, although she had found English spoken quite widely in Thailand.

When the office closed at six, she walked to the corner where she noticed again the small spirit house in front of the Visitor's Bureau. Erick had said that people working for the tourist bureau brought offerings. Since tours of Thailand were to be her specialty, it seemed only fitting to do her part. She placed a lighted candle in the dollhouse-sized shrine.

There was just one item remaining on her list. She took a taxi to the Dusit Thani to leave a note for Marvin. She couldn't leave without a word, even though he deserved none. He was a person of such regular habit, she knew he would be at dinner and that there was no risk of running into him.

Wendy had a little trouble convincing the clerk to put her brief note in Marvin's box. Since Marvin was in the hotel, he couldn't understand why she didn't deliver the message in person. She finally persuaded him that Marvin would be in the dining room and that she didn't want to disturb him. The clerk looked at her dubiously, as if he doubted that such a pretty girl would be a disturbance or that anyone would be having dinner as early as six o'clock. The traditional dinner hour in Thailand, as in most warm countries, is much later. But he smiled slyly and put the note in the appropriate pigeon hole.

Wendy turned instinctively toward the express elevator to the observation tower but, remembering it adjoined the dining room, changed her mind. She just wasn't up to an encounter with Marvin.

Her mission accomplished, Wendy stopped on the steps to feed peanuts to the hotel's baby elephant—a thank-you for the help an elephant had given in finding Erick.

"Any friend of Tiny is a friend of mine," said a hopeful American voice behind her.

Wendy was in no mood to become involved with a lonely American looking for a friendly face from home. With a deliberately aloof look she turned to confront a tall, grinning, red-haired man.

"Mike O'Connor!"

"The little green-eyed leprechaun," he said, holding out a large hand which completely engulfed hers.

"What are you doing in Bangkok?"

"Trying to be a knight on a white horse, I guess—but as usual my timing was off."

"I seem to be having the same problem," she replied with more bitterness than she had intended.

"How about drowning our sorrows together?" When she seemed about to refuse, he hurried on. "Or dinner? I have a friend who dances at one of the Thai restaurants. I really would like to see her before I go back to Bali."

"Sumnieng?"

"Oh, you've met Sumnieng. How is she?"

"She is being acclaimed one of the most talented dancers in Bangkok—so beautiful, such a marvelous person," said Wendy with enthusiasm. "I would like to see her dance again before I leave, but we'd be lucky to get a table on such short notice."

"So you're leaving too. When?"

"Tomorrow morning."

"Then it's agreed, we will say our farewells to Bangkok tonight at the Baan Thong. Don't worry about the reservation—I have a friend."

"You sound like the Major."

"So you've met the whole crew—I should have known."

Changing the subject, Wendy asked, "Can we stop by the Siam so I can freshen up? It's been a long day."

"Meet me in the bar," he said when they arrived at her hotel, "and if you take longer than two drinks' time, you could be sorry you accepted the invitation."

Although she didn't take Mike's warning too seriously, Wendy showered and dressed quickly. Selecting the right clothes was no problem—a green dress for Mike, one with a full skirt for sitting on the floor cushions of the Baan Thong. She noted the contrast between the blue sapphire twinkling at her throat and the green dress, and replaced the pendant with carved jade beads.

When Wendy entered the cocktail lounge, Mike was staring morosely into a half-empty glass. "Better have one while I finish this," he said, patting the stool beside him.

Wendy ordered the banana liqueur that is a specialty of Thailand.

"I thought that was for after dinner," he teased, his mood brightening.

"Among the sophisticated I suppose it is, but it smells so good, tastes sweet and cool, and I like the way it shimmers crystal clear over ice. It'll drown sorrows as well as the whiskey you're drinking."

"An Irish lass who scorns good whiskey," replied Mike in a deep brogue.

"I still have one friend who hasn't forgotten me. We have our dinner reservations," he said as he tossed down the rest of the whiskey and waited for Wendy to finish sipping her drink.

Wendy felt memories begin to nag at her as they crossed the bridge and entered the Bann Thong restaurant where she had first met Jane, the Major, and Paul.

"So I'm not your one true love," complained Mike with mock injury when they had been seated at a front-row table and given their order. "You took off the sapphire with the perfect star," he explained in answer to Wendy's puzzled look.

Involuntarily her hand went to her throat and she blushed with confusion.

"I bought one like that for a girl once—lot of good it did," he complained. "Jane?"

He nodded miserably.

"Is she why you are here?"

Again he nodded. "When I heard on the radio that Erick was lost, I pictured

Jane all alone, feeling abandoned—a repeat of all the bad times after Jimmy was killed—so I caught the first flight for Bangkok. But there was a tropical storm and I didn't arrive until this morning.''

"And by that time Erick had been rescued," prompted Wendy.

"Not only that, but when I got to the hospital to see Jane, they told me she was gone for the day with one of her patients. I thought I'd drop in to see Erick and congratulate him, but he was gone too. That age-old story, best pal and best gal.'' He stopped abruptly as he saw the pained look on Wendy's face. ''Guess you don't need me adding my troubles to your own.''

"That's all right. I already knew the story. I was there too, must have just missed you," she said, grateful for the concern in his eyes. Even in his own misery he was not insensitive to her unhappiness.

"I must be out of my mind mooning about another girl when I'm having dinner with the prettiest colleen outside of the Emerald Isle.''

"Thanks, Mike, my ego needed that," said Wendy, her green eyes recapturing some of their usual sparkle.

"In romantic geometry, does that make us a square or a double triangle?'' he asked.

Wendy smiled. If misery loved company, she certainly had some of the best.

Attractively arranged Thai dishes began to arrive. The beautiful girls in silk sarongs dropped effortlessly to their knees in spite of the huge trays they carried, and arranged the dishes on the low teak table. Determined not to act like a schoolgirl who demonstrates her heartbreak by nibbling at her food, Wendy attacked the delicious morsels with enthusiasm.

"The condemned man ate a hearty meal," quipped Mike as he demolished a dish of crisped duck sprinkled with ground peanuts.

As they finished the last bite of fresh melon, the houselights dimmed and the entertainment began. As before, the polite applause which marked the end of the opening number swelled to an ovation as Sumnieng appeared. Wendy sat entranced as she watched the beautiful girl perform the ancient rituals.

"Whew! She is something," enthused Mike when the number was completed. "Guess I have spent my share of time watching temple dancers and others throughout the Orient, but I have never seen anyone to match her beauty and grace.

"Who is the Stagedoor Johnny at the front table? His eyes followed Sumnieng like he'd seen every performance she ever gave," said Mike when Sumnieng had concluded her final number and the applause had died down.

"You didn't know Paul Hess?" Wendy asked with surprise. "I guess he joined the squadron after you left. I think you are right about his seeing every performance when he's not flying. Those are his parents sitting with him, just arrived yesterday to meet Sumnieng. From what I saw, they may not let Paul come home if he doesn't bring Sumnieng and Urai with him.''

"I'm glad; she deserves some happiness," said Mike. "Have you seen Urai? She was the cutest baby I ever saw.''

"She is a perfect little doll, a miniature of her mother. She has an absolute hangup on American daddies. I guess she has had a full squadron of them.''

"Wish I could see her and Sumnieng too, but I have reservations on the early-morning flight to Bali. They haven't changed the rules about going backstage, have they?''

"Afraid not. Sounds like you are an old-timer here.''

"Jane and I used to . . .'' replied Mike but his voice trailed off.

"Sorry,'' said Wendy, the moments of forgetfulness shattered by their mutual memories.

"The perfect dramatic conclusion for our soap opera tragedy,'' said Mike when the rain began to come down in sheets as they waited under the covered portico for a taxi.

Streetlights became dim blurs through the deluge of water. In a matter of minutes the street was running full of water from curb to curb. All traffic stopped and people huddled under whatever shelter they could find. With almost unbearable longing, Wendy recalled the tropical storm on Mooréa when she and Erick had huddled in a cave behind a rock.

"Hey, are you cold?'' asked Mike, slipping a protective arm around her shoulders as he noticed her shiver. "It won't be this bad for long.''

Wendy wasn't sure whether he meant the rain or the misery that they shared.

14

Wendy quickly completed the packing which she had neglected for her dinner with Mike the previous evening. She made a final check of the room and picked up the twinkling star sapphire pendant from her dressing table, where she had laid it the night before. She started to put it in her purse but, realizing that wearing a valuable piece of jewelry is safer than carrying it in a purse or suitcase, she put it on. Glancing at her watch, she saw that there were still two hours before she needed to leave for the airport. The rain-washed freshness of the day looked so inviting from the window of her room that she decided to take a walk.

As she stepped out onto the lawn surrounding the hotel, the fresh morning air was filled with the chattering of monkeys and the calls of myna birds from the garden. "Erick says you will like the garden,'' Tahn had told her the day she arrived. She crossed the rain-swollen *klong* and entered the beckoning garden. The honey-colored monkeys, who considered it their duty to inspect all visitors, frolicked along the path in front of her. Brilliant pink and turquoise cockatoos darted from the trees. The delicate petals of night blooming cereuses were gently closing, their life cycle spent. A sweet, spicy fragrance filled the air, and she followed the scent to the base of a tall tree from whose branches spilled a cascade of purple orchids. She hadn't realized that orchids smelled so sweet in their native state. As she watched, a small black form scooted up the tree and broke off one of the blooms, placed it in his teeth like a pirate's dagger, and came scooting back down. The white-ruffed monkey Erick called the General presented the orchid to Wendy with all the solemnity of a prom date. Just as seriously, she rewarded him with the peanuts which had spilled into her purse from the bag she had given the baby elephant. "Thank you for the bon voyage,'' she told him, tucking the orchid in her hair Tahitian fashion.

In the tranquility of the classic Siamese garden, loneliness enveloped her again.

She felt as if her first day in Bangkok were a film running in reverse. She smiled crookedly as she imagined herself being pulled backward up the stairs of the plane and into her seat, then the plane flying backward to Tahiti—back to the bliss of those first carefree days with Erick. As she came around the corner by the lotus pond where he had been waiting that first day, the imaginary film broke; other lovers locked in embrace stood in their place. Was she destined always to be a spectator to someone else's love? Tears welling up in her eyes, she turned her head away, but in that instant she recognized that the trim blonde eagerly kissing the tall man who held her was Jane! But the man who held her close was not Erick—it was Mike! In confusion, Wendy tried to retreat behind a tall Croton, but in spite of Mike's preoccupation, he had seen her.

"You're too late, little leprechaun. I've already found the pot of gold at the end of the rainbow," he said with a wide grin spreading across his handsome Irish face.

"Wendy, we were looking for you," added Jane, flushed with happiness and looking less composed, less professional than Wendy had ever seen her.

"We couldn't let you go without letting you know how well the charm of a perfect sapphire star works, even if they are sometimes awfully slow," Mike continued.

"What happened?" Wendy asked, trying to conceal her surprise at the turn of events.

"We were all in the staff lounge talking about the plans for the Kau Clinic to be built on the timber reserve. Kau is the boy Erick rescued," explained Jane. "His father is a foreman with the teak company, and he and other company officials were so pleased with the rescue and the stories about the boy and his elephant that the company is establishing the clinic in Kau's honor. Erick and the Major were invited to the ceremonies at the Ministry of Health yesterday when the grant was presented. I'll be in charge of training the nurses," said Jane with professional pride.

"That's where everyone was yesterday when we went calling," added Mike with a wink.

"What a boost for your work," said Wendy, still wondering what it all had to do with reuniting Jane and Mike.

"While we were still talking about it," continued Jane, "Paul came in to tell us about his engagement to Sumnieng. He casually mentioned seeing you at the Baan Thong with a big red-headed American who Sumnieng said was an old friend of mine. I may not be Irish, but I really exploded." Jane looked searchingly from Wendy to Mike to be sure her earlier suspicions were not true. "I haven't worked such a miserable shift since I joined the army."

"Woman must work, and man must wait," said Mike, still grinning.

"You're going to stay here?" Wendy asked surprised.

"If I can find a razor and clean shirt big enough to fit me. My luggage is on its way back to Bali."

"Did you miss the plane?"

"I was in line to board when this wench come running up, threw her arms around me, and said, 'please don't go.' What could a frustrated knight in shining armor do?"

"He picked me up and carried me out of the terminal with all those people looking at us and smiling,'' said Jane, as embarrassed as a schoolgirl. ''To think it took me two years to find the three magic words 'please don't go.' ''

''You never seemed to need me before,'' said Mike. ''When I heard Erick was missing, I thought you might, so I came flying back to Bangkok, and almost blew it again in a fit of jealousy.'' He kept one arm around her protectively as he spoke.

''We're being married tomorrow. Can't you stay over for the wedding?'' asked Jane with a radiance which foretold what a beautiful bride she would be.

''I—I can't,'' stammered Wendy. ''I have a business appointment in Hong Kong I wouldn't be able to postpone,'' she lied, not too convincingly. The thought of a wedding no longer upset her, but Erick would be there and she just couldn't bear to watch him valiantly trying to hide the hurt of losing Jane to Mike. She wanted no part of holding the hand of a man on the rebound. She had learned her lesson about love based on less than total commitment.

With a look of quick understanding, Mike said, ''Then let us take you to the airport.''

''If you showed up there again with two women, that would really confuse things,'' said Wendy, trying desperately for a light touch. ''Thanks, but the airport limo is picking me up in ten minutes.'' She kissed Jane's cheek and held out her hand to Mike, who squeezed it gently. Then she turned and resolutely walked away. Her pace became more and more rapid as the shrubbery hid her from the happy lovers. As the contrast of her own hopeless love crushed in on her, she ran blindly up the path toward the *klong*.

''Not so fast, I'm flying on one wing,'' called the familiar voice she thought she might never hear again.

Flying wasn't a bad description, Wendy thought as she turned to see Erick coming toward her with surprising speed and agility, in spite of his crutches. She longed to rush into his arms and hold him in a close embrace that would need no crutches for support. They had not needed them in the magic moment when he limped down the steps of the rescue helicopter and caught her in his arms—but that was before she had seen the look that told her he was in love with Jane. In a torment of conflicting emotions, she waited.

His headlong rush toward her stopped just as hers had done, as if halted by an invisible barrier.

''What are you doing here?'' she asked in a reasonably steady voice.

''Playing hookey,'' he answered, pausing to catch his breath. ''When I called, the switchboard operator said you had checked out.''

''How did you know where to find me?''

''Chai was at the desk when I arrived. He said you hadn't left yet. I hoped you would come to the garden to say good-bye to the General and his friends on such a beautiful morning.'' He shifted his position awkwardly. ''I've got to get off these damn things.'' He dropped smoothly to a stone bench beneath a plumeria tree and, taking her hand gently, pulled her down beside him.

''You were right about the General, he picked this farewell gift,'' she said, indicating the orchid in her hair.

''I wondered who my new competition was. He is a very smart monkey— that's how he got to be General. But I can't let him get ahead of me,'' he said, pulling a small box from his pocket. The box contained a tiny gold elephant, its trunk raised as if trumpeting.

"Oh, Erick, he's beautiful!" she said, throwing her arms around his neck and kissing him lightly on the cheek.

He let the opportunity she offered pass. "A replacement for the forget-me-not you gave Kokay. Elephants are for remembering too."

"How could I forget the elephants of Thailand when one helped locate you?" She was struggling vainly to keep her voice light and not betray the deep longing she felt. "How did you know the flower I gave Kokay was a forget-me-not?"

"I noticed it when you added it to your charm bracelet the night afer we first met in Tahiti. I knew it meant someone back home was waiting for you—not an encouraging sign."

"You certainly are observant."

"I try not to miss a detail where you're concerned," he said. Then, watching her face closely, he asked, "Was it from the man who just came to Bangkok, Marvin Mortimer?"

She smiled inwardly, pleased that he had been concerned enough about his competition to find out the name. She nodded. "We were to have been married."

"It's over?"

"It was a mistake from the start." She handed the little gold elephant back to him and indicated the empty place on her bracelet. "Please put it on."

"I see it's not the only new remembrance," he said as he finished attaching the charm to her bracelet and raised his hand to touch the gleaming star of the pendant at her throat. "From Mike?" he asked.

"How did you know I've seen Mike?"

"I was in the hospital staff room when Paul came in to announce his engagement to Sumnieng, and mentioned seeing you at the Baan Thong with Mike. I don't think I have ever seen Jane so upset. I have seen her in all kinds of emergencies in the last five years, but it was the first time I have ever seen her cry."

"What did she do?"

"She was on duty last night. She straightened everything her hands touched, ran needless errands, paced, and moped. When she went off duty I persuaded her to call the Dusit Thani where he always stayed, but when she called, he had already left for the airport. I reminded her that check-in time is two hours ahead of departure on international flights. She must have made it. I just passed them on the path." He chuckled, a deep throaty sound that sent a shiver through her.

"I thought Jane was in love with you, she seemed so distressed when you were missing. She sure acted like a woman waiting for the man she loves."

"She was waiting to see if I could keep my promise again," he said quietly.

"Your promise?"

"When our first assignments were up after Jimmy Thompson was killed, each of us—Tom, Mike, and I—went off to work out the shock and pain in our own way, leaving the Major and Jane with a couple of raw replacements to carry on the work of the squadron. Paul was one of them. Jane was discouraged and desperate when I got back from Tom's wedding. I told her then that I agreed our work was more important than anything else in the world, and I could always be counted on to come back and help."

"So Jane *was* the girl in Bangkok Migin told me you came back for?"

"How you women do talk. Yes, it was Jane, but not for the reason Migin and Niki assumed. She was also why it was so important for me to get released from that assignment to the Pentagon. What a reunion it was. You should have seen the look of triumph Jane gave me when I made it back with the boy."

"I did. That's when I knew you were in love with her."

"In love with Jane? You mistook admiration and mutual interest for love. So did I at first. When we all came to Bangkok, I was one of the pack of Jane's eager suitors. Then I realized it was all a matter of ego, competing to be the choice of the most popular girl in the crowd. Once I realized that, I began to grow up—to find real meaning in my work and my relationships with people, both men and women, American and Thai. Sumnieng and Jimmy helped me learn the real meaning of love."

How could he be so understanding, so able to communicate with everyone but her, she wondered.

He turned his head away a moment, then continued. "I've known I was in love with you since that day on Mooréa when the flash flood almost snatched you away from me. When I came down the steps and found you waiting after the helicopter rescue, I hoped for one wild moment that I could have it both ways—do the work that is my way of life, and come home to find you waiting. But when I saw the tears in your beautiful green eyes at the hospital, I knew I couldn't risk bringing you sorrow, asking you to endure the waiting and anguish this life might bring you."

"What kind of china doll do you think I am?" she demanded, her green eyes blazing and the charms on her bracelet jangling as she pulled free of the arm encircling her. "Do you think Jane is the only woman with the courage and self-reliance to share a life of danger and uncertainty?"

"When your Irish temper explodes, you're like a kitten with its back arched," he said, stroking her hair and silencing her outburst with a kiss.

It would be so easy to return his kiss, to nestle in his arms and leave the big questions of their lives unsettled while he played the role of noble protector. Defying every instinct of her surging emotions, Wendy pulled away from his embrace, determined to face the issue.

"I've seen you stand up to whatever came your way, from tropic storms to missing helicopters, and that's part of the girl I love. But because I love you, I want to make you happy, not someday bring you sorrow." He pressed his lips to her throat at the V formed by the star-sapphire pendant.

Trembling with desire, she pressed his head to her and stroked his temples. Her pulse pounded in her throat beneath the pendant, just as the legend had foretold. But the legend had only promised that her love would be true, not that they would find happiness together. Mike had said: "Sometimes the magic works awfully slow," but she couldn't risk the waiting.

Softly she said, "Mike says being needed and wanted makes everything else unimportant. Jane found the magic formula for that."

Erick raised his head and looked at her for a long, searching moment. "I think her phrase was 'please don't go.' Stay in Thailand, Wendy, and marry me."

In answer she moved into his arms and raised her lips to his. He crushed her to him almost roughly and pressed his mouth to hers in the long, fulfilling kiss from which they had both held back too often. Waves of happiness spread through her, sweeping away all doubt and filling all the lonely corners of her heart.

The Wedding Journey

by Marjorie Eatock

1

Victoria Landam was afraid.

In all her twenty sheltered years she'd never known such fear—until now.

In a way it was her own fault. She had traveled for weeks just to get from England to this dreary, rain-rutted frontier in America. In all that time she had defiantly ignored what lay at her journey's end.

Now the journey was within hours of being over. She couldn't ignore much longer its final purpose: marrying Paul Winterthur. And she was so scared, she was sick.

With every creaking turn of its enormous wheels, the carriage was taking her nearer and nearer to a man she hardly remembered, a man whom she'd not even seen since 1819—four long years ago! It was taking her to a stranger's house— a stranger named Will Clark, who was arranging for her to marry Paul this night. This very night! It was taking her through the fast-sifting minutes of her girlhood's last hours as, alone in the swaying, stuffy interior, frightened beyond words, she was getting sick to her stomach again.

The first time she'd been ill was on that crowded, filthy boat waddling up the Mississippi. The delicate Landam stomach had rebelled against heavy, greasy food, tobacco spittle, the stench of human excrement, and dirty, swarming flies. But there the agony of being disgustingly sick in the midst of strangers had been eased by a kind traveling companion.

Here she had no Mrs. Devery. She'd been left behind in St. Louis just this morning. "Bring no attendants," Paul had written, and she hadn't. Paul expected to be obeyed—she remembered *that* well enough! But what she wouldn't have given for Mrs. Devery's gentle hands right now!

Swallowing desperately, she faced the inevitable alone. The rain-rutted trail and the nauseous swaying of the carriage was going to take its inexorable toll. And soon. For all her heavy traveling dress she was clammy, shaking. That too familiar taste of bitter gall was in her mouth. Panic-stricken, she thrust up a gloved fist and beat frantically on the trap.

It opened. The driver's friendly, stubbled face appeared.

"Yes, miss?"

"Please stop! I don't feel well!"

That was self-evident.

He said briefly, "Hang on!"

The trap banged shut. The carriage lurched as he whoaed mightily, sawing at the reins. They'd started down a rocky slope to a creek bed; the horses' feet were almost in the water of the ford before he brought them up short.

Victoria leaned weakly into a corner, more desperately concerned with keeping her breakfast in place than her possessions. Her old plaid cape slid to the floor, followed by her portmanteau (which popped open) and her furled parasol.

But Victoria was beyond all trivialities.

The carriage tilted as the driver scrambled with an audible grunt from his perch and opened the door. She gave no resistance as he lifted her out almost bodily and supported her heaving shoulders with rough, gentle hands. She was too occupied with depositing the remains of Tremont House's best upon the cold November earth.

"My goodness!" he was saying. "My goodness! Poor little lady! Cough 'er up, miss, all that stuff! You'll be better for it!"

Finally, gasping and weak, she leaned against a friendly cedar tree. He made a hurried trip to the creek, returned with his creased neck-scarf dripping with icy water. It felt heavenly on her cheeks and eyes. Ashamed, humiliated, she said in a shaking voice, "Oh, thank you! You are so kind. . . ."

"And you're about done up, miss. I thought you was a mite pale when I called for you this morning—such a little bit of a maid to have come that perishing long way! You're just tuckered. That's all."

His eyes were concerned; he was patting her shoulder with a fatherly paw. Once again, even in her distress, she was amazed at the free and easy directness of these people. Still, it was she that must remember: Lady Victoria, only daughter of the late Earl of Landam, was no more. It was just—Victoria Landam.

She managed a weak smile. "I'll be all right. Truly," she said in that clear, English voice he found so pleasant to hear.

He nodded. "Sure. We're but a few miles from home now. You just walk around a bit. Take your time. They won't even be looking down the road for another half hour."

Unsteadily she found her way to the edge of the creek, dipped the scarf again, and laved her clammy forehead. Crouching pained her stomach inside the tightly laced corselet. She shifted with the pain, went off balance, and collapsed in a heap like some enormous brown velvet mushroom.

There she stayed without the will to move.

Before her rose the unfriendly rocks and ledges of the creek bank. On its lip grew gray, scrubby brush. Beyond, a clump of cottonwood trees etched themselves stark and black against the cold, gun-metal sky. *Why don't I die right here,* she wondered blearily. *It would solve everything. I wouldn't have the humiliation of telling Paul how Papa bankrupted us, I wouldn't have to hide my love for his cousin Owen.*

And I could forget that I am a thief!

I must have been quite mad. But there the necklace lay, in a heap of jewels on Lady Fandley's dressing table—my mother's necklace. And Lady Fandley had so much; I, so little! After the sale there'd been nothing left as a dowry to take to Paul!

If she hadn't been so patronizing, if she hadn't slurred my darling father, I wouldn't have taken it. Lord Fandley had been kindness itself. . . .

But rationalizing was of no help now, and Victoria knew it. She'd slipped the necklace into her bosom, felt it burn her breasts as she'd said farewell to the new lord of Landam Hall, almost breaking down as Lord Fandley had secretly pressed a small roll of money into her hand.

She'd opened her mouth then to speak—willing to throw herself on the mercy of this understanding gentleman who'd been her father's friend. But then she'd caught the cruel, satisfied eyes of his wife—eyes that gloated at seeing a Landam brought so low. Her stupid pride had surged up. She'd departed without a word.

So here she was, in this chill wilderness, a bankrupt thief, sick and frightened, on her way to marry a stranger. Death would be a relief. . . .

Robert, the driver, observed his passenger shrewdly, also keeping an eye on the western sun, which shone thinly through a gap in stringy clouds. True, General Clark's place was only a few miles off, but he had no appetite for driving this trail after nightfall. The Sauks were friendly enough, yet there was always the chance of being waylaid by some thieving Winnebago—and they'd as soon lift a scalp as look at a fellow, particularly, he added to himself, if that fellow was driving a rig loaded with white man's gear, as he was.

The old carriage was fairly groaning with four big fancy trunks, a hide bandbox, and a bunch of other gewgaws—not including the portmanteau inside. *Did it take all that to get an English lady hitched?* Robert wondered. (He grinned. His Mirandy had come to him with an extra shift, some go-to-meeting shoes, and a cooking pot.) *Worse, the poor little thing was going to marry Paul Winterthur. What a downright, wasting shame! She seemed like a real nice lady despite her funny hat and fancy duds.*

The wheel horse snorted and shuffled his big feet. Robert murmured, "There, boy, there," soothingly. He walked around to the other side of the carriage, took a private swallow of brandy, and wiped his mouth with the back of his hand. He'd give the girl a bit longer. *White as a sheet she'd gone, with shaky pins. Let her get her breath back. No bigger'n a minute around the waist she was. Laced to hell. Helping her out of the carriage had been like taking holt of cast iron. . . .*

The cold creek water ran cleanly over shallow rocks, glinting and shining, no different from the brooks of home. The sound of its purling soothed Victoria, but she wouldn't allow herself to remember England. There was too much pain in looking back, seeing again the raw earth covering her beloved, spendthrift father's grave in Landam churchyard, recalling how many nights she'd cried in her sleep for Owen, whom she'd sent away forever. Retrospect was a luxury she could ill afford. She must look ahead—to the future. The future was all she had left.

Her head swam; the creek bank and the fringe of trees danced before her. She pressed cold hands to her temples, closed her eyes, tried to picture her future, tried to picture Paul.

Again, again, all she could see was Owen!

A tiny moan escaped her lips, a sound of desperation. *Oh, God, please,* she cried out silently, *I must not think of him! I dare not! Give me Paul's face! Let me not remember just a vague, handsome shadow! Give me substance! Give me the thrill I felt at the Hunt Ball when I wore the Landam sapphires and Paul danced with me for the first time! Give me the first time he came to call, the first time he kissed me! Surely a man's arms, the feel of his mouth—surely those are things not to be forgotten!*

They weren't forgotten. But they weren't Paul's arms, and it wasn't Paul's mouth. Paul had gone to America. It was Owen she remembered. Owen. . . .

And the danger to Victoria's future was part of her nightmare. Owen was here in this wilderness also.

Owen was with Paul, working for Paul, on Paul's estate. His own dissipations had thrown him on his cousin's bounty. "I have made him overseer," Paul had written.

> What else can I do? He seems to have wasted his entire inheritance, turning up here without a shilling in very ragged pockets. However the outdoor life seems to suit him very well, and to my relief I find he does not expect me to entertain him socially. The rougher class of locals thinks him a fine fellow. He also appears enamoured of a young female named Thalia—a good match, if he can swing it. All old Greenwood's holdings will descend on his only chick—and she does have a fine pair of flashing black eyes. . . .

A fine pair of crystal blue ones stared hopelessly at the flowing creek. So obviously Owen had forgotten.

If she could only forget it too! But it was burned on her memory—that autumn evening in England when they'd quarreled so bitterly.

She thought he'd understood she couldn't break her troth to Paul. He hadn't understood—not at all. When she refused again, he'd shouted awful things about his cousin, things she'd covered her ears so as not to hear. He'd called Paul a sadist, a misanthrope, a cold-blooded, fortune-seeking megalomaniac—terms she could hardly comprehend but felt obliged to protest. Her defense had enraged him further. He'd grabbed her shoulders in big hands that hurt, glared down at her, angrily asked if she'd never questioned why an exquisite coxcomb like Paul Winterthur had suddenly found it so necessary to run off to a raw, uncivilized country halfway around the world.

It was the shaking that did it. The chilling shaft of his query got lost in her outrage. She'd slapped him hard, with all her strength.

And he'd suddenly stepped away, dropped his arms, made a funny little bow, and stalked across the lawn out of sight.

She'd cried all night, knowing he would never come back. Not Owen.

Then next week her father had died unexpectedly, plunging his only child into the humiliation of shouldering his enormous gambling debts.

There had been no word from Owen. Dimly, through her grief and worry, she heard he'd also left the country. A few kind friends such as Lord Fandley had offered assistance ("and well they should," her nanny had grumbled indignantly, "seeing as how t'was them that had led her father into such disgrace!") but nothing could disguise the fact she was, in the end, totally indigent.

Paul's letter instructing that she come at once to marry him had been accepted with blind relief. She'd clung to its gift of renewed respectability as if letting go would let her drown. All fears, doubts, questions had been shoved numbly to the back of her mind.

Until now.

The day of reckoning was at hand. If, as her tearful nanny had said, weeping, she'd made an awful mistake, it was too late. Too late to wonder about the terrible things Owen had thrown at her about his cousin. (She must say that they were not true; she must believe in their spuriousness.) Too late to wonder whether, had Paul known of her penniless state, he would have still wanted to marry her. (But Paul *has* money; she must not think him so grasping.) Too late to wonder why, after four almost casual years, she had suddenly become so ardently important to him. Too late to wonder why she must come in the hard month of November, not the easier ones of spring. Too late for everything.

She was here; this was her wedding journey. Tonight, this very evening, in the midst of strangers, she would become the wife of a stranger, and later go with him to his new estate in the Illinois wilderness. Father was dead, Landam Hall was sold. She could never go back—not now, not branded a thief as she surely must be.

There was nothing to do but go forward—with her double burden of guilt, with her aching fears and nightmarish doubts—forward to Paul Winterthur.

So she'd best get on with it.

She arose awkwardly, bobbling, but got herself erect, smoothed down the heavy skirts, straightened the tall, swept-brimmed hat. The image in the clear pool of water aped her moves—a pale image with heavy, lavender-smudged blue eyes, and ash-fair hair that looped modestly over her ears and disappeared into the hat.

The water also showed another face, friendly, stubbled, and ruddy, looming up behind her.

Limp felt hat in hand, the driver said, "Best we get on, miss. The sun'll sink fast now. It's them bluffs yon side of the river. I thought you might like a drink."

He stooped, scooped water in a battered tin cup, and held it out.

Victoria murmured, "You're very kind," and drank sparingly. Icy water on an invalid stomach might not be too fine an idea. Yet her throat was tight and hot, and it did taste good although smacking inexplicably of brandy. Then, lifting her skirts, she went back to the dusty carriage. The horses stamped in their traces, looking at her impatiently.

"They smell Indian," Robert explained. "No, miss, don't be alarmed," because she'd audibly caught her breath. "Old Black Hawk, he's up river palavering Keo-Kuk, and most of the Sauk, they wouldn't do nothing to rattle General Clark. They think he's a mighty fine white man. But this here crossing is used a lot. There's usually a hunting camp in the cottonwoods yonder. Up we go!"

Gently he boosted her on to te merino-covered seat. "Kiver up warm, now," he went on. "It begins to get real chilly this late in the day." He restored the portmanteau and the plaid cape to their places and handed up her scattered possessions. The genteel, furled parasol was touched with an almost reverent hand.

"My mam had one o' them," he said. "Back in Kaintuck. No, no. T'warn't neither. T'was here. Pa traded a plew of beaver for it at LaClede's Landing. Mam was fair as a lily—like you, miss. It was her pure joy and treasure. We buried it with her the spring she died of the milk-sick. All set? The trail'll smooth out considerable on the other side."

He closed the door, shutting her into the dim interior. The carriage groaned as he mounted. He clucked to the team. The swaying jolt began again as the team splish-splashed through the creek and up the rough bank. True to his words, however, the bouncing then seemed to ease.

Victoria pulled her old plaid cape around her and huddled into a dark corner, eyes shut. Rid of its greasy burden, her stomach felt better. She'd walked fairly strongly back to the carriage. But her heart was beating like a trip-hammer, going *thud-thud-thud* against the painful laces.

It couldn't be far now.

One journey would end, and another begin. *Oh, God. I am so afraid. . . .*

Must we marry tonight? she thought. If she could have only one good sleep, she argued (knowing full well she was only dodging the primal reality of Paul Winterthur's bed), one short rest in single comfort with a light omelet in her poor stomach and perhaps a little wine.

Then she could cope. She knew she could. She could forget the stink of that packet boat, with its coarse, roistering, foul-mouthed rivermen, drinking and shouting and making love to their dirty slatterns right outside her airless berth. She could wipe out the sight of the beaten black men, half naked, manacled over festering sores, chained together, shuffling along the St. Louis wharves like driven cattle. She could forget the rough-clad traders in strange fur hats, spitting and laughing. She could remember only the tall, feathered Indians, wound in bright, dirty blankets, knee-deep in bundles of half-scraped pelt. . . .

Suddenly, unbidden, another memory came back. There had been a girl on the wharf, then later in the lobby of Tremont House, a girl with gypsy-black eyes who had stared insolently at her tall hat, her tired face—a girl who had laughed when the hat had proved too tall for the Tremont portal and got knocked askew.

Weary as she'd been, the laughter had stuck in Victoria's craw; no woman enjoys being laughed at. The staring had been impudent enough. The girl had some way managed to infer that Victoria was a spectacle, a monkey out of a cage. When she'd turned up again, at the hotel, to resume her staring, Victoria had been hard put to preserve her ladylike demeanor. Thank God, in this enormous country, they'd never need to meet anymore!

The tight lacing was actively hurting her now. Victoria put her bare hands to the taut buttons of her traveling jacket, thought unhappily, *Tomorrow I'll have to let out one eyelet. Perhaps that will help.* She could almost count every jewel in the necklace as it cut into her tender midriff.

Then an appalling thought made all others pale: *What if tomorrow there's no maid? I can't lace myself. Who will do it?*

The answer was as frightening: Paul would be her husband. Paul. . . .

Red flooded her white face; she covered it with cold fingers. In courtship Paul had contented himself with light kisses on the nape of her neck, her fingers. She had been contented too, happy just to be the chosen of the London season's most coveted catch. Only once had she looked into his cool eyes and found them hot, seen the leashed tiger looking back. It had frightened her then, but the unleashing seemed so remote.

Now it was not and she was ill with the thought of it.

Through the dim, dusty window the land rocked by inexorably, gray and brown and sere. They were trotting briskly now, crossing an open stretch of prairie. The bottoms, Paul had called them, with enormous bluffs looming in the west, blue humps against the low sun. Suddenly the huge wheels echoed on masonry. Leaning forward, she had a brief glimpse of a stone bridge and buildings ahead. Then the pain of stricture made her gasp and drop back.

Her hands made futile tidying gestures, straightening the cravat of her jacket, settling the swept-brimmed hat with its grouse feathers. Thank God she hadn't cried. But there'd been no tears. They were shed long ago.

What was she going to say? The truth: *Paul, please, I'm so frightened, I'm ill—give me some time! You're a stranger now, and I'm terrified! So many things have happened, so many things gone wrong. . . .*

Yet she must not embarrass him before his friends. She knew that very well. Paul could encompass almost anything but affront to his pride.

No matter now; it was too late. They'd arrived.

Suddenly, clearly, even as the carriage rocked to a stop and she heard the driver whoaing, saying cheerfully, "Evenin', General. One cargo and lady, delivered safe!"—even then she saw her father before her in her mind, pictured his handsome, raddled face, his long fingers sweeping the whole enormous pile of chips to the center of the gaming table. "With my shield, or on it, gentlemen!" he'd say.

And that was what she must remember: With her shield, or on it!

She took a deep breath, steadied her shaking lips, reached into her bag, and donned another pair of gloves, hurriedly smoothing each kid finger. "Ladies," her Scottish nurse had drummed into her, "do not offer naked hands. 'Tis not decent."

The door opened.

Silhouetted against the setting sun was such an elegant figure that her heart stopped—dead.

Then the man spoke. He had a warm, pleasant voice. He was not Paul.

Her heart beat again.

"Welcome, Lady Victoria," he was saying, reaching out, steadying her as she descended. "I'm Will Clark. This is my wife, Harriet. Our house is yours."

"My dear, we are so glad to have you." Harriet Clark was pleasant also, her eyes curious but her handclasp warm. "Do come along. The men will get your things, and I know you are tired to death! Such a tedious journey."

Beyond the carriage block the lawn stretched upward, rough beneath Victoria's feet but filled with statuary—until one moved, and she realized the statues were very real and all of them Indian in various stages of comfort, some lounging, some standing. There was an air of smoke, of cook fires, encircling the large, brick Federal house and on the western side the tall, forked tops of lodge poles pierced the haze.

Madam Clark saw her discomfiture, squeezed her arm encouragingly. "You'll get used to them," she said, almost laughing. "It's a way of life. This is Dragging Canoe's village. They stopped to see my husband; he's Director of Indians, you know. They'll wander on tomorrow. They want to keep ahead of the snow."

Her arm about Victoria's shoulders, she guided her up wide stone steps into a lamplit hall. A thin, quick black woman in dark linsey divested her of her plaid cape. Through an arch, polished furniture reflected tongues of flame from a leaping fire. A number of people were sitting about comfortably. Conversation ceased, heads turned as they entered, and Victoria saw blurred faces, strange faces, but smiling.

None of the faces belonged to Paul.

Her tongue seemed stuck to the roof of her mouth. With difficulty she made it work. Her heart beating as fast as a frantic bird's, she asked, "Paul?"

"Not here just yet. Are you all right, my dear?"

Victoria had grabbed at the back of a chair. Now she stood still, holding herself steady, trying to firm her clear voice. "Yes. Yes, quite. Thank you. It has been—" and she was parroting her hostess —"such a tedious journey." But the shaking was not what Harriet Clark thought, not disappointment. In anguish Victoria recognized it for what it really was: relief. A reprieve.

Madam Clark was saying, "We do expect them shortly. It's a ten-day trip at best—and the weather upriver has been very bad—winds, rain, ice storms. Trees snapped in the cold like straws, our traders tell us. The Indians predict a hard winter. 'Big snow,' they say. If they know. Will says they do. I know Dragging Canoe has never been through here so early before." She was just making talk while her kind eyes assessed the pale-faced, frail-looking young woman before her. *God help us,* she thought to herself. *She'll never last. I'd like to wring that man's neck!* Aloud she said, "But don't worry. If Paul wants to come, he will. He generally does what he wants. He is," she added quietly (even a little acidly) "a very—positive young man. As I'm sure you know."

"Yes," said Victoria, and tried to smile. Warmth was flowing into her body again—warmth because Paul was not there. "You're so kind to take me in."

"Nonsense, it's our pleasure. In this country, my dear, we all help one another or we don't survive. You needn't meet our friends now; there's plenty of time. Let Nancy take you upstairs to your room. I had a fire built this morning. I hope you'll be comfortable. Do try to get a little rest before the ceremony."

The simple word *ceremony* froze Victoria again. Numbly she said, "Thank you."

Nancy was the black servant, with sharp eyes beneath a neatly tied head cloth. She murmured, "This way, miss," in a soft, slurring voice. Victoria followed her through the arch into the large drawing room, blindly answering the various bows and curtsies as she went. The walnut staircase was polished, and was bent out of sight on the first landing. She welcomed the dim hush of the upper hall although the carpet was rag and the plaster merely whitewashed.

Nancy opened a door and stood aside. "In here, miss."

There was a warm fire and Victoria went to it like a homing pigeon. The servant folded her plaid on the long, comfortable seat of the settle that faced the fire, then showed her the humbler amenities—the commode, the wash basin, the bathing screen. Victoria was hardly listening but Nancy was not affronted. She realized this fragile-looking young guest was ready to drop with weariness. Saying gently, "Here, miss," she guided her to the settle, made her sit, put up her feet, and plumped the pillow at her back.

"Could I bring you up a little hot something?"

Victoria said, "Oh, thank you. I would be so grateful."

The door closed behind the servant. Victoria stared at the flames. Desperately she thought, *I must get hold of myself! I must! I* chose *to come here! I must meet the consequences!*

Father's death, the loss of my fortune, the miserable journey—I've allowed those things to put everything else askew, out of proportion. I've lost my perspective!

Paul is no ogre! He has honorably asked me to marry him! We've both changed somewhat, of course. Four years is a long time. But I was enchanted with him in England; why am I afraid of him now?

The answer came sadly: *Because in England I was a child, dazzled with his attentions.*

And I had not yet met Owen.

(Owen, whose enormous frame and bright, Irish grin had filled the doorway at a friend's fashionable assembly . . . Owen, just back from the Continental and newly mustered out of his regiment, pockets full of coin and time on his hands . . . Owen, who hadn't known she was betrothed, and no one else saw fit nor reason to mention it. . . . Until too late. Too late.)

Memories both painful and dangerous came rushing back. Grimly Victoria realized, *I cannot do this, I cannot allow myself to remember!*

She started to rise. Finding herself light-headed, the room spinning, she sat down again. All right. She'd sit just a moment longer, just until Nancy came back. She would make her treacherous mind a blank. A total blank.

It was such a relief not to be jolting about. . . .

But she couldn't sit. She couldn't. She stood up again, more steadily this time, plucked the pins from her hat, and tossed it, plumes streaming, on the mountainous posterbed.

Were all the servants black? How did one deal with black servants? She probably should ask. Paul might well have black servants for her.

Was Nancy a slave? Illinois was a free state, but some people did have slaves with them. Did Paul?

If he does, she decided innocently, *I'll ask him not to.* Nanny had always said if you paid a good wage, you'd get good help. So if she offered enough money and ran his household smoothly, Paul surely wouldn't mind not having slaves. . . .

She freed herself of the tight jacket, loosed her cravat, and unbuttoned the top of her waist down to the white lace of her camisole. How lovely to be alone— totally alone—in a large, clean, quiet room!

The hat had crushed the soft mass of her hair. She undid the long pins, let it tumble down, shaking her head like a filly tossing her mane. Madam Clark, she recalled, had had her hair done up very simply in a sort of provincial knot. She could probably manage that if it was the mode. It was a new country; she must do what they did. Paul must not be ashamed of his wife.

Everything she did, from this day on, would be for Paul, she promised herself. England was behind; Paul was her future.

She shook the ashen hair back, straightened her shoulders resolutely. Feeling clear-headed at last, she told herself, *One step at a time. That's how anything may be got through. One step at a time. My next step is to have Nancy unlace me so I can get into my dressing sacque.*

There was a knock at the door.

Nancy, she thought. She called, "Come in."

The door opened.

It was not Nancy.
It was Owen.

2

He stood in the open doorway almost blocking it shut, the same Owen Verinder, yet not the same. The dandy Owen she knew would never have worn such scuffed boots, nor the huge travel-stained capote belted about his large waist—yet the eyes were Owen's—granite-gray and steadily cold.

She said, "Oh," grasping like a schoolgirl at the gaping top of her waist. But he seemed not even to notice. All he said, in a tired, flat voice, was "So you did come."

Buttoning was futile. The gesture would only draw attention where she wanted none drawn. She dropped her hands, answered as flatly, "Of course. Paul needs me."

"I'll say he does." But there was a strange sound to the words—not derisive, not mocking—just strange. "Four years. Four long years." His eyes had not left her face. "You're different."

She turned away, twisting the long tail of hair up into a loose knot, skewering it with a pin, pushing down the sleeves of her waist. Over her shoulder she said, "I'm tired."

"No. It's more than that."

He moved at last, brushing by her, making the high settle creak as he sat on it, extending his boots to the fire. They were soaking wet. "*I'm* tired. Ten days traveling. Ten days through sleet and ice. Brush camps. No niceties. Are you sure you want to hack it, Victoria?"

He was prodding her, digging—as though it hadn't been four years, as though their own grievous parting had been yesterday. Angrily she said, "It's not your affair."

He snorted. "Little do you know!"

That strange tone was in his voice again. Suddenly she stiffened. "You've told Paul about—about us."

"Vick, Vick! How can you say that! Gentlemen do not kiss and tell!" Then the sneer turned grim. "Of course that was part of the problem, wasn't it? Owen Verinder, third son, was hardly gentleman enough for Lady Victoria—not when Winterthur, Earl of Clattham, was to be had for the taking."

"Owen, you know that isn't true!"

He heaved off one enormous boot, poured water from it on the fire, listened to the hiss. His voice dead again, he answered, "I know it doesn't matter. Not now."

She took a deep breath, put her hands to the hurt on her midriff, commanded her own voice to be equally quiet.

"You're right. Where's Paul?"

"Not coming."

"Not—" The words pulled the floor from beneath her feet. She grabbed at the back of the settle to keep from falling. Owen never even looked around; he was occupied with removing the second boot.

"Paul broke his leg. Can't travel. Be calm, Victoria. Never fear. There will be a proxy for him tonight. You'll get your wedding if you wish—right on schedule."

She raised her head proudly, walked around the end of the settle, and faced him.

"I do wish. Owen—why are you here?"

"Haven't you heard? When Muhammad cannot come to the mountain, one takes the mountain to Muhammad. And from the looks of that ton of nonsense strapped on Will Clark's carriage, the word *mountain* may be understating it."

She ignored that. "No, Owen. I mean why you? Why not someone else? You didn't have to come."

"As a matter of fact," he answered soberly, "I did. Don't try to find an answer, Vick. You'll be better without. Just look upon me as the instrument designed to carry you to your beloved."

"All right," she said. "I will. But an—instrument—didn't have to come up here to my room. You could have sent word you'd arrived. Word, in fact, would have sufficed nicely."

She was trying to use sarcasm to put distance between them. If she succeeded, she couldn't tell. He still hadn't looked at her, not since he'd sat before the fire. He said, now, "But I'm solicitous of your welfare, Vick. Harriet said you looked—puny."

He could not have selected an adjective to irritate her more. Crisply she said, "Bosh!"

"Not bosh. She's right." And he went right on, over her indignation: "Also, if you're worried about proprieties, love, don't. They're different out here. They even change with the terrain."

"Mine shan't."

"Dear Vick. Dear, queenly, rigid, proper Vick. Would you like to place a wager on it?"

She caught her breath. "A wager! Of course—a wager. Indeed. I see you haven't changed much at all."

He didn't rise to the bait. He only stared at the fire again without moving. She looked down at his enormous bulk, saw he needed a shave, that his thick, tawny hair was rough, straying over the thrown-back hood of his damp capote. Where were the tailored coats, the flashing rings, the polished boots that had made Paul's slender elegance seem almost—effete? Owen had always brought immense energy into a room: old ladies had loved his teasing, his attention, his Irish grin; and the bucks of the realm, his open-handedness—profligacy, Paul had called it. And of course Paul had been right.

His deep voice interrupted her thoughts: "Anyway, I needed to talk to you."

"About what, pray?"

" 'About what, pray?' " He mimicked her rudely. "God! What a prig you've become! About changing your mind. About going back home, back where you belong!"

The anger that began to smolder in her was defensive anger feeding on fear—fear of exposing herself, fear of discovery. She couldn't change her mind. She couldn't go back. Coldly, because of those things, because of being so afraid, she answered, "I presume you have reasons."

"Reasons! Good God!"

For the first time since sitting he looked at her again, twisting a quarter turn to do it, supporting himself on one massive arm. The firelight flickered across his blunt face, found every new line, every rocklike plane. If she was different, so was he.

"I have reasons," he said. Then he laughed—a short, harsh laugh. "But what can I say of them? Where should I begin? And even more pertinently—what would you believe? Forget it. If you must accept anyone's pack of lies, it probably better be his—it might be your only salvation."

"Owen—"

"I said forget it! Do what you damned please. You would, anyway. Just understand it won't be easy. There's no Savoy between here and Paul's place, Vick."

That he should underrate her so, doubt her strength, assume—high-handedly *assume*—that she'd buckle under trouble—this angered her. Deeply. Truly. In a stiff voice she replied, "Listen to me, Owen. Listen well. I came here to marry Paul. I am going to join him on his estate—"

"His what?"

"His estate!"

He snorted again—this time it *was* derisive, *was* mocking, but she didn't notice. She went on tensely: "If you don't take me there, someone else will. Do I make myself clear?"

"Very clear, Vick. You always have."

He began hoisting himself to his stocking feet, leaving a large damp splotch on the cushions. "But have you ever questioned, Victoria, why that after four damned lackadaisical years Paul suddenly calls for you to come now? Why he has timed it so your first few months will be hard, cold, winter months, when he so easily could have waited until spring?"

"He needs me!" She said it defiantly.

He answered savagely, "He sure as hell does!"

He was standing now, towering over her. Close. Too close. She was aware of her gaping silk waist, the drift of lace camisole against the beginning curve of soft breasts. She was also aware of the deep ache inside her this wasteful, heedless giant caused, had always caused, beside which Paul's gentle, tactful lovemaking had paled. The traitorous pulse began to beat at the base of her throat. She stepped back, covering it with her hand. He knew.

Yet he didn't move. Quietly, almost whispering, he said, "I told you four years ago, Vick. I don't trespass."

She turned away in desperation, went to the window, pulled open the heavy, flame-patterned curtains, looked out unseeing over the lodge poles to the distant bluff line.

To her, still softly, still not moving, he went on. "And yes, indeed. Paul needs you. I'll take you to him."

She answered recklessly, defiantly: "So Paul is not different—Paul has not changed!"

There was a short silence. Then he laughed—the same abrupt laughter. "Paul," he said, "is—exactly what he has always been."

With a light tap the door opened and the servant came in with the tray. Behind her was Harriet Clark saying, "Sorry we took so long, Victoria, but I'm very particular about my tea. Owen, dear, I'm sure you want something stronger. You'll find Will waiting in the study—and do change those socks!"

Owen Verinder smiled, then bowed. "Ladies," he said, and, boots in hand, went out into the hall. They could hear his feet squelching as he walked. Harriet Clark laughed.

"If he wasn't so big, he'd be dead of exposure," she said. Pulling a small slipper chair over near the tray, she sat down with a whisper of petticoats. "Nancy, light the candles, then you may go. Oh, Victoria, do tell Nancy what of your luggage you require. Owen is insisting on an early-morning start, so there's not much value in hauling it all upstairs. How awful about Paul's accident." (Was there a subtle change in the tone of her voice also, or could Victoria be suddenly too acute?) "But don't fret. We'll manage; my Will has it all figured out. Yes, Job?"—this to a tall, black manservant in the doorway.

Victoria was saying to Nancy, "Just the portmanteau, please, and the corded trunk." Behind her Madam Clark went to the door, exchanged a few words, then returned, a vexed look on her face.

"Fiddle!" she said. "Job says Thalia's arrived. Why in the world is she here?"

"Thalia?"

"Thalia Greenwood. She just rode in from Saint Louis. An independent, headstrong child. I'll wager money she's left school, means to persuade Owen to take her back up-river with you. The Greenwoods settled near Paul."

"Yes," said Victoria slowly. "I know." Sitting down, she accepted the cup of tea, and sipped from it.

Frowning, Harriet Clark poured her own, picked it up but still didn't drink. "Just when things were going so well," she murmured.

"Will—will Owen let her come?"

"I don't know. I really don't know. There are a lot of things—" She stopped, made a conscious effort to smile. "I doubt that he will. You don't need Thalia up there with the rest of you right now. Well. Anyway." And she sipped her tea, then put down the cup. "I just wanted to tell you what we have planned. Then you may alter as you choose, of course. Reverend Allen will arrive at seven thirty or so; he's riding over from Edwardsville. We're saying the ceremony at eight, dinner at nine."

"That's—that's fine. You're being very kind."

"My dear, I'm loving it. Our social life out here is rather thin this time of year. Will your gown need a press?"

"My gown?"

"Your wedding gown."

"Oh! Well—" She hesitated. How lovingly Nurse had packed that gown, layered in muslin and sprinkled with lavender, yet even then Victoria had felt—unreal. Not at all like a bride. And she certainly didn't feel like one now. "Should I wear it? I mean, without Paul—"

"My dear, don't disappoint us—and don't deny yourself. This is your wedding whether Paul is here or not."

What a cold truth that was. With your shield or on it, Vick.

Victoria nodded. "Of course. You're quite right. And I fear it will need pressing badly."

"I'll have Nancy heat the irons and Susan do the pressing. They're very careful. Oh—Thalia!"

Thalia Greenwood came tumultuously into the room. She was small, quick, with heavy, dark hair and angry eyes. She wore a dark green riding dress and was brandishing a crop. "Harriet, Owen says he won't take me home! You must make him change his mind! I won't stay in Saint Louis, I won't go back to that silly school! If he leaves me, he'll be sorry!"

"Thalia!" said Harriet Clark again, and this time her voice was crisp. "Mind your manners!"

The girl stopped dead still, said, "Oh!"

Victoria said, "Oh!" also.

That rude child in St. Louis had been Thalia Greenwood.

Thalia spoke first, swallowing hard, using a different, precise, finishing-school voice: "Lady Victoria."

With a sick sense of trouble, Victoria said, "How do you do?"

"Very well, thank you." *How proper the words, how mincing.* Yet there was hostility in the room thick enough to slice. *I have an enemy,* Victoria realized, *and I'm not certain why.*

Owen. It must be Owen. But I'm marrying Paul. She knows I'm marrying Paul. . . . Unless—oh, God! Surely Owen hasn't told her anything about—himself and me. . . .

Harriet Clark put her empty cup on its thin saucer and stood up. Her lips were firm. "Lady Victoria needs her rest," she said. "Come along, child. We'll leave the bride alone."

Thalia caught her breath. "Bride? But—Paul's not here—"

"Isn't it unfortunate?" said Madam Clark. "But there'll be a wedding, nonetheless. By proxy, Thalia. Proxy."

The small, pretty girl said again: "Oh!" Victoria could have sworn tears started in the huge, dark eyes—but she couldn't be sure, because Thalia whirled and left as precipitately as she'd come. Madam Clark sighed.

"I could have done without her very nicely," she said. "Fiddle! Well, I am going to leave you alone. Call for Nancy when you want her. I'm afraid we don't yet have the amenity of bells."

"Thank you. You're very kind."

The door shut, then opened again. "Oh, dear," said Harriet Clark. "I almost forgot. Robert brought my husband a note from a Mrs. Devery saying your father died—just recently, I believe. My condolences."

"Thank you."

"I'm sure it saddened your journey. Have you no brothers or sisters?"

"No. No one. I'm quite alone."

The poor child looked almost defenseless, standing there. Harriet Clark felt an unreasonable surge of wishing Paul Winterthur were at the bottom of the sea. But of course it was none of her affair. She murmured something else inconsequential but consoling, and again closed the door.

Inside it Victoria began to pace—restlessly, blindly, unseeing, like a cat in its cage.

She hadn't bargained on seeing Owen again so soon.

In her head she'd imagined something quite different: Lady Winterthur, safe in her role as Paul's wife, extending a queenly hand, murmuring polite nothings about it being nice to meet again, do try to come dine with us some evening. . . .

Not this! She could smell nothing but danger from Owen, danger all around her—

"Miss? Can I help you?"

Nancy had entered unheard. She added softly, "I knocked."

Victoria stopped her pacing, sighed. "Would you unlace me?" She stepped in one movement from the encumbrance of heavy skirt and petticoats and leaned against the tall bedpost. The dark maid's fingers were quick, and the sudden release of pressure almost exquisite.

"Mercy," said Victoria almost moaning. "Thank you, Nancy. That's all."

"Miss Harriet said you had a gown—"

"Oh. In the trunk."

She turned away, not really wanting to look at it. "There's a veil too. On the bottom. Do what you can."

Nancy rose from her knees, arms full of crumpled, creamy billows. "It's mighty pretty."

Unaware of the servant's curious eyes on the corselet she still clutched to her slender, long-legged body in the thin silk shift, Victoria pulled the dressing sacque from her portmanteau with one hand, shaking it out. "Thank you," she said. "I will rest now. Give me until half past the hour, please."

"Yes, miss. I'll wake you."

The door shut again.

Then Victoria dropped the corselet on the floor, its laces dangling, went to the mirror, lifted the silk shift. On her white midriff was the angry red outline of the leather packet.

But where else could she carry it? Where else would be safe?

On the boat she hadn't worried about its being in her portmanteau. But out here in this godforsaken country. . . .

She dropped the skirts of the shift, shrugged on the dressing sacque, untaped the packet from the inside of the corselet and unfolded it on top of the chest below the mirror. First came the Winterthur betrothal ring—a heavy cluster of rubies. Reluctantly she put it on. It was too large; it weighted the hand that went on unwrapping the pad of chamois until in the candlelight five diamond-circled sapphires shot blue flame from their filigree setting.

"Landam's Luck," Papa had called the necklace.

Victoria hated it. Too many times had she seen it in the hands of the brokers, buying her father's way out of misfortune. Too many times had it lain among the chips on a gaming table. What terrible, twisted impulse had made her pluck it from among Lady Fandley's tawdry trinkets and run away? Was it knowing Paul's admiration for it? Was it feeling every husband should have a dowry, and she had nothing? Was it the vague memory of the sapphires, years and years ago, on her own young mother's beautiful throat, coupled with the vision of them on Lady Fandley's scrag?

She didn't know. She didn't know. But one wild action had made her a thief. Eventually she would have to tell Paul.

She shivered, thinking of it. Her midriff felt abraded, and deliberately she put her mind away from the theft, to another problem: Perhaps if she wrapped the harsh leather in a handkerchief. . . .

From somewhere in the house a clock boomed the hour.

Oh, God, she thought. *Time goes so fast.* At nine o'clock she'd be married to Paul. Irrevocably married, even though he wasn't here. Then there would be ten days' travel. With Owen. Constantly with Owen. How different her wedding journey was going to be from what she'd thought!

What if on the trail to Paul's she just—disappeared?

3

It was ridiculous, it was absurd. She must have been not quite sane. Perhaps there had been witchery in the blue fire of the sapphires, because at that moment it seemed a solution.

If she disappeared, she'd not have to go into Paul Winterthur's bed, not have to be a dutiful wife, not have to confess her guilty secret to him, not have to hope he'd understand.

If she disappeared, Owen Verinder could no longer tear her inside to bits as he'd done before, and now, and could forever do.

Owen had never understood what it was like for a Landam to give his word! Whatever Papa had been, whatever mistakes he'd made, he'd never violated his sacred word of honor . . . even when it had been almost all they'd had left!

How could she break her word to Paul—especially when he'd been thousands of miles away? How could she break it now before all his friends? Even if she wanted to. . . .

Somehow, in the midst of this feverish muddle, she drifted off into restless sleep, holding her aching stomach tightly. What she dreamed and what she truly heard became mixed in her head. Paul's voice—Owen's voice—no, no, Paul's, because he called her *Victoria.* Owen, in that deep, rich bass of his had never said anything but *Vick.*

"Victoria," Paul said. "Victoria. I need your—"

Your what?

"Your money."

No, no, impossible. Paul had money.

"Your love."

But that was Owen, picking her up, tossing her high in his arms like a doll, laughing in delight like a young boy at the discovery that he loved her, never dreaming of defeat, saying incredulously, "I need you! Do you hear? You're my life's love, Vick!"

Yet the face she saw was Paul's face—chiseled, clean-boned, calm, hair so pale, it was like a silver helmet, and the voice was his—crisp, pure, the cultured accents of Balliol: "I'll build an empire, Victoria. You'll be queen!"

"She'll be dead!"

Whose voice was that?

"Dead, dead, dead," it repeated, and the word echoed in Victoria's brain, turning her on the settle, causing her to screw up her face like a little girl.

She didn't know the voice, but now in her dreams she was running, she was terrified, frantic, and someone was chasing her. Owen was commanding sternly, "Stop saying that, you idiot!" But still she must stumble on, gasping and sick with fear, for hands were clutching the flying skirts of her robe, the same hateful voice was saying, "I won't, I won't let it happen; I swear I'll kill her first, I'll kill her dead!" It was that girl's voice—Thalia—screaming—and Thalia's awful hands on her!

Victoria screamed, twisted—and opened her eyes to see Nancy staggering back from her flailing arms, saying urgently, "Miss! Miss! Wake up! You're dreaming, miss!"

"Oh!" said Victoria, and struggled to her feet, shocked, dismayed. "Nancy, did I hurt you? I am so sorry!"

"No, miss," said Nancy, recovering her composure. "But the hants were sure chasin' you! Are you all right now?"

Victoria sank back on the settle, panting, trying to slow her racing heart. Slowly the dream dimmed—the voices, the jumbled faces, the menacing, unbelievable words. Of course they were unbelievable. For what reason would anyone want her dead? "Yes," she said. With both hands she rubbed her face hard, pushing long fingers back through tumbled hair, shaking it—the familiar gesture she'd made all her life of a high-strung filly tossing its mane. "What time is it?"

"Time for your bath, miss. Job done filled the tin tub. Miss Harriet says to take a long 'un; you'll not get another on the trail. Them creeks is mighty cold this time of year."

The black woman was bustling about, laying out towels, poking the fire. "Oh," she said suddenly. "I 'most forgot. A note from Mr. Owen."

Victoria took the fold of paper, murmured, "Thank you," leaned to reach into her petit-point bag for her spectacles. She really didn't want to know what else Owen Verinder had to say but she supposed she must.

The exhilaration from her ideas of escape had faded with the wild dreaming. Feeling sapped, languid again, she perched the awkward lenses on the bridge of her slender Landam nose. Owen's scrawl came into focus.

"Vick," he'd written.

> nce there are to be guests who ask embarrassing questions, here are a few answers. Paul broke his leg in a fall from horseback while he was riding alone. It isn't a bad break. He set it himself, and expects to be using the leg in six weeks.

Victoria felt herself blushing, both from annoyance and shame. She *hadn't* asked about Paul's accident, *hadn't* shown concern. And of course it *had* to be Owen who found the chink in her armor!

Nancy's soft voice interposed gently, "Best use the water whilst it's hot. I'd be pleased to help you, miss."

Victoria began to say yes, then she remembered the red welts on her middle. All servants talk. She'd probably better bathe herself. She shook her head, saying instead, "But you may lay out my things. I'd appreciate that."

She went behind the folding screen, dropped her robe, peeled off the thin shift and eased her tired body into the warm tub. Hair. She'd forgotten to twig up her hair.

"Nancy, may I have some hairpins, please?"

A black arm came discreetly around the screen. "Your dress is done, miss. Susan will bring it up shortly."

"Oh," said Victoria, and reality dimmed the pleasure of getting clean. Politely she asked, "Did it come out all right?"

"Yes, miss," said Nancy and was glad the lady couldn't see her face. That damned wildfire, Miss Thalia, running smack into Job just as he was carrying a full decanter of wine past the ironing board! Land, there'd been a panic!

But most of it had gone on the floor, and what few splatters Susan couldn't sponge off wouldn't show. They hoped.

Behind the screen Victoria tried to get between her shoulder blades with her loofah, gave it up. At least most of the grime was gone—she could see it floating on top of the water. Disgusting. Like a cat, she hated being dirty.

Standing up, she poured the rest of the now tepid water over her shivering body, stepped out, toweled, shook lavender between her breasts and down her rounded thighs. Looser yet on her cold finger, the betrothal ring slipped off, rolled. Sighing, Victoria retrieved it, put it back. The plagued thing!

Soft voices mingling told her her wedding gown had arrived.

For one moment there was a cold knot in her stomach.

Then she forced herself to relax.

It's a charade, she told herself. *A charade with no meaning, something I must walk through.*

My wedding will be when I am with Paul.

How foolish it had been to think of running away! Her entire adult life had been ordered and directed to mingle with Paul Winterthur's life.

Fatigue had made her silly—fatigue and illness, and the cruel necessities of leaving home.

And Owen.

Tonight Owen Verinder had upset her, confused her, played on her childish fears.

She must not allow him to do it again.

Holding the corselet tight against her shift-clad body, she stepped around the screen and turned her back to Nancy to be laced. She'd forgotten to wrap the packet in her handkerchief, but with Nancy watching, it was too late now. She'd just have to bear it.

Nancy was deft and quick but she didn't lace very well.

Breathlessly, clinging to the bedpost, Victoria said, "More, Nancy. I'm sure you lace Madam Clark tighter than that."

"Miss Harriet don't lace, miss."

"Doesn't lace!" With difficulty Victoria stifled the shock in her voice. Nurse had always said the only women who went about with bellies flopping were drabs and actresses.

"No'm. Never laces when she's in a family way."

"Oh. I see." What Victoria didn't see was Nancy's curious look at her as she put her hands on her own waist, holding grimly as the strings tightened.

"Sick as a heifer with heaves," the driver had said in the kitchen. "She could hardly wait to get out."

He'd drained his tankard, wiped his mouth. "Hear tell the bridegroom ain't coming."

Job, turning the spit, said, "Broke his laig."

"Well. Ain't that a shame."

"It sounds mighty like," said Susan from the ironing table, "you don't particular care for Mr. Winterthur, Robert."

"He ain't m' favorite. Give me a hunk of that jack cheese, Nancy—I wet my whistle, now my belly's growling. Thankee. No, gentlemen—and ladies. He ain't m' favorite. Welshing on wages and a chop across the back with a riding crop ain't my idee of real winnin' ways."

"He's in the weeds," said Job from the turnspit. "I heard the master tell the missus at table."

"In-deed!" said Robert, and his bushy eyebrows rose. "You mean what I just delivered was a fresh bankroll—in skirts?"

Susan had leaned over to Nancy across the billows of creamy peau de soie. She whispered, "What's 'weeds'?"

Robert heard her and laughed. "Broke!" he said. "Busted. Well, now. That do put a different light on things. No wonder little Greenwood's nose is out of joint. Bet she never thought Milord would prefer bucks to boobies!"

Nancy remembered all this as she tugged and her dark eyes were thoughtful, her mind on very female matters. . . .

Totally unaware of the interesting ideas solidifying in the dark woman's kerchiefed head, Victoria pursued her own thoughts as she made her toilette. Uppermost in her mind was getting this travesty over with so she could go to bed. Madam Clark poked in her head briefly. Garnets swung from her ears, but her gown was covered with a protective coarse linen smock. She smiled approval of Victoria's high, simply twisted hair.

"My dear," she said, "you do look lovely! Now, Nancy, mind. We've run a strip of new linsey from the landing to the drawing room—that's for the bride. If anyone else walks on it I'll skin them alive! When she's ready, take Lady Victoria to the top of the stairs out of sight—then you run down the back way and give old Mr. Robinson the nod. He'll start the pump organ. That's your signal, Victoria. My William will meet you at the foot of the staircase and escort you from there. I'm sorry we can't have an Anglican service, but Reverend Allen is very nice, really he is."

She paused. "Best of luck, my dear," she said, then, "Oh, fiddle! I always cry at weddings!" and rustled out of sight.

The veil was a large square of Nottingham lace.

For a moment, looking through it, Victoria saw herself in the mirror. Then with a defiant gesture she lifted the part that covered her face and flung it back. This single, unplanned movement may have saved her life. But at the moment all she could think was, *I am not a misty-eyed bride!*

Nancy arose from arranging the flow of cream-colored skirts, smoothed the wrinkles from her own starched apron.

"There," she said. "I reckon we're ready. About on time too."

With steady, cold hands Victoria reached for her small white prayer book.

"Thank you, Nancy," she said. "You'd better go, then. I'll be at the head of the stairs."

As she lifted her skirts through the door, she noticed for the first time the sounds of laughter and happy voices seeping up from the drawing room.

My wedding, she thought bitterly. *My guests. And I don't even know them. . . .*

The hall was dim, cool, lit only by flickering candles in brass sconces at the landing. Her gown whispered softly as she put one foot before the other and went toward it. It was almost as if someone had wound a tight spring in her back.

Four steps down, then a square of landing where the stairs reversed.

Below, the voices and laughter suddenly ceased. An organ began a thin, sweet, reedy melody. Her stomach constricted; she shivered. But there was no going back.

With your shield, or on it, Victoria.

Then she saw something. Just a shine, a sudden glimmer in the flicker of a candle.

She froze, absurdly poised with one foot lifted. She looked again—unbelievingly. And it was still there—something patently, unmistakably meant to hurt her. Her. Not another person. Madam Clark had said no one else was allowed on the new strip of linsey.

Two steps down a thin wire stretched across the riser. Ankle-high.

What if she hadn't looked first? What if the candle hadn't flickered, hadn't caught the gleam?

At best she would have gone ass over applecart—a ludicrous, humiliating descent. At worse she might have been badly injured. Even killed.

Now she was no longer cold, no longer a wound-up toy. Angrily she bent down, yanked at the tight, fine wire. It snapped; she was left with a piece in her hand.

Guitar string!

Down below, the organ began sounding a little insistent. There was a groundswell of whispers.

Victoria, very pale, very angry, tucked the small tangle of wire in her bosom. Her head went up, her nostrils pinched. Holding the banister tightly, she turned the corner, coming into view of the assembly.

A blurred sea of faces looked up. At the foot General Clark stood anxiously. When he saw her, he smiled. A friendly smile. An encouraging one.

She fastened her eyes on that smile. She took her hand from the safety of the banister. She began to descend.

At the bottom he offered his arm. She put her fingers on it. They were icy cold. He glanced at her sharply, placed his warm ones on top of them. Together they walked through the aisle of people toward a blur of cedar boughs, the sharp white of a clergyman's stock. For the rest of her life she would remember the snowy collar like a beacon in the fog, the spicy smell of evergreens.

Then General Clark was releasing her, urging her feet forward, stepping back. Another hand came out, took hers, A large hand.

She looked up into the sober, expressionless face of Owen Verinder.

Owen was the proxy!

Gone were the stained capote, the wet boots, the rough head. He wore dark brown, neatly cut, his jaw fresh-shaven, the tawny hair brushed back, showing copper in the firelight. Gently, insistently, he pulled her to his side, turned her toward the minister, steadied her with the breadth of his shoulder, the hard warmth of his hand,

The hour was late, the enticing smell of coffee flowed from the dining room. The hungry clergyman, having ridden hard without any dinner, pared the ceremony considerably to the satisfaction of all. Through a haze Victoria heard her own voice saying, "I, Victoria. . . "; heard Owen's deep, calm tones answering, "I, Paul. . . ."

But it wasn't Paul. It was Owen.

The minister closed his Bible with a snap, said, "You may now salute the bride."

Owen turned her toward him. Her breath stuck. She helplessly closed her eyes.

She felt his warm lips—chastely pecking her forehead.

Around them laughter broke out, a burst of applause. Strangers pressed forward with smiling faces, murmured words of congratulation. Harriet Clark embraced her warmly; her husband caught Victoria in a bear hug; between the two of them they began to introduce their friends, and names buzzed in Victoria's ears like flies: Nicholas Hansen, Nathaniel Pope, John Shaw (a very dark, stocky man with an ugly, oddly attractive face), Judge and Mrs. Reynolds. Victoria bowed, numbly, unhearing. Then Owen took her hand again, turning her to a chair by a table. Dipping a pen in an inkwell, he said laughing, "That was the window dressing, my lady. This is the real part—the register. Harriet and Will have already done us the honor of being witnesses. But you aren't committed, love, until you sign."

The elaborate, printed certificate blurred before her eyes. She couldn't read it. Owen knew she couldn't. Not without her spectacles. He laughed again, guided her hand with his. She wrote, for the last time, *Victoria Landam*.

With a flourish he signed on Paul's line.

The clergyman said sharply, "But—" then stopped. Owen was waving the document in the air to dry, neatly folding it, tucking it away inside his waistcoat.

Victoria looked up at him. All her fears, her anger—her resolution—sounded in her clear voice: "Now I am committed."

He loomed over her, his deep chest and wide shoulders seeming to go on forever, his big body a monolith encased in brown velveteen. There was an odd sound in his deep voice, an inexplicable sound—almost like triumph.

"Yes, my dearest Vick," he said. "You most certainly are."

4

The wedding guests hadn't driven all the way out to the Clarks' ménage to go to bed early. They dined lavishly—entire hams, racks of beef ribs dripping smoky juice, platters of succulent little quail. And they talked—rivers of talk, washing by Victoria's ears like spring freshets, accompanied by pounding fists and great gusts of laughter that made the cut-tin chandeliers dance.

Owen sat among them, his cravat loosened, a tankard in one big hand. His responsibilities toward Victoria seemed to have ended with a few formal toasts at the dining table.

Thalia Greenwood was conspicuous by her absence. It was just as well. Knowing no one else who so patently disliked her enough to do her harm, Victoria's suspicions had settled on Thalia as unerring as a homing pigeon's.

What if the girl went with them tomorrow? What if she wheedles Owen into taking her?

I can't have it, Victoria promised herself. *I won't have it. I've troubles enough without shouldering Owen's.*

Her head ached abominably. Everyone was being very kind and she wanted to scream. It was awful of her. But the leather packet hurt; the skin must be rubbed raw. She could hardly keep her hands away, but there was no easement except getting the corselet off.

Mrs. Nathaniel Pope gave her the excuse she needed. A motherly lady, she leaned forward, touching Victoria's cheek with a cool hand, asking, "My dear, are you well?"

Harriet Clark turned around then, her eyes concerned. Beneath the protective linen cover she'd worn a lovely garnet-colored moiré. It rustled as she moved, catching peacock hues from the candlelight, and she, too, touched Victoria's cheek, painfully mindful of what Nancy had said. *Oh, dear,* she thought to herself, *could she be right?* Aloud she said, "I don't mean to interfere, Victoria—but the uptrail is just now really frightful. Does Owen know—" *Fiddle!* Harriet thought. *That was not very diplomatic!* "I mean—does he realize how—unwell you are?"

A bit stiffly Victoria answered, "I haven't felt it—his concern."

"Of course not. Yet—"

"I'm certain I can manage."

Oh, my dear, said Harriet—but to herself. She was sure this delicate young woman had no concept of the grueling trip ahead of her, and for the second time she heartily wished she could wring Paul Winterthur's arrogant neck. But what could one do?

She decided. She summoned Nancy to escort the bride upstairs and she went looking for Owen Verinder. Owen had sense.

But Victoria found him first, making her manners as she progressed through the welter of guests toward the stairs. He had one large, polished boot on the first riser and was leaning against the newel talking to the stocky Mr. Shaw. He turned as she approached, swinging the tankard so it splashed. His face was flushed, his eyes blank—all danger signs.

Please, Owen. Please. Don't embarrass me. . . . "Good night, Mr. Shaw."

"Madam." His ugly face broke into an attractive smile as he bowed over her hand. "I wish you much joy."

"Thank you."

Then—very carefully—she went on, "Good night, Owen."

"Good night, my love. Don't wait up."

She felt the hot blood sweep her face, and he grinned—an impudent, reckless grin. She tried to go by calmly, with dignity, but two steps high the hem of her gown caught on something and Nancy had to kneel to free it. As she waited, not looking, she realized with relief that the two men had resumed their conversation.

Indistinctly she heard John Shaw say in a low voice, "Owen, that lily maid! Can't you delay? It's not only the weather, man—you know the word is out she's carrying gold! I tell you, I'm not certain how much control I have! There's so much ill feeling toward Winterthur, and good God, all it would take would be a few well-placed shots!"

Nancy said, "There we are, miss," and Victoria moved on up the stairs. She was puzzled; she'd caught only the words *control* and *shots* clearly. She asked, "Nancy, *what* is that man?"

"What?" Now it was Nancy's turn to puzzle. "I can't rightly say *what*. He's—sort of like the boss of Pike County, Mr. Shaw is. He owns half of it. The 'breeds and the Indians, they follow him like dogs, 'cause he's mighty good to them. And he's got the whole Boone clan in his pocket—he fought alongside the old man, y'see. Now some folks, they're a-scairt of him on account of his bully-boys. But I ain't. He can be ornery, but he's fair. Not like—" She stopped. "Miss Harriet says I shouldn't judge," she finished lamely.

But Victoria was totally unaware that Nancy had almost maligned her new husband. They were on the landing. She stopped and pointed down. "What's that, Nancy?"

Nancy bent, touched the shining, short fillip of wire. It was still looped on the stair spindle. "Land. I don't know. Looks like something was tied to it."

"Something was," said Victoria grimly. "Leave it there."

Nancy straightened. "Can't get it anyway—not without my scissors. Job, he'll find it, cleaning in the morning."

The new bride was already going down the hall, her skirts and her veil billowing mistily behind her. Nancy shrugged and followed. She was curious to see the lady in her room, pulling out the long curtains, ducking to look under the bed—like she was expectin' someone to pop out at her!

She knew she was right as Victoria straightened, asking, "Can the door be locked?"

Incredulously Nancy said, "Miss?"

"The door to the hall. Can it be locked?"

"No, miss. But we'uns do intend to knock. Miss Harriet gets mighty upset if we forgets." She waited, but Victoria said no more about it. With a deep, almost pathetic sigh she asked, "Please, will you undo me, Nancy? I am so tired."

"Oh, yes, miss."

Nancy loosened the laces tenderly. *Poor lady,* she thought. Leaning against the bedpost, Victoria went on with great casualness, "Who plays guitar in this household?"

Land! In England did them lords and ladies get sung to sleep? Aloud, Nancy answered, "Bunch of folks. One of the gem'mun who came down-trail with Mr. Owen. Dalverez—he's master's overseer. That Thalia. My man, Job— though he plays banjo mostly."

Her lips ominous, Victoria picked it up: "Miss Greenwood?"

"Yes'm. She learns all kinds of fancy things in that school. But if they're going to make a lady of *her* I reckon their work's cut out for 'm!"

"I didn't see her at dinner."

"No. She warn't. She got into big trouble. Mr. Owen, he spanked her butt and sent her to her room—begging your pardon, miss,'' because Victoria was staring at her in disbelief.

"He what?"

But Nancy ducked her neat head, looked embarrassed. "Missus says my tongue runs," she mumbled. Victoria kindly let it pass. She'd heard anyway.

"How old is Miss Greenwood?"

"Seventeen. Eighteen, shortly."

Nancy turned down the silk patchwork counterpane, smoothed the plump pillows. "There you are, miss." Then she hesitated, pursed her lips, and asked very cautiously, "Could I get you something soothing, miss? You feeling poorly and all. Missus, she's got a potion guaranteed to soothe, let a lady sleep. We— we been though this before."

What had they been through before? Victoria wondered. *Another wedding?* But she didn't really care. She nodded, clutching the corselet to her, eager for the black woman to be gone.

"May I repack your pretty gown?"

"In the morning. Morning will be fine."

"Yes, miss. I'll be back right shortly."

The door closed, and in one motion Victoria dropped the corselet, looked down with dismay. There was blood on the leather, blood on her shift. The bright diamond on her midriff was now not only red, but bleeding.

She couldn't hide it there anymore; she couldn't stand it. There had to be another place.

She put a clean handkerchief on the abrasion, pulled her long dressing sacque about her. Tying it loosely, she glanced around. Where? Where would the necklace be safe? After the incident with the guitar string she didn't trust anyone.

The old plaid cape! She'd brought it because it was warm, useful, and Paul's gift. What better place to conceal his dowry?

She went to her portmanteau, kicking aside the abandoned skirts of her wedding gown. Somewhere old nurse had packed a little sewing kit. . . .

As she bent to look, the crumpled coil of wire fell from between her breasts, and slipped into the portmanteau. She stopped a moment, her searching hand arrested.

Should she tell Owen?

No. At least not yet.

Just be on her guard.

Because she didn't wish to be interrupted, she took the small slipper chair, pushed it up beneath the wooden doorhandle. Then she spread the cape on the bed, looked at it thoughtfully. Not the hood. The necklace was heavy.

The hem then.

She donned her spectacles. As she snipped and sewed, the awkward betrothal ring kept turning under, getting in her way. She was very tempted to put it with the necklace. Yet taking off the betrothal ring left nothing on her hand but the very new, very plain gold band. Somehow—somehow she wasn't ready for the sight of that. And the betrothal ring did hide it very nicely.

For the first time she thought: *Strange the band should be so—plain: a mere circle of gold.*

It wasn't really like Paul at all. . . .

"Miss!"

It was Nancy, tapping at the door. And she wasn't through, she wasn't nearly through!

She called out, "Could you just leave it in the hall, please? I'm—I'm occupied." Let her think she was on the commode; that was all right.

"Yes, miss," said Nancy through the door panel. "It's here on the tray. Mind, you drink it down. . . . It'll get that 'poorly' feeling."

"I will. Thank you."

"Good night, Mrs. Winterthur."

Mrs. Winterthur.

Oh, God, thought Victoria, *I should be so proud, so happy—not torn up like this!*

Papa always sensed how I felt, he'd hate to see me now. But her father hadn't wanted her to marry Paul. He'd said she didn't know Paul well enough. . . .

(The spectacles slid down her slender nose; she shoved them up again and her sewing came back into focus.)

She hoped—she prayed—that, wherever Papa was, he realized she'd been in a trap of his own making. That she'd had no other choice. . . .

When she finally finished, her hands ached from poking the small needle through heavy fabric. But the stretched necklace made only a long, discreet lump in the bottom hem, and she was satisfied.

Downstairs the party noises were diminishing. Her fire was burning low. She'd lighted a fresh candle to sew by; now it was guttering. The room was so quiet, she could hear a mouse gnawing in the wall.

Sudden light footsteps in the hallway caught her ear. Nancy! She'd forgotten the sleeping draught.

Staying very still, she heard the steps pause. Stop. Then go lightly by. Nancy probably thought she was asleep.

But I'd best bring it in, she told herself. It was, after all, a kindness.

She removed the chair quietly, cracked the door, looked out. The hall was dim, the low candles smoking a little. At her feet was a tray; on it a stemmed goblet.

Reluctantly she brought the goblet inside. The nostrum was dark, and it smelled bitter.

A strong sense of obligation made her sip. She swallowed with difficulty. The stuff was dreadful. Silently she apologized to her hostess and threw the rest in the fire.

Then, slipping off the dressing sacque, she lifted the silk shift and took away the handkerchief. It was spotted, but the bleeding had stopped. Nancy had laid her long, ruffled nightdress on the settle to warm by the fire, but suddenly she was too tired to struggle with its ribbons and loops. She climbed up the two steps in her shift, crawled between the delicious privilege of lavender-scented sheets.

Vaguely she remembered she hadn't replaced the slipper chair. In her dreams she imagined she had.

She'd no idea how long she'd lain there in oblivion, only that time had passed. Once she had a foggy sense of being looked upon. Nancy, probably. She stayed still, feigned sleep, and the feeling went away.

There were more footsteps in the hall, a muffled snatch of voices and laughter. In the fireplace the big log finally burned through, fell apart with a bright shower of sparks. A mouse gnawed.

Frost began to pattern the ironwork on the windows. Outside the last of the kitchen servants sucked a dram of leftover wine against the cold and trotted across the lawn to his quarters. His flailing feet found an obstacle. Reeling, he caught his balance, cursed, kicked. The recumbent Sauk merely grunted, rolled out of the way.

The thin sliver of a waning moon laced stark tree branches against a hard, glassy sky as Victoria opened her eyes.

Owen was standing at the side of the bed.

5

Owen's shirt was open, his cravat askew, and he smelled rankly of whiskey.

A primitive sense of survival made her voice indignant: "What are you doing here?"

"I'm your husband."

"You are not!"

"I was a good enough proxy at the ceremony; why not in the bedchamber?"

"Owen, you are talking nonsense. Now get out of here!"

But he didn't move. He continued to stare down at her. In the half shadows he loomed like a mountain. The firelight caught his eyes, making them glitter. She didn't move either. She hardly breathed.

Thoughtfully he said, "What if I were very rich and *Paul* was very poor? Would that make the difference, Victoria?"

"Are you?"

"No."

"And Paul *is* rich."

"He is now," he answered.

But the words made no sense. Owen made no sense.

She said coldly, "You're drunk."

He shrugged. He put out a big hand, gently touched her throat with his fingertips. She pushed the hand away, pulled the counterpane to her chin. He laughed, and yanked it down again. It was the laughter that really frightened her; it was strange, sardonic, and it wasn't Owen. In a whisper she reminded him, "You said you didn't trespass."

"I don't, love. I never cross a property line. But, my dear, when the lines are down—"

His hand was back, caressing her throat, pushing behind her head nestling into the warm, soft hair. She twisted away and said indignantly, "What are you talking about?"

The low firelight outlined his wide frame, made his hair shine as he bent. Again she caught the reek of whiskey and again she said, "You're drunk!"

"Very perspicacious." His deep voice handled the word without a slur, commending her sarcastically. "I'm drunk. Harriet says you're pregnant. Does that make us even?"

He mistook her gasp of total outrage for dismay and shook his head. "Vick, Vick. For four years I've remembered you, I've fantasized, I've hungered, I've kicked myself for being a damned fool. Yet I was proud too. Because I'd been a gentleman." The very tone of his voice made the word a mockery. "But now, my love, since you seem to have been passing it around, I think I'll have some."

She said tensely, "I have not been 'passing it around'!"

He ignored her. The hand slid slowly from behind her head, down across the soft velvet of a breast, and on to her stomach. "Who was it, Vick? Say his cursed name so I'll know who bested me!" The fingers dug suddenly; she cried out in pain and he didn't care. "God!" he said savagely between clenched teeth, "I'd like to tear it out by the roots!"

She grabbed with both hands, pushing against him, sliding away, trying to rise on one elbow.

"You listen to me!" she said furiously to the face now inches from hers. "How dare you say such things? How dare you? True or not, it is none of your business nor anyone else's in this—this busybody household! I'm sure I thank them for being so concerned!"

He was too huge, too strong. His other hand whipped out, caught her shoulder, pinning her. His quiet voice had a catlike purr. "And I'm concerned too, Victoria."

"Then show it! Go find out who tried to kill me on the stairs!"

It was a frantic shot, born of desperation. His searching mouth was on her cheek, sliding toward her own. She knew she had to stop him now or she was lost.

Unbelievably it worked. He froze. After a long, tense moment he lifted his head and said harshly, "I warn you—don't lie to me, Vick!"

"I am not lying."

She didn't dare move. His hand still lay beneath the covers on her body, warm, heavy, barely arrested in its seeking. She had to hold him with her voice. "There was a wire stretched across the stairs where the linsey began. A guitar wire. I nearly fell."

"I don't believe you."

"Look on the stairs."

He pulled away and went toward the hall in giant strides. She seized the moment to scramble from the bed and wind herself in the long dressing gown. For one frantic second she thought of trying to bar the door. But that would be useless. Self-defeating. He was drunk; he'd only batter it down and the entire household would know.

Her breath was coming in pants. She waited. It was what she had to do.

He came back, shutting the door, and leaning against it with his arms folded. He was like some sort of mocking tribune.

"Try again, Vick."

So it was gone. She might have known it would be. Desperately she said, "Nancy saw it!" then, realizing that that way led to exposure, she made herself meet his cynical smile and say with steady eyes, "There's another piece. It broke off in my hand. It's in the portmanteau."

This time he believed her. When he returned again, the bit of guitar string in his hand, all the liquor had drained out of him.

He said heavily, "I'll take care of this."

So he knew who had done it; he'd known immediately. And because he did, she did. She said, "That girl!"

"What girl?"

"Thalia."

He started, looked at her with narrow, almost angry eyes. "Why Thalia? What do you know about her?"

Stubbornly she answered, "I know she's after you."

"Indeed!"

"Don't pretend stupidity. Of course she is. Paul said so. In his letters."

"How well my cousin is up on my affairs! What else has he told you, fair Vick?"

"Owen, stay with the point!"

"Which is what? Instruct me."

Her hands clenched. Damn him! "Which is telling your piece of skirt she has no rival in me!"

His strong brows arched. "I do thank you, Vick. That's very noble. Too bad you're on the wrong track."

She stamped her foot. "You *know* what I'm trying to say!"

"But you don't. Anyway, she'll be no further problem. I'll see to that."

"Madam Clark says she wants to go with us."

"She's not. She's going back to that Saint Louis school where her father put her. And if she bucks, I may tie this string around her neck. My God," he said suddenly, and all the hostility faded. "Vick—she could have killed you!"

His arms unfolded, fell to his sides like dead weights. His wide shoulders sagged; his lined face looked careworn. Victoria realized for the first time that the gay, engaging rascal with the crackling vitality, the ne'er-do-well who never thought about the morrow—that Owen was gone. This was a new man, a different man.

Yet not a stranger. Not yet a stranger.

He was still the Owen she'd known so well. She knew that too, poignantly, as he went on in the same slow, painful voice, "If you could have seen yourself . . . coming down those stairs. Like a queen. Head high. White as death, frightened as a deer, yet the most beautiful, desirable woman I have ever seen since—since one autumn four long, barren years ago. . . ."

He stopped because his voice was shaking.

That small, traitorous pulse began to quiver at the base of her throat again; once more she put her hand to it. But this time he came to her, took the hand away, bent, placed his gentle mouth on that delicate, fluttering hollow.

What could not be won by force could be taken by sweetness. With a helpless half sob she reached with both arms to bring his rough, tawny head to hers. His hands slid softly beneath her robe, her shift, cupped the velvet, warm delights of her breasts, stroked them softly. Urgently against the scented heat of her bare throat he whispered, "Vick, don't stop me this time. . . . Please, Vick. . . . It can't matter so much. . . . Not now. . . ."

She stiffened.

Not now!

What he meant by those words—what he was thinking—came to her, came to her in a bitter flood of comprehension. She thrust him away. When he resisted, unbelieving, she struck him viciously, hard as she could with the flat of her hand. The sound of the blow was like a clap of thunder.

He put his fingers to his jaw where it was already reddening. He stared at her a moment with narrow, granite eyes, muttered something filthy between set teeth. Then he reached out.

She ran.

But there was nowhere to go.

He stood, waiting.

Panting, she seized the candlestick. It was brass, heavy. She wheeled, opened her mouth to scream because he'd lost all privilege, all human rights in those two filthy words.

But the scream never came.

Something else was happening to her, something beyond Owen, something she could not understand, could not control.

Her stomach had knotted—knotted as though squeezed in a clawed hand. The pain was excruciating, unbelievable. Her face went gray-green, frozen into a grimace that drew the lips back over her teeth. Her stomach tore again, cramped in agony, drew her double. While Owen watched, transfixed, she whispered like an animal in pain, half turning.

He said, "My God, Vick—"

Clutching at the table, she went to her knees. Strangling, coughing, she was spewing a stringy, bloody, black viscous mass on the carpet.

With one enormous stride he scooped her up, carried her constricted body to the china basin, turned her tortured face, and held her while she vomited again and again until, spent and white, she lay back limply in his arms, eyes closed, her shallow breathing like a leaf fluttering in the wind.

"Vick," he said then, and his voice shook. "Vick, hang on, I'll fetch someone, we'll get help, please, Vick, you can't die—"

Her eyes opened suddenly, very red-rimmed, very bleary, very blue.

"I am not dying!" she whispered. Her voice was faint, but it surged with defiance. "I won't! Not until I settle with whoever is trying to do this to me!"

To his bewildered face she said, "The drink! Something was in the damned drink!"

"Vick, a pregnant woman—"

"Pregnant be damned!" she croaked indignantly. "I was poisoned!"

"Vick—"

"I can taste it! Almonds! I should have known it then! Thank God I didn't drink the whole thing or I would be dead! There stands the glass; go see for yourself, you big buffoon!"

He lowered her awkwardly from his knees to the settle, put one finger in the goblet, smelled, and placed it on his tongue. His face told her she spoke the truth.

"I told you," she cried in weak triumph. "And I'll tell you something else! You'd better get to your little darling before I do, Owen Verinder, because I am going to tear her limb from limb!"

But he was shaking his head. "No," he said.

She was so angry, her voice squeaked. "No! What do you mean, no? Really, Owen!"

"No!" he repeated, and in the firelight his eyes were suddenly implacable points of rock. "The guitar string—perhaps. She's a spoiled child; she doesn't think, she acts. But this—"

He took a huge draught of air. "No, Vick," he said again. "No. This happened after the ceremony. Right? After."

She wiped the dampness from her forehead with shaking fingers, gaped at him crossly. "Whatever difference does that make?"

"*After* made you Paul's wife," he said harshly, "and I'm afraid that fact makes all the difference in the world."

He bent over her again and said, "Hang on."

"What?"

"Dammit, hang on. I'm going to put you back to bed. Don't be an ass, Vick; now I have other things to do."

He carried her as easily as a rag doll, slid her beneath the rumpled covers, dropping the dressing gown on the floor and pulling the counterpane to her chin. "How are you now? All right?"

She nodded.

"Certain?"

"Yes!" she said in a snappish croak. With her tousled hair and pale, scowling face, she looked like a sulky child.

He nodded, satisfied, and stood erect. "We'll have to get this mess cleaned up. I'll see if Nancy's still awake. And I want her to sleep in here, not leave you alone. Not one minute. Do you understand?"

Stubbornly she mumbled, "I don't want her."

"Would you rather have me?"

At the expression on her wan face he smiled, rather grimly. "I thought not."

Turning on his heel, he spraddled his long legs, stooped his head to see in the mirror on the chest, fastened his shirt, straightened his cravat, and smoothed his rough head. "Must keep up appearances," he said, but there was no humor in it.

The small tangle of guitar string lay on the floor. He picked it up, stuffed it in his pocket, and went to the door. For such an overlarge man he walked lightly, on cat feet.

"Good night, Lady Winterthur," he said, and was gone.

6

Outside Victoria's door Owen Verinder's entire demeanor changed. His jaw tightened, his eyes narrowed, his fists balled, and he looked what he was: a very angry and a very frightened man.

So there had *been someone behind them on the trail!* he thought. It had been a sense rather than sight, a feeling as elusive as smoke. Yet Owen had learned early that many frontiersmen weren't sociable; he'd chalked up his unease to the edge he felt going to meet Vick, soothed himself with the delusion that if anything overt was meant, it would have happened somewhere on the trek.

But he had been wrong. Now he knew he'd been wrong. Whoever had been back there—he'd not been just another suspicious trapper preferring his own company to that of strangers—he'd been going to meet Vick too.

And he'd found her.

Now. Who the devil was it? Which one of Paul's enemies?

Owen took a deep breath, a savage rasp of air, grimacing, and shook his head. Then he set off down the silent hall in huge strides.

Thank God for men like Will Clark! In answer to Owen's low voice at the door Will slid quickly from the high tester-bed. He stuffed his nightshirt into his trousers, dispatched Nancy to Victoria's room, sent her husband, Job, to sit outside the door, quieted his own wife's sleepy questions, and returned to the large young man restlessly pacing the ten-by-ten of his untidy study.

"Nancy's taken charge," he said soothingly. He poured a clear, shining dram of whiskey, handed it to Owen. "Victoria will be fine. Now. What is going on around here?"

Owen nursed the whiskey, not wanting it. Quietly, making himself calm, he told Will about the guitar string.

Clark's eyes narrowed angrily. "I'll take care of Thalia, Owen."

"No, by God! She has to learn—"

His host cut him off. "Yes, indeed. She does. But she also has to get over this hopeless attachment for Winterthur. Drink up, man, then tell me about the poison. That can't have been Thalia; she's not been let out of her room since the wedding."

Owen tossed off the dram, put down the empty cup. His eyes very cold, very angry; he repeated what he knew.

Clark turned, stirred up the fire, stared at it tensely. Over his shoulder he said, "You know they say Victoria is carrying gold to Winterthur. Is she?"

"Hell, I don't know! I'm not in her confidence." Then Owen tried to temper his truculence. "The word came down from Paul: no outriders, no escort; try not to draw attention."

"The man's an idiot!"

"Tell me about him."

Clark put down the poker and turned. "But robbery, lad, would happen along the trail. This is a personal assault here, in my house, with nothing apparent to gain but the lady's death. Who would that please? I mean, of course, besides Thalia, because Thalia has had no opportunity to do anything since the wedding."

Owen looked at him loweringly, heavy brows drawn. "Paul!" he said savagely. "If he could arrange to get Vick's money without having to bother with Vick, it would suit him fine. He could marry Thalia too, and double his winnings when her old man dies."

Gently Clark asked, "Don't you think he has that in mind?"

As Owen's head jerked up, he went on, "His choice of seasons, Owen, the route he's chosen. You know the primitive conditions under which she'll have to live, regardless of what high-flown nonsense he's fed her. Look at that delicate child! She'll not last a year! He doesn't intend for her to live very long. Good God, man, even the proxy works for him! If she dies along the trail, he's still her husband—and most definitely her heir!"

Owen clenched his fists. "What can I do?"

"Send her back. That's safest. The marriage can be voided."

"She won't go."

"Not even if you told her the truth?"

Owen stared at him mutely, hands still clenched.

Clark continued, "The truth being that you are more than half in love with the girl yourself. Come, come, Verinder. I'm getting old but not daft! I could never understand why an intelligent, able young man like you should come into these parts and deliberately subjugate yourself to a sadistic tyrant—cousin or not! Tonight I saw the reason. You knew she would come."

"Yes." The answer was tight-lipped, the face not friendly.

Clark put his hand on the broad, rigid shoulder. "I've half a fancy she'd go back—if you went with her."

"You're wrong. Her head's stuffed full of family honor and sacred oaths." Then his shoulder sagged, and Owen sighed, anger draining out of him. "She has no idea what he's like, Will."

"Will you tell her?"

"She'll not believe me."

"Then the task," said the older man clearly, "would appear self-complicated. So be it." He reached up to the mantelpiece, took down a long clay pipe, hesitated, then put it back. "Very well. My original question: Whom would her death please? I think that Paul, being miles away with a broken leg, can be safely discounted. But remember, it appears to be a personal thing."

Owen frowned. "Jupiter disappeared after Paul's flogging."

Clark shook his head. "Not Jupe. Word has it he was one of the blacks going north with Sparrow Hawk toward Fort Dearborn. Besides, Jupiter's revenge would be more primitive, and directed toward Paul's person, not his wife's. Victoria, I presume, has no pursuing demons, and has hardly been in this country long enough to make enemies. I'd guess a white man, Owen, a man who thinks Winterthur loves his bride."

Owen said, "Oh, my God. Mersey."

"Who?"

"Mercedes. I don't know the rest. He's French. And Cree."

"Oh, yes. I know him now. His woman shot herself. Lord! The honorable Paul didn't have a hand in that!"

Owen nodded grimly. "Mersey was with me, cutting timber. Paul said she 'didn't know her place.' He paraded her naked before the field hands." He took a deep breath. "When we came back, she was dead. Everyone knew how Mersey worshiped his woman. When he disappeared, not taking anything with him but his Hawken gun, we all figured Paul was finally in for it. Paul thought so too, although he'd never admit the fact."

"What happened?"

"Nothing. Absolutely nothing. And it's been two months or more." Owen sat down on a wide, cane-bottomed chair that creaked with his weight, stared up at his host with eyes that didn't see him at all. "But this—this sounds like it could be Mersey. His sort of revenge. Paul's wife for his. Damn me, Will— I felt as though I was being followed downtrail. Yet I never thought of Mercedes; I had about decided he was dead too."

Will Clark shook his head slowly. "No," he said. "He's alive. He's here. Or was. Hold on!" Only his firm hand on Owen's shoulder kept the big man from coming up out of his seat. "Victoria will be all right, Owen! Job won't let Jesus Christ into that room without my say-so!"

"Will, I don't want to tangle with Mersey; he's to be pitied. But I won't take a chance with Vick's life—"

"Nor I, you young idiot! All I know is that Mercedes turned up here the day before you did, looking as if he could stand a square meal. If you can be sensible, come along. We'll find out where he is now."

Victoria hadn't been so cosseted and soothed in months. When at last her tired, racked body drifted off to sleep, it was with hot stones on her cold feet, a soft, goose-down comforter tucked about her shoulders and Harriet Clark tiptoeing away, leaving Nancy knitting by the light of the low fire. To the counterpoint of clicking needles and popping beechwood, the hot, sweet wine took its toll. The poison that had purged her body also purged her mind. Drowsily it refused reality, turtled back into its own mental goose down.

In a vague way she knew it was raining. She loved rain—dreary, November rain, dashing against the tall Gothic windows of Landam Hall, soft, warm rain that burst the white blossoms in the hedgerows. Rain had caught them in the garden once—she and Owen—and Owen had scooped her up, running with his burden into the domed shelter of a repose. There he'd kissed her for the first time, laughing. Then not laughing. . . .

Once she heard Owen's voice. He was asking about someone named Mersey. "Job," he said earnestly, "have you seen him?" *Job. Who was Job?* A soft voice answered, "Yes. I seen 'em. He was here, sleeping in old Red Fish's lodge and carrying f'ar wood for the missus. It takes a mint of fuel for these here upstairs f'arplaces. The drafts is set wrong. But about midnight he come through the kitchen like the devil was after him. Susan, she thought she'd heard someone go through the door; she rises up and there he was, just goin'. She calls, but he don't answer—gits his horse and lights out. Po' fellow—real unsettled in his mind since his lady died. . . ."

Victoria's eyes were heavy, so heavy. She couldn't open them although she tried, and the rest of the conversation drifted beyond her. Time floated by, shapeless as a cloud. . . .

Suddenly she was awake. And hungry. She moved in the huge bed, raised herself on one elbow. Her eyelids obeyed; they opened on gray light, a small black child sitting cross-legged on the rag carpet, stringing dried apples from the basket beside her.

Victoria's movement caught the youngster's attention. Her eyes widened. Then with a tooth-flashing smile she scrambled to her feet, ran to the door, and cried, "Mam! Mam!"

In seconds Nancy came rustling in, hurried to the bedside, put her dark hand on Victoria's brow. "Good morning, Mrs. Winterthur. My, we're cool as a cucumber! That's fine." To the youngster poking her dark head around her starched apron she said, "Run for Miss Harriet, Peggy. Say Mrs. Winterthur's better."

Peggy obediently departed, catching up an apple slice to chew as she went. Victoria said apologetically, "I didn't mean to sleep all day."

"You didn't sleep all day, ma'am. You slept all two days. Miss Harriet said you were just plain worn out.'' Then, as she saw Victoria's horrified face, she said, ''Don't fret, miss. Mr. Owen said it didn't matter how much time it took as long as you got well again. Could you eat a bite now? You need to get your strength up.''

Victoria nodded—a little sheepishly because she was so hungry. As she did so, Harriet Clark came rustling in, throwing off a fringed shawl as she came. ''It is cold!'' she said. ''I've been helping Will hand out tea and sugar. Dragging Canoe has decided to go. That's the noise you hear. They loaf for days, then suddenly everything is in a tangle because they must leave on the hour. My dear, you look much better.''

She felt Victoria's brow as, for the first time, Victoria became aware of the rattles, yells, and curses drifting in from downstairs. ''On top of everything else,'' Mrs. Clark was saying, ''you were simply worn out! That's what I told Owen—not that he listened. And if the Sauk's medicine is right, I said, and there is a big snow coming, so much the better. I'd love to keep you *here* all winter, safe and sound. When I think of you and your valuables on that dangerous trail—'' She stopped, a light flush of embarrassment, of being too forward, on her pleasant face.

Victoria, sensing once again the heavy guilt of the stolen necklace, felt her own elation fade. She said a little stiffly, ''How kind you are! But it's not possible to stay, of course. I'm certain Owen has told you. He'll manage capably, I'm sure. And I feel I must get to Paul. It's very difficult to run both a household and an estate efficiently—Papa found that out. I want to lift Paul's burden— although by now he probably has his servants well trained. With a good staff one can cope nicely, don't you think?''

Harriet Clark said, ''Oh, my dear—'' then stopped. ''Of course,'' she finished pleasantly, but the expression she turned to Owen as he entered was a helpless one.

''Of course,'' Owen said, to no one in particular. ''How are you, Vick?''

''Much better, thank you.'' There was caution in her voice, caution that only he heard, that only he understood, but she couldn't help it. There was no larger danger to her resolutions in the entire wilderness that Harriet Clark talked of than Owen Verinder. She knew it now, and she must not allow herself to forget. Owen would deal with whoever meant to harm her—she must deal with Owen. It was really as simple as that.

He lounged before her, hands thrust deep into the front of some sort of stained leather weskit, tawny hair trailing back over the folds of a rough, knotted neck- scarf. She caught herself wondering if returning to the shabby trail-kit was deliberate, if he thought making himself a stranger to her would put distance between them. Well. He needn't worry. . . .

She said bravely, ''Whenever you want to travel . . .''

He shrugged. His eyes looked veiled. ''I did hear you decline a winter's hospitality?''

''You did indeed. Madam Clark is very kind, but it's not practical. Is it, Owen?'' She would make him say it, make him agree, underscore the fact she was Paul's wife and must go to Paul.

He merely shrugged again.

Nancy had gone to the door and taken a tray from a servant. It gave off wonderful smells! *How positively carnal I am,* Victoria thought ruefully. Nancy put the tray on the table, and while Harriet punched up the pillows at Victoria's back, brought her a dampened cloth and a hairbrush. Expertly she drew the brush through the soft mane of fair hair, coaxing it in damp curls around Victoria's ears. Owen turned away abruptly, and as she said, "See how cosseted I am! Perhaps I should reconsider, Owen!" he merely grunted. He picked up the three-tined fork, tasted the soft, buttered egg, the ham, even the creamy porridge, drank from her cup of tea. The movement was so casual, so idle—yet, with a sudden chill of truth, Victoria realized it was not casual, not idle at all. It had purpose. And it brought back the cold fact someone had tried to hurt her!

Madam Clark fussed at him: "Owen! Stop that! If you're so hungry, I'll have Susan bring you some!"

He grinned at her. "Never mind," he said. "I'm going down to the kitchen and stoke up with Robert shortly. Susan promised us fried pies when the Sauks are gone."

Harriet anchored the tray firmly on Victoria's lap. "Did Will tell you Shonnewwek wants to go back with you?"

As hungry as she was, Victoria's fork stopped halfway to her mouth. "An—Indian?"

Owen nodded. "Spice Bush. That's English for *Shonnewwek.* Will told me. That's fine. I can use him." The rather grim sound of his voice was suddenly split by a grin. "He says he has 'much pain in belly.' "

Harriet snorted. "He means 'heart.' But it's more likely in his cooking pot. His squaw stayed up at Ross's station for the winter, and I don't think Shonnewwek likes fending for himself. I should get myself back down to the yard. Owen, make her eat every bite."

She patted Victoria's free hand and bustled out. Owen lowered himself into the slipper chair, which groaned. When the door shut, his face seemed to close with it. In an almost expressionless voice he said, "We should go today, Vick. At least we can get across on the ferry and be ready for the bluffs tomorrow."

"Whatever you say, Owen."

He hoisted up the sole of an enormous boot, examined the surface minutely. In the same polite voice he went on, "Will is loaning us Robert to drive your carriage. But you must realize that if it snows, we may have to leave the carriage and finish on horseback. Can you—somewhat—condense your goods and chattels?"

She turned, looking at him in dismay. What could she possibly leave behind? She faltered, "My—my ball gowns. . . ."

To his enormous and everlasting credit he did not laugh. Instead he replied gravely, "Very good. It would be much better to leave them here, Vick, than to see them next spring on some fat squaw—which would happen if we had to cache them along the trail. Indians have insatiable curiosity, love, and there are no ownership labels in the wilderness. What else?"

There was a dab of porridge on her chin and she looked very like a little girl. Troubled, she said, "There's linens and flatware, and candlesticks, and my mother's epergne—"

"Leave them," he said. "You'll manage until spring without the epergne also." A careful note crept into his voice. "Best leave your other—valuables too."

The look she gave him was almost guilty. "I don't want Paul to be—ashamed of me," she said. "He does expect . . . certain things."

A wave of anger went over him. He stood up abruptly. She saw his face close, and without thinking, she cried, "Owen, please try to understand!"

He answered savagely, "I'll never understand!"

He turned to go and she caught at his sleeve. "Owen, wait! Can't we at least be friends?"

He froze. His face almost frightened her. It was dark, stony, his eyes slitted. In a silky voice he answered, "Friends, is it? You want a piece of everyone, don't you? Well, love, I'll show you the only kind of friends we can be."

He stooped, and her hands came up to push him away. But they couldn't. One arm half lifted her from the bed toward the hungry demand of his mouth. The fingers of the other pushed at the silk of her loose gown, freed the creamy globes of her breasts, cupped them, stroked them, while his mouth slid down the curve of her throat, hurrying toward their softpointed sweetness.

Then suddenly he was aware that his shirt was wet, that tears were slipping silently from beneath the fringed lashes of the face turned against it. He realized she was lying in his arms, supine. Unmoving.

He said violently, "Goddammit all to hell!" He almost flung her back against the pillows. "This takes two or it won't wash, Victoria! Are there going to be two?"

She couldn't answer. She lay very still, not daring to answer. She could hear his tortured breathing.

"If," he said between his teeth, "it wasn't for that bastard in your belly, Vick, there'd be two! Poor little sod; I won't bruise him up. It's not his fault. But you, missy, you remember this well: I'll hold. I can. For a while. But you damned well better stop letting me into your bedchamber when you're half dressed!"

That registered. The patent unfairness of it brought her upright, eyes wet but flashing. Then she said, "Oh!" and grabbed the bedclothes up around her ears. "*Letting* you!" she cried furiously. "*Letting* you, my hat! *Barging* is the word! Who do you think you are, Owen Verinder?"

He folded his arms, towering over her. And his voice went very quiet. "I know who I am," he said. "I know what I want. I also know I most generally get it." He went to the door.

While she stared at him, speechless, he made a courtly bow. "It will be a long, cold journey, Lady Winterthur," he said. "You'd better dress for it. Whatever mode you choose."

7

He had closed the door very quietly behind him.

After a long battle with her racing heart, Victoria slid slowly from the bed. The cold beneath her bare feet was the cold she'd heard in Owen's voice. Yet there'd been heat behind the cold, there'd been unleashed tigers hurling themselves against thin bars.

And deep inside her there had been tigers answering.

Had he just given her the one humiliating weapon she held against him? Owen had a genuine respect for life—life in any form, even beginning. She remembered so well his angry tenderness toward a little maid who'd been seduced, abandoned, and then discharged by her employer. He'd begged his aunt to reconsider, but Paul's mother was an adamant woman. The poor girl had then been found dead by the roadside, shot.

Owen's anger had been frightful. He could be a very frightening man. . . .

"Poor little sod," he'd just said. "I'll not bruise him up." Suddenly the full force of that statement hit her and her face flamed, but her body went weak. What an awful weapon she must use, then! Owen had changed. He was no longer a whole-hearted, ingenuous youth in an over-large frame. He was a man with a muscular body that breathed power. And she was no longer sixteen, but a woman . . . a woman who was married to someone else: There was the truth no matter how her heart raced, no matter how much the warm mounds and curves of her own body cried out for the force of his.

Pregnant she must be, and carry it like a shield!

But the Clarks! She couldn't explain herself there either, then, not even privately! She couldn't disclose the necklace!

Guilt slid over her again, guilt no longer rationalized by the memory of Lady Fandley's shabby, humiliating treatment of her helpless guest. She was a common thief. Perhaps Lady Fandley had already prevailed over her gentler husband to set the dogs on her trail.

Somehow Victoria would get the purchase price, somehow she'd send it back to him! The idea of telling Paul drenched her with shame—but "beggars can't be choosers"—a singularly relevant aphorism, she thought grimly, and not very comforting to a girl already in an embarrassingly hypocritical position with her kind and anxious hosts!

What could she say to the Clarks?

Nothing, she decided. Absolutely nothing.

The indelicacy of bringing up such a subject made her shrink. Explaining that she was *not* pregnant seemed fully as difficult as explaining how she could be such a thing. In her experience ladies did not seek out such matters. Besides, the next time she saw the Clarks it would be with her husband, she would be obviously *not* pregnant, and if desired, Harriet Clark and she could have a good laugh. If until then they must regard Paul as cuckolded, so be it. She was beginning to doubt seriously if such things really mattered out here in the wilderness anyway!

Victoria took a deep breath, quite sobered with resolutions. *I am twenty years old,* she thought. *At home that's quite an old maid. If I can't keep my own counsel now, I never shall.*

She straightened, and her bare foot stepped on something hard—mud from Owen's boot. Despite herself, the memory came flooding back: the feel of his mouth; his gentle fingers; the hard, tight warmth of his encircling arms.

"Oh damn!" she said aloud in a voice that would have shocked her nanny, and fled to the cold reality of the open window.

Below her, the Clarks' lawn was pockmarked with dead campfires trailing thin curls of smoke. A few tumbled lodgepoles and large splotches of bare, iron-hard earth were being nosed over by half a dozen lean hound dogs, their bristling hackles raised. Beyond the stake fence, stretching far across the bottoms, marched the motley members of the Saukee village. Blanketed braves on shaggy ponies with feathered lances flying led the way. Next the young bucks, defiantly half naked in the cold November air, and a few favored maidens mounted behind them spearheaded the main body. This spread across the crushed and broken grassland like a draggled tail. In its ranks fat squaws trudged, sending piercing screams of abuse after the horses that were stolidly pulling lodgepole travois, and a shifting prism of children darting to and fro. The rear was brought up by two dozen yapping, snapping yellow curs. Dragging Canoe was heading south in all his casual disarray.

Victoria looked down on them in wonder, seeing in her mind's eye the lawns of Landam Hall: velvet-green to the lush, herbacious borders, bright summer blooms in their carefully regimented order. How could Harriet Clark bear this continual assault on her household?

Her eye was further drawn to a figure of barbaric splendor remaining at the Clarks' gate. This Indian was blanket-wrapped to his knees, where soft-fringed leather boots, beaded and painted, finished the rather long trip to the desecrated ground. The top of his head was shaved to the crown. There, a bushy fetlock was bound by rawhide and pierced with an enormous, white-tipped feather that waved in the cold breeze. He was quite tall and well formed; however, the "noble savage" image dimmed somewhat in Victoria's eyes as the man directed an enormous brown stream of tobacco against the whitewashed gatepost.

She said, "Ugh," and turned away. Surely Paul would not expect her to put up with that sort of thing on his estate!

The sight of the carriage being pulled around to the hitching block with her boxes still tied on top brought her back to necessities. She put on her robe, winding the sash about her waist. With the robe belling behind her, she went to the hall door and called, "Nancy!"

"Be right there, miss."

Nancy's voice answered from somewhere around the bend of the stairs. Victoria nodded, turned—and found herself face to face with Thalia Greenwood.

Thalia wore the same dark green riding habit and a jaunty hat, but in the gray light of the hall her dark eyes were enormous in a white, sullen face. For a moment she stared at Victoria, who willfully stared back, and the tension between them was tight as a wire. Then Thalia laughed—scornfully, as her eyes swept Victoria up and down. "My God!" she said. "Why am I worried? Coming down on you would be like lying on a picket fence—especially to a man who likes soft boobies and bums as he does!"

It was a totally unexpected attack, a sort of rude infighting Victoria had never encountered before in her whole life! Anger flooded her; she sucked in her breath and the furious words almost came out: "He's not complained yet!"

Thank God they weren't said! Thank God Thalia had already turned on her booted heel, slammed the door of her room!

Weakly Victoria went back to her own room, stared appalled at the pale, angry breathing face in the mirror. Never in Lady Victoria's life had she ever even thought of such words—beyond actually saying them! What was this low-minded, rustic country doing to her—and so soon?

But on the other hand, no one had ever tried to hurt her before—badly, maliciously, as that girl had done. It was a good thing she was to be sent packing to St. Louis!

Nancy's entry forced Victoria to be calm. When bathed, laced, and buttoned, she descended the stairs; the civilized gentlewoman was in charge again.

It was her intent to make some hard, practical choices among her myriad possessions. To her dismay she found them already made. The burly driver was cording two small trunks on top of the carriage with another box she couldn't identify. The rest of her baggage sat abandoned on the wet lawn.

Angrily she began, "Owen, what have you done—" but he cut across her indignation: "Take off that fool hat."

"What?"

"Take off that fool hat!" Not waiting, he took it off himself, tossing it summarily on top of the abandoned trunks.

"Owen Verinder—"

"It won't keep you warm, Vick. Fashion doesn't mean a thing when your ears are freezing."

"I have my plaid!"

"And thank God for it; it's the only sensible thing you do have. Harriet is loaning you a hood and some mufflers. Be a good child and put one on."

His air of command was insufferable, but the wind had a cutting edge. Meekly she obeyed, winding the long ends around her throat, tucking in the loosened strands of pale hair. It was warmer, and she needn't let pride make her foolish.

Only where the lodges had been was the ground dry, and the gray air smelled of soaked bark and acrid smoke. It went into her lungs, raw and cold. Harriet Clark, herself shawl-swathed, came out of the house with a bundle of blankets. She nodded approval at the muffler, and handed the blankets to Owen, who put them inside the carriage. She said, "I hate to admit it, but the Indians are so often right. Please try to get across the prairie before it snows, Owen."

From on top of the carriage Robert laughed.

"If anyone has snuff with the Almighty, you do, ma'am," he said. "Why don't you take care of the snow for us?"

Harriet blushed. "I'll pray," she said. "Truly I will."

Owen grinned at her. "With my compass, Shonnewwek's instinct for a warm bed, and your prayers, we can't go wrong," he said.

General Clark emerged with Job, who carried a wicker basket. His eyes were serious, his pleasant face sober.

"There's wine and cheese and chicken and roast pheasant," he said. Owen whistled.

"Good God. I expected to introduce Vick to hoecake and jackrabbit."

"You may do that too," said Clark, "before it's over. Are you ready to move out? It's a fair trip just to the ferry and for my own comfort I want you on the other side of the Miss' before nightfall. I feel ice in my bones."

"Thanks," said Owen drily. They shook hands warmly. Victoria found herself embraced by Madam Clark, her slightly stilted words of gratitude brushed aside. The general handed her into the carriage and Nancy mounded her in blankets, pushing hot wrapped stones beneath her feet. From the stables at the back of the house stalked the same tall Indian Victoria had noticed from her window. He led two mounts, one a tough, small pony, and the other a long-legged buckskin with a saddle. The reins of that one he handed silently to Owen. Then, turning to Clark, he spoke in a soft, liquid language. The general replied in kind and they clasped fingers in a stiff, almost ritualistic shake of farewell. The Indian swung up on his pony. Ludicrously his long legs almost touched the ground.

Owen had kissed Harriet Clark affectionately, sweeping her up high in his arms. Now he handed her, still aloft, to her husband, turned and put one foot in his stirrup.

For a moment his motion was stopped. Frozen.

Then he put the foot back on the ground and asked in a cold, quiet voice, "Where the hell do you think you're going?"

Thalia Greenwood had come from behind the tall brick house. She rode a chestnut mare that curvetted nervously as it passed the impassive Indian. A blanket-wrapped bundle was tied behind her saddle. Her face was pale, her voice thin: "I'm going with you."

"You are not."

"Owen—"

"You heard me. I have troubles enough."

The dark eyes blazed. "I won't be half the trouble she is!"

The *she* was eloquent. Owen's face set in stone. He took one step toward her. In a voice barely heard by the others he said, "You turn that mare and you get yourself moving toward Saint Louis."

Huge tears brimmed up, began to slip down the white cheeks. "Owen, please—"

He lifted his hand to smack the chestnut's flank. He didn't see the green-clad arm flash, but he was quick enough to fend the slashing quirt from his face. The chestnut reared, plunged and, goaded, took off at a dead run down the trail, the little figure laid low along her neck and the full habit flowing out behind. Water dashed from the flying hooves.

In the vacuum she left behind, Harriet took a deep, audible breath. "You're right," she said. "You're totally right, Owen. But—what *is* to become of her?"

His face still tight, Owen swung astride his own horse. "Let's hope that school puts some sense in her," he said. "But it's not likely. Let's go, Robert."

The driver clucked to his team and the big wheels of the carriage lurched into that swaying jolt so familiar to Victoria. Owen and the erect Sauk moved ahead, their horses' feet *plop-plopping* through the wet. Robert followed. Victoria waved until the tall brick house was lost in the gray mist; then she leaned back, eyes closed, gulping back her own unexpected tears.

As they crossed the stone bridge, Owen eyed the creek water. It was running high and clear, and ice gleamed along the ledges. Not good. Not good at all. The wind, as they breasted into it, was painfully cold. Shonnewwek had already turtled his blanket up about his ears. Owen pulled his capote hood over his hat. Robert had started to whistle, but he soon stopped as the chill reached his lungs. They rode in the silence of a dozen noises—the wet spray as water dashed from sixteen hooves and rolled from the carriage wheels, the clink and jingle of harness, the creak of leather springs, the snorting of horses torn from warm stables as they saw their breath mist in plumes on the morning air.

Suddenly, high overhead, geese honked. Looking up, they saw a ragged V darting uncertainly through the gray sky.

"Bad," said Shonnewwek. "Bad sign. We hurry."

Owen nodded. Robert "gee-upped" to his team, and the carriage lumbered a little faster.

Inside, Victoria felt the pace increase. She didn't hear the geese; it would have meant nothing if she had. But she leaned forward, peering out the small window, clearing the mist with one gloved hand.

There was nothing to be seen but gray sky and endless land, its tall, dry grasses laid over by wind and glistening with water. She leaned back again, and realized the carriage was draughty. Wind made little whistles through the trap and around the windows. However, her feet were warm, and with her plaid cape drawn around her shoulders, she was fairly comfortable. Shutting her eyes, she thought without regret of Thalia Greenwood riding toward St. Louis. Sulking, no doubt, and livid with jealousy.

There had certainly been no affection in the voice with which Owen had scored the girl off! Victoria would not allow herself to admit how that pleased her—such thoughts were not only dangerous but undignified. That Owen apparently also blew hot and cold in his flirtations was not her concern, either, she decided virtuously. However, when such unmitigated hatred spewed out in things like that guitar string—then they could not be ignored. Owen had not denied the girl loved him; the fact probably fed his enormous vanity, yet he was sensible enough to realize both women together on one trip would be untenable.

I can understand, Victoria told herself from her new height of resolute maturity. *Women—young or old—sense rivalry. Thalia sensed it in me—but she's too obsessed with Owen to realize that he and I are through, that I am Paul's wife now, and must not permit any—* She stopped, flushing at the word that came to mind, her heart whipping at the picture it conjured: *intimacies.* No, no, she couldn't say that, not even in her private thoughts! Relationship! That was better: she must not permit any relationship—

She stopped again, changing *must* not to *will* not.

Owen was an old friend—she had to concede the permissions of friendship. But it had to stop there!

"Vick?"

She'd been so totally submerged in her desperate word games, she failed to see the door open; and Owen, bending from horseback, thrusting his face inside, threw her into a complete voiceless panic.

She gasped, then, in a shaking voice, said, "Owen!"

"Vick, love, who did you expect?" Then, entirely misunderstanding her fast breath, he said, "Vick, Vick, trust me! My God, you surely know anyone getting in here to hurt you will have to come over my dead body!"

Faintly, but in indignation, she replied, "Don't be heroic! You just startled me!"

Heroics having been far from his intent, his jaw set ominously. "Sorry!" he snapped, and slammed the door.

Conscious of feeling injured, and aware of how childish the feeling was, Owen resumed his place ahead of the carriage with Shonnewwek, who was chewing solemnly on a ragged strip of dried beef. The geese still wheeled above, and the cold air was so wet, he could almost taste it on his lips as the day wore on.

The line of scrub willows and towering cottonwoods was a welcome sight. It meant the riverbank; and shortly they were going down to it on brush laid across sucking mud so deep, it was treacherous. Victoria had half drowsed, but the sudden, violent rocking of the carriage brought her up sharply, holding on with both hands.

At last the motion stopped. The door opened again. Owen's face, encircled by his capote hood, looked at her coldly, and his voice was short. "All right?"

She nodded, and let go her frantic clutch at the carriage sides. "Where— where are we?"

"The ferry slip."

Bang! went a burst of noise right at her ear. She cried out, involuntarily thrusting her hands toward Owen. He caught them both in his. "Good old Owen," he said wryly. "The protector. Not too bright, but very reliable."

She ignored that. "What was it?"

"The ferry's on the other side. Shonnewwek fired a shot to bring it back. You're to stay in the carriage when we load. I don't want you underfoot."

It was not a request but a command. She went rigid, very aware of the strong hands holding hers, not letting go. "I'm stiff. I need to walk around."

"There's a station on the other side. We'll put up there for the night, and you can do all the walking around you want."

He looked down at his hands and suddenly seemed surprised to find them holding hers. "Oh," he said. "Sorry. Old habits are hard to break."

He smiled, showing too many teeth, dropped her hands, and shut the door. She heard his feet squishing away.

The hot stones were cold and her cramped legs ached. Resentfully she waited, listening. It seemed hours before a hailing voice announced the ferryman.

Chains rattled; overhead, Robert shook his reins. There was a sickening dip as he drove forward onto the pitching lip of the raftlike ferry. From her window Victoria could see nothing but roiled, scuddy water, rising up and down, up and down. It couldn't be a river! It was like a lake, an ocean! And there was no rail on this ferry—nothing between her and those enormous, chopping waves. In sudden panic she thought, *If this thing goes under, I'm a rat in a trap.*

She scrambled to the door, flung it open, thrust her feet down blindly. The surface of close-lined logs was slimy slick. Helplessly she skidded, her arms trapped by her cape, arrested only by the alert Shonnewwek. Then he slipped, grunting in alarm. It took Owen, with a sound purchase around a wooden upright, to catch them both just as the hungry river lapped the bulk of her skirts.

Wordlessly angry, he thrust her back up inside the carriage, slamming the door on her white face. Scolding would have to wait. The horses were sliding all over, held only by their tethers. Robert was busy helping the young ferryman, lending his heft to the steering oar.

"Pap's sick," the boy panted. "He's been sick three days past—since some damned fool swiped the ferry in the night and he had to swim the horses over to get it. Ol' river's mighty cold. Heave right, mister, or that snag'll swamp us!"

Robert heaved with a will.

"There," the boy said. His lips were blue and his teeth were chattering. "Now we'll make quiet water. Mam said I shouldn't bring 'er out. But I just purely can't leave strangers on the south bank when it's comin' up mean weather. Pap wouldn't. Hang on; we're going to jolt!''

The entire ferry shuddered as it ground its lip into the mud. The boy hopped out, took quick turns around an old cottonwood bole before it could slip back, then threw down a battered gangplank. "Best lead your horses," he called. "The team too. We can roll the carriage off and hitch it back on the bank. Pap had a span of mules bolt last week—they tangled their traces and put a wagon over the side. 'Most lost it all. It's deep here.''

Victoria felt the carriage move forward again, jolting over logs so rough, she set her teeth to keep her jaw from rattling. Then it stopped, the door opened, and in the gathering gloom she saw Owen's face.

"Now you may walk," he said grimly.

She climbed out, her stiff legs awkward, almost falling against him. "Where?"

"Up the bank to the station," he replied. "It's not far and it will help you get the kinks out.''

She moved away, staggered, and caught helplessly at his arm.

"Just a moment," she said. "Just a moment. I'll be all right.''

He waited with ill-concealed impatience, his eyes not on her but the surrounding dark. A gust of wind blew out her plaid cape like a sail. She gathered it close trying to shut out the cold. Night was falling fast. Too fast. Then she raised her eyes and understood why.

They'd reached the bluff line. It towered over them, shutting off the waning daylight, rising in wave after wave of tangled brush and monster trees and crumbling limestone, like an enormous, ancient monolith. The tiny star of light in the station window seemed a mere pea caught in its roots. The ferry slip was on a narrow ledge that, even as they looked, the river seemed bent on chewing away.

Victoria shivered. Forgetting the constraint between them, she asked, "Owen, how do we get around this thing?"

"My dearest Vick," he answered flatly, "we do not get around. We go up it. Then we go down it. Wherever we can go up and down. And," he added, "if we are lucky we keep ahead of the ice. Move along, Lady Winterthur. The first to arrive get the beds at the station. And if you have to share, I'd on the whole rather have it me than Shonnewwek. He has a squaw."

8

In the dimming light behind them Robert led his team over to the carriage, backed them between the traces. Shonnewwek started up the stiff ruts of the trail with his little pony and Owen's mount. Hoisting himself to the box, Robert chirruped, flapping his reins. The carriage creaked into motion, throwing muddy water from its wheels. The ferryboy loped along beside it, one hand on the door panel as it tilted precariously, his long, unkempt hair tossing in the wind, wet to the knees and panting with his exertion.

Victoria said indignantly, "He's too young, he shouldn't be doing that!"

Owen shrugged. "Out here you do what you can," he said. His hand tightened on her elbow. "All right. Come along. This way."

For the first time she noticed he'd taken his long rifle from its sheath on his saddle, was carrying it loosely, by the middle, his fingers curved around the trigger loop. "Owen, aren't these people honest?"

He shrugged again. "It's all in your point of view," he answered, which was ridiculous. "Watch out." The warning meant a gnarled tree-root, which she obligingly tripped over anyway, only his hand keeping her from going down. Wisely she decided to save her breath for what he seemed to feel was a path; she couldn't see it! Wet cedar branches brushed her face, rocks bore into her boot soles, the earth crumbled and caved beneath her. They came to a ledge; he took it with a single wide step of his long leg, reached down for her. She grabbed at a wiry tussock and pulled; it came loose in her hand, showering her face with wet dirt. She sputtered like an angry kitten, "I could have ridden!"

He yanked her up on his ledge with a wrench that caught her close, hard against his side, so hard she could feel his tight thigh muscles, the keen outline of a sheathed knife. Beneath the glistening wet capote hood his eyes were narrowed, cold.

"Listen, Vick," he said tautly, "like it or not, I'm master on this trip! You disobeyed me once and almost got drowned. Do it again and you may get us all killed. Don't question me! Understand?"

"Let me go."

He bored: "Do you understand?"

"Yes! Yes! Let me go!"

He did, so abruptly that she almost fell again.

"It's easy from here," he went on calmly, as though the blaze had not been in his deep voice. Grasping her cold hand, he walked ahead, leading her like a sulky child. The low cedar branches brushed his head, showering water on her. She took it with compressed lips. The ground beneath her was springy with needles, and ahead she could glimpse the weathered log corner of a building. Horses were nickering too, traces jingling, and dogs barking stormily. One huge, slick hound suddenly bounded toward them, ears laid back, teeth bared. Heightening his viciousness was a livid white scar, running from crown to nose.

Owen snapped, "Stand still!"

To the beast he said, "All right, Pedro, all right. . . ."

The animal skidded to a stop, stretched his scarred nose out cautiously. Victoria hardly breathed.

Then the tail wagged, the ears came up. Pedro gave Owen's hand a friendly bunt as if to say, "Sorry, I didn't know it was you," wheeled, and loped back to join the fray around the horses' heels.

"Oh. . . ." Victoria said, on a long sigh. "He recognized you."

"Yes."

"Paul had a dog named Pedro."

"That's the dog. He ran away. He's a ferryboat dog now."

"Paul doesn't want him back?"

"Paul doesn't want to see him again." And he didn't explain. They'd reached the high-lofted, double cabin. Beyond it, by some lean-to stables, the carriage, the horses and the dogs were milling. Robert was cursing, laying about with his boot. Shonnewwek, feet tucked up on his pony's back, was gazing from his inelegant perch with a look of unconcern. The cabin door burst open, and a tall, thin woman with a corn broom charged forth, screaming and flailing; the dogs fled like chaff in the wind and Owen, saying, "Inside!" in Victoria's ear, hustled her across the open threshold.

Still holding her arm, he swept the small crowded room with his eyes, strode to the partition, raised the blanket, and scanned the next room. Only then, dropping the blanket back into place, did he let go. He also slid his fingers from the trigger loop of his rifle, clasping it loosely by the barrel, butt on the puncheon floor.

A bundled-up man by the deep fireplace said weakly, "'Pears you're a mite restless today, Owen."

"Times are hard, Reuben," Owen answered with a carelessness Victoria knew he didn't feel. "How are you?"

"Puny. Got the heaves in my chest. You ain't totin' some of that good whiskey from Clark's Job, be you?"

"You think it might perk you up?"

"Or I'd die happy. Set a spell, ma'am. My old woman'll be in shortly. She's got her hands full, she and the boy, with me laid low. How many in your party, Owen? We might have to put another chunk of bear in the stew."

"Three of us."

Victoria said quickly, "Four—the Indian."

"Indians don't count, ma'am. They grub for themselves." The ferryman took a fit of coughing, leaned over, and spit in the fire. He was small and wiry and balding; his coloring was feverish. Owen handed him a dipper of water from the bucket by the door. "Much traffic, Reuben?"

The man's eyes went to the loft, but it was such a flicker neither Owen nor Victoria saw it. He occupied himself in haste, drinking greedily. "Thankee, Owen. No, not to mention. No travelers here." He said that positively. "The dogs have been barking around, but I figure it's some laggard Sauks trying to catch up with the village."

There was a half-log bench drawn to the fire. Victoria sat on the end of it, feet in the ashes, trying to wring water from her saturated dress-tail. Heavy smells assaulted her nose—pungencies from the strings of onion and garlic overhead, smoke from the poorly drawing fire, a rich, brothy miasma from the blackened, bubbling pot on its crane. She took her mind from the fact that it was bear in that pot, tried to forget the fine, overlaying stench of wet dog and sweaty men, put her mind, instead, on a bed for the night. She didn't believe Owen, of course—that nonsense about Shonnewwek. But where was it? Perhaps beyond the hanging blanket. . . .

Her eye was caught by some writing, chalked on a smoothed slab by the door. Written by a crude hand, it read:

RATES
1 PERSON 25¢
1 HORSE 25¢
EACH HEAD CATTLE OVER A YEAR 25¢
EVERY HOG, SHEEP, GOAT 6$\frac{1}{2}$¢
WAGON, FOUR WHEELS 50¢
1CWT DEAD LUMBER 6$\frac{1}{4}$¢

Then below in a line was scrawled: 1 MEAL 25¢, LODGING PER NIGHT 12^1/2¢, HORSEKEEPING PER DAY 37^1/2¢. FRENCH BARBERING ON REQUEST.

Sudden laughter welled up inside Victoria as she remembered her father's French barber—his cascading laces, his waxed mustaches, the delicate high heels on his shoes. If Monsieur Debeq could only see her now!

Laughter was followed swiftly by depression—if her father could only see her now: draggled, wet, untidy hair frizzed across a dirty forehead, Savile Row boots streaked with mud and ashes. He hadn't meant this to happen! She couldn't blame him, she should have, herself, seen approaching disaster. . . .

The door opened, ending her sober soliloquy, admitting the tall woman with her corn broom; the wiry young boy; Robert, with mud to his eyebrows; Shonnewwek, whose deerskin shoepacs were squishing water; and the large scarred dog, who wormed his way through the forest of wet legs right to the warm hearth, where he proceeded to shake his soaked fur all over everyone.

Reuben dodged back, roaring, "Get that damned beast out of here!"

Quietly his son said, "Come, Pedro. Down," and bedded his dog around the chimney breast with his back against the warm stones. His dark eyes gave little sympathy to Victoria, who was trying to mop muddy water with a minuscule handkerchief.

Owen was counting out bit pieces to the lady of the house, whose tongue worked agonizingly as she added. This transaction completed to her satisfaction, she dropped the money with a clink inside her dress and turned her attention to Victoria.

She said brusquely, "Best you come with me before you float."

Victoria rewarded everyone by turning agonizingly pink. Wordlessly she followed her hostess, leaving a chorus of unfeeling guffaws. On her return she found the male entourage feeding themselves amply from calabash bowls of the stew.

"Help yourself," said Owen shortly, tipping his to get the last of the broth. "Then go to bed. We have to move out of here before sunrise. You're short a child, Reub. Where's Sarah?"

"In t' loft."

"Sick?"

"Ague," said the father, and "Fever," said the mother, and then looked at each other.

"You know," said Madam Reuben, taking it up. "Fever and chills. She ain't a healthy youngun. I got her bedded down warm; it's about all I can do. Here you are, lady." She turned from the pot with a lavish helping of stew, held it out kindly to Victoria. "Menfolks ain't very gallant out here. This is what you do: Tear off a piece of corncake, see. Dip in, kind of using the corncake for a shovel. It ain't dainty, but it fills the belly."

Her broad, tired face was sympathetic. Victoria murmured her thanks and followed instructions. It was greasy and dripping, and she knew without a look that that horrid Owen Verinder was grinning at her.

Well. He could just grin! Defiantly, putting out of her mind all thoughts of the wine and the roasted pheasant in the wicker basket on the carriage seat, she ate it, progressing with increasing desperation through the enormous portion. Suddenly she found Owen's big hand coming out, removing the calabash.

"That's enough," he said, and surprisingly he sounded kind, caring. "You'll be sick."

"It's very good."

"Yes, Vick. I know it is." Stretching out a long arm, he put the bowl on the floor by Pedro, who quietly swallowed the rest. "You're not well, yet. You'd better go to bed. I'll bring some blankets from the carriage."

Hoisting his huge frame aloft, he went out with Shonnewwek, who was contentedly sucking on something that looked like meat but smelled disgusting. Madam Reuben said, "Come along, m'dear."

She thrust aside the hanging, pointed through the doorway to the other side.

This part of the double cabin was tinier yet, with a fireplace at the farther end, a dirt floor, and no windows. From each of the two corner ends low wooden frames were built out on two sides, meeting at stout saplings firmly driven into the sod. Sagging rope laced the primitive beds; a tumbled heap of dubious bedclothing ornamented one. The other was empty, and the woman indicated it with a sweep of a worn hand.

"There you be," she said cheerfully. "T'other belongs to my man and me. We most always rent it out too, but him feeling puny, I figure he needs his bed. Your menfolk can have shakedowns on the floor by the fire."

Owen brushed by, dropped an armful of blankets on the gray old ropes. "Wrap up good," he said and grinned—that same, almost mocking grin that was starting to annoy her. "I've slept there; your backside always freezes."

They both turned, the blanket over the doorway dropped, and Victoria was left alone.

No light but the fire, no nightclothes, no robe, no way to wash. No one to unlace her.

She could call Madam Reuben, but somehow she shrank from the idea.

Then she'd sleep in her laces! It certainly would solve the problem of tomorrow morning.

She hurriedly slipped out of her heavy skirt, tried to arrange it along the hearth so it would dry with her boots and stockings. The waist and jacket went neatly folded beneath the bed. Then, shivering in her bare feet and long petticoats, she spread two blankets, jumping nervously at every burst of laughter from the other room, lay down, pulled the third blanket over her and her old plaid over that.

It was like lying in a hammock. And her neck was going to ache.

Grimly she reached out a bare arm, got her jacket, rolled it into a ball, and stuck it beneath her head. Much better. Covered to the chin, she stared up wide-eyed at the smoky, cobwebby ceiling, imagining horrid, crawly things dropping down on her, and told herself she'd never go to sleep, never in a million years.

She went to sleep.

Out in the other room pipes were being smoked, Madam Reuben sharing hers with her husband, who coughed but persisted.

"So that's Mrs. Winterthur," she said. "I ain't never seen a real English lady before."

Owen smiled, a little wryly. "They put their drawers on one leg at a time just like you do, Betsy."

"She 'pears a mite delicate."

"She is," he answered, and this time he didn't smile. Reuben leaned over, got a coal from the fire, relighted his wife's long, clay calumet. "So Winterthur broke his leg. Reckon it didn't hurt many feelings. You never said—is it bad?"

Owen shrugged. "I don't know. I wasn't with him when he broke it. The word just came down I was to come get Victoria. We're not precisely—chums. I do my work, I draw my pay."

"When you can," said Robert plainly. The big Englishman shot him a sudden cold look, and he subsided, leaning back, wiggling his toes through the holes in his socks as he warmed his feet on the fender.

"I seen one of his big dun mares," Billy said suddenly, as he stretched out on the floor, his head on Pedro's warm flank. "Up on the trail. Clear as paint. That'd be the day you crossed."

Inside the leather vest Owen's chest tightened. Casually he puffed smoke, leaned, stroked the dog's dark head. The boy went on, "Couldn't tell the rider. Too dark. I hallooed, but didn't get no answer. And I knowed it to be Winterthur's mare; Pedro was growling."

"Now I tol' you," said his father. "That 'breed rides one of them mares. What's his name—Mersey. And that's who it had to be, because Mersey always crosses upriver at the Indian fording and he sure as hell didn't take the ferry here. Lessen," he added, "he was the rascal that took it at night. And I doubt that. He ain't hardly got the heft for it."

His wife abruptly knocked her dottle on the hearth. "Finish your pipes," she said. "This house is closing down."

In ten minutes the entire ménage was bedded.

Owen, Robert, and the boy, Billy, lay like large sausages, their feet toward the fire as it burned through the heart of the night log, drying their boots, sending small curls of steam from wet garments. Billy got up, let out a restless Pedro, fell immediately back to sleep again. It began to rain—first a light patter like mice feet, then a persistent drum on the shake roof.

Outside Shonnewwek made a grunt of disgust, moved himself into the lean-to among the warm horses. It never entered his head to take shelter in the white man's carriage. It was too close, too penned. A man must breathe. . . .

Pedro ambled by and bared his teeth, but it was a perfunctory gesture, a duty, and they both knew it. Besides, there were strange smells, familiar smells intensified by the rain, smells that raised the hackles on his neck. Quiet as a shadow, he slipped away to investigate.

Inside the cabin Victoria was suddenly wide awake, horrified to find a long form burrowing in beside her. She sucked in her breath to scream, found a large hand on her mouth, Owen's quiet voice whispering, "Shut up, Vick. This is no assault on your virtue. That damned floor is crawling with fleas and roaches. Go back to sleep; you're safe as in church."

The frame shook as he flailed his length about, trying to get comfortable. She clung to the rough log wall on her side, almost hanging suspended, trying not to touch him. Her reward was losing her pillow. Exasperated, she twitched it back, lost her grip, slid downhill. They bumped hips. He put a hand out, felt, asked in an incredulous voice, "Good God, Vick, what have you got on? You feel like a pewter jug-handle!"

"My laces," she hissed back, "and keep your hands to yourself!"

He mumbled, "Grow up!", flounced on his side, his back to her.

Still as a mouse, she waited.

In the other bed both Reubens were snoring, a bucksaw cacophony that reamed the ears. But finally she thought she could hear Owen breathing deeply. Bit by bit, then, she let her body relax against his backside. He was warm; he was so deliciously warm. . . .

But just when she was drifting off, he turned again, like a child, sighing, gathered her into his arms, buried his nose and chin in her soft hair. Stiff once more, hardly breathing again, she waited.

He was so relaxed, so still, Victoria thought. *He must be asleep.*

Cradled as she was, one hand lay caught beneath her, the other doubled against his chest. His twisting and turning had brought the shirt from his trousers; her palm lay on bare skin. The deep, steady beating of his heart against her cheek lulled her too. Her palm moved, in innocent sensuousness, liking the strong feel of his flat, lean belly muscles, the silk mat of hair on his broad chest. Her fingers entwined gently, softly.

Then a deep, thick voice said in her ear, "Vick, if you don't mean it, don't do it."

She snatched back her hand as though burned, almost scrambled to the log wall, losing covers and pillow as she fled.

After a long, tense moment Owen's hand reached out, pulled the blankets back over her. A little wearily he said, "Good night, Vick," hoisted himself erect and went back into the other room.

Left alone, Victoria stared at the ceiling. Scalding tears ran down her pale cheeks and dried only when she finally let sheer exhaustion take her back to sleep.

9

Victoria awakened once again to the sound of drumming rain, the hissing drip of the leak over the chimney piece, the distant whistling of young Reuben calling, "Here, Pedro, here, Pedro!"

The room was as dark as ever, but she was quite alone; it must be morning. Yet for a moment she could not make herself move. She could only huddle there beneath the warm covers in a total and desolate misery. How could she have let him go last night! How could she have lain like a lump allowing him to return to the fleas and roaches. She shuddered, a wave of revulsion shaking her whole body. Owen—who had always smelled of soap and scrubbing, not sartorially perfect like Paul who had seemed faintly perfumed but—but clean!

She struggled to a sitting posture, her petticoats bunched about her waist, her loosened hair flowing across her shoulders. She felt ashamed, humiliated. Petty.

Yet perhaps things were better this way. Perhaps she'd best leave well enough alone.

Snatches of conversation from the other room spurred her into movement. Still sitting, she buttoned on her waist, smoothed down the petticoats, swung pale feet to the cold floor and hurried into her stiffly dried skirt. Only then—feeling decently clad—did she sit down again for shoes and stockings.

These were beautifully warm, but there was a fine pepper-spray of holes where popping cinders had taken their toll. But it couldn't be helped. She put on her boots, caked with a sort of claylike mud, and stood erect, moving her slender back inside the stiff lacing. It had been like sleeping in a tube. *A pewter jug-handle,* she thought inevitably, and blushed.

She needed a wash, but it was so cold, she almost didn't mind. The cumbersome jeweled ring on her flnger flashed as she hurriedly twigged up her hair, skewering the knot with four pins—all she could find. Then, shivering, she hurried through the blanket-hung doorway.

It was just daylight. Rain was falling in a gray curtain all around. The men were hunched over tin cups of bitter-smelling chicory coffee. Their eyes swivelled as she entered but their faces remained set in the sort of blank expression a man has in early morning when he's already stiff and tired, yet knows it's going to be a long, long day.

Madam Reuben was bent over the blazing fire, stirring some indefinable mess with a wooden spoon. "Morning," she said briefly. "Coffee's on the fender."

It was then that Victoria missed Owen among the faces, and her heart skipped a beat. It was absurd even thinking he'd leave her, that he'd go away and let Robert take her on to Paul—yet what would she do if he did?

This useless speculation was ended when he came in, bringing a cold, raw blast of air with him, dripping rain from the brim of his hat, taking a glistening piece of canvas from his broad shoulders and chucking it into a corner.

"There's a light streak in the west," he said, holding his hands to the fire, rubbing them. "Maybe it will let up. Damn, it's cold. Good morning, Vick."

"Good morning." She hesitated. "Can we go?"

"We have to go. Better rain than ice, I guess. We'll take the left trail. Blue Creek is coming down in a torrent over the right one. No luck, Bill?" This to the young Reuben, coming in behind him, shivering and wet, his hair plastered lank to his thin face.

Billy said, "None. I've looked everywhere."

"He'll turn up," said his mother. She was ladling what appeared to be gray glue and handing it around in the same calabashes. "Pedro don't get lost. He's smart."

Robert was putting a sizable dollop of honey in his bowl. He handed the pot on to Victoria. She saw quite a few bits of dismembered bee still swirling in the pale amber, felt her stomach roll, and hastily passed it on to Owen. She murmured, "I don't think I'm hungry," and he didn't urge her to eat.

The door opened again, and Shonnewwek, dipping his head beneath the low lintel, came inside. He said something in his own language to Owen, and Victoria saw Owen's eyes narrow, his jaw set.

Madam Reuben brushed by, called, "You feel like eatin' something, Sarry?"

A small voice from the loft answered, "Yes, ma'am." Two skinny girl-legs in limp calico began to descend the ladder by the wall. Abruptly Owen put down his bowl; both he and the Sauk stalked back out into the rain.

"It's letting up," said Billy, following them to the door. He stood watching, and Victoria sensed a feeling of unease among the three of the adult Reubens.

But it missed the burly Robert. Cheerily scraping out his bowl for the third time he said, "Mighty fine porridge, missus. But I expect I'd best go see to my team."

Sarah Reuben was pale, thin, and lavishly adorned with freckles. She took the calabash from her mother by feel, unable to tear her wide eyes from cataloging every bit of Victoria's hair, face, figure, and costume. Finally, in a loud whisper she said, "She's purty. I don't care what anybody says!"

Victoria smiled, said, "Thank you, Sarah," not noticing her flustered mother.

But as she went back into the other room to gather the blankets, she heard a distinct smack, and Sarah began to cry. And when she came out with her armload, the child was gone.

Owen was in the cabin again, and his face looked lined, set. He took the blankets from Victoria, said, "It's getting lighter. Let's move out."

When Victoria finished her manners with the Reubens, she turned and found the carriage hardly two feet from the open door. She was acute enough to realize it wasn't totally to keep her dry because Owen was carrying his long gun again. As he helped her inside, she whispered anxiously, "Owen, what's wrong? What happened?"

"Shonnewwek found signs. Someone was around the horses last night. Whoever it was, he was pretty trail-wise because Shonnewwek didn't hear—and he's damned piqued about it. They took a bottle of wine and the pheasant."

She caught her breath. "From the carriage! Owen, why didn't the dogs bark?"

"Where was Pedro? That's what worries me. There's blood beneath a cedar where the rain hasn't washed, and some dog hair. Shonnewwek's gone on uptrail. We'd better move after him."

Decisively he shut the door on her worried face.

She stood up, and despite the rain, lifted the trap. Robert's ruddy face smiled down at her. "Don't fret, missus. Ol' Spice Bush, he's got his dander up now— whoever was around, he'll nail 'em. Best sit down and stay dry."

He had a gun across his knees!

Victoria obeyed, mostly because her own knees were shaking. On the seat beside her was the wicker basket, its fastenings still undone. She didn't even want to touch it.

Traces jingled, Robert shouted, "Hi-ya!" and the carriage lurched forward, bumping over the stiff ruts of the cabin compound. Victoria was glad she hadn't eaten any breakfast.

As the day lightened, the rain turned to a fine mist, beading every bush, every boulder, every tree. At first Owen rode beside the carriage, his gun balanced before him on the saddle. Then the trail narrowed and he dropped behind, disdaining the hood that would cover his cold ears. Once he stopped, turned, one hand on his mount's broad rump, and listened. Nothing. Where was Mersey? How long would he wait? Or—what was he waiting for?

He nudged the horse up again.

They were in thick timber now. Gnarled trees hung with naked grapevines crowded for space among the hickories and honey locust. They were traversing an ancient waterway sided with moss and dead roots. The horses picked their way cautiously, scuffling through the dead leaves, avoiding the rain-slick limestone, the treacherous, loose gravel. The worn banks were sometimes chest-high, sometimes over Owen's head.

He'd be glad when they got out of this stretch. It was good for the carriage to travel but he felt uneasy, hemmed in.

A crashing in the brush brought him up in his stirrups, gun ready but too late. A big buck deer sailed across the ravine almost above his hat, thundered on through the thickets.

He was relieved, and not relieved. What had spooked the buck? And where the living hell was Shonnewwek? And what had happened to Pedro? That bothered him almost as much as anything. . . .

There was daylight and a break in the trees ahead. They were coming to that big wash where, years ago, half the bluff had tumbled down, leaving the face looking as though some giant had taken a bite and then spewed it.

Owen urged his mount past the carriage, trying to avoid the slapping mud of the big wheels. He glanced in as he edged by, caught a brief glimpse of Vick's face staring straight ahead, felt his heart turn over. She was Paul's girl; that's all there was to it. Whatever happened back home to get her in this state, whatever happened now with Paul Winterthur, he'd just have to weather it, learn to live with it.

The carriage lurched out of the waterway, its wheels protesting, slipping on the soapstone ledge. Robert was whoaing his team, setting the long, wooden brake to keep them from rolling backward. Owen rode out in front and saw Shonnewwek sitting passively on his shaggy pony.

In his hands he held reins. At the other end of the reins was a chestnut mare. On the mare sat Thalia Greenwood.

The explosion was so loud it shot the crows from the cedars: "GODDAMMIT ALL TO HELL!"

She held her ground. "At least you can't send me back."

"I'm sure tempted!"

He cocked a long leg across his saddle bow and glared at her. "Don't push me."

"I want to go home."

"I know what you want to do! I'm not that much of a fool, miss."

"I'll either go with you or I'll follow. You can't stop me."

He stared at her, sick with anger. He'd like to drop her down the nearest pothole; but on the other hand he knew that now she was his responsibility too. He wouldn't be able to bear the sight of old man Greenwood's face if anything happened to his daughter. She was all he had left.

He said accusingly, "You were in the loft, weren't you? I should have remembered this wasn't the season for ague. And you took the wine and the meat."

Defiantly she said, "I was hungry. And I needed something for the trail. Reuben couldn't spare much."

"The dogs knew you. That's why they didn't bark." But he knew his talk was only procrastination. He sighed from his boot tops, puffing wind like a grampus. At least she was better than worrying about Mersey out there, dogging his trail. "All right. But you listen and you obey or I'll spank your butt again and you know damn well I can!"

She yelled, "Yippee!" like a little child, spurred her horse to his side, threw her arms around him in a hug. Owen caught a sudden sideview of Victoria's face in the carriage pane. On purest impulse he caught Thalia closer, planted a large, impassioned smack on her mouth.

Her surprise was complete, and not totally pleasant, but he didn't care. It might serve to keep the young miss in her place—and it might throw a little shock into Vick.

At least, he noted, letting go, Victoria's face was no longer at the window. Thalia was sputtering, rubbing her mouth. Owen grinned; he felt almost jolly.

"Let's move," he said, throwing his massive leg back over his horse's neck, sticking it in the stirrup. "You first, so I can keep an eye on you."

Still watching him a bit uncertainly, she went ahead. Owen followed single file. Robert chirruped to his team, and the tall Sauk fell in behind.

They were riding the ridge left by the huge rockfall. Far below, the broad band of the Mississippi flowed silently, almost obscured by mist. The sky was gray, pressing down with the strange, tangible weight of wetness. The rain had stopped but it was cold. Too cold.

And it would be colder at the top.

He sheathed his rifle, pulled the hood of his capote over cold ears, nudged his mount until the horse's nose was almost on the chestnut's tail. "Thalia."

"What?"

She didn't look around.

He asked, "What happened to Pedro?"

Then she did, half turning. She'd abandoned the green habit for a much more sensible garb, and she was riding astride, a knitted cap covering her hair. Inside the damp wool frame her face was puzzled. "I didn't see Pedro."

"Not at all?"

"Not at all." She giggled. "I sneaked by old Spice Bush close enough to touch, though."

He frowned, fell back.

She stayed, turned a moment, then straightened, and said to the large tumble of yellow boulders ahead of her, "Owen—"

He grunted.

"Why did you kiss me?"

He merely grunted again. It wasn't important now.

But she persisted. "Why? You've never so much as looked at me before." Then, suddenly, she made her own conclusion. She whipped around again and her face was indignant. "I know! It's that—drooping lily back there! Isn't it?"

"Or because I haven't had any woman for a long time."

That scored. He saw uncertainty on her face.

"Oh," she said. "You wouldn't dare!"

He laughed. That made her even more uncertain. She faced forward again and her back was rigid. *Damn Paul,* Owen thought. *How far had he tried with her?*

Owen suspected it was too far. He'd suspected it for a year—especially after Paul's high-handedness really sent his fortune skidding and old Greenwood made it patently clear that Greenwood money was not available through his daughter! When Thalia was suddenly bundled off to school, and Paul did not object, Owen's attention had sharpened further. The rudely luscious girl had always seemed to him to be incongruous as a choice for the polished Paul; however, he assumed it could be lonely on Olympus too.

Then Owen had discovered the truth: Victoria was coming, and Paul needed the jealously adoring embarrassment of Thalia Greenwood removed. The fact

Owen *didn't* know was what promise Paul had made to Thalia to effect the removal. *That* worried him.

"Owen!" said Robert, and he was pointing up ahead with his whip to where the ridge turned into the wind and they would leave the shelter of the bluff face. Owen looked, and his heart sank.

One small ray of sun had pierced the overcast and was touching the ragged cedars. They glistened: ice. Damn. Now they walked. In fact Robert was pulling up the horses. Shonnewwek waited for Owen. He saw the gleam of freezing branches, nodded, put one hand to his blanketed chest, then swept it back down the trail.

Owen cursed.

One man, the sign meant, on the trail behind them.

Then the Sauk made another gesture: *softly, softly.*

One man, on the trail behind them—and he didn't want to be seen.

Mersey. Damn it. Was it Mersey?

It had to be.

Didn't it?

Who else?

10

Inside the carriage Victoria sat stiffly. She was numb with cold, and numb with something else—a primitive sense of violation. Of loss. It had been all very well to calmly sit alone and make fatuous, patronizing resolutions, complimenting herself on her maturity. But the real, hateful sight of Owen caught in Thalia's arms was something quite different! He had kissed her and had obviously enjoyed it, and it had been like a hard punch in Victoria's stomach!

She was coping not at all with the thoughts that reeled through her brain: *Thalia has tried to kill me, but right now I could kill her! I could cut her in bleeding pieces and throw the rags away!*

Desperately she closed her eyes, tried to calm herself, tried to reason with the spewing hatred that was racking her body: *He's not mine; I have no right; I gave him up; I am married to Paul!*

I must not feel like this! I cannot allow it to rule me!

She was committed. What if the bitter truth was that she was using Paul—that, when one eliminated the self-imposed deception that prated of integrity, the divine sacrament of betrothal, nothing was left but the fact Paul had offered an escape hatch, a rabbit burrow, and she had dived into it like a frightened mouse!

Now she knew it was an awful price to pay for pride. The image of Owen's arms around Thalia Greenwood was burned on her brain!

And what could she do? What could she do?

Nothing!

Her father's voice echoed in her ears: *With your shield, or on it, Victoria.*

Bleakly she said the words to herself, twisting the heavy betrothal ring on her finger, blinking back the hot tears. She was cold, she was dirty, she was hungry; her body ached from the jolting, and her lacing hurt.

I can't cry, she thought desperately, screwing up her face, taking deep breaths in gulps. *I can't! Owen mustn't know he can hurt me. Neither of them must know. Please, God, let me at least save myself that. . . .*

And let him forget that girl who tried to kill me—tried twice! Let him forget.

I won't. But if he thinks he has two women to pleasure with now, he can *forget that!*

She opened her portmanteau, found her hand mirror, defiantly went to work with hairbrush, clean handkerchief and spit. Just in time too, for as she finished, the carriage stopped again, the door opened, and Owen looked in.

Calmly she closed the portmanteau lid, coolly she said, "I see there's a new member of our entourage."

"Yes," he answered briefly and extended his gloved hand. "Come out, Vick. We have to walk a piece."

She said, "One moment."

She opened the lid again, pulled off the betrothal ring, dropped it inside. Then she offered the hand to him, and the plain gold wedding band shone new and bright.

For herself it was the drawing of a real property line beyond which all other lines had paled. If Owen noticed, or understood, or even cared to understand, she couldn't tell. But it didn't matter. The lines were hers, not his.

He said merely, "Put on your gloves. And bring your plaid. It's very cold."

She meant to descend elegantly, with élan, very much the Lady Winterthur. But even that was against her. The narrow step was slick. She slipped, scraped her shin cruelly and would have fallen had not Owen caught her. Distinctly she heard a tinkle of laughter. Compressing her lips against the pain, she shook herself loose, murmured, "I'm sorry. I'm so stiff."

He said, "It's starting to ice. We've a ways to go before we can camp. But I don't want you in the carriage in case it slides. Take my arm."

"I can manage."

"Take my arm!" Then he added, coldly, "Mind me, Vick. Of all things, you must not fall."

She'd forgotten: he thought she was carrying a child. Feeling painfully hypocritical, she obeyed, and could not prevent her heart's quickening at the smooth slide of muscle beneath her fingers.

With his free hand, Owen led his mount. Behind them, Robert picked his way carefully between his team. Ahead, Thalia preceded her chestnut, balancing herself with the cautious use of a tall sapling. Shonnewwek's pony was riderless, the Indian nowhere to be seen.

At first, it wasn't bad. The incline was gradual, and the trail half filled with autumn's dead leaves. Then it turned again, and Victoria found herself crossing another weather-scoured ridge. The wind was like the blade of a knife in her lungs. The land dropped away so sharply on both sides that she could gaze down into the tops of trees, then away, far beyond, into trackless, rolling infinity. The gray sphere of space and sky was so awesome, she hardly believed her eyes; the sight chilled her heart as the wind her breath. She was almost glad to look at her feet again, to cope with the smaller danger of the glazing path.

Suddenly Robert was shouting, "Whoa, whoa, steady there!" She heard the scraping, rattling sound of rolling rocks, turned, saw the back of the carriage slowly, inexorably slipping sideways. Owen snapped, "Stand still!" He dropped her arm, ran, skidding and sliding, past the huge helpless wheels, found a purchase for his feet, and put his big shoulder against the frame. The team was frightened, snorting, wanting to run, not pull. Robert held them, soothed them, but still it was no use; Victoria could see it wasn't any use.

She couldn't just stand!

She scrambled down the slope by Owen, found leverage for her feet on a gnarled root, put her hands desperately against the wooden boot of the carriage. She was hardly aware that the shape at her side was Thalia until she saw the girl's black, caped coat. Thalia cried, "Hold on!" She stripped off the coat, stuffed it beneath the sliding wheel. "Pull, Robert, pull!"

Robert called, "Gee-up, Blaze, gee-up, Toby, good fellows, gee-up, boys—"

The wheel caught, found traction on the heavy coat, moved, and she stuffed more as Owen threw his shoulder into it. The carriage lunged, then skewered back up on the ridgetop so suddenly, the nearest horse almost went down in the traces and Owen had to grab at Victoria or she would have been the one to roll and bounce and shatter all the hundreds of feet to the bottom.

The team was standing quietly now, their heads drooped, their sides heaving. Robert came, helped Victoria up, then Owen, who leaned gasping against the corner of the carriage, his face a tortured gray. Thalia stooped, picked up her dirty, wrinkled coat, shook it out, put it back on.

Robert said soberly, "I guess you earned your passage, miss."

Thalia only gave him a grave nod, but Victoria could sense the triumph in her. Owen's breathing eased. He straightened, shoved the damp hair from his eyes, put his hood back up. Hoarsely he said, "That's a good trick, Thale."

"Learned it from my father."

But the use of the girl's familiar name, the look that passed between them— they weren't missed by Victoria.

And when Owen croaked, "Let's just lick this ridge, then make camp," it was as though she wasn't there.

Slowly, cautiously, Thalia went back to her place ahead of the patiently standing chestnut, Robert took up the reins of his team again, and Owen turned to Victoria.

"Take my arm."

With total surprise she saw his eyes were blazing in his drained face. She said, "You're angry at me!"

"You disobeyed me!"

"But . . . you needed help. . . . I just meant to—"

She stopped. It was useless. He said, through set teeth, "You idiot, can't you learn anything? Don't you realize that both of us could have gone ass over applecart clear down to the Mississippi?"

She wouldn't cry. She absolutely wouldn't. There were too many eyes and ears, smug ones, curious ones. She pressed her shaking mouth together, swallowed hard and said nothing. But her eyes showed her hurt.

He looked away sharply, smacked his hand against the back of the carriage, and said, "Oh, hell! Move on, Robert!"

Slowly, cautiously, they got under way again.

Blood was trickling down inside Victoria's boot where the leather rubbed her lacerated shin, but she couldn't stop, couldn't let anyone know, and tried desperately not to limp. It seemed ages, eons before the huge, tumbled boulders and cedar scrub of the other side was within her reach.

Just as her weary feet touched the dry, glistening scurf of pine needles a fierce, glowing ball of red burst forth in the low, western sky. *My God,* she thought dimly, *the day is gone!*

Her first sensation was relief. They'd stop now, they'd make camp; Owen had said so. And her raw ankle stung, her body ached; she was terribly cold. Then as she looked ahead, anxiously scanning the huge, comfortless boulders, the scragling cedar clinging precariously to loose scree, her next dismayed thought was: *Where? Where would they stop?* There was no sign of habitation, only cedar and more cedar, pierced now and then by a soaring pine.

The wind picked up suddenly, blowing fine ice crystals against her face. High overhead a hawk circled, soundless against the empty sky. Owen had dropped her arm, was marching along withdrawn, silent. She'd never felt so lonely in her life.

Owen looked up, saw the bird. "Buzzard," he said. Robert looked too, and nodded. Thalia said, "Something dead in the brush. See—there's another."

Victoria was hardly listening. She was numbly absorbed in placing one foot before the other foot in a pattern, one, two, three, to the swinging, relentless single stride of Owen's foot. Only the tip of her nose, a stiffened ashy puff of hair, and part of a cheek showed beyond Harriet Clark's muffler. But the nose was pink and faintly moist, and the cheek was very pale.

His heart smote him. He longed to pick her up, carry her the last few yards, warm her cheek with his, feel her arms around his neck. But he must not; he knew he must not, and besides he needed his arms free. He was uneasy. Nothing moved around them, not even a crow squawking, and that should be good—yet it wasn't. And old Shonnewwek ought to be in sight behind them. . . .

Robert mirrored his thoughts: "Where's Spice Bush? Shouldn't he be showing up?" Robert had seen the signs; he knew.

Owen shrugged. "I told him where we'd be," he said.

"The cave?"

"Yes."

"Sure hope it's empty. I'm too damned tared to squabble with a bobcat."

Cave! That word penetrated. Victoria broke the rhythm of her pace and stumbled. Owen expected her to sleep in a cave with—with wild animals in it!

Owen found a grin for her horrified face.

"We'll make certain it's not occupied," he said as though soothing a child.

They were among the pines now, their feet crisp on the turf. Up ahead Thalia had dropped her horse's reins, was sweeping dead sticks into a bundle. She reached overhead, pulled down a grapevine, severed a length with a tiny knife blade, wound it around the bundle. As they approached, she said, "Hey, Robert, get me a light."

The driver stopped his team, tossed her his tinderbox. With calm efficiency she struck a spark, ignited the ends of the faggots, glanced at Victoria.

Victoria should have been warned, but she was too busy hating the girl for her capable manner, for her insouciant assumption of comradeship with the men.

Suddenly Thalia turned, tossed the blazing bundle behind her. For a flash the brief blazing arc lit up like day a large gaping hole.

There was one second of nothing.

Then from the cave poured thousands of angry, squeaking bats, swooping and soaring, beating their rubbery wings. For Victoria it was a nightmare. She screamed, ran to Owen, frantically burrowed like a small mouse into his arms, inside his stiff capote, sobbing against his warm chest.

He held her, rocked her like a baby, saying, "Vick, Vick, love, it's all right. . . ." And he could have killed Thalia as she stood there laughing.

Sweetly she said, "All clear."

Shuddering, hiccuping, Victoria said, "Don't make me go in there . . . don't, Owen. . . ."

"Vick, they won't be back. I know; I've laid over here half a dozen times. Listen to me." He lifted her face with his hand. "I promise you. It's all right."

Tears sparkled on the fringy lashes as she searched his eyes with hers. Then she gave a sad sort of sigh, stepped back, snuffled. "I'm sorry," she said. "Whatever you say."

"Good girl. Come on; I'll show you."

The cavern was larger than the door and higher at the back, where water ran softly down limestone, pooled and trickled out on one side of the opening. A slanted bar of light shone from its incept on the arched ceiling. Beneath was an old fire-ring of black stones where Robert was already piling small twigs and branches.

"We'll just have you a fine warm blaze in a minute, ma'am," he said cheerfully. "'Twill likely hearten everybody."

When he saw her looking suspiciously at a small side gallery that led into blackness, he added, "That ain't nothing. It peters out about ten foot back in a heap of old bones. Animal, ma'am. I figure it used to be some bear's larder years ago. We all throw dry wood into it, handy like."

"I'll bring the blankets," Owen said. He dropped her arm, patted it reassuringly, and went out. She heard his voice, low, angry, and Thalia's loud, defiant, "You can't make me!" But when she came in, carrying her saddle, her pretty face was flushed and sullen.

Owen followed with his, and an armload of blankets from the carriage. He dropped the saddle by the fire-ring, where Robert was coaxing a bright flame from grass and twigs, took his gun, propped it just inside the entrance.

The driver fanned his fire with his old felt hat, asked quietly, "Any sign of Shonnewwek?"

"Not yet. Pull the carriage back in the scrub before you unhitch; we don't need to issue invitations."

Everyone seemed to know what to do but Victoria. Owen reached into a crevice, extracted a battered, smoked coffeepot, put it beneath the water to fill. Robert was expertly building his fire, adding to it stick by stick like an Indian lodge. With knowledgeable ease Thalia picked up one of the blankets, draped it across the outside opening, and secured the upper corners.

But reeling with fatigue, Victoria found she didn't mind doing nothing. She sat down on Owen's saddle, stripped off her dirty gloves, stretched cold hands to the fire. After a while she'd take off her boot. But not now. Not now.

Her hands were too heavy for her wrists. She put them on her knees, her feet crossed beneath her like a small girl. Robert went outside; the flap of the blanket created a draft and sent sparks careening wildly up through the ceiling hole. She watched them in a sort of stupor, still staring after they were gone, unaware of Thalia's look of contempt, Owen's of concern.

Robert came back in, caught Owen's eye, shook his head. Thalia said brightly, "Wait until we feed. Then he'll turn up."

But Robert said slowly, "How about my having a look-see—so long as there's daylight."

After a moment Owen nodded, and followed him out.

Alone in the cavern Victoria stared at the fire. Thalia stared at Victoria. *One push,* Thalia thought with enormous longing, *one push and she'd be in the fire. I'd say she fell. They'd never know different. Not for sure. . . .*

But Owen came back inside alone. He was carrying the wicker basket from the carriage. He gave Thalia a sharp look, which she returned innocently, grateful she hadn't moved. Then he knelt by Victoria, opened the basket, took out the remaining wine bottle. It popped hollowly as he pulled the cork with his teeth, poured red wine into a tin cup, and said gently, "Vick, drink this."

He put it in her hands, urged it toward her face. She drank slowly, almost with reluctance, but she drank. He reached into the basket again, found half a chicken wrapped in a towel, callously tore out only the finest white meat, laid it on one of Harriet Clark's napkins. "And eat. Mind me!"

Behind him Thalia muttered, "I suppose the rest of us peasants get hoecake and fatback."

Without even looking, he said, "Shut up, Thalia." But Victoria's tired eyes widened; she said, "Oh!" and hastily put down the cup.

Scowling, he made her pick it up again. "I said, mind me! If you get sick any more, it will be that much harder on the rest of us. Besides, she's had her share."

He stayed with her, hunkered on his heels in the dirt, until she'd eaten everything he'd asked her to eat and had a bit more animation in her face. Then gently he got her to lie down, her head on the saddle, and her plaid spread over her. She was asleep almost at once.

For a moment he stayed where he was, not touching her, just looking.

His feelings about the baby were very ambivalent; he couldn't help that. He was a man; he felt cheated. But the burning resentment was gone, leaving behind only smoldering anger for whomever was responsible.

Any hope that she'd confide in him he'd certainly buggered up himself. Yet he'd felt, almost from the first, that she was on the run.

From what? Owen wondered. *The father of the child?* That was logical. But there was more. He knew in his bones that there had to be something else—something bad enough that she'd been willing to face Paul's outraged indignation at having a pregnant bride. Damaged merchandise: That's what she'd be to Winterthur.

Damn Winterthur! he said to himself. *Why couldn't he have broken his neck instead of his leg? Why couldn't Mersey have gone gunning for him instead of stalking his wife?*

And while he was at it, why couldn't he himself have been more reasonable back there at Clark's—and less the brassy young ass who thought Vick would fall into his arms like a plum in the intimacy of a long journey!

Intimacy, my foot! Owen acknowledged wearily, standing erect. *I've handled things so damned badly, I'm fortunate we're still speaking.*

And I don't want to hurt Mersey! If only Shonnewwek can find him, bring him here. Then we can talk; I'll make him understand. Poor clod. . . .

If it is Mersey.

But it had to be him. Who else could it be?

Thalia had been responsible for the guitar string all right, and he'd settled that account in a way she'd remember for a long time! Or at least he hoped so.

But she couldn't have had anything to do with the poison because she'd been locked in her room without a stitch of clothing. (Punishment for a spoiled brat like Thalia had to be pretty direct.)

However, he must not forget that she regarded Paul Winterthur as her possession and Vick as a serious threat. The guitar string demonstrated that. . . . He wished he could tell Victoria the truth—that Paul was Thalia's lover—but he was afraid. Vick's confidence in him was too poor; it might well backlash as just more scurrility on his part and send her running even faster to Paul.

The water had boiled while he'd moped. Thalia had stirred in cornmeal, fashioned little hoecakes, patted them on the hot rocks around the fire-ring. Now she was rinsing the pot and setting it to fill again. She looked at him sullenly as he rose, stretching to such a huge height, the linsey shirt popped from his trousers.

"What a slob you are, Owen. I suppose we do have coffee."

"In my saddlebag."

He got it for her, tossed her the cloth bag. Putting his shirttails back, he watched her with narrow eyes. She was a pretty piece. No doubt of that. Olive skin, dark eyes, a cloud of black hair. A shapely, curved, and untrammeled body. No laces there. *Obviously,* he thought, catching the sensuous movement of her breasts as she stood erect and smoothed down heavy skirts.

And spoiled rotten. Her father had never denied her a thing; those who worked for him never dared. Paul must have promised her something very potent to get her out of the way! Was it as Will had said: a guarantee that Vick wouldn't live very long?

She caught his gaze, glared back. In a hard voice, he asked her, "Did Paul give you permission to come home?"

She stiffened. "I don't need permission!"

He waited, only letting patent amusement show on his face. She added defiantly, "I do what I want! He doesn't—he doesn't own me!"

"Neither does he like being disobeyed."

"I don't care. I want to be home!"

He leaned against the wall, crossed his arms and his legs, grinned. He said deliberately, "It's going to be a little crowded in his bed."

She gasped and clenched her fists. Then it boiled out: "How could I stay away?"

"How indeed?"

"I didn't know what she was like! When I promised to stay away, I didn't know!" Her hands were opening and closing like pulses. "I went down on the wharf to see—and there she stood—there she stood, Owen—a piece of everything he's missed, longed for, talked about: the balls, the hunts, the gardens, the teas—''

''And?''

''And I couldn't take a chance!'' Then her voice fell, placated: ''Owen, can't you understand?''

''Will he?''

''Won't you help me? Sure you will!''

''Thalia,'' said Owen coldly, ''I wouldn't touch you with a pole.''

''I didn't mean to hurt her—not very much!''

He said a coarse word and told her where to put it, then straightened and went to the entrance. Robert had been gone about long enough. At least for his comfort.

It was growing dark outside, and misty cold. The horses were bunched together for warmth, ghostly plumes curling from their nostrils as they breathed.

Shonnewwek's pony stood a little to one side, munching tough watergrass. Suddenly he tossed his head; his ears rose. And Owen heard it too: crunching footsteps in the mist.

He whistled—a wild, piercing whistle, a night bird's cry.

The footsteps stopped. Robert's voice came through the gloom.

''Halloo,'' it said. ''I'm too winded to whistle back. Come bear a hand. I got old Shonnewwek here.''

Owen reached inside, grasped his gun. ''Will,'' he said.

''Clark,'' said Robert, answering the sign. ''It's only me. And it ain't slick now; the mist took the glaze off. Come on; he's bleedin'.''

''He took a shot right above the ear,'' he said as Owen appeared, leaned and hoisted the sagging Indian's other arm across his own shoulder. ''One in the rib. Grazes, both of them, but it took him out. I would have passed right on by except I heard a dog raising Cain.''

Shonnewwek was a dead weight. His shoepacs made twin trails in the dirt as they got him inside to the fire, laid him down. His jaunty feather was askew and his deerskin tunic stiff with blood.

''Look at that,'' said Robert, peeling it up. ''That, and this here.'' He turned Shonnewwek's head by the brushy crown, pointed to the long bloody score. ''What do you think?''

''Pistol,'' said Owen curtly. His eyes were narrowed.

Robert nodded. ''Now what damned hunter hunts with a pistol?''

''It wasn't a hunter,'' said Owen. And at that moment he would have given half his life to know who it was. Mersey had a Hawken gun. Didn't he?

He asked, ''How long ago?''

Robert shrugged. ''Hard to say. Not too long. The ice wasn't melted under him.''

Owen cursed. ''We should have known when we saw the buzzards!''

Robert shook his head. ''Nope,'' he said. ''Them buzzards are still out yander. They're on to something else.''

11

Thalia was standing over them, a half-eaten hoecake in her hand.

"Dirty beast," she said, and stirred the Indian with her toe.

Owen failed to realize she showed no curiosity whatsoever about who had shot him. He was, at that moment, more concerned with current problems and acted on them by reaching up beneath her heavy skirt. She yipped in indignant surprise and tried to move away. He held on by one ankle, using the other hand to open the caseknife clenched between his teeth. Through it he mumbled irritably, "Hold still, dammit!" and proceeded to saw a long cut in one of her voluminous petticoats. When ripped off, the swatch provided four yards of excellent bandage.

"I knew them tarnal things was good for somethin'," said Robert, laughing. Gently he lifted the unconscious Sauk so Owen could wind the cloth around his chest.

As they finished, the Sauk stirred; his eyes opened, widened, flicked from man to man. With an effort he said something in his own language. Robert bent close, listened. Owen, whose own knowledge of Sauk was very smattering, could only wait. Beside him Thalia waited also. If he had been looking, he would have seen that her hand was clenched on the forgotten hoecake, and that her eyes were frightened.

The soft words stopped. Robert prompted. Shonnewwek shook his head and the blood began to flow again. He put a hand to it, looked at the red, fumbled at the top of the deerskin tunic crumpled up beneath his armpits. Robert said, "Holt on," drew out a small leather pouch fastened by a thong around the Indian's neck.

"His medicine," he said.

Shonnewwek extracted a dried, dark brown leaf, like a plantain, pressed it shakily against his head wound. The red trickle ceased. Satisfied, he resumed his narrative, Robert putting in a word here and there. Shortly he stopped again, with a sigh, and put out both hands in the sign of *no more.*

"And there ain't much to begin with," said Robert, sitting back on his haunches. "Some white men went across here about two days ago—John Shaw's bunch, probably, heading back up for Cole's Grove. He thinks he recognized the Frenchy's mule tracks among 'em. Then two other white men."

"Together?"

Robert shook his head. "They didn't seem to be. Anyway, one of them doubled back, like to let us get ahead. He figures that's the one that got him."

Owen swore softly. "Did he see anything before he went down?"

"No."

Over his head Thalia made a tiny noise, a sound that might have been relief. "The noble red man," she said derisively. "Get him away from the fire. He stinks, and the heat makes it worse."

They ignored her. Robert said, "He thinks he remembers coming to once with something licking his head. Like a dog. And that's what led me to him. I thought I heard a dog bark, although when I got to Shonnewwek, there warn't no dog."

Owen reached out, turned the Indian's head. Down his jawline, disturbing the soil of quite a few days, were some curiously clean striations.

A wild beast, licking blood? But Robert had heard a dog. Varmints don't bark. A dog, then. Yet Indian dogs showed no particular allegiance.

Pedro?

If so, then Pedro was still alive.

And if he was still alive, and it had been Pedro—where had he gone? And why?

Shonnewwek disturbed Owen's thought processes by grunting and reaching out one hand. Owen put a hoecake in it and stood up, suddenly aware of aching thigh muscles and enveloped in a clouded, pressing sense of peril. Victoria still slept, like a tired kitten, one hand curled beneath her chin. Thalia was turning hoecakes, a look on her dark, pretty face that was almost smug. Robert still sat on his haunches, hands on knees, staring thoughtfully at the munching Indian.

"Owen," he said, "we ain't carrying plews nor stores. What have we got somebody'd want? Coin? Is that what it is?"

"Or just Paul Winterthur's wife."

"Ah," Robert said, and sucked musingly on his hollow tooth. "So it's either robbery or evening a score."

"Or both."

"And either way the lady loses. Poor little lady."

Thalia laughed rudely, from her place by the fire. "Poor little lady," she mimicked, "dining on roast and wine while the rest of us eat trail grub. And if you want some of it, you'd better start. Shonnewwek's eaten half already. I'm not making any more either. I'm tired."

They ignored her, but she didn't mind. She sat down comfortably, pillowing her arm on her saddle and watched them help Shonnewwek stretch out on his blanket, farther away from the fire. Robert gave him a drink from his jug, poured more into his and Owen's tin cups, and topped them off with boiling coffee. Then he hacked off some strips of side pork to sizzle and curl on the same rocks that had baked the hoecakes. That done, he sat on his own blanket and chewed in contented silence, dribbling crumbs down his stained vest.

Owen couldn't seem to stay still. He alternated between listening intently at the blanketed entrance to standing at Victoria's feet, looking down at her.

Thalia watched him, in part with a contempt born of secret knowledge (hugging its sweet confidence to her breast), and in part intrigued by his sudden attention, this day, to her genus female. At home she could recall at least half a dozen settlers' daughters who would gladly have found themselves in Owen's bed— and had, if you believed Paul. Paul had always been contemptuous of his huge cousin, and, as an echo, so had she. Yet at the moment she found him rather . . . appealing. Was it simply a primitive rivalry between her and that drooping lily beneath the blankets—or was it that, having not been kissed or caressed for weeks, she suddenly realized how she'd missed such attentions? Owen was not Paul—but he had an arrogance that was like Paul's. . . .

Whatever, it had a certain dangerous attraction. She said, "Owen, for heaven's sake, sit down. You're making me nervous."

He ignored her. To Robert he said, "You stand first watch?"

"Reckon I will." Robert stretched out a long arm, drew his rifle into his lap, checked its prime. "By God, next time I get to Saint Louis, I'm going to have me a Hawken gun. Ever shoot one of them, Owen? Nice and light and tougher'n a boot.''

"Mersey has one." Owen didn't want to talk about Mersey, nor think about him. He drained the blackened old pot into his cup, set it beneath the drip of water to fill. Behind him he heard Robert say cheerfully, "Well, howdy, ma'am. Feelin' a mite better?"

Victoria had awakened and was sitting up, trying to tidy her hair. The fire had pinkened her cheeks, curled the damp hair around her ears. In her clear voice she said apologetically, "I shouldn't have gone to sleep! I'm so sorry; I don't mean to be a burden!"

Thalia's short laugh was covered by Owen's brusque, "You need the rest," and Robert's, "Best thing you could have done, ma'am." Their tenderness infuriated Thalia. Her dark eyes blazed, but she covered it with a pseudosweet voice:

"Would you like to go—you know, my lady? We can take a short turn in the picture gallery." Her hand indicated the black hole of the other cave. Victoria gasped, "Oh, yes—please, let's do."

She got to her feet unsteadily as Thalia stuck a faggot into the fire and arose herself. With the burning ember and her wickedly sparkling eyes she looked like an avenging Fury. The warning hairs prickled on the back of Owen's neck.

He caught her hand as she passed him. "Thalia," he said softly, viciously. "It's worth your life if you harm her."

She believed him. There was no mistake; he meant every word. Even as Victoria crouched, helpless and vulnerable beneath her, and she raised the deadly torch, the sound of his voice stayed the lethal blow.

So—not this time. There'd be another. She could wait.

When they reentered the flickering light of the main cavern, Robert was gone, Shonnewwek lay in the shadows, snoring sibilantly, and Owen sat by the fire staring at the smoke as it sucked up the hole by the dripping water. Victoria shivered; the dark gallery had been damp and cold with strange, unseen textures crunching beneath her feet. Owen glanced at her sharply, upended his tin cup so the dregs hissed into the fire, then poured a short portion of the fresh-made coffee.

"Drink this," he said, "and get back under your blankets. We can't stay here beyond dawn."

She sipped. It was bitter, and despite herself she made a face. Thalia laughed.

"Sorry, my lady. We seem to be fresh out of China tea."

Owen said coldly, "Shut up, Thalia."

With dogged determination Victoria drank it all. The enmity between her and Thalia might be an unalterable fact, but there was no use adding to Owen's burden. And the heat of the coffee was spreading from her stomach, warming her. She thrust the cup at him.

"May I have a little more, please?"

He poured, turned back, found her staring with patent dismay at her dirty hand.

"Oh, Owen," she said, and the sound she made was shaky, but it was also laughter. "I must look like I did the day Papa's roan hunter tossed me into the compost."

The swift, wild surge of love for her almost got him. He couldn't touch her, couldn't smile back. He didn't dare. Instead he said briefly, "At least you smell better. Go back to sleep."

She didn't understand the reason, but she felt the rebuff.

She and Owen couldn't even be friends! Not anymore. Putting the cup carefully on the dry, powdery cave floor, she sat down stiffly on her blanket, pulled her old cape around her shoulders, half turned away from them both—the stranger, Owen, and the hateful girl.

She knew at once she couldn't sit that way long. She hadn't been unlaced for two days; her stays were digging into her ribs cruelly. And the blood from her lacerated shin had dried the stocking to the foot. The sitting attitude was tearing the stocking loose and it hurt no matter how she shifted.

But she was not going to let Owen know, not going to expose herself anymore! It was bad enough to be dirty and wrinkled and frowsy-headed from that damned hood while Thalia was rose-cheeked and smooth, with her black curls shining like a raven's wing—

Oh, stop! she commanded herself, dismayed. She couldn't allow thoughts like that! She had to keep facts in their proper slots. She was Paul Winterthur's wife now.

But she didn't feel like Paul Winterthur's wife. And that was the danger.

She picked up the tin cup, drank hastily. A mistake. The coffee very nearly came right back up. Horrified, she fought the urge, and won. *Thank God,* she thought. Weak with relief, she abandoned the cup, lay down, curled beneath her cape. The long, sinuous ridge of the necklace in the hem should have given her comfort, but it didn't; it only hurt her knees. She twisted, trying to find a restful position.

There didn't seem to be one.

In the shadows Shonnewwek's snores had turned to a series of grunts. Owen bent over Victoria. Between slitted eyelids she couldn't see his face, only his hands as he spread another blanket, pushing the edge beneath her fanny. On the other side of the fire Thalia said softly, "Now will you tuck me in?"

Owen ignored her. He put more dry wood on the fire, laying it carefully so it would burn low with heat but little flame. Then he stuck his head out into the frosty air, talked to Robert a moment, picked up his rifle leaning by the entrance, came back to the fire, laid the rifle on the ground by Thalia and said very quietly, "Move over."

"What?"

"Move over, dammit."

"She's got your blanket; sleep with her."

"I know where she is. I want to know where you are. The simplest thing is to sleep with you." He shoved at her rudely with his knee, lowered his big body to the ground with a weary sigh.

She turned, rose on one elbow, spread a corner of the blanket over his shoulder. It was a humble, submissive gesture; it was also open provocation. Her breasts brushed his chest and the scent of her own warm body assailed his nostrils.

Owen sighed. He certainly had a talent for the wrong place and the wrong time. He said, "No, thanks," and arrested the wandering hand.

She nestled sinuously against him. "At least," she murmured in his ear, "we can keep each other warm."

This time he captured the hand, took it outside the blanket and held on to it. But she was right about the heat. He hadn't really been warm all day, and the gentle radiation from her snuggling body was so soporific, he found himself unable to keep his eyes open. Within mere moments he was asleep.

Finding no response to the wandering caress of her other hand, Thalia gave up in disgust. She tried to pull loose the one clasped in his. His grip tightened. He'd meant it about wanting to know where she was; even in sleep he wasn't letting go. Half turning, she suddenly caught, from the tail of her eye, an edifying sight: the outraged, incredulous stare of two wide blue ones from across the smoldering fire.

She turned again, deliberately cuddled herself against Owen, emitted a very audible warm-woman sigh. *Shocked, was she, that English priss! I'll give her something to be shocked about!* She slid her free hand slowly, sensuously down the blanket on Owen's thigh, then beneath the blanket. She left it there, allowing English imagination to do the rest, and, quite satisfied with herself, she went to sleep also.

On the other side of the fire Victoria lay stiff, rigid. Emotions tore at her she hardly dare name.

She hadn't been able to hear the whispers of those two beneath their blanket, but it hadn't been necessary to hear. The result was patent.

There was no fair play in Victoria, no recollection of having turned the same man from her own bed the night before, no calm self-reminders that Paul had, after all, told her Owen was carrying on with that—that—(Vick, here, said a very succinct word that would have shocked her nanny)—and absolutely no memory of having told herself firmly not too long before that after all she was now Paul Winterthur's wife.

The entire day's hardship culminated inside her aching head—a burden of unreasoning misery. She could only fashion one idea in her addled brain: When Paul had sent Owen for her, he'd never meant it to be like this!

The illogic in her reasoning she ignored. Or perhaps she was simply past logic. She had not, after all, been other than harried and humiliated for months. And there does come, inevitably, a breaking point.

Like a wounded child nursing a secret hurt, she waited, lying very still. The activity across the fire had ceased, although he still held her hand.

How solicitous, Victoria thought in a sort of shrewish passion. With caution she raised herself on one elbow.

Behind her Shonnewwek grunted, snorted, flailed around, then went quiet again with a sound like pain. The fire crackled faintly; the water ran in a thin, glistening stream down the far wall. The smoke curled up and out of sight. Nothing else moved.

Quietly Victoria edged her feet beneath her, stood erect. Ignoring the pain in her ankle and her gouging laces, she thought, *At least there's something to be said about sleeping in one's clothes!*

She bundled her tousled hair back into the wool hood, tied it beneath her chin, and swung the plaid cape about her shoulders. Quietly she slipped through the hanging blanket into the outside.

But the draft of cold air—brief as it was—awakened Owen. He raised up, saw immediately that Vick was gone, spoke a soundless curse. Easing himself away from Thalia, he hoisted his aching frame erect, picked up his rifle, and followed.

He paused a moment, blinking, adjusting his eyes to the dark. Although there was an ominous bank of clouds riding low in the west, overhead it was clear, with a few bright stars diamond-pricking a black-glass sky. His tethered horse, glimpsing him, blew softly through his nostrils, making a white plume of his warm breath. At the flutter, the two figures by the side of the carriage turned— Robert's with a gesture of relief, Victoria's with a sort of balked defiance.

Immensely relieved at the sight of her, Owen went toward them. As he moved, the relief was replaced by a sort of grumpy anger. *Damn the girl, anyway!*

To Robert he said, "My turn. Go catch some shut-eye."

With alacrity the burly driver obeyed. As the blanket dropped behind him, Owen leaned his rifle against the carriage and said with what he thought was splendid self-restraint, "What the hell are you doing out here?"

She tossed her head, and even with the hair bundled up inside the hood it was the same familiar gesture—a young filly flipping her mane. Or Lady Victoria, drawing herself away from the ragtags.

The anger burgeoned inside him. The part that she could arouse by being bewildered, tired, and sweet was not the part that panted to be loosed now at the sight of her defiant face. That part was compounded by his own fears, his weariness, his own complex feelings. And it would only take a touch, a nudge, to let it go.

He stopped in his tracks. He said very, very reasonably, "It's cold out here. And you need your rest. Get back inside."

She answered as if from a great distance, "I want Robert to take me on. Now. Tonight."

He stared at her. "You're out of your mind."

"Nonetheless." Her low voice was as icy as the wind. "I command him to take me."

"Command!" It spurted from him: mirthless laughter. "Dear Vick, wake up. You have the wrong country. Over here you *ask* people, and if you're smart, you *ask* them damned nicely!"

"Then I'll *ask* him. I'll make it worth his time. Or Paul will, when we arrive."

Consciously or unconsciously she was using Paul's name as a shield, and aware of it or not, she saw Owen's eyes narrow, his mouth go thin.

He replied coldly, "I assure you, love, there is not enough cash between the two of you to induce Robert's going down that trail tonight. He dislikes being shot at. So do I."

Now it was her turn to stare. Lips hardly moving, she said, "You're being absurd to frighten me. I thought better of you than that, Owen."

He swallowed his anger at her cool, superior voice by reminding himself: *She doesn't know about Shonnewwek.* Very calmly he answered, "Spice Bush is lying in there with two holes in him, Vick, and he didn't acquire them in a coconut shy."

"Two—" She stopped. "You're serious. It's true."

"It's true."

"Who did it? Why?"

"I don't know." Mersey had been old Shonnewwek's friend. "Please. Go to bed, like a good child."

He didn't mean to sound patronizing; he was just damned tired and cold and worried and sick of arguing. She was standing there with the wind lifting lightly at a fringe of hair, and her brows arched, defying him. If she didn't shut up, he knew how he was going to shut her up, and the devil take them both!

She said icily, "I shan't go back in there! I hate that place."

He said, "Fine. I'll keep you warm!" With a swift force that almost took her breath he pulled her up into his arms against his chest, within reach of his wind-chilled and searching mouth. At first, with her hands trapped in her cape, she resisted fiercely. But he tamed her with his mouth, as gently sweet as his arms were relentless. And helplessly she responded. He felt her lips soften, her body mold to his body!

And he laughed. He couldn't help it. He laughed, deep in his chest, the triumphant, joyous, male sound of a conqueror.

The slivered moon kept Victoria from seeing his face, but she both understood and totally misunderstood the laughter. When his arms tightened about what was rightfully his, they found they held an empty cape. Victoria was a wraith speeding past the astonished horses, through the frozen brambles, and out of sight. Only the sound of crunching gravel and the outraged squawk of a night bird marked her path until Owen, galvanized from frozen surprise into cursing action, took after her.

Victoria's course was blind, merely unseen, insane flight, a little like the lemming that goes until it dies. She blundered into the trees and fell headlong over rocks, picked herself up and charged on, sobbing, scratched, cold, insensate. She hardly knew her scrabbling feet had stepped off into nothing. But when her body pitched forward and rolled, hit a mattress of fir, bounced, fell again, and began to slide steeply down, down, down, a helpless bundle—her reason returned, preservation came alive, and she clawed at roots, rocks, anything to stop her vicious descent.

Whatever she finally slammed into almost knocked her breath out. But she grabbed hold and clung, not daring to move, fighting to get air in her pumping lungs. The hood had fallen back, its ties twisted about her neck almost strangling her, but she was afraid to let go what tenuous grip she had, frightened she was on a ledge, imagining below her the sheer drops she'd seen that morning on the trail.

The rolling bank of clouds had risen, a forward wisp engulfing the ragged moon. In the absolute black she had her one moment of total self-condemnation, cursing her selfish, bloody small-mindedness. Then she heard Owen's voice overhead, and she answered, weeping this time at the sheer relief of being found, wanting nothing more in the whole world than to have around her the arms of the man she'd been running from.

She was at the bottom of an enormous wash, scored years ago by a huge, tumbling boulder, since eroded pitilessly by the rush of seasonal rains. Standing on the rim, trying to warm the air in the cold bellows of his lungs, Owen could glimpse her vaguely, a lighter black in the blackness against what appeared to be tangled roots.

Torn between a livid desire to spank her and an aching need to hold her to him, to never let her go again, he began his own descent. A thin prick of the obscured moon gave him increasing light as the clouds moved on. He was grateful for it, but dared not wish for more. Darkness could be more protection against a hostile wilderness than the rifle slung across his back.

In a rattle of gravel he slid the last yard, landing on his knees almost in her lap. Now she came up into his arms willingly, but it was a child's willingness, a child's gratitude at being rescued, and he bitterly wanted none of that. Besides, things weren't right here. Something was strange. The shapes and shadows behind her were assuming postures that raised the hair on the back of his neck. He loosed a hand, put it out tentatively.

He said, "Good God!"

As she turned to look, the last slice of moon shook free. Too late he tried to turn her head. She saw.

Victoria had been lying in the frozen arms of a very dead man.

12

That he was dead was incontrovertible. He was white with frost rime—his clothes, his face, his staring eyes, the gaping wound in his head.

Owen heaved himself to his feet, holding Victoria close against him. Half of him soothed her, caressing the frantic face burrowing into his shoulder. The other half looked at the dead man with sick speculation.

It was Mersey. No doubt about that. And he'd been dead at least a day. The protruding leg bones and the position of his gun showed plainly the reason for his death. A helpless man doesn't leave himself either to starve or be mauled to death by varmints if he can help it. One steady shot and it was all over.

So what was bothering him? There was the gun. There was the hole.

Owen turned Victoria away. He said gently, "All right, Vick. Enough. We can't help him. We do have to climb out of here."

She nodded, stepping back, digging both fists in her eyes like a child. "I know. I know."

"Don't look around. You needn't. Are you hurt?"

"N-n-no. Just scratched." Despite her efforts her teeth were chattering. He started to take off his capote; she stopped him. "I'm not cold. Not yet. I'm just—scared. Owen, I *fell* on him!"

"He was past hurting, Vick."

"Poor man. Oh, poor man."

"Come on, love. Put one foot here, and the other on that rock where it sticks out. I'll climb behind you."

He had second thoughts. He went back, picked up Mersey's gun, twisted it in the sling of his own. As Robert had said, a Hawken gun was not to be taken lightly. And besides—something about Mersey still bothered him. . . .

It was a hard climb. Long before they reached the top, Victoria had to rest, exhausted, while he sheltered her shaking body with his, holding her safely against the cold face of the limestone strata. She said, gasping, "Owen, must we just leave him there? It seems so cruel!"

Life is cruel. The frontier is cruel. God, Owen thought, *what sickeningly pat phrases for a man who had once sweated and laughed and teased him from the other end of a bucksaw.* Mersey had been a happy man. Once. Instead of all that garbage, Owen answered only, "Don't worry, Vick. Put it out of your mind."

How simple to say! Forget Mersey, lying back there, frost-rimed, his dead mouth agape. How hard to do it! Owen knew he never would. But a man had to establish priorities. . . .

It seemed hours before they reached the top. There the wind was blowing sharply, soughing through the pines. He opened his warm capote, then took her inside against him, savoring the movement of her body next to his as he directed her stumbling feet back down the slope toward the cave mouth.

Everything was quiet. Nothing seemed changed. He scouted the small clearing, then let her come from her place by the horses, wrapped the cold cape about her shoulders, pushed her inside. Quietly he whispered, "Send Robert out."

Robert was a snoring lump, lying with his feet to the fire. Cautiously Victoria touched him with one chilly hand. His eyes popped open. She whispered, "Owen wants you."

Groaning, he hoisted himself erect, grasped the rifle by his side and went out, tugging on his heavy surcoat as he was going. (Thalia saw him go, her eyes slitted, her body tense.)

Victoria sat—collapsed—on her blanket; she was disheveled, scratched, bruised, and dirtier than ever, with her hair full of pine needles and a jagged tear in her skirt. Her fingertips were abraded from clawing at the sharp limestone. She held them out, shaking, to the fire. Her stays hurt as she bent, and her ankle throbbed. And for what? Nothing to be proud of! Resistance that crumbled like putty in the arms of a man who, only ten minutes before, had been stroking the body of a slut who had tried to kill her! A useless, futile flight! A fall into the cold lap of a dead man!

Totally miserable, she huddled beneath her plaid cape, looking at the fire through a prickling blur. What a disgusting spectacle she'd made of herself!

Then that man—that cold, stiff, frost-covered dead man—

She shivered and put grimy hands up to hide the sight.

This awful, lowering unforgiving country! How could she learn to live here? But she must. There was nowhere else to go.

Almost consumed with the longing to howl like a homeless dog, she lay down again, pulling the cape over her face. She courted the blessed darkness, needing oblivion for both her humiliation and her aching body.

Outside Robert was handling the Hawken gun, its short stock, its light, octagonal barrel. "So we don't worry about Mersey no more."

"No."

"But we do worry about who potted Shonnewwek— particularly since it wasn't Mersey. What do you think, Owen: the gold? Is someone thinkin' on robbing our little lady?"

Owen nodded. *It had to be that now. What else was there?*

It began to sleet, rattling noisily through the pines, pricking the faces they turned up to it. Robert mumbled, "Oh, hell, sometimes nothin' works!" Owen shivered, thinking of the cold, dead face of his friend in the ravine, the ice striking it, eroding the rime. But what could he do?

His charge was the living. And it was all his. The band of immigrants at Ross's would wait for him ten days before they got restless. Ten days was too long to wait for help. He'd called Robert out with the idea of moving on. But that was impractical now. The moon had been smothered in storm clouds. They couldn't even see the trail, and with this weather they'd be as likely to go over the edge as to travel it. They needed daylight to pass across the big dropoff. Damn. Any other time but fall flood-time they could have gone upriver and traversed the flatlands. It seemed almost as if Paul had wanted Vick to have as hazardous a trip as possible. But Paul never thought of anyone's comfort but his own. . . .

He sent Robert back inside, crawled between the wheels of the carriage out of the sleet, and settled himself as best he could.

So that's what the buzzards had found: Mersey. Had he been following them? If so, how had he got ahead? What had landed him in that ravine with two broken legs and a hole in his head? And since he'd lit out of Clark's about midnight, how had he discovered Paul's wife wasn't dead after all? Or had Owen been on the wrong track from the beginning?

It couldn't have been Mersey who had shot the Sauk; Mersey didn't have a pistol. And Mersey had been dead already. . . .

Then Owen said to himself, *Oh, goddamn!* He knew then what had bothered him in the ravine: the Hawken gun had lain by Mersey's right hand. His right temple was blasted. Mersey had been left-handed.

Cold washed Owen, a cold chillier than the ground. The game, far from solved, had become more deadly. He'd felt that, given the chance, he could reason with Mersey. There was no reasoning with a shadow who shot to kill. . . .

Dawn found the sleet turned again to rain, sending a sluice of swollen creekwater raging downward, tearing its banks. Inside the cave the trickle of water was now a jet. Robert had awakened in a puddle and was moodily drinking coffee while his sodden coat steamed between two sticks near the fire. Shonnewwek sat upright on his blanket, chewing on a lump of stringy dried meat. Between bites he singsonged a dreary chant designed to ease the pain in his head. Victoria was dispiritedly trying to comb pine needles from her tangled hair. Her eyes were ringed with violet, and her shoulders slumped. Thalia still lay in a calm sleep.

They looked up quickly as Owen stalked inside, his own face as gloomy as the weather. He prodded Thalia with a rude, booted toe, took the tin cup of coffee from Robert, and said curtly, "It seems to be letting up. Let's go."

They made an unhappy cavalcade as they struck out again. Owen led, leading his horse, striding along through the mud like an angry giant. Thalia followed, groggy and cross, atop her chestnut mare. Traces jingling, the carriage horses plodded behind her; Robert sat, a huddled lump, on the box. Shonnewwek trailed, painfully erect, astride his pony, still singing his medicine song beneath his breath. Inside the jolting carriage Victoria braced herself with aching arms and wished she were dead. She hadn't known it was possible for one body to have so many hurts.

She'd wanted to walk, hoping to work out some of the stiffness. But Owen, his eyes unconsciously on her belt buckle, had insisted she ride; and, painfully aware of living a lie, she'd acceded rather than add to his burdens which, this morning, seemed to be heavier than usual.

They climbed up and up through the cold gray morning mists. Then suddenly they were going down—far down, Victoria realized as she crashed to the floor, her portmanteau sliding painfully into her rib cage. She'd just pushed herself grimly back up on the seat, bracing the portmanteau in place with her elbow when the carriage lurched to a stop. Robert was sawing reins, shouting, "Whoa! Whoa!" and somewhere out in front of him Owen was saying distinctly, "God-dammit all to hell!"

She thrust her head out and saw them all grouped at the edge of a rushing brown torrent, tearing downward, carrying bobbing chunks of soil and random bush roots as it went.

Thalia said in amazement, "This creekbed is always dry! There's never been water in it, never in all the years we've crossed the bluff!"

Robert answered crossly, "Well, that ain't buttermilk."

Owen tossed back the hood of his capote, enveloped them all in one glare. "We'll have to ford it. We can't wait for the freshet to go down." Crisply he organized them. Robert was to stay aloft and manage his team. Owen and Shonnewwek would flank the carriage, keeping it upright. Thalia was to get inside with Victoria.

"No!" Thalia's voice rang out in the thin morning air. "I won't!" With one swift motion she spurred her mount down the bank and into the swift stream. The problem was current, not depth. It caught her up and swept her a few yards downward. Then the chestnut found its feet, scrambled up the opposite bank. She came cantering back, wringing out her skirttail with one hand, and jeering at the rest of them.

With a snort of annoyance Owen ignored her. While the Indian and he rode their mounts close to the carriage side, Robert urged his nervous team into the cascading water. It boiled, brown and ugly, up their ankles. It tugged and sucked at their knees, then, without warning, went to their bellies as they sank in an eddying hole. The carriage lurched heavily toward Owen, lipping water at the window as he struggled frantically to hold it upright. He was losing it, he knew he was losing it, when suddenly Thalia was there, drenched as a rat in the whirling tide, the chestnut treading strongly beneath her. Her small meed of strength was all it needed, coupled with the team's frightened surge toward the opposite bank. In one moment the crisis was over, and the carriage, streaming water, was lurching up the other bank.

Owen and Thalia followed. Both of them were wet, but Owen's capote shed damp like a seal. Muddy water striped Thalia's face and hair, and ballooned the heavy skirts of her habit. On the high bank the cold wind hit them again, slicing like a knife, and her teeth began to chatter.

Owen said curtly, "Now climb in the carriage, dammit! You've got to get dry."

"No!" she said again sharply, and whipped her horse to a canter beyond his reach. "I won't!"

He felt a little more charitable toward her this morning; after all, she had saved Vick a wetting. He said, "Damn me, Thale, Vick won't bite!"

"No, but I might!"

"Be reasonable!"

Her answer was to wheel the chestnut. "I'm not getting in that carriage! I'll freeze first!"

He gave up. She could go to the devil then. Opening the carriage door, he leaned inside. Victoria's pale face looked up at him and smiled faintly. "I'm fine," she said to his unanswered question. "But Owen, she's going to catch her death!"

"If she thinks I'll chase her, she's crazy."

His callous words gave Victoria a cruel satisfaction but made her action quite virtuous as she bundled up a blanket and handed it out. He shrugged, shut the carriage door, cantered closer to Thalia, and tossed it to her. Then he turned and rode back. When he looked at her again, she had the blanket wrapped around her.

Owen had more pressing problems. It had started to rain, and there were slivers of ice in it. Damn. Just down below through the trees they'd come to the bad spot—that narrow ledge that dropped off to nothing. And there was no other way to go.

Well. They'd just have to chance it. Far to the west those clouds held snow— he was certain.

They had to beat the snow across the prairie. He didn't want to think about not making it. He'd been on the prairie in a snowstorm. He knew the thick, cold smother, where all shapes altered, where landmarks disappeared in a gray cotton curtain; where horses floundered and fell and lost men, who lay down to die within yards of an unseen haven.

He pulled his hood up to cover his head, said urgently, "Let's move."

Obediently Robert shook his reins over his horses' backs. The carriage groaned into motion. Owen and Shonnewwek fell behind. They all followed the bundled form of Thalia on her chestnut through the naked, whining willows and down the stiff, slippery trail into a belt of jack oaks and pine.

Here the mat of ancient needles underfoot slid at their step, as treacherous as the ice. Overhead, the pine boughs moaned with the cutting wind, and small birds huddled quietly, unseen, their breast feathers fluffed.

Robert said, "Cheerful as a graveyard, ain't it?"

"What?"

He raised his voice. "I said, cheerful as a graveyard! I'm lost. What's next? A flat piece, I hope. I ain't never been further than the cave before."

"Forget the flat piece. There's a ledge coming up. Short, but nasty. We'll have to walk our horses."

"Loverly," said Robert glumly. "This place ain't so great. I'm wearing the damn brake out to keep us from climbing my team's hinny right now. And in case you ain't noticed, the yon side of this wagon path already slopes to hell."

"I've noticed," answered Owen. "Slow it down all you can."

"I have." Robert's voice was grim. The carriage was pulling funny. It must be those slick needles. "Ain't there no other way to go but this?"

Owen shook his head. "A big rockslide last spring filled the old trail. Boulders the size of a house."

"Land! What causes them things?"

"Freezing and thawing, I suppose. The cracks get bigger and bigger, then the whole chunk lets go."

"Ain't that called a—" and he hesitated over the strange word—"a *avalanche*?"

Owen shook his head. "An avalanche usually is snow, or ice, or earth. This is just rock. Rolling over and over. I saw one once. From the distance. It scared the hell out of me."

Inside the carriage their voices came to Victoria only as distant murmurs. She was crouched into an uncomfortable bend, trying gingerly to work her boot and stocking from her lacerated shin. The stays in her corselet dug inflexibly into her, cutting off her wind, sending her back against the merino, gasping, chin up, her lips blue. *Oh, God,* she mouthed silently. *If I ever get that thing off me, I'll never lace again!*

Far too uncomfortable to be shocked at her unladylike thoughts, she cocked her ankle up on the other knee, stared down past her cheekbones, stretched her arms and tried peeling the boot again without bending.

It finally came off, revealing a sad, tattered stocking, caked with brown blood and firmly stuck.

Loverly, she thought, unconsciously echoing Robert. *I've nothing to soak it with. Best I leave well enough alone until I get home—*

Home! The word struck her like a blow, left her staring at the stocking with eyes that no longer saw. *Home.* Paul's. That was her home now. That's where she was going.

She shuddered, unable to hold it back.

I won't think about it.

You have to think. You must.

Not now. Later. . . .

Later, she repeated firmly, pushing aside the sick fear that glossed sweat on her brow. *Right now I'm going to put a clean stocking over the dirty one so it won't rub, then get my boot back in place.*

The boot was a struggle, leaving her exhausted. Limp against the rocking seat-back, she thought dimly, *I must brush my hair.*

That had been Nanny's chore. She'd brushed with long, strong strokes that left it in shining pale waves.

Once Owen had come unexpectedly in the morning. Nanny, who liked him, had let her run downstairs, her hair streaming behind like a schoolgirl's. Delighted, Owen had played with it, letting it slide silkily across his big arm like a waterfall, tying it in two tails beneath her round chin. . . .

Then he'd suddenly caught her close, so close she'd felt his heart thump, buried his face in the sinuous mass. She'd turned her mouth for his, but he'd never kissed her. Instead, he'd thrust her away forcefully, savagely. His deep voice had been thick: "Put up your hair, Vick."

She hadn't understood then. She understood now and— her own heart thumping— she put her hands to her head and jerked them away, repelled at the frowze, the mats.

Dear God, what a harridan I must be! Victoria thought. *Wrinkled and dirty, unwashed, scruffy. . . .*

Desperately she scrabbled inside her portmanteau, went to work with the tortoise-backed boar's-hair brush. Tears came to her eyes, but she winked them away to see the tangles she pulled before the Landam nose, grimly sorting out what she could and tearing viciously at what she couldn't.

In a vague way she was aware pine needles were no longer scraping the carriage sides, that their place had been taken by a different sort of underbrush. The jolting and rocking too were now such a part of motion that the discomfort had moved to an unconscious plane, something merely to be endured. Yet a new sound caught her ear, such a tortured screek of wood on wood below her feet that, alarmed, she rose halfway, hanging on, reaching for the trap.

At that moment, with a ripping, smashing lurch, the entire carriage dropped down on the back corner, the front rising up and pulling the horses off balance. Grabbing for his own seat, Robert was shouting and sawing the reins over her head, scrambling wildly as the box threatened to tip completely on its side.

Victoria screamed. She clung with terrified fingers as the carriage seemed to go mad. It bounced and jolted sideways, sparks flying as metal ground on rock. Glass shattered, varnished wood flew in splintered pieces. Her portmanteau shot through the air, striking her cruelly, jerking loose her hands. She tumbled like a rag doll from seat to floor; then, as the equipage turned completely over, she plummeted helplessly into the broken roof. Her portmanteau followed, banging her shoulder, popping open, spewing its contents helter-skelter on her; a ragged bush jammed upward through a gaping split in the top. The final thing she knew was that an enormous horse-hoof was crashing through wood and merino like tissue paper, directly at her face! She threw herself aside, came in solid contact with the ironwork of the seatlocker, and remembered no more.

At the last moment Robert had jumped, landing on one knee, and rolled as far as the reins in his hands would permit. Not letting go, he panted, "My God, my God!" and scrambled clear just as the whole box went on its back with an awful scream of tortured wood. His horses had been inexorably towed in reverse down the rocky slope. To his horror he saw them fall in a tangle of traces. He staggered towards them but was jerked off his own feet again as the pitch of the carriage yanked their hindquarters into the air then dropped them heavily on the wreckage.

At the same time Robert jumped clear, just as startled birds shot from the trees and the equipage took its first crazy lunge, Owen had thrown himself from his horse, leaped to the door, tried with all his massive strength to hold it upright—to no avail! When it turned turtle, he went with it, sprawling like a puppet. The wheel horse's hoof scored his leg; he saw its whitened eyes flash past and heard the eggshell sound as its huge feet splintered the floorboards.

To him nothing else existed but Victoria. That Shonnewwek had been off his pony like a panther, was even then clambering the wreckage, grasping the horses' heads, Owen cared not. As the Indian's hands soothed their plunging necks, as he blew on their laid-back ears, eased them down, down, down, past the idly spinning wheels to familiar earth, Owen had pitched himself belly first over the capsized carriage. Scrambling up from the torn ground, dropping on the bloody knee that gaped through torn trousers, he wrenched at the bent and broken door. It was jammed—but nothing could stop him. He tore it off its hinges, flung it over his shoulder, thrust half his body inside.

Victoria was a silent huddle, buried in debris.

Mortally afraid, terrorized beyond sensibility, Owen crouched over her, oblivious to anything else. He was not aware of what he was saying if, indeed, he was saying anything. Tenderly he pushed off the crumpled plaid, found the white face, cradled it in his dirty, scratched hands, tried to form words, could only croak, "Vick, Vick. . . ."

Incredibly the heavy lids fluttered. Her eyes opened, stared at him blankly. Then with a gasp, a sob, she flung her arms around his neck, pulling him down to her, saying into his wet capote only his name: "Owen, Owen, Owen. . . ."

Trying to make his voice steady, he said, "Listen, heart's dearest, I have to get you out of here. Can you move? Are you pinned?"

She wouldn't let go of his neck, but her muffled words reassured him: "I think I can move. Wait."

In the tangle of her cape and the torn merino of the seat-back, he saw her knees waggle.

"Ouch!" she said, grimacing. "No—it's all right. I'm just banged where something hit me. I—I guess I'm in one piece."

He started wriggling out through the crunching shards. "Watch the glass. Can you follow?"

Gingerly, pushing the tangled hair from her eyes, she came after him on all fours. When he could stand erect, he pulled her up with him, into his arms. Just to hold her again, hold her safe a moment—that's all he asked.

She took a long, shuddering breath against his chest, then tilted her head back, looked at him. "What happened?"

"I'm not sure."

Shonnewwek was still holding the team, soothing them softly. Their sides heaved, but their heads were down. A tangle of cut traces trailed from their sweaty shoulders and blood dripped from a gash on the wheel horse's leg.

Seeing Owen and Victoria emerge safely, Robert sagged to a seat on the ground. He mopped his face with a ragged bandanna. Hoarsely he said, "That was mean!"

The rain began again, an insidious patter.

It dappled the sides of the broken carriage, the dust on their pale, dirty faces, slid crookedly through the sweat on the horses' gleaming sides.

Miserably Owen said, "Damn! Just what we need!"

He led Victoria to a tumble of rocks by the trail, turned one over with a powerful shove of his booted foot, sat her down on the dry side. "Are you sure you're all right?"

"Yes. Yes, I'm fine." *Fine* being a relative term, of course.

He limped back to the carriage, pulled out a blanket, shook the splinters from it and bundled its width about her shoulders and head. Robert had hoisted himself painfully to his feet. With an eye to first things first, he located his horses' blankets where they'd been pitched from the carriage box, and covered the team's steaming sides. Then he retrieved his felt hat from a sticky perch on a scrub pine and clapped it on his own wet head. At the far-flung sight of the rest of their gear, scattered thither and yon down the wet, brushy slope, he sighed.

The spinning carriage wheels were winding down.

With fear gone exasperation set in. He glowered at them. Then suddenly his eyes narrowed and a curious purple-red began to suffuse his usually easygoing countenance.

He hoisted himself up high enough on the battered frame to look closely, not at the three remaining wheels, but at the place where the fourth had been. In a voice like thunder he said, "Owen! Come here!"

The rags flapping on his bloody knee, Owen limped over. He said, "I know. The axles are bent to hell. We'll have to leave her."

"That's not what I mean." Robert pointed a stubby finger. "Look where that wheel was. The damned cotter pin's gone."

"Broken off."

"Broken off, hell! Gone, I said! Took!"

"You're mistaken."

Belligerently the driver thrust his red jaw forward like the prow of a barge. "Looky here, Owen Verinder, I've kept up this here rig for the general nigh to three years now! *My* cotter pins don't jist *go*. It was took, I say, and b' God, I stand behind sayin' it!"

They looked at each other, glance for glance, while the chill rain beaded their drawn brows and dripped dismally from the rear brim of Robert's thrust-back hat.

Robert added angrily, "And something else too. I 'low I know who took it. I saw her sneak outside last night, but I thought I heard voices and figured you all were talking."

"Thalia!"

"That's right, mister. It ain't no trick to slip a cotter pin if the hub's tight. That there wheel will stay put for quite a while—maybe, if the fording hadn't loosened it, clear to that big drop-off you've been talking about. And who do you recollect wouldn't get inside this here carriage this morning, not if'n she froze plumb to death!"

Huddled beneath the damp blanket on her dry rock, Victoria heard Owen's deep voice raised in a now familiar chant: "Goddammit all to hell!"

She saw him reach his buckskin mount in two strides, fling himself upward. Down the trail Thalia was just poking back into view. As he charged toward her at a dead lope, she stiffened, tried to turn her horse. The buckskin was swifter.

Not even dismounting, he reached across and dragged the girl off bodily, holding her in midair, and shaking her so savagely, her head flopped.

Not understanding, Victoria half rose in protest. She found herself restrained by Robert's dirty hand.

"No, ma'am. Let him be."

"What did she do?"

Robert told her.

She stared at him aghast, incredulous. "We could have been killed!"

"Yes, ma'am. And I reckon if that wheel had held just a mite longer, there wouldn't have been any question about it." Still scowling, Robert took off his old hat, thwacked it against his knee, jammed it back in place again. Then he took solace in savagely biting off a huge chew of plug tobacco.

Shonnewwek had settled his own dirty blanket over his topknot again. From the folds shot an eloquent hand.

Robert shrugged, gave him the remainder. "I guess you earned it," he said sourly.

Shonnewwek agreed. He shoved the entire plug in his mouth. Masticating loudly, his curious eyes watched Owen and the girl. *White men were strange*, he thought. In his lodge that woman would have been traded for a good pony long ago.

As the sodden little trio held their places by the wrecked carriage, they saw Owen set Thalia back in her saddle with a jolt that must have cracked her spine. He smacked the chestnut's rump with the flat of his hand. The sound echoed up the trail. The chestnut took off at a run and disappeared around the bend.

Slowly, Owen came riding back to them. His eyes were stony; his face set. He swung down, and without another word about Thalia Greenwood, said to them all, "We'll use the team for pack. Vick, you'll ride behind me, and Robert behind Shonnewwek. We'll have to make a lot of track before it starts to snow."

There was no question who commanded the expedition. Not daring to protest, Victoria watched her chattels get decimated again. Most of them were tied in merino bundles and hoisted high into the misty branches of a tall sycamore. The poor remainder went on the backs of the nervous team, along with what little Robert could retrieve of their scattered, dirt-covered and rain-wet food supply.

The driver salved the bleeding scrape on his wheel horse's foreleg while Owen retreated behind a tree and emerged, shivering, in a different pair of pants. He smelled faintly of horse, and Victoria realized the same salve had served his abraded knee. She stood up as he came to her, brushing bits of dirt and shard from her increasingly disreputable skirts.

He loomed over her and frowned down. His voice sounded harsh. "Are you certain you're all right? Can you travel?"

His tone angered her. "As if I had a choice. All right, Owen. I insisted I come! I put you into this condition! I take the blame for it!"

"Don't be a fool," he rasped, and reached for the reins of his buckskin. He swung up, put down a hand. "Step on my boot, and I'll pull."

She gaped up at him, and her pale face went pink. "Owen, please! I can't! I've never ridden astride; my skirts—"

Suddenly he grinned—the grin she'd seen before, which showed all his teeth. "Now don't tell me," he said quietly, "that you're solid from the waist down and run on castors because I know better, Vick."

As her face flamed even more brightly, he swung down again. Before she could guess his actions, he stooped, reached a swift hand beneath her skirts, grasped the rear hem and brought the entire mass of petticoats forward like a huge baby napkin.

"There," he said. "Now you're a proper frontier lass. Hang on to that, and don't give me any more nonsense."

This time, as he reached down his hand, she took it, put her shabby boot on his. Her chin was set, and she wouldn't meet his eyes. He swung her up behind him, went on calmly, "Put your arms around my waist, your head on my back, and pull the blanket over you. There's nothing you need to see, and it will be a hell of a lot warmer for both of us."

Her seething indignation communicated itself clear through the back of his clammy coat. He ignored it. Loosening his gun butt in its sheath, he kneed the buckskin into a walk.

Thalia hadn't denied she'd tampered with the carriage wheel. In fact she'd laughed, and he'd been hard pressed then, not to break her neck. But now the anger was gone; nothing remained but worry: worry about the unknown. Weather and trail hazards he could handle; sneaking shadows were something else.

13

Once more the rain had degenerated into a fine, cold mist. Owen tugged his hatbrim low, covered the crown with the hood of his capote, and stared straight ahead beneath the wet-beaded felt. He was letting the horse pick its way delicately, and the pace was slow. It had to be. Double weight was hard on all the animals.

His gaze was still stony-eyed, but almost unseeing. Strength had flowed through him like a jet when the carriage went over; now he was sapped. He fought it, knowing this was no time to let up, to be off guard.

Mersey had not killed himself. He was as certain of that as though he'd seen the deed.

Nor had Mersey shot Shonnewwek—yet shot he had been. Why? Because Shonnewwek had got too close to someone else—someone who could not afford to be recognized?

All along, Owen should have recognized that there were two shadows behind them. It was the second who had stolen the ferry—not Mercedes, who had taken the Indian crossing. It was the second who had used a pistol on the Sauk. Not Mercedes; he'd often said pistols were ladies' weapons. Who could the second be?

John Shaw had been right. Many men in Pike County disliked Paul Winterthur; a few actively hated him. He was arrogant and cruel. There'd been a lot of talk of revenge. Owen had dismissed most of it as whiskey talk; still, Paul was sitting there in his draughty, unfinished manor house, waiting for his wealthy bride. That bride was an English lady, daughter of a lord! God only knew how many gold coins and treasures frontier imagination had put inside all her boxes and trunks! And the fact that Paul had not sent outriders, an armed escort, would just seem like more of his arrogance!

Vick *was* a plum for the plucking! Why had he never taken it seriously? Robbery, hostage—or both!

Unconsciously one hand went to cover the two smaller ones clasped about his middle. *Back to checkmate*, he thought grimly. *Back to the unknown.* . . .

If he could only put a name on the shadow! He had a futile feeling that he knew all the facts, that if he weren't so damned dense, he could put them together and the proper name would fall in its slot!

He considered turning back, then dismissed the idea. The high bluffs were no place to get caught in a snow; they'd starve. Better to get on across the prairie to that abandoned cabin. That was a place to hole up while Robert went on for reinforcements. It had both food and fuel.

In the meantime, he realized more futilely than ever, he was doing all he damned well could. If their enemy was single, open attack wasn't likely; it would be three against one. Night camp was the time to worry. . . .

Nonetheless, he pulled out his rifle, laid it across the saddle again. Frontier shooting was quite different from bagging partridge in a party of gentlemen, but he had to admit: he'd adapted very well. Better than Paul, who broke into a sweat when he held a long gun.

Let Paul call it an "accident" if he wished. The pretty little chambermaid was still dead. And if it were an accident, Paul had certainly nipped out of England in a hurry. . . .

Victoria was an unmoving weight against his back, and her hands had gone loose. Perhaps she was asleep: good. It was hard to tell from the gray sky, but his stomach told him it was past midday. They'd lost a lot of valuable time. . . .

The trees had gotten thin, more ragged. In half an hour, they'd emerged from cover completely. The small cavalcade picked its way downward through long, wet grass, gray-brown and dying. Owen said, "Whoa!"

Robert said, "Oh, my God." Then he added, "This is what you were talkin' about."

Owen nodded. The driver pursed his lips. He said soberly, "It'd be fine if I was an eagle."

Centuries before, the earth had thrust up an enormous bow of limestone strata. Its clifflike sheerness now walled the entire west face of the bluff. Behind them was the torturous track down which they'd come. In front was a fissured, eroding drop of hundreds of feet to brown, trackless prairie. Robert asked incredulously, "You mean you've always come this way?"

"No, no." Owen waved his arm north. "There used to be a dry creek yonder until a rockslide filled it this spring. And if the river wasn't so high, we could have gone on up to Pilot's Bluff and crossed there. But the flatlands flooded three weeks ago in the night. Washed everybody down to Cairo."

A soft flow of Sauk came from Shonnewwek. Robert said, "That's dandy news." To Owen he interpreted with a grimace, "Ol' Spice Bush says they drove a war party of Cree over the edge here a few years back. A good time had by all. Except the Cree, I suppose. I'll tell you all something: I'm going to walk for a ways." He suited action to words by sliding backward off the Indian pony's round rump.

"We all are." Owen dismounted, lifted his arms for Victoria, helped her down. For a moment, groggy and half asleep, she leaned against him as one would against a tall, substantial tree. Then, suddenly aware of what she was doing, she straightened, moved away.

Robert had uncorked his jug, taken a draught, passed it. Owen hesitated, then poured some out for Victoria. She took an obedient drink, coughed, spewed, but definitely shed the sleepy look. He nodded. "I thought that would wake you up." He took her hand in one of his and the reins of his horse in the other. "Come on. Watch your step."

They seemed to have left the mist in the trees, but the wind was even more cutting and very cold. Dreary, rolling banks of cloud burgeoned fast across the western sky. It blew in gusts, sailing Victoria's blanket far out behind her, finding her ankles, reddening her Landam nose. She clutched the blanket more tightly, clung to Owen's hand, wished for the gloves in her portmanteau. The wind blew his hood back, worried at the broad brim of the hat clamped on his brow.

Shonnewwek led, stopping now and then, studying his footing with impassive eyes. On his pony's unshod heels was Owen, his rifle slung across his broad back, leading Victoria and his mount, whose soft whickers of protest she echoed silently, biting her lip. Each step on her ankle was agony. Behind them Robert trailed, wrapped in his greatcoat like a grizzly bear, using the long butt of his rifle as a staff and chirruping encouragingly to his team.

Suddenly he skidded, losing his footing, yelling uselessly, "Whoa! Whoa!" as he slid under Victoria, then Owen, toppling them like skittles. After one brief, frightening moment Owen caught an outcropping with his boot and the team, having obediently whoaed, accomplished the rest.

Shonnewwek waited calmly while they sorted themselves out with much groaning and cursing. There was a gleam in his eye that was almost amusement. But he made no comment, only shot an enormous brown stream of tobacco juice against the escarpment, where it steamed and ran.

Owen put his arm about Victoria and asked anxiously, "Are you all right?"

She pulled away. "Am I all right? Am I all right?" She mimicked him savagely, her voice high and thin. "Can't you ask anything else? No! I'm not all right! I'm cold and hungry and tired and scared and I want a bath and m-m-my hair clean—" Then the tears came, streaming down her cheeks, and humiliated, ashamed, she put her scratched hands to them, mumbling, "Oh, I'm sorry! I'm so sorry. . . ."

Wordless, Owen reached out his arm again; this time she came willingly, blindly against his chest. One cold hand left her face, stretched, caught at Robert's rough sleeve, tugged like a child. Hiccupping, she said, "You're both so kind— I'll try not to be such a bloody nuisance. . . ."

"Poor lady," Robert mumbled, touched. "It's all right. Poor lady."

The Sauk waited with no comprehension, only patience. Suddenly something caught his ear. He listened carefully, frowned, laid his hand on Owen's shoulder.

"Horse," he said.

"Where?"

The Indian gestured: *ahead.*

"Probably that idiot Thalia." Nonetheless, Owen slung his gun from his back. His eyes were narrow, cold.

Shonnewwek made the sign for *wait.* Soft-footed, he glided out of sight. But the wind had hardly time to dry Victoria's face before he returned, looking disgusted, and beckoned them on.

"Is it Thalia?"

He nodded. The blanket had slipped from his nobbled head and the tattered feather waved in the wind as he made a stolid announcement in Sauk. Owen turned to Robert.

"What did he say?"

Robert was frowning, bushy brows drawn. "That she's—'sick on head.' That doesn't make sense. Wait a minute." Leaning his long gun against the boulder at his elbow, he used both words and hands. Shonnewwek responded, touching his forehead and making the sign of a horse. Robert's face cleared. "Oh," he said. "He thinks her horse threw her. Anyway, she's lying just off the trail with her scalp bunged up."

Owen grimaced and said a word new to Victoria but obviously both pungent and unclean. "All right, let's go. We'll have a look, although I'd rather patch up an asp."

He reslung his own gun across his back, picked up the buckskin's reins and Victoria's hand. The Indian stalked ahead, arms wrapped in his blanket, the fringe on his shoepacs fluttering, and Robert, with his laden team, brought up the rear.

He was muttering, "That girl ain't nothing but bad news. Ain't never seen a child so born to trouble. . . ."

They were nearing the end of the limestone projection. It had began to turn a little south now, curving under a brown, dead-vine covered outcropping like a mustache beneath a hairy nose. Robert noticed the pack on his wheel horse was slipping a little. He stopped, tightened it, and also took a consoling pull from his small jug.

Clark's Job made damned good corn whiskey, he thought, wiping his mouth and pushing forward again. *It sure warmed up a man's insides when he had the willies. . . .*

The rest had gone around the bend. He was beginning to follow when suddenly, with a rattle and a bounce, a handful of loose rocks and gravel fell on the track before him.

He stopped dead, looked upward keenly with his gun at the ready. But he saw nothing. Bushes and boulders. Gray sky.

A varmint maybe. Or a dog. He whistled.

"Here, Pedro," he said. "Hey, boy! Pedro! Is that you?"

Silence.

Robert shrugged. He chirruped to his team and moved forward again, step by step. Damn. He'd be glad when they made the prairie. It might be wide and lonesome, but it didn't slide out from under a fellow. *I 'low I'll stay at Ross's until the rivers go down and go back overland*, Robert thought. *I don't cotton much to the bluff country.*

He was around the outcrop now, where the limestone strata, with a lift and a twist, turned itself into a sort of jutting roof. Far below he could see the rough trail angling down between towering piles of sandstone and the knobby roots of wind-crippled scrub oak. He could see Verinder and the lady, too, crouched together over something—Thalia, probably. There was her chestnut cropping dead grass with old Spice Bush stalking it. They could use the horse, but he didn't have much use for the girl. . . .

Thalia was still breathing, but it was harsh. Her eyes were shut, her face waxen and scored with dirt and brush scratches. She had rolled quite a ways. The scrape on her scalp was minimal. The real problem was that she was still wet and very, very cold.

Owen realized he had no choice. She couldn't be left here, as he'd left Mersey. They had to take her along.

He rose to his full, towering height, looked down at her, frowning. The chestnut was skittish, but Thalia had been born on horseback! He found it hard to believe she'd been thrown.

Victoria, still kneeling, glanced up at his stern face and was conscious of some very ambivalent thoughts: This girl had tried to kill her three times. Because of Owen. She'd been available and willing when Victoria had rebuffed his passions! Victoria had seen them making love beneath that blanket; she'd never forgive the arrogant blatancy of it!

As much as Thalia hated her, Victoria hated Thalia—wicked and sinful though it might be! Right now, she could easily walk away and leave the little hussy without a backward glance!

But it would not be humane. There would be death on Victoria's conscience. God only knew, she didn't need that!

She made herself say, "Owen, we have to do something."

He wrestled with it, pulling off his big hat, running long fingers through the tawny hair beneath it, putting it on again. Hell. They couldn't stop to build a fire here and get her warm. There wasn't time. He absolutely mustn't risk getting caught in heavy snow on this side of the prairie. There were no settlers, not a station for miles, and damned little game. They'd all starve. Or freeze.

"She may have some broken bones," Victoria said.

"I don't think so. But we can't worry about it now. If we only had something dry to put on her—"

"My cape!"

"What?"

"My cape. It's warm and it's dry, and I don't need it—truly, I don't. The blanket is quite enough. We can put her in the cape and Robert can ride the horse and hold her. I know he'll do it."

Robert, not pleased, opened his mouth to say so, encountered two blue eyes in a very dirty face, and discovered—helplessly—that he would indeed.

Victoria knelt again. "Here. Let's get this off."

"Get what off?"

"This heavy coat. That's what's wet, Owen; it's held water like a sponge. Be careful—watch her head."

Owen shook his, then gave way. Working swiftly, they pulled the unconscious girl from her own garment, rolled her like a rug into the plaid cape. Shonnewwek had come up, leading the chestnut, and now stood looking far off across the valley, chewing like a ruminant, and detached from the whole affair. Reluctantly Robert swung into Thalia's saddle.

"All right. Heave her to me."

For all her slenderness Thalia was a very sturdy girl. Owen grunted as he lifted her, almost losing his balance. Her head fell back against his arm, and suddenly a shock went through him colder than the air.

Victoria's clear voice asked, "Owen, what is it? Is she bleeding?"

"No. No, she's not." If he sounded short, he was sorry. He looked at her again, swiftly, to be certain of what he saw, then away, so neither Vick nor Robert would be drawn to the same thing.

There were livid marks on Thalia's throat.

Like fingers.

What if Thalia hadn't fallen?

What if she'd been thrown away like a rag doll?

Who then? And why? Why Thalia?

Vick, he could understand. Not Thale.

The thoughts shot through his mind as he carried her over, handed her limply up to Robert. Robert, grumbling under his breath, noticed nothing, but Victoria did as he returned to her.

"Owen—what is it?"

He answered almost angrily, "Nothing. Nothing! Move out, Bob. We've lost enough time."

Robert said sourly, "Giddap." The chestnut, curvetting resentfully at the double burden, threw her head back and walled her eyes. He banged her with his heels. "Stop that, damn you!"

Not at all in accord they started moving in a downward direction.

Whatever he was munching, Shonnewwek thrust it back in the murky recesses of his blanket, picked up the reins of the pack horses, and mounted his own tough little pony. Owen saw a girth loose and tightened it, glad of the chance to have a moment to think.

Thalia had run smack into someone on the trail ahead— someone who had tried to kill her—or thought he had killed her. Someone Thalia knew, or he'd not got close enough to put his hands around her neck. . . .

And another thing struck Owen: from the back! Those livid bruises on her throat had not been thumb bruises. . . .

Someone, then, that Thalia trusted.

Not a nice idea, Owen acknowledged to himself. Victoria was standing by the buckskin. Her skirts were wet and draggled. She was holding the blanket over her head like an old woman's shawl, and she looked very, very cold.

"There's an old cabin across the prairie," he told her, and because he was afraid of what he was feeling, his voice was cold too. "I'll build a fire, there, Vick. We'll all get dried out."

Dried out was a myth. She couldn't remember being dry. Or warm. She looked at him steadily. "How long until we get to Paul's?"

He turned, swung up into the saddle, reached down his hand. He'd put his gloves on again. The leather was stiff with the cold, and the hand looked like a mailed fist.

She put her own hand into it, her boot on his, started to climb up behind. He shook his head, lifted her easily up before him. "You get the front seat this time," he said. "The wind will be behind us." Also, if they were attacked, it would likely come from behind or overhead; this way he had more control.

Finally, as he flicked his reins and they began to move downward, he answered her question. "It depends on the weather. I want to make it on into Ross's Settlement tomorrow. That's a day's journey. If the weather gets bad, we'd better take the fork and lay up at Cole's Grove with John Shaw. Any way you look at it, there's still six more days' travel after that into the upcountry. But take heart, Vick. Ross's ends the bluffs. I left a wagon there, and we'll pick up more people and supplies."

"What—sort of people?"

"Immigrants. Looking for grassland. John sold them some of his military tract. They're waiting for us at Ross's. I told him I'd guide them on upstate."

She didn't reply. She was sitting erect, not allowing herself to lean against him. But his arm was around her waist. *My God*, he thought, *she's still laced! The little fool!*

He didn't know much about babies, but he did know lacing couldn't be good for anyone! *Tonight*, he promised himself grimly, *tonight, damn me, she'll take that laced thing off!*

A small, angry stream fell from above, and dashed itself across the trail before them. It was new, carrying roots and grasses with it. Robert had forded already, and his mount began to jog on the sharpening incline. Behind Owen Shonnewwek said something sharply.

Owen paid no attention. The dashing water was noisy, and besides, he was amusing himself by letting his spread fingers stroke Vick's stiffly self-conscious belly rhythmically, sensuously. The little sod's first lullaby, he thought. . . .

Shonnewwek shouted. Owen still couldn't hear for the hurtling cascade. He reined in, muttering, and half turned in his saddle. The Sauk, head lowered, was charging straight for him!

Victoria screamed and threw her arms around his neck, pinning the hand that reached for his rifle. Before the startled buckskin could obey the pressure of his knees, Shonnewwek was by him, his dark face in a grimace.

Eagle feather flying, blanket flapping loose, his sinewy torso leaned forward, grasping at the buckskin's bridle. His little pony stopped short, bracing all four feet. The buckskin jerked backward, rearing with a terrified whinny. Owen was almost unhorsed, taking Victoria with him. Cursing, hanging on for dear life, digging for the knife on his thigh, he vowed to kill that crazy Indian!

Only then did he sense an enormous shadow. Only then did he feel the rush of dank wind on his cheek.

End over end, the monolithic juggernaut crashed by, showering them all with flying gravel, with a shower of mangled saplings. Lesser chunks followed, bouncing after it down the new path cut by the raging stream. It struck a small escarpment half submerged in the water and sent up a blinding spray. Ahead, distorted by the glassy sheet of wet, Owen caught one brief glimpse of Robert's terrified face. Then it was gone, blotted by the smashing boulders. Sick at heart, Owen shut his eyes.

Like a receding roll of thunder the rockslide went on, diminishing until the last burst of noise at the bottom was like a faraway salvo. Then silence fell—a frightening silence in which the rushing gurgle of the stream was almost delicate.

Owen willed himself, set and ashen-faced, to open his eyes. Victoria was still pressed against him, clutching tightly. He held her that way a moment, trying to still her shaking, then said gently, "Get off here a moment, Vick. I have to go down and see."

Even as she slid to the ground, the incredible thing happened. They both heard it—a faint "Hallo!" from below on the trail.

Robert grinned as they came down to him—a shaken grin from a very tallow-colored face.

"It was that close!" he said, measuring with the hand that didn't clutch at Thalia. "That close! I'll not cuss this here chestnut nag, not no more! I put the heel to 'er and she jumped, I'll tell you! Damn, Owen! I heard varmints up on the ridge, but I sure didn't 'low they were big enough to set that one loose!"

Owen turned, looked back up the long slope. The fresh scar of the behemoth's path was easily seen as it followed the streambed. That and nothing else.

But he felt cold. He felt as if he'd never be warm again.

14

Owen turned the other way in his saddle, rising a little in the stirrups. Far below he could see the boulder where it had finally come to rest amid the bulky shards of others—mammoth, battered eggs in an ancient nest. It was easily distinguishable by its sharp edges, but getting to it would take at least a half hour or so—and for what? What would he expect to find? Pry marks? Good God. He was getting positively paranoid, finding enemies in every tree. . . .

Robert interrupted his thoughts, muttering nervously, "Let's get out of here."

In front of Owen, Victoria stirred. Her clear voice sounded muffled: "How's Thalia?"

"Still breathing. Hey, Owen, hold my horse a minute whilst I switch sides. M'arm's going to sleep."

"Sure." Callous or not, Owen's mind wasn't on Thalia's welfare at the moment—simply because there was nothing he could do. He waited patiently while Robert made the change. Thalia's face came partly into view, waxen, her lashes half-moons of black on her cheeks, her mouth dropped with the effort of breathing. Victoria looked at her and tried to feel sorry.

She said, "If we could only get to a doctor—"

Owen laughed, a short, ironic bark. "This country is a bit shy of doctors, Vick."

A note of panic crept into her voice: "Then—what do you do?"

Oh, God, the baby, he thought. *And I had to open my big mouth.* "There are people, love. They may not have shingles to hang, but they know what to do." *When you can find them*, he added, bitterly, to himself.

Victoria's mind had been far from babies. It had gone from that awful frozen man in the ravine to Thalia's advancing case of exposure and on to the simplicity of her own lacerated shin. "Of course," she said firmly, "Paul must have one on his estate."

Owen had reached for Thalia's limp, cold hand, found the pulse reedy. "One what?"

"Doctor. I mean—one has to look after one's workers. It's an obligation."

His brows lowered, Owen turned and looked angrily at the bland curve of her cheek. He'd about had a craw full of this "estate" business! But the hot, revealing words wouldn't come. Damn. Besides, a cold windy trail was no place for a lecture. To Robert he said shortly, "Let's go."

Robert nodded, touched the rather subdued chestnut with his knees and moved out ahead. Shifting his reins to the hand that held Thalia, he reached into the deep, wet side pocket of his greatcoat with the other. What he brought to view had once been corn dodger; now it was a sodden, crumbling lump covered with lint and tobacco. "Hell," he said morosely, "and my stummick's rubbing my back bone."

He ate it anyway, from the cupped palm of his hand, getting his mustache and scarf full of crumbs.

Owen paid no attention. He was looking anxiously ahead at the sinking rim of the far hills as they picked their way slowly down. Water splattered from their horses' hooves as they entered the brown current of the same creek they'd forded with near disaster that morning.

Its flow was turgid and grumbling now, as the freshet dashed into it, bringing mud and debris from above. The opposite bank was caved and crumbling. The exposed roots of the crowning willows were hung with wisps of dead grass from the bluff top, and they blew in the wind like wet hanks of hair.

There was a deep cut in the bank, scored by the ancient scramblings of a million buffalo. Owen looked at it closely, saw no recent signs of horses nor men; nonetheless, he signaled Shonnewwek to go ahead and fell in behind with Robert at the rear. No order was safe. There was nothing but calculated risk. Putting Vick in the middle was all he could do.

She was sitting before him in grim silence. Her two muddy boots stuck out above his like a child's, her back was eloquently rigid, but there was no blanket in the world that could disguise the fact it was Vick's body his was cradling in the big old remuda saddle. He thought ruefully, *Damn. Half the people in this world are women; why is Vick the only one who stirs me?* He knew he was attractive. In the last four years he had been not quite celibate. But Vick was still the one who turned his heart to jelly.

"Are you hungry?"

"No. Thank you." What a cold little monosyllable *no* could be! How sorry she was she'd said it when she heard him chewing something behind her. And it was too late then; silly vanity wouldn't allow a change of mind.

It had only been a small tailpiece from a roll of plum leather anyway; hardly enough to keep Owen's stomach from growling. He searched his deep pocket in vain for more. Thank God he'd had sense enough to leave a cache of food up ahead. They'd go pretty hungry tonight without it. The carriage accident had squashed the wicker basket, breaking the wine bottle into the remains of the meat, and the grub box had bounced half a mile down the slope, dumping everything into the dirt.

Behind him suddenly Robert groaned.

"Tophet!" he was saying in disgust. "I declare we are all witched! I ain't never been on such a trip! Will you look at that!"

"That" was a large snowflake drifting idly down from the leaden sky. Before it could melt on the chestnut's ear, it was followed by companions. Owen glanced up, sick at heart. This could be a very real disaster. Shonnewwek, his shoulders already whitening, gestured urgently from the high bank on the other side.

Victoria gasped in pain as Owen's arm tightened, but he never heard. He was urging his horse up the rough cut. She could hear Robert cursing under his breath, and the two pack horses jingling as they scrambled awkwardly for footing.

Beyond the fringe of brown willows was an enormous wallow, with huge buffalo pats frozen to the ground like huge polka dots. From there two dim wagon ruts plunged into the broken and tangled ranks of prairie grass. They took this trail, whispering and crunching the dry, dead growth. Far, far away on the other side Victoria could barely see a blue line of hill. That's where they were going, that's where Owen had promised her warmth and rest.

To her dismay, even as she looked, the blue line turned to gray and disappeared.

"Damn," Owen was saying softly between his teeth, behind her. "Damn, damn, damn."

The snowflakes were thicker now, large and fluffy and floating. Gentle. Frail.

"Oh, it's coming," said Robert behind them. "It's coming good. Got your bearing, Owen? I sure as hell don't want to be lost in this."

"Here." Owen stuck the reins into Victoria's hands, reached between them deep into his capote. He hauled out a worn leather pouch on a thong, extracted a small, tarnished brass compass, glanced behind and then ahead. "See what you get," he said, taking it from his neck and handing it back.

Robert verified the bearing and returned the compass with a sigh of relief, shifting his heavy burden uncomfortably. "I sure don't want to get lost out here like ol' Mose Grimmel."

"What happened to Mose Grimmel?" Victoria's voice was sharp.

"Nothing," answered Robert, "until spring. He had a nice long sleep until the Indians found him. By that time, though, the varmints had had their turn. Not much left for the widder, but soon as she seen that blue-glass eye she said, 'That's Mose, all right.' Hey, Spice Bush!" he called, rising a little in his stirrups, "you still carrying that thing?"

Shonnewwek indicated that he was. Robert went on, "The widder let him keep it, seeing as how she had little use for it herself. Her eyes being brown. Law! Look at that blamed stuff come!"

The snow was advancing towards them like a curtain. Hardly fifty feet in front of the horses the ground was turning white.

And it was so soft, so silent. There was not a cup of wind now. No birds wheeled overhead. The sky was like a pewter bowl, inverted, pressing down on them. They were pygmies moving under an enormous dome.

Father's paperweight, Victoria thought suddenly. The one on his baronial desk. It bore the title FALLING SNOW, and for a treat he used to let his little girl shake it up then watch the snow cover the tiny people.

But never over their heads. She'd tried and tried, but never would it cover their heads. . . .

It had been soundless, though. Like this. Even the horses' hooves seemed muted.

And the grass was no longer rank but laid low, ravaged and trackless.

"Buffalo herd," Owen said in anticipation of her question. He held his compass in his free hand, was keeping an eye straight ahead on Shonnewwek. His long legs dangling incongruously three inches above the ground on either side of his ambling pony, the Sauk was like a prow in the deepening white.

It was snowing furiously now, wet against their faces, sticking to their sides, muting Shonnewwek's tracks almost before Owen's covered them. Robert had moved up anxiously, the chestnut's nose almost on the buckskin's tail.

Snow covered the compass dial. Owen rubbed it free with his elbow. Shonnewwek had stopped and was looking back, pointing with one arm. Owen shook his head, gestured left. The Indian shrugged, moved to one side, and let Owen go ahead.

Robert snorted sarcastically but kept his remarks to himself. Shonnewwek had unfailing instinct all right, but it was in his stomach. He'd already taken that hunk of dried meat from his tunic and was gnawing imperturbably. "Here," Robert said, holding out the reins to his team. "Take these buckos. This jesse is getting heavy again."

Awkwardly he shifted his load, pulled the cape hood down so the snow wouldn't drift onto Thalia's white face. She hadn't improved any at all as far as he could see, but then she didn't seem to have worsened either.

The snow was up around their ankles now as they moved farther into it. No good. No good at all. He had made a joke about Mose Grimmel, but it really wasn't a joke.

Probably hadn't been particularly funny to Mose either, he thought wryly. "Owen!"

"What?"

"You travel thisaway. How far across?"

"Far enough."

"Ought we to have stayed where we was?"

Victoria drew in her breath sharply. Robert was questioning Owen's judgment! How dare he question Owen's judgment? Robert was just a—a hireling!

But in Owen's calm voice she learned another lesson about this new country. "No," he said. "I left firewood and provender on the other side. We can hole up for a week at least—if we need to. I figure that's better than hunkering down cold and hungry in a buffalo swale."

Robert nodded, accepting it. "How much daylight we got left?"

"About two hours. It ought to be enough."

"This stuff starts getting deep, the horses are going to be mighty tired."

"Then you and I will walk. And we'll shed some more pack."

Owen's deep voice was clear; the rest of him was shadowy up ahead. The snow had started to swirl around them. Robert urged his mount closer, wondered glumly how much of what Owen said was real and how much was just to buck up the little lady.

He turned a bit in his saddle, reaching out for the reins of his team.

They weren't there!

He cursed heartily, the blood thumping in his neck, and squinted back through the snow.

He could barely make out Shonnewwek's silhouette.

"Hey!" he shouted, and there was anger in his voice. "Get up here!"

The Sauk banged his knees against his pony's flanks, ambled up, put the reins in Robert's hand. His slitted black eyes glittered beneath his snowy blanket, but he said nothing, merely falling back into place.

Robert didn't like it. Not at all. Two fine horses would be pretty nice for a trader like Spice Bush. It would be damned easy just to fade off in this mush and not be seen again.

It was not that he didn't trust Shonnewwek but—to come right down to it— he didn't trust him. "Never did trust no damned Indian," he muttered to himself. And they were General Clark's horses. He'd already lost Will Clark his carriage; he sure as hell wouldn't want to lose his team too!

Behind him Shonnewwek began to sing again, his dismal voice curiously flattened by the snow. *Oh, well. A bellerin' Sauk was better than no horses*, Robert philosophized.

The snow deepened. The fluffy flakes had turned to thick ones, heavy with water, and so dense, it was almost like a wall. Owen took the coil of rope from his saddle, secured one end to the pommel and passed it back to Robert, who did the same, securing another length to his team then handing the end to the Indian, who accepted it gravely.

A wind had sprung up, pushing the white surface into little drifts and windrows, obstacles they had to cross transversely. The buckskin's head was down; he was plodding along doggedly but with sudden decision Owen threw his leg over, and against Victoria's protest, slid off into the snow.

Robert did the same. The pace quickened perceptibly. The horses were big, but so were the men. Whatever the Sauk's thoughts were—probably derisive, Owen knew—he stayed as he was, and his tough little pony seemed none the worse for it.

The snow was getting deeper, sometimes to their knees, and dark was coming on. There was no avoiding that— Owen had to squint now to see his compass.

Oh, God, he thought anxiously. *Did I make a mistake? Would it have been better back in the swale?*

Overhead Victoria was just a bundled shape in the gloom, but through the muffling of the storm Owen could hear Thalia's stertorous breathing. It was harder, if anything. Robert had tied her in the saddle, but he had to keep a hand on her to keep her from swaying off. She'd not said one word since they'd picked her up. If she knew anything, then she was faking—but that she was seriously ill was no fake.

She could die. And there would be small comfort to old man Greenwood in knowing that she'd willfully brought it on herself. But Thalia's death might solve a serious problem for Paul. She was far too jealous to be discreet, and one could reason more handily with a firecracker.

And something else suddenly slid into Owen's mind, disturbing him: Will Clark's remark about the proxy marriage making Victoria's husband her heir whether the marriage had been consummated or not. *Even if they were robbed on the trail and Vick died, Paul wouldn't lose everything*, Owen reasoned. *He'd even own Landam Hall!*

God knew, Owen had never wanted Victoria's money—only Victoria! How the sleek-legged, dark haired women on the Continent and the lusty, willing Kentish lasses had paled against the sweet, crystal fragility of Victoria Landam. How many, many pounds of his own inheritance had he paid into old Landam's pockets, knowing full well that Victoria's only bulwark against poverty was her mother's money—and that her father was quite willing to dip into that too, if his daughter would allow it. Damn the man! He'd like to have his two hands on him now—promising to mend his ways, to look after Victoria properly, blathering about the Landam honor! He'd looked after her, all right! Here she was, cold, frail, scared, and carrying some other man's child! He'd promised too—promised to take her to Paul. He would—because she had to see the man in all his tarnished fraudulence before she'd come back to Owen with no halfway measures. Owen had become a man on this frontier, and was no longer satisfied with flirtatious teasing. He wanted all of Victoria!

There was snow on his hatbrim, in his eyebrows, settling softly against his mouth. He tasted it, suddenly realized with a physical shock that God, he was hungry! It had been a long time since breakfast, and a skimpy breakfast at that. . . .

Now that he'd thought of it, he was almost light-headed. None of that nonsense!

He couldn't afford it. Surely on a frame of his size there was enough fat to carry him through a little deprivation.

Check the compass. . . .

Darkening. . . .

He could still see though, and made a small change in his direction. Funny old Shonnewwek, lolloping along back there in the spectral whiteness. He must be hurting; he was singing his song again and it came eerily through the snow. Could he find the way in this stuff if he had to? Shonnewwek had always been content to let others do the work, and Owen had discovered long ago that the infallible Indian instinct was a lot of Bow Street scrum.

There was a piece of foxfire in his saddlebag. Would it glow enough to light the compass dial?

Plod, plod, plod. The snow was deeper, heavier, weighting his boots. Right foot. Left foot. Vick a swaying shape above him. Robert and the horses close behind.

Tired as he was, Owen grinned. The chestnut's nose was almost up the buckskin's fanny. Robert didn't much favor getting separated.

Disaster sometimes requires only a catalyst. Owen's was a large owl, blundering out of the snow, thumping into Victoria, flailing his broad wings frantically to get away as—jerked from her somnambulistic state—she screamed and fought it off. The owl fell, flapping and squawking, on the neck of the buckskin. The buckskin reared, neighing shrilly. Owen yanked at his reins, knowing the plunging animal would bolt if he could, put one foot into the soft, treacherous snow of a prairie-dog burrow, felt the keen pain as his ankle twisted, went down as if poleaxed. For one black moment he saw nothing but a vast belly and thrashing hooves descending like a crusher. How he managed to roll from under, he never knew.

But he did. Half smothered in the snow, he scrambled erect, felt that searing pain again, and fell to one knee. Victoria, good horsewoman that she was, kept her seat, kept her head, and quieted her quivering mount until he succumbed to Robert's heavy hand on his bridle. Then she slid off, stumbling through the half seen drifts. "Owen! Are you all right?"

He was sitting now, mingling groans and curses, nursing his foot. It was swelling already, filling his boot, but not broken. At least he didn't think so. Gritting his teeth he said, "Goddammit all to hell!"

"Are you all right?"

She was on her knees in the snow beside him now, brushing it away to cup his face, demanding an answer.

He jerked himself away like an irascible child. "Yes! Yes! Except I've bunged up my damned ankle and—dammit! Dammit! Don't move! I've dropped the damned compass!"

15

It was a moment Victoria would remember all her life, a scene etched so clearly that twenty years later she could still shiver recalling it: the cold, gray-blue world with snow falling so thickly, it was like a ragged scrim between her and Owen. Behind them the horses curvetted nervously, stomping the heavy drifts, fluttering their nostrils. The anxious bulk of Robert, bending past her to Owen, gave off a rank musk of perspiration, wool, and whiskey; Robert had been taking solace in his jug. And somewhere in the nether gloom Shonnewwek resumed his plaintive keen song: "*Ai-o-ey-ey-ey. . . .*"

Somewhere in her middle, past the draggled coat and crumpled waist, past the ribs bruised to numbness by laces, past the stomach shrunken and aching with sickness, somewhere inside there a red spark began to glow.

This bloody country wasn't going to beat her!

"Then it's lost," she said of the compass, in a voice so crisp, it even surprised her. "There's not a bit of use in looking; we've either smashed it or scuffled it deeper into the snow or it's flown out there somewhere and is covered up already." Her hand waved at the gloom around them. "Can you stand, Owen?"

He could, dragging himself erect with Robert's arm, and balancing on his rifle butt. White-lipped, he muttered, "I'm fine," but she wasn't deceived.

"Don't sauce me, Owen Verinder. It's your turn to ride. Unless we stay right here until morning. Could we, Robert?"

She ignored Owen's sputtering, turned to Robert, putting a bare, cold, very small hand on his arm. He could see her face upturned in the dim, and her eyes, widened by weariness, were huge, dark smudges. He answered uneasily, "I suppose we could. There's blankets, and if we all huddled together like sheep. . . ."

"Sheep manage." Her clear voice sounded thoughtful. "I remember my father's herdsman talking about sheep out in heavy snow on the downs. They lay down together and even though the snow covers them, their breath makes a sort of cave over their heads."

Robert muttered unhappily, "I ain't no damned sheep."

Her temper flared. The cool, well-bred Lady Victoria stood off in the snow somewhere amazedly eying her ratty-haired, soggy-skirted replacement snuffle a runny nose and spit defiantly, "Then you say something better!"

Suddenly she spun on the shadowy silhouette on the droop-headed pony. "Or you! Sitting there like a slug! Shame!"

Shonnewwek gave an astonished grunt.

Furiously she demanded, "Well, are you an Indian, or aren't you? Letting us get lost and not lifting a finger! I guarantee General Clark will be sorry he called you *friend*!"

Of course he didn't catch half of what she said, but her tone was unmistakable and the name *General Clark* held an importance of its own.

With a snort of disgust the Sauk swung stiffly from his pony, dropped the rope twisted in its scrubby mane, and stalked off into the gloom.

Victoria stared after him in dismay.

"Oh dear," she said, "I didn't mean for him to leave—"

"He's not leaving," said Owen shortly. A numbness was spreading up his leg, blessed because it eased the pain—yet he sure as hell didn't want the damned thing to freeze.

Bewildered, she asked, "Then . . . what—"

"I don't know. But he's got something up his sleeve." Galled at his own incapacity, chagrined at Vick's taking command, yet Owen found himself rejoicing at the spirit that was back in her voice. He shifted himself gingerly, peered around. "Maybe we can't find the compass, but I'd surely like my hat."

She glanced around, saw it edgewise in a drift, grabbed it, dumped out the snow, reached up with both hands, and jammed it down on his frosted bare head.

"There!" she said acidly. And aping a country servant, she added, "And will there be anything else ye be wantin', sir?"

He caught one of the bare hands, brushed it lightly across his mouth. "Oh, yes," he said softly. "But I'll wait."

She couldn't even see his face, but once again the sense of being owned, possessed by him washed over her as palpably as a warm wave.

Alarmed, she jerked her hand away and stepped back. There was danger for her in this big man far more wounding than ice and snow—constant danger, and she mustn't forget it.

Her breath short, faint heat on her cheeks, she turned aside, yanked on her wet gloves, said to Robert in a rather muffled voice, "How's Thalia?"

"Still breathing." He'd been peering through the gloom for a sight of the Sauk. Seeing nothing, he went on rather plaintively, "Ain't there anything to eat? I swan, my stummick's growing to my hip pockets."

When Victoria had jerked away, Owen had laughed—softly, to himself. He took two tentative steps, leaning on his rifle. His strength seemed to have been renewed. "Check Thalia's saddlebags. She's country-savvy. Maybe she's got something."

Robert obeyed with alacrity, but there wasn't much—an almost empty cornmeal bag and a small lump wrapped in linen. He put it to his nose. "Cheese!" he said happily. Fishing out his caseknife, he hacked off small chunks, handed them around on the point of the blade.

Victoria was much too bemused with other thoughts to realize that a proper servant would have handed the whole mass over to Owen, and accepted whatever Owen chose to give back. She'd heard Owen laugh, recognized the conceited self-confidence in his laughter. Grimly she realized her errors in the past days. Beset by her troubles, it had been so easy to take shelter in his arms—even when they'd still been warm from holding Thalia! He'd every reason to think she had no propriety! She'd shown none.

How could she face Paul? How could she grace his home as Lady Winterthur when on the trail she'd acted a slattern?

Fists clenched inside the wet gloves, she made herself promises she intended to keep.

Owen had heaved himself awkwardly around to the other side of the chestnut. In a gentle voice he said, "Thalia?" Reaching up, he shook her a little. "Thalia, answer me."

She moved her slack mouth. "Wa— Wa—"

He swung up behind her, eased the limp head against his chest. Unscrewing his canteen he let her have a small drink. Not much. She was not cold anymore, but burning with fever.

"Wa—"

"No. No more. Later. What happened to you?"

"Did you fall?" Robert asked eagerly, and silently, Owen cursed him for leading an answer. It came too, patly: "Yes. Fa'."

Whatever she might have said if unguided was lost.

She stirred against his chest. "Ropes. Hurt."

"We found you on the trail. Before it started to snow. We had to push on, so Robert tied you on your horse." Owen was trying to measure her awareness. But she was sick; there remained no question about that. He went on, "If you can ride, we'll take them off."

A faint nod. Very faint. But there was a sort of weak alertness about her that didn't deceive Owen. He swung down again, and loosed her binding. But he didn't hand over the reins. God knew he could happily do without her, yet neither did he want her frozen body on his conscience.

Shonnewwek passed in the gloom as though they weren't there. Outside the mashed wallow of their feet he knelt, pawing at the snow until he'd cleared a spot. Then as they watched, squinting through the blue-white dark, he lowered his head. The rather fat expanse of his rear arose in some eminence, the soiled, wet deerskin fringe stuck down with wetness.

Robert said, "What the hell?"

"He's listening," said Owen shortly.

"Out here? For what—the Second Coming?"

"I don't know for what." Owen frowned. "We can't be too far from the other side."

Still in silence the Sauk arose, advanced a few more paces, and repeated the performance. Victoria looked at the cheese in her hand, still stuck on Robert's caseknife. Moving through the snow that was now wet and squashy beneath their trampling feet, she went to Thalia's side, said gently, "Would you like this?" and held it up.

A hand came down slowly, took the knife, moved it mouthward. Feeling smugly virtuous, Victoria glanced about to see if Shonnewwek was still at his mysterious work. She had no intimation of the arm that suddenly went up, then plunged down viciously.

She only knew that she was abruptly sprawled in the wet snow, and Owen was grappling with a muffled shape atop the chestnut—a shape that first snarled, then broke into hoarse, rasping, helpless tears.

Owen was saying furiously, "Give it to me! Give it to me or I'll break your arm!"

The caseknife sailed overhead, almost grazing the Sauk's topknot.

Owen grated, "You little wildcat! By all that's holy I ought to finish you off myself!"

From the snow Victoria found herself crying, "Owen, no! Don't! It's not her fault!"

He spun around, looked down at her. "Not her fault! Vick, you're crazy!"

Hopelessly, she said, "You don't understand!"

"Well, I understand this: that, even half sick, she's as dangerous as a cobra!"

"Let her alone, Owen. Please. I ask it."

His hat had fallen off again. He shook his tawny, snow-dusted head, stepped back, picked it up, and jammed it in place.

"All right, Robert," he said. He was very, very angry. "We must humor

Lady Winterthur. Tie her, though. Tie her damned hands and any other part that moves. I'd rather travel with the cholera.''

Shonnewwek, who had followed his own path, oblivious of the white men's vagaries, suddenly gave a grunt of satisfaction.

Sitting back on his haunches he beckoned imperially. "Verinder.''

Owen put down his hand, yanked Victoria to her feet, dropped the hand, picked up his rifle from where it had fallen and hobbled over. He knelt painfully at the Indian's side, maneuvered so he could put one ear to the frozen patch of bared ground.

Nothing.

He turned his head, tried the other ear.

"I'll be damned,'' he said. "Water.''

"What?''

"Water. Running water.''

Robert said truculently, "I ain't thirsty.''

Owen sat back on his one good foot, the other stuck straight out in front. He said to the Indian, "The creek. Right? Damn. Ask him, Robert. There's a small creek, runs out from the timber about half a mile until the prairie soaks it up. Little Blue. Ask him if that's what he's found.''

The soft, mellifluous Sauk flowed between them. Owen caught one phrase: *P'tit bleu*. He said, "That's it. That's the one. If he can locate it . . . and we follow upstream, we're only a twenty-minute trek away from a warm fire.''

Shonnewwek stood up, readjusted the blanket over his tattered hairknot. A little smugly he nodded, picked up his pony's rope-lead, and plowed off through the snow into the dark. With some disarray they followed meekly, close together.

Like mice, Victoria thought, *after the Pied Piper*. Not a comforting allusion, she realized, recalling the fate of the mice. But surely Shonnewwek was to be trusted. At least Owen seemed to think so. . . .

Owen hobbled painfully through a drift almost breast-high. Victoria floundered after him, with Robert, Thalia on the chestnut, and the pack team close behind. The world had closed in on them almost totally, leaving nothing but blurred shapes seen through eyes that were slitted to keep out the snow.

Like blind *mice,* Victoria amended wearily. The snow was exhausting and her brief spate of courage began to wear thin against the agonizing rack of those laces and the lacerating rub of her boot on her shin. She began to pant, then realized they were all panting, even the horses. Sweat began to trickle out from beneath her hood; blood drummed in her ears. *Oh!* she was saying to herself, in rhythm with her plodding feet, *Oh, oh, oh!*

Owen stopped so abruptly, she smacked into his broad back, almost tumbling them both.

Ahead Shonnewwek grunted again, this time with satisfaction. He lifted one wet shoepac and brought it slamming down. There was a soft breaking sound, then another sound more welcome—the unseen gurgle of swift-running water.

"By God,'' said Robert in her ear, almost with awe. "He's found it. Which way, Owen?''

"Left,'' said Owen. "Mount up. It can't be too far.''

Robert said, "I don't know if I can trust this jesse in front of me.''

"If she makes a move, break her neck.''

Owen's voice was grim. He meant it. He swung up on the buckskin with a groan, reached down a hand for Victoria.

"I'd rather walk, Owen."

"Don't be an idiot, Vick," he said and pulled her up willy-nilly. His good knee nudged the horse forward, and one strong arm encircled her waist. "I'll make you a promise," he said in her ear quietly, "that tonight we'll get those damned laces off."

She didn't answer. He shrugged, perversely satisfied with feeling her body tense, and let it go at that.

Even with the stream to guide them they had no intimation of where they were, except that the wind grew stronger, gustier, blowing great needlelike wafts of snow in their faces.

"We must be close," Owen shouted back, cupping his mouth. "There's a big gap in the timber. It always blows through there like thunder. Make sure you're tied secure; it would be damned foolish to lose anything this near shelter."

Robert nodded. He replied, but the wind tossed back his words. He felt for the rope looped in a half hitch on the saddle horn. It was fine. He reached back by touch, and found the other end secure on the first pack animal. All right. Where his wheel horse came, the other would follow.

Only dimly could he glimpse Owen up ahead. He couldn't see Shonnewwek at all. But by Tophet! He'd vote for the Sauk's coming in and sleeping by the fire like white folks this night—even if he did smell like a pet 'coon!

Warmed by this charity, he took a firm, encircling grip on the supine bundle that was Thalia, closed his eyes, and left the horse to do the following.

Owen discovered they were in the cottonwoods by the simple process of running into one. The blessed numbness in his leg was gone, supplanted by living fire, shooting clear up into his hip. *Good God,* he thought blearily, *if Paul's leg hurt like mine does, then he's a damned sight braver man than I to set it himself!*

The sudden scrape of branches brought him out of his haze. He reached down, felt a rough bole. *Cottonwood, all right.* The creek was on his left, then, and the wind screaming through the cut on the right. The old cabin should be almost dead ahead. It ought to be hard to miss since the land had been cleared around it.

He tried to make his voice normal. God, he hurt! "Almost there, Vick."

She nodded. He felt the hood waggle beneath his chin. His belly was warm where she'd sat against it—the only warm place on him except that hellfire leg. *By all that's holy,* he said to himself with dangerous virtue, *if a man is supposed to win his woman by his deeds, then I sure as hell have won her!*

His horse stumbled, then righted himself. The old well-sweep loomed like a snow-crusted arm: they'd made it. There was the cabin. But he reckoned it wouldn't do much good to tell Vick this was Mose Grimmel's old place.

He slid down, gritting his teeth against the pain, muttered, "Stay there." Using the rough cabin wall for a prop, he worked his way along until he felt the deep cut in the logs and one sagging leather hinge. He called out hoarsely into the howling wind, "Robert!"

Robert's dark shape blundered forward; together they scooped off snow, pulled at the slab door until it opened enough to pour out the dank chill of an empty house.

"I got m' tinder," Robert gasped. "Where's the chimney?"

"Left!" Owen shouted in his ear. "There's wood piled. I'll get Vick!"

Robert disappeared. Owen heard a hearty curse as he stumbled over some unseen object. Owen turned back, braced himself, held up his arms.

It was no time for nonsense. She slid down into them, he bundled her into the pitch dark, felt along the rope for the chestnut and Thalia.

Above the wind he said, "I damned well ought to let you stay out here and freeze!"

If she replied, he didn't hear—nor care. He untied the rope knots, gnawing at them with his teeth, and pulled her off roughly. She slid right on down in a heap on the snow. Painfully he bent, got an arm around her, half carried, half dragged her across the drifts, dumped her inside, leaned against the doorframe, panting.

There was a thin, bright wisp at the far end, and the black silhouette of a hand feeding it twigs slowly and tenderly. To that wisp he said in a rasp, "You'll have to get the horses. You and Shonnewwek. I'm played out. Put them in the other half of this place. It's good shelter, and there's still some old fodder there."

Robert fed another, larger stick, and a flame shot up, dancing. There was a comforting sound of crackle and actual warmth. Victoria, in a heap by his knees, put her hands out to it almost unbelievingly. She found to her dismay that silent tears were running down her cheeks.

"There, little lady," said Robert, getting stiffly to his feet. "Just keep on like that. A stick at a time. See? She'll go fine if you don't get in a hurry. I'd best look after the beasts."

Turtling his head into his collar again, he stepped over Thalia, put his shoulder to the door. The wind whirled in; Owen heard old leaves skittering across the packed dirt floor. Then it shut again.

He half sat, half lay, in a sort of stupor, struggling to pull his mind and his body together, slow the big thumping pump of his heart, and contend with the fiery club of the foot that was held by his boot as though it were in a vise.

The door reopened a crack. A squeeze of wind blew snow across him. Through it Robert said, "Where's Shonnewwek?"

Owen frowned, trying to think. He actually hadn't seen the Sauk for half an hour. "Can't you find him?"

"No. And I'll tell you something else I can't find! One of my horses! That thieving varmint—"

"What about his pony?"

"Oh he's here—miserable little nag with the dry heaves! I got him. But I ain't got Toby! And don't tell me he came untied because he sure as hell didn't!"

The door shut again on Robert's wrathful voice. Owen sat still a moment, staring at where it had been.

So Shonnewwek was gone.

It was not really strange. Even in just four years Owen had learned that an Indian goes when and where the whim took him. That he'd taken a horse was not remarkable. He'd done the white party a service; it had seemed to him, probably, a fair exchange.

If he'd gone of his own choice.

Had their shadowy enemy come ahead of them to this refuge in the snow?

16

His heart was gradually stopping its mad lunge inside his chest. Owen sat up, careful not to move his leg, glanced down the musty, dark little room at Victoria. She was still crouched by the burgeoning fire, feeding it with an almost empty, mindless motion as though hypnotized by her own movements. Flames were licking up the back of the blackened old fireplace now; it was ready for a fair-sized log, but Robert could do it. He wasn't going to even try getting himself erect. Not just yet.

He was gripped by a sort of apathy, a deadness, a suspension of activity. He knew he had to shake it off. There were things to be done.

Thalia lay, a shapeless plaid bundle, by his good leg. He touched her, prodding with his toe. She didn't move. Maybe she was dead. He didn't think so. One of the flames flickered high, lighting her face; it was flushed with fever.

The hood had slipped from Victoria's head; her hair shone, tousled and pale. The same flame silhouetted the aquiline Landam nose, the slim elegance of her long fingers. Lady Victoria! What did she think she was doing here in this ruined place, sitting in the dirt, cold and hungry? Why had he let her leave the Clarks'? He must have been insane!

He took his eyes away from her because just seeing her delicate frailty was a reproach, let them travel slowly the length of the half dark cabin. Mose had never had a palace. There were no windows; the roof sagged. It was dirty and dank and smelled like varmints. Suddenly, viewing it through Vick's feelings, it was intolerable. She must hate him. How could she do else? Look what he'd put her through!

At least there was food; at least she'd have a good meal. There was wine in his cache, and meat for roasting, a loaf of excellent bread, and a pat of new-made butter.

He looked up toward the webby, smoke-blackened rafters—and his breath stopped, jamming inside his chest.

The cache was gone!

Frantically he heaved himself erect. His breathing started again but with such violence, his head spun, and he had to grab hold. Robert came back in, dropped his load, and pulled the door shut behind him. He glimpsed Owen's contorted face, said, "Great Tophet, man, sit down!"

Owen shook his head, gritting his teeth. "The cache," he gasped, pointing.

In dismay Robert murmured, "Glory. That ain't good news. Gone, is it?"

Owen nodded. "Rafters," he muttered, "Not there."

The two men looked at each other a moment, then Robert's brushy eyebrows raised. "This country," he said, "is getting too much damned riffraff in it! I may just think about movin' me and Mirandy on to where we'll be shet of the no-accounts and the thievin' Indians! You stay put. I'll look."

It was gone, of course.

But Robert found two things: the rope that had bound it to the crossbeams and the wine bottle—the object he'd kicked in the dark and sent rolling under an old puncheon bench.

"Cut," he said of the rope. "And look you there!"

He pointed, and in the flaring light Owen could see where the wine had been allowed to gurgle itself away uselessly on the packed dirt floor. He added, "That wasn't no thievin' Indian."

Owen stooped painfully, and picked up the cork.

"And no hunting knife dug this out," he said hoarsely. "The bastard used a corkscrew!"

He turned, smashed his fist against the cold log wall once, twice, in impotent, helpless fury. *You think you're so smart,* he told himself, *you think you're so damned smart! Then everything turns to ash!*

Robert was pondering.

"A corkscrew," he repeated, puzzled. "A corkscrew. Well. At least we ain't been robbed by no ordinary, flea-bitten lowlife."

He scuffed the dirty green bottle with his cowhide toe, then with a sudden motion kicked it back into the corner.

"It appears," he said sadly, "as if we postpone our Sunday dinner." He looked up at the sagging shoulders of the big man before him, shrugged. "We're not so bad off. I still have a bit of salt pork in my bag. There's a gill of cornmeal in Thalia's. You got coffee. Let's us fry up a meal and things won't look so bad. My paw always said a full belly cured a lot of troubles."

Owen swung around. He saw that for all Robert's brave words he was facing facts. If they got snowbound their difficulties were compounded. In deep snow all the animals took cover; hunting would be virtually nil. Firewood could get to be a struggle of its own. And their company was composed of one frail girl, one sick one, one man with a game leg and Robert, who knew his country— but not this part.

Owen thought bitterly, *No wonder Shonnewwek decamped.* It burst from him involuntarily: "Why did I let her come?"

Robert patted the big arm. "Come now, lad," he said, gently. "She would, y'know. And she's got sand, that little lady."

"She's going to need it," Owen replied grimly. He turned and looked down at their traps on the floor. "All right. What did Spice Bush leave us?"

"Whatever was on Blaze. Blankets, some of her faradiddles, that wee trunk she sets such store by." He turned away to the fire, said, "Hey there, ma'am, how about helping me spread a pallet or two? We ought to move this young hussy here closer to the warm, I reckon. And Verinder better get his boot off or he'll be in for it. Gangrene gets kind of nasty."

Victoria started as though coming back from a long way off. She scrambled up from the huddle of her blanket and came to them, her wet skirt sweeping a soggy trail across the floor. One look at his drawn face and she knew how painful it must be.

Unaware of the clean streaks that ran down the smuts on her own face and the story they told, she put her arm around Owen's back, saying, "Lean on us. We'll get you to the fire. Robert, if you'll spread a blanket for Thalia, Owen may sit on mine."

Owen hobbled between them, smiling even through the pain at the casual disregard of his two hundred and thirty pounds. With a gasp he sat down in the leaping circle of warmth. She knelt before him, looking aghast at the leg that ballooned above the battered boot.

"Owen, is it broken?"

He shook his head. "I don't think so. Vick, you can't get that boot off. Let Robert do it."

Robert had spread one of the horse blankets near the hearth, carried Thalia over, laid her down. Her face was flushed; her eyes closed. They could hear her teeth chattering.

Owen said, "Untie her hands. Cover her with all the gear we can spare. She's a strong little wench; she'll probably make it."

Normally Victoria would have been upset at his callousness. Now she hardly noticed. Her entire attention was for Owen.

Robert obeyed, burying Thalia beneath a mound, then he sat on his haunches by Victoria. "Give me your caseknife. A prairie dog's got mine by now."

Gently he cut the threads of the sideseam, spread the top of the boot. The sudden release of pressure was so easing that Owen said "Ahhh" involuntarily, followed by an equally involuntary groan as Robert worked the foot.

"You're right," Robert said cheerfully. "T'ain't broke. Hurts worse than a break, don't it? I'll get some snow. Packin's the thing to bring a swelling down, and when the snow melts, you can have yourself a nice hands-and-face wash, ma'am. Then I figure you might fry up some grub."

Owen frowned; Victoria swiftly put her hand on his, warning him. "I'll try," she said, "but you'll have to help." She found it unnecessary to mention her cooking expertise consisted sheerly of lavish, creamy omelets for her father's cronies after a large evening at the gambling tables. Besides, the very thought of light, fluffy eggs made her weak.

Robert was looking around, trying to turn up something that even vaguely resembled a container that might hold snow. Victoria divined his thoughts. She went through the flickering shadows to her portmanteau, unlatched it, and with one motion dumped the contents on the ground. "There," she said triumphantly. "This will do."

Robert said, "Oh, ma'am!" at the iridescent shot-silk lining, but Owen only nodded.

"Good girl," he said, and grimaced, closing his eyes involuntarily as he moved the foot.

So much for sacrifice, she thought ruefully, moving to scoop up her possessions as Robert went out the door. She opened the folds of a thin lawn-chemise, laid on it her brush, her spectacles, various little artifices and perfumes, tied the corners into a bundle. The sweet smell of lavender almost made her giddy. *Oh, God,* she said to herself, *that's what* clean *is like. . . .*

Robert reentered on a gust of snow. His grizzled face looked set; she asked swiftly, "Robert, what's wrong?"

But he only shook his head, answered, "The storm's letting up a little. It's getting blamed cold out there."

By the fire Owen nodded. It would as soon as it stopped snowing. He lifted his leg with his hands, set his teeth as Robert slid the snow-fled portmanteau beneath it, piled more snow on top.

"Now then," Robert said. "All packed up like a side of beef. Best we think of eating next, I reckon."

He bustled around—there was no other word for it but *bustling*—getting a nub of bacon from his saddlebag, haggling it into slices on his knee, showing Victoria how to twist them over the length of his ramrod, which he propped like a fishing pole above the fire. The drip of its fat into the flames made her realize how hungry she was. Robert was hurriedly coaxing snow to melt in his hat. Then he caught some of the fat, dumped in the cornmeal and coarse salt, stirred it all together with a stick. "Now, ma'am," he said to Vick. "If you'll make some little balls of this and mash them on the hearth rock, where they'll brown, I'll see what else I can find."

Victoria nodded. She tried to wash her hands with snow, got them cold and wet and perhaps a little cleaner. She glanced at Owen anxiously. He was leaning back, his eyes closed, deep lines around his mouth. She crawled around him trying not to joggle as she got nearer to the fire with Robert's hat.

The cornmeal didn't want to stick together. To her dismay she was getting more between her fingers than in a ball. Robert glanced over, said judiciously, "Bit more water, ma'am."

She swallowed, angry at herself. *Any woman would have known that!*

With a little snow, they went better, and she patted them out, absorbed in making them round and neat. *Like playing Patty Pans,* she thought wryly.

Robert was grumbling, "Tarnation! My stummick sure could use some coffee! The least that damned Sauk could have done was leave us the coffeepot!"

Victoria sat back on her heels, grimacing as the stays dug her ribs. "He's gone?"

"Yes, ma'am."

In dismay she said, "Oh, Robert, I didn't mean to make him angry!"

"Now don't you go thinkin' that, ma'am. There ain't no reliance in a Sauk. He just saw the chance to horse-trade, that's all." His old felt was drying by the fire; he shook out the crumbs and stuck it on his head again. "Turn them cakes easy, ma'am." He handed her the knife blade, but not before she said, "Ow!" and jerked her fingers back.

Owen's leg was melting the snow. Robert reached in to the portmanteau with Owen's tin cup, scooped it full, poured in a careful amount of coffee grounds, set it on the hearth to boil.

"A cup at a time," he said cheerfully, "but it's better than none."

The cakes wanted to break and crumble. Gritting her teeth, Victoria slid the knife blade beneath them cautiously. One broke, tumbled into the dirt. She said, "Oh I've ruined it!" but Robert picked the little cake up, dusted it, and ate it all with such speed that suddenly she realized how hungry he must be.

They hadn't eaten—not really eaten—since Reuben's station! She had—oh, indeed, she had—wine and roast white meat!

Robert was bustling again. He righted the puncheon bench, set it before the fire, spread his dubious neck scarf on it and with a flourish slid the bits of crisp sidemeat off his ramrod onto the scarf. Neatly he dealt out the hoecakes—two apiece for Owen and Victoria, one for himself, said cheerfully, "Now! How's that for style?"

For the first time it dawned on Victoria: that's all there was to eat. This wasn't an entrée, or a first course. This was it!

Heedlessly she said, "But I thought—"

She stopped. But Owen's eyes were open. Bitterly he finished for her, "That there was food here. There was, Vick. But someone—" He hesitated only slightly, chose different words. No need to frighten her more, although to him the desecration of the cache was almost malignant. "Someone took it," he finished.

Then, completely misinterpreting the appalled look on her face, he said angrily, "I told you we'd be far from the Savoy, Vick!"

Her mouth went tight. Choking back answering anger, she got stiffly to her feet, went past them to her small trunk that lay in the shadows. Opening the lid, she dug down beneath the soft robe, the clean, folded garments—dug with her cold, chapped hands. From the bottom she lifted out a heavy, paper-wrapped lump shaped like a large turnip. Carrying it on her palms as if it were a head on a salver, she went back to the bench, knelt, put it down, and began to peel the wrappings.

A lovely smell hit their noses—a winy smell, rife with citron and raisins.

"Oh, Lord!" said Owen, and despite his leg, he straightened, scraping back the tawny hair from his incredulous eyes. "It can't be!"

Almost in awe Robert said, "Plum pudding, I know it's plum pudding. My grandmaw made one once back in Kentuck."

She'd come to the stiff brown pudding bag. She untwisted the top, pulling it down to the dark, glistening rich-smelling ball. "Nanny gave it to me," she said. "Well—she really sent it to Owen." Which was true. Paul had considered plum pudding indigestible. But Owen and her nanny had sat by the fire one late autumn evening and eaten a whole one by themselves—liberally laced with brandy sauce.

They were still staring, as though witnessing a miracle.

"Well!" she demanded. "Aren't you going to eat it?"

Robert put out his big paw of a hand. "Just put a piece right there, ma'am," he said, "and you'll see whether I will or no!"

Owen elected to wait, eating his sidemeat and hoecakes first, and there was no more nonsense about "not the Savoy." Victoria presided at the cutting as neatly as though she were at her own tea table, oblivious of her tear-stained cheeks, her crumpled traveling habit. The heat put a little pink in her cheeks, made her open the throat of her waist; and she was so obviously pleased at having been useful, Owen wanted to reach over and hug her.

They ate half, then Owen said gently, "Wrap it up again."

She didn't ask why. She just obeyed, soberly, without looking at him.

Robert sat back on his haunches, glanced from her to Owen, trying to catch his eye. When he succeeded, Owen said, "Vick, look to Thalia, will you? I think she's too sick to be dangerous, but be careful."

As soon as he dared, Robert said softly, "I've been waiting to tell you. The horses is gone."

All the ease left Owen's face. "Wandered off?"

Robert shook his burly head. "Took," he said.

"Indian?"

"Not likely. Heeled boots; I saw the prints before the snow filled 'm. We got us a problem, Owen."

Owen nodded grimly. They had, indeed. More than he'd thought. The shadows were fast turning to substance.

In a quiet voice he asked, "When did you miss them?"

"When I went for the snow. I started off to look, madder than a buzzsaw. I figured it was old Spice Bush again, you see, and I was going to have his topknot clear down to his knees! Then I saw the boot marks. I'll tell you; the hair went up on the back of my neck like a cornered pup. Indians don't bother with boots, and a white feller stealing your nags, he ain't set on being too friendly!" His voice had risen; he lowered it self-consciously. "You figure it's the same one what took the cache?"

Owen nodded. His eyes were slitted; the firelight caught a cold glitter through the narrow cracks. With his set face and big body he looked formidable. Robert had the fleeting thought that he was glad he was on Verinder's side. He said slowly, "Then this ain't no chance stealin'. Somebody's gettin' us ready to pluck." His own eyes slid to Victoria, then back again. "I reckon it don't really matter—but *is* she carryin' gold to Winterthur? Folks think she is."

"I don't know. I've never asked. But you're right: it doesn't matter, if whoever's out there thinks so." Either way, they'd all be killed. The dead can't talk.

Robert said slowly, "On the other hand there's the little Greenwood jesse. Her paw's worth a mint, and he's *got* money. Not like Winterthur."

But this wasn't going to be an ordinary robbery. The enemy wasn't interested in hostages. He'd had his chance with Thalia out on the trail and left her for dead.

Owen shook his head. "We've got to keep ourselves from being picked off one by one."

"That's easy. Stay inside. Of course, then we starve."

The voice was flippant, but neither of them saw the humor. Owen shifted painfully, let his eyes roam the cabin. No windows. One door. Hell!

The nearest help was John Shaw at Cole's Grove. But anyone trying to sneak out the door might be gunned down. It was too big a chance to take if there was an alternative. . . .

His eyes lit on the far end of the long room where Robert had found the puncheon bench. His heart quickened. That was the west side, away from the stables, away from the fireplace heat, and if Mose Grimmel tracked like everyone else, it was also near the garden plot. If his own memory served him, there was a plum thicket there, too, that had been left as a windbreak.

"Root cellar!" he said.

Robert started. "What?"

"A root cellar. Bob, go see if you can find a hole in the floor down there. It'll be under something. And if we're lucky, it's the kind Mose could put his potatoes in from the outside and his wife could get them from the inside."

"Tophet," said Robert softly. "I never thought of that."

Victoria had sat down by Thalia on the floor by the fire, her knees drawn up, her head in her hands. Lulled by the warmth, she was drowsing; weariness had taken over.

Careful not to wake her, Robert thrust a short billet in the flame, got it blazing, bore it to the rear of the cabin. Owen could see him on his knees.

"Find anything?"

"Not yet. Wait. Yes, I have. Yes, sir!"

He was digging like a hound dog, pulling out dead fireweed and moldy straw. Owen could hear him panting. The billet burned away. Vaguely in the gloom his burly shape could be seen diminishing eerily as he thrust his feet into the hole he'd cleared and lowered his torso. Then things fell quiet because Robert was being quiet, and Owen could only wait, hoping.

The seconds ticked in his mind, dragging themselves like a rusty clock. If Robert could get away, make it to John's at Cole's Grove. . . .

Robert was back, smelling of mold and cold dirt, shaking soil and bits of straw from his coat.

"I'd make a damned good mole," he said, "if I do say so myself. But it's there, Owen. Sort of fallen in, and I had to burrow through a bit of snow—but not much. There's a copse of crabapple or something, kind of shelters that side."

He hunkered down by Owen. "Figurin' it's the door being watched," he went on, "I'll be clean out of sight and ought to get away slicker 'n mud. But you got to tell me where to go."

There was obviously no question in his mind what had to be done; all he wanted to know was how to do it.

Not for the first time, Owen felt both amazed and touched by the tough insouciance of the people he'd found in this new land. Nodding, he hitched his body into a curve, picked up a short stick of firewood. "Here," he said, drawing in the ancient dirt of the floor. "Remember, I said the wind always comes through the draw? Walk into it. Always walk into it. There's a wagon track of sorts at the bottom where Johnny Wood hauls timber down into the Grove. It crosses a creek. You follow that creek right into the settlement. Not the road; you'll lose it in the snow. The creek. The first bridge you bang your head on, you're in Cole's Grove."

"What'll I tell them?"

"What you can. John won't be surprised. He tried to warn me off at the Clarks'."

Robert grinned, a little wryly, stood up. "All right," he said. "The night ain't gettin' any younger." He took his rifle, checked its prime, refastened the front of his heavy greatcoat. Soberly Owen handed up the shapeless felt hat. He grimaced. He said between his teeth, "Goddammit all to hell!"

Robert shrugged. "T'ain't your fault," he said. He took the hand Owen held out to him. "Hold the fort. I'll be as quick as I can."

All Owen could make of his going were the few grunts as Robert eased himself down into the cold pit. Then there was silence—a thick, oppressive silence that he tried so hard to pierce with his ears that he felt they were strained away from his head.

Once he thought he heard the horses neigh as though they weren't too far-off and there was a varmint among them. Then the big fire log cracked, shooting blue flames up the chimney. One piece rolled down, scattering wild sparks, and smacked against the end of another.

Had there been another crack, from outside, echoing the firelog? Had it been just his imagination?

17

The tumbling fire log awakened Victoria. She said, "Oh!", jerked her head up, looked guilty. Owen was leaning back, his eyes closed, but she had a sense of his not sleeping but listening. For what? She glanced around. "Where's Robert?"

"He went on to Cole's Grove. He'll bring back a wagon."

"Is it far?"

"No. Not if it isn't snowing. Not if you know the way."

There were now no sounds at all from outside. The snow deadened everything, and it was too soft and wet to squeak. Owen opened his eyes and found Victoria looking at him.

"Is there a doctor?"

"Where?"

"Where Robert went."

"Of sorts."

Now she wished she hadn't mentioned doctors. He was looking directly at her—a long look she'd rather not meet. She turned away, picked up Robert's scarf, and dipped it in the melting snow around his ankle. She said, in a carefully matter-of-fact voice, "The swelling is going down," wrung out the scarf, and went over to Thalia, putting the cold, clammy scarf on the girl's hot forehead.

She could feel Owen's eyes on the back of her head. She could almost see him behind her, half reclining, one booted leg straight out like a tree trunk, the other cocked up in the portmanteau. His dirty shirt was open to his vest, letting the fine mat of chest hair glint red in the firelight. His stubble of beard glinted too, and she heard the rasp as he passed his hand over it, saying casually—too casually—"I need barbering."

"I need washing." It was just a comment, just conversation tossed over her shoulder as she picked up the scarf, found it hot, waved it in the air to cool it, and put it back again.

But he said, "All right. I'll shave. You wash."

His voice had a strange sound to it—a sound she couldn't identify.

Suddenly it struck her: For all practical purposes, they were alone. She and Owen. With full force his remark about the evening and her laces surged back. She tensed. He couldn't have been serious! Yet how well she knew Owen seldom said anything he didn't mean.

Wondering how best to distract him (but also terribly aware that the big man with the tawny hair couldn't be distracted at all if he didn't wish to be), she said, "I'm sure Paul would find us both a disgrace! If he'd walk in here right now, I'd just die!"

She was dipping the scarf back in the icy water. At the name *Paul*, she saw the yellow-and-purple foot jerk. It was such a sudden movement that, perforce, she looked at him, found him looking at her. His eyes were slitted, his face ashen.

Alarmed, she said, "Owen! What is it?"

He answered only, "Oh, my God," in an unbelieving voice, shaking his tawny head as though to clear cobwebs. "My God," he said again, and closed his eyes. "What a dunderhead I've been! What an ox!"

His brain felt as though it was reeling. Vaguely he heard her clear voice: "What are you talking about?"

He wanted to shout it at her: "You spoke the truth! If Paul Winterthur walked in here right now, you would die!"

But he couldn't say that—not even if it was the truth—which he knew, now, it was!

He had been blinded by the premise that Paul was miles away with a broken leg. Everything had hung on Paul's being miles away with a broken leg. Yet there was no proof of that other than Paul's own written word—which, Owen admitted ruefully, he'd been all too eager to accept because he'd wanted to see Victoria first.

Once he removed the false premise, then everything made a terrible sense. Who needed Victoria's money but not Victoria? Who knew being married by proxy made a husband an heir? Who shot only with a pistol, rode a dun horse, was hated by the dog Pedro, and carried the affectation of a golden corkscrew?

Who never meant for his bride to reach her destination?

Paul, Paul, all Paul!

Yet Owen had allowed Mersey to mislead him—poor, maligned Mersey, who'd probably glimpsed Paul in the Clark house and followed him to his own untimely death.

He was not misled now. It was Paul Winterthur out there in the dark and cold, and Owen could almost laugh because he knew how uncomfortable he must be, because he knew how Paul hated discomfort. This trip must have put him through the hoops!

And he could almost laugh because Owen Verinder was not afraid of Paul Winterthur!

Puzzled, not a little peeved, Victoria had shrugged and turned away. All right if he didn't want to answer; she didn't care!

She bent over Thalia again. The girl was in the deep sleep of high fever, breathing through parted, parched lips. Victoria bent to moisten them with the scarf and grimaced as her stays bit into her midriff.

Behind her Owen spoke. Inexplicably his voice sounded almost gay, as though a burden had fallen from him. "Vick," he said, "you silly sausage, will you take those damned things off or shall I?"

That was not good—not good at all. She needed no contact with Owen, particularly when he sounded like that—male and dominant and sure of himself! She put the scarf on Thalia's forehead again, brushing back the dank, black hair. She didn't look around. Coolly she answered in her primmest voice, "Don't be ridiculous. But I do wish I could have a wash."

Behind her he was hoisting himself to one leg, grunting. His giant shadow sprawled across her, and her hands froze on Thalia's head. Her breath came in short spurts because her heart was whipping. But Owen was only putting another log on the fire. He shoved the portmanteau closer with its load of half melted snow.

"Maybe we can get us some wash water."

She waited for him to sit again, but he didn't. He stood, a monolith on one leg, staring down into the flames as they crackled upward. Water dripped from his purple, naked foot, but he seemed oblivious. The big hand that braced him against the rough stone of the fireplace was working its brown fingers in a sort of rhythm as though he were studying, sorting, and settling something in his mind.

Suddenly he wheeled. She stiffened. But he went past her, limped into the long dark shadows. A thick plank, hand-hewn, rested against the wall by the door. He picked it up, dropped it into the two slots, barring the entrance, wiggled it thoughtfully, chose a short log from the pile and wedged that beneath the bar.

Curiosity compelled her to ask: "Whyever did you do that? What about Robert?"

He answered casually, "Robert won't be back until tomorrow. And the wind's picking up. If this door blew open, love, you'd awaken under two feet of snow."

It didn't totally satisfy her, but she let it go. He limped back, bent over her. She felt his warm breath on her cheek, but he was only reaching out, taking the scarf.

"Here," he said. He scooped a large handful of snow, rolled it into the scarf, replaced it. "Now, come away from her. I don't trust Thalia. And surely you're not forgetting what she tried to do to you."

Victoria had known what she could do with the scarf; it had seemed more important to have something to occupy her hands. She stood up, replied in a voice as stiff as her body, "Of course I haven't. But I can't just let her lie there like a hurt kitten!"

He straightened himself with a grunt, his hand on her shoulder for support. She was very aware of each finger as it clasped her, but he didn't seem to be. He was staring downward, and his face seemed sorrowful. "Yes," he said gently. "That's exactly what she is, Vick. A spoiled, cosseted, undisciplined kitten—who has gotten hurt."

There was nothing in his voice but regret. No affection, no caring—not even a sound of gratitude. What sort of man had this wild country turned Owen Verinder into?

Or had he always been like that—always been a selfish, taking, greedy male?

"Sit down, Owen," she said, making her own voice calm, detached, "You'll have that ankle swelling up again. Now sit down!"

She only wanted loose, wanted that possessive hand off her shoulder!

He grinned at her, the first time she'd seen him grin in three days. "Bossy little wench, aren't you?" he said.

But he sat with a lurch, easing the ankle up onto one of the fire logs. "All right, Lady Victoria," he said. "I'm down. Now you'll have to go find my shaving gear in my saddlebag."

"Well, I'll *do* that," she said—then stopped, realizing her overhearty affirmative might raise the question of what she *wouldn't* do. He didn't seem to notice. As she went swiftly into the shadows toward his saddle, he called a little plaintively, "And have you a looking glass?"

The knobby little bundle tied in a dubious square of towel was not the elegant gentleman's toilet set she'd been accustomed to, but Owen seemed perfectly content. He set out his worn tools, propped the tiny mirror against the fireplace stone, scooped cold water into his tin cup, and began to rasp away. A small bit of slimy soft soap produced a yellow lather. He wiped it in whiskered globs on the side of a log as he worked.

He seemed totally absorbed.

Quietly Victoria moved back into the shadows. She unbuttoned her jacket, dropped it down, put one arm into the sleeve of her long dressing robe as she worked off the waist sleeve from the other, then reversed the process, dropping the dingy, crumpled waist. Clutching the robe around her, she sent a surreptitious glance at Owen.

His head was up; he was working on his massive chin.

Reassured, she reached back behind her for her stays.

She met total defeat. Too many days had passed, too many twisting, bending days. The laces had turned to small, hard knots. She was trapped inside.

And now that relief had seemed so near she found her numb tolerance gone. She wanted them off. Off! She wanted to breathe again, to bend without hurting!

Her arms ached with their fumbling struggle and despite herself a small, frustrated gasp escaped her.

Owen laid down his razor. Wiping his hands, he turned, said with infinite patience, "Silly little ass. Come here."

He said again, firmly, "Vick, come here."

Common sense told her it was better to obey as though accepting an ordinary favor than play the twittering virgin.

Meekly she came, stood before him presenting her back, dropping the robe from her shoulders to her waist. After all, she told herself sternly, you still have on all your petticoats and the chemise!

He hoisted himself erect, bracing his shoulder against the wall, reached out, then stopped. His hands were shaking. She was so white, so dainty. So vulnerable. Tousled as it was, the pale hair shone silky in the firelight, trailing over her shoulder and the grime had not reached the smooth mold of her back.

He forced himself to say, "You have a very dirty neck," and reached down his thigh for his sheath knife.

She protested, "What are you doing?" but he went on, cutting the knots ruthlessly.

She said in dismay, "I'll never get it on again!" and he replied cheerfully, "You're damned right!"

"Owen, stop it!"

But suddenly the very bottom knot was severed and the abrupt relief was so profound that she could only sigh as the instrument of torture fell away from her abused body. The sigh was followed by a scream as Owen calmly reached around and with one swift, deft motion consigned the garment, stays, laces and all, to the gulping flames.

"Owen!" But it was too late. Furious, indignant, she turned on him, blue eyes blazing in her streaked face. Her soft breasts, untrammeled now, surged with the motion, swelling voluptuously beneath the thin chemise. But he didn't notice. His incredulous eyes were glued to her waist line. Red-streaked, creased, bruised though it was, there was a hollow V between her ribs, and her belly was concave.

Frontier life might not have polished Owen Verinder's manners, but it had taught him a few basic things about time and babies.

He said in a voice so staggered, it was barely audible, "You are not pregnant!" It was like a dash of cold water—sudden and shocking.

She whipped away from him, struggling with both arms to pull the robe back up on her shoulders. In an awful voice he said, "Victoria!"

Frantically she cried, "I never said I was! I've never had control over what you *thought*! I never meant to—Owen let me go!"

He had lurched forward, turned her, holding her almost at arm's length but with her own two arms trapped in the robe sleeves. He was gazing at her with such a look in his eyes that she couldn't bear it. She closed her own. She said despairingly, "Owen, please let me go."

He bent his head. His mouth slid down her cheek, her warm throat, kissed the soft fluttering pulse there, surged on. His arms shifted, raising her. Then he answered her, his deep voice a whisper, muffled in the sweet cleft of her breasts. "Do you mean it, Vick? Say it now, or not at all!"

The tigers are loosed, Victoria thought, *the tigers are loosed, and it's too late.* "No," she whispered. "No, no. . . ." The robe fell with a gentle sigh to the floor as her own arms came free and she lifted them—not to push him away—but to free her soft breasts from the chemise, to hold them up to his searching kisses, to cradle his rough, tawny head while her whole body dissolved against his. He said into that scented, doubly curved valley, "Vick, you're mine, you've always been mine, let any other man lay a hand on you and I'll kill him, I swear it. . . ." And all she could answer over and over again was his name. But it was enough. She clung blindly, hardly knowing when her petticoats slipped down to a drift of tattered ruffles at her feet, knowing full well that the sudden press of his hard, naked thighs against her woman's softness was the supreme demand of her life, a demand she could answer, that she would answer, and must, moving against him in a response that brought one brief gasp of pain, then a storm of paradise.

Owen Verinder was much too accomplished a lover, and despite his own compelling, headlong urgency, he was deft, not savage. He leaned against the log wall, oblivious of the rough bark boring holes in his shoulder, holding his love, unwilling to let her go. Their breathing slowed together. Holding his tender mouth against her cheek, he said softly, "I won't say I'm sorry! God, I'm not sorry. But I promise you, heart's dearest, soon there will be proper sheets and a proper bed and a husband without a game leg."

He was not even really aware of what he was saying. She was clasped in his arms, warm and pliant. She had satisfied some deep, male necessity inside him beyond the act of love, some part that had to know she was his without force or compulsion. He had taken, but he had given too, given a part of him he'd always held back because it was Victoria's. Now Victoria had it. "My love," he said against her hair, "my darling, my wife. . . ."

She stiffened.

She said, "Oh, dear God!" and tried to pull away. "What have I done?"

His deep voice was calm. "You have loved me, heart's dearest, as I have loved you."

"I'm not your wife! I'm Paul's wife!"

She tore herself away, and suddenly understanding, he let her go. She scooped her robe up around her, stared at him with eyes he could hardly bear because they were terrified.

"I've cheated him," she whispered. "I've cheated him, and I've had so little to bring to him anyway! What am I to do, what am I to do?"

She was almost in a frenzy, shaking and twisting her hands. Hurting because she was hurting, he said gently, "Vick, love, come here." He was reaching with two fingers inside his vest.

"Owen, I can't. Don't ask me. . . . Please, Owen. . . ."

He had drawn out a folded, creased square of paper.

Gently he held it to her.

"Do you know what this is?"

She squinted.

"No."

"Then come here and see. No—first get your spectacles. Then come, my darling bat. This time I want you to see."

"See what?"

"What you must! Your spectacles, love."

Reluctantly she turned, pulling on the robe, winding the cord about her waist. He lived a long, long moment as she pawed through her bundle. He knew she was delaying, trying to calm herself. But at last she straightened, and came slowly toward him, the awkward lenses perched on her Landam nose.

Purposely not touching her, he merely handed over the paper, pointing with one finger. "What does this say? Read it to me."

Unsure, trembling, she read, " 'Joined this day, by writ of Holy Matrimony, Victoria Landam and—' " She stopped. She looked up at him, not believing. She faltered, " '—and Owen Verinder'!"

He nodded.

"But the proxy ceremony—"

"There was no proxy, love. All the way downtrail I knew there wouldn't be. I knew I wouldn't let you go again. That's my mother's wedding ring on your finger, Vick—and you're my wife."

"I'm not married to Paul!"

"Nor will you ever be as long as there's breath in my body. You're mine."

"But you were taking me to Paul!"

"I knew you would go. And anything I tried to say seemed to work aganst me." He reached out with his good hand, touched the pale curve of her cheek.

She didn't move away, but neither did she turn her face into the hand. Her eyes were still unsure. She said shakily, "What if you'd been wrong? What if I really loved Paul?"

Gravely he replied, "Look in my eyes, Vick, and tell me that you do."

She didn't drop her gaze, but now it mirrored helplessness. She knew so well he'd kept his word all along about staying away from her. But it had not kept him from using every circumstance—weariness, fear, even poor Thalia—that might possibly send her running to him. And she had, she had; she'd responded every time. In his mind he'd really taken no chance at all.

Resentfully, she said, "You've not been fair, Owen."

"I never meant to be fair." Then he added with as much of an apology as she'd ever get, "But I'll make it up to you." He held out his arms hungrily, wanting her. With almost a sob she went into them, knowing she couldn't resist him. Not any more, not now, she told herself, closing her mind to the future. He was whispering against her lifted throat, "And you must learn, O wife, that this sort of action will get you in trouble with me whether there's a proper bed or not. . . ."

He was so heedlessly male, living for the moment, and she allowed herself to be swept along with him, whispering back, "I don't care about the bed."

"But a proper bed is nice," he said, some time later, putting his aching ankle back up on the fire log, but keeping her in the bend of his arm as they lay together on the blanket. "It's still a promise. I'll show you how nice as soon as I can. Ross's has beds." He closed her eyes with his mouth, saying, "Sleep if you can, heart's dearest."

He knew Paul would not force the door. A frontal attack would place his own elegant person in too much jeopardy. And whatever Paul did, even murder, must be done grandly, with style. It was certain: Winterthur would bide his time in chill discomfort until morning. While inside the cabin—ah, inside, Owen thought, smiling to himself, his despised cousin was clasped in his bride's warm arms, having only to turn his head to taste the sweet honey of her breasts.

Desire surged in him again. It had never been like this before, not with any other woman. *I would,* he realized with a thundering heart, *risk the fires of hell to make love to Vick even one more time!* He caught her closer, saw her half open her eyes, and let himself drown in the look that was there. Her hand lay on his lean, powerful thigh. He guided her hand gently, felt the fingers turn from shyness to pleasure, and he washed out onto the spun-gold firmament of her satin response.

Now it was a long time before he let her slide to the blanket beside him. Her misty eyes followed as he lifted his ankle to the fire log once more, grimacing. She asked swiftly, "Owen, am I hurting you?"

He laughed. He couldn't help laughing. "Heart's dearest," he said, "Every man should have such pain! Good God, the way I feel, I'll survive to be another Methuselah!"

There was a small silence. Then she whispered timidly, "Ought I be ashamed? I don't feel ashamed. It's just—what you make me want to do. . . ."

"Then heaven keep me from changing my ways," he murmured softly. He kissed her softly. "My wife," he said, and the depth of his feelings made him incautious. He added, "Poor old Winterthur." And he felt Victoria stiffen. Just a little.

She said, "Oh!" in a stifled, small voice. Suddenly she was back in the present; suddenly she was flooded with a terrible wash of remorse. Paul!

The square hardness of Owen's chin was nuzzling the top of her head. "Poor Paul," he said. "Cuckolded out of his bride and her money in one swoop."

He was unfortunate in his choice of words, and doubly unfortunate in allowing the fatuous sound to enter his voice. He was so completely satisfied, he was forgetting how very little about Paul Winterthur's mindless arrogance Victoria really knew.

The word *cuckolded* jarred her; *money* drove a shaft of ice straight into her heart.

In a voice that sounded faraway, she said, "Oh, dear God."

Totally misunderstanding the tone of her words, ignoring all the danger signals, Owen went on calmly, "Don't feel sorry for him, Vick. He deserves no sympathy. God knows, I tried to tell you in England."

"What did you try to tell me, Owen?"

"What he was like! That he'd been the lover of every high-priced courtesan on the Continent, that a little baa-lamb like you, sweet and dear as you are, my darling, would never have even caught his depraved eye, had you not had money! A great deal of money—which, God knows, he needs now more than ever before!"

She was frozen—almost enough to die, almost enough that her stiff lips did not want to work. She made them work. She whispered desperately, "Paul loved me. He wanted me to come here because he loved me, he needed me!"

It wasn't that she forgot how she'd been using Paul. It was that the idea of his using *her* toppled her entire card house of self-esteem, took her last shred of personal worth!

All the things she had suffered to get over here to Paul were for naught! All the promises she'd made to herself about being a good, dutiful wife, all the sacrifices, the humiliations—they were as nothing! They hadn't mattered; they had never mattered. She may as well have not made them!

And while her bruised ego was still reeling from that stark truth, Owen said with brutal sincerity, "Paul Winterthur loves your money, Vick. He needs your money—more desperately than I can say. And he will go to any length to get it."

What he meant to say, though reluctantly, was that Paul Winterthur was outside right then—ready to go to any length. But his overabundance of knowledge had betrayed him into sheer obtuseness. And as complete as his victory had been, so was it now reversed into loss.

He had no idea where his words had winged in her distressed and humiliated mind—until in a voice of deadly evenness she asked "And who else do I know who has squandered his patrimony, gambled away his birthright, has been reduced to the level of a cowherd and badly needs a rich wife?"

He couldn't believe his ears. Aghast, he said, "I suppose you mean me. But Vick, you don't understand—"

"But I do understand! I do! I do!"

He stopped because she'd torn herself from his arms, scrambled to her feet, and retreated, stumbling, to the middle of the cold floor. Her voice was choked.

She cried out, "Oh! Oh, what a besotted fool I have been! God, forgive me! Paul, forgive me! And that poor child, there—" her finger shot like an arrow toward Thalia, motionless on her pallet "—that child who loves you! Dupes, all of us!"

"Vick, for God's sake—"

"How dare you! What sort of unfeeling animal are you, Owen Verinder? Making love to me while she lies there helpless! Saying those things about Paul—a man whom you have indeed cuckolded—and betrayed, tricking his betrothed with the lowest of tricks, and for what? For what? Money! Money! Oh!" She ended in a sort of helpless, impotent agony: "Oh! Have I a revelation for you!"

Shocked, staggered beyond measure, Owen braced his arms, bunching his shoulders to raise himself up. Frantically she glanced around, grabbed his rifle, and leveled it at him. The tears ran down her face, making new runnels in the dirt.

"Don't move," she whispered. "Please don't move, Owen. Or I'll have to shoot you."

18

He had to be careful. He knew he had to be careful. She could really hurt him, or worse, herself. Either way they'd both be in deep trouble—far deeper than she realized.

Silently he cursed himself for being so naive. So stupid. A few careless words and he'd lost all he had gained. Her money meant little to him; indeed, he'd agonized that she might think it did. Now look what his mouth had done. Would she ever believe him again?

He said steadily, "I love you, Vick. That's the beginning. And the end of it. For me. Whatever happens—I love you."

"And I'm your wife."

She said it with a sort of horror. Nothing had ever hurt him more.

He answered soberly, "Yes. You are."

"Not Paul's. Yours. Your rich wife."

Suddenly she began to laugh, helplessly, thinly, the tears still streaking her cheeks. The barrel of the gun lowered, but still he dared not move.

"Oh, God!" she gasped. "What a joke! What a joke!"

He pulled his good leg under him and the barrel came up.

"Stop!"

He stopped. Almost mildly he admonished, "Will *you* stop waving that thing around!"

"I know how to shoot it!"

"I know you know! That's what's worrying me. Victoria, for God's sake, be sensible!"

"I am being sensible. I am going to keep you away from me until tomorrow, when Robert comes back. Then I shall find Paul and throw myself on his mercy."

She meant it. She meant everything she said.

He swallowed his fear, his anger, but in the flickering firelight his ruddy face looked white. He said, "Your word is sufficient to keep me away from you, Vick. It always has been. It is now. Put the rifle down."

She looked at him a long moment, then very slowly lowered the barrel, turned, leaned the rifle back against the wall. He should have felt triumphant, but he didn't. Her shoulders slumped, her face wore a look of total defeat.

One step at a time. That's all he could safely take.

She said to him in a display of misery he could not touch, "What have I done? What have I done? He'll turn me away."

The *he* was obvious. Grimly he said, "He'll not."

"He will. Now he will. Oh, you don't know, you can't know the trouble I'm in!'' Her eyes were shut, she was holding herself with both her own arms, rocking. ''And I cannot go back, I can never go back. . . .''

''Vick—'' Then he stopped.

There was really nothing to say.

In Victoria's eyes he had not only violated another man's honor, he had also done it for gain.

And suddenly it angered him, angered him beyond expression that she should think so, that she didn't know him, didn't trust him any better than that! All the things that he might say to defend himself had been rising like weeds—eager, thrusting.

But he wouldn't say them. Stubbornly, he thought, *The hell with it!* He had his pride too. When this was over, let her beg!

He had said, ''Vick—'' and stopped. Now he said it again, but this time his voice sounded harsh, cold.

''As you will,'' he said.

It surprised her. She lifted her head, looked at him uncertainly, and he took a certain wicked pleasure in returning pain for pain.

''It bids to be a long night,'' he went on. ''And since you obviously wish to avoid further contact with me, I suggest you make some sort of bed and lie on it. Tomorrow may be a very difficult day.''

She turned like a chastened child, went slowly toward her trunk. With great deliberateness he folded his capote, thrust it beneath his head, crossed his arms on his vest, and shut his eyes.

But through slits he watched her.

She came from the shadows with a sponge bag. A little ostentatiously she ignored his recumbent form, kneeling by the barely warmed water in the portmanteau, washing her face and arms with a sliver of soap that put a sweet smell of lavender in the air. Then she sat on the puncheon bench, took off one boot and stocking, then the other. The second one gave her trouble; she grimaced and he saw dried blood, realized that at some time she'd hurt herself and said nothing. Carefully she bathed her white feet, put on clean stockings, pointing her toes, drawing them up with the classic grace of women donning hose all over the world.

Thalia moaned. Victoria went to her quickly, stooped, refreshed the cold scarf, and put it back. Resuming her seat before the fire, she cinched the robe tighter about her waist, took a brush from the bag, and began to wrestle with the vexatious mats in her hair.

This took a long time. Despite himself, the warmth and the stillness extracted their toll. Owen dozed off. When he aroused again, he found she'd washed the long pale mane and was now fluffing and combing it dry before the fire.

The sight of a pretty woman quietly brushing her hair can be one of the most sensuous in the world. There is the fluid sweep down the length of the tress; the movement of hip and breast; the sleeve falling back from the white, round arm. The combed locks lie shining down her back, or nestle in soft curls against her throat. Even her pushing her own fingers through the silkiness is exciting.

Owen felt desire grow in him, long-leashed desire that had had a taste of paradise just a short time ago. His breath quickened; his muscles tensed.

Then she gave herself away—just one, swift, secret glance sidewise, but it told him: she knew she was being watched. Each provocative movement of her body was deliberate. She meant for him to be aroused, she meant for him to come up off his duff like a stud horse and force himself on her! And why? He knew why. To help her forget that first time, when there'd been no coercion! To salve her wounded virtue!

To be able to tell Winterthur she was raped!

Owen's fingers curved, bit into the palms of his hands. *No,* he told his aching body, his drumming brain. *No!* He stayed where he was. He didn't move. He didn't dare. But he opened his eyes and he looked at her steadily.

The next time she glanced, there were his eyes.

The brush faltered. She bit her lower lip, almost convulsively, color flooded her face, her throat. With one movement she arose, gathering up brush and sponge bag, walked away slowly with a sort of defiant dignity. But in the shadows by her trunk he could see her shoulders shake, knew she was crying.

He didn't say a word, not even when she came quietly back, arranged a blanket before the fire, and lay down on it, turning away from him.

Owen had no particular fears about going to sleep. Very probably Paul Winterthur meant to create the illusion of robbery. When their dead bodies were found, stiff and frozen in the snow, they would be stripped of valuables—especially those of the late "poor Lady Winterthur." To achieve this effect safely, however, he must pick them off one by one—preferably the men first, as the greatest danger to him, and then the women. Even Thalia would die. Owen had no doubt, now, that Paul had gone too far to permit any sort of witness.

Eventually they had to emerge from the cabin; Winterthur had only to wait. What he might not know was that Owen had put a name and a face on the enemy—and that the precious element of surprise was gone. The "camp" was alarmed.

Owen hugged this knowledge to himself as he twisted and folded his long frame fruitlessly, trying to find ease on the hard floor, some pose of comfort for the dull pain in his ankle. Knowledge was a poor substitute for Vick's pliant warmth; his mind cried out in protest against the injustice of her charges. But his pride would not let him relent his attitude one whit. At last, worn and sapped, needing the rest, he slept.

Not far behind came Victoria. Drowsiness won, unasked. She didn't want sleep; she fought it. But her exhausted system knew far better than she what was needed, and she slept also.

For three hours there was no sound in the half dark cabin but the sharp pop of the wall logs as the cold clutched them. Tiny feet skittered in quick dashes across the pounded dirt toward the tallowy scent of drying lather. One small shadow veered away, its whiskers twitching excitedly at a new smell. It sat impudently in the very shade of Owen's enormous cowhide boot and dined on a crumb of plum pudding.

Suddenly the farthermost lump stirred. Six shadows zipped for safety, and crouched in the dark, small hearts pumping. A hand wavered out, found a smelly scarf, dried and noxious, on a forehead hot again with another surge of fever. The hand flung the scarf into the fire. Dark eyes opened, looked around with no recognition, no reason, only a primitive, insatiable urge to get outside, to find the blessed cool of the snow.

Cautiously, weakly, Thalia struggled to her feet while twelve beady brown eyes watched. Dropping the enfolding blanket in a huddle, she staggered toward the door. Victoria's cape tripped her feet, but she'd worn it so long, it seemed a part of her. Her fingers were plucking at the throat of her waist, longing for the feel of cold air on the hot, dry skin of her breast.

The door wouldn't open. Why wouldn't it open? Squinting, she saw the bar, then the brace.

It was almost too much for her. But her tugging made her fall sideways, and the angle of her sprawl tore the dirt around the brace's foot. It fell beneath her.

She lay there a moment on the cold earth, blinded by the cape hood, panting. Then she crawled to her feet again, lifted the bar with both arms, dropped it on the dirt, tugged at the sagging door. With a scrunch and a sift of snow it opened to the first gray streaks of early day.

She was free!

Whether it was the *thunk* of the dropping bar, the rasp of the door, or the sudden draft of bitter cold, both Owen and Victoria wakened. Owen came to full consciousness in a snap, rolling, his hand on his rifle, his good leg kicking free of the blanket. Victoria roused more slowly, her eyes sleep-fogged, rising on one shaky elbow. But the two of them saw an open door through which came a dingy bar of light, the tree-filtered essence of the dawn's chill pearl.

Only Owen noticed that Thalia was gone.

Fear shot through his frame. He scrambled to his feet, pain sending bolts of fire up the calf of his leg, made a limping leap toward the open threshold, saying over his shoulder hoarsely, "Vick, stay there, stay down, mind me!"

He hardly made the doorway, hardly had time to focus on the hooded plaid cape wavering across the snow. From the fringe of trees beyond the ruined well sweep came the sharp crack of a gun. On the thin air the sound echoed like a fusillade, sending frightened birds squawking upward to wheel indignantly in the sky. Thalia's arms flew upward too. Then she pitched forward without a sound upon her face.

And Owen—on the clear, cold winter air—Owen heard the sound of laughter.

Paul thought it was Victoria in the plaid cape! But Owen knew better. Owen knew the game was scarcely played out—it had just begun.

Thalia moved. She made a sound like a sigh.

Frantically Owen glanced around. The empty wine bottle lay by his bare foot. He picked it up, threw it as high, hard, and fast as he could, across the clearing into the trees. It struck the trunk of an oak with a loud *thunk*. Almost on its heels came the sharp whine of a bullet.

His ploy had worked. Paul had fired his second pistol. He had about thirty seconds to get Thalia back into the cabin before he could reload. Two giant limps scattered the frozen crust of snow as he bolted for her, bending low past the well sweep, trying to stay beneath the cover of the plum thicket.

Thalia hadn't moved again. As he scooped her up, bright red blood gushed, steaming, into the snow. She was dead; he knew it instantly. He turned and ran for the doorway—and once again Victoria disobeyed him.

She appeared there, pale hair streaming, the white V where her breast plunged into the rose-colored robe like a magnet, a ready-made bull's eye. In agony, lunging toward her like a wounded bear, he cried, "Get down! Get down!"

A third shot rang out. It slammed into him like a battering ram. He thought, *"Oh, God!"* and made one supreme effort, gained the doorway gasping, "Bar it!"

He pitched to his knees, dropping Thalia to the dirt. His bared chest and leather vest were bloodied where he'd carried her. He could feel his own hot blood dripping down his back. He thought dimly, *I must stay with it, I must!*

And could not.

Behind him a terrified Victoria was struggling with the heavy bar. Before she could seat it, the door burst inward, sending her reeling like a ninepin against the opposite wall.

Again the early morning light streamed inside.

Silhouetted against it, legs braced apart, silver head gleaming, stood Paul Winterthur.

A different Paul—elegant coat torn and soiled, elegantly heeled boots scuffed, lean cheeks unshaven.

But Victoria didn't see that. She didn't see one hand loosely holding a smoking pistol, the other cocking its venal mate. She saw only a miracle: Paul!

Casting herself into his arms, against his rumpled stock, clinging, she cried out his name, "Paul! Paul!" She sobbed, "Help us! Help us! He's hurt!"

Paul put around her tightly the arm with the discharged gun. The other did not waver from the enormous bulk of Owen Verinder, lying still in the dirt. In a clear, cool voice, a voice she remembered well, he replied, "Oh, indeed."

She tried to pull away, found she could not.

Uncomprehendingly she reached up, caught at the aesthetic lines of his face, attempting to turn it to her. She was gabbling frantically, "Listen! Listen to me! He's dying—Owen's dying!"

"My dear Victoria," he said, and reaching out, poked Owen in the back with the tip of a scuffed boot. "Since the fat is now in the fire, as they say, I find that fact devoutly to be wished."

Stunned, unbelieving, her voice froze. She stared.

"You have both given me," he went on coldly, "an inordinate amount of trouble."

"What do you mean?"

Now he turned, now he looked at her, and she shrank from what she saw.

He said, "It was an excellent plan—well conceived and well executed—until I ran afoul of the bunglers! That Mercedes—the temerity of him, challenging my right to do what I liked! And Thalia—disobeying me! I can't have disobedience, you know—although, considering all of you I think I shall regret Thalia the most."

But suddenly she wasn't listening, she was looking. With a gasp she said, "You have no broken leg!"

"Of course not. But only you and I know that now. The others are dead. Or will be shortly. Stand still, my dearest," he said sharply as he felt her stiffen. "Be the passive, pretty little play-toy I always thought you to be. We're neither quite up to the scratch sartorially, this morning, but I shall pretend if you will."

Self-preservation made her stand very still, but anguish turned her head downward toward Owen. Her voice shaking, she asked, "What are you going to do?"

"Get my breath back. And you're as good a hostage as any in case that bourgeois hulk on the floor decides to stir."

"Paul—I don't understand any of this. What do you want?"

"You shan't like it if I tell you, my dear. Let's have it be a surprise."

"You wanted me to come! You sent for me!"

"Oh, I did. Indeed I did."

There was a cold satin sound to his voice. She met his eyes—and suddenly she knew, without question: Owen had been right. She said, "Oh, dear God. How blind I've been."

The aristocratic brows arched. "It's one of your virtues I valued," he said. "Would that Thalia had possessed more of it. She loved me a bit more than was convenient; it made her overanxious."

In shock Victoria said, "She loved you—"

"Obsessively, I fear. Regardless of how I told her what you really were to me—a prim, unawakened little prude, I said, but she was mad with jealousy. With that wire on the stairs she almost ruined my entire plan. I had to be married to you, you see—if only by proxy. But looking at you now, dear Victoria—" and his arm shifted higher, his hand forced her chin up, pressing her cheek into the cold pistol butt "—I wonder. Are you still unawakened?"

She tried to make her voice cold: "Let me go."

"Impossible. I've few choices left; that's not one of them."

The corners of his thin mouth upturned suddenly. The other hand with its deadly burden raised, passed across the swell of her breasts, moved downward. She felt the stiff prod of the barrel between her thighs.

His eyes had not left hers. Thoughtfully he mused, "Four years is a long time. A long time, my betrothed. Perhaps now there are possibilities to be explored before we part. Oh, definitely before we part. Necrophilia is not one of my passions."

Horror swept her, surpassing fear, and more than horror: revulsion.

"My God," she whispered. "This is what I have struggled and fought to come to? Oh, what a joke. What an awful, awful mummery!"

The pistol came up, went into the V of her robe, pressed against her stomach while the free fingers cupped a breast, stroked softly. His thin mouth opened, showing wet teeth; his breath had quickened.

"Why," he asked, "should you say that?"

But he wasn't really listening, didn't really care. Thalia was dead, Owen dying on the floor, and she was going to die too, after he'd satisfied himself in her. His hard knee was already forcing itself between her legs, his head was coming down, his slitted eyes on her mouth.

She had to shock him. She blurted, "There isn't any money!"

He stopped dead still, like a statue. Only his eyes were alive and sparkling, considering her. He said, gently, "Oh, my dear. That won't work. It won't keep you alive. I'm the one who must live, Victoria. I'm going to be a king! And queens," he added softly, "are cheaply had."

His hard, cruel fingers squeezed her jaws, forcing open her mouth. His head came closer, his tongue like a red, licentious prod. She screamed, twisting, writhing like a trapped animal, forcing him to give up the lure of her inviting breasts to hold her rigidly in place, to keep her from slipping away. Panting and cursing, he struggled with her, forgetting Owen Verinder on the floor—until one large hand encircled his entire knee, and with all the strength he had left, Owen yanked, bringing Winterthur crashing down on top of him, Victoria sprawling free, and both pistols spinning into the dirt of the cold floor.

She scrambled up wildly, having only time to reach for one and level it. Owen's left arm was useless; he couldn't hold his cousin. Paul wrenched away, kicked Owen viciously, regained his feet with the other pistol in his grasp, looked at Victoria and laughed.

Then she knew: she had the empty gun.

She screamed once more and threw it at him.

He dodged easily, laughing at her stark terror. His thin mouth curled in amusement. He leveled his pistol, holding it steadily in both hands.

It was almost the last thing he ever did.

19

The dog, Pedro, had waited a long time for revenge. His shoulder was painful and barely healed from the cutting lash of Paul's crop at the ferry station. His pads were worn and sore, for he'd traveled many weary miles in silent, unremitting pursuit. Few rabbits could not elude a dog in deep snow, and his belly was empty too; it had complained as he'd crawled on it cautiously closer and closer to the open cabin door.

His enemy had known he was behind him. All the time he'd known. There had been curses and stones and shots. Pedro had grown adept at dodging, at disappearing like a gray wraith. Robert had never seen him crouched by Shonnewwek. Mercedes, his body already cooling, hadn't felt the sad lick of a friend. Winterthur had not been allowed to catch more than a glimpse, yet he'd never forgotten there was vengeance on his trail.

Until now! Now, in the open doorway, he'd dropped his guard.

Ninety pounds of hurtling hate, Pedro launched himself.

Victoria caught only sound; her eyes were shut with terror.

Paul Winterthur sensed motion. He whirled, and had one horrifying vision of airborne fury, of bleeding paws and bared teeth, before he crashed to the floor. Too late he tried to shield himself from the slashing fangs that tore and riddled his soiled shirt before sinking into his throat.

The pistol dropped unheeded; the impact discharged it into the wall. Desperately Paul rolled away, tearing the ravening beast from him, throwing the clawing bundle of manic fury with one superhuman effort against the stones of the fireplace.

The dog dropped, kicked, was still. Paul turned to Victoria, bedabbled hands succoring the red tears in his throat. His eyes were wide, uncertain, like a child's. He formed *Victoria* with drained lips, a horrid, grotesque mockery of speech. Then the blood gushed in a fountain from his mouth and neck and he fell into the reeking pool.

Dead. Victoria knew he was dead. Thalia was dead. Owen was dead—Owen!

She scrambled across the floor, threw herself down, gathering his limp bulk against her breast, cradling his tawny head, her cheek against the enormous purple bruise where Paul's boot had struck him. She was like that still, moaning and rocking, when Shonnewwek stalked in the door.

He stopped, grunted in surprise. His black eyes flicked the room, the people, assessing the carnage, the possibilities for Shonnewwek. Then, behind him, another voice said a rude pungency and stocky, swarthy John Shaw swung down from his horse.

He added, "Looks like we're a little late."

Following him, a huge French-Canadian slid from his small, brown mule, half a dozen other horsemen dismounting also, their booted feet packing the snow, their horses snorting, tossing their heads, their bridles jingling.

The black-bearded Canuck murmured something in liquid patois, following Shaw across the threshold.

Shaw replied, "God, I can't tell who's alive except the lady. Not Winterthur; I'll swear to that."

He knelt beside Victoria, gently touching her shoulder, saying urgently, "Ma'am . . . ma'am. . . ."

She paused her rocking, looked at him with blank blue eyes. "He's dead," she said simply. "Go away."

"He's not," said Shaw. He repeated louder, to penetrate. "I said he's not! Owen Verinder is too damned big for Winterthur to kill! Move aside, ma'am, I'll have a look. Madam! I tell you—he's breathing! He's alive!"

She stared, first at him, then at the silent face in her arms. "Oh!" she said, and again, "Oh!" as though suddenly sliding back into reality. "Oh, help me! Please, help me!"

She suffered Owen's being drawn from her lap, the blood-soaked shirt being torn rudely from his back and arm, but she would not move, she would not go away. Brisk words brought another man to Shaw's side, kneeling, another man who had just drawn a blanket decently up over Thalia Greenwood's waxen face. The large French Canadian had found Pedro and was carrying the limp form out into the yard.

John Shaw glanced up, asked, "Is he dead?"

The Canuck shrugged.

John said, "Save him if you can. He's collected his dues; he'll be a good dog now."

Two other men silently scooped Paul Winterthur into a second blanket and carried him out. Another kicked dirt with his heavy shoepac until the large pool of viscous blood was blotted. There was a certain efficiency to it all, as though they'd done these things before.

Owen Verinder suddenly reentered the world with an irritated "Ow!" as his wound was probed.

Shaw grinned. "What did I tell you, ma'am," he said. "He's too big to die. But with that hole in him he's going to be meaner than a rattlesnake for a few days. For God's sake, Verinder," he went on, suddenly shifting his direction. "You knew he was out there! How'd you let him get the jump?"

Owen ignored that for more pertinent things. In weak amazement he rejoined, "How the hell did you get here, John?"

"Shonnewwek. He drifted into Cole's Grove last night on the back of one of Will Clark's horses. Since one of my lads recognized it he obviously had lost a trade, so he mentioned it might be useful if we came over and looked in on you."

Owen turned his head gingerly and looked at the Sauk. He had unerringly searched out the only edible in the place, and was standing before the dying fire munching plum pudding with every indication of pleasure. Hearing his name, he said, "Good," and rubbed his belly, looking pointedly at Victoria.

But Victoria was a heap on the floor, hands tightly clasped, looking at no one. Her world had fallen in; it lay in pieces around her. Limp, bewildered, her mind could only engender disjointed thoughts: Those were frightening. Above all things she wanted to crawl away and hide.

Owen grunted in pain as they bandaged him, nodded his head at the Sauk. "Did he know about Winterthur?"

"Spice Bush? It's doubtful; he just plays the wind."

Then Owen remembered Robert. In vast relief, he said, "Bob got through, then."

John shook his head. "Not exactly," he replied.

Owen froze. "What do you mean—not exactly?"

"Winterthur saw his tracks, trailed him to the cut, put one shot in the back of his leg, and another in his whiskey bottle." John grinned. "I think that hurt the worst. He was afraid of the glass and had to strain it through his hat to drink."

"Where did you find him?"

"Hell, he found us. Crippling along on his rifle barrel and drunk as a lord! One of my lads took him on in to Ross's. Winterthur had left him for dead." Shaw paused, uncorked the demijohn handed to him, poured a dram into a pannikin, and said gently, "Here, ma'am; it will do you good." Then he passed the jug to Owen, who slung it expertly over his undamaged shoulder and drank from the narrow neck. "So you were looking for us?"

John shrugged. "In effect. The word had drifted back from Winterthur's place that he wasn't where he was supposed to be. I found that curious—especially for a man with a broken leg, who liked his comforts. Begging your pardon, ma'am," he said to Victoria.

She nodded, mostly because it seemed to be expected of her, took a polite sip of the whiskey. It was surprisingly smooth, and the cool liquid turned to fire in her stomach. The warmth was vaguely comforting; she took another sip.

John Shaw stood erect, grunting with the effort, and looked down at Owen, his dark brows drawn in his swarthy face. "You can't travel horseback with that hole in you, Verinder. We'll ride on into Ross's with the—" he hesitated, and then supplied a more delicate word than had first come to mind "—the deceased. This is Leonard Ross's bailiwick; I'll give him a chance to practice his sheriffing. My lads will bring back a sled. I do hope, ma'am." And now his piercing eyes turned to Victoria. He gave a short, courtly bow. "Indeed, I beg you accept my hospitality at Cole's Grove. At least until—the weather settles."

What a diplomatic phrase: *until the weather settles.*

Victoria raised her tired blue eyes to his, replied in a toneless voice, "Thank you very much.'' She lowered her head to take another comforting drink, but found Owen's one good hand removing the pannikin.

He drank the remainder himself. ''John is leaving you to defend my virtue until the sled comes,'' he told her coolly, ''and you won't be much good if you're tiddled. Any rations on you, John? Our dining was a bit scant last night.''

Shaw nodded. He was not just a little relieved to hear Verinder assume the responsibility for poor, wraithlike Lady Winterthur. That there was more to this affair than met the eye, he didn't doubt; Winterthur's death would hardly cause wholesale mourning. Still, it did rather leave Victoria high and dry.

He moved to the door and glanced around. One of his men had built up the fire. Another had found the horses tied far down in the brush, brought them back to shelter and given them fodder. The dog was on a blanket. His eyes were open, and his pink tongue licked gratefully at the water cupped in the Frenchman's large hand.

''Put him by the fire,'' John said, ''and he can ride in the sled too.''

Pedro was carried inside and deposited gently on the warm, packed dirt of the hearth.

Owen said, ''Good dog, Pedro.''

The battered, scarred hound skewed his eyes sideways. He saw Owen and gave a feeble thump of his tail. Then he closed his eyes. He was very tired.

With a lot of jingling and shouting, Shaw's men mounted up and moved across the soiled snow toward the pristine white of the timber. John said his casual farewell, swung his stocky figure aloft, and followed them. The trees were very black, the snow very white. The sun was high, making dazzles before Victoria's eyes.

She got up, closed the door against the cold that filled her lungs like ice, but did not bar it. Then turning, she walked slowly back to the fire and stood looking at it, her back to Owen.

She still wore the rose-colored robe, but it was pulled closely now, covering her throat. As she stared, she reached back, gathered up her hair, twisted it, remembered she had no pins, and let it fall again. As though her throat were dry, she swallowed convulsively, the slender throat constricting. ''Owen.''

''Yes, Vick.''

''You were right, of course. About Paul. Everything.''

''No. Not everything. I never thought he'd try to kill Thalia.''

''You couldn't have known. Only Paul knew that. Still, if I hadn't come, he'd be alive. Thalia too.''

Suddenly she turned; her eyes accused him. She said reproachfully, ''You should have told me about Thalia, Owen!''

He shook his head, and even the angry purple bruise where Paul had kicked him couldn't disguise the soberness in his eyes. ''Vick, Vick! You thought you were married to the man. How could I tell you he was Thalia's lover?''

''But I hated her so!''

''Would you have hated her any less?''

She stared at him a moment, then put her hands to her eyes and turned back to the fire. The sound of muffled weeping made him ache. He added quietly, ''I thought your troubles were sufficient without that, Vick. And you were being, you know, not quite honest with me.''

She took a deep, shuddering breath. "I know. I was wrong. Oh, dear God, Owen, I have been wrong about so many things. I haven't been right since my father died!"

"Vick, no one is faulting you."

"They should. They will when they know."

"Then they don't have to know! Goddammit all to hell, Vick!" He started up, and pain tore at him. He dropped with a thud and said much more mildly, "What are you talking about?"

She spun around. Her wet eyes were huge in her pale face. "I haven't any money! How's that for a start?"

"It's a damned good one." He was trying not to let her see how he hurt, but nothing could disguise the patches of sweat on his forehead. Holding his voice steady as he could he went on, "Give me a bit of the whiskey, will you, Vick?"

Something in his tone caught her. She stopped, bent closer, squinted, then cried out, "Owen! Are you all right?"

If he hadn't hurt so much, he would have laughed. Other than a game leg, a hole in his shoulder, and an eye rapidly swelling shut, he guessed he was fine. "The whiskey, Vick."

"Oh! Oh, yes!"

She poured into the pannikin, slopping it, and knelt by his side in the dirt. "Here—let me hold it for you." She put the rim to his lips and her breath was sweet on his face. He drank slowly; it steadied him. Then before she could move away, he caught at her hand. It stiffened in his, but he didn't let go.

"Vick," he said. "My love. Listen to me. About the money: I don't want it; I have never wanted it; and if you don't believe me, then our marriage has very little chance."

She didn't pull away, but the hand was like ice.

She said, "It hasn't, anyway, Owen. It hasn't. The best thing you can do is let me go."

The muscles around his heart tightened, making his entire shoulder hurt. He said, "Never," and curled his strong fingers about hers. "I know there's something wrong, Vick. I've known it all along. Tell me."

She shut her eyes, but the tears came anyway, slipping crookedly down her cheeks. "I can't. I'm so ashamed."

"Tell me, Vick."

His voice was so calm, so sure. The tips of his fingers stroked hers, gently, softly.

She thought, *I can't lie, he has to know*! And she blurted it: "I'm a thief! Before I left England, I—I stole something!"

It was the last thing he expected. It left him blank, and it showed on his face. She misunderstood.

It's happened, she told herself: *I'm losing him.* Numbly she went on drymouthed, "I stole the Landam necklace."

He stared. She groped for words, but in the face of his stare none came. She faltered and went silent kneeling there, wishing she were dead.

Then he said in a whisper, "Oh, my darling. Oh my precious Vick. What hell you have been through."

He dropped his head, put her cold hand to his cheek, saying savagely, "I'm sorry. I'm sorry, Vick. I'd no idea—I only meant to help. . . ."

That made no sense. She could only sit by him miserably, beaten, looking at him with hopeless eyes. She said, "They'll find me. I know they will. Sometime."

Desperately he tried to marshal his forces, think it through. He asked, "Who, Vick? Forgive me the questions, love, but it's important. From whom did you— take the necklace?"

She made her lips form words. "Lord Fandley. Or Lady Fandley. It was just—lying there in the midst of a tangle—bracelets, eardrops—everything, all together. She cared nothing for it. She'd been—horrid to me. And I hardly had enough money for my passage. I was frightened, Owen, so frightened! Then when Lord Fandley said good-bye, he put money in my hand, enough for almost everything. I felt terrible. I would have given it back, but she was there. And I couldn't. I couldn't. God knows, I've paid for it since. . . ."

He said gently, "Where is the necklace, Vick?"

"Sewn into my cape."

He tried to rise, and his legs failed. Holding his side, he said, "Bring me my capote."

It was her turn to stare. He insisted. "Go on. Get it."

The heavy, hooded capote lay on the floor, where it had cushioned his head. She picked it up, handed it over. Stretching painfully to unsheath his hunting knife, he began to pick at the neck seam.

Something began to appear, something that caught the firelight and flashed a million rainbows across his leather vest. She caught her breath and said, unbelievingly, "It can't be. It's impossible. I thought it was sewn in my cape. How did you get it?"

From its long hiding place he gently drew the delicate filigree, set with blazing sapphires. Quietly he said, "I didn't. You never had it."

"But I did! I do!"

"No, Vick. You had the paste one—the copy."

"The paste—" She faltered. "I didn't know there was one." With a soft puff of the robe, she sank to her knees again at his side, and her eyes held a different sort of trouble. He took a deep breath, and another sip of the whiskey.

"Listen, love. Do you remember the week I left England?"

She hesitated, and bit her lower lip. "Yes."

"I met your father. He was in bad shape. The tables had gone against him and the brokers were getting nasty. I bought the necklace."

She gasped. "He never told me."

"Of course not. That was my stipulation. And you know your father never broke his word of honor."

"No. He didn't."

There was little point in saying that Lord Landam had not been quite as ethical in other areas; Owen, in fact, had had to insist on an appraisal before he took possession.

He made an effort to gloss over the situation: "Fandley was along that day. Your father also owed him. A trifling amount, he said. But he had a fancy for owning the paste." (Bless the old roué; his fancy had been keeping Landam out of further trouble by trying to palm off the paste as real!)

Victoria asked blankly, "Why would he want the paste?"

Owen shrugged. "A rude joke on Lady Fandley, I'm afraid. They don't get on, you know. It tickled him to see her wearing dross and putting on airs. I don't think Bow Street will be after you, Vick."

"But when they found the necklace gone!"

"Perhaps the joke turned, and he had to buy her a real one! He'd not dare admit it was paste, love; she controls the pursestrings, you know."

She looked down at the bauble in her hands. "Oh, Owen, was it a lot of money?"

"Almost all I had," he said, and almost grinned. "If Paul wrote you that I'd landed in this country with empty pockets, he was absolutely right."

She looked at it a moment longer. All her life it had caused her little but anguish. With sudden resolution she held it out in both hands. "It's yours."

He reached out, but took the hands, not the necklace. "Only if you call it your dowry, Vick."

"Owen, you needn't. Please—"

"Hush. Listen to me a moment. This may as well be said here, heart's dearest, in this place with blood on the floor, where you went to sleep hungry last night. I was going to wait. But I've been at John's place. He has a carpet and real stairs. Those things might deceive you into forgetting. So I'll take my chances and say it now."

His hand held hers lightly. It was his body that was tense. "I have to be honest. You have to understand. I'm going to stay here, Victoria. In this country. I love you. You're my wife. God willing, you'll be my wife the rest of my days. But—but if you go back home to England—you go alone."

He meant every word—more than he'd ever meant anything in his life. And nothing had ever been so important.

She knew it. For a moment dismay flooded her. She looked around at the dirt floor, the chinked walls, the smoky fireplace; she remembered the jolting climbs, the bats, the bitter cold, the greasy food. She remembered the sound of shots on the cold morning air, and strange men in cowhide boots kicking dirt to soak up Paul Winterthur's blood.

She asked in a careful voice, "Did Paul really have an 'estate'?"

He'd turned from her because he couldn't bear to look. He poured the pannikin full of whiskey again, recorked the demijohn, lifted the pannikin and drank— all with one hand. As carefully as she, because he had no idea how the wind blew, he answered, "Paul had an enormous, unfinished house with chalk marks on the floor to show where the library ended and the ballroom began. He had no books, and gave no balls."

"It was just a—dream."

"An overblown dream. Had he given up the idea of an empire, and come down off Olympus, he could have done very well. I shall."

It was a statement of fact. He turned, went through the uncorking and pouring again. He was hardly aware of what he was doing. Victoria stared at him, saying to herself, *Sweet clean linen, china plates, roses, damask chairs, hot buttered scones, servants who move as soft as silk. . . .*

It was a picture of home, but the picture wouldn't come, because Owen was there instead. Owen was before her, with his big body, battered face, tawny hair, steady eyes.

Owen was *home*.

She said, "Owen—"

Had he won or lost? In a voice quiet as death he answered, "Yes, Vick?"

She sighed. What an obstinate, arrogant man he was! How could she live with a person like that?

How could she not?

She said, "Are there proper beds where we are going?"

It was certainly not what he'd expected. Bewildered, he wiped his mouth and put down the pannikin. "At John's? Yes. Three or four."

"Will you explain to him about the proxy?"

"Of course."

"Then one will do," she said. "For us, I mean."

She put herself inside the bend of his only working arm. It worked very well. On the whole she was satisfied.

Owen could barely see, now, from that one eye. He bent his tawny head, aimed for her mouth, kissed her Landam nose. He was half drunk, but the pain had dulled and he'd never been so content. He whispered in her ear, "I think I'm even going to miss him."

"Who?"

"The little sod."

She was blushing; he could feel heat against his unbruised cheek. He thought to himself, *But not for long*.

He shut his one good eye. Holding his wife against him, he drifted into healing sleep, thinking about proper beds. And proper places. And better times.

EPILOGUE

She was only seventeen, devastatingly pretty, and much more intent on enchanting the gangling swain around her than meeting a visiting celebrity. In fact she protested.

Nonetheless, her tall father took her firmly by the elbow and led her, her silk flounces whispering, right into the midst of the lounging knot of gentlemen who had been laughing and slapping their knees all evening.

"Mr. Lincoln," he said, "may I present my daughter, Victoria?"

Mr. Lincoln arose. It was more like unfolding himself, and at the end of it he towered even over her tall father—no mean trick. From this enormous height, he smiled down as she made her best curtsy. (Mother was a fanatic about proper curtsies.) "Such a regal name," he said, "for such a dainty child."

Vicky grinned, and from her mother's delicate face shone her father's roguish eyes. "Daddy calls me 'Sod,'" she said, and was rewarded by seeing her handsome parent color to the roots of his beard. "It has something to do with my mother's wedding journey," she added helpfully.

Caught between exasperation and laughter, Owen Verinder sighed. "All right," he said. "Run along, imp."

It worked again, Vicky thought, obeying happily.

I wonder if Mother will ever tell me why. . . .

No Time for Love

by Lori Herter

1

Lorelei put aside her violin, having mastered the difficult passages in the Brahms symphony to her satisfaction. Glancing at the living room wall-clock, she was astonished to find it was already five thirty P.M. Quickly she switched on the portable color television, which stood on a low cabinet, and sat down on the couch opposite to watch the local evening news.

As a reporter began to discuss the impact of a current truck strike on Chicago's economy, Lorelei's mind soon drifted away to a topic far more important to her. She played with the Chicago Philharmonic Orchestra and only yesterday morning had auditioned, along with others, for the vacant second chair of the first violin section. The elderly man who had held that place for so long had retired.

Now, in her mind's eye, she relived the audition again for perhaps the hundredth time. She could see herself hesitantly walking out onto the bare stage and smiling vaguely at the white-haired conductor and those sitting with him in the empty concert hall. Trying to block any extraneous thoughts from her mind, she began playing the selected passages of music she had placed on the stand in front of her. The first notes projected clearly, resonantly echoing through the large hall. To her pleasurable surprise, she continued playing through to the end with much confidence and finesse.

The conductor was smiling and nodded to her as she finished. He seemed pleased. Out of the corner of her eye, for she dared not look directly, she observed the dark-haired man next to him. The blue eyes she had so often covertly observed were glaring at her. Quickly she tucked her violin under her arm, picked up the music, and strode offstage before her composure could turn to panic.

Lorelei had been able to keep calm during this audition because she felt there was no chance she would be selected. Those with whom she had competed were fine musicians with long years of experience in the orchestra. In fact, the only reason she had chosen to enter the competition was to get more practice in auditioning, which she thought would be helpful for similar occasions in the future. Due to her unexpected calmness, however, she had performed unusually well. Did she have a chance after all? she wondered.

Lorelei's reverie was suddenly broken and her attention brought back to the television screen when the newscaster pronounced a name all too familiar to her. "Today for our Windy City Celebrity feature our reporter, Jim Hanley, has taped an interview with Peter Sutherland, the concertmaster for the Chicago Philharmonic. Jim?"

The television camera focused on a young man with a bright smile who spoke with a great deal of enthusiasm. "Thank you, Bob. In the past, only avid classical music buffs would have been familiar with the name of the concertmaster of Chicago's world-renowned orchestra. But Peter Sutherland is changing all that. He is young, handsome, sophisticated, and incredibly talented. This has caused him to become somewhat of a heartthrob to Chicago's female concertgoers and a sought-after, if reluctant, guest at the elite parties of the city's social set. I asked him about all this and more at his elegant apartment on Lake Shore Drive, overlooking Lake Michigan.''

If anyone had been observing Lorelei, they would have been amused, for she was sitting bolt upright, eyes wide and mouth open, staring motionless at her television. As the tape of the interview was about to start, she quickly got up and sat down on the carpeted floor directly in front of the set, eyes glued to the screen.

The television camera made a brief sweep of a beautifully furnished apartment and then settled on two men: the reporter, Jim Hanley, and an uncommonly handsome, dark-complected man with blue eyes, Peter Sutherland. They were sitting comfortably on a couch and turned toward each other.

"I must say, Mr. Sutherland, I was surprised to find you have a slight accent," the reporter began.

Sutherland gave a disarming smile. "Yes," he said in softly cultured tones, "people keep telling me I have an accent. I don't believe it, of course." He paused while Hanley chuckled a bit. "I was born and raised in Montreal. My father was American and my mother French Canadian, so I grew up speaking both English and French." Sutherland raised his dark eyebrows slightly. "Perhaps I also speak French with an English accent," he added, his blue eyes issuing an engaging, if somewhat world-weary, amusement.

Lorelei compressed her lips and shook her head ruefully at this. How charming he could be when he wanted!

The reporter continued. "Does your American heritage explain your preference for wearing blue jeans to orchestra rehearsals? I notice you have them on even now."

Sutherland laughed softly. "I find jeans more comfortable than anything else, and it's a welcome change from the formal white tie and tails we must wear for each concert."

"I see," said Hanley, smiling. "You're thirty-five years old, is that correct?" Sutherland nodded. "Isn't that unusually young to be the concertmaster of a major orchestra?"

"Yes, I have been very fortunate."

"I'm sure your great talent as a virtuoso violinist had something to do with it," the reporter prodded.

Sutherland only smiled slightly and inclined his head with polite modesty.

"Now, I know the concertmaster is the lead violinist and sits in the first chair of the violin section at the conductor's left. He also plays any violin solos required by the music. What other duties does the concertmaster have?" Hanley asked.

"Well, he must work out the best bowing, that is, which notes should be played up-bow and which down-bow, and the style of bowing for all passages of music the string sections play. He must see to it that all the players know and understand them."

"Why is that important?"

"The quality of sound is much better if all are bowing in unison. The style of bowing affects the phrasing and dynamics of the music."

"Any other duties?"

"I rehearse the string sections individually, if necessary, and occasionally assist in conducting at rehearsals. Alexander Markham, our conductor, has also allowed me some say as to which players will play at which stand, according to their ability."

Lorelei's eyes hardened, for this she understood only too well.

"That brings me to another question I wanted to ask you." Hanley paused momentarily before he went on. "As you know, there has been some controversy concerning a woman cellist in the orchestra. In fact, the concert hall has been picketed several times by the women's rights group, Working Women. They claim the orchestra kept her from being promoted to principal cellist because she is female. Do you have any comment on this issue?"

Sutherland's demeanor became quite serious, the look with which Lorelei was very familiar. "I was not a part of that particular decision. I must say, however, that I concur completely. While the individual in question has a great deal of talent, there was someone else in her section who was more worthy of the promotion."

"And that person is a man . . . "

"Yes, that's true. Out of over one hundred players in the orchestra, only five are women. I wish there were more. But to continue to achieve the highest quality of music, the orchestra must promote only according to ability. This lady did not have the best talent available to us for that position. I suppose Working Women would disagree, but they are not professional musicians. It was the Philharmonic's decision to make, and I think it was the right one."

Lorelei listened intently to this speech and had mixed feelings. While she wished to support members of her own sex, she knew for a fact that the crochety and sometimes obnoxious woman who had started the dispute did not have as much talent as the man who was promoted over her. Still, when she had passed the women picketing in front of the concert hall, she secretly felt an affinity with the group, for she, too, was a working woman in an organization run totally by men.

"If I may ask one last question," Hanley continued. "You are probably one of the most eligible bachelors in town and are invited to many gatherings of Chicago's social elite. Yet one very seldom sees your name mentioned in the society columns of the newspapers. Why is that?"

Sutherland relaxed again to a slight smile. "I have devoted my life to music, and music is extremely demanding. I take my responsibilities in the orchestra very seriously, and I'm afraid that I'm quite ambitious for my career. I simply don't have time for parties."

"Chicago's hostesses will be sad to hear that," Hanley said with a pleasant grin. "Thank you very much for giving us some of your valuable time for this interview, Mr. Sutherland. You are certainly one of our city's most talented and engaging personalities."

"Thank you," responded Sutherland with studied modesty. "I've enjoyed it."

A commercial came on the screen next and Lorelei turned the set off. She did not want to be distracted while she considered what she had just seen.

To her annoyance, she was not allowed much time for reflection, as ten minutes later her telephone rang. Somewhat irritated, she walked over to the small side table next to the couch and picked up the receiver.

"Hello?"

"Miss Lawrence?"

"Yes."

"This is Peter Sutherland."

Lorelei almost dopped the phone. He had never called her before and she did not recognize his voice from the few words he had spoken. Recovering, she blurted out, "I just saw you on television!"

There was a long pause on the other end, then, "You mean they showed the interview today?"

"Yes! Didn't you see it?"

"No, I've just come from a meeting. The reporter told me he didn't know when it would be shown. They shot it a few days ago; I guess I forgot all about it."

Lorelei was amazed that anyone could forget such a thing. "It's a shame you missed it," she said.

"Yes," he replied absently, then asked with some hesitation, "How was it?"

Was he actually asking for her opinion? "You . . . it was very good. You answered the questions well. . . ." Her voice trailed off and she was at a loss as to what to say. It was difficult to be flattering and businesslike at the same time. Whenever she had spoken to him in the past, and those occasions were few, she had always found herself unnerved by his presence. Speaking to him over the phone was not much better.

"I had a reason for calling you," he said abruptly, as though she had purposely distracted him from his original intent. "The meeting I've just come from was with Mr. Markham and the others who listened to the auditions yesterday. It was decided that you should be assigned to the second chair position."

There was silence as Lorelei absorbed this unbelievable statement. "Are you there?" he asked.

"Yes." Her voice was breathless.

"I feel I must also tell you that I did not agree with this decision. You played unusually well yesterday—equal to the best of those with whom you competed. But I don't think you regularly perform at such a high standard. Also, you're not as experienced as some of the others. I feel these things should be considered when promoting someone to assistant concertmaster."

Lorelei listened silently, concentrating on every word as he continued. "The others wanted to use the opportunity to promote a woman in hopes of subduing the bad publicity the orchestra has been subjected to lately. They're worried our patrons won't donate as much money this year if the complaints from the women's movement aren't stopped. You played very well and they felt they could justifiably promote you. But as I said, I don't agree for the reasons I've mentioned." For a moment there was silence on both sides. "You're just too inexperienced and young," he reiterated, trying to fill the void.

There was another pause as Lorelei considered pointing out that he was also quite young when he became concertmaster. "I see," she finally said. "I appreciate your telling me the circumstances surrounding the decision," she added stiffly.

"I thought I should tell you, because I feel you may not last long at first stand—unless, of course, you can continue to play at a superior level."

And put up with sitting next to you, she thought vengefully. "I understand. Thank you." She said this with amazing diplomacy.

There was another space of silence. "I expect you to be on time for rehearsal tomorrow."

"Of course." *I always am,* she yearned to add, but tactfully kept it to herself. Another pause. "Well . . . good-bye, then."

"Good-bye," she answered carefully, not wanting to reveal by her tone of voice how relieved she was the conversation was over.

About half an hour later, Lorelei was still contemplating what Sutherland had told her, when she heard the key turn in the door to her apartment. In swept her ever-cheerful roommate, Rosemary Hart, coming home from some last-minute grocery shopping. She was an attractive brunette with warm, dark-brown eyes and a healthy, glowing complexion. She and Lorelei had been close friends throughout college and had shared an apartment ever since graduation. Rosemary had studied accounting and now worked at a large bank in downtown Chicago.

"What's the matter? You look rather dazed," she said, putting down her parcels.

"I've just found out about the audition. I'm to be promoted to the first stand! Can you believe it?"

"Of course I can," Rosemary said as she rushed to Lorelei and gave her a hug. "I'm so happy for you! I knew if you didn't let your nerves get the better of you, you'd have it made," she preached. "Didn't I tell you you always underestimate yourself?"

"Maybe you're right," Lorelei said with a laugh. "I was so sure I didn't have a chance, I was as cool as a cucumber. Of course our glorious leader, Mr. Sutherland, maintained my promotion was a bone to throw to the women's rights watchdogs," she added with some sarcasm. "But even he said I played equal to the best of those with whom I competed," she said, quoting him with a fair imitation of his accent.

Rosemary's eyes danced. "Was he the one who told you the news?"

"Yes," Lorelei said, her voice full of oppression. "And now I have to sit with him all the time."

"Do you!" responded Rosemary with a perceptive smile. She cast an intent and knowing look at her friend, but Lorelei chose to ignore it and lowered her eyes.

2

The next day Lorelei walked self-consciously, violin and bow in hand, onto the stage of the concert hall, having left her carrying case and jacket in her locker. It was the same stage on which she had auditioned. Empty then, today it looked more familiar with music stands and chairs set in an organized array, forming a half circle around the conductor's podium.

About half of her fellow first violinists were already at their places, and she shyly nodded to them as she threaded her way between chairs toward the center of the stage. She passed the third stand where she had been sitting for about a year now. She had persistently worked her way forward to that position from the last stand of the second violins where she had started seven years ago, even before she had finished college. Ever since her promotion into the first violins four years ago, she always felt she must have reached her highest level at each step in her forward progression. She never dreamed—it seemed utterly impossible— she would ever reach such a high position in the orchestra as she was to take today.

The conductor, Alexander Markham, was stepping up to his podium and smiled as she approached. He had pure white hair, worn rather long, and a ruddy complexion. Though seventy, he exuded the vibrance and fitness of a healthy fifty-year-old and apparently had no intention of retiring for some time. He took her free hand and kissed her cheek when she reached him.

"I take it you have been told," he said.

"Yes, thank you so much . . ."

"Now, now, no thank yous. You deserve it. Besides, I like to have such a pretty girl sitting closer to me." A fatherly smile crossed his face as she blushed.

Inwardly she knew she should not mention what was on her mind, but something compelled her to proceed. "Mr. Sutherland said—"

"*Mister* Sutherland? So formal?" he gently teased.

"Peter," she corrected with another blush. "He said I was promoted mainly because of the bad publicity about discrimination against women."

Mr. Markham's expression changed. "He shouldn't have told you that," he said quietly. "Since he has . . . yes, it's true. But I have confidence in your ability, even though you are a little inexperienced. Don't concern yourself with the reasons for this promotion," he admonished, shaking a finger at her. "This is a wonderful opportunity for you—for your career. Take full advantage of it. You have a chance to show that women can perform as well as men in the music world—and prove us male chauvinists wrong," he added with a wry smile.

She smiled back and replied with all the assurance she could muster, "I will."

"Good. Now take your new seat." He pointed to the second chair at first stand. She did so, giving him a pleased look.

Settling herself, she put her handbag next to her chair on the wood floor, laid her bow across the ledge of the music stand, and placed her violin in the traditional resting position, tucked under her right arm.

She turned to her right and gazed across the still vacant chair next to her, out into the large, well-proportioned hall. The layered balconies and expansive main floor were all silent and empty except for a couple of workmen at the back, who were apparently checking some wiring.

Lorelei shifted a little farther to the right and noticed Henry Morrison sitting in the chair behind the concertmaster's. A pang of conscience came over her. Henry had been her partner back at the third stand, and now she was sitting ahead of him. Fearing she might have lost a friend, she gave him a hesitant hello.

Henry was a slightly paunchy man of about fifty-five, not too tall, with receding brown hair. He looked up from tightening his bow, a distant expression locked in his usually inquisitive hazel eyes, and said, "Well, I see you had to show me up."

Lorelei's face fell and she said with concern, "No, I didn't . . ."

"I was only kidding," he said, putting on a broad grin as he reached over to pat her arm. Lorelei smiled with relief. He was always joking; she should have guessed. "My congratulations!" he said. "I could tell you played better than any of the rest of us, except Peter, of course. Naturally, I wasn't going to let anyone know, but they managed to figure it out."

"Oh, Henry!" she said with amusement, discounting his half-serious assertions. "I see you were promoted, too!"

"Yes, second stand! Frankly, I was surprised. I was prepared to end my career sawing away at the third."

"*I'm* not surprised," Lorelei said.

"Come on, now, don't make me blush—it might be bad for my high blood pressure."

"You don't have high blood pressure," she chided gently.

"You think you'll be able to keep yours down, sitting next to Peter the Magnificent?"

Lorelei had to laugh at the appellation. "Really, I wish I could continue to sit with you. We worked well together and had a lot of fun."

"Now, Lorelei, you shouldn't prefer to sit with a balding, middle-aged, married man when you can have a young, handsome bachelor who's making a name for himself. Just imagine, you'll be the envy of all those women who pack the hall at Friday matinees to swoon every time he breaks a hair on his bow."

"It's no use trying to play matchmaker, Henry. With the choice of women he has, he wouldn't bother with me."

"You may be wrong about that. I think you're just a late bloomer. Besides, with a name like Lorelei, you're destined to be a glamor girl someday."

Lorelei rolled her eyes in exasperation. "I wish you'd stop saying things like that. You have as many empty-headed, romantic notions as my mother. It was her idea to call me Lorelei."

"I'm not romantic. I'm just stating what I see in you. Underneath that schoolgirl exterior is a beautiful, elegant young woman."

"I think you need glasses, Henry."

"All right. I won't say any more. Just remember what I predicted."

"You say it so often, I don't see how I could forget," she said with a smile as she turned forward to face her music stand again.

Lorelei was always at a loss to know how he could say such things. Whenever she studied herself in the mirror, all she saw was a rather thin, moderately tall girl with lifeless dark blond hair. She invariably wore her long hair severely tied back with a scarf, as she was unable to do anything else with it. She constantly lamented over her colorless complexion, pale green eyes, and light lashes. Once, at Rosemary's behest, she had attempted using some of her roommate's makeup to accentuate her features, but she thought the result looked artificial and never tried again. While she admired stylish clothes, she felt out of place wearing them, so she stuck to her unimaginative wardrobe, little changed since school days. Thus, Lorelei's general appearance remained unadorned and unremarkable, much to her dismay.

Fortunately there were others, like Henry, who were able to perceive Lorelei's attributes in a clearer light, undimmed by her cocoon of self-deprecation. To them, she was a fragile young woman of ethereal grace, with large, luminous eyes and a haunting innocence. They noted her childlike face, completely unlined, and her lovely, well-formed features. She had a small nose, perfectly straight, and full lips that gave her mouth a soft, sweet expression. Her small hands were beautifully shaped, and she had long, graceful legs that were usually kept hidden under slacks or a long skirt.

Her incredible look of innocence stemmed from the simple fact that she had never experienced much of life. While still a child, studying violin, she had discovered a love of music and had spent hours and hours practicing by herself at the expense of other, more social, activities. During adolescence she had been terribly thin, and the boys at her school, bound to the unbending partialities of youth, had shown little interest. Her figure had filled out more when she reached maturity, but by then the habit of shyness was formed and she did little to seek out the attentions of men.

Through perseverance she excelled in her music, though she did not feel she had the vivacity and mental stamina to become a solo performer. She had been thrilled when admitted to the Philharmonic at quite a young age and was perfectly content to remain one of its nameless members.

She did not meet many men now. Her life was contained in the orchestra, composed mostly of older, married men. Rosemary, who always had a boyfriend, occasionally lined up a date for her, but these never worked out. It seemed Lorelei found most men rather uninspiring, or at least she had since the day Peter Sutherland left a brief but notable career as a soloist to become concertmaster of the Chicago Philharmonic. That was three years ago, and since that time, all other men had faded to gray when compared with him.

Peter Sutherland. A commonplace name to most, but to Lorelei it held an almost mystical quality when she pronounced it to herself, alone in her bed at night. She might impugn her mother for being romantic, but the truth was she was just the same, if not worse. She often chided herself for the time she spent weaving daydreams around Peter, dreams in which he was kind, gentle, attentive, sensitive to her every nuance of passing emotion.

Why should she imagine him this way? she wondered. In reality, he paid little attention to anyone, least of all her. He was always polite, but in an aloof and businesslike way. When social occasions required, he obligingly put forth a practiced charm, but Lorelei always suspected, as she guardedly observed him, that under his veneer of social poise he was bored stiff.

As for his manner toward her, it seemed as though he took pains never to notice her shy presence. Those times when she approached him to ask for clarification of the type of bowing he wanted or some other question regarding the music, he invariably gave her a clear but terse answer, never looking at her directly. Then he would continue with whatever he had been doing as though she had turned into thin air.

She noticed him in casual conversation with a few of the other men from time to time. He seemed to like Henry, but then, everyone liked Henry. For the most part, he kept to himself. She liked to think that his aloof behavior was due more to a constant preoccupation with work rather than arrogance. This idea was bolstered by the fact that lately he had become somewhat absentminded, as when he had forgotten all about his own television interview.

Thoughts of Peter occupied Lorelei's mind as, with increasing nervousness, she waited for the rehearsal to begin. She was distracted by the usual commotion caused when Rachel Logan awkwardly carried her cello to her seat. She was a small woman, rather stooped with age, with gray hair and quick, darting eyes that pierced through her bifocals. As she sat down, there was the customary spatter of complaints: The stand was too high, her chair was unsteady, the hall was too cold. Lorelei sighed to herself, realizing she now sat nearer the cello section and would be within closer range of hearing the constant complaining. She had to admit, though, that it was probably Rachel's charges of discrimination that brought Lorelei to sit at her present position.

She was reminded of the telephone conversation with Peter and tension continued to creep over her, insidiously tightening the muscles in her slender neck and shoulders. He would come in soon. Where was he? she wondered restlessly. It wasn't like him to be late. What would he say, if anything? Would he still be as arrogant as he was over the phone?

Anxiety beginning to gain control, she rubbed a tremulous forefinger along the side of her nose, her tensing nerves needing an outlet in motion, however small. She noticed her bow still resting on the heavy metal music stand. Quickly her right arm shot out to retrieve it so it would not be in his way when he finally arrived. She was loath to antagonize him in any way. He would probably resent her very presence, she feared, since he thought her so unworthy.

At last he strode up from behind, walking in the narrow space along the edge of the stage. Lorelei fairly jumped when she first caught a glimpse of him. It was probably due to her apprehension, but he seemed even taller than usual. He was wearing his customary well-cut blue jeans, closely fitted to his lean, muscular legs and narrow hips, and a casual shirt of lighter blue, which hung from broad shoulders. He moved with a languid, easy stride of manly grace and erect carriage. His hair was a very dark brown, brushed smoothly over his high forehead from a side part and cut a little long so that it ruffled against his collar at the back. His French heritage was reflected in the dark tones of his skin coloring. The clear blue eyes, made even more vivid by the contrast to his complexion, were set above high angular cheekbones and a long narrow nose. His smooth mouth was neither full nor thin and, on those rare occasions when he smiled, revealed perfectly even, white teeth.

He placed a large folder on the stand and nodded to the conductor. "Well, glad you could make it," the spry old gentleman said with amused sarcasm.

"Sorry. I was halfway here when I realized I had forgotten something."

"It's just starting time now, so there's no need to apologize. What did you forget?"

Sutherland gave a swift sigh of consternation and replied, "The folder of music." With a slight lift of his hand he indicated the music he had been carrying.

"I'm glad you remembered it," said Mr. Markham dryly.

Panic swept over Lorelei as Sutherland placed a hand on the back of his chair, moving it slightly before he sat down. "Hello, Miss Lawrence," he said in a cool, impersonal tone, keeping his eyes on the music as he arranged it on the stand in front of them.

Lorelei was too shaken by his presence to make any response. She sat motionless, holding tightly to her instrument, and anxiously waited for Mr. Markham to start the rehearsal.

The conductor began with a short update on the plans underway for the concert tour of Europe to take place in late spring. An itinerary was being finalized by the tour's planning committee, he said, and would be distributed to the orchestra members shortly.

He sat down on the high-backed stool used only for rehearsals, then gave a sign to the oboe to sound an A for tuning. The rest of the orchestra tuned their individual instruments to the note. Holding a slender white baton in his right hand, Alexander Markham raised both arms to call the orchestra to attention, and the musicians readily brought their instruments to playing position.

Lorelei, in her nervous state, accidentally hit the metal tightening screw at the bottom of her bow to the side of her violin, causing a small, sharp sound. Peter cast her a furtive, ominous glance, filling her with trepidation. Embarrassed, she hurriedly put her violin under her chin, arranged her fingers over the strings on the neck of the instrument for the first note, and positioned her bow. Eyes on the conductor, she waited for his downbeat and, when it came, began to play.

In the opening measures, she was immediately aware of the strong vibrant sound coming from Peter's violin. Compared to his, her playing sounded weak and tenuous. But as they made their way through the *Roman Carnival Overture* by Berlioz, the necessity of concentrating on the music and the action of playing, which was second nature, caused her self-consciousness to gradually ebb away. Soon she was performing with her usual precision and fortitude.

At the end of the overture, the conductor began to make comments to the orchestra members. He directed attention to certain passages he wanted played more pianissimo and to another place where he expected more of a crescendo. Then he worked exclusively with the woodwinds for a few minutes.

While Mr. Markham spoke, Lorelei noticed Peter feeling his shirt pocket, then his pants pocket. He lifted the music from the stand slightly and looked under it. Next, he looked at the floor all around him. Finally, he leaned toward her, eyes downcast, and asked in a low voice if she had a pencil. Lorelei had already taken one out of her handbag, so she quickly handed it to him. Out of habit from sitting with Henry, she had prepared to mark the conductor's directions on the music herself, but then thought better of it.

Peter pressed the tip of the pencil to the paper lying against the metal stand and immediately broke the point. Exhaling sharply through his nose, he tossed the pencil down onto the stand's ledge. "Do you have another one?"

Hurriedly, she fished through her bag and dug out a short stub of a pencil with a worn-down eraser. He looked at it as if it were a vile thing, but nevertheless took it and marked the music.

The two movements of Schubert's *Unfinished Symphony* were rehearsed next, after which the conductor again stopped to give directions designed to achieve the quality of sound he had in mind. Peter, having apparently forgotten where he had put the pencil he had used, began looking about him once more. Lorelei had kept track of his every movement, so she shyly pointed a slender finger toward his shirt pocket. He reached in, retrieved it, and began writing. Soon he let out a sigh of exasperation, put down the pencil, and began searching again.

"What's the matter?" Lorelei asked hesitantly.

"Where's that other pencil with the good eraser?"

She leaned forward and pushed the music upward a bit, revealing the broken-tipped pencil that had been hidden from view between the sheets of paper. Peter swiftly grabbed for it, and as he did, his long brown fingers slid over and covered for an instant the small hand that was already there. Feeling the warmth of his touch, Lorelei drew back her hand as if stung. He hesitated a fraction of a second, then picked up the pencil and began erasing as though nothing had happened. Lorelei lowered her eyes to her lap in the hope of hiding her confusion as her breathing quickened and her heart began pounding.

When the conductor had finished his comments, he called for a fifteen minute break. Peter immediately got up and walked away. Some of the others began to stand up and move around, and many headed slowly offstage to the large, carpeted locker room and lounge downstairs.

Lorelei stayed where she was, still recovering. A gentle, feminine voice roused her and she turned to find Mary Morrison, Henry's wife, standing near her chair. Mary played the flute. She and Henry were the only married couple within the orchestra. A few years younger than her husband, she was a lovely, slender woman with delicate features and light-brown hair attractively streaked with gray. "I wanted to offer my congratulations," Mary said.

"Don't bother, I already did," interrupted a male voice. "She'll just get a swelled head." It was Henry, speaking to his wife.

"That's impossible; she's far too modest," replied Mary with calm assurance.

Henry reached his wife's side and affectionately laid a careless arm over her shoulder. Lorelei had always admired the deep respect between them and their easy understanding of one another. Outwardly, their personalities were quite different. He was always wisecracking and full of good fun; she was much more refined, very gracious, and poised. Somehow there was a natural balance between them that enabled them to take life's offerings in stride.

"So, how's it going?" Henry asked Lorelei when she had thanked Mary.

"Oh, pretty well," Lorelei replied.

"I see already he can't keep his hands off you," Henry remarked. A look of dismay came over Lorelei's face; he had apparently seen what had happened. "Peter was holding her hand during the rehearsal," Henry explained matter-of-factly, answering his wife's inquiring look.

"He was not! He just accidentally touched my hand when we both reached for a pencil," Lorelei hurried to contradict.

"How do you know it was accidental?" Henry asked.

"He wouldn't have done it on purpose!"

"Oh, I don't know. I think he's got some hot French blood under that cool exterior," he said speculatively.

"Well, *I* certainly wouldn't be the one to bring it to a boil," said Lorelei derisively.

"Who can tell? I thought he seemed a little nervous, losing pencils all over the place."

"Henry, weren't you paying any attention at all to your own music?" asked Lorelei.

"The show was better up ahead."

Lorelei gave a pleading look of exasperation to Mary. "Henry, don't upset her," said Mary soothingly. "This is her first day at her new place and she's probably a little nervous, so don't add to it."

"I know why she's nervous," Henry plunged on. "She's had a crush on Peter for a long time." He scrutinized Lorelei's face to see what effect his words would have.

Lorelei sat perfectly still. "Why do you say that?" she said, carefully maintaining an even tone in her voice.

"It would be impossible to sit next to you for a whole year and not notice in whose direction your eyes are focused" was his gentle reply.

Lorelei didn't know whether to deny or admit the truth. Until now, she had genuinely believed that her feelings for Peter had not been perceived by others. Knowing Henry as she did, however, she realized that he would probably get it out of her one way or another.

"Okay, I suppose you could say I'm slightly attracted to him," she said, trying to make light of it.

"Slightly?" he asked, looking her directly in the eye.

Lorelei's eyes fell to the floor. She never was any good at deception. With concern, she glanced about and said, "Do you think anyone else has figured it out?" thereby tacitly admitting the truth of his statement.

"Oh, I doubt it," he replied comfortingly. "I just noticed because I'm around you so much and because I'm nosy."

Lorelei made a little, pleading smile. "You won't tell anyone, will you?"

"Don't worry, I won't."

"I'll see he doesn't," put in Mary, casting her husband an urgent look.

Henry's eyes were directed at someone who was approaching. "Oh, there you are, Peter," he said with emphasis on the name, apparently to alert Lorelei, who was facing the opposite way. She stiffened slightly. "I was just saying to Lorelei," he continued, "that if you two should need a third pencil, I have an extra one." Lorelei, unobserved, lifted her eyes to the ceiling.

His mouth slowly forming a hesitant smile, Peter said, "Thanks, but I think we'll be able to manage."

"How's Lorelei doing at her new post?" Henry asked with enthusiasm.

The smile left Peter's face. "Fine," he said quietly. Then, for the first time, turning his eyes directly to Lorelei, he said, "There were a few things I wanted to go over with you."

"Well, in that case, we'll leave you two alone," Henry said affably, and he and his wife moved away.

Lorelei wasn't sure what to expect as Peter took his seat beside her. She watched as he turned the pages of the *Unfinished Symphony* back to the beginning. Working his way through, he pointed out various sections where he thought her style could be improved. Here, she should take longer bow strokes; this could be played more legato; he suggested the second position for fingering instead of the third in another place. It seemed like a private lesson.

Lorelei listened intently and mentally stored all his recommendations. This was no easy task, for his voice, as always, had a disturbing effect on her. It was low and had a curious faraway quality, yet it seemed to draw all attention to itself and softly envelop the listener with its lulling gentleness. It was unlikely any woman could withstand its mesmerizing effect on the senses. Even had he not been handsome, the voice alone, combined with his captivating accent, would have been adequate to beguile any woman to do his bidding. Lorelei struggled to concentrate as the gently modulated tone of his voice continually beckoned her mind to wander.

Soon Mr. Markham returned to the podium and the second half of the rehearsal began. It went smoothly enough, the search for a pencil becoming necessary only once.

The concert that night, as usual, brought quite a change in the appearance of the orchestra members. Instead of the casual clothes in assorted colors worn at rehearsals, women were dressed completely in black and men in white tie and tails. Such rigid formality made even Henry look dignified.

It was customary in the Chicago Philharmonic for the musicians to filter out on stage at their leisure before the concert started, instead of filing out all at one time. Lorelei was again rather nervous, this being her first concert at first stand, so she decided to leave the locker room area and walk onstage early to get the feel of it.

The concert hall was already half full and people were coming through the doors at the rear in a continuous stream to take their seats. The balconies were filling also. There was a soft undercurrent of noise as people talked and moved about, coupled with a jumbled mixture of musical notes from the instruments of those few players already onstage warming up.

Lorelei sat down and opened her music. After tuning her violin, she began to run through a few difficult passages. She was wearing a long black velvet skirt and a long-sleeved black blouse of lightweight silk with loose ruffles running down the front and at the wrist. Her hair was tied back over her high collar with a black silk scarf. She looked charming enough, but had the schoolgirl quality Henry had noted.

Time passed quickly. Soon most of the players were onstage, and a degree of tension permeated the air as they anticipated the approaching performance. All at once the audience began to applaud and suddenly Peter was there looking magnificent in formal attire. The white of his shirt, vest, and bow tie contrasted strikingly with his dark skin; and the well-fitting, swallow-tailed coat gave him a graceful dignity.

He sat down, taking no notice of Lorelei's presence or of the audience's response to his appearance onstage. After arranging the music on the stand, he began to run through a few passages on his violin by memory. Now everyone except Mr. Markham was onstage and the audience was beginning to grow quiet with expectation.

At a sign from someone offstage, Peter rose from his seat, his back to the audience, and signaled to the oboe to sound the A for tuning. The woodwinds picked up the note, then the brass, and finally the strings. When the tuning was finished, Peter seated himself again. The houselights dimmed, and precisely forty seconds later Mr. Markham stepped onstage from the left rear of the orchestra and walked down the narrow aisle between the first and second violin sections. As he approached the podium, eager and enthusiastic applause resounded through the hall. Briefly he acknowledged the response, then turned to the orchestra and raised his arms authoritatively. The orchestra snapped to attention, all eyes upon him. He gave the downbeat, and the *Roman Carnival Overture* began.

The first half of the program went very well. At intermission, Lorelei followed Henry and the other players downstairs to the lounge area to relax briefly and talk with friends. Peter went to the private dressing room allotted to him as concertmaster.

In fifteen minutes they were back onstage waiting for Mr. Markham. Lorelei was looking forward to the second half of the concert, because *Scheherazade*, a symphonic suite by Rimsky-Korsakov, was to be performed. This had always been her favorite work. The composer had based this exotic, romantic suite on the tales of *The Arabian Nights*. There was a recurring theme throughout its four movements that was written for solo violin and, therefore, played by Peter Sutherland. The piece had been worked on at rehearsal, but in a rather clinical manner with several stops by the conductor, so she had not had a chance to really enjoy it.

In a moment Mr. Markham reappeared onstage as the audience applauded, and the orchestra prepared to play *Scheherazade*. Outwardly Peter looked calm, but Lorelei sensed that every fiber of his being was locked in concentration on the music and the conductor.

Mr. Markham gave the downbeat, the opening notes were played by the orchestra, and then came the first solo passage. From Peter's violin came forth a sinuous, beguiling musical strain, beautifully executed by the hands of a master musician. Lorelei thrilled to the sound so close to her and marveled at the effortless way he performed when thousands of eyes were riveted upon him. She had played a number of recitals when she was studying music, but the potential of her talent had always been diminished on those occasions by her nervousness in front of an audience. How Peter could play so obliviously of the staring mass of people astonished her.

The orchestra made its way through the first two movements, accented with repetitions of the solo theme. The third movement, called "The Young Prince and the Young Princess," contained a tender and sweetly sensitive melody, carried by the violins, which profoundly moved Lorelei. In her romantic mind, she felt as though she and Peter were united as they played the lovely strain together.

Following this were more vibrant solo passages and then, at the end of the fourth movement, Peter played the final exquisitely haunting, plaintive phrases. Lorelei stole a glance at him as he performed. His head was bent to the side and over the instrument; his eyes were closed. She was touched by the infinitely tender expression on his face. A tiny, innocent voice within her dared to wonder if it was the way he looked when he was making love to a woman.

She followed the final measures on the page in front of her through watery eyes. When his last, clear, shimmering note had faded away, there was a moment of total silence. Suddenly the audience broke into thunderous applause, punctuated with shouts of "Bravo! Bravo!" With a satisfied smile, Mr. Markham motioned for Peter to stand, and, as he did, the applause increased markedly. Lorelei, emotions already high, was moved to tears by the adulation. How she admired this man!

The conductor indicated the entire orchestra should stand, and Lorelei did so, surreptitiously wiping her eyes. Mr. Markham walked over to Peter and shook his hand. To Lorelei's surprise, he next took her hand as Peter watched.

When the conductor had moved away, she turned and looked up at Peter. His unblinking gaze was still upon her, studying her moist eyes. Overcoming shyness, she smiled up at him, silently hoping to communicate to him the joy she felt in their shared musical experience and her sincere admiration for him. He did not smile back, but continued to stare deeply into her eyes, as though considering something intangible he had found in their misty depths. Mesmerized by the intense gaze that held hers, Lorelei was disturbed by a strange, elusive sadness she perceived somehow within the transparent blue of his eyes. Her smile faded and her responsive eyes took on a concerned, sympathetic warmth.

They looked at one another for a timeless instant, no longer conscious of the applauding audience or of the others on stage. But the seemingly endless moment was abruptly broken. As though suddenly aware of himself, Peter dropped his gaze to the floor and faced forward again. Like the last, evanescent notes of *Scheherazade*, the fleeting, but compelling, force that had drawn them to one another was gone.

Mr. Markham took a final bow and walked offstage. As the applause at last began to die down and the musicians made ready to go, Peter turned and walked away. She saw him no more that night.

3

Weeks went by, filled with the usual heavy schedule of rehearsals and concerts. Lorelei and Peter gradually fell into an easy but businesslike partnership. She began to regularly take a supply of sharpened pencils with her to rehearsals, for inevitably, as soon as Peter laid hands on one, the point was broken or it went astray. Before long, he was also forgetting to bring a mute, the small attachment sometimes placed on the bridge of the violin to create a muffled sound. He had begun to borrow them from players around him, so Lorelei started to keep a small supply of them along with the pencils. She was well rewarded for her efforts, however, as he continued to offer advice on her style and technique of playing.

Peter's forgetfulness reached a low point—Henry considered it the high point of the day—when, before one rehearsal, he opened his violin case backstage and discovered it was empty. After he had recovered from the initial shock, Peter explained, with unaccustomed chagrin, that he had taken the violin out to practice at his apartment. Later, when he had picked up the closed case to go to rehearsal, he never realized he hadn't replaced the instrument.

Henry, who had earlier dubbed him "Peter the Magnificent," now changed it to "Peter the Absentminded." Those who had gathered round laughed at the joke, including Sutherland, who made some comment about "getting old." To Lorelei's extreme embarrassment, Henry retorted, "You're not *that* old. I think you're just distracted by the fascinating creature who sits next to you." Lorelei blushed. Peter's color intensified slightly, and he seemed to search his brain for some appropriate response. He finally managed a polite, but mumbled, "Maybe so." Henry opened his mouth to speak again, but was quelled by a sharp look from Lorelei.

It was a few weeks later that Lorelei observed her twenty-seventh birthday. She was readying herself to go out and celebrate with John Benchley, a young dentist she had met shortly after her promotion and had since casually dated.

Rosemary was helping Lorelei zip up her dress, a long green gown that matched her eyes. The design was more sophisticated than Lorelei ordinarily wore, this because Rosemary had been with her while shopping for it and had influenced her choice. Since John was to take Lorelei to a fashionable new French restaurant on the Near North Side of Chicago, Rosemary had helped her fasten her long hair in a stylish knot on top of her head, so that she looked quite pretty for the occasion.

"Well, I guess you're about ready," Rosemary said, fastening the hook and eye above the zipper.

"Thanks. John should be here soon."

"How well do you like John? You've been dating him a while now," Rosemary carefully asked.

"Oh, I like him, of course. He's always pleasant and good company. Bright and intelligent, too. But, to be honest, I guess my feelings for him don't go much further than that. We always get along very well, but somehow there's no spark there. Do you know what I mean?"

Rosemary nodded that she did.

"I often wonder why he keeps asking me out," Lorelei continued. "Sometimes I think I should stop seeing him, but then I consider the alternative—sitting at home—so I accept his invitations."

The doorbell rang twice.

"That must be him!" Rosemary said with unexpected nervousness. "Well, I hope that . . . I hope you have a nice time . . . that you like the restaurant . . . "

"Thanks," Lorelei said, curious about Rosemary's confusion. "You're going to say hello to him, aren't you?"

"No, not tonight. I . . . I have to call my mother before it gets too late."

"You called her last night."

"Well . . . I said I'd call her again tonight."

The doorbell sounded once more.

"You'd better go!" Rosemary said urgently.

Not having time to get to the bottom of her friend's unusual behavior, Lorelei went to the front door. Rosemary quickly shut herself into her own bedroom.

John appeared, dressed in a smart suit, with a bouquet of flowers for Lorelei. After he had offered a few compliments on her appearance, they left to go downtown.

Lorelei had never been at the new, expensive restaurant he was taking her to, though she had recently read about it in the papers after a few visiting celebrities were seen there. It had quickly become the newest "in" place for Chicago's resident social set, and therefore, was a favorite haunt for local gossip columnists, eager to report who was being seen with whom. She felt a little out of place as they entered the elegant restaurant, but was determined to enjoy her birthday.

The decor was completely blue and white. Blue velvet hung in graceful canopies from the ceiling. The thick carpet, the plush soft chairs, and the wallpaper, velvety to the touch, were also blue. The tablecloths and napkins, blindingly white, made the carefully laid silver service sparkle. There were candles and a rose at every table, and small lamps with opaque white shades were placed strategically, giving off a soft glow.

Lorelei was taken slightly aback when, after they were seated at a small table, the waiter solicitously asked her if she wanted a footstool for her feet. Stifling a giggle rising in her throat, she managed to decline politely.

The elaborate wine list and menu took some time to look over, but at last their selections were made and ordered.

John appeared to be inexplicably edgy as they waited for the first course. He was a pleasant-looking man of about thirty with light brown hair and eyes. His manner was usually calm and sociable, so his present fidgeting with his silverware and napkin puzzled Lorelei.

He soon noticed her studying him and said, "I was going to wait till after dinner, but maybe it would be better to say it now." He paused a while and then went on. "We've been dating for some time now, Lorelei, and I have to say I've sincerely enjoyed your company. When we first met, I thought something serious might develop between us, but as time went on, it seemed as though we became more like good friends than lovers. Do you feel that, too?"

After some hesitation, Lorelei nodded affirmatively.

He was quiet for a few moments, apparently formulating what he wanted to say next. "Last week . . . remember there was a mix-up about that date we were to have? I showed up at your apartment, and it turned out you were off at some college campus with the Philharmonic, playing a special concert?"

"Yes, I felt so badly when Rosemary told me you had come. For some reason I thought the date was for the next night."

"Yes, Rosemary . . ." John continued. "She and I had a long talk that night. By the end of the evening we had discovered that we'd been attracted to one another for some time, but neither of us had ever said anything out of loyalty to you. We each thought it over for a few days and then I called her at her office." He kept his eyes on his wineglass as he spoke. "We decided that I should tell you as soon as possible that she and I wanted to start seeing one another. I suppose your birthday wasn't the ideal day to pick, but I didn't know how soon I'd see you again and I didn't want to put it off any longer."

Lorelei smiled at him and noted a secret feeling of relief within herself. "That's okay, John. I'm very pleased for you both. Now that I think about it, you two seem quite well suited to each other."

John relaxed visibly. "Thanks, Lorelei. It's typical of you to be so understanding. Other girls would be jealous, even though they weren't in love with the man involved."

"Oh, nonsense," Lorelei said. Then she added, "It's too bad Rosemary didn't come. We could have celebrated my birthday and your budding romance all together."

"I suggested she come along, but she didn't want to. I think she was worried you'd be hurt or angry with her."

Candlelight Romances

"Oh, I see. That's a shame—it would have been fun for the three of us to be together."

As the wine was kept flowing and the dinner progressed, Lorelei and John found themselves in a lighthearted discussion of how they met.

"I remember I was sitting in your waiting room wondering with trepidation what the new dentist would be like. I had been so happy with Dr. Shiller, when he decided to move to California. You took over his office and a neighbor told me you had put in all new equipment. I was shaking in my boots thinking what I would be in for."

"That new equipment made things a lot more comfortable for my patients," John reminded her.

"Yes, but people are always afraid of the unknown," said Lorelei.

"Wasn't that the day you had a run-in with that weird character?"

"That's right, you rescued me. I was sitting there minding my own business when this man came in and sat next to me. He seemed nice enough and was well dressed. I had my violin along, because I had to go to a rehearsal afterward, and he asked me about it. I started telling him how long I had studied music and that I played with the Chicago Philharmonic. He seemed to be listening very attentively, and then before I knew it, he had his hands all over me."

John was laughing. "I remember hearing this high little voice in the other room saying, 'Will you please keep your hands to yourself! If you don't leave me alone, I'll call the police!' "

Lorelei joined in the amusement. "Then you came in with one of those sharp dental instruments in your hand, gave him a mean look, and he bolted for the door." They were both convulsed with laughter for a while, and she added, "I guess you lost a patient as a result."

"That kind of patient I can do without." After a moment's reflection, John said, "Maybe that's why we were so attracted to each other in the beginning. You were a damsel in distress!"

"And you were my knight in shining armor—with a dental pick instead of a sword," she added, laughing again. Gradually, she grew more serious. "Being too romantic isn't good, I guess. It can cause people to deceive themselves, to see something in someone else that isn't really there."

"That's true," said John.

"Well, it's all worked out for the best," Lorelei said, brightening up. "If you hadn't started dating me, you wouldn't have met Rosemary."

As she spoke, her attention was arrested by a very striking young woman who was being led by the maitre d' to a table. She had long, beautiful, toffee-colored hair that fell around her shoulders. Her curvaceous figure was tastefully, yet provocatively, revealed by a modish clinging gown with a plunging neckline. She was tall and her face had lovely features, but there was an air of superiority about her that indicated wealth and position. She looked as though she had always gotten everything she had ever wanted in life and had grown to expect it as her right.

It was only when the woman turned to the man following her that Lorelei realized with a shock who her escort was and encountered his sharp, blue-eyed gaze. Peter had seen Lorelei first, and his eyes were steadily upon her as he walked to his table. Shaken, she managed to give him a slight nod with her head. He returned the gesture, then cast his unsmiling eyes upon John for a moment.

When he reached the table, he sat down with his back to them, much to Lorelei's relief. It was a blow seeing him with another woman, though she had heard many rumors about his dating members of the social set. To watch him there, at ease in the elegant restaurant, conversing with such a beautiful female, put her into a sudden depression. She felt inadequate and insignificant.

She and John had just finished dinner, so she asked John if they could leave. She did not want to be in a position to observe Peter and his dinner companion any longer than necessary.

John agreed and they left the table. When they reached the entrance, she looked back, and again her glance met the blue eyes across the room. She turned quickly and walked out.

When they arrived back at Lorelei's apartment, they were greeted by an anxious, dark-haired girl, whose worried gaze went from Lorelei to John and back again.

Lorelei gave Rosemary a big smile and a hug. "Don't worry, everything's fine and I'm happy about you two. I only wish you had told me sooner, so we all could have gone out together."

Rosemary, her eyes a little watery, smiled her thanks.

"Well, now *I'm* going to be the one to run off to my room and leave you to talk alone for a while," Lorelei said. Turning, she added, "Thank you for a lovely evening, John," and gave him a peck on the cheek. She left them to themselves and went to her room, where her thoughts soon returned to Peter and his beautiful companion.

One morning, a few days later, Lorelei sat curled up in an easy chair reading a magazine. Rosemary was stretched out on the couch with a colorful afghan covering her. She had developed a bad cold and had stayed home from work that day to nurse it.

Without a hint of forewarning, a look of miserable depression suddenly came across Lorelei's face. She threw the magazine in her hands to the floor, where it landed with a sharp slap. Sliding her hips forward to the very edge of the seat, she stretched her legs in front of her and leaned far back into the soft chair, so that only her shoulders, neck, and head rested against the back. She folded her arms over her chest and her expression became a glum pout.

Watching her, Rosemary said, "What on earth is the matter with you?"

"I was looking at this new woman's magazine"—indicating with her eyes what she had thrown to the floor—"that's supposed to be so sophisticated, called *Foxy Female*."

"I've heard about it."

"Well, according to them, any woman over eighteen who is still . . . inexperienced . . . is regarded as an 'old virgin.' I suppose they would consider me 'ancient.' "

Rosemary laughed. "Don't take it so seriously. They just print stuff like that so they'll sell a lot of copies."

"I suppose so, but I do have the feeling that life is passing me by," said Lorelei dejectedly.

"How are things going with Peter Sutherland? And don't try pretending you aren't interested in him," Rosemary admonished.

"You figured it out, too! I didn't realize I wore my heart on my sleeve so much," Lorelei lamented.

"Well, there is a certain light that comes into your eyes whenever you talk about him, and that's quite a bit."

Lorelei gave a long, sad sigh. "When I was out with John for my birthday, I saw him at the restaurant with another woman. She was gorgeous." Her expression suddenly changed. "I forgot! I was going to check the gossip columns."

She got up and hunted for the newspapers of the last few days. When she had collected them, she quickly searched through the pages.

"Here it is! 'Peter Sutherland, concertmaster with the Chicago Philharmonic, was seen dining at the Near North's most fashionable restaurant with Candy Bradshaw, only daughter of steel tycoon Harold Preston Bradshaw the Third.'"

"Wow!" exclaimed Rosemary. "He really gets around!"

Lorelei nodded in agreement and seemed to sink deeper into her depressed state. "Meanwhile, I've been sitting here turning into an 'old virgin,'" she said sarcastically.

"It's easy enough to remedy that," Rosemary said lightly. "Just go and hang around the singles bars on Rush Street for a while."

Lorelei snickered at the prospect. "I would fit in really well with all the swingers there," she said with bite in her sarcasm. "No, I don't think that lifestyle's for me."

"No," agreed Rosemary, "but you'll have to do something to pull yourself out of your depression. Nothing will ever happen if you sit at home moping."

"I know, Rosemary, but I haven't any idea—"

"Wait a minute!" Rosemary interrupted. "I know just the thing! A girl at my office went to a chic new hairstyling salon on North Michigan Avenue. She came in looking marvelous and couldn't praise her hairstylist enough. He gave her lots of advice on how to handle her hair. She gave me the address and phone number for the place. I'll get it."

With that she threw aside her afghan and, grabbing a tissue for her runny nose, went into her bedroom. She came out a second later with her purse and withdrew a small piece of paper. "Here it is. She said to ask for Tony."

Lorelei took the slip of paper hesitantly. "It must be awfully expensive if it's on North Michigan Avenue."

"That's true, but you just got a raise in pay with your promotion," Rosemary pointed out. "Besides," she added with a smile, "you've always been Miss Moneybags because you spend so little on clothes."

Blocked at this avenue of retreat, Lorelei searched her brain, but was hard put to find another good reason for not taking Rosemary's advice. She looked at her friend and, in a little voice, said, "What'll they do to me?"

"That I don't know. I would just ask this Tony to do whatever he thinks is best with your hair. You know you need a change, Lorelei. Here, I'll dial the number for you."

Rosemary picked up the telephone receiver, handed it to Lorelei, and dialed. Soon a brief conversation ensued between Lorelei and a voice at the other end of the line. She replaced the receiver and cast a dazed look at Rosemary. "The receptionist said ordinarily I would have to wait two weeks to get an appointment, but she had had a cancellation from one of Tony's clients.''

"So when are you going?" Rosemary asked eagerly.

"Today, at one o'clock."

"Wonderful! Now you don't have any time to talk yourself out of it. You'd better hurry up or you'll be late!"

Lorelei took the commuter train, which ran near her suburban apartment, into downtown Chicago. About an hour later she was sitting in front of a large mirror in the stylishly decorated salon. There were bright, modern designs painted on the walls, and loads of assorted green plants hanging from baskets and sitting on the windowsills.

"What did you want done?" asked Tony, a young man with dark hair, brown eyes, and a quick manner.

"I'm not sure. I was hoping you could suggest something," Lorelei answered.

Tony studied her features and general bone structure with a practiced eye. He removed the scarf tying her hair and examined the long tresses, which reached the middle of her back.

"Here's what I would suggest," he began. "Your hair color is what is unkindly referred to as dishwater blond. I would brighten it by using a bleaching solution on very small sections scattered through your hair, leaving the rest its natural color. You would wind up with a mixture of half light blond and half dark blond, creating a sunstreaked effect."

"Bleach?" said Lorelei in a small, tight voice.

"It won't damage your hair, if that's what you're worried about. Your color is light enough that the solution won't have to be left on for long."

"I'm afraid it would look artificial," she said.

"It would look perfectly natural on you," he answered. "I bet you were a towhead when you were a kid, weren't you?"

"Yes."

"Even now, your hair would probably lighten up if you spent some time in the sun, but it doesn't look like you do that much," he said, eyeing her pale complexion. "All this process would do is make you look like you went swimming a lot at Oak Street Beach. Better, in fact, since the blonding would be more evenly distributed."

Lorelei doubtfully regarded her image in the mirror.

"Now, about the haircut . . . " Tony continued, as if the previous matter were settled. "We'll cut it below shoulder length and layer it, and we'll give you some long bangs, too. Okay?"

"Well . . . if you think so . . .''

If Lorelei had been told what she would go through over the next two hours, she might never have stepped in the building. At one point her head was an intricate mass of bleaching solution, cellophane, and hair clips, with wisps of hair sticking out all over. *I look like a Martian*, she thought. A towel was wrapped about her head, and she was placed under a hair dryer. Then, clips and cellophane were removed and the hair washed and rinsed.

Tony combed through it and cut it with precision. As he blew the hair dry with a hand-held dryer and went over it with a curling iron, he explained what he was doing so she could recreate the hairstyle herself at home.

"Well? How do you like it?" he asked when he was finished.

Lorelei was speechless. She could hardly recognize the woman facing her in the mirror. Instead of the lifeless hair that had hung about her head and neck, there was a carefree mass of loose waves and curls that stood away from her face, framing it. Each lock had bright highlights that shone as the hair bounced when she moved her head. The long bangs were flipped back over her forehead and somehow transmitted a slightly mischievous look to her innocent eyes. In the back, the hair was smooth near the top, but soon cascaded into a buoyant jumble of loose curls that fell gypsylike about her shoulders. "It's wonderful," she finally managed to say. "I can't believe it's my hair. There's so much of it."

"The bleaching process gives hair more body. You'll find it easier to manage, too. The style may look a bit overpowering now, but when you get a little makeup on, your features will stand out more and you'll look terrific."

Dismay came into Lorelei's eyes.

"Now you're going to tell me you don't wear makeup," he said. "Somehow, I suspected that. All right, come with me!"

Hardly giving her time to grab her handbag, he took her by the wrist and led her to a small enclosure in another part of the salon.

"This is Martha," he said, introducing her to a stylish woman of about forty. "She handles our special cosmetic line."

Martha smiled and looked Lorelei over as Tony left. "Marvelous hairstyle he gave you," she said in a low, earthy voice. "It brings out the angles in your face so well."

As Martha studied her countenance a bit longer, Lorelei considered with some trepidation the numerous shelves about them, packed with assorted sizes of small bottles and tubes.

Her perusal completed, Martha said, "Honey, ordinarily I try to interest my customers in our whole line of cosmetics, but your skin is so flawless and your coloring so delicate, it would be a crime to cover it up. You do need a little color on your cheeks and some light eye makeup, though."

She selected a pink blusher, and eyeliner, mascara, and shadow in shades suitable for a pale blonde, then applied them to Lorelei's face. Once Lorelei had seen the results of Martha's work in a mirror, she purchased the cosmetics used without hesitation.

She was so happily befuddled over her new appearance that she didn't even flinch when given the total bill. She gaily wrote out a check for a substantial sum and left the salon.

She proceeded down busy North Michigan Avenue, crowded with shoppers, to Water Tower Place, a tall building of more than sixty stories, constructed of white marble. Named for the old Water Tower that stands across the street— the Gothic-type structure that was one of the few buildings to survive Chicago's great fire of 1871—the new skyscraper houses, in several floors at its base, two large, expensive department stores and dozens of small shops and boutiques.

When Lorelei left Water Tower Place some time later, it was only because she feared she may have depleted her checking account. Her arms were full of parcels, which included two long, black gowns for concert performances and a variety of modish casual clothes.

It was one of the first warm spring days in the Windy City, and Lorelei wanted to walk the long distance to the train station, but the weight and number of her parcels changed her mind. As she stood on the corner trying to arrange her packages so as to have a free hand to hail a cab, she was startled by a loud wolf whistle from a passing truck driver. Shortly after that, a gentlemanly young man came to her assistance and flagged down a taxi for her. Later, as she walked through the huge, bustling train station, she received many admiring glances from amongst the rush-hour swarm of businessmen on their way home from work. She felt ill at ease with so much attention and wondered if she could get used to it.

Rosemary's mouth dropped open when Lorelei finally walked through the door of their apartment and put down her packages. "Lor-e-lei!" The name rolled off Rosemary's tongue at the speed molasses drips from a spoon. "Lorelei!" she repeated as she moved in a slow circle around her roommate, studying her with astonished eyes.

"I know what my name is, Rosemary! What do you think?"

"Tony must be a genius! You look just gorgeous!" she answered with awe in her voice. "Your hair is so bright, and that style makes you look so glamorous! Why, you're even wearing makeup!"

"The woman at the salon helped me with it," Lorelei eagerly told her. "I was surprised it turned out so well. When I tried it before—"

"That's because you were using *my* makeup. It's suited to my darker coloring, so it looked harsh on you," Rosemary explained. Then, as a new thought entered her mind, she exclaimed excitedly, "Oh, Lorelei! Wait till Peter sees you!"

The next day when she entered the locker room where musicians were readying their instruments for rehearsal, she unconsciously held her breath. Reaction came swiftly. Soon she was surrounded by a laughing, smiling group, doling out compliments so fast, she had no time to respond. Even Rachel, who never had a good word about anything, told Lorelei that she looked much healthier now and should have changed her hairstyle long ago. Mary Morrison said she looked like a cover girl for a magazine. At that, a few of the men drew a rousing response from their cohorts with playful suggestions that she might look good on the centerfold of some magazines. A little shocked, Lorelei rolled her wide eyes to the ceiling and there was more laughter all around.

She was not offended, knowing the comments were made in good fun. Rather, she was warmed by the fact that so many people took an interest in her.

Henry, who had been out in the hallway talking to a violist, came in to see what all the commotion was. When he realized the beautiful blonde was Lorelei, he made his way through the group clustered about her. With a broad smile on his face, he pointed a forefinger at her nose. "See?" he said proudly. "Didn't I tell you you'd turn into a glamorous, exotic creature someday?"

Lorelei laughed. "Yes, Henry, you did say that."

"You've more than met my expectations! You look . . . Hey! Is Peter here yet?"

"Haven't seen him," replied several of the others.

"Henry . . . " Lorelei began to admonish him. She spent the next few minutes gently, but earnestly, begging him not to say anything in front of Peter that might cause embarrassment. As she was finishing, she noticed that the banter among the musicians had tapered off and the group had become strangely silent. Instinctively, she sensed who must have come into the room from the doorway at her back. She turned a bit to take a careful glance in that direction.

Peter was entering the locker room in his usual preoccupied manner—eyes on the floor, violin case in his left hand, haphazardly unbuttoning his brown suede jacket with his right. He must have sensed from the bated silence that something was up, for all at once he turned his eyes toward the group. His attention was immediately caught by the lovely blonde who was just turning around in the opposite direction.

"We have a new player here, Peter," Henry said invitingly.

"We do?" Peter said with some surprise.

As the persons between them made way, Peter approached the unknown beauty with interest. When he was directly at her side, Lorelei turned to face him squarely. She watched the look of wondering admiration in his eyes change to shock and then anger.

"What the hell did you do?" he said sharply. "Who said you could wear your hair like that?"

"I didn't know I needed anyone's permission," she answered.

"You can't keep it like that!"

"Why not?"

"Because . . . you . . . you look like a gypsy!"

"So—I look like a gypsy," Lorelei responded, failing to comprehend his line of reasoning.

He took a step closer, looming over her like a disciplining parent over a naughty child, while a clenched fist rose to his hip. "Perhaps you don't understand," he began with clearly enunciated sarcasm. "The Chicago Philharmonic is a very prestigious, cultural institution. Our sole purpose for existing is to make high quality music, not to put on a show. I might remind you that the reason we all dress in black is so individual players won't be noticed. We function as a unit. The last thing we need is a flashy blonde with a wild hairdo drawing everyone's attention to herself!"

Henry, whose eyes had been eagerly darting from one to the other, as though he were watching a tennis match, interrupted. "Oh, I don't think it would be so bad, Peter. Think of all those men in our audiences who are only there because their wives dragged them. If they have a beautiful blonde to look at, they might be able to stay awake."

Peter shot him a menacing look, then turned again to Lorelei. "You'll have to change it back!"

She looked at him incredulously. "I can't change it back. It's been cut for this style."

"I've seen hairstyles like that on other women. There's nothing so uncommon about it," put in one of the other men.

"Yes, why are you making such a fuss, Peter? She looks fine," added someone else.

"Why don't we wait and see if Mr. Markham objects to it?" was a third suggestion, with which everyone but Peter voiced agreement.

General opinion against him, Peter glared at Lorelei, a small muscle near his mouth twitching. His eyes traveled down to her newly purchased clothing. She was wearing tan denim jeans, which clung snugly to her slender hips and thighs, and a close-fitting shirt of coordinating colors, which subtly revealed the tender curves of her lithe body. His lips parted slightly and slowly his eyes came back up to meet hers.

"Why are you wearing *that?*" he said in a soft undertone that breathed rage.

"I assumed since you wear jeans all the time, it was acceptable for me to do so," she answered coolly.

"Don't be impudent!" he snarled, eyes flashing.

"You don't have any right to tell me what to wear," she countered with daring boldness.

He glared at her threateningly, then, perhaps realizing he had no ground to stand on, he abruptly turned and stalked off to his dressing room.

After he was gone, Lorelei became aware that her hands were trembling, and tears began to well in her eyes.

"He'll calm down," said Henry, trying to comfort her.

"I don't understand why he's so angry," she said, a tremor in her voice.

Henry smiled to himself and merely replied, "We'd better get up on stage for rehearsal."

In a few minutes they were all at their places waiting for the conductor. Lorelei, looking pale and contrite, toyed with her bow as Peter kept a stony silence next to her. She looked up apprehensively when Mr. Markham approached the podium.

The white-haired gentleman gave her a random glance, then looked again. He smiled broadly. "Why, Lorelei, you look lovely. Very pretty!" He pretended to tidy his hair and tuck in his shirt. "If I had known I would be in the presence of such a beautiful young lady, I would have taken more care with my appearance today," he said.

Lorelei smiled while her fellow players laughed at Mr. Markham's gentle humor. Peter, meanwhile, leaned stiffly against the back of his chair, his eyes focused on some point in space. From then on the rehearsal progressed as usual, except for Peter's glacial silence.

That evening for the concert Lorelei wore one of her new black gowns. It had long sleeves and was tightly fitted about the waist and bodice, emphasizing the lines of her slender figure. The scooped neckline was by no means low, but it did reveal her long graceful neck and delicate collarbones. The contrast of the black with her newly bright hair was stunning.

When she encountered Peter in the locker room, he tautly cast his eyes over her from head to toe. As he raised his eyes back to hers, she glared at him, silently issuing a challenge. He returned her hard stare momentarily and then turned away.

They did not speak to one another that night, nor any time during the next two weeks. Pencils were passed and received in silence. Eyes were cast in all directions but toward each other.

By the latter half of the second week, she thought she had begun to detect a softening on his part. Finally, at the concert on Friday night, he dourly greeted her with, "Hello, gypsy." She smiled. At last things would go back to normal, she thought.

During the intermission she managed to subdue caution and straightforwardly asked him if he still disapproved of her hairstyle. He took a moment before he answered, then flatly said, "Yes." Raising his eyebrows slightly with resignation, he added, "But apparently it doesn't matter much what my opinion is."

Wanting to prove him wrong, Lorelei busied herself all Saturday afternoon trying various alternatives of arranging her hair. With Rosemary's help, she came upon a way of sweeping the hair off her face in an upward fashion and pinning it into a roll at the back of her head. Some loose curls could not be kept from falling forward to frame her face, but the style was much more subdued than before. She pinned an artificial flower of black velvet at one side of the roll.

She got out her other new dress. This one had a turn-of-the-century look with a ruffled yoke and high collar of black lace. It fit tightly at her tiny waist and widened into a full skirt. The sleeves were long with lacy cuffs.

When she arrived for the Saturday night concert, she anxiously checked herself in a mirror first, then boldly knocked on Peter's dressing room door. When he opened it, she said shyly, "I wanted to know if you approved of my appearance tonight."

A seldom-seen warmth stole into his eyes and he smiled. Then, quite unexpectedly, he reached out with one arm, clasped his hand to the back of her waist, and pulled her into the small room, shoving the door closed with his foot. He put his hands on her slender shoulders and made her turn about slowly. Having thoroughly examined her by the time she was facing him again, he said with mock pomposity, "I approve."

As they stood smiling at one another, he lifted his left hand to her face, putting her chin between his thumb and forefinger. He turned her head to the side so he could inspect the black velvet flower once more. "I like that," he said. Turning her head so she faced him again, he added in his soft low voice, "You're very lovely, Lorelei."

It was the first time he had ever called her by her given name, and that, combined with the tone of his voice, caused a troubling shyness to come over her. She could not look at him, and her eyes came to rest on his white shirt instead of the clear blue eyes.

His hand moved from her chin to the side of her face. Slowly, gently, he ran his thumb across the soft, smooth skin of her cheek. She began to tremble a bit. Eyes still locked on his shirt, she felt the whole palm of his hand press softly against the side of her head and was touched within by its warmth. She felt something press against her forehead. Was it a kiss?

"You'd better get your violin ready," said the soft voice. His hands had come down to her elbows and she started to back away from him. Gathering her courage, she looked up into his face. He smiled down and she saw the warmth, even tenderness, in his eyes. She gazed at him in shy wonder for a moment, hardly believing what she saw. Slowly, she turned away from him and left the room.

As she drove home after the concert—she preferred to use her car rather than take the train at night—her thoughts dwelt happily upon her successful evening with Peter. During intermission he had lingered about her, making pleasant conversation, and he had made a special point of saying good-bye to her when the concert was over. Never before had he shown her so much attention. Could it be possible he was as attracted to her as she was to him? Perhaps it was her change in appearance that had finally made him take notice, she thought.

The disturbing image of Candy Bradshaw came into her mind. She pushed it away, telling herself it could be possible that they were no longer seeing one another. Perhaps he had shown interest because now he was free of Candy and wanted to date her.

When she reached home, she pulled her car into the parking lot connected to the small, modern apartment house. As she was about to leave her vehicle, she noticed a light-colored sports car, which had been following her for some time, stop in front of her building. She waited to see if it was someone else who lived there, but no one got out. Darkness prevented her from seeing the face of the driver. The unknown car remained a moment longer and then drove off.

Lorelei had become a little concerned, as it was night and she was alone. She shook off her fears, however, when the thought occurred to her that it could have been some Saturday-night partygoer who was having difficulty reading the address of the building in the dark. This explanation eased her mind, and she hurried to her door, anxious to see if Rosemary was home from her date yet, so she could tell her of her success with Peter.

4

Monday, as usual, was a free day, there being no rehearsals or concerts scheduled. Lorelei decided to go downtown to the Loop, Chicago's central business district, to do some shopping in the huge department stores along State Street. She spent the morning comparing prices before selecting a travel iron and some other items she thought she would need for the fast-approaching concert tour of Europe.

Her shopping completed, she had lunch in a crowded department store restaurant. Afterward she did not feel like returning home so early in the afternoon and decided to visit the city's impressive Art Institute. It must have been at least two years, she estimated, since she had last been there.

Her golden curls blowing loosely in the brisk wind coming off Lake Michigan, she turned down Adams Street and crossed the broad sidewalks and pavement of Michigan Avenue. Approaching the Art Institute, she walked up the steps to the entrance, guarded on either side by two huge sculptured lions. Once inside, she checked her parcels and coat, paid the fee, and climbed the elaborate marble staircase to the upper level. She went to that section containing the institute's large collection of French Impressionist paintings, which she had long admired.

Slowly she made her way through several of the small connected galleries, lit naturally by glassed-in ceilings, and viewed some of the works of Renoir, Monet, and Van Gogh. One room had a display, blocked off at the center, of antique European furniture, and she stopped to examine a small lady's writing desk made of beautifully finished wood and inlaid with an ornate flower pattern. The small card placed nearby indicated it was French and of the eighteenth century. She was wondering what kind of wood it was made of when her thoughts were interrupted by voices that seemed to be approaching from the next gallery.

"You certainly take me to some of the most prosaic places!" a woman's voice was saying. "I don't know how many times my mother insisted on taking me here when I was a child to look at these same dull paintings. Why can't we go someplace more interesting?"

A low, mildly accented voice casually replied, "If you don't like the places I take you to, why don't you go out with someone else?"

Lorelei straightened up and listened intently. She was almost sure it was Peter's voice. The suspicion was confirmed when she heard the woman speak again, this time in a cooing tone.

"Surely, Peter, you can think of something better to do. You haven't taken me to see the view of Lake Michigan from your apartment lately. . . ." Her voice was becoming suggestive.

Somehow Lorelei had little doubt it was Candy Bradshaw speaking. Her heart sinking, she suddenly found herself wishing she hadn't decided to visit the art museum. She took a few hurried steps toward the opposite door, hoping to avoid an encounter with them, but in the next second they had entered the room.

It was now too late to complete her escape without drawing attention to herself. She stopped in front of a Louis Fifteenth armchair and pretended to study the flowered design of its blue-gray upholstery, all the while fervently praying they would pass behind her and go on to the next room without noticing her. She regretted having put her hair back into the loose, full-blown style that morning, making it quite unlikely that she could go unobserved by Peter.

Several endless seconds passed as she stood feigning interest in the large chair. Suddenly a masculine voice near her ear made her jump.

"Who is this blond gypsy? Someone I know?"

Lorelei's mouth mechanically formed a smile, while her heart began racing unsteadily. She turned and looked up into bright blue eyes gazing at her in amusement.

"Do you come to the Art Institute often?" he asked with what seemed to be genuine interest.

"I used to. I haven't been here lately, though," she answered as Candy Bradshaw approached.

"Aren't you going to introduce me, Peter?" the young woman asked in a condescending tone as she took possession of his arm.

Candy Bradshaw was wearing a skirt and a casual, but obviously expensive, blouse, with several of the top buttons left provocatively undone. She looked Lorelei up and down, as though examining a bug through a magnifying glass, making her feel unkempt in her new jeans and tucked-in knit top.

Peter made brief introductions and explained that Lorelei was his stand partner in the Philharmonic.

"I see," Candy said looking down her nose, though she was not much taller than Lorelei. "Strange, I don't remember seeing you at the last concert I attended."

"She's made herself more conspicuous lately," Peter said sardonically.

Lorelei was feeling increasingly uneasy in their presence and decided it would be best if she separated herself from them as quickly as possible. She used the first excuse that came in mind.

"There were a few more things I wanted to see here before I leave," she explained self-consciously. "It was a pleasure to meet you, Miss Bradshaw. See you at rehearsal, Peter."

Sutherland did not respond verbally, but stared at her, his expression serious. The look in his eyes was unfathomable.

She forced herself to give them both a brief smile and turned to go.

"Well, she certainly is in a hurry," she overheard Candy say as she walked through the doorway into the next gallery. A wave of embarrassment swept over Lorelei, and she began to realize how gauche she must have appeared, abruptly leaving them after so short a conversation. How foolish and awkward she probably seemed to Peter, when compared to his sophisticated and haughty companion. Her eyes became glassy. Well, there was no use thinking about it, she lectured herself. She couldn't change what she had done. She might as well just see what she had come to see and leave.

She decided there was only one more painting she really wanted to look for, and then she would go downstairs to visit the Thorne Rooms. After passing through several small galleries, she finally came upon Claude Monet's *Old St. Lazare Station, Paris* hanging near a corner in a room containing still more French Impressionist paintings.

Lorelei smiled a little as she approached it, as if recognizing an old friend. She never had understood why she liked it so well. It was simply a painting of a spacious old railroad station with a black engine puffing smoke and a line of people waiting to board the train. She thought it must be the predominant colors of green, gray, and blue that instilled the painting with a certain tranquil quality that she always felt when she looked at it.

"Do you like this one?" a male voice behind her inquired as she stood in front of it.

Lorelei turned quickly. It was Peter, and he was alone. It took a moment before she could answer. "Yes, it's always been my favorite," she said, steadying herself from the shock of seeing him again.

"I noticed it, too, the first time I came here. What do you like about it?"

"I'm not sure," she answered.

Peter studied the painting for a while. "It has an airy quality from the billowing smoke"—he raised a hand to indicate a portion of the painting—"and there's a sense of static movement, an impression of patience, perhaps, in the people waiting about. But, still, there's something more . . ."

"A feeling of peace . . . tranquility . . . " Lorelei ventured.

"I think that's it," he said. "The feeling of peace that comes from a sense of purpose. The train is ready to leave for a certain destination and those people waiting to board all know where they're going and why. It leaves one with a feeling of order, security, and therefore, serenity."

Lorelei had never thought of it that way. She was contemplating his words when she became aware, from a slight movement, that his hand was at her waist. Thus brought back to the here and now, she edged away from him a bit.

"Where's your . . . friend?" she asked.

He looked at her blankly.

"Candy Bradshaw," she said.

"Oh . . . she had to make a telephone call or something."

There was silence between them for a moment. "What else do you look at when you come here?" he asked.

"I like some of the other paintings by the French Impressionists—*On the*

Terrace by Renoir, for instance. I always go and see the Thorne Rooms downstairs, too.''

"The Thorne Rooms?''

"Yes, those are . . .'' she began, but was interrupted.

"So here you are, Peter. I asked you to stay in that other room and wait for me,'' Candy complained as she walked in.

"Did you?'' he replied absently.

"I don't know what's the matter with you lately! Your mind is always elsewhere. . . .'' Candy noticed Lorelei and her eyes darkened ominously. She took Peter's arm and said authoritatively, "I think it's time we leave. We've been here long enough!''

"Lorelei was just going to tell me about the Thorne Rooms,'' he said in a voice that was excessively calm.

"Oh, Lord!'' exclaimed Candy impatiently.

Peter steadily looked to Lorelei, as if waiting for her to speak.

"They're miniature rooms showing American and European interiors from various historical periods,'' Lorelei explained.

"Yes, I was dragged through them regularly,'' said Candy with disgust. "My mother thought it imperative that I know the difference between Chippendale and Regency furniture.''

"Sounds fascinating to me,'' Peter said with determined amiability. "I don't have time to come here often—I must have missed them. Why don't you show us the way, Lorelei?''

Lorelei looked at Candy and almost shuddered at the daggerlike gaze fixed upon her. With a sense of foreboding she began to guide them in the correct direction. Leading them down the staircase, she silently wondered if Peter was aware of the role in which he seemed to be placing her—that of the Other Woman. Was he doing it on purpose?

At last they descended to ground level and Lorelei led them through the glass doors that were the entrance to the Thorne Rooms, named for the woman who had created them. Peter paid the small extra fee to an attendant behind a desk just inside.

Ahead of them was a long, darkened, rectangular room. It was divided lengthwise by a very thick partition into two aisles, which were connected at either end. Along the aisles on both sides were lighted windows between eye and shoulder level. Running just beneath the windows were long railings. It was getting to be late in the day and there were only a few other visitors there, a small group that was nearing the end of the exhibit.

Lorelei and Peter took their time looking into the first several windows at the beautiful miniature replicas depicting rooms of English design from the Tudor through the Victorian periods. Lorelei noted with satisfaction that Peter's attention was completely absorbed by each fascinating display. Eagerly they pointed out to one another the tiny chandeliers, clocks, dishes, candlesticks and holders, miniature paintings, and tapestries, in addition to the furniture, copied from originals with perfect detail. Light had been made to appear as though it were entering through the tiny windows within each of the rooms, which ranged from cottage interiors to the halls and salons of great mansions.

"We don't need to worry about missing anything in Europe because of our tight schedule," Peter joked. "We can see it all here."

Their third companion, who had apparently been forgotten, let out an audible sigh. "Peter, you aren't going to go around to all of these windows, are you?" she asked tiredly.

"Why not?" he answered without turning from the miniature room he was perusing.

"You're only a quarter of the way through. We'll be here till the place closes," Candy whined.

"So?" was his only reply.

Lorelei glanced at the young socialite and, with uneasiness, noted in the girl's petulant expression the unmistakable signs of an oncoming explosion of temper.

"Peter, I want to leave now!" Candy demanded, a defiant tilt to her jaw.

The man she was addressing turned toward her and leaned languidly against the railing. Lorelei could see only his profile, but sensed his eyes must be conveying something at odds with his leisurely stance, for she noticed Candy's determined expression change. The woman seemed to be bracing herself. In a chilling voice, with slow emphasis on each word, he replied, "Candy, you are free to leave anytime you wish."

Candy's lower lip trembled slightly. "Are you coming with me?" she asked stubbornly.

An unblinking stare was Peter's reply.

"All right, then, I *will* leave," she said in a hoarse whisper. "It'll be the last you'll see of me!" She turned abruptly, ran down the aisle and out the glass doors.

Lorelei looked after Candy, stunned by the scene just played in front of her. Her gaze fell to her hands clutching the railing; she wondered how much her presence had precipitated their argument.

"Don't worry about her. She's just a spoiled rich girl who expects to get her own way all the time," Peter said in an easy tone of voice.

Lorelei looked up at him. She was surprised to find that he seemed to be completely undisturbed. There were no signs of anger, sadness, worry, or remorse. It was as though nothing had happened. "But she said she would never see you again," Lorelei emphasized.

"So she did," Peter responded.

"Doesn't that bother you?"

"Should it? Who knows if it's true?"

Lorelei was taken aback by the casualness of his replies. "I guess I don't understand, Peter," she said hesitantly. "If you think so little of her, why do you see her?"

He looked at her vaguely, as though uncertain of the meaning of her question. Shrugging his shoulders lightly, he said, "Because she's there. Why not?"

Lorelei was dumbfounded. What did he mean? His answer made no sense. She longed to pursue the matter more deeply, but felt she would be out of place to do so and said nothing further.

They continued on, looking at more of the miniature rooms, but Lorelei's mind was no longer on the tiny exhibits. Her thoughts were engaged in contemplating this newly revealed facet of Peter's personality. She had always hoped the aloof, cool nature he often displayed was not truly a part of his inner character. But if this were so, how could he be so uncaring toward a woman he had apparently been seeing for some time? Lorelei had no liking for Candy, but the fact that he could treat any woman with such disregard disturbed her.

"Because she's there" had been his answer to her question. She noted the similarity to the traditional response given when someone was asked why he had climbed a mountain. A cold feeling crept over her. Did Peter regard a woman as merely something to conquer? And if that were true, was she his next conquest? Why had he been showering so much attention on her lately?

A hand was gently shaking her by the shoulder. "What's the matter, Lorelei? Don't be so troubled by a little temper tantrum," Peter said soothingly.

She looked up into his face, dimly lit in the darkness by the soft light of the window they were standing near. He was smiling at her as if slightly amused, but there was also concern in his eyes. "Lorelei," he said, his voice beguiling and caressing, "you're so sweet and gentle, such a sheltered little girl. You're not used to seeing arguments and dealing with people who think only of themselves. So innocent—you need protection from things you don't understand."

She searched his face with wide eyes full of wonder. His soft, hypnotic voice played in her ear, scattering her thoughts, confusing her. He made her feel like a small child, and she wanted him to give her the protection of which he spoke.

"Come," he said, turning her toward the window. "You haven't been looking at the exhibit. Don't you like this one?"

She looked through the glass at a miniature English drawing room of the 1930s with modern-day decor. "Yes," she answered, "it looks so comfortable and elegant."

"It could have been in London, I suppose," he said, moving in back of her. He gently leaned forward, his chest resting against her back, looking through the window from over her left shoulder. His arms stretched forward on either side of her to grasp the railing, locking her in place so she could not move away from him. She felt enveloped by him, mentally and physically. "Have you ever been to London?" he asked softly, his warm breath on her ear.

"No . . . I mean, yes. Rosemary . . . my roommate and I took a vacation there a couple of years ago," she said, desperately trying to keep her wits about her.

"How did you like it?"

"Oh, I loved it," she answered shyly. "We saw several plays and took the Underground to all the famous sights—The Tower, Trafalgar Square, Buckingham Palace . . ."

"Have you been anywhere else in Europe?"

"No, just London," she replied.

"Then you must be looking forward to our concert tour," he said, moving around to her left to see her face. He put his arm about her waist and slipped his left hand over hers, which was clutching tightly to the rail in front of her.

"Yes," she answered unsteadily. "Have . . . have you ever been to Europe?"

His gaze was soft and unwavering upon her. "Yes," he whispered as his eyes lowered to her mouth. Sensing what was about to happen, Lorelei instinctively tried to back away, but his arm tightened around her, keeping her close. She almost stopped breathing as time began to move in slow motion. His other arm went round her and slowly his face lowered to hers. She was trembling as their lips met. He held her more tightly and her tremors stopped.

He kept her clasped to him for what seemed an endless time. She began to feel herself growing limp in his arms. The tightness of his hold had kept her from breathing sufficiently, and she made a feeble attempt to push herself away. It had no effect at first, but then he took his mouth from hers and relaxed his arms around her. She leaned against him, her head on his shoulder, gasping for breath. Vaguely, she noticed that his breathing was labored too.

They clung to one another for quite a while until they were calmer. He moved her away from him just a little so he could look into her face.

"Are you all right?" he asked softly.

She nodded she was as she looked up at him. His eyes held concern, but their expression quickly changed to one of tenderness and longing as they gazed into hers. Drawing her close, he kissed her again, but more gently this time. She felt the insistent pressure and movement of his lips over hers, as his hands moved slowly up and down the length of her slender back. Caressingly, he brought one hand up and tangled his fingers in the loose, blond curls flowing over her neck and shoulders.

At last he ended the kiss and placed his hands on her upper arms. He looked down at her, but she could not meet his eyes. Realization of what was happening made her shy and embarrassed. Her gaze settled on the print shirt he was wearing under his denim jacket. It was unbuttoned at the neck, allowing a glimpse of the dark hair on his chest, so she lowered her eyes even farther to the last button, just above his belt buckle.

"Poor Lorelei, always so shy," he murmured, then kissed her forehead. "Aren't you going to look at me?"

She shook her head negatively.

"I didn't realize my shirts were so fascinating."

As she gave a weak little laugh, he put one hand at the top of her head and began mussing her hair. She protested, laughing, and raised both her hands in an attempt to tidy it. While she was thus engaged, he surreptitiously dug his fingers into the soft flesh beneath her rib cage. "You aren't ticklish, are you?" he asked, his voice full of mischief.

"Yes!" she said, laughing, as she pushed the offending hand away, only to be attacked from the other side by his free hand. Soon it seemed she was battling him from all directions and was laughing so hard, she could barely breathe.

At last he stopped and she leaned against him to recover from the onslaught. He enfolded her in his arms again and gently rocked her back and forth.

In a little while she looked up at him and several moments passed as they gazed lingeringly at one another. Lorelei had never known such a feeling of sheer joy, and her happiness was complete when she saw the same emotion mirrored in the clear, blue warmth of his eyes.

As if he couldn't contain himself, he stooped, tightening his arms beneath her hips, and lifted her off the ground, leaving her legs dangling. Slowly, he turned round, smiling up at her as she clung to him, laughing, with her arms about his neck.

"Peter!" she protested. "Put me down!"

"Why?"

"This is an art museum. We aren't supposed to be carrying on like this," she said, her voice broken by giggles.

"Well!" he said with mock gravity. "Somebody call a guard!"

He let her down till her feet touched the floor again. She kept her arms around his neck as he continued to press her against him. Her face tilted up toward his, she parted her lips slightly, and he bent his head to kiss her once more.

"Peter?" The sound of a woman's voice gradually broke into her consciousness. It seemed to come from around the corner of the thick partition. "Peter?" it called again. Lorelei pushed herself away from him.

A second later Candy Bradshaw appeared. She walked up to Peter and took his arm with both hands. He looked at her as though she were a stranger.

"Peter, please," Candy said in a choked voice, "may I speak to you a moment?" She had obviously been crying. "I . . . I want to apologize." Peter lowered his eyes to the floor, his face a mask. Candy tugged at his arm. "Could we go outside to the hallway?" she pleaded after a furtive glance at Lorelei. "Please, Peter, just for a little while?"

He stood perfectly still for a moment, his expression maddeningly enigmatic. Then without even an inkling of a glance in Lorelei's direction, he began to walk slowly toward the glass doors, Candy still clutching his arm. Lorelei turned away. She did not want to watch.

When they had left the exhibit room, Lorelei remained alone in the dim light, feeling unreal, as if suddenly thrown into an emotional vacuum. Trying to pull together her confused thoughts, she sought desperately to reason out what had happened. Had those moments of joy with Peter been imagined? she asked herself. No, came the firm answer. He had been there. He had shared them with her. But why was he gone now, and with someone else?

Slowly, she walked to the glass doors, her thought processes beginning to return to order. Perhaps she would be able to make some sense of it all later, she told herself, when she could once again think clearly—see things rationally. There must be some reasonable explanation for Peter's behaving as he did.

She hesitated a moment, then opened the door and passed through into the large hallway outside. She looked around and saw Peter some distance away with Candy. The girl was still clinging hopefully to his arm, looking up at him as she spoke, her anxious eyes full of earnest intent.

But Peter did not seem to be listening. His eyes were cast downward and his thoughts appeared to be focused somewhere deep within himself. Lorelei turned away and hurried up the staircase, completely unnoticed by either of them. Blindly, she rushed to the main entrance, collected her coat and parcels, and left the building.

5

Lorelei lay in her bed that night pondering the unsettling events of the day, but was still unable to come to any conclusion about Peter's unusual conduct. Earlier, she had related the story to Rosemary, but her roommate could offer little insight, except to say that while Peter certainly appeared to be attracted to her, it might only be in a physical way. The fact that he had so unceremoniously left her for Candy, Rosemary had suggested gently but realistically, clouded any hope that his feelings for Lorelei were of a deeper nature.

But Lorelei found this hard to believe. She still felt the arms that had held her close and remembered the joy and warmth she had seen in his eyes. These were enough to persuade her of the sincerity of his attentions.

Her mind relentlessly worked to invent reasons that could explain his actions. Perhaps it was only because he had been startled by Candy's unexpected reappearance, she speculated, that he had walked out without a word or glance. Candy, after all, had been his date in the first place. He probably had felt some obligation to listen to her apology and see her home. Perhaps he had decided to tell her that he cared for someone else, and his mind had been preoccupied with that unpleasant task. But if this were all true, Lorelei wondered, why hadn't he called her to explain himself?

Other, more troubling, possibilities also entered Lorelei's mind. Maybe Rosemary was right in saying he had only been drawn to her physically. Maybe he really did care for Candy, and so had gone back to her in the end. Perhaps he had even been using her to make Candy jealous. If that was the case, his scheme had obviously worked. Still, it had singularly struck Lorelei that he cared very little about the woman.

She recalled the cold, disquieting fears that had overcome her after witnessing their argument. Could it be true that he did look upon women as conquests? Perhaps he had merely regarded her as a new diversion, having become bored with his present girl friend. After so easily conquering her heart, had he already cast her aside? Did she mean as little to him as Candy?

A worse possibility occurred to her. She and Candy might be only two of a number of women he kept within easy reach for his own amusement. If gossip were to be believed, he knew many women, and certainly he was capable of holding a woman's attention for as long as it suited him. What female could resist his looks, his assured manner, his persuasive lovemaking technique? Even a rich, beautiful young socialite like Candy, who must have men standing in line, had apparently succumbed to his charms, if her abject apology to him was any indication.

But no, Lorelei reassured herself, he could not be the careless playboy she was imagining. She was getting carried away with negative thoughts. She must dwell on the positive aspects—the look in his eyes, the gentleness of his touch, the concern in his expression. The truth lay somewhere in these, not in the ominous improbabilities her mind had conjured up, she told herself.

The next morning Lorelei was in an odd state of uneasy happiness. Though she tried to maintain her positive outlook about the new state of affairs between herself and Peter, the less pleasant alternatives kept edging into her thoughts.

About mid-morning the doorbell rang. A delivery man asked for Lorelei Lawrence, then extended to her a large vase full of lovely white roses. Surprised and delighted, she eagerly took the flowers, thanking the young man profusely. She had no doubt they were from Peter.

Breathlessly, she set the vase on a table and looked among the flowers for a card, but could not find one. She checked the carpet and the hallway outside the door, but none was there either. Thinking it must have been lost en route, she called the floral shop whose name was printed on a small attached tag. The florist checked the order, then politely informed her that there was no card—the sender had wished to remain anonymous.

Anonymous! Why didn't he want her to know he had sent them? How silly, she thought. He must have known she would guess who they were from, for no one else would have done such a thing. After all, it was well past her birthday.

Maybe he was being playful—wanting her to guess, waiting to see if she said anything. Or could it be part of some plan he had to apologize for leaving her at the art museum? Perhaps he felt so bad that he was afraid to speak to her for fear she would be angry, so he sent flowers to soften her mood. Later he would acknowledge that he had sent them and make his apology. Yes, it must be something like that, she conjectured.

After dressing for rehearsal, she ate a quick lunch at home, then rushed to catch the commuter train going downtown. Over the half-hour ride she dreamily gazed out the window at the passing suburban neighborhoods, but did not really see them. Her mind could dwell only on Peter and white roses.

When she arrived at the concert hall, she saw Peter just as she entered the locker room. He had his violin in hand and was about to go up to the stage. She smiled brightly at him, but he merely cast a fleeting look in her direction before continuing on his way.

Assuming he was apprehensive about seeing her, she readied her instrument as fast as she could, then hurried upstairs onto the stage. She walked to first stand where he was already seated, intently concentrating on the music he was playing.

He continued to play even after she had taken her seat, so she touched him lightly on the arm to attract his attention. He paused midbow and glanced at her.

"Hello, Peter," she said gaily.

He nodded briefly, without smiling, and resumed playing. An uneasiness began to creep into Lorelei's stomach. She touched his arm, more firmly this time. He stopped his bow again. "Yes," he said with great impatience.

"I . . . wanted to ask you something," she said, trying to keep the fear out of her voice.

"Well?"

"Did . . . did you . . . send me flowers?"

"What!" His expression was hard and incredulous. "I have never sent flowers to a woman in my life. There's certainly no reason I would send any to you!" he said angrily. He resumed his playing with a vengeance, whipping his bow across the violin strings and coldly shutting her off from further conversation.

It was as if Lorelei had received a physical blow. The stage seemed to swim about her for a moment. She turned ice cold and her hands began to tremble. With what finality her illusions had been shattered! Peter was, indeed, all the terrible things she had feared and not the kind, loving man she had imagined. Obviously, he cared not a jot for her. He had only used her—either for momentary pleasure, or to make Candy jealous.

It was probably the former reason, she decided when she began to regain her equilibrium. Women, it appeared, were no more to him than fleeting sources of amusement—unimportant and easily cast aside, she bitterly concluded. And what a pragmatist he was in dealing with them! It was just too bad if a woman like

Candy foolishly overstepped her place. He merely sent her packing until she was willing to toe the line and come crawling back. If she didn't, it was of no consequence; he could easily find another to fill the gap, as he had demonstrated.

She actually could feel sorry for Candy now. There was no hope for the poor woman. She was obviously in love with a man who thought no more of her than of a used handkerchief. *At least I realized what he was before it was too late,* Lorelei thought, ruefully congratulating herself. *At least* I'm *not in love with him.*

She played mechanically through the long rehearsal, eyes kept rigidly on the page of music in front of her. From time to time, however, she had to blink hard to clear away the blurriness that made the notes swim on the page before her.

Lorelei's attitude toward Peter solidified into an uncaring coolness during the weeks that followed, while the orchestra was preparing for its European tour. His demeanor was about the same toward her. She consciously made him ask her for pencils and mutes instead of foreseeing his needs and automatically supplying them, as she used to do. The only reason she continued to serve him at all was to make work at rehearsals go more smoothly; she felt she owed the orchestra that much. Peter, for his part, made his requests coldly, as if it were her duty to play personal secretary for him.

She went back to wearing her hair in the gypsy style for concerts, to his clear displeasure. Twice he ordered her to change the style, but she merely stared icily back at him until he seethed with impotent anger. She would not grovel at his feet to please him as Candy had!

Meanwhile the question of who sent the white roses remained a mystery. A growing mystery. She continued to receive similar bouquets, sometimes twice a week. After a while there were notes attached, always unsigned. "From one who admires you from afar," said the first one. This was followed by other insipid and trite sayings, as: "You are like the first flower of spring"; "You are perfect, like a white rose"; "I see you at every concert and worship you." When she received the last one, "You and I could make beautiful music together," Lorelei was becoming very uneasy.

"It must be someone who's spotted you in the orchestra and has become enamored," surmised John Benchley, who was over to dinner one night at Rosemary's invitation.

"Maybe, but how would he have any idea where I live?" said Lorelei.

"You're the only woman in the first violins. He could have gotten your name from the program they hand out at each concert. Then he could have looked it up in the phone book," suggested Rosemary.

"But I could be living anywhere in Chicago or the suburbs—that's several million people. How would he find the right local phone book?" Lorelei asked.

"That's a good point," said John. "Maybe it's someone in this neighborhood, who knows you live here. You said the flowers always come from a local shop?"

"Yes, in fact it's the one about a block from your office," Lorelei said.

"Hmmm," said John, ruminating. "One of my patients is a recently retired policeman, named Retherford. He lives in this area. When he was in last week, I got the impression he had a lot of free time and not enough to keep him busy. Maybe he wouldn't mind looking into the matter. This guy hasn't done anything yet except send you notes and white roses, but you can't be too careful. The notes are getting more ardent—who knows what he's leading up to? Do you mind if I ask Retherford to see what he can do?''

"Oh, no," replied Lorelei, "I'd be grateful for any help—if he doesn't mind, that is."

"Frankly, I think he'd be glad to have something to do. He still has a lot of friends on the force, too. He probably could get some help from them that you wouldn't get on your own. I have his number in my office records. I'll call him tomorrow," John said.

He sat silently a moment, thinking. "You know," he added, "I just had an idea as to who it could be. Remember the masher you ran into at my office? You said you told him you played with the Chicago Philharmonic. Maybe he's started going to the concerts to see you."

"But that was months ago," Lorelei pointed out. "The flowers have only been coming for a few weeks."

"Shortly after you made yourself over into a femme fatale," put in Rosemary. "Maybe he doesn't want to 'admire you from afar' anymore."

"I should still have that man's name and address in my records. I'll look it up and give the information to Retherford as a possibility," said John.

"Have him find out if the man drives a light-colored sports car," said Lorelei. "I think one may have followed me home from a concert one night. The car was right behind me all the way and stopped in front of our building for a few seconds. That was right before I got the first bouquet of flowers, too, now that I think of it. Maybe he was checking to be sure he had the right address."

"This is sounding worse all the time," John said, shaking his head.

Within a week a great deal of information had been obtained through the retired police officer. John told them about it when he came to pick up Rosemary for a date one evening.

"It is the masher you met at my office, Lorelei," he said. "His name is Walter Booth and he lives about a mile from here. Retherford checked his driver's license. He drives a white Fiat and his handwriting matches those notes you gave me from the flowers. He also checked at the floral shop and they confirmed it was him from their records."

Lorelei listened with a worried expression on her childlike face.

"I'm afraid that's not all. He's been picked up two or three times by police for molesting women. Nothing serious, though—at least not so far. He's connected with a rather wealthy family and they've always been able to get him off with a good lawyer."

"Did Mr. Retherford have any suggestions as to what I should do?" asked Lorelei.

"Well, since you're about to leave for Europe, he said to just go ahead on the trip and forget about it for now. He's going to try shadowing the guy for a while, hoping to learn his habits and perhaps even catch him in the act of bothering some other unsuspecting woman. He figures if he can make a charge stick, it may at least force Booth to get psychiatric care, which he probably needs."

"It's nice of him to go to all that trouble for me," said Lorelei.

"He said he doesn't mind a bit," replied John. "In fact, he's been quite enthusiastic about it and has started thinking about doing some work for a private detective agency. He likes being active again. Besides, he's also interested in classical music, though he never had time to go to many concerts. He just went to one with his wife a couple of weeks ago, though, and remembered you. He said, 'Is she the gorgeous blond with all the hair?' I said, 'Yup, that's her,' and he said, 'I can see why this guy has a problem!' "

Lorelei laughed. "Tell him I can get free tickets for next season, if he'd like them."

"He'd love it, I'm sure. I'll tell him," said John. "By the way, is that another bouquet over there on the table?"

"Yes," said Lorelei, with a sigh of depression. "Here's the card that was attached to it," she said, picking it up and handing it to him.

It read: "How can I exist without seeing you while you're gone? Don't forget me—I won't forget you."

6

On a sunny morning a few days later, Lorelei was feverishly occupied trying to close her large suitcase. Having eliminated much of what she had originally wanted to take with her to Europe, she was now down to what she considered the absolute minimum. This was not including her black concert dresses, which had been packed the day before in wardrobe trunks with other players' formal clothing to be shipped on the plane separately. Her violin had also been placed with others in large, specially designed cases used by the Philharmonic whenever they were on tour.

The orchestra had traveled from time to time to other cities in the United States, but this was its first trip to Europe. The extensive tour was intended to definitely establish the Philharmonic as one of the world's leading orchestras. It was already touted to be so in the United States, but it was necessary to prove its reputation in Europe as well.

At last, after some tricky rearranging, she managed to close her suitcase. She checked her carry-on luggage and handbag to be certain that she hadn't forgotten anything and finally concluded she was ready.

John and Rosemary drove her to O'Hare Airport that afternoon and they said their good-byes in the International Terminal. Lorelei found her way to the correct departure gate where many musicians had already gathered, waiting to board the specially chartered plane bound for Amsterdam, the first stop on a lengthy itinerary.

"Hello, Lorelei." She turned to find Mary Morrison smiling at her. "We were wondering if you'd be here soon. Henry thought maybe you would like to sit with us on the plane. There will probably be three seats across."

"That would be great! Thank you," said Lorelei.

"Henry decided to buy some film before we leave the airport. He should be back pretty soon now," Mary explained. She and Lorelei continued in pleasant conversation until Henry joined them. He was, as always, in a jovial mood, and their conversation soon became liberally interspersed with laughter.

It was during one of these lighter moments that Lorelei first noticed Peter. He was standing with others some distance away, but was looking directly at her. She returned his stare. As if awakening to reality, he turned to those he was with and joined in their conversation.

"Maybe you'd rather sit with him," said Henry, who hadn't missed a thing.

"No, I really would rather not," Lorelei answered, sounding quite definite in her tone of voice.

Henry looked at her curiously, but said no more.

They continued to chat amiably for about ten minutes until their attentions were drawn to a television film crew that had come down the hall and was moving into the crowd of musicians. Lorelei recognized Jim Hanley, the young reporter who had taped the interview with Peter some months ago. Wasting no time, Hanley looked about him quickly, then walked directly to Sutherland. The two men shook hands and spoke a few words. Then with a gesture indicating Peter should remain where he was, Hanley moved through the crowd purposefully to Mr. Markham. After a brief conversation, the conductor and reporter walked back to where Peter was standing. Hanley looked keenly about him once again until he set eyes on Lorelei. Straightaway he hastened toward her.

"Oh, no!" Lorelei moaned.

"I'll bet he wants to interview you!" Mary said, excitement in her voice.

The newsman strode up to her, hand extended, saying, "I'm Jim Hanley, WKG Television News. May I ask your name?"

"Lorelei Lawrence," she replied, shaking his hand.

"You sit with Peter Sutherland now, don't you?"

"Yes."

"Would you mind joining us for a TV interview?"

"Well, I'd rather not . . ." Lorelei said, discomfitted.

"Oh, go ahead," Henry encouraged her.

"It'll only take a minute," Hanley assured her, cupping his hand under her elbow to lead her toward Peter and Mr. Markham.

Reluctantly she walked with him to the others. The TV crew was readying its equipment as he placed her next to Peter. After a brief check with the men operating the camera and sound, he began the interview, speaking into the camera.

"I'm here at O'Hare's International Terminal with Alexander Markham and members of the Chicago Philharmonic, who are about to leave for their well-publicized concert tour of Europe." He turned to Mr. Markham. "Mr. Markham, you are, of course, the noted conductor of the Philharmonic. What does this tour mean to the orchestra and to Chicago?" He held the microphone toward the white-haired gentleman.

"We very much welcome this exposure to European audiences who have not had the opportunity of hearing us, and we hope our performances abroad will make Chicagoans proud of its resident orchestra," Mr. Markham responded.

"Will the tour help to secure the Philharmonic's reputation as one of the best symphonies in the world?"

"At the moment we are thinking only in terms of doing our best," Mr. Markham replied with a diplomatic smile.

"Thank you, sir," Hanley said, then turned to Peter. "Here we have Peter Sutherland, who is concertmaster of the Philharmonic. I had the pleasure of interviewing you a few months ago. We discussed equal opportunities for women in the orchestra, which was an issue at that time. I attended a concert recently and noticed that you have a rather lovely young lady as a stand partner now." He motioned toward Lorelei and the cameraman focused on her momentarily, then turned the camera back on Peter. "How do you feel about having to work so closely with a woman?" Hanley asked.

"I welcome the opportunity," Peter said in the most gentlemanly manner. Lorelei slowly raised her eyes to the ceiling.

Hanley grinned with a slight glint in his eye. "Isn't it a little hard to concentrate when sitting next to such a pretty blonde?" he asked Peter.

Peter took a breath, then turned on one of his radiant smiles. "I just try to keep my eyes on the music," he answered good-naturedly.

"It must be difficult," Hanley said as he moved on to Lorelei and the camera was turned toward her again. "And here is the lady in question. Your name is Lorelei Lawrence?"

Lorelei nodded that he was correct.

"Do you feel that women are being treated equally in the orchestra?" Hanley asked. He held the microphone in front of her mouth.

Lorelei unconsciously took a step backward, but was kept from moving any further by a firm hand at her back. "Yes, I think the Philharmonic is doing its best to be fair to women," she said, regaining her nerve from some inner resource she didn't know she had.

"Do you think there should be more women in the symphony?"

"Yes, and I think there will be more in the future," she managed to respond with conviction.

"You must be looking forward to this tour."

"I certainly am," she said amiably.

"I can't resist one more question. You sit with one of Chicago's most sought-after bachelors, Miss Lawrence—by the way, is it Miss or Mrs.?"

Sensing what he was about, Lorelei, with sudden presence of mind, replied, "It's *Ms*. Lawrence."

The reporter was startled for a fraction of a second, then said, "You don't want to tell us your marital status?"

"Is it important?" Lorelei countered with a steady smile.

"Well, I know better than to argue that point with a woman these days," Hanley said laughing. "Let me just ask: Do you like working with Peter Sutherland?"

Lorelei increased the wattage of her smile. "It's been quite an experience."

"Thank you," the reporter replied. To Lorelei's relief, he turned back to Mr. Markham to ask some final questions regarding the tour's itinerary.

The interview finished, Hanley thanked all three and shook hands. There was a hint of respect in his eyes when he came to Lorelei, as if he knew he had been foiled. "Would you tell me now if you're married or single?" he asked with a hopeful grin.

"I don't think I'd better—I don't trust you," she answered with a smile that bordered on flirtation.

"Okay, Ms. Lawrence. Thanks for the interview." He kept her hand in his a little longer than necessary, and his eyes lingered over her face momentarily before he walked away.

When he was gone, she turned and found she was under the surveillance of a taut pair of disapproving blue eyes. Without hesitation, she coolly moved out of Peter's presence and back to where Henry and Mary were standing.

They were eager to know about the interview, so Lorelei gave them a word-for-word account.

"Sounds like you handled it very well," Mary complimented her.

"Thanks. I'm surprised my brain was able to function. I thought I would be at a loss for words."

"So the reporter sensed a romance between you and Peter, too," Henry commented.

"I'm afraid he was mistaken," Lorelei said tersely and changed the subject.

They passed the time in conversation as several people with badges marked "Press" moved about asking questions of the orchestra members and Mr. Markham. When a few approached Henry and Mary, Lorelei skillfully maneuvered herself away until they were gone. She was not anxious to be included in any more interviews for the moment.

After what seemed an interminable wait, it was finally time to board the plane. Lorelei was feeling anxious and stuck close to Henry and Mary.

Henry selected a row of seats near the center of the plane. "Why don't you sit by the window, Lorelei," he suggested.

"Oh, no. Let Mary sit there."

"I'd rather have the aisle seat," Mary said. "I wanted to walk around and talk to some of the others later on."

"Then you sit by the window, Henry. I'd just as soon not look out—it makes me nervous," Lorelei said.

"Makes you nervous! Are you afraid of flying?" Henry asked.

"Well, a little . . ."

"Then you sit by the window, young lady! It's the best way to overcome your fears," he ordered.

Mary laughed softly as Lorelei edged her way toward the window seat. "Henry won't admit it, but he doesn't like to look out the window either. He always takes white-knuckle flights, too."

Lorelei turned on Henry. "Is that true?"

He looked a little sheepish. "I'll sit there if you like," he offered.

"No, that's okay, I'm already here," Lorelei obliged him.

"I'm glad you finally got it settled," a low voice muttered.

"Oh, sorry, Peter. Didn't realize we were blocking the aisle," Henry apologized.

Peter smiled to himself and moved on toward the back of the plane.

When they were settled in their seats and the hand luggage was properly stowed away, Henry said, "You're sure you wouldn't rather be sitting with Peter? I could try to arrange it somehow."

"No, thank you!" Lorelei said with emphasis. "I'd rather have a *pleasant* trip talking with you and Mary."

"I thought I'd detected a coolness between you two lately. What's wrong? Don't you like him anymore?" Henry asked.

"Let's say I've become disillusioned," Lorelei said. "I used to have some silly romantic ideas about him. Now I see him for what he is."

"And what's that?"

"A man who looks upon women as playthings to be toyed with and then discarded," Lorelei answered somewhat acidly.

"My goodness!" Henry exclaimed. "What made you come to that conclusion?"

"Oh . . . just a minor incident that revealed his true character," Lorelei answered, purposely avoiding detail.

Conversation ceased as the airplane was preparing for takeoff. When they felt the craft beginning to accelerate, Henry and Lorelei unconsciously gripped the armrests and turned apprehensive eyes toward the window in spite of themselves. Soon they could feel the plane was airborn and watched, fascinated, as the ground dropped away below them and buildings, roads, and fields grew smaller and smaller.

"It's never so bad as I think it will be," Lorelei noted.

"No," agreed Henry. "I try not to think about it, though. Let's get back to Peter. You may be judging him a little harshly. A lot of men play around when they're young. Then they meet one woman who changes their attitude—blows their mind, as you young people say."

Lorelei laughed. "I'm not that young anymore, Henry."

"Oh, come on! How old are you?"

"Twenty-seven."

He looked at her incredulously. "You're putting me on. You look more like seventeen."

"Would you like to see my passport for proof?"

Henry smiled. "Well, I guess you have been in the orchestra for quite a while at that." His eyes narrowed. "You know, you'd better get on the stick and find yourself a husband. You'll be an old maid before long!"

"Times are changing, Henry," his wife said, coming to Lorelei's aid. "Women don't think in those terms anymore. Many young women these days are pursuing a career and have no thought of marriage."

"That's right," Lorelei agreed.

"Oh, no!" Henry moaned. "Don't tell me you don't want to get married. It's fine to have a career, but you should have more in life than that. It's too bad marriage has been so maligned lately. I think it's great. Mary and I have been married for almost thirty years and we've been very happy. Right?" he said, turning to his wife.

Mary's eyes widened slightly and she smiled at him. "I always thought so. I never knew you had such well-formed opinions on the subject, dear."

Henry's mouth formed a small smile and he lowered his eyes in embarrassment. "Yeah, well . . . " he said, reaching over to touch his wife's hand. He turned back to Lorelei. "You really don't want to get married?"

"Sure, I'd like to get married," Lorelei said, quite moved by the obvious affection between them. "But it may not happen. Maybe I'll never meet anyone I'd want to live with for the rest of my life. In that case I might as well concentrate on my career and make the most of it. Being single isn't the end of the world, after all. If I did marry, it would have to be to someone I could respect and who had sincere regard for me."

"What about Peter—he doesn't fill the bill?" Henry asked.

Lorelei sighed deeply. "I don't think he has any real feelings for other people," she said. "He's more like a computerized robot programmed to play the violin.

He may blow a fuse occasionally, but that's about the extent of his emotional capacity.''

Henry was startled by her words. "I can't believe you're saying such things about him. If he's so computerized, why is he so absentminded?''

"Faulty wiring maybe?''

Henry laughed, shaking his head. "You're hard, Lorelei,'' he chided. "So it's all over between you two?''

"There was never anything to begin with.''

"I thought you were in love with him,'' Henry persisted.

"Love? I never said that.''

"You didn't have to. It was written all over your face.''

"Well,'' Lorelei allowed, "he's handsome and he has a few other qualities that are fascinating to women. I may have been taken in by his shallow charms for a while, but now I know better.''

"So that's the end of the orchestra's hot romance. Looks like this will be a boring trip!''

"Oh, Henry!'' said Lorelei, laughing.

Henry turned to his left and noticed his wife's seat was vacant. "What happened to Mary?''

"I saw her get up a minute ago. She mentioned earlier that she wanted to talk to some of the others.''

"Oh, that's right. Several players have been to Europe before, and she wanted to get some hints as to what we should see.''

"Are you going to try to squeeze in a lot of sightseeing?'' Lorelei asked.

"As much as we can with our tight schedule. You're welcome to come with us wherever we go, by the way,'' Henry invited.

Lorelei was thanking him when Peter unexpectedly moved past them up the aisle, toward the front of the plane. He was carrying some music and Lorelei assumed he was probably on his way to speak to Mr. Markham about some matter.

"He certainly is conscientious,'' Henry said, having come to the same conclusion. Oddly, he continued to look in Peter's direction, though the concertmaster was no longer in view. Lorelei sensed the wheels clicking in Henry's brain and wondered what he was up to.

A couple of minutes passed, and then Henry casually rose from his seat and said in an offhand manner, "I think I'll go see what Mary's doing. Be back in a while.''

Thus Lorelei was left with only herself for company. After about five minutes, she noticed Peter walk by again, apparently on his way back to his seat. Her mind lapsing into a curious void, she languidly turned her head toward the window. The breathtaking view caught her a bit by surprise. Soon her drooping spirit was uplifted as she marveled at the vast, rolling blanket of white clouds beneath the plane and the limitless blue above.

Her quiet reverie was jarred by a familiar voice. "Do you mind if I sit here for a while?''

It was Peter, looking tall and arrogant as he stared down at her from the aisle, his music still under his arm. Yet there was an odd trace of humility in his manner as he explained, "Someone has taken my seat for the moment, and these are the only ones left vacant."

Lorelei made a brief, affirmative nod. She felt quite sure she could correctly guess who was occupying his seat.

As Peter settled himself next to her, she promptly reached below for her handbag and withdrew a paperback book. She opened it and began to read, all the while conscious that Peter was observing her every action.

"What are you reading?" he finally asked. Lorelei thought she detected a slightly acrid tone in his voice.

"*Pride and Prejudice.*"

"Jane Austen? I read that at school when I was in my teens," he said dismissively. "It was required."

"So did I," Lorelei replied without taking her eyes off the printed words.

"You're reading a book you've already read?" he taunted, as if insinuating she had lost her intelligence.

"It's my favorite novel and I enjoy rereading it every few years. Is that all right with you?" she answered, a challenging undertone in her voice.

"If you have to read, you would do better to choose a book on the life of a great composer or something else in the music field," he pontificated.

"No doubt that's what you read," she muttered, eyes still on her book.

"When I have time. I certainly wouldn't bother with a foolish romantic novel."

"Well. Good for you," Lorelei said with cool acidity.

He quietly took in her last response and with a disgruntled sigh opened the music lying on his lap. Quickly he began turning the pages with sharp, resolute movements. "You wouldn't be so eager to read if Henry were still here," he said, almost to himself.

Lorelei ignored this last remark and tried to concentrate on her book. She had managed to read through a long paragraph when she sensed another interruption coming. Peter was going through his ritualistic search of his pockets, the floor, and the seat. Lorelei pressed two fingers to her lips and began to steel herself for a confrontation. This time, she decided, she was going to take a stand. She was in the mood. Keeping her eyes steadily on her book, she waited for it. It came.

"Do you have a pencil?"

Carefully, she placed a forefinger between the pages to mark her place and lowered the book to her lap. "Peter," she said, trying to ignore how bright a blue his eyes appeared as they reflected the sunlight streaming through the window, "I think it's time I made it clear that I am not required to function as your secretary. We aren't even at a rehearsal, and you're expecting me to supply you with pencils. Well, I'm sorry, but I'm not going to do it. You'll just have to fend for yourself. Now, I'd like to read my book in peace, without further interruptions—if you don't mind!"

The blue eyes widened in astonishment. "You certainly are crabby today! Traveling must not agree with you. All right, keep your damn pencils. I can manage," he said in an angry tone.

As Lorelei snappishly reopened her book, Peter leaned across the empty seat on his other side and asked those sitting across the aisle if anyone had a pencil. After some searching, one of the three men came up with a pen, but Peter refused it, saying ink could not be erased. He stood up, sank one knee into the seat, and draped himself over the back of his chair to ask the people in the row behind them. They could do no better.

"Why don't you ask Lorelei," a second violinist suggested. "I thought she always kept a lot of pencils with her."

"Apparently she's going on strike," Peter said waspishly. "Doesn't like her working conditions or something."

"Oh, all right, Peter!" Lorelei said, exasperated. "You'll bother everyone on the plane!" She reached for her handbag as Peter sat down again. "Here!" she said, throwing a pencil at his chest. "And here's another one, so you won't have to ask me again when you break the point on the first one!"

With defensive action, Peter clutched at the onslaught of pencils hitting smartly against his sweater.

"Now, is there anything else you'll need?" Lorelei continued caustically. "An extra eraser, perhaps? How about a mute? Maybe you were planning to practice your violin on the flight over. I know you don't like to waste time!"

Peter stared at her, an odd, questioning look in his eyes. "What's the matter with you? Why are you so upset over a pencil?"

Lorelei jerked open her book and pretended to read. The printed words began to run together through the angry tears forming in her eyes.

"You haven't said a decent word to me for . . ." Peter stopped mid-sentence. He snatched up the music and the pencils and threw them onto the empty seat next to him. With a long sigh he pushed himself back against his high cushioned seat and stared straight ahead in injured silence.

The sunlight was beginning to fade as the plane approached darkness over the North Atlantic. Light conversation and laughter could be heard from other parts of the cabin over the drone of the engines. Rachel's voice came through from a distance complaining to a flight attendant about a cold draft on her neck. The crackling of ice and tinkling sound of glass hitting glass indicated the crew was slowly moving down the aisle passing out drinks.

There was only silence between Lorelei and Peter. She had put down her book and was looking out the window at the clouds below, now softly colored by the receding sunlight. She had grown calmer and was beginning to wish she hadn't created such a stir.

Without warning, the aircraft took a downward lurch, then regained itself. Immediately there was increased excitement in the voices of the other passengers. Lorelei anxiously looked around the inner walls of the plane, as if hoping it would hold together. The "Fasten Seat Belt" signs flashed on. She checked her belt, then turned to Peter, who was watching her closely.

"You don't have your seat belt fastened," she pointed out diffidently.

As he secured the belt around him he said calmly, "Don't be afraid; they handle air pockets like that all the time."

The flight was becoming bumpy now. Lorelei looked out the window and leaned forward so that she could see the wing of the aircraft. Urgently she turned back to Peter, quite agitated. "The wing of the plane is bouncing," she told him with great concern.

"Don't worry, it won't fall off," he said, smiling, as though speaking to a small child.

The captain came over the loudspeaker and said in an impassive voice, "We are experiencing some air turbulence. Please make sure your seat belts are secured. We also ask that you remain seated. We'll try to find some smoother air at a different altitude so you can have an undisturbed dinner later on. Hope you enjoy the remainder of the flight."

"There, you see?" Peter said. "He doesn't seem very worried, does he? I think he's more concerned about dinner."

Lorelei nodded in agreement, but anxiety still showed in her eyes and serious expression.

"I know what you need," Peter said, unbuckling his seat belt. He stood up and moved toward the aisle.

"You're supposed to remain seated," Lorelei admonished him.

"Well, don't tell anybody, then," he said and disappeared down the aisle.

Within several minutes he had returned, carrying two glasses and a bottle of champagne. He sat down, putting the bottle aside for a moment, and fastened his seat belt just as Lorelei was about to remind him to. He handed her a glass and filled it, then poured his own.

"How did you get champagne?" she asked.

"They're going to serve it with dinner."

"They gave you a whole bottle?"

"Sure."

Lorelei pictured him flashing blue eyes and white teeth at some weak-willed stewardess, who probably offered him two bottles. At that point, two young flight attendants pulled the cart with ice and drinks up to their row. One was about to ask what they would like when she noticed the champagne. She seemed rather surprised, but smiled and said, "I see you're taken care of," and moved on. Lorelei looked askance at Peter.

"Drink up," he said, gently pushing the glass in her hand toward her mouth.

About half an hour later, Lorelei was feeling quite calm and enveloped by a warm glow.

"Traveling by plane is fun," she said, looking around with bright eyes. "How long does it last . . . the trip . . . I mean the flight? I mean how long will we be on the plane?" She realized she wasn't making much sense, so she just smiled happily into Peter's blue eyes.

"About eight hours. I hope they serve dinner pretty soon," Peter said, raising himself up a little to look down the aisle.

"Could I have some more, please?" Lorelei asked, holding out her empty glass.

"I think you'd better hold off until we eat something," he answered.

"I only had two glasses."

"I know, but that appears to have been more than enough."

"How come you wear a sweater and blue jeans on a plane trip to Europe?" Lorelei asked, totally unconcerned about changing the subject so abruptly.

"It's the most sensible thing to wear when one must sit for so long in cramped quarters. Aren't you a little uncomfortable in that?" he said, looking over her tailored yellow pants suit.

"I am getting a little warm in this jacket," she admitted. "Did they turn up the temperature in here?"

Peter smiled. "That's from the champagne. Hey! What are you doing?"

"Taking it off."

"Oh, I didn't realize you were wearing a sweater underneath," he said with obvious relief. He leaned over and helped her ease the jacket off. There was a little confusion when she tried to pull the sleeve over her wineglass, but he took it from her hand momentarily so the coat could be removed.

"That's much better," he said as he eyed her matching yellow short-sleeved sweater. It had a V-neck, causing it to be hidden from view under the jacket, and it molded itself well to her slender torso.

Soon dinner was served on compact trays, with champagne poured freely by the flight attendants. While her lighthearted mood continued, Lorelei asked Peter questions about his background as they ate. He told her he had been playing violin since age five, had studied music all his life, and that he was also proficient at viola, cello, and piano. He had developed an interest in music through his mother, who was a fine pianist.

Lorelei asked him about growing up in Montreal.

"In some ways Montreal is like Chicago," he said. "It's a city of industry, commerce, and finance. That's how my father wound up there. He had a job with a large Chicago company that had a branch office in Montreal. He was transferred there and soon met my mother, who was of French descent. She spoke very little English and he spoke very little French at first, but somehow they managed to communicate well enough to get married. I grew up speaking both languages."

"That's why you have an accent, then," Lorelei said.

Peter let out an audible sigh. "I don't really have an accent, do I? We moved back to Chicago when I was a teen-ager. I should think I would have lost it by now."

"Well, you do pronounce certain words differently and you don't have the flat, matter-of-fact manner of speaking that's typical of a Chicagoan. Maybe part of it is due to your voice."

"My voice?"

"Yes, it's kind of soft and cultured and . . . well . . . you have a nice speaking voice," she finished quickly, realizing she was saying too much. She certainly did not want to betray how much his voice could affect her libido. She mentally instructed herself to be more careful; the champagne had obviously loosened her tongue.

"Thanks," he said lightly. He sank a fork into his pie and added, "You have a rather distinctive voice, too."

"I do?"

"Yes, you sound like a little kid," he said dryly, without breaking concentration on the piece of pie.

She studied his profile a moment, but didn't know what to make of the comment.

"Do your parents still live in Chicago?" she asked, continuing the original topic of conversation.

"No, they've both died. What about yours?"

"My parents retired to Phoenix a few years ago for health reasons."

"So you're on your own now? Oh, no, you have a roommate, don't you? What do you two do, share the housework?"

"Sort of." A muted smile twitched across Lorelei's mouth. "Do you do your own cooking and cleaning?" she asked, maintaining a straight face.

"Are you kidding?" he asked with disdain. "I have a maid service to keep up the apartment and I eat out most of the time."

"Somehow I couldn't picture you behind a vacuum cleaner. Don't you get tired of eating out, though?"

"Well, occasionally I make a sandwich or one of those frozen dinners. A lot of times I just open up a can of tuna and eat it plain."

"Really?" she said, eyes wide with surprise. "I thought I was the only one who did that. I like canned salmon, too. . . ."

Peter was looking at her, perplexed. "You mean you don't cook yourself a meal?"

"No, I hate to cook," she said. "Rosemary and I have an arrangement—she shops and makes the meals and I take care of the other housework. I usually have to make do at lunchtime, though."

Peter studied her, as if through new eyes. "From your appearance—that is, your former appearance—I had assumed you were the type that liked to spend all day in the kitchen making sugar cookies."

His image of her was rather a letdown. She never realized she had appeared to be that much of an old-fashioned goody-two-shoes. "No, I'd like doing that about as much as you would," she told him.

With a warm, broad smile, he placed a hand on her shoulder and gave her a gentle shove back and forth. "You're all right, Lorelei! Anybody who's willing to eat tuna from the can rather than waste time cooking is okay in my book."

Though she wouldn't denigrate cooking as being a waste of time, she was glad to have gained some respect in his eyes for whatever reason. Pleased with this open, friendly manner, she smiled back at him. Perhaps once they got to know one another better . . .

"Excuse me," a feminine voice said. Lorelei looked up to an attractive, auburn-haired flight attendant who was holding a bottle of champagne and directing her attention to Peter. She seemed shy and a little nervous. "There's a bottle left. Would you like it?" she said, extending the champagne to him.

"Fine. Thanks!" he replied. The young woman's face became crestfallen as she saw his hand leaving Lorelei's shoulder to accept the bottle. She gave a weak "You're welcome" and hurried away, clearly disillusioned.

He *had* obtained the champagne by flirting with a stewardess, Lorelei thought, realizing her suspicions were correct. So. Another conquest. Another vulnerable female carelessly used. The thought sobered Lorelei from the last vestige of euphoria created by the wine and Peter's amiability.

Something cold and wet was pushed against her hand. Peter was giving her a full glass of champagne. "We have another bottle to polish off," he said, encouraging her to drink. Hesitantly, she lifted the glass to her mouth.

After their dinner trays were collected, Lorelei continued to ask him questions about himself. Due to the champagne, perhaps, he was in an unusually talkative mood, and she felt she would do well to take advantage of it. She wanted to understand what motivated him if she could.

"Do you ever compose music?" she asked.

"Occasionally, but my main ambition now is to be a conductor. I decided some time ago that that was a greater challenge to me than performing as a soloist. I stopped doing solo work and joined an orchestra again for that reason. I felt it would be wise to actually play with a symphony for a few years in order to be able to conduct more effectively."

"Is that why Mr. Markham used to have you conduct at some of the rehearsals?"

"Yes, he seems to look upon me as a protégé. We've been under so much pressure preparing for this tour, there's been no opportunity for me to take over any rehearsals lately. I've been conducting some smaller orchestras in the Chicago area from time to time, however. I'm still pretty young, I guess. I get impatient waiting for my career to develop. Sometimes I wish I were old and my goals were all accomplished. Then I could relax a little."

He stopped as he noticed Lorelei's serious and intent expression. He smiled self-consciously. "I'm sorry, I don't usually talk about myself so much. I don't know why I am now. . . ." His voice trailed off and he seemed to become preoccupied with some troubling thought.

"I don't mind," Lorelei said, encouraging him to continue.

He cast her a quick, guarded look, then his face broke into a sociable smile. "No, I've been boring you long enough already. What about you? What are your ambitions?"

Lorelei tried to hide her disappointment; she didn't want to talk about herself. "Oh, I guess I don't have any ambitions, really. I'm happy where I am. In fact, I never expected to progress as far as I have in the orchestra." She finished her glass of champagne.

"You mean at your young age, you've reached the pinnacle of your career?" he said, refilling her glass. "You don't want to go any further?"

"Many orchestra members stay at one position for years and years," she said defensively. "Where is there for me to go anyway? I'm playing first stand in one of the world's best orchestras."

"You could aim for concertmaster—or rather, concertmistress. I won't stay there forever, as I said. You could be the first woman to hold the position in the Philharmonic's history."

"I don't think I'd want that. I . . . don't have the stamina for it," she said, wishing he would change the subject. She liked things the way they were, and it pained her to think of him no longer being there. Playing with the orchestra would seem like an empty exercise without him around, she realized. It had been for so long, now, that she had looked forward to each rehearsal much more because he would be there than for the love of playing music. Even though they had lately been on bad terms with one another, she was now becoming conscious that her motivation for continuing with the orchestra had still remained the same.

"Well, build the stamina, then," Peter said sternly. "What's the purpose of life if you have no ambition, no plans for the future?"

She thought a moment and replied, "You may have a point, but I think there's something to be said for just enjoying life. I'm content with my job as it is. Being burdened with more responsibility wouldn't make me any happier. I don't want to just eat, sleep, and think music. There must be more to life than that."

Peter regarded her quizzically. Finally he said, "I suppose it's because you're

a woman. You probably would prefer to get married and have a pack of kids.''
There was a touch of derision in his voice.

"Not necessarily," she said. "I wouldn't want a lot of kids, and as for marriage . . . well, who knows?"

"Indeed," he said aridly. "Well, if you don't get married, then you might as well aim for first chair. What else is there for you to do?"

His blunt logic made her self-conscious. To concentrate on her career was the same conclusion she had come to in her earlier conversation with Henry, she noted with irony. She was now quite aware that her heart wasn't really in it. "I don't have that much talent," she said, trying a new tack.

"You can play as well as I do."

She looked at him, startled. "I cannot."

Peter smiled patiently at her. "Yes, you can. All you need is more confidence in yourself. I have to admit I've been pleasantly surprised. When you were first promoted, I didn't think you had the technical ability. You're always so self-effacing, one tends to underestimate you, as you do yourself."

"You've been giving me advice, sometimes," she said, suddenly shy.

"Only on minor points. I would suggest, though, that you try to put more emotion into your playing. It will come better as you gain confidence."

"More emotion?"

"Yes, more feeling . . . passion. You tend to play a little mechanically," he said.

Lorelei accepted his advice without comment, but her mind was activated. She had told Henry she thought Peter had all the feelings of a robot. Now he was criticizing *her* for not putting enough emotion into her playing. Was that somehow a revelation of his inner self? Instead of wasting his emotions on people, did he channel them all into music?

"By the way," he said, interrupting her thoughts, "I've been meaning to tell you something, and I never get around to it. You know, don't you, that you should always be prepared to play any of the solo passages I have to play. If, for some reason, I can't perform—illness, or whatever—you would have to take over at first chair."

Lorelei became uneasy and rubbed her nose. "Yes, I guess I knew that when I was promoted. Nothing like that will happen, though. You're never sick," she said, directing him a smile.

"You should be prepared anyway," he cautioned.

Lorelei nodded in agreement. The movie screens were being lowered in the cabin of the plane, and Lorelei was glad for the distraction. The movie was to be a comedy and she hoped it would lighten the atmosphere, which was becoming increasingly serious and unsettling—for her, at any rate.

Peter and Lorelei put on their headsets and plugged them into the armrests of their seats. He refilled their glasses as the lights inside the cabin were turned off and the movie began.

It was one of those motion pictures that looks promising at the start and goes steadily downhill. At least it seemed so to Lorelei. By the time she finished her champagne, she was very drowsy and having trouble keeping her eyes open. She laid her head back against the cushioned top of the seat to relax a moment.

The next thing she knew, a masculine hand was on her arm and her head was on Peter's shoulder.

"Are you sleepy?" came his soft, soothing voice, as one would ask a little child an obvious question.

"I'm sorry," she said, embarrassed. "It must be all that champagne." She looked into his face and saw his smile in the darkness. The bright blue of his eyes was lost in the dim light, but they remained luminous and compelling.

Gently he removed the headset that had fallen from her ears to her neck. She felt a warm tingle as his fingers brushed her bare skin. Again, the silky voice crept into her ear.

"Maybe you'd better go to sleep. I'll get a blanket."

Soundlessly he got up. She could see the stretch of his lean body as he reached up to the compartment above their seats. He brought down a blanket and a pillow, then sat down in the aisle seat, leaving the middle chair vacant. He pushed up the two movable armrests between them so they were flush with the seat backs. He reached toward her with an outstretched arm.

"Come. You can lie across these two seats."

She started to move toward him, then stopped midway. "How will you sleep?"

"I can sleep sitting up," he said, gently coaxing her the rest of the way. He placed the pillow against his thigh, and she settled her head into it, curling her body comfortably over the two seats. She lay on her side facing away from him, and he spread the blanket over her, pulling it up to her ear. Gently his long fingers smoothed her hair away from her face and neck, causing sweet sensations to run through her nervous system.

She felt him lean over her, and his mouth whispered near her ear, "Are you comfortable?" She nodded she was, and he responded with a subtle rocking motion of his hand on her shoulder. He leaned back in his seat, but his hand remained where it was. She could feel its weight and warmth through the blanket. *How will I ever sleep?* she silently wondered, deeply disturbed by his physical nearness to her.

She closed her eyes. She could hear the monotonous drone of the engines. Everything else was quiet. Strangely, she felt as if she had been on the plane forever. There was no past, no future. It was as though the aircraft were speeding through some sort of endless limbo, moving toward an unknown destination that it would never reach. But, more strange still, she didn't care. She felt warmed and protected by the hand gently resting on her shoulder. She was with Peter and nothing else mattered. Soon the sound of the engines was gone. She had drifted into the oblivion of sleep.

Lorelei had slept for perhaps two hours, when again she became aware of the steady drone of the plane's engines. She opened her eyes, and it took a moment before she recognized her surroundings. Lifting her head from the pillow a bit, she could hear a few muffled snores from nearby passengers. Apparently the film was over and everyone was asleep.

Her muscles were cramped from having been in one position for so long, and one leg was going numb from lack of circulation. She began to turn over onto her back and, as she did, felt something move against her neck. It was Peter's hand, which had still been resting gently on her shoulder.

She pressed her head back into the pillow and looked upward toward his face.

He was asleep, his head tilted to one side and resting against the curved edge of the seat back. A dark lock of hair had fallen across his forehead, and the serenity of his sleeping expression softened the angular face, making him appear almost boyish.

He stirred fitfully in his sleep, and the hand that had been unintentionally pushed aside moved languidly across Lorelei's throat and came to rest carelessly over the collarbone and base of her neck. It lay warm against her delicate skin. In a responsive impulse not to be denied, she brought her own hand up to touch him. Her fingertips lightly explored the smooth skin and dark masculine hair on the back of his hand. She could sense the potential strength in the hard muscles and long bones.

His large hand tightened almost imperceptibly beneath her touch. Soon it moved knowingly to her cheek and, with gentle pressure, turned her head toward him. She lifted her eyes to his face again. He was looking at her with subtle, sleepy eyes. The corners of his mouth were drawn back a little, deepening small lines in his smooth cheeks.

Her mouth was parted as she strained to tilt her head back in order to see him. He extended his thumb and moved it caressively back and forth over her yielding lips. Almost of itself, her mouth responded with a faint puckering motion.

All at once she felt his two strong hands placed under her arms. Slowly, by sheer muscular strength, he lifted her upward and toward him, as the blanket slipped away. When her hip had been drawn up to his thigh, the pillow having fallen to the floor, and her face was a few inches from his, he held her suspended for a moment like a helpless kitten. His longing eyes surveyed her lovely features, while she placed her hands on his shoulders to steady herself. When she touched him, she saw his eyes wince sensually just before he drew her up the last little distance and their lips met. She felt herself being released to sink down against his chest, and his arms folded snugly around her.

At last securely within his grasp, his lips grew more insistent. He pressed her head back and the kiss became deeper and more intimate. She was devastated by his superior masculine strength, but had no wish to fight it. She sensed a crying need within her, which she had never before experienced, and, frighteningly, the desire to yield to whatever he demanded.

His mouth left hers and traveled to her chin and down her throat. She arched her neck to experience more fully the pressure of his warm, moist lips moving slowly across her sensitive skin.

Her arms were about his neck now, causing some cleavage to show at the V-neck of her sweater. She felt his hold tighten, lifting her upward slightly, and she gave a small gasp when his mouth pressed into her soft flesh. In wayward opposition to her careful upbringing and pristine life-style, she longed to tear the sweater away from her body and expose more of her feminine curves to his seeking mouth.

He returned ardently to her lips, pulling her body toward him in an effort to hold her even closer. The slight change in her precarious position made her feel uncomfortably off-balance, and she pushed herself away briefly, shifting around until she sat upright in the chair next to him. She turned to Peter again, smiling, and met troubled eyes searching hers. He seemed anxious, uneasy that she had pulled away from him, but her smile and shining eyes reassured him. His expression warming, he pulled her close so that the full length of her thigh was against his. "Don't go away," he whispered before he kissed her again.

Lorelei eagerly submitted, wrapping her arms around his neck once more. As the kiss continued, she felt his hand run caressingly down the side of her body to her waist. It moved slowly over her hip and thigh and then back again, making her flesh quiver beneath her thin clothing. Finally, its warmth came to rest under her arm, against the side of her breast.

Her breathing was becoming unsteady from the expert work of his hands. She took her mouth from his and nestled her cheek against the side of his neck. Opening her eyes dreamily, she noticed a hint of soft sunlight coming through the windows on the other side of the plane. She drew herself away from Peter a little and saw he was staring out of their window. Turning her head, she observed that the sunrise was brighter from that direction. When she looked back at him, he seemed miles away as his gaze continued on the brightening sky.

She lifted her small hand to his neck and slid it down his dark, warm skin to just beneath the open shirt collar under his sweater. At her gentle caress, his complete attention was drawn once again to her. With a slow sigh of pleasure, he pressed her close and placed his mouth on hers. Their kiss was long and sweet, and Lorelei wished it would never end.

"Ladies and gentlemen, we hope you've had a pleasant sleep," came a flight attendant's voice over the loudspeaker, startling them from their blissful preoccupation. "A continental breakfast will be served shortly. We will be landing in Amsterdam in approximately one and a half hours," the voice advised.

Lorelei and Peter drew away from each other, groping their way back to reality. She looked up at him and saw his gaze was directed out the window again. But reason was coming back to him. His expression became ominously troubled, then hardened into anger. Fiercely he turned his eyes on her for an instant, and in that moment she saw violence in their blazing depths.

He leaned back in his seat and rubbed his hands roughly over his face. Lorelei cowered as she heard him swear savagely under his breath. He got up, angrily snatching the music he had brought with him, and strode off down the aisle without further notice.

Lorelei was left stunned and alone. Yet she knew what had happened. It was simply history repeating itself. She should have been more wary—not let herself get involved with him again. But now, she realized, it was too late. She was in love—and it was too late.

Tears started in her eyes, and she moved over to the window seat to hide from people who were beginning to move through the aisle. She looked out at the brightening sunshine and tried to compose herself, but the sorry tears kept coming. Why did she let herself fall in love with him? she asked in desperation.

"Boy, Sutherland is sure a grouch in the morning." It was Henry, coming back to take his original seat. Lorelei kept her face to the window. "He practically yanked me out of the chair before I was even awake, saying he wanted his seat back. I never saw him in such a stew."

He looked at Lorelei and immediately seemed to sense something was wrong. He leaned forward. "You're crying! What's the matter?"

Lorelei hid her face in her hands and fought back the urge to sob.

"Calm down. Nothing can be that bad," Henry said, trying to console her. "Did you two have an argument?"

She pulled her hands from her face, wiping away the tears, and shook her head negatively.

Quietly, Henry surveyed her, taking in her mussed hair, the disheveled sweater, and the slightly swollen, sensual look about her mouth. He withdrew his eyes, as if not wanting to invade her privacy any further. But she sensed his thoughts, and with some shame began to tidy her appearance.

After several moments, Henry turned to her and carefully asked, "He didn't . . . take advantage of you, did he?"

Lorelei managed a weak smile. In a small, broken voice she said, "No, Henry. Nothing really happened. Nothing . . . really."

"You love him, though, don't you?" he asked gently.

Lorelei gave a small affirmative nod as her mouth constricted and her eyes refilled with tears.

Henry touched her arm. "I'm sorry, Lorelei. This is probably my fault. I contrived it so you and he would be alone together. That's the last time I try any matchmaking," he vowed with chagrin.

7

The arrival at the vast, modern Amsterdam International Airport was a bewilderment to Lorelei's distracted mind. There was the passport check, customs inspection, greetings from city officials, questions by reporters, all to the accompaniment of departure announcements in English and Dutch over the airport's loudspeaker system.

Her hand luggage, camera, and shoulderbag seemed to grow heavier, and she struggled with them as everyone walked to the buses waiting to go into Amsterdam. While they rode toward the city, momentary glimpses of the flat, verdant countryside, seen through tired, troubled eyes, imprinted into her consciousness.

Finally they were brought to their hotel, where they were escorted to a special room in which refreshments were served along with more greetings and speeches by government officials and other VIPs. Lorelei would have been able to recall very little of what was said. She was totally unable to concentrate on the momentous words attributed to the occasion.

At last, room keys were distributed to the musicians by the hotel's efficient management. Henry and Mary accompanied Lorelei to her room, then proceeded to their own.

Lorelei wearily dropped her baggage to the carpeted floor and noted that the rest of her luggage had already been brought to her room. Somewhat comforted that her belongings were all together in one place again, she sank down onto the bed and lay perfectly quiet for some time. Her body still seemed to vibrate within from the long hours of travel, accentuated by insufficient sleep and the confusion of arrival.

But more than that, it was the recognition of her hopeless love for a man apparently incapable of returning the emotion that sapped her of strength. There was no use in even thinking about it, her conscience repeated over and over.

She had played the fool. She had allowed him to use her once again, and again he had callously cast her aside. He had even had the effrontery to be angry about it, as though she alone were to blame for what had happened between them.

The only thing to do was to try to forget him. But how could she forget a man with whom she worked so closely, a man to whom she longed to run, regardless of how he treated her? Nevertheless, she must; it was the only way. She must avoid seeing him outside of rehearsals and concerts and, when obligated to work with him, try to ignore his presence. The insurmountable pain and difficulty of the task leaned heavily upon her, and she buried her face in the pillow.

She must have drifted off to sleep for some minutes and was startled by a knock at her door. It came again.

"Lorelei, are you there?"

She recognized Henry's voice and hurriedly rose to unlock the door.

"We were afraid you'd gone out," Mary said when the door had been swung aside.

"We're going to grab some lunch downstairs and then take a boat trip down the canals. Do you want to come?" Henry asked.

Still feeling drained, Lorelei responded, "No, I don't think so. I'm kind of tired—jet lag, I guess."

"You know, we only have a few days in Amsterdam," Henry pointed out. "There's a rehearsal tomorrow morning, a concert tomorrow night, and matinee and evening concerts the next day. That doesn't leave much time for sight-seeing. Don't you want to take advantage of this free time?"

Lorelei was hard put to form an argument against his precise reasoning. "There's the formal dinner they're having for us tonight. I thought I should rest up for that."

"How rested do you need to be to eat?" Henry asked.

"Why don't you join us for lunch downstairs, at least," Mary coaxed. "Then afterward you can see how you feel about the boat ride."

"Yes, you hardly touched your breakfast on the plane—not that it was much of a breakfast, anyway. You probably feel washed out because you haven't eaten," Henry added.

It was becoming clear to Lorelei that she wasn't going to be allowed to have her way. She understood, too, that they knew she was upset and didn't want her to be alone, so she felt almost obliged to accede to their kindly efforts to cheer her up. She managed a smile. "Okay, you talked me into it. Let me comb my hair and I'll be right with you."

She did feel considerably revived—physically, at any rate—after lunch at the hotel's sandwich shop and was willing to accompany them on the boat ride. She hoped the distraction would serve to keep her mind occupied and away from her troubles. Henry asked a hotel clerk where the nearest dock was and hustled his two attractive companions off to find it.

Before very long they were seated aboard a sleek, glass-enclosed tour boat cruising gracefully down Amsterdam's placid canals. The tour guide, who was proficient in several languages, described the bridges, buildings, and churches along the way. They silently glided past row upon row of tall, narrow, brick buildings that looked as though they had been squashed together by some giant hands, for there was little or no space between them. The fronts facing the canals were covered with a neat grid pattern of large windows, some covered with curtains, others left bare.

These were formerly the elegant homes of seventeenth-century merchants, now converted into offices, apartments, restaurants, and shops. Thus, while accommodating to the twentieth century, the city had still remained essentially unchanged in appearance since the seventeenth and eighteenth centuries.

The dignity and harmonious order of the city's architecture acted as a soothing balm for Lorelei's distressed state of mind. Soon she was able to feel her innate resilience coming to her rescue. There was so much beauty in the world, so much to see and do, why let one person upset her, she reasoned. Planting that premise firmly in mind, she began to enjoy the rest of the afternoon.

The canal boat headed out into the city's large harbor, busy with freighters and liners from many nations, before returning to its starting point. It was still not too late in the afternoon when they reached the dock again, so at Mary's suggestion, they did some shopping, then stopped for a snack at an irresistible pastry shop they had passed along the way.

They returned to the hotel early enough for Lorelei to have time to bathe and touch up her hair with her curling iron, making use of the transformer she had purchased in Chicago to accommodate the appliance to Europe's 220-volt electrical outlets. She put on a lightweight floor-length dress with a bright floral pattern, applied a little makeup, and soon looked her usual strikingly attractive self.

The dinner, held in the orchestra's honor, was at a restaurant housed in one of the many historic buildings that were formerly canal mansions. The interior had been kept authentically Dutch in design, but had been modernized a bit to accommodate present-day conveniences. Lorelei found herself able to enjoy the atmosphere and the elegant meal immensely while Henry and Mary and a few of the other players kept her pleasantly amused with their easy banter.

She had caught a glimpse of Peter when they entered, but did not see him during dinner. Luckily, Lorelei mused, it was not hard to keep her distance from him in a crowd of over one hundred convivial orchestra members who were out to enjoy themselves.

Since the restaurant was not too far from their hotel, Henry suggested the three of them walk back. It turned out to be a marvelous idea, for the patrician facades and foliage along the canals were floodlit at night, making the old city look beautifully romantic.

After a full Dutch breakfast at the hotel the next morning, a meal comprised of several types of bread, butter, cheese, sliced meat, a boiled egg, and tea, they were off for rehearsal at the Concertgebouw, an historic concert hall considered to be one of the most acoustically perfect in the world.

The object of the rehearsal was not so much to practice the music, since the orchestra was by now thoroughly rehearsed, but to get the feel of the unfamiliar hall and adapt themselves to its particular acoustics. It might be necessary for certain sections to play more forcefully, or more softly, since the sound might project differently here than in their concert hall in Chicago. Individual players might hear themselves in an unfamiliar way as they performed together, and various personal adjustments by the members would have to be made.

From a musical point of view, the rehearsal went quite well. The atmosphere at first stand, however, was distinctly frigid. Lorelei and Peter did not so much as look at one another during the entire rehearsal. When the inevitable time came that Peter needed a pencil, Lorelei frostily laid one on the ledge of the music stand rather than hand it to him. He took it without acknowledgment, as though it had somehow appeared of its own accord. When the rehearsal was over, they had not exchanged even one word and moved off as if each had been sitting alone.

In the afternoon Lorelei accompanied Henry and Mary on a whirlwind tour of Amsterdam, including the impressive Rijksmuseum with its treasury of Dutch paintings that Lorelei greatly admired.

Their last stop was Rembrandt's house, the seventeenth-century brick home where the great artist lived for many years. It now housed hundreds of his etchings and drawings. Lorelei and the Morrisons were upstairs in the room at the front of the house studying drawings displayed in a low glass case when Lorelei happened to look up to see Peter entering the doorway. He was alone. Quietly she turned away before he had time to notice her and walked a few steps to a large window. She pretended to look out onto the street below.

"Hi, Peter. Taking in the sights?" she heard Henry say.

There was a low, indistinct response. She turned her head toward them momentarily, but Peter did not acknowledge her presence, though she felt sure he must have seen her by then. She returned her gaze out the window as the small talk continued, kept alive mainly by Henry and Mary. The sunlight was shining softly into the room from the window, and it shimmered through Lorelei's fluffed mass of loose, flaxen curls, giving her hair a gossamerlike appearance.

After a few minutes she heard the quiet conversation stop. Henry approached her and asked if she was ready to leave. She nodded in agreement and the three of them left, leaving Peter behind.

When they were about a block from the building, Henry looked briefly down the sidewalk behind them, then said to Lorelei in a conspiratorial manner, "What exactly is going on between you and Peter?"

"Nothing, why?" Lorelei was somewhat surprised by the question.

"Well, at rehearsal this morning you both seemed to be on separate icebergs, and just now you certainly kept your distance from one another. Yet, the whole time Mary and I were talking to him, he kept looking in your direction. And he had an odd expression in his eyes—you know, the sick-calf look . . ."

"Oh, Henry, you're imagining things!" Lorelei interrupted crossly. She did not want him to be entertaining any more thoughts of inveigling a match between them.

"No, I'm not. Didn't he, Mary?"

"I did notice a touch of sadness in his eyes," Mary agreed. "In fact, I felt a little sorry for him."

"Besides that," Henry said, "he had a hard time keeping his mind on the conversation. Twice, I had to repeat a question I had asked him."

"He is absentminded," Lorelei pointed out.

"No, it was more than that," Henry maintained. "His attention was focused on you."

Lorelei would have remained silent, but Henry was obviously waiting for a response. "I don't know," she said softly. "I can't understand him. His behavior is erratic and inconsistent and . . . well, I just don't know."

"I don't think Peter understands, either," Mary quietly added.

The first concert was a triumph. The audience cheered and applauded wildly and gave the Philharmonic's concert tour a glorious start. When their stay in Amsterdam was over, the orchestra continued on through the Scandinavian countries, with concerts in Oslo, Stockholm, Helsinki, and Copenhagen, receiving enthusiastic ovations after every performance.

Between rehearsals and concerts, Lorelei accompanied the Morrisons on what Henry referred to as their "tornado tour" of each city. They became expert at seeing as much as possible in the shortest amount of time, with intricate combinations of travel by foot, streetcar, or taxi. In fact they were beginning to be looked upon with awe by some of the other orchestra members who were not so efficient and, therefore, did not see as much.

Meanwhile, the relationship between Lorelei and Peter remained frozen, at least outwardly. She was growing tired of the total silence between them. She wished the strain could be eased a bit so they could discuss occasional problems concerning the music and performances, and thus at least make their business association less awkward. Sometimes she sensed a similar inclination on his part, but neither seemed willing to make the first move, so the chilly distance between them remained.

It was on the morning of the last day in Copenhagen when Lorelei and Mary were standing in the hotel lobby waiting for Henry to cash a traveler's check. They were going to spend the day sight-seeing, planning to return in time for dinner and the concert that night. Lorelei was surprised to see Peter emerge from one of the elevators at the edge of the lobby. He looked about him grimly, and when he saw Lorelei, he moved toward her purposefully.

"We have a problem," he said when he came up to her. "Mr. Markham got word during the night that his brother has died suddenly in New York. He's flying there this morning to be with the family. He thinks he'll be back in time for the first concert in Cologne."

"What about tonight's concert?" asked Henry, who had arrived in time to hear most of the news.

"He wants me to conduct it," Peter said. "Would you and Mary try to contact as many of the others as you can? Perhaps the hotel personnel will help. I'm trying to arrange a late afternoon rehearsal, since I haven't conducted the orchestra recently."

"Sure," Henry replied. "It's still early—probably a lot of them haven't left the hotel yet. Let's get going, Mary."

"Thanks," Peter said, looking after the couple, who were hurrying off. He turned back to Lorelei. "This means you'll have to take my place at first chair."

Lorelei nodded that she understood.

He looked at her intently. "We're playing *Scheherazade* again tonight. You'll have to do the solo violin passages."

Lorelei felt the blood drain from her face. She looked at him in horror. "No, Peter, I can't," she whispered.

"There's no reason why you can't," he said curtly. He took her by the hand and began pulling her toward the elevators, saying, "I'll go over it with you."

Once inside the elevator he asked, "What's your room number?" When she did not answer, due to shock, he shook her and repeated his question.

"Five twelve," she responded after a moment.

"I'm on the seventh floor. Go to your room and get out your violin. I'll be there in a few minutes."

When the elevator reached the fifth floor, he pushed her out and repeated his instructions before the doors closed again. Numbly, she walked to her room. There must be some way out of this, her mind kept repeating. She fumbled for her key, unlocked the door, and walked in. The bed was freshly made and she sat down to think. There must be some way . . .

All too soon there came a knock at her door. She let Peter in. He was carrying music and his violin. Lacking a stand, he propped the pages of music on the knobs of the armoire.

"Get out your violin!" he ordered sharply when he saw she hadn't yet done so.

"Peter, I can't play it. I get too nervous in front of large audiences. I'll ruin it," she wailed.

"Lorelei"—his voice was becoming hard and threatening—"you'll play it, and you'll pay it well."

"Why can't you change the program?" she asked in a shaky voice.

"You remember we had a great deal of trouble adapting to the acoustics in the concert hall here, and a lot of rebalancing was done so the wind section didn't drown out the strings. We're prepared for this program. We can't throw in something we haven't rehearsed in that hall—especially with a replacement conductor," he said sternly. "Now, get out your violin!"

Seeing no alternative, she obeyed him. By the time her instrument and bow were ready, she was near tears.

"Don't cry!" he ordered harshly. "We don't have time for hysterics! Now, start here at the beginning."

They spent more than two solid hours rehearsing the solo parts. He gave her many instructions, played along with her, then had her do it alone. By the time they finished, she felt somewhat more confident about her ability to play it well.

"You're doing fine," Peter said, putting away his instrument. "Go over it several times by yourself. If you have any problem, call me. I'll be in my room going over the scores. The rehearsal should be around four o'clock—I'll let you know for sure."

"Peter, what if I should pass out onstage from fright?" Lorelei asked quite seriously.

"Then we'll leave you lying on the floor, and Henry can play it." He looked at her and gave a little smile. "Don't worry, you'll be all right."

"What if I make a mistake?"

"You won't. Even if you did, the audience and critics would probably be willing to forgive a cute little blonde anything."

This statement somehow cut through her fears and struck a feminist chord within. However her performance might be judged, she wanted it to be on her ability, not her appearance. After all, she wasn't just a stage decoration.

Peter was looking at her as if he knew his words had hit home. "See you later," he said, then left.

Lorelei spent most of the afternoon refining and perfecting the solo passages. As far as her ability to play the music was concerned, she felt fully prepared by rehearsal time. Performing in front of a large audience would be another matter.

When she walked onto the stage, the hall seemed to have enlarged to twice the size it had been when they performed there the night before. Self-consciously, she sat in Peter's usual place. Henry moved up to her second chair position. He and Mary had managed to contact most of the orchestra members, and there were only a few places vacant when the rehearsal started.

Peter, looking pressured and tense, began with a few comments. He repeated the facts creating the situation, then said that he intended to conduct the program in the same manner as Mr. Markham, so there would be no eleventh-hour changes. He recited the order of the program, and Lorelei was relieved that *Scheherazade* was to be played at the end of the first half, before intermission. At least she wouldn't have to look forward to the ordeal through the whole concert.

They began playing through the selected pieces in order. The first went quite smoothly. Peter's manner of conducting was clear and precise, and he did maintain the same tempi and style of musical interpretation as Mr. Markham had used.

Lorelei, as could be expected, was apprehensive when they began *Scheherazade*. The fine quality of sound coming from her violin as she played the first solo passage almost surprised her. Soon, self-confidence began to overcome her lack of assurance, and she found herself performing perfectly through all four movements.

She was greatly relieved, nevertheless, to finally come to the end. Immediately upon finishing the final high, delicate note, she lowered her violin to her lap, dropped her right arm so the tip of her bow scraped the floor, leaned back against the chair and blew out a long sigh of relief that puffed her cheeks.

Applause and scattered laughter brought her to attention, and she looked at Peter. He was standing, hands on hips, staring at her. There was amusement in his eyes and a slight movement of his throat muscles indicated he was stifling a laugh.

"That was fine, Lorelei," he said, "but you'll have to find a classier finish."

She straightened up and looked at him questioningly, not understanding his meaning.

He sat down on the conductor's chair behind him saying, "When I finish playing, do I do this?" He slouched limply in the chair, sprawling his arms and legs in all directions and heaving a big sigh in exaggerated imitation of Lorelei's pose.

There was laughter from everyone onstage while Lorelei cupped her hand over her mouth to hide her embarrassment. Henry, sitting next to her, was in stitches.

When everyone had settled down, Peter resumed the rehearsal, and it continued without further event. When it was over, Lorelei rose to leave. There were only about two hours left before the performance, and she had to return to the hotel to dress, as did everyone. Peter came up behind her as she was walking offstage.

"You played very well, Lorelei—as I expected," he said.

She smiled weakly. "I hope I can do as well tonight. I suppose the hall will be packed again. Peter, how do you keep from getting nervous in front of big audiences?''

''When did I ever say I didn't get nervous? A person would be a fool not to be apprehensive about appearing onstage. I just ignore it and play anyway.''

''I'm afraid I'll freeze and my fingers will stop working. Or maybe I'll skip a line of music.''

''It won't happen,'' he said with assurance. Lorelei wished she could be as confident in that statement as he was.

To her surprise, he accompanied her back to the hotel. Along the way he described a few traditional methods some performers used for controlling stage jitters. ''I've tried them all and none of them worked for me,'' he said as they entered the lobby, ''but you may find them helpful.''

It occurred to Lorelei, belatedly, that Peter was also burdened with having to perform well. In fact, the success or failure of the concert was largely in his hands. Suddenly, she felt guilty. They had been speaking only of her problems. ''The rehearsal went well. You seem to have things under control,'' she said diffidently.

''I hope so.''

They entered the elevator. ''Are you nervous, too?'' she asked hesitantly.

He shrugged his shoulders. ''If the orchestra falters badly because I miss giving a cue or take the wrong tempo, it could well mean the end of my brief career as a conductor. I would start worrying if I thought too much about that possibility—so, I just concentrate on doing the job well.''

The elevator reached the fifth floor. Lorelei lightly touched his forearm with her hand. ''You never make a mistake,'' she said softly, as the doors were sliding open.

She saw a shyness come into his eyes before he quickly dropped his gaze to the floor. He smiled gently and gave her a little push, saying, ''This is your floor.'' Quickly, she walked out into the hall and turned to meet his blue eyes once more before the doors closed again.

Once in her room, she bathed and dressed. She was too nervous to eat, so she didn't bother about having dinner.

Peter's earlier comment about the audience looking upon her as ''a cute little blonde'' influenced her decision to wear her more conservative black dress with the high, old-fashioned collar. She decided it would be better to subdue her hair a bit, so she tied it with a black ribbon at the back of her neck, much as she used to do. Now, however, the appearance was somewhat different, for the curls bunched together and flowed down her long neck like a waterfall instead of hanging limply down her back. The shorter locks in front curled softly about her face. She wished she could have put it up into a roll, as she had once done to please Peter, but was too nervous to tackle the project. After looking at her newly created hairstyle in the mirror, she decided it was, indeed, substantially less flamboyant than the gypsy style and made her look less of a showpiece. Maybe Peter had been right to complain about her hair, she reflected. She wanted to look capable tonight, not cute.

Time sped by. Soon she was backstage at the concert hall again. She supposed that since she was serving as concert-mistress, it would be all right for her to use the private dressing room Peter had been using. The door was slightly ajar, so she pushed it aside and walked in on Peter, who was going over the conductor's scores.

"I'm sorry," she said. "I thought you'd go to the room Mr. Markham used."

"You're right, I guess I should have. I'm a creature of habit," he said with a little smile. His eyes revealed some strain from tension, but otherwise he appeared calm. "How are you holding up?"

"I feel pretty jittery—and tired, all at the same time," she said, setting down her violin case.

"That's normal," he replied.

"How are you?"

"About the same as you."

She lowered her eyes and said in a desperate whisper, "I wish it were all over."

"It will be, soon." He walked over to her and put his arms around her comfortingly. Her arms encircled his waist under his formal black coat and she clung to him like a child, her cheek against his white shirt.

"I feel better when you hold me," she murmured.

"So do I," she heard him say, almost inaudibly.

They held the embrace for a few moments before she had to pull away. "I'd better get ready," she said as she picked up her violin case.

"You can stay here. I'll go to the other room." He collected his music and placed a reassuring hand on her shoulder before he walked out.

In a short time she found herself once more onstage sitting next to Henry, but now the huge empty hall had become a sea of faces. She began to feel panicky and rigidly fought to maintain control of herself.

At the proper time she rose, as Peter always did, to give the signal for tuning. When all instruments had tuned to the oboe's A, an announcement was made in Danish. Lorelei recognized Peter's and Mr. Markham's names in the foreign accent and assumed it was an explanation for the elder conductor's absence and an introduction for Peter. The audience was clearly disappointed, but there was polite applause as Peter strode onstage. After bowing briefly to the audience, he stepped up onto the podium. He picked up the baton and raised his arms as the orchestra brought their instruments to playing position. At his firm downbeat, they began the first piece.

Almost before Lorelei realized it, they had played through it. During the enthusiastic applause that followed, Henry changed the music on their stand to *Scheherazade*. Lorelei mentally braced herself as the applause stopped. She looked to Peter and encountered his questioning eyes. "Are you ready?" they silently asked. She gave a slight nod and placed the violin under her chin.

He turned forward and gave the downbeat. The opening measures of low, heavy chords were played. Eyes moving quickly over the notes, she watched and counted, occasionally looking up momentarily to check the rhythm of Peter's baton.

Soon they came to her entrance. Fingers correctly placed on the string, she played the first high tenuous note and continued through the sinuous solo passage. The notes came forth smooth, clear, and beguiling, as Peter had taught her to play them.

When she had finished the passage, she relaxed a trifle, taking comfort in the knowledge that her fingers still worked, her bow did not catch on the strings, she was still in control. She could actually function under the stress. If she could do the first passage, she knew she could do the rest.

As she and the orchestra continued flawlessly through the four movements, Lorelei became the captivating focal point of the performance. Small, frail, almost childlike with her golden hair and innocent, intent face, she was visually as enchanting as the music being created.

It was with pleasure and no small relief that she played the final notes. The sudden burst of applause took her by surprise. Henry leaned over and patted her on the back as the clamor continued. Remembering herself, she looked up to Peter. He was smiling and eagerly motioning for her to stand up. She did so with painful modesty, keeping her eyes to the floor as the applause increased.

Peter walked over to where she was standing and extended his hand. Quickly, she transferred her bow to her left hand, already holding her violin, and placed her right hand in his. He pressed it warmly between both his hands and looked down at her, smiling, his eyes full of pride. Then, releasing it, he stepped back toward center stage and motioned for the entire orchestra to stand for recognition. As they did so, he turned toward the audience and bowed, then strode offstage for the intermission. The applause still continued, even as the musicians began to file off.

"Am I glad that's over!" Lorelei said to Henry as they entered the backstage area.

"You did a great job, Lorelei! I'm really impressed. You'll be giving old Peter a run for his money from now on."

"No, I won't—" She left off as she suddenly felt herself being pulled away by a firm hand at her waist. She was turned round and shook by her shoulders.

"You did it, kid!" Peter said jubilantly.

He put his hands under her arms and lifted her high off the floor. Holding her violin and bow away from her to protect them as he whirled her about in a half-circle, she exclaimed, "Peter, be careful!"

Gently, his strong arms set her down again. He placed his hands on her slender shoulders and peered intently into her wide, green eyes. "Wasn't I right? Didn't I tell you you could do it?" he exclaimed.

Lorelei smiled shyly and nodded. "I couldn't have done it without you, though," she told him in a small voice.

He chuckled to himself and replied, "Sweetheart, you *wouldn't* have done it without me!" He looked at his watch. "I'd better go over the scores a little before the second half," he said. Giving her a last little shove on the shoulder, he added with sincerity, "You did an outstanding job, Lorelei. I'm proud of you!" He smiled at her, then walked off to his private room.

Lorelei stood rather stunned for a moment. Were her ears deceiving her? Had he really called her sweetheart? She turned around and noticed there were a number of orchestra members standing about, smiling, eagerly observing all that was going on. At her regard, they self-consciously began to move away, except, of course, for Henry.

"Well, well, well!" he said knowingly. "I guess the war between you two is over—*sweetheart!*"

Lorelei smiled. "A battle, maybe. Probably not the war. I'm glad we're talking to each other again, anyway."

"It looked to me like there was a lot more than just talk—"

"Henry," she interrupted with some exasperation, "don't make more of it than it is. He's in good spirits because the first half went well. Tomorrow he may give me the cold shoulder again."

"Okay," Henry said with resignation, but as he moved off, he looked back over his shoulder and added, "Don't forget to invite me to the wedding." A sigh of vexation was the only response Lorelei could make.

The second half of the concert went as well as the first. More relaxed now, Lorelei was able to take better notice of Peter as he conducted. Standing erect and tall, he seemed born to the elegance of white tie and tails. Through the precise, but flowing, movements of his arms and his keen eye, he commanded authority and easily maintained control, extracting a fine performance from the army of musicians under him. He seemed to be so much in his own element, Lorelei observed with deep admiration.

The end of the concert was marked by thunderous applause, and Peter was required to return to the stage for several more bows before the audience was placated. Later, backstage, he was surrounded by dozens of wellwishers offering congratulations. Lorelei was moved to see the adulation, knowing how much he deserved it.

There were also quite a number who came over to compliment Lorelei on her performance, and she thanked them in her shy manner. One was a rather handsome man, with an accent that was distinctly French, whose name she did not quite catch in the clamorous atmosphere. He mentioned something about seeing the orchestra again later on when they got to Paris. She assumed that he was probably somehow involved with organizing their stay in that city. He smiled at her warmly, saying he would look forward to their next meeting, and then walked over to join the group gathered around Peter.

Her innate modesty severely buffeted by so much praise, Lorelei began to feel ill at ease. When she saw the Morrisons leaving, she hurried to catch up with them, eager to escape.

When they got back to the hotel, Henry and Mary asked her to join them for a drink in the bar off of the lobby, but feeling rather wrung out from the events of the long day, she declined and went up to her room.

About half an hour later, her telephone rang. It was Henry saying that most of the orchestra members were down in the hotel bar celebrating and everyone was asking where she was. "Don't you want to come?" he cajoled. Realizing she didn't really want to be left out, she agreed to go down and join them.

As soon as she reached the lobby, she could hear the jovial chatter and laughter coming from the bar. A cheer went up from her fellow players when she entered the dark, crowded room. She smiled and greeted those she passed as she made her way through, looking either for Henry or an empty seat, whichever she came to first.

"Over here, Lorelei!" she heard Henry's voice calling from the other end of the room. As she moved in that direction, she saw he was sitting around a small table with Mary, a couple of violists, and—Peter. She began to wonder what Henry's real reason was for asking her to come down.

When she arrived at their table, she looked around to see if there was an empty chair, and Henry started to rise to give her his. Peter, sitting across from him, quickly put out a restraining arm.

"No, don't get up especially for her, Henry. Women nowadays consider that chauvinistic behavior," Peter cautioned him. "She can sit here." With a sudden, swift movement, he pulled her down onto his lap.

A hearty cheer went up from some overeager male observers close by, Henry being the loudest. Red-faced, Lorelei made a movement to get out of Peter's grasp, but his firm hands at her waist did not allow her to budge.

"Comfortable?" Peter mocked, obviously gloating over his superior male strength.

Still embarrassed, Lorelei kept her eyes on her hands, folded ladylike in her lap, and did not answer.

"Would you like something to drink?" Peter asked in a more congenial tone.

She would have answered no, but noticed a waiter coming toward them and felt obliged to order something. "Ginger ale," she told Peter, remembering what had happened the last time she imbibed an alcoholic beverage with him.

"Really?" he said with incredulity. "A ginger ale for the little girl," he told the waiter with excessive politeness.

He leaned back in his chair and cast his eyes slowly over Lorelei's features. "Is something wrong?" she asked self-consciously.

"You've got your hair different," he answered, drawing his brows together in displeasure. He straightened up and tilted his head to see the bow at the back of her head. She felt a small tug. Suddenly her hair loosened and fell forward over her neck and shoulders, not without help from Peter, who ruffled it with a back and forth movement of his hand.

"That's better," he said pontifically. He took the black ribbon he had removed and draped it carelessly over the top of her head.

"I thought you didn't like my hair down like this," she said, pulling the ribbon from her head and placing it in her lap. "You said I looked like a gypsy."

"I suppose I've gotten used to it," he said, lowering his eyes.

Her ginger ale came. She set it on the table and turned her head toward the others, pretending to be interested in their conversation. All the while her mind was on the strong hands clasped about her waist and her nearness to the man she found irresistibly attractive.

After several minutes passed, Peter shook her a little to regain her attention. "How come you're so quiet?" he asked.

"Tired, I guess," she replied casually as her mind raced. What a stupid question! What was she supposed to say? Didn't he remember what happened the last time they were this close? Had he already forgotten how he had kissed her on the plane? Were they always to carry on as if that never occurred?

A new train of thought entered her brain. Perhaps he had changed his mind and wanted to take up where he had left off. Was that why he was toying with her now?

A number of the others were beginning to leave, remarking about their early flight the next morning to Cologne, Germany. Lorelei and Peter rose to leave also and trailed the others across the lobby to the elevators. They entered one together, and Peter accompanied her out when they came to the fifth floor.

Silently, they walked alone down the long corridor toward her room. Lorelei's heart was pounding. What would he do? Would he kiss her good night? Would he want to come in with her? She cast a furtive glance at his profile. He appeared to be deep in thought and unaware of her—a posture she had seen before. What did he think about when he was like this?

She had to call his attention to the fact that they had arrived at her room. Trying to hide her nervousness, she turned the key in the lock and opened the door, then looked up at him.

He seemed slightly ill at ease. "Good night, Lorelei," he said. He touched her wrist with his fingertips. "Thanks for doing such a fine job tonight. See you tomorrow." He turned and walked back toward the elevators before she could even respond.

She went into her room, locked the door, and threw the key onto the dresser, where it landed with a loud clink. The man was a veritable chameleon!

After a few minutes' consideration, she decided to be grateful that at least they were on friendly terms. There was no reason to wish for anything more, she decided, reminding herself of past resolutions she had made regarding Peter.

8

Mr. Markham rejoined the Philharmonic in Cologne, where the orchestra gave performances over three days. Peter and Lorelei began a period of easy partnership at first stand, their relationship being neither distant nor overly friendly. It was a welcome comfort to Lorelei to have things going normally for a change.

As usual, she spent her free time touring Cologne and its huge cathedral with the Morrisons. At the end of their stay in that city, the orchestra was scheduled to take a day-long boat trip down the Rhine River to Mainz, followed by a short bus trip to Frankfurt, the next city on their itinerary. It was their one totally free day during the entire trip with no scheduled concert duties and nothing to do but relax and enjoy the scenery.

As might be expected, everyone was in unusually high spirits as the orchestra members were waiting at the riverboat dock in the cool morning air. Lorelei was sitting at one end of a bench next to Henry and Mary. Henry was busy reading a tour book he had purchased that gave information on all the castles, towns, and other points of interest they were to see as they traveled down the river. Peter was standing a number of yards away talking to Mr. Markham.

Waiting to board along with the musicians were small groups of tourists of various nationalities, but most were German. As Lorelei sat serenely, her long, slender legs gracefully crossed, absently dangling a delicate low-heeled sandal from one arched foot, she soon realized she had become an object of admiration for three healthy-looking young German men standing some distance away. Tall and fair-haired, they appeared to be around twenty years of age.

"Looks like you have some admirers," said Henry, who of course hadn't failed to notice anything.

"They look a little young to me," Lorelei told him with a chuckle.

"Well, at your age you can't be too choosy, you know," he said, smiling while he waited for her reaction.

"Thanks a lot!" she responded, trying to look indignant through her laughter.

"Why don't you flirt back, or walk over and start a conversation. Might light a fire under Peter," Henry suggested.

"Look, things are going fine right now. I don't want any more trouble," she said firmly.

"Doesn't look like there's much going on to me. He seems to have cooled down since Copenhagen."

"Well, at least we're still speaking to each other," Lorelei pointed out. "That's something."

"Big deal."

Lorelei was spared further analysis of her love life, as the large river steamer they were to board was now drawing up to the dock. In a little while, they were comfortably seated outside on the broad bow of the clean, efficient steamer, and plying up the river. They watched the passing picturesque scenes of tidy, charming German villages scattered along the shore against a backdrop of terraced vineyards and wooded hilltops, some with ancient stone castles perched on top of them.

"It certainly is a gorgeous day for this trip," Mary was saying.

"Yeah," responded Henry, whose nose was in his guide book.

Mary shook her head. "You're going to miss half of what you're so anxious to see if you try to read everything in that book. Why don't you just sit back and enjoy it?" she suggested.

"I guess you're right," he conceded. "If only we'd had more time, I could have read it beforehand." He closed the book and eased back into his chair. For a while, the three were silent as they absorbed the sunshine and the beauty of the passing scenery. But, inevitably, with a mind as busy as Henry's, the quiet did not last.

"By the way, Lorelei," he said, turning to her, "whatever happened when Peter took you back to your room that night in Copenhagen?"

"Henry, don't be so nosy," his wife gently chided.

"Oh, Lorelei doesn't mind," he blithely assured Mary, then turned back and waited for a reply to his question.

Lorelei took a deep breath and let it out in a long sigh, both at being expected to answer such a query, and at the answer itself. "Nothing," she told him.

"What? He was hanging all over you in the bar . . ."

"I know, but on the way up to my room he went into one of his mentally preoccupied states, and then he turned into a perfect gentleman," Lorelei said.

"I wonder what his problem is," Henry mused. "Where is he, anyway?"

"I don't know. I haven't seen him since we boarded. He's probably on the other side of the boat—it seems like he deliberately tries to avoid me sometimes." As she said this, a touch of rancor showed in her voice. "But I don't care," she went on, trying to lighten her tone. "He's too treacherous to get involved with, anyway. It's best like this."

"Now, come on. You don't believe that for a minute."

Lorelei would have refuted Henry's assertion but saw Mr. Markham approaching her. Soon the conductor was next to her, stooping down to speak in her ear, his white hair blowing about in the light wind. "I've been meaning to talk to you ever since I got back," he said. "Peter and many others have been telling me what a fine job you did in Copenhagen. I wanted to give you my thanks and congratulate you. I had every confidence you would come through for us. I'm told that both you and Peter were noted by the critics as having performed extraordinarily well, especially under the circumstances.''

"Thank you," she said, flustered. "It was Peter who helped me do it."

Mr. Markham smiled. "Yes, he has a way of moving people to get things done, doesn't he? Very dedicated. He'll be a great conductor someday. But he didn't play *Scheherazade* for you, don't forget that!''

"All right," she responded with a smile, then grew serious. "I'd like to express my condolences on the death of your brother."

"Yes, it was rather a shock. But he was quite a bit older than me and one has to expect such things. I'm glad for this tour—keeps my mind occupied." He stood up and in a more jovial tone added, "Enjoy the day. It's back to work tomorrow, you know," then moved on toward the other side of the boat.

The next hour or so passed uneventfully. When it became late morning, Henry suggested they go inside and get something to eat. They walked toward the center of the craft and entered the enclosed dining area with enameled wooden tables and large windows all around. Lorelei walked through the doorway first, and soon afterward there was quite a bit of noise and commotion coming from a table she had passed on her left. She turned to see what was going on. Seated, more or less, at the table were the three Germans who had drawn her attention earlier. Strewn about them were numerous empty beer bottles, some even rolling on the floor.

"Fräulein, Fräulein!" one of them exuberantly called to her when she turned around. Quickly she faced the other way again and continued walking until she came to an empty table at about the middle of the room. Here she took a seat facing away from them while Henry and Mary sat down opposite her.

"That's quite a reception committee!" Mary said, laughing.

Lorelei, who was flattered and amused, but mostly embarrassed, could only shake her head in response.

Henry leaned forward with a sly smile and said, "Good timing, Lorelei. Look who's a few tables in back of us. He saw the whole thing."

Lorelei leaned a bit to the side to look past Henry. Farther down the aisle she could see Peter sitting alone at a table with a glass of beer, concentrating on the sheets of music that were spread out in front of him. "Don't tell me he's working!" she said with dismay. "Doesn't he ever quit?"

"Only when you distract him. He didn't look too happy about the response you got from those young Germans," Henry said, obviously pleased.

Bratwurst and beer were ordered for lunch. Lorelei decided to check her handbag to see how much cash she had in German marks. "Oh, no," she exclaimed when she noticed the inside of her bag was a mess of gooey chocolate. She extracted a partially eaten candy bar, which had slipped half out of its wrapper, and laid the soft melting mess on the table. She cleaned her handbag as best she could with a facial tissue, saying ruefully to Mary, "I should have known it would melt in the hot sun. Now my hands are all sticky, too."

"We passed by a door marked 'Damen' just before we came in. You could wash them there," Mary suggested.

"I guess I'll have to," she replied. A thought came to her and she slumped in her chair a bit. "That means I'll have to pass by those Germans again."

"Great!" said Henry. "Make the most of it. Give them a nice smile and raise your skirt a little so they get a good look at your legs."

"Oh, Henry, be quiet!" Lorelei said, ready to throw the chocolate bar at him. She got up and resolutely began to walk toward the entrance, keeping her eyes steadfastly focused on a point beyond the doorway.

"Fräulein, Fräulein! Come here!" came the throaty voices when she neared the Germans' table. As eager hands stretched toward her, she veered away to avoid them, bumping against the table on her other side. Embarrassed, she made a quick apology to those who were seated there and hurried through the door toward the ladies' room.

She took more time than necessary to wash her hands, not being anxious to reappear in the dining area. It had to be done, however, if she was going to eat. Gathering her fortitude, she once more walked through the door into the room. A quick glance at the dreaded group of young men told her they were anticipating her return. One held out his beer glass to her while another spread both arms toward her, palms up, saying loudly as she hurriedly passed by, "Fräulein, I love you!" Blushing with embarrassment, she moved quickly back to her table as people she passed were laughing and smiling.

Henry's grin almost reached to the top of his balding head. "Perfect, Lorelei! You don't need any more coaching from me." He leaned forward conspiratorially. "I glanced back at Peter, and you should have seen the look—"

"Lorelei, what the hell are you doing?" Peter interrupted, having come up from behind Henry. "Do you enjoy parading yourself in front of a bunch of drunken men?" He looked at her sternly, expecting an answer.

"I had to wash my hands," she defended herself. "I got chocolate all over them. See?" she said, pointing to her melted candy bar.

"Oh, that was just an excuse," Henry eagerly interjected. "You know how she likes to flirt."

"Henry!" Lorelei exclaimed, outraged.

"Can't you keep her out of trouble?" Peter demanded.

"She's not my responsibility," Henry disclaimed with a wave of his hand. "*You're* her stand partner."

Lorelei was beginning to feel like a mischievous brat for whom no one wanted to baby-sit. "I'm of age! I can take care of myself!" she proclaimed hotly.

"Well, you're not doing a very good job!" Peter retorted. He took a deep breath and shrugged his shoulders. "I guess I'd better join you," he said with resignation, "so you don't look unattached. I'll be right back." He headed toward his table.

While Mary regarded her with a sympathetic gaze, Henry, looking very smug, gave Lorelei an exaggerated wink of his eye.

"Henry, I thought you said, just before we landed in Amsterdam, that you weren't going to play matchmaker anymore," Lorelei reminded him, narrowing her eyes.

"Me?" he replied with a studied innocence. "No, you must be mistaken. I would never have said anything like that."

Exhaling a long sigh of exasperation, Lorelei lifted her glass of beer, delivered while she was gone. She took a sip and got a mouthful of foam.

Meanwhile, Peter quickly returned and sat next to her, setting his half-empty glass on the table along with his folder of music.

"Don't let me keep you from your work," she remarked coolly.

"I have to eat anyway," he said. "I'll go back to it after lunch."

"Haven't you bothered to watch the scenery at all?" she asked.

"Sure, I look out the window from time to time," he casually replied.

Lorelei was too perturbed to attempt making any further comment. Peter ordered a lunch and their meal progressed without any added conversation from her side. By the time they had finished eating, however, her good humor had been brought around again, thanks to a few amusing quips from Henry. Even Peter had become relaxed and he seemed to be genuinely enjoying both the passing scenery outside and the company.

"Well, what do you say we go out on deck again? The view's better there than looking through this window," Henry suggested. The two women readily agreed. "How about you, Peter? Why don't you join us?" Henry cajoled.

Peter hesitated, eyeing his music. He seemed on the fence, and Lorelei felt he would probably refuse the invitation. Finally he cocked his head to one side and said, "Oh, all right. Why not?" giving her a pleasant surprise.

All four rose and moved toward the entrance. Peter kept close to Lorelei as they passed the young Germans' table. His protective manner had become unnecessary, though, since all three had dozed off, their heads propped up on their hands or resting on the tabletop.

"I imagine they'll be out for the rest of the day," Peter said with disdain. "They spent the whole morning drinking."

"They're just having fun. I was like that once," Henry reminisced. "They'll probably get off at Bingen to see how much wine they can drink. It's one of Germany's chief winemaking cities. In fact our word *binge* comes from Bingen. At least that's what it said in my guide book. I should get that out again."

By this time they were outside, taking seats toward the front of the boat facing the shore. "I wonder where we are now," Henry said as he began flipping through his book.

"How did they know to speak to me in English?" Lorelei pondered aloud, referring to the few phrases the Germans had spoken.

Peter, sitting next to her, said, "Europeans seem pretty adept at recognizing Americans at first glance. Besides you could hardly be anything else."

"What do you mean?" she asked.

"Tall, slender, long legs, stylish clothes, and blond hair," he recited. "You're almost a Hollywood cliché."

Lorelei did not quite know what to make of this comment, but was pleased that he had taken inventory.

"She just draws them like flies," put in Henry, still leafing through his guide book. "Well, I'll be darned!" he said, struck by something he read on one of the pages. "Did you know you have a namesake rock, Lorelei?"

"A what?"

"According to this, there's a steep cliff, four hundred thirty-three feet high, that overlooks some dangerous narrows of the Rhine and is purported to have a remarkable echo. Its location is near Saint Goar, where the river takes a sharp curve."

"And it's called *Lorelei*?" she asked with surprise.

"Yes. There's a legend connected with it. Here, I'll read what it says: 'In the commonest form of the story associated with it, Lorelei was a maiden who threw herself into the river in despair over an unfaithful lover.' "

"How depressing," Lorelei said.

"Wait, there's more," Henry continued. " 'She became a siren and lived on the rock, luring sailors to shipwreck on the reefs below with her seductive singing.' " He looked up from the book. "You see? With a name like that, it's no wonder you can't keep men away." He switched his glance to the man next to her. "Right, Peter?"

"I guess so," Peter answered noncommittally.

Lorelei shot Henry a threatening look, keeping him from pursuing his obvious train of thought. "Have we passed it yet?" she asked, deflecting the subject a bit.

"I don't think so," Henry said, turning to the map in his book. "No, according to this, it would come more toward the end of the trip, but we may be approaching it pretty soon. I think I'll ask around and find out where we are." With that, he rose from the seat and walked away.

Not very much time had passed before he was back again. "I asked Rachel Logan. She's back there with a big map of the river in front of her and has been keeping track of everything. For once she's come in handy. She says that little stone tower up there on the hill"—he pointed to a ruin they were passing—"is Burg Maus, or Castle of the Mouse. Pretty soon we'll be coming to another one called Burg Katz—like cat and mouse. Saint Goar is across the river from Burg Katz, so the Lorelei rock should be right after that."

They eagerly watched the passing shoreline and looked ahead up the river. After a little time they approached another picturesque castle built high atop a steep hill. "I think that's Burg Katz," Henry said. "It was supposed to have been built in thirteen ninety-three." He leaned forward and looked ahead of the ship. "Look, there's a steep cliff coming up. I'll bet that's it!" he said with confidence.

All four eagerly looked toward the massive, sparsely vegetated rock looming before them. "Somehow it doesn't look as romantic as it sounds," Lorelei said, disappointed.

"Why not?" asked Peter.

"It's so big and hulky looking," she said, studying the formation.

Peter grinned down at her. "No, it doesn't bear much resemblance to you, does it?"

She smiled shyly, looking up into his bright blue eyes, noting the humor dancing within them. His dark hair had blown softly over his forehead and he had a kind of contented look that she rarely saw in his face. The lines around his eyes and mouth conveyed a relaxed, good-natured disposition, instead of the somewhat weary, preoccupied look he usually carried. If only he could always be like this, she silently wished.

She looked back to the rock and her mind strayed to her legendary namesake who had thrown herself into the Rhine over a fickle lover. An ominous feeling overcame her, the image of Candy Bradshaw intruded into her thoughts, and her expression grew melancholy.

"What's the matter?" Peter asked softly as he brushed windblown strands of hair from her face.

"I was just thinking I'd hate to live up there," she replied.

Several hours later, all four were having dinner together at a restaurant in Frankfurt. Henry, Mary and Lorelei were discussing what sights they could see the next day, before their scheduled rehearsal in the afternoon. Peter did not take part in the conversation. When their morning tour was finally planned, Henry said, "Why don't you come along, Peter?"

"No, I should do some practicing," he said, but his manner seemed indecisive.

"Oh, come on," said Henry. "How much practicing do you need to do? You already play everything perfectly."

"One can always improve," Peter replied with a smile. "Besides, I don't know if I'd be up to one of your 'tornado tours.' From what I've heard, they sound pretty grueling."

"Lorelei manages to keep up, and she's just a frail little thing. You couldn't be outdone by her, could you?" Henry challenged.

"Well, that's true," Peter answered with masculine conceit. He looked down at his plate and toyed with his fork a bit. "Okay, I'll come," he said at last.

Lorelei averted her eyes, afraid they would reveal the happiness she felt.

The next morning when they all met for breakfast, she half expected Peter to say he had changed his mind. He hadn't. He seemed relaxed as they set out to tour the city. Lorelei was happy just to be near him and not to have to wonder, as she always had, what he did when they were apart. They became a cheerful quartet as they walked about, admiring the sights and laughing at Henry's ever-flowing wit.

9

After Frankfurt, the orchestra continued on to Munich, then Vienna, and after that, Milan. Peter continued to join Lorelei and the Morrisons for every sight-seeing excursion they made. All the while, Lorelei grew more and more aware that her attachment to him was becoming even stronger. She thought she sensed that he liked her company, too. This was not from anything he said, but rather from the way he always looked for her reaction to whatever was happening and his protective manner toward her as they walked around the foreign cities. She began to forget her bitter past experiences with him and dared to hope once more that he cared for her as much as she loved him.

By the time they reached Milan, however, the idyllic ambiance among the four was beginning to show signs of wear. Peter, for no reason apparent to Lorelei, seemed to become restless and discontented. Strangely, there were also subtle signs of animosity toward Henry, which did not stem from any actual dispute between the two men.

"It's really frustrating," Henry was saying, between mouthfuls of fettuccine as they were lunching at a small restaurant. "The Sforzesco Castle and that huge park it's located in took so much time to see this morning that we had to race through the Duomo, which is only the fourth largest cathedral in the world. We didn't even have time to go up to the roof to see the view. Now we have to wolf down lunch so we can squeeze in that church that has Da Vinci's 'The Last Supper' before we have to be at rehearsal.''

"Henry, this isn't supposed to be a vacation,'' Peter interjected sarcastically. "This trip is part of our job—it's work!''

"I had heard a rumor to that effect,'' Henry responded.

"At least we're playing at La Scala opera house, so we don't have to worry about missing that,'' Mary put in optimistically.

"I wish we had more free time scheduled, like that day we took the trip down the Rhine,'' Henry continued. "That was great.''

"All except for that rock I'm named after,'' said Lorelei.

"I thought that was the best part!'' Henry objected.

"It depressed me, finding my name comes from that stark, ominous-looking old cliff. And that story about the girl throwing herself into the river . . .''

"The second part was good, though—where she turned into a siren who lured men to destruction by her seductive singing,'' Henry said. "It suits you.''

Lorelei laughed. "Me, a siren? I can't even sing.''

"Well, all you need to do is say hello in that little-girl voice of yours,'' Henry explained. "You don't have to sing to make men fall at your feet.''

"Oh, Henry! Don't be silly,'' she said, subduing her laughter.

"Sure,'' he went on, "and that's only if they haven't succumbed just from looking at you. In fact, you're so dangerous to men, I think somebody ought to take you out of circulation. Don't you think so, Peter?''

Peter, who appeared to be engrossed in his own thoughts, seemed caught off guard by the question. He opened his mouth as if to speak, then said nothing.

"Now, let's not get carried away, Henry,'' Lorelei quickly interjected, hoping Peter had not caught his drift.

"I told you long ago it would be this way, Lorelei,'' Henry preached. "Don't blame me if you can't handle all the poor beggars crashing on your reefs.''

"Oh, Henry, will you stop . . .'' Lorelei said, becoming a bit peeved.

"'Oh, Henry! Oh, Henry!''' a mimicking voice interrupted. "I don't know how many times I heard 'Oh, Henry' behind me when you two used to sit together,'' Peter complained in a nettled tone.

Henry regarded the younger man thoughtfully for a moment. "You must have well-attuned ears to be aware of what was said two stands in back of you over all the noise at rehearsals.''

A brief but uneasy silence followed as Peter and Henry eyed one another, seemingly communicating on some level that did not require language.

"Maybe we should go and see 'The Last Supper,' '' Lorelei broke in with a small voice, hoping to dissipate the tense atmosphere.

"Go ahead,'' Peter said coldly. "I've seen enough for today!'' Tossing his napkin on the table, he rose and walked out.

"Maybe someday he'll wake up,'' she heard Henry mutter with cutting sarcasm when Peter had left. Looking across the table at him, she realized it was the first time she had ever seen Henry angry. What was happening? Why was everyone suddenly so put out?

She looked at Mary, who still remained calm, as always. Don't worry, Mary's serene and knowing eyes seemed to say. It will all come right in the end.

It was after rehearsal that afternoon when a well-dressed, dark-haired Italian, perhaps somewhat younger than Peter, approached Lorelei as she was putting her violin back into its case. He apparently was some representative of La Scala, and she had seen him looking at her earlier. While he was outwardly quite charming as he made polite conversation, the way his eyes traveled over her body clearly indicated to Lorelei that he had something else on his mind.

"Perhaps you will care to join me for a late dinner after the concert tonight?" he said in heavily accented English.

"No, I . . . uh . . . this tour has been so strenuous, I make it a point not to stay out late," Lorelei prevaricated.

"But perhaps for this one time, you could make an exception?" he persisted.

"No, thank you, really I can't . . ."

"Actually, the young lady has a date with me tonight. She's too polite to say so," Peter interrupted as he approached from behind and put an arm around Lorelei.

"I see," said the Italian with chagrin. *"Scusi,"* he added, and with a slight inclination of his head, moved away.

"Thanks, Peter," Lorelei said, grateful for his intervention.

"I didn't think you'd want to tangle with him. You should be more careful how you dress. There've been men looking you over all day," Peter said crossly, indicating the form-fitting, scoop-neck knit top she wore over her skirt.

"It was pretty warm today," she said in her own defense.

"Well, if you don't want men like him following you around, you'd better learn to suffer the heat," he said with finality.

Later, when she was alone in her hotel room, a mischievous idea entered her head. *He did say that we had a date, even if it was only to shoo off the other man,* she thought. *Why not take him up on it?*

When the concert was over that night, she coquettishly cornered him as he was leaving. "So, where are we going tonight, Peter?"

"What?" he said, looking at her blankly.

"Earlier you said we had a date tonight."

"That was only to get rid of that Italian," he said quietly, but firmly.

"Oh, but I had been planning on it," she said, pretending disappointment.

Peter's eyes hardened. "Lorelei, don't play a flirt with me. There's something I'd better make clear to you. We may sit together and even sight-see together, but we are not 'going together.' Ours is a professional friendship, nothing more. Do you understand?" He was deadly serious.

"Of course. I was only kidding," she said, managing to feign a careless demeanor.

"I hope so," he replied curtly, then turned on his heel and left her.

A wave of embarrassment swept over her, made all the more acute by the knowledge that she had brought it on herself. *He might have been more tactful,* she thought spitefully.

By the time she was in her hotel room, spite and shame had given way to hopeless depression. He had rejected her once again, this time quite clearly and without emotion. There was no longer any question of where she stood, and though there was still no explanation for his past behavior, now it was certain she had no future with him. She wished she had stuck to her past resolutions and put him out of her mind. She was now more attracted to him than ever and forgetting him would only be that much more difficult. Oh, why hadn't she kept her guard up? Why did she always fall so easily under his spell, leaving herself so open to his inevitable rejection? Had love so weakened her that she had lost her common sense? Even her self-respect? Now she had stooped to trickery to try to get a date with him! Well, if she had no more pride than that, she deserved what she got, she reproached herself, even as the tears of misery fell.

The orchestra flew on to Paris, where it was to give performances over several days. The tour was nearing an end at last. There was only London left on the itinerary, then home to Chicago. Lorelei was not sorry to see the trip coming to an end. Once she was home she would not have to see Peter so much and maintaining a "professional friendship" with him would not be such a strain.

In Paris the touring party became a threesome again when Peter showed no interest in accompanying them. Lorelei sorely missed him as she and the Morrisons spent time exploring the romantic "City of Light" during the first couple of days after their arrival. Notre Dame, the Eiffel Tower, the Champs-Élysées— she wished she could have shared them all with him. Paris was the last place she would have wanted to be left unattached. Paris, she had always heard, was made for lovers. Indeed, it seemed so to Lorelei. With the breathtaking grandeur of its broad avenues, stately white buildings, lovely fountains, and famous landmarks, it was surely the most beautiful city she had ever seen.

After a day that had included a rehearsal in the morning and an exploration of the Louvre in the afternoon, Lorelei decided to bathe and wash her hair to look fresh for the concert that evening. She was standing in front of the mirror in her bathrobe finishing a blow-dry of her hair when she thought she heard a knock at her door. She turned off the hair dryer and listened. It came again. Overlapping her robe to cover herself better and tying the belt tighter around her waist, she walked to the door and opened it.

"You're finally back," Peter said, giving her a preoccupied glance before unceremoniously walking into her hotel room. "I made several bowing changes in the Beethoven and wanted you to be aware of them before the concert. I've already seen most of the other violinists."

He spread out a copy of the music on her dresser. Lorelei quietly stood next to him as he explained the changes he wanted made. "Any questions?" he asked when he had finished, looking directly at her for the first time.

"No, I think I understand," she said, raising her eyes to his. He was staring at her strangely, as if suddenly his mind were no longer on the music, which only a moment ago had been of such importance. She looked at him questioningly.

"Is that . . . perfume you're wearing?" he asked, his eyes motionless upon her.

Puzzled for a moment, she replied, "I just washed my hair. It's probably the scented shampoo."

His eyes traveled over her hair, loose and free from the blow-drying. "It looks different," he said softly, raising a hand to stroke the locks, which fell smoothly about her neck and shoulder.

"I haven't curled it yet," she responded, becoming uneasy under his touch. She drew back slightly, but he took a step toward her. The blue eyes moved down to her robe. She sensed from the subtle change in his expression that he had become fully aware she had nothing on underneath. His eyes moved back to hers and she saw the longing in them she had seen before. With both arms he drew her against him. "No, Peter," she whispered just before his mouth covered hers in a hard embrace.

He kept her locked against him for a long while as his hands moved roughly over her. When at last he released her, the expert work of his hands and lips had left her weak and only dimly aware of what was happening. She did not even realize that her robe had loosened from around her body and the overlapping lapels she had been so careful to secure had pulled apart, revealing the soft inner curves of her breasts. Shakily, she took in a deep, long breath as Peter's deft hands easily slipped under the material to caress the warm softness beneath. As his mouth came down upon hers again he slid his hands up to her shoulders and pushed away the robe so that it fell down her back and arms, leaving her uncovered to the waist, where the tie belt still held.

She felt herself being lifted off the floor by two strong arms. He carried her to the bed and laid her upon it crosswise. Urgently he tugged at the buttons of his shirt and then pulled it apart, exposing his muscular chest covered with dark brown hair. He threw himself down upon her, pinning her beneath him as he kissed her passionately.

Perhaps it was her innocent, instinctive fear of such unbridled male desire that quickly brought Lorelei to her senses. With all her might she tried to push him off, but her strength was inadequate.

"Peter!" she cried after she had managed to wrench her mouth away from his. "Peter, stop! Don't do this!" She was able to direct a sharp blow to his ear that, together with her cries, seemed to bring him to reality. He pushed himself away and she quickly sat up, pulling her robe protectively about her. She eyed him warily as she tried to control her labored breathing. He looked at her as if stunned. Soon his expressive eyes unguardedly revealed an inner torment of anger and disbelief. He drew away and stood up, steadily keeping his eyes upon her small huddled form as if she were a cunning enemy.

"By God, you *are* a siren, aren't you!" he said in a low, hoarse voice. "Work your sorcery on someone else, will you?" With three long strides he reached the door and slammed it shut behind him.

Tears followed shock as Lorelei sat alone on the bed, still clutching the robe about her with trembling hands. That he could have used her this way! And what right had he to blame her? She was the one who had been taken advantage of and forced to defend herself! He had actually tried to make love to her. Yet a few days ago he had wanted her friendship only. Some friend, to treat her in such a way!

As she dried her eyes, a new determination began to steel her faltering strength. This newest episode with Peter was far too serious to try to push aside, as she had always done up to now. She had had enough of his unpredictable behavior; she vowed to confront him.

By the time she was knocking on his dressing room door before the concert that night, she was mentally well prepared to face him. "I want to speak to you," she said with unaccustomed firmness when he had opened the door.

Anger edged his voice and blazed in his eyes. "I'm preparing for the concert. Don't bother me now!" He started to shut the door, but she pushed against it and managed to wedge herself halfway over the threshold between the frame and the door.

"I'll talk to you later!" he said, anger increasing as he tried to force her out.

Using all the strength she could muster to keep her ground, she replied, "Later means never, doesn't it? No, Peter, you'll speak to me now! Let me in, unless you want the rest of the orchestra to hear this!"

She saw his eyes flare at her just before he turned away, allowing her to enter the room. She shut the door and turned to him, but he kept his back to her and picked up his violin and bow.

"You owe me an explanation, Peter."

"For what?"

"For what! You know as well as I do what happened in my room this afternoon."

"You're making a mountain out of a molehill. Nothing happened of any consequence," he said coldly.

"Only because I stopped you!" she said, incredulous at his callousness. "In Milan you said there was nothing between us. Today you almost forced yourself on me! Why, Peter?" It was all she could do to keep emotion from getting the better of her.

He turned to face her in a cold rage, barely kept under control. "What do you expect to happen when you come to the door half dressed? I'm only human!"

"Half dressed! I was wearing a robe . . ."

"Which you didn't take any pains to keep around you."

"You're twisting the truth! You're the one who took it off!" she accused, beginning to cry in spite of herself.

"You didn't do much to prevent me, did you? Now, leave me alone!" He turned away and began to play forcefully on the violin as if to shut her out. She grabbed at his arm to make him stop.

"Why do you treat me like this, Peter? It isn't the first time you've held me and kissed me and then become angry and tossed me aside!"

"Get out of here!" he raged.

"I want to know why!" she exclaimed, undaunted.

"How am I supposed to resist a flashy blonde who continually flaunts herself around me in seductive clothes, always playing the innocent with that little-girl voice! You get what you ask for!"

"That's not true," she said, shock turning her voice to a whisper. "You're making me out to be cheap!"

"Get out!" he cried. "Don't come near me anymore!" He began to play again, though the sounds he produced were uneven and lacking control. She watched him a moment, her anger mounting at the disparaging innuendos he had made about her character. His continuing disregard provoked her beyond control. With a quick movement of her arm she reached up, grabbed the upper part of the bow as it moved over the violin, yanked it from his hand, and threw it to the floor. It landed sharply, loosening some of the horsehairs, which fanned out over the carpet.

Peter grew livid with an anger that bordered on violence. "Have you lost your senses! Do you know how much that bow is worth?"

"Yes," she hissed, almost shaking with rage, "and if you ever come near me again—if you so much as lay a finger on me—I'll break it over your head!

Your precious violin, too!'' She turned abruptly, stepping over the wounded bow as she headed toward the door. She faced him again, briefly. ''I hate you, Peter! I hate you with all my heart!'' she said, glaring her wrath at him before she slammed the door in his face.

Somehow they made it through the concert, each in isolated anger as they sat together. Peter seemed to have the most difficulty in functioning. His usually precise manner of playing had become very unsteady. At one point Lorelei noticed he lost his place momentarily and missed a full measure of the music before he regained himself. She was glad for the orchestra's sake that he did not have any solo passages to play that night.

Afterward, when she was backstage putting away her instrument, she saw a man, who looked vaguely familiar, coming toward her from Mr. Markham's dressing room. He had apparently been one of the usual bevy of well-wishers who greeted the renowned conductor after every performance. Wracking her brain, she tried to remember where she had seen him before, as he continued to approach. He was quite handsome, with brown hair that was graying at the temples.

''We meet again, Miss Lawrence,'' he said with a rich and beautiful French accent, pronouncing her name with equal emphasis on both syllables.

''Yes,'' she said, still unable to place him.

''I fear you don't remember me,'' he said with a smile. ''We met briefly backstage in Copenhagen . . .''

''Oh, yes! It was the night that Peter . . . that Mr. Markham was away . . .''

''And you played *Scheherazade* so beautifully.''

''Thank you,'' she said diffidently. ''I'm sorry, I don't think I ever caught your name—it was so noisy backstage that night.''

''Indeed it was. My name is Marc Forestier.''

''Marc Forestier . . .'' she repeated, her voice trailing off in disbelief. ''The famous pianist?''

''I'm afraid so,'' he said with a sympathic laugh, amused at her charmingly candid reaction.

Lorelei blushed. ''I'm so embarrassed. I have one of your recordings. I should have recognized you from your picture on the album cover.''

''It's perfectly understandable. I never photograph well,'' he assured her. ''Tell me, have you seen much of Paris during your stay here?'' he said, beginning to move with her toward the exit door.

''Oh, yes. I've been sight-seeing every day. It's very beautiful.''

''Even more beautiful at night. Have you been out at all in the evening?'' he asked.

''No, just to go back and forth from the concert hall.''

''If you will permit me to escort you, I would be happy to show you the sights. You really shouldn't leave Paris without a ride down the Seine in a *bateau-mouche* when the city is aglow with lights.''

The prospect sounded enchanting, and since Lorelei had nothing better to do than go back to her hotel room and mentally rehash her falling-out with Peter, she decided to accept. ''It sounds wonderful . . .'' she began.

''Pardon me,'' interrupted an excessively polite male voice. ''So nice to see you again, Mr. Forestier,'' Peter said, extending his hand.

"Ah, Mr. Sutherland. The pleasure is all mine. The performance was outstanding tonight . . ."

"It's very kind of you to say so," Peter said with oppressive charm. "I have to speak to Miss Lawrence for a moment. Will you excuse us?"

"But of course. I'll wait for you here," Forestier told Lorelei as Peter was grasping her tightly by the wrist. He pulled her away quite a distance.

"What do you want?" she asked, angrily pulling her arm out of his grip.

"You aren't going out with him, are you?" Peter asked urgently, apparently having eavesdropped on their conversation.

"Why not?"

"That man is in his middle forties. He may be old enough to be your father. And he's not only known for his musical talent, but also for his dalliances with a large assortment of women."

"He seemed nice enough to me. Besides, what do you care who I go out with?"

"Of course he's charming," Peter said, ignoring her question. "Otherwise he wouldn't attract so many women. You don't know what you may be getting into—you're very naive!"

Now she was naive! The variety of his impressions of her was certainly perplexing! "He's just going to show me around the city," she said, growing tired of arguing with him.

"Sure, and then he'll want to show you his apartment. You're so innocent, you can't even figure that out," he said in an emotional tone of voice that resembled anger, but was more like desperation. "How will you take care of yourself when you're there alone with him and he wants you to stay the night?"

"You may recall," she said hotly, "that I've lately had some practice fighting off an overly aggressive male. Thanks to that experience, I'm quite confident I can handle myself. Besides, I may *want* to spend the night with *him*," she added tauntingly, hoping to repay the hurt he had given her.

The stricken look in his eyes told her she had hit her mark. It surprised her. She hadn't thought she had the power to hurt him. He seemed so wounded that she wanted to comfort him, to tell him the truth—that she hadn't really meant what she said.

"Lorelei," he implored, taking her hands in his, "don't go with him! Please don't go with him!"

"Does it really matter to you, Peter?" she asked earnestly, looking into his eyes.

"What?" He seemed confused and dropped her hands. "Matter? Of course not. I . . . I'm just trying to warn you for your own good. I don't give a damn what you do!" He seemed angry again. "Go on! Go with him if you like! What the hell do I care!"

Lorelei watched him in an almost clinical way. "Good night, Peter," she said softly, before turning away from him. As she walked back toward Forestier, she heard Peter call her name from the distance she had put between them. Her eyes moistened slightly, but she did not turn around.

She smiled when she reached Marc. "I'm ready to go now," she said, taking his arm. Together they walked out into the cool night air along a street bright with lights and cars rushing by. Somehow it seemed unreal.

"What would you like to see first?" Marc asked a few minutes later as he was assisting Lorelei into his expensive-looking sports car.

"Oh, anywhere you want to go," she said, trying to make herself interested in their excursion. "I'd like to see the Eiffel Tower. I've always seen pictures of it at night with the lights shining on it."

"Very well, we'll go in that direction, but I'll take the most scenic route," he said, smiling.

He drove first to Place de la Concorde, the large square near the Tuileries Gardens where the Egyptian obelisk is located. Lorelei had seen it during the day, but now it was much more beautiful with lights making the needlelike structure stand out against the darkness and playing on the water gushing from the fountains.

He drove down the wide and elegant Champs-Élysées toward the Arc de Triomphe, the magnificent huge stone arch built to commemorate Napoleon's military victories. It was awe-inspiring when illuminated by bright floodlights. From there he drove toward the Seine and found a spot to park. After helping Lorelei out of the car, he led her down a street and then up some steps. They came around a building and then suddenly it was there—the Eiffel Tower shining brightly against the clear night sky, just on the other side of the river. In front of them the Trocadero fountains played as if vying for attention. Lovely though they were, they were no match for the graceful tower. It stood there, quietly beckoning, like a huge, glittering toy. Shehad been impressed when she had seen it in the daytime, but now it seemed magical.

"It's just beautiful," she said in a hushed voice.

"Yes, it is," Marc said, as if pleasantly surprised. "Living here, I never pay much attention to it, but with you I see it through new eyes." He was looking at Lorelei now, studying her wide-eyed expression as she gazed at the famous landmark.

After several more minutes, he took her gently by the arm and led her down to the riverbank to stroll along the cobblestone walkway.

"I've never been to Chicago. I imagine it must be an attractive city," Marc said.

"Nothing like this," Lorelei responded.

"Oh, come now. What about all those—what do they call them—skyscrapers?"

"Yes, we do have those. It is kind of pretty along Lake Shore Drive, especially at night. The lake is on one side and the tall buildings, all lit up, on the other. That's where Peter lives . . . on Lake Shore Drive. . . ." Her voice trailed off as Peter's image entered her mind. Catching herself, she shook off the unwelcome thoughts.

"Here we are," Marc was saying. They had arrived at a boat dock along the river. He bought a couple of tickets and hurried her toward a sight-seeing boat, the *bateau-mouche,* that was just about to depart. He assisted her in boarding, which was a little difficult with her long black gown, and led her to two empty seats.

As the boat moved along, he pointed out various buildings and bridges. The lights from the structures reflected on the tranquil waters in a peaceful, multicolored glow.

To maintain conversation and keep her mind off other matters, she asked Marc a few questions about himself. He told her he had just finished a concert tour of his own, which was why he had been in Copenhagen several weeks ago. He was a Parisian by birth and had traveled widely.

As she listened to him speak, she decided she liked him. He was pleasant, calm, and easy to be with. Perhaps it was due to his age, but she sensed he had come to terms with life and had a great deal of understanding. He was also experienced, charming, and sophisticated, however, and it was not hard for her to believe that many women found him attractive.

When the boat ride was over, he suggested they have some coffee at one of the outdoor cafés along the Champs-Élysées. He knew of one that would still be open. Lorelei readily agreed.

In a little while they were sitting at a small table, in the night air, watching occasional passersby along the magnificent tree-lined avenue.

"I know it isn't polite to ask," Marc was saying, "but how old are you, Lorelei?"

"Twenty-seven," she answered.

He shook his head slightly. "You seem even younger." He fingered his cup absently, as if toying with some idea. Lorelei wondered a bit uneasily what he had on his mind.

"I have an apartment near here on the Avenue Foch. It overlooks much of the city, including the Eiffel Tower. We could be there in a few minutes. Would you . . . like to see it?" He seemed slightly ill at ease as he spoke the last words.

Even though she had been forewarned, Lorelei was rather shaken. She had never actually been asked to a man's apartment before, and the fact that the man was famous, a "star" of the musical world, was even more unsettling. Keeping her eyes cast downward, she said, "No . . . thank you . . . but . . . I don't think I'd better."

Marc smiled and placed a hand over hers. "Somehow I thought you would say that. You can't blame a man for trying."

Lorelei smiled back at him and relaxed a bit, glad that he accepted her refusal without argument. Marc regarded her thoughtfully.

"It's strange," he said, "but . . . in a way I would have been disappointed if you had agreed."

"You mean you didn't really want me to come?" she asked, conscious of a perverse pang of disappointment within.

"Oh, yes, I did. You can't realize how much. You're very beautiful . . . enchanting. I haven't been able to take my mind off you since I saw you on stage in Copenhagen. But part of your charm is your sweet innocence, and, though I want you, I . . . I don't want to take that away from you."

It caused Lorelei some embarrassment to know that her lack of experience was so obvious. "It's funny," she said ruefully, "when you're innocent, everyone wants to keep you that way. I've noticed that even other women won't tell certain jokes around me."

Forestier laughed. "I have a feeling you won't remain that way for long. I'm not the only moth who's attracted to your flame. Peter Sutherland, for instance. He didn't want you to come with me tonight, did he?"

"No," she answered after some hesitation. "I'm sorry, I was hoping you hadn't seen that."

"Oh, I can't blame him. I would want to keep you for myself too, were I as deeply in love as he is."

"You think he loves me?"

"It was obvious during your performance in Copenhagen. And tonight, well . . ." he said, spreading his hands outward in a self-explanatory gesture.

"He keeps saying that there's nothing between us."

"Then he's lying—either to you or himself."

It was almost 3:00 A.M. when they arrived back at Lorelei's hotel. "I'm sorry to have kept you so late. You're flying on to London tomorrow, aren't you?" Marc said apologetically, as they stood outside her room.

"Maybe I can sleep on the plane," she said. "I've enjoyed our evening together, Marc. Thank you."

He looked at her warmly. "I don't like to say good-bye to such a lovely thing. If only I had been a little younger and you. . . . Well," he said, laughing at himself, "*c'est la vie!* Perhaps we will meet again one day. I wish you well, Lorelei." Taking her by the waist, he kissed her gently on the mouth, and after a last lingering look, he left her.

She was smiling softly to herself as she entered her room and turned on the light. She walked to the window and looked dreamily at the Paris streets below.

A sharp knock sounded at her door. "Who is it?" she asked when she had reached it.

"Peter. Let me in."

"Not now—it's too late!"

"Let me in!" he said forcefully, rattling the doorknob.

She began to fear that he would disturb other hotel guests and opened the door cautiously. He burst into the room.

"It's three o'clock! Why did you stay out so late with him?" he said in a voice that was dangerously low. He was wearing blue jeans and a disheveled shirt that was half undone. His dark hair was mussed and his red-rimmed eyes had a wild, anguished look about them.

Lorelei's instincts warned her to take care, but something compelled her to stand up to him. "How do you know what time I came in?"

"My room is just down the hall."

"What did you do—listen at the door?" she exclaimed with disgust.

"Yes! Where did you go with him? What did you do?" he said as if ready to lunge at her.

"Why do you want to know?" she shot back.

He rushed toward her and grasped her upper arms in a bruising grip. "He asked you to his apartment, didn't he? Didn't he?" he said, shaking her like a rag doll.

"Yes!" was all she could get out.

He stopped the violent motion and looked at her, his eyes filled with pain. "I knew it," he said in a choked voice. "Why did you do it? Why?" Before she could give any response, he was shoving her back toward the bed and pushing her down onto it. "You little slut!" he said viciously. "You wouldn't let *me* touch you, but you'd give yourself to a perfect stranger! If he can have you, so can I!'' He began tearing at her dress, ripping a sleeve.

"No, Peter! Let me explain . . .'' she said as she tried to fight him off.

"I don't need explanations! I know what you are!'' His fingers found the zipper at her back and pulled it down. He pushed the unfastened dress off her frail shoulders, revealing a delicate, black lace bra. "I see you were dressed for the occasion,'' he said with cruel sarcasm.

Lorelei began to cry as her exhausting efforts to defend herself were proving completely inadequate against his superior strength. "Peter, please listen!'' she pleaded. "Nothing happened!''

He stopped and looked at her. "You said he asked you to his apartment!''

"Yes, but I didn't go.''

"Then what exactly did you do all night?'' he said tauntingly.

"We went around the city . . .''

"I don't believe you. A man like that wouldn't waste his time showing you the sights!''

"It's true!''

"And I suppose he just accepted it when you refused to go to his place . . .''

"He did! He's a gentleman—not like you!'' she choked out.

"Was he a gentleman in bed, too?'' he said caustically as he resumed pulling at her dress with even more violence.

With no more stamina left to fight, she began to sob. "I didn't sleep with him,'' she cried, almost incoherently. "I've never been with any man!'' She covered her face with her hands and wept uncontrollably. "I've never . . . been with any man . . .''

He did not touch her for several minutes as she continued sobbing. Then, gently, he took her into his arms and held her trembling form against him, burying his face in her tousled hair. "I'm sorry, darling, I believe you,'' he whispered. "Don't cry. I won't hurt you.''

She wiped away her tears with her hands. Slowly, he lifted his head and she looked up into his face. His eyes were wet and a tear was coursing down his gaunt cheek. "I'm sorry,'' he repeated, looking gravely into her eyes.

"Peter,'' she implored, "why do you do these things?''

He lowered his eyes and slowly got up. He walked toward the foot of the bed and then turned toward her. "Because I'm in love with you,'' he said softly. "I'm so in love, I don't know what to do anymore.'' He sat down on the corner of the bed at a little distance from her and continued. "I guess I've loved you for a long time, only I didn't know it. Even before we sat together at the same stand, I found you distracting. That was the real reason I didn't want you to be promoted, though I couldn't admit it to myself. Still, I knew I wouldn't be able to think straight with you so close. And I was right; my mind was so much on you, I became forgetful about my work. Then''—he sighed in consternation and looked at her—"you had to turn yourself into a beauty. It became hopeless. Though I tried to fight my wanting you, something would always draw us together and my desire would get the better of me. I'd blame you and become angry and, naturally, you'd stop speaking to me. How I hated those cold silences between us! And I began to be jealous of any man who came near you. Even Henry.''

"Henry?'' she said with surprise.

"Yes, he always makes you laugh. I felt I had to vie with him for your attention. And I began to dislike him because he saw through me. He knew I loved you."

"But you kept denying that you cared for me," she said.

"I desperately wanted to believe that I didn't. But tonight, waiting for you to come back, imagining you with Forestier—I had to finally admit to myself that I do love you, more than I ever thought it was possible to love a woman."

Lorelei smiled as tears streamed down her cheeks. Quickly pulling her torn dress over herself again, she moved to sit next to him. "I love you, too, Peter," she said, gently grasping his arm as he looked down at her.

He kissed her cheek and wiped away her tears. "I know you do, sweetheart," he said softly. "That's what makes this so difficult. I don't want to hurt you any more than I have already."

"What do you mean?" she said, her expression becoming serious.

He cast his eyes to the wall across the room. "The problem is that I don't want to get married." He looked back at her as she withdrew her hands from his arm. "That's why I tried so hard to convince myself that I didn't care for you. It wasn't part of my plans to become seriously involved with a woman."

Lorelei looked at him questioningly. "I don't understand . . ."

He took a deep breath. "When I was still very young—fourteen or fifteen— I decided to make music my career. Even then, I was ambitious. I decided I wanted to make it to the top of the profession. I began to make plans in order to accomplish my goals and I've stuck to them with good results all these years. My plans, however, never included a wife or any other sort of permanent involvement with a woman. I wanted to remain independent so I wouldn't have to make compromises that might affect my career. Wives have a way of changing things, you know. Besides, I devote most of my time to music, so any woman would undoubtedly feel neglected and jealous of my work. I'm just not good husband material."

"What about Candy?" Lorelei asked.

"Who? Oh. . . ." He rose and walked to the window. "She was just the latest in a long line of women I've known. I never intended to cut myself off completely from the opposite sex—I'm still a healthy male with normal needs. But I always chose women who were sophisticated and willing to take such relationships lightly. I made it clear to them from the beginning that I had no intention of becoming serious. Of course, there were always a few, like Candy, who wound up wanting me to come home and meet Daddy," he said with derision.

"I thought she was in love with you."

"Candy? She's mostly in love with herself—a spoiled brat. She was just upset that I wouldn't be at her beck and call like everyone else she knows." He looked away from the window and back at Lorelei, who was staring at the floor. "All that has nothing to do with you," he said in a softer tone. "You're the girl I never wanted to meet. With you there can only be marriage, and that I can't offer you. It would mean disaster. You understand, don't you?"

"Yes," she said, her voice barely a whisper. "What do we do?"

"I don't know, Lorelei. I wish I did." Both were quiet for some minutes, then Peter broke the silence. "Perhaps now that we understand one another, we can deal with it better. Maybe we can just continue as we have been—working together . . .''

"A professional friendship?" she said, quoting the term he had used in Milan.

"No, more than that. I'm in love with you . . ."

"A platonic love affair?"

"Yes, I suppose . . . something like that."

"How do we prevent it from developing into more than that? Do you really think we could keep it platonic forever—based on past experience?" she asked.

"I don't know. We can try . . ."

Lorelei was sitting rigidly on the edge of the bed. "It won't work, Peter," she said in a tight voice. "The best thing for us to do is to never see each other again."

He paled and looked at her with unbelieving eyes. "What! You can't mean that!" In a moment he was kneeling on the floor in front of her, grasping her hands in his. "Don't say that, Lorelei. We can work it out . . ."

"I don't see how, Peter," she said in a small voice as tears formed in her eyes.

"Look, sweetheart, it's very late. We've had a bad day and we're both upset and tired, so let's not think about it any more tonight. We'll talk more tomorrow, okay?" He brightened his tone of voice. "We can sit together on the plane. You won't mind being with me instead of Henry, will you?" he said, as if attempting to distract a crying child.

Her mouth formed the word *no* and she gave a tremulous smile, even as tears flowed down her cheeks.

He leaned forward and put his arms around her, holding her close. "Everything will work out all right, you'll see. Don't cry anymore," he said softly, his head next to hers. "I love you so much." Gently, he kissed her lips and after admonishing her to get some sleep, he quietly left her room.

Later, in bed and alone in the darkness, Lorelei for the first time thought deeply about her future. Her former, romantic nature had suddenly vanished; she dealt only with harsh reality now. She had learned that nebulous, wishful thinking could not make things right. She must at last take her life into her own hands; she must make plans of her own. Hours later, when the final, fearful decision had at last been made, she fell asleep.

10

"Well, look what we have here!" Henry said the next morning as they were waiting to board the buses to take them to the airport. "You two holding hands? Did I miss something?"

"I'm going to take her away from you for this flight," Peter said, releasing Lorelei's hand and putting his arm around her, "if you can spare her."

"Oh, be my guest!" Henry said jovially, glancing at Lorelei. She gave a little smile, but there was a steadfast seriousness in her eyes that was not lost on Henry. He looked at her curiously and she dropped her gaze to the ground.

Through the bus ride and the wait at the airport, Peter also seemed to be aware of the subtle change in Lorelei and he hung about her vigilantly. When they finally were sitting alone together on the plane, he asked, "What's the matter, Lorelei? Is it what we discussed last night?"

"Yes," she answered and after a pause, added, "have you thought of any solutions?"

"I think we should just go on as we have been," he said. "We'll be together at rehearsals and concerts; we can also go out for dinner, to the theater, visit the Art Institute . . ."

"Remember what happened there, Peter?"

"Yes," he answered reluctantly.

"How long do you think it would be before I wound up becoming your mistress? How long before I'd be getting in your way?"

"That isn't what I want for you," he said sharply. "I said we would keep it platonic, and I meant it."

Lorelei gave a sigh. "All right, let's suppose that that's possible. What would you do—keep all your other women, too?"

"You make it sound as though I had a whole stable of them," he said irritably. "I don't know—you're the only one that I love . . ."

"But you probably wouldn't be willing to remain celibate out of deference to me. I would have to accept the fact that you would see other women." She looked directly at him, waiting for a response.

He shifted uneasily in his chair. "Yes, I suppose so," he quietly admitted.

"You're probably figuring that I would never have affairs with other men, and you'd be right—I don't intend to. But what if I got married?"

His eyes became troubled. "What do you mean? How could you marry someone else if you love me? You wouldn't marry someone you didn't love."

"No, I guess not," she allowed. "But that's why this won't work, Peter. Unlike you, I *want* to marry, and I never will if I go on year after year carrying a torch for you, whether our relationship stays platonic or not. I want a commitment, something for the future that I can build on." She looked at him. He was staring tensely at the back of the seat ahead of him. "That's why I've come to a decision." Her voice became a bit unsteady, and she made an effort to speak in a firmer, more deliberate tone. "I have to separate myself from you permanently, so that I can hope one day to forget you and be free to love someone else— someone who will want me for his wife."

She took a deep breath before continuing. "I overheard some of the others saying that the London Symphony will be losing a few of its first violinists through retirement and they'll be auditioning for replacements soon. I'm going to stay on in London after our concert tour is over and see if I can try out for a position with them. I'm pretty well qualified now—I think there's a good chance that they'll hire me. If not, there are several other orchestras in London I can try. In any case, I intend to start a new life."

Peter's blazing eyes ripped her apart. "That's the most ridiculous thing I ever heard! You don't know how to take care of yourself—you're still like a little girl. You think you can move to a large city in a foreign country and make it on your own? You must be out of your head!"

"I don't think I'm quite as naive as I may appear," she said in her own defense. "It's about time I learned to be on my own, anyway. I can't remain a little girl forever."

"Why move to a foreign country? Why not somewhere else in the United States?"

"I want to be as far away from you as possible. If I were to remain anywhere in the States, I doubt if you'd leave me alone."

"You're right, I wouldn't! I'll never let go of you! You think an ocean could keep me away?"

"I hope your common sense will keep you away. It won't work, Peter. There can never be anything but unhappiness for both of us!" She blinked back hot tears and steadied her breathing.

"I don't believe you'll do what you say," Peter told her, his voice full of feeling. "If you love me, you won't leave me."

"I love you, Peter. But when this concert tour is over, we'll never see each other again," she said with deep conviction, as though it were already fact.

"No, you won't," he said quietly and with equal certainty. "When the time comes, you won't be able to watch me, Henry, and the others fly back to Chicago leaving you behind, all alone. You'll change your mind." He was looking at her now with assurance. Gently, he brought up his hand and caressingly stroked the hair that fell along her neck. Her eyes softened vulnerably at his touch. He pulled her toward him. His mouth close to hers, he whispered, "You'll never leave me." As his lips came down on hers, she wondered if he was right.

Several hours later, while the orchestra members were waiting in the lobby of their elegant London hotel for room assignments, a clerk moved through the group asking for Miss Lorelei Lawrence. When he finally found her, he gave her an urgent message. John Benchley had called twice from the United States asking if she had arrived. He left word that she should call him immediately upon receiving the message—it was of utmost importance. Lorelei asked where she could make the call, and the clerk led her to an available telephone and gave her instructions for placing an overseas call.

"Who is John Benchley?" Peter, who had followed her, was asking.

"A friend of mine," Lorelei informed him as she was waiting for the call to go through.

"And why would he be so anxious to speak to you?" Peter said, eyes flashing darkly into her own.

Recognizing familiar signs of jealousy, she answered, "He probably wants to tell me he and my roommate are engaged." Peter seemed to relax a bit and they waited in silence until John's voice came on the other line.

"Lorelei?"

"Yes, it's me. How are you?"

"Fine. I'm glad I got hold of you. Listen, I have a lot to tell you, so I won't waste any time. First of all, Rosemary and I are going to be married at the end of the summer . . ."

"I knew it! Congratulations! You're getting a wonderful girl."

"I know. She wanted me to tell you to plan on being her maid of honor at the wedding."

Lorelei was silent for a moment as sadness came over her. "I . . . I may not be able to, John. I won't be coming back to Chicago. I'm going to stay in London. In fact, I was going to ask Rosemary to have my belongings shipped over."

"I don't understand . . ."

"It's too much to go into now," she said, avoiding the glaring blue eyes that were watching her intently. "I'll write and explain it all."

"Well . . . all right. I just hope you're doing the right thing. There's something I have to tell you. Remember Walter Booth?"

"That man who sent me all the flowers?"

"Yes. Our ex-policeman, Retherford, who's been keeping an eye on him for us found out he's on his way to London. In fact, he's probably there already. He left on a flight yesterday. The guy's been hanging around your apartment a lot. Even Rosemary's seen him. He parks his car in front and just sits there and stares at the building. Looks like he's got a case on you—you'd better be careful. Don't walk around alone and don't let anybody into your room. You can't tell what he'll do, especially if he's gone all the way to London just to see you. As far as we know, he doesn't have any other reason to go there just at this time. Is there anyone you can room with while you're there?"

"No, I don't think so," Lorelei answered slowly, trying to think calmly after such disconcerting news. "The other women are all married and have their husbands along—except for Rachel Logan, but she made a big point of wanting to room alone before we left."

"You might be wise to ask her to share a room. It's better than being by yourself," John said. "We couldn't contact the London police about it because there just isn't enough to go on, so you're pretty much on your own. It would be best to take all precautions. Well, I'd better hang up now—these calls are expensive. Just be careful, will you, Lorelei?"

"I will, John. Thanks for warning me. Good-bye."

"What was that all about?" Peter asked, eyeing her pale face as she replaced the telephone receiver. She gave him a brief summary of the events that had happened before she left: the masher in John's office, the flowers, the notes. Then she repeated what John had just told her.

Peter reflected on what she told him for several moments. "Why don't you room with me?" he suggested.

"Don't be ridiculous."

"I'm not. You may be in danger and you need protection."

"I'll ask Rachel to share my room," Lorelei said.

"She probably wouldn't agree to it. How much help would she be if you were in trouble, anyway?"

"I'm not sharing a room with you, Peter," she firmly declared.

"Lorelei, I don't have any ulterior motive in this, if that's what you're thinking. No one else need know about it. We can take two rooms, but you can come and stay in mine. I'll sleep on the floor."

"Oh, sure. You know darn well how long that would last . . ."

"All right," Peter said, putting up a hand to quell her protests, "I have another idea. Why don't we get adjoining rooms? That way we'll be separate, but I'd be close by if you need help."

"I guess that would be okay," Lorelei responded, but after much hesitation.

Peter smiled. "You're so suspicious," he said, putting his arms around her. "I'll be a gentleman from now on, I promise. Wait here and I'll make the arrangements,'' he said softly, then kissed her on the mouth before moving a short distance away to the reception desk.

Lorelei was embarrassed at his being so openly affectionate with her and looked around at the few remaining orchestra members still in the lobby. None of them appeared to have noticed. Fortunately, Henry was no longer about, for he certainly wouldn't have missed it, Lorelei noted, giving silent thanks. Since she would be leaving the orchestra soon, she hoped the ill-fated romance between herself and Peter would not become a source for gossip after she was gone.

Peter was back shortly with two keys, and together he and Lorelei followed a bellboy up to their rooms. The luggage was put into her room first and she was left alone for a few minutes as Peter was installed into the room next door. She heard him tipping the man through her open front door and saw the bellhop walk away. She waited a moment, expecting Peter to come in, but instead heard a knock on another door which she had supposed to be a closet. Quickly she rose to open it and was astounded to find Peter on the other side of a double doorway.

"Nice arrangement, isn't it?" he said brightly.

"You didn't say the rooms would be attached!" she said, horrified.

"I said adjoining rooms, didn't I?"

"I thought that only meant they would be next to each other."

Peter smiled and shook his head. "You sure would be easy to put something over on . . ."

"Yes that's just what you did, isn't it?" she accused.

"No, Lorelei, I thought you understood. What good would it do merely to have two rooms next to one another? This way, if we keep these doors open, I can always get in if you need help."

"And even if I don't!"

"Oh, come on! Why do you always think I'm trying to seduce you? Don't judge me by the way I behaved in Paris. When I came into your room that afternoon, I didn't foresee anything would happen. I didn't understand then how I felt about you and my emotions got out of control. I've got myself together, now, and I assure you, you have nothing to worry about."

"Yes, now you're so together you've worked out a strategy to lead me into an affair with you! You think once we've started making love, I wouldn't stay here in London and leave you."

Peter was visibly angry. "I had no such ideas! It disturbs me that you think I would be so underhanded. I promise I won't touch you. I won't even come into your room unless you ask me. But you must leave this door open, otherwise if someone else gets in, I won't be able to help you. Do you understand?"

Lorelei was silent as she weighed her alternatives. "Maybe we're getting carried away about nothing," she said at last. "We don't know that he'd actually try and come after me. How would he know which room I was in—or even which hotel? He may have come to London for some other reason. It would be pretty farfetched to think he'd travel all that way just to see me. The tour's almost over, so wouldn't he figure I'd be going back soon anyway?"

"If he were a rational person, he would," Peter answered. "But a rational person doesn't molest girls while waiting to see a dentist, doesn't send cryptic, anonymous notes, and doesn't sit in a car staring at an apartment building for hours. And it wouldn't be any trick to find you. The newspapers often publish at what hotel the Philharmonic is staying. I asked the clerk downstairs not to divulge your room number to anyone and to alert the house detectives. But that doesn't mean a clever man couldn't get to you. All he'd need to do is cross someone's palm with a little money. Your friend John was right, Lorelei. You need to take every precaution.''

He looked intently at her, as if to ascertain whether his words had made any impression, but she avoided his eyes.

"I don't believe it!'' he said. "You're actually more afraid of me than of this maniac who's been following you around. Or is it yourself you don't trust?'' The blue eyes penetrated her own. She looked at him irresolutely, unable to form a response.

They were interrupted by a light knock at the hallway door, which was still ajar. "Are you Miss Lawrence?'' a young man asked. At her nod, he said, "These are for you,'' and held out a large bouquet of white roses.

Lorelei stood motionless, eyes fixed with dread on the delicate white flowers. Peter moved quickly to the door and accepted them for her. As the young man left down the hall, Peter nudged the door closed and set the bouquet on the dresser. He extracted a small envelope from among the roses and opened it. After looking at the enclosed card, he asked, "Shall I read it?''

"Yes'' was the faint reply.

Peter held the card in front of him. " 'You have been away from me too long. At last I am near you again. We will meet soon, my love.' '' He extended the card to Lorelei. "Very sweet. Still think you don't want to have me around?''

The remainder of the day was heavily scheduled with a rehearsal in midafternoon, a concert in the evening, followed by an after-concert soirée. It was during a break at the rehearsal that Lorelei approached Mr. Markham. She told him of her plan to leave the Philharmonic and stay in London. "This is the end of the concert season, so I don't think I'll be putting you in a bind,'' she explained.

"No, of course not,'' the elderly gentleman replied, "but I didn't realize you had any thought of leaving us. I hope you haven't been unhappy.''

"No, not at all,'' she told him sincerely. "It's for . . . personal reasons. I just feel that this would be better for me.''

"I see. We'll be very sorry to lose you. I hope you'll think about this a while longer before making any final decision. After your fine performance in Copenhagen, I think you know you would have a bright future with the Philharmonic if you stay with us.''

"Thank you. It's kind of you to say so, but . . . I can't stay.'' She hid her hands behind her back as she spoke. She didn't want him to see that they were trembling.

"You said you were hoping to join the London Symphony,'' Mr. Markham said quietly. "I understand they'll be needing some violinists. In fact, I may be able to help you there. I'm well acquainted with their conductor and others who manage the Symphony's affairs. Stay here a moment and let me make a telephone call.''

He returned several minutes later. "I called their offices and pulled a few strings for you. They assumed you would be leaving England in a few days with the Philharmonic and offered to audition you now. It's an unusual arrangement, but I think they were very interested and didn't want to chance making you wait for the formal auditions. Since Copenhagen, you've become known in the music world, young lady."

Lorelei was surprised at the statement and blushed, but managed a polite "Thank you."

"At any rate," Mr. Markham continued, "with this arrangement, if you don't like their offer—and I'm sure they'll make you one—you can still return to Chicago with us. And don't accept anything until you see me again. It may be I can make you a better offer. All right?"

"All right," she said with a smile. She didn't want to explain that her reason for leaving the orchestra had nothing to do with money or working conditions.

"Here's a name and telephone number to call," he said, handing her a small piece of paper. "The man I spoke with suggested you make arrangements to come in tomorrow or the next day. He was anxious to hear from you."

She thanked him wholeheartedly and returned to her seat onstage with bolstered confidence that her hopes of living and working in London could become a reality.

"What were you discussing for so long with Mr. Markham?" Peter asked when she sat down.

She told him she would explain later, knowing her reply would anger him. In addition, she did not want to be dissuaded from her plans, and Peter would certainly make every effort to do that.

Peter, she noticed, had begun to dog her every step, ostensibly as her self-appointed bodyguard. But there was a possessive look in his eye that told her his wary vigil over her also served his own purposes. It was only when she was alone in her room—though the connecting doors leading to Peter's room were left ajar as he had insisted—and getting ready for an early dinner that she had opportunity to make the important phone call.

The man from the London Symphony she spoke with was, indeed, very pleased that she contacted him and he made arrangements for her to audition in the morning. That being accomplished, and without Peter's knowledge or interference, she was able to relax for the moment.

She and Peter dined with the Morrisons that evening in the hotel's elegant restaurant. Enjoying the English atmosphere, Lorelei decided it would not be difficult for her to adjust to the polite manner of the British people and the stately yet somehow very lively city of London.

She had thought, even while on her first visit to the city with Rosemary, that if an American wanted to live abroad, London was an ideal choice. There was no language problem and the people were friendly. In addition, London had, in the Underground, a wonderfully laid out public transportation system serving all parts of the city. This led Lorelei to believe that she need not even own an automobile if she could find an apartment in the metropolitan area. Also, London had a reputation for being a "safe" city, a place where one need not fear for one's life when walking about after dark. This was no small consolation for a woman alone.

But even as these positive thoughts flowed through her head, she could not shake off a heavy feeling of sadness. As she sat at the table with Peter at her side, listening to Henry's familiar quips and complaints of lack of time for sight-seeing, it was only with great difficulty that she kept the tears from her eyes.

Throughout the concert that evening, Lorelei found herself scanning, when she could, the multitude of faces in the audience. She had the disquieting feeling that her unwelcome admirer was probably among them. For the past several weeks she had enjoyed freedom from worry over that problem. To have to deal with it now, in addition to the task of putting her life in order, was beginning to be more than her nerves could bear. It was difficult to concentrate on the intricacies of the music when her personal world was in such upheaval, and her playing became erratic and uneven.

Peter noticed her unsteady performance and made solicitous efforts to comfort and ease her mind during the intermission. But this did not offer any solace; rather, it caused more pain. Now, when Peter was so gentle, sensitive, and loving—all those qualities she had hoped he would have during those long quiet years when she had secretly loved him—now she must put herself away from him if she was ever to hope for fulfillment and happiness in her life.

When the concert was finally over, she felt obligated to attend the soirée being given for the orchestra, though her head was beginning to ache and she did not feel up to making polite conversation with dignitaries and rubbing shoulders with royalty. Peter kept close by and when the earliest opportunity availed itself, he quietly left the festivities with her and took her back to the hotel.

With a protective arm around her, he led her through the lobby and up to their rooms. "Maybe you'd better get some sleep. You look pretty tired," he told her after making a careful inspection of both their rooms.

"I don't think I'll be able to," she replied.

"Still worrying about Booth, aren't you? Look, maybe nothing will come of it after all. He may just show up backstage after tomorrow's concert and want to shake your hand. Try to think about something else for a while. How about if I order you some tea? It might help you sleep . . ." Peter offered.

"Okay," she answered. Within seconds he was on the telephone asking for room service.

"You said you had a headache earlier. Is it still there?" he asked when he had completed the call.

"Yes, only it's worse now," she answered with a wan smile.

"Did you bring any aspirin with you?"

"No, I don't usually need it for anything."

"Me either. I'd better go down and get you some. They probably sell it in the hotel somewhere."

"That's all right, Peter, don't bother . . ." she protested.

"No, I have to take care of you," he said, smiling. "I'll go now. Don't let anyone in unless you know who it is. I'll be back as soon as I can." He kissed her on the forehead and walked to the door. "Lock up after me and fasten the chain," he cautioned before leaving. She did as he instructed.

In about ten minutes there was a knock at her door and a male voice outside said, "Room service." She opened the door without unfastening the chain and peered into the hallway. Seeing a uniformed young man with a tray, she undid the chain and allowed him to enter. Hurrying to find her handbag, she took out her change purse and gave him a tip. With a brief thank you he left, closing the door behind him as Lorelei was replacing the purse in her handbag.

After a few seconds there came another knock. Wondering if the young man had forgotten something, she moved toward the door, but before she reached it, it swung open. Suddenly, she was facing a man in his forties, somewhat overweight, of medium height and plain appearance. She recognized him immediately as the same man who had attempted to molest her in John's office.

Instinctively, she backed away. He closed the door and walked toward her. There was a smile on his lips, but his breathing was labored and audible, and his eyes held an odd, disconcerting look. Lorelei was terrified.

"You got my flowers . . ." he said, motioning to the white roses on the dresser. "You liked them, didn't you? I ordered them white again, just like all the others." He paused, as if waiting for some reply, but Lorelei said nothing. "Did you read the note? I said I'd come . . . I came all the way from Chicago . . . just to see you. . . ." The smile faded and he seemed troubled by her lack of response.

"Why?" Lorelei whispered, fearing he would become agitated if she said nothing. She continued to move slowly away from him and toward the door leading to Peter's room. If she could just get into his room she could lock his door from the other side and be safe.

"I couldn't wait anymore—you've been gone so long. And you won't be in any concerts all summer. I wanted to watch you play once more . . . you're so beautiful when you're playing." The smile returned and a glint entered his eye, which sickened Lorelei. "Besides, you live with that other girl back home. Here we can be alone . . ."

"How did you find me?" she asked, hoping to keep him distracted as she continued to edge toward the door.

"I knew what hotel the orchestra was at. I waited in the lobby this morning and followed the man who delivered my flowers to your room. I decided to come back after the concert and surprise you." His expression changed. "Hey, where are you going?"

Quickly, she made a bolt for the door. She was halfway through when she felt herself being pulled back into her own room. "Peter!" she cried, desperately hoping somehow he would be there.

Booth shoved her toward her bed and closed her door, thus preventing Peter from being able to enter her room when he did return.

Realizing her plight, she ran toward the door leading to the outer hallway. He reached it just as she did and held it shut, then fastened the chain and locked it. As he was securing the door, she started to move away, but he grabbed her by the arm.

"Stay put!" he said, breathing heavily. "Why are you trying to run away from me? Who's staying in that room next door?"

"Peter Sutherland. He'll be back any minute!" she said boldly, trying to act as if she weren't afraid.

Booth's expression was alarming. "That's that guy you sit with, isn't it? I saw you with him this morning in the lobby. You let him kiss you. And I saw you come back with him tonight." His voice was rising. "Why are you hanging around him? You were supposed to wait for me! I told you not to forget me!

Don't you remember that last note I sent?'' His chin and lower lip began to tremble and his eyes held an almost frightened aspect.

"Why do you think I would wait for you?" she said. "I don't even know you—except for that day you attacked me in the dentist's office!"

His eyes took on a pleading look and he breathed in quick, shallow gasps. He twisted his hands together. "I hoped you wouldn't remember that when you saw me . . . I sent all those flowers . . . I wanted you to like me. Look. . . .'' He got down on his knees in front of her, clasping his hands about her waist. "Look . . . see? I'm apologizing. Do you forgive me? I shouldn't have acted that way, not with you. You're so beautiful! I started sending the flowers— white ones—pure like you. I tried to court you like a gentleman. I want you to be *my* girl." Lorelei, filled with repulsion and pity at this plaintive onslaught, tried to move out of his grasp.

Suddenly there was a violent shaking of the door to Peter's room. "Lorelei! Are you all right!" Peter yelled as he pounded on it.

Seeing Booth was momentarily distracted as he looked in the direction of the noise, Lorelei gathered all her strength and forcefully jerked her knee up against his chin and neck, knocking his head back. His hold on her loosened and she fled from his grasp. She ran to the door and opened it. The instant she did, Peter shot into the room. He ran directly to Booth, who was getting up, and knocked him to the floor. Turning him facedown, he pinned the intruder to the ground by twisting the man's arms across his back.

"Call the hotel operator! Tell them to get someone up here and send for the police," Peter instructed Lorelei as he continued to hold Booth down.

"No! Don't do that!" Booth cried against the floor. "I didn't mean any harm!"

"Be quiet!" Peter said harshly.

"Lorelei—no!" Booth wailed as she was dialing the phone. "I wasn't going to hurt you!"

She ignored the man's pleas and did as Peter had told her. Within moments of speaking to the operator, a hotel security man was at the door. Lorelei let him in and he immediately went to assist Peter. Soon two more security men from the hotel appeared and not long after that, the police.

The frenzied scene that followed was very distressing for Lorelei. Hurriedly she and Peter were questioned about what had transpired as Booth, now near hysterics and behaving wildly, was forcibly taken away by four officers.

The police asked Lorelei and Sutherland to accompany them to headquarters for further questioning and to sign forms. Peter comfortingly kept hold of her hand during the ride to the station. Once there, she was asked further questions regarding her previous encounters with Booth and described with great detail what had happened when he had entered her room. She assured them that she had not actually been harmed in any way. Though she hoped that she would never see or hear of Walter Booth again, she felt sorry for him and did not wish for him to be dealt with severely.

When at last they were finished with the procedures and were waiting to be taken back to the hotel, the officer with whom they had been speaking received a telephone call. Lorelei could tell from his conversation that it concerned Booth.

"Well, that finishes that," the officer said quietly as he replaced the receiver.

Lorelei looked at him with questioning eyes. "Walter Booth is dead. He apparently suffered a heart attack while he was being interrogated. He died before he reached the hospital."

Lorelei was stunned. She helplessly looked to Peter, whose countenance held a serious, introverted expression. "How old was he?" he asked the officer.

"According to his passport, he was forty-six. Not really very old, was he?"

"No, not old at all . . ." Peter replied.

11

They were silent as they were driven back to the hotel. When they were once more inside Lorelei's room, she turned to Peter in tears and buried her face against his chest.

"I feel like it's all my fault . . . like I killed him," she said brokenly.

He put his arms around her and stroked her hair. "How can you think that?" he said, trying to soothe her. "He came into your room uninvited—you had to protect yourself. And he had bothered you before."

"I know, but he probably didn't intend any harm."

"Lorelei, you don't know that," Peter softly chided her. "He obviously had mental problems. No one knows what he might have done if he hadn't been stopped. He tried to keep you locked in here with him, didn't he?"

"But he did it because he liked me. He became upset when I turned against him . . ."

Peter grasped her by the shoulders and shook her gently. "He was a sick man! It's all right to be sorry for him, but you shouldn't feel guilty. No one knew he had a weak heart. I was the one who pinned him down. If you're to blame, so am I."

"I guess you're right," she said, wiping her eyes. "It's just that he came here because he was so attracted to me. I'm going to let my hair grow back to the way it was. Being beautiful has brought me nothing but trouble."

Peter smiled. "Don't be silly. You're beautiful no matter what you do, and there's nothing that will change the way men react. We'll all crash on the rocks below, just as in Henry's old legend. Now, try to forget what's happened. We'll be back home in Chicago soon, and all this will be behind us."

A feeling of heaviness came over Lorelei. Slowly, she walked away from him to sit on the edge of the bed. "Peter, I've told you, I won't be going back to Chicago . . ."

"Don't start *that* again," he said with irritation. "I don't want to hear any more about your crazy plans to stay on here. You're coming back to the States with the rest of us and that's all there is to it."

"You can't make me go with you. It's my life and I can do what I want," she said with determination.

"Have you thought about this rationally?" he asked, making an effort to keep his voice calm. "What if the London Symphony doesn't accept you? What will you do here with no job? You don't even have a place to stay! If you would use that head of yours and think through this harebrained scheme, you would see that it's totally absurd!"   .

"I have thought it through," she told him. "I have an appointment with some people from the London Symphony early tomorrow morning. Mr. Markham seemed sure they would make me an offer. If they don't, there are several other major orchestras in London. Since my qualifications are good—and I've even attracted some attention in musical circles, thanks to you—I'm not all that worried about finding work. As for an apartment, I was going to start looking—"

"All right! All right!" Peter interrupted. "I get the picture. So you can make it on your own. What are you trying to prove?"

"Peter, we've been through all this! We're in love, but you don't want to get married. Where does that leave me?"

"The same place it leaves me," he retorted. "I realize we have a problem, but that doesn't mean we can't work it out. Running away doesn't solve anything."

She sighed and bowed her head, moving it from side to side in dismay. "You're such a dreamer, Peter. I always thought I was, but you're a worse case than me. First you tried to make yourself believe you didn't care for me. Now you think you can solve a problem to which there's no solution. Wishing doesn't make things so."

"How can you be sure there's no solution? You haven't even tried!"

"I've told you, I don't want to become involved in any kind of long relationship that leads nowhere. That might be fine for some people, but not for me. The only way I'll have any chance of getting what I want is to break away from you completely and try to forget." She stopped speaking a moment as her voice became choked and her eyes filled with tears. Then she added with self-inflicted sarcasm, "Besides, I'm not that young anymore and I won't always be attractive. I'd better find a husband while I'm still marketable."

She stared dully at the floor, glassy-eyed, her chin trembling slightly. Peter was silent. His expression deep and intent, he began slowly pacing back and forth over the clear space of carpeting in front of her. After several minutes, he walked over to the window and stood in front of it a long while, staring out. "What now?" Lorelei wondered tiredly as she sat on the edge of the bed.

Finally he moved away from the window and came to stand near her. "All right, you win," he said in a voice devoid of emotion. "I can't stand to be without you, so I guess I'll have to marry you."

Lorelei's posture sagged listlessly and she made no response.

"What's the matter?" he asked with a mixture of surprise and irritation. "Isn't that what you want?"

"What do you mean, I win? You sound like you've just given yourself a life sentence," she said cuttingly.

"Do you expect me to get down on my knees and make some flowery proposal? I said I'd marry you, for God's sake—"

"I don't expect anything," she interrupted. "Obviously you still don't like the idea of being married. You're just giving in to keep me around."

"Is there anything a mortal man can do to please you?" he flung at her in lofty sarcasm.

"Peter, listen to me. You should marry because you want to, not because it's the only way out. You said once that you weren't good husband material and, unfortunately, I think you were right. You'd always look upon a wife as a weight

around your neck, interfering with your plans, keeping you from your work. I
don't want to become your ball and chain.''

"You've interfered with my plans already! Marriage won't make much difference," he sourly replied.

"Well, if I'm such a nuisance to you, it's best I get out of your life!''

"I didn't mean it that way . . .''

"It doesn't matter," she said. "Don't you see we wouldn't be happy? You
would grow to resent my intrusion in your life, and I would always feel I was
competing with your career for attention. It wouldn't be long before our love
turned to hate." She looked at him in tender earnest. "Let's end it, Peter. While
we still like each other. There's no other way for us," she told him in a hushed,
but persuasive voice.

She tried to read the clear eyes staring steadily into her own, but was unable
to interpret what she saw in their blue stillness. It was an almost vacant, unseeing
expression, but with an odd hint of rebellion. After several moments, he suddenly
dropped his gaze. Without a word, he turned away, walked to his room, and
sharply closed his door, sealing himself off from her.

She looked sadly through her open door at the barrier he had put between
them. At last it was done. The final break had been made. It was over.

She sluggishly changed into a long white nightgown, put off the light, and
got into bed. Stretching out under the covers, she forced a yawn, trying to entice
herself to drowsiness. But for a long time she remained awake, though she was
extremely tired.

The next day was the beginning of a new existence—the beginning of the end
of her old life. The last concert was that evening. The following morning they
would all fly home, and she would be left on her own.

It wasn't the fact that she would be alone in a foreign country that played on
her mind, nor the need to make new friends and start a new job. It was cutting
herself off from her former friends and co-workers that was so painful. The fact
that she would probably not be present at Rosemary's wedding made her feel
as though she were abandoning a treasured companion. The two girls had shared
so much over the past years, it seemed wrong not to be with her on such an
important day in her life.

To leave her fellow Philharmonic members, whom she had grown to respect
and love, was also difficult. She would no doubt come to like the musicians in
her new orchestra, but it was unlikely she would ever find Henry's counterpart.
Somehow he had always managed to buck up her spirits when she was low, and
though at times he could be vexing, he had a way of pointing her nose in the
right direction while keeping her amused. She would miss his open, friendly
manner and the way he had taken special interest in her, even if it was in part
for his own diversion.

But more than this, it was separating herself from Peter that gnawed at her
very soul. Peter, the man she had admired for so long, the only man she had
ever loved, must be forgotten. How could she accomplish the impossible? How
could she ever hope to love again, knowing he existed, however far away?

His looks, his voice, his touch—these could never be duplicated in another.
She loved even his faults, for they were unique and part of his character. His
forgetfulness was adorable, his jealous nature amused her, and his contrariness

in the face of reality was touching. These were balanced by his strength, intelligence, and ability to take command. Indeed, it was his capacity for controlling others—particularly women—that tore her heart, for she did not doubt he would comfort himself with others. His way with women was irresistible. To never again feel his arms about her, to never have shared his bed were torments almost impossible to bear.

Tears began to stream down Lorelei's cheeks and into her hair. Soon she was sobbing uncontrollably. Much later, when she was totally exhausted from convulsive weeping and she had no tears left, she at last fell asleep.

Even her sleep was disturbed by vivid dreams. She saw herself wandering aimlessly through the night, searching London's misty streets. She stopped everyone she encountered to ask for help in her quest, but she could make no one understand what it was she was looking for. It seemed she did not know herself. Finally she came to an old man with sharp blue eyes that seemed to sear through her. He told her in a harsh voice that she should go home. She would find what she wanted there. She became very angry and denied what he said was true, but he remained adamant. It began to rain as she continued to argue violently with him. Soon it was pouring, and he walked away in disgust, leaving her alone in the downpour. She began to cry out of sheer frustration. The wind grew stronger and she had no protection from the heavy torrents of water beating down on her.

Blinded by the wind, she became confused, lost, and frightened. Suddenly, and from nowhere, she felt herself enveloped by a comforting warmth. Vaguely she sensed a soft voice speaking to her, leading her to shelter. Now she was clinging to someone and could not let go, while the voice became clearer and more distinct.

"Wake up, Lorelei. It's just a bad dream."

With a start, she opened her eyes and was completely undone by the sight that greeted her. Her small hand was pressed into the thick, matted hair of a man's chest. Her cheek was nestled against the smooth skin of his shoulder, and she felt herself lying full length against his lean, masculine body.

She hurriedly pushed herself away, though strong arms kept her within reach, and looked into his face. Her shocked eyes were met by smiling blue ones gazing cheerfully back at her.

"Peter! What are you doing here?"

"I . . . uh . . . couldn't sleep," he answered with only token sheepishness.

"You weren't supposed to come into my room! You said you wouldn't!"

"I guess I forgot," he said, incredible innocence luminating from eyes that had brightened to baby-blue.

She twisted out of his grasp and pushed herself to the other side of the double bed. "How long have you been here?" she asked with horror, noticing he was under the covers with her.

"Oh, about an hour, I suppose," he said as he propped himself to a sitting position against the pillow. "I had dozed off, but you woke me up with your nightmare. You rolled up against me." Some of the innocence left his eyes as he uttered the last sentence.

"Why did you come in here, Peter?" she asked plaintively. "It's over between us."

"Sweetheart, it will never be over between us. I'm going to marry you."

"No . . ."

"Yes. If I have to drag you kicking and screaming to the altar, you'll be my wife!"

Something about the way he said the words made her pause. She studied his face as he calmly regarded her. He seemed unusually composed and content—almost carefree. His eyes were radiant with a light that was not a mere reflection of the morning sunshine streaming through the window. It was the look of joy she had seen only once before—the first time he had kissed her, long ago, in the Thorne Rooms of the Art Institute.

Inexplicably, Lorelei responded by dropping her gaze from him to the mussed sheets. In a shy and hesitant manner, she said, "I . . . don't understand . . ." as her eyes crept up to meet his once more.

He was smiling and looking at her curiously. "You turn shy at the oddest times," he said, reaching for her hand. "What don't you understand?"

"You seem . . . different. And why are you here?"

"I'm here because. . . . Well, let me start at the beginning. When I left you last night, I was at my wit's end. What you said made sense. There seemed to be no way I could have you. But, still, something within me wouldn't accept that. I knew there was a solution, if only I could work it out. I was up all night wrestling with my thoughts until finally, near dawn, the answer came. I realized I was actually bored with my life. You were the only bright spot in my tedious and predictable existence. That's partly why I liked to be around you so much."

"What was the other part?" Lorelei asked, wanting to have complete understanding.

He seemed a bit surprised by the question. "What do you think?" he responded, as though he expected her to know. She looked at him with wide, perplexed eyes. Peter laughed softly at her and shook his head. "Because I liked to gaze at your tender little body and watch the way your hair falls over your shoulders. . . ." His voice softened to oblivion as he stared at her, the longing creeping into his eyes. Lorelei blushed and bowed her head.

"Now you've distracted me," he complained. "Will you please be quiet until I'm finished?"

"Okay," she meekly replied.

"Where was I?"

"You were bored . . ."

"Yes. I realized I wasn't happy. And after seeing Booth die so miserably and so young, I was keenly aware how short life can be. I asked myself, what good was it to achieve the highest accolades of the music world if my life was empty? Was that really any accomplishment? So I began to wonder why I was discontent. Everything was moving according to my plans; I should have been satisfied. Then it struck me: It was my damn plans that were holding me prisoner in an unhappy life-style and keeping me from you. Suddenly I saw how foolish I'd been, clinging to ideas I had formed when only a teen-ager, before I knew anything of life. How absurd it was to never have reexamined my priorities in all these years. I was so enmeshed in habit, I had stopped thinking." He paused and cast his eyes downward in quiet annoyance, still angry with himself.

"So," he continued, "I simply decided to throw it all out." His hard expression faded and he smiled. "You know, it was like a great weight had been lifted from my shoulders. Suddenly, I was liberated—no longer obligated to follow my self-imposed life script. I could actually allow myself time for love. I stood by the window and watched the sun come up, and I never before experienced such a feeling of peace and joy. At last there were no obstacles between us."

He stopped speaking and his manner became hesitant. He dropped his eyes from Lorelei's watery gaze and explained almost apologetically, "I wanted to tell you. I opened the door slightly and looked into your room. You were sound asleep. Having been up all night, I was afraid if I lay down I would doze off. I might not wake up until after you had left for your appointment with the London Symphony. So. . . ." At last he looked suitably sheepish. "It occurred to me that if I fell asleep next to you, I would be sure to be awakened before you left." He feigned a docile, innocent expression as he waited for her response.

Lorelei had to laugh at his pretense, her eyes already brimming with tears of joy. She moved to him and threw her arms around his neck, her slender torso leaning against his muscular chest. "Oh, Peter, I'm so happy!" she gushed. "Are you sure you won't mind being married? I won't be a burden?" she asked, wanting to be assured once more.

"If anything has to be a burden, it should be my job, not you. All my plans will revolve around you from now on. Our life together is what really matters." He watched lovingly as she vainly tried to hold back further tears from springing to her eyes. "Is it okay then? You haven't agreed to marry me yet," he said, running his hands caressively over her back.

"Yes," she answered in a choked whisper. He held her tighter against him and covered her tremulous lips with his mouth. When the long, gentle kiss was over, she languidly placed her head on his shoulder, her silky hair brushing against his bare skin. They clung to each other in contented, blissful silence for a long while.

Dreamily opening her eyes, she hazily studied her hand resting against his muscular upper arm. Slowly she ran her palm over the smooth, bronze skin, sensing the firmness beneath. She lifted her head away and moved her hand carefully over his shoulder and up along his neck, feeling the rise and fall of every contour. She looked into his face and saw by his expression that he was enjoying her exploration. She smiled at him softly and hesitantly inclined her head toward him, pressing her mouth to his with childlike timidity.

He accepted her kiss eagerly. His strong, sensitive hands wandered over the gentle curves of her body. She could feel their warmth as they slid over the thin material of her nightgown, pressing through to the supple flesh beneath. She reveled in the masculine embrace enveloping her and it made her crave for more. Her breathing becoming unsteady; she was losing touch with her surroundings, wanting only him. Her mouth still fast on his, she urgently pressed herself more firmly against his chest, sensually delighting in the feel as her soft contours yielded to his hard body.

Suddenly he wrenched her away from him. "What are you doing!" he said, breathing heavily. She looked at him, not comprehending. "I thought you'd want to wait until we're married—don't you?"

"Yes," she answered, nodding her head.

"Well, do you think I'm made of stone?"

"We were just kissing . . ." she said lamely.

"Sweetheart, you should know better than that. Have you forgotten what happened in Paris?"

"But you said you were in control now. That's what you told me when I objected to the adjoining rooms," she responded.

"Only if I'm not tried too hard!" he said with an exasperated breath.

"I'm sorry," she said, reaching out a hand to touch him.

"Just stay back a minute, would you!" he said, edging away from her. "Here I thought I was marrying a shy, reticent little girl. Where did you learn that?" he asked, attempting to recover his composure.

"Nowhere. You just bring it out in me," she answered with a pouting little smile. "I was never this way before, so it must be your fault."

Peter laughed. "Blame me, will you! You don't know what you do to me."

In a moment he surprised her by relenting. "Oh, you're right," he said. "I shouldn't have let things get carried away, since you're too naive to understand your own power. I should have remembered how responsive you were on that long plane trip to Amsterdam. I couldn't get it out of my mind for weeks. . . ." He stopped speaking as his thoughts wandered. Then he looked at her and let out an impatient sigh. "I guess it was pretty foolish of me to think we could ever remain platonic. I'd better get out of here while I still have my head together." He pulled away the covers and slid his long legs over the edge of the bed to the floor.

"Peter!" she exclaimed, breaking into laughter.

"What's the matter?"

"Do you always wear blue jeans to bed?" she said between giggles.

"Very amusing!" he said, pretending to be indignant. "Actually, young lady, I don't wear anything to bed. I just threw these on so I wouldn't shock you."

Her green eyes opened wide. "How will I get any sleep at night?" she said with wonder.

"What do you mean?"

She slid over next to him. "You have such a handsome physique, I don't see how I could take my mind off it if you're lying there next to me. . . ." She broke off as she was distracted by his eyes looking knowingly into hers. With a smile she dropped her eyes to his intriguing chest. She reached out to touch once more the soft dark hair that had startled her so when she had awakened in his arms. Inquisitively, she moved her gentle fingers across the smooth, warm skin.

"Lorelei!" he remonstrated, taking her hand away. "Will you stop!"

"I don't want to," she pouted.

"You'd better learn to behave yourself or you won't be wearing white at our wedding!"

"Yes, sir," she said with dejected obedience. "How soon can we be married?"

"That's what I was wondering. I don't even know what has to be done, since I had expected to remain single."

"Rosemary and John are getting married at the end of the summer. They can clue us in when we get back."

"End of the summer!" Peter exclaimed. "We'll have to see if we can beat that. I had the impression John was pretty efficient. What's taking them so long?''

Lorelei laughed. ''He is efficient, but he has a little more patience than you—a calmer nature.''

''I see! Perhaps you should steal him away from your friend, since you admire him so,'' Peter said, feigning jealousy.

''Actually, she stole him from me. He was the one I was with that night at the restaurant when you walked in with Candy.''

The pretended jealousy was beginning to turn real. ''Yes, I always wanted to know who that was,'' he said dryly. ''How did he wind up with Rosemary?''

Lorelei smiled gently. ''Nothing ever developed between us and he became attracted to her. As for me . . . well . . . I only had eyes for you.''

His expression softened and he took her in his arms and held her a moment. ''And I'm always a jealous hothead,'' he said. ''I'll try to be more patient.''

''I love you the way you are,'' she replied. ''Besides, you'll never have any reason to be jealous.''

''I'd better not!'' he said, trying to look menacing through the joy sparkling in his eyes. He briefly pressed his mouth to hers, then gently pulled away from her clinging arms. ''There's something we have to do today, sweetheart. Besides, being alone together like this is too risky.'' He rose to his feet and began walking toward his room. ''I'll give you half an hour to get ready for breakfast,'' he said as he reached the door. ''And call the London Symphony and tell them you won't be coming!'' he added sternly.

''What are you going to do?''

''Now? Take a cold shower!'' he said, giving her a blameful look.

She smiled with delight. ''I mean after breakfast.''

''I'll tell you later. Just get ready.''

''Is that what I think it is?'' Henry was saying with astonishment as he inspected the large diamond solitaire gleaming on Lorelei's left hand. They were backstage shortly before the final London concert.

''Yes, it's an engagement ring,'' she told him eagerly.

''You mean Peter actually popped the question? When did all this happen? How come I wasn't in on it?'' Henry protested.

''You must be losing your touch, Henry,'' said a low voice with quiet sarcasm. Peter approached from behind Henry and claimed Lorelei, putting an arm about her waist.

''Well, I think I have a right to complain,'' Henry said, tongue-in-cheek. ''With all the work I've done trying to throw you two together, you could have at least let me overhear the proposal.''

''Next you'll want to come along on our honeymoon,'' Peter said sardonically.

''Why, thanks! Where are you going, so I'll know what to pack?'' Henry blithely responded.

Lorelei laughed while Peter looked exasperated. ''When we decide, we'll be sure *not* to let you know,'' he said.

''When's the wedding?''

''Sometime before the summer's over,'' Lorelei answered.

''Long before summer's over,'' Peter added.

A sly look came over Henry's face. He cast his eyes over to Peter, giving him a man-to-man look. "Can't take it anymore, eh?"

Peter's color heightened just a shade and he took a deep breath, hiding an encroaching smile, before he said, "Don't you have to rosin your bow or something?"

Lorelei laughed and leaned up to kiss Peter on the cheek. He looked down at her affectionately, then bent to press his lips to hers.

"Good grief!" Henry exclaimed. "Don't tell me we'll have to watch this kind of mush from now on!"

"You don't have to look," Peter reminded him.

"Are you kidding? I wouldn't miss it for anything," Henry replied with a satisfied grin.

Morning Rose, Evening Savage

by Amii Lorin

1

Tara's fingers flew over the keys of the humming Olivetti, her eyes steady on the letter she was transcribing. So intent was her concentration, she didn't hear the office door open and she glanced up with a start when the morning mail was dropped onto the corner of her desk.

"Coffee's just about ready, Tara," Jeannie, the young file clerk and head coffee-maker, caroled brightly. "I'll be back with it in a minute, okay?"

Fingers hovering over the keys, Tara nodded and returned the smile of the pretty, eager teen-ager.

"Yes, thank you. I'm just finishing the last of the letters David left. I can take a few minutes and relax with my coffee while I go through the mail."

Jeannie nodded and bounced out of the office and Tara went back to the keyboard. She finished the letter, placed it on top of the others she'd typed that morning, then flexed her fingers and arched her back in a stretching motion.

Glancing at the clock, she noted it was nine forty and she'd been typing steadily since eight. On entering her office at her usual time, a few minutes before eight, she'd found her typewriter uncovered and a piece of paper rolled into it on which her boss had typed:

> Tara,
>   I have an early appointment. Type up these letters
> ashed off last night, if you can decipher them. I should
> be in the office around ten.
>
>   David

Tara smiled to herself. *Decipher* had been the correct word. Though David's architectural drawings were a beautiful sight to behold, one might suspect from his handwriting he was a doctor.

Tara had come to work for the young architect on leaving secretarial college four years ago and the atmosphere had always been informal. From the first day it had been *Tara* and *David,* never *Miss Schmitt* and *Mr. Jennings.* There had been a smaller staff at the time as David had just begun receiving recognition for his work, but as David's reputation grew, so had his staff. Yet the informality remained.

Jeannie delivered the coffee and, after taking a careful sip, Tara gave a small, contented sigh. From the very first day she had considered herself fortunate in finding this job. She enjoyed the work, earned an excellent salary, and, perhaps the best of all, she had made firm friendships with David and his wife, Sallie.

Sallie had acted as David's secretary until she was in her seventh month of pregnancy with their first child. She had remained in the office one week after Tara started, to show her the office procedure. In that short time they discovered a rapport that grew into a strong bond between them.

As for David, Tara freely admitted to herself that, if he had not been married, she would have made a play for him. David Jennings was one of the few men Tara really liked. His looks were commonplace. Tall and thin, almost to the point of gauntness, he had thinning, sandy-colored hair and wore dark-framed glasses. His manner was gentle, with a smile that could melt the core of an iceberg. At the same time he was a brilliant architect and an unabashed workaholic.

Tara rose and walked around the desk to ease her cramped legs, then stood with her back to the door as she flipped through the mail. The office door opened then closed quietly and Tara went stiff at the sound of the new familiar, deeply masculine voice of David's newest, and so far most important, client. "I understand you're looking around for a prosperous man to marry. Would I fill the requirements?"

Shock, followed by swift anger at the softly insolent tone, stiffened her spine even more. Jerking her head up, she turned swiftly to glare into the handsome, mocking face of Aleksei Rykovsky.

"If you are trying to be funny," Tara snapped, "you are failing miserably."

Eyes as deeply blue and glittering as sapphires roamed her face slowly, studying with amusement the high angry color in her creamy cheeks, the flash of sparks in her dark brown eyes, the way she flipped back her long silvery gold hair in agitation.

"Not at all," he finally answered in a silky smooth tone. "I am completely serious. Have I been misinformed about your avowed intention to marry a man who is—uh—well-off?"

Tara was not a small girl, standing five feet nine in her three-inch heels, yet she had to tilt back her head to look into his face. *And what a face,* she thought sourly. For any one man to possess such a devastatingly rugged handsomeness was unfair to the rest of the male population in general and to the whole of the female population in particular. The face was the icing on the cake, being at the top of a long, muscularly lean body that exuded pure male vitality and sensuousness. And as if that were not enough, a full head of crisp, blue-black wavy hair was a blatant invitation to feminine fingers. *Too bad,* Tara thought in the same sour vein, *his personality is a complete turnoff.* She did not appreciate the masterful type.

"No," she finally managed to answer, forcing herself to meet that steady blue gaze. "You have not been misinformed."

"Well, then," he drawled, "all we have to do is set the date."

Tara felt the flash of angry color touch her skin. If there was anything she hated more than an arrogant man, it was to be made the object of his humor. She breathed in deeply, trying to keep a rein on her growing temper. For David's sake, she could not afford to antagonize this man.

"You've had your little joke for the day, Mr. Rykovsky," she said through stiff lips, "now if you'll excuse me, I have work to do and—"

"Morning, Tara." David's cheerful voice preceded him into the room. The rest of him followed, a warm smile lightening his otherwise nondescript face. "Have any trouble with my chicken scratches?"

"Not too much." Tara smiled at her boss, sighing in relief at his appearance. "They're all typed and ready for your signature."

David grinned at the other man as she handed him the neatly typed sheets. "Every busy man should have a Tara in his office, Alek." Then, turning, he walked to the door of his own office. Before following, Alek leaned close to Tara and whispered, "I can think of a better place to have you." Then he moved quickly up behind David, who turned and said, "Alek and I are going to be closeted the rest of the day, Tara. I don't want to be disturbed unless it's something you think absolutely must have my attention."

Struck speechless by Alek's whispered words, she nodded dumbly, then stood still, watching the door close. Tara's thoughts exploded. *How dared he, that— that arrogant, overbearing, conceited—*words failed her. Unclenching her hands, flexing stiff, achy fingers, she made a concentrated effort at control. The emotions raging through her were an equal mixture of anger and humiliation. Anger at his audacity at using her to sharpen his—to her mind—twisted wit. Humiliation at the fact that the basis of his attack was true: she *had* promised herself she'd marry a prosperous man. And although it was ten years since she'd made the vow, she had not changed her mind in the least.

Legs still shaky, Tara walked slowly around her desk and sank into her chair. In a burst of activity she got busy with the work at hand only to pause moments later to stare unseeingly at her typewriter.

She had been fourteen when she'd made that vow, a not unusual thing at that romantic age. Most young girls have been known to declare dreamily that they will marry rich men. But, unlike other girls, Tara had had no dreams of a prince charming with gold-lined pockets. Quite the contrary. She had viewed the prospect realistically. A handsome Prince Charming she didn't need; actual wealth she didn't need. What she had decided she wanted was a reasonably prosperous man and, of equal importance, one who would not be a tyrant. She had already, at the tender age of fourteen, seen enough of the type of man who, to feed his own ego, had to be forever boss. She had seen him in her male teachers, in the fathers of most of her friends, and in her own father.

Tara shuddered as a picture of her mother thrust its unwelcome way into her mind. Trying to dispel the unwanted image, she got to work. She was only partially successful, for throughout the rest of the day incidents and scenes from her childhood flashed in and out of her mind. And her mother was in every one: her beauty fading over the years; her bright eyes growing dim and shadowed with worry; her flashing smile turning into a mere twist of once full lips that had felt the bite of teeth too often; and, possibly the worst of all, shoulders starting to bow with the weight of hardship and far too little appreciation.

Not for me, Tara had told herself while still in her ninth year of school. *Not for me the scrimping and scraping to make ends meet but rarely even coming close. Not for me the tyrant who would be absolute master in his home, punishing his wife for his own inadequacies.*

She had indulged in no wild dreams or flights of fancy, but had planned carefully and well. She had been blessed with beauty of both face and body and she nurtured it rigidly, getting plenty of rest and exercise and being very careful of what she ate. She had worked at baby-sitting and as a mother's helper from the time she was thirteen, giving most of her earnings to her mother, but always managing to put aside a few dollars for herself. At sixteen she got a regular job working part-time after school in the winter and full-time in the summer. She paid a rather high board at home and hoarded the rest of her money like a miser. She studied hard, receiving high grades in school. After graduation she had applied at and was accepted into a highly reputable secretarial college in Philadelphia, whose curriculum included courses on charm and personal appearance. She bolstered her funds by working part-time at Gimbels department store. It had not been easy. In fact it had been very difficult. But it had paid off. When she left secretarial school at twenty, she came home to Allentown a beautiful, poised, well-groomed, excellently trained secretary.

She was hired for the first job she applied for, the one in David's office. That had been four years ago. The first two of those years she lived at home, wanting to ease the burden on her mother. But the situation became increasingly more impossible. She found it harder to except her father's dictates. She was no longer a green girl, but a well turned-out, highly paid young woman and she could no longer bear being told when to come and when to go, when to speak and when to be silent. A few days after her twenty-second birthday she packed her things and left her father's house for good.

She did not actively hate her father. Herman Schmitt did the best he could within the range of his own knowledge and understanding. What his firstborn daughter resented was that he'd never made an effort to widen his vision past what he'd learned of life from his own straight-laced, Pennsylvania Dutch parents. And more important still, she resented his marrying a lovely, laughing, blond-haired girl and turning her into a nervous, drawn-faced, gray-haired, timid mouse.

No. No. No. Not for Tara this type of man and life. Over the years her resolve had strengthened. It had not taken long for her co-workers and few close friends to ascertain her goals. She rarely dated and then only with carefully selected young men. She was wise enough to realize one had little control over the unpredictable emotion called love. So she operated within the premise that she could not become vulnerable to the wrong man if she had no contact with him. None of the men she'd dated over the years had left an impression on her, and at the present time she wasn't seeing anyone.

She had no idea who had enlightened Aleksei Rykovsky as to her intentions. Who it was did not even matter. What did matter was that that hateful man had used it to amuse himself at her expense.

Tara had felt an immediate antagonism toward him from the day, a few months ago, that David had introduced her to him. He wore his breeding, wealth, and self-confidence like a banner. Arrogance etched every fine, aristocratic feature of his dark-skinned, handsome face. This man, she had thought at once, was probably the most bossy of any boss she had ever met. She hadn't liked him then; she liked him even less now.

The afternoon wore on, her thoughts and memories occasionally jarred by the sound of a low, masculine voice that sometimes filtered through the closed door.

Tara greeted quitting time with a sigh of weariness, and slid one slim hand under the heavy fall of silver-blond hair to rub the back of her neck. She tidied her desk, covered her typewriter, slipped into her lightweight suede jacket, scooped up her shoulder bag, and left the office with unusual haste. As she walked to the parking lot, she drew deep lungsful of crisp October air in an attempt to clear her mind of the afternoon cobwebs. She unlocked the door of her six-month-old blue Camaro and, her sense of well-being returning, she slid behind the wheel, started the engine, and drove off the parking lot and into the crowded line of homebound traffic. In her preoccupied state she didn't hear the low roar of the engine being started up after hers, or notice the shimmery, beetle-green Thunderbird that followed her off the lot.

Fifteen minutes later she had left the heavier traffic and five minutes after that she parked the car on the quiet street in front of her apartment house. Thanking the Fates it was Friday, she locked the car, slung the handbag strap over her shoulder, and hurried across the sidewalk and through the street door of the apartment, unaware of the same Thunderbird parked two cars away from her own.

Dashing up the stairs, she swung into the hall, heading for her second floor apartment, then stopped dead in her tracks. Leaning against the wall next to her front door was the cause of her suddenly intense headache. Looking for all the world like he owned the place stood one totally relaxed Aleksei Rykovsky.

Tara felt anger reignite and the flame propelled her forward. She stopped a foot from him, brown eyes smoldering. "What are you doing here?"

Dark eyebrows went up in exaggerated surprise. "I thought we had things to discuss." His voice flowed over her like smooth honey, and she felt a tiny shiver slide along her spine.

"We have nothing to discuss," she snapped irritably. "Now, if you'll excuse me, I'm tired." She had turned and unlocked the door while she was speaking, preparing to step inside and close the door in his face, when his voice stopped her. "Of course if you're afraid to talk to me . . ."

Tara turned, her eyes frosty, her face mirroring contempt. "I'm not afraid to talk to any man. What is it you have to say?"

"I usually don't hold conversations in hallways. May I come in?" The taunting amusement in his voice grated on her nerves and, with an exclamation of annoyance, she flung open the door, then spun around and walked into the living room.

On hearing the door close with a soft click, she drew a deep breath for control then turned to watch him come slowly across the room to her.

"What do you want?"

"You."

Tara's breath was drawn in on an audible gasp. "Are you out of your mind?"

"No more than most. If I'm not mistaken, I proposed marriage to you today. I came for an answer."

"No."

"Why?"

Really angry now, Tara was finding it difficult keeping her voice down. "I told you this morning I don't think you're funny. Aren't you carrrying this joke a bit too far?"

"And I told you this morning I was not trying to be funny." His own tone wasn't quite as smooth. "I mean it. Will you marry me?"

Tara brushed her hand across her eyes in disbelief. "Why? I mean, why are you asking me to marry you?"

He stepped closer to her, brought up one hand to brush long brown fingers across her soft cheek. "Fair question," he murmured, "but I've already answered it. You're a beautiful, desirable woman. I want you. Would you let me set you up in an apartment in my building?"

"No." It was a soft explosive uttered at the same time she moved back, away from his caressing, oddly disturbing fingers.

"I thought not." He laughed low in his throat, arching one mocking brow at her as she moved away from him. "If the only way I can have you is through marriage," he shrugged, "I'll marry you. I should more than meet your requirements of a prosperous man. I'm a very, very prosperous man."

Tara shivered in revulsion. This man's arrogance was beyond belief.

"Get out of here." Her voice had dropped to a whisper, and she was shaking in anger.

"Tara."

"If you don't get out of here, I'll call the super and have you thrown out." Fighting for control, she spoke through clenched teeth.

Dark blue eyes, bright and glittering with anger, stared into hers; then he moved so quickly, she was left speechless. His hands shot out and caught her face, drawing her up to him. Up. Up, until she was almost dangling on tiptoes inches below his face. She could do no more with her hands than grasp his waist for support, and her voice was a barely strangled gasp.

"What do you think you're—"

Closing the inches that separated them, he caught her open mouth with his, sending a shaft of sensation Tara later told herself was disgust through her body that left the tips of her fingers and toes tingling. His lips were firm, cool, and insistent and, to her horror, she felt her own begin to respond.

Alek's mouth released her slowly. Then with his lips still almost touching hers, she felt his cool breath mingle with hers as he murmured words in a strange language Tara thought must be Russian. His mouth brushed hers roughly before he lifted his head, and his even more darkened blue eyes stared into her soft brown ones, wide with confusion and a hint of fear. "All right, pansy eyes, I'll go," he said softly, then more firmly, "but think about what I said. I could give you a very comfortable life, Tara."

He released her so suddenly, she almost fell, and before she could form a retort, he was across the room and out the door. Trembling with reaction, lips parted to draw deep, steadying breaths, she glanced around the room as if seeking reassurance from familiar things. *No one in his right mind would say and do the things he had,* she thought wildly. Moving a little unsteadily, she walked to the sofa and sank into it, resting her head back and closing her eyes. *The man had to be mad.* The thought jolted her memory back to something David had said months ago.

Tara had had dinner with David and Sallie and they'd been sitting comfortably in the living room with their coffee when Sallie mentioned Aleksei Rykovsky. Tara had grimaced with distaste and, with a rueful smile, David shook his head. "I don't understand why you don't like him, Tara. Most people do, you know."

Although David and Sallie had long been aware of Tara's preference for well-off men and in fact had introduced her to a few (believing she had an ingrained fear of being poor due to her upbringing), they had no idea of her aversion to the masterful type.

Tara had sighed, reluctant to answer, yet knowing she had to say something. "Oh, I don't know. It's just, well, he seems so damned sure of himself. So completely *in charge. The*"—and here she waved her hand around as if trying to pluck the word out of the air—"*boss,* so to speak. It annoys me."

"I don't know why it should," came David's gentle-voiced reply. "I've never heard him boss you. And anyway, he is the boss. You know what designing his new plant means to me, Tara. This is what I've been waiting for ever since I opened my own office. This is the biggest challenge I've had so far, and Alek has very definite ideas on what he does and does not want. My God, girl, you've seen the proposed budget. In my view, any man who can afford to build a new plant at that cost without batting an eye damned well deserves to be boss."

David's tone had become unusually severe toward the end of his admonition to Tara, and when he finished, the room grew taut with a strained silence.

In an obvious attempt to lighten the mood, Sallie turned to David with a soft laugh. "Darling, within the last few weeks I've heard several people refer to him as 'the Mad Russian.' Do you have any idea why?"

David's laughter echoed his wife's, and when he answered, all traces of his previous harshness were gone. "Yes, sweets, I do know why. But don't be alarmed; they don't mean crazy-mad. It seems Alek has acquired a reputation for accepting difficult jobs with a close delivery date. Real squeakers, so to speak. The way I hear it, he has, so far, always managed to deliver top quality work—on time. When he first started this practice, those who are in a position to know were heard to say the man was mad to take on such impossible job orders. Ergo—the title *Mad Russian* evolved."

Sallie gave an exaggerated sigh of relief. "Well, that's good to know. I was beginning to think perhaps his attic light was out."

Opening her eyes, Tara shuddered and sat up, Sallie's words of months ago ringing in her ears. After Aleksei Rykovsky's behavior this evening, Tara was inclined to disregard David's explanation and go with Sallie's. In Tara's opinion the Mad Russian's attic light was definitely out.

Reaction was setting in. Tara felt tight and jumpy all over and, glancing down, she stared vacantly at her trembling hands. Closing her eyes, she swallowed around the dryness in her throat and bit hard on her lower lip.

Suddenly she had to move, needed the feeling of some sort of purposeful action. Moving almost jerkily, she went into the kitchen to the cabinet where she kept her cleaning materials. Grasping a dustcloth and a can of spray wax, she returned to the living room.

Slowly, methodically, she applied herself to waxing every piece of wooden furniture in the room. There were not all that many pieces, for it wasn't a very large room. But what there was was well chosen, reflecting Tara's quiet good taste. Not an edge or corner was missed and from there Tara went into the bedroom and proceeded to give the same treatment to the furniture there.

When, finally, she had to admit to herself there was not one square inch of wood left without a double coat of wax, she returned to the kitchen and replaced the cloth and can.

Straightening from the low cabinet, she stood motionless a moment then said aloud, wonderingly, "What am I doing?" But without allowing any answers to filter through, she was moving again, going to the sink to wash her hands.

Uneasy, because she didn't know why, Tara didn't want to think at all just then. Least of all about *him*.

With single-minded purpose she broiled a small steak, tossed an equally small salad, and brewed half a pot of coffee. Twenty-five minutes after she had seated herself at the small kitchen table, she swallowed the last of her third cup of coffee then stood up and carried her plate to the sink to scrape most of her meal into the garbage disposal.

Tara washed up slowly and carefully, wiping the table, countertops, and stove free of the tiniest imagined spot. When she finally flicked the light switch off, she left the darkened room even more neat and sparkling than usual.

Still moving with the same single-minded purpose, she went to the bathroom, stripped, stepped under the shower, and brought all her concentration to bear on shampooing her long, heavy fall of silver-blond hair.

Later, dressed in nightie and terry robe, she sat in front of her makeup mirror—brush in one hand, blow dryer in the other—and stared with unseeing eyes into the glass. In her mind's eye grew a sharp picture of two glittering dark blue eyes and inside her head, as clearly as a few hours earlier, that deep masculine voice said: "You're a beautiful, desirable woman. I want you."

A shudder went through her body, and she watched, almost blankly, her pale, slim hand grasp the handle of the dryer to still its shaking.

He was beyond her experience. His manner—everything about him—was an unknown. She had gone out with a few carefully selected young men. She had been kissed, thoroughly, by all of them. Most had made a play toward a more intimate relationship. Yet none had shocked or upset her as this man had, with seemingly little effort.

Tara felt vaguely frightened even now, hours later, and she wasn't quite sure why. Was she overreacting? She didn't think so. People who were hitting on all cylinders didn't behave as he had. Did they?

From their first meeting she had felt uncomfortable and strangely on edge whenever he was around, either in the office or on the building site, and now, Tara told herself, she knew why. Not only was he autocratic and arrogant, which were bad enough in themselves, but he also had a streak of erraticism. The thing that puzzled her was, if she had sensed this in the man, why hadn't David and the others?

2

Tara had a depressing weekend. Not only was she shaken, at odd hours of the day and night, by thoughts of Aleksei Rykovsky's strange behavior, she made the mistake of choosing this weekend to visit her mother.

She walked into her father's house Sunday after dinner to find her mother in tears, her father bellowing at her younger sister, Betsy, and the twenty-one-year-old Betsy screaming back that she was packing her clothes and moving in with her boyfriend.

Tara groaned softly as she hurried across the room to her mother. *This was all I needed to make my weekend complete,* she thought wearily. At that moment she would not have been shocked or surprised if her mother told her her eighteen-year-old brother George had a girl in trouble and that her fourteen-year-old-brother Karl had taken their father's car and smashed it.

"Tara." Her mother grasped her arms agitatedly. "Please go talk to your sister. She'll listen to you. I'll die of shame if she moves in with Kenny. And your father will be impossible to live with."

So what else is new, Tara thought resignedly. But she smoothed her mother's once beautiful hair, then gently removed her clutching hands. "All right, Mama, I'll go see what I can do. But will you tell me what this is all about first?" As she was speaking she drew her mother into the kitchen, enabling them to talk without having to shout over the din from the second floor.

In the comparative quiet of the kitchen, Marlene Schmitt drew a deep breath before beginning her explanations. "Well, it started Friday," she began and Tara thought swiftly, didn't everything? "Your father told Betsy that with inflation and all, he'd have to raise her board. She was very upset because she herself hasn't had a raise in pay for some time. Then yesterday they had an argument just before Kenny came for her to go to a movie. He said her room looked like a pigsty, and it was time she cleaned it." Tara felt a flash of irritation. It was true that Betsy was a little careless with her things, but her room did not look like a pigsty.

"They barely spoke to each other all morning." Her mother's eyes filled with tears, and she twisted her hands nervously. "I guess it's my fault. I was late with dinner, and Betsy asked if she could skip drying the dishes since Kenny was picking her up soon and she had to get ready. Your father exploded. He told her she was not allowed to go with Kenny today and could only see him two nights a week from now on."

"For heaven's sake, Mother, Betsy's twenty-one years old," Tara exclaimed indignantly.

"That's exactly what she said to him. But he told her that she was in his house, and as long as she remained under his roof, she'd do as he said. That's when she said she wouldn't stay here any longer. That she was moving in with Kenny. Oh, Tara, please stop her."

"Okay, okay, calm down. I said I'd do what I can. And you're not to blame yourself just because dinner was late. I'll talk to him too, if I can, and try to make him see reason."

Several hours later Tara collapsed onto her own sofa with a sigh of exhaustion. After long talks with both her sister and father that would have put a diplomat to shame, she had finally procured a peace settlement of sorts. She smiled ruefully, acknowledging the fact that George had been the one who swayed her father. He had entered the house, and the argument, and declared firmly in favor of Betsy. That her eighteen-year-old brother's opinion was held in higher esteem by her father than her own did not surprise Tara. To a man like her father the judgment of almost any male held more value than that of a female. With bitter amusement Tara thought her father would fall over one Aleksei Rykovsky, seeing in him the absolute top dog of dominant men. Her amusement faded as she considered the probability of encountering that same top dog in the office tomorrow.

After Friday night, what could they possibly say to each other? How could they work together if need be?

Thankfully her fears were proved groundless—at least through Wednesday—as the "head honcho," as Tara now thought of him, hadn't appeared.

A mystery did, though, in the form of a single, long-stemmed white rose that was delivered to her at the office Monday morning and each morning after that. When Jeannie brought the first one to her, Tara was at first delighted. The rose was perfectly shaped and beautiful; its scent heady, almost sensual. As Tara searched through the tissue paper in the florist box, Jeannie sighed enviously. "You must have a secret admirer, Tara. The delivery man said there was no card and wouldn't even take a tip. Said he'd already been tipped. Do you have any idea who it's from?"

Tara shook her head slowly. "No, but I'll probably find out before too long." Then smiling teasingly at the younger girl, she added, "And you'll be the first to know, I promise."

Jeannie flashed her an impish grin as she left the office, and Tara sat staring broodingly at the rose. Who could have sent it? The first name to jump into her mind was Aleksei Rykovsky, but she dismissed that at once. Much too subtle for the head honcho; he apparently went in for caveman tactics. Who then? Terry Connors? She mused on the young draftsman in the outer office a few moments, then shook her head decisively. Not Terry. He probably wouldn't think of it, especially after the way she'd spoken to him the last time he'd asked her out. She'd been honest to the point of bluntness. Although he was an attractive young man with talent and a promising future, he was more in love with himself than he could be with any one woman. In so many words she'd told him just that. He'd barely spoken to her since and then only in the office. He lived in an apartment just down the street from hers, and she'd passed him a few times going to and from her apartment and her car. At those times he'd nodded curtly, not speaking. So scratch Terry.

Names kept bouncing in and out of her mind as she hunted up the summer bud vase she'd shoved to the back of her personal desk drawer, and one by one she rejected them. Finally, running out of prospects, she gave up.

She went through the same mental gyrations on Tuesday morning. When the rose was delivered on Wednesday morning, she decided to stop trying to solve the puzzle and just enjoy it.

As she prepared for bed Wednesday night Tara realized the advent of the morning rose had taken the edge off her nervousness about meeting Aleksei Rykovsky in the office. She also told herself the man was probably feeling ridiculous about his behavior and had not come to David's office because he was embarrassed to face her. She should have known better.

She was at the filing cabinet Thursday morning when David, with a pleasant good morning, breezed through her small office on the way to his own. Tara looked up, but before she had a chance to voice a return greeting, two strong hands gripped her shoulders and a caressing voice said, "Morning, darling," as she was turned around and held against a hard, muscular chest. She saw gleaming blue eyes, gave a startled "Oh," then went warm all over as Aleksei Rykovsky's firm mouth covered hers. Again that odd, tingling sensation touched the tips of her fingers and toes but before she could react to push him away, he lifted his head. "I missed that this morning, sleepyhead." While caressing, his tone also held a touch of possession, and Tara was left speechless. He laughed softly as he moved away from her with obvious reluctance to join David, who still stood in the doorway with a patently interested look on his face.

Flushed with embarrassment, wide-eyed in confusion, Tara faced David. "I— I . . .''

David shook his head slowly, smiled gently, and closed the door between the two offices.

Anger flushed her cheeks even more brightly as she stared at the closed door. Who did he think he was, kissing her like that? And what in the world did he mean, he'd missed that this morning?

At lunchtime, instead of having lunch at her desk as she usually did, Tara left the office and walked. Ever since her teens, whenever she was troubled or had a particularly knotty problem to work out, she walked. She started out at a good pace, her long slender legs eating up the city blocks rapidly. Anger stirred her blood and kept the adrenaline pumping.

This man, this Rykovsky, was beginning to drive her wild. *Banish him,* she told herself severely. *Push him out of your mind completely.* Not an easy thing to do. Mocking blue eyes in a handsome face were beginning to haunt her. Why had he suddenly set out to bedevil her? Had she slipped up, let her dislike and disapproval of him show? If she had, she couldn't think when. For David's sake she had worked hard at always displaying a cool, efficient, respectful attitude toward him.

She could not think of one instance during the last few months when she had let her mask drop even at the times—and there had been several during office meetings and on the new plant site—when his overbearing superiority, his enormous self-confidence and arrogance, had made her hand itch with the desire to slap his haughty, patrician face. She had controlled the urge by removing herself from his presence on one pretext or another.

Sighing softly, Tara shook her head in defeat. She had no idea why he was attacking her. She had avoided his type like the plague and so could not fathom what his motivation could possibly be.

Tara had been striding along at a good clip, oblivious to her surroundings and the gloriously warm fall day. The dry, crackling sound of leaves being crushed underfoot cracked the door of her consciousness; the happy ripple of young children laughing pushed it open.

Glancing around. she shortened her stride; then she stopped completely. She was passing the park, the still deep-green, well tended grass partially obscured now by the heavy fall of leaves from the various types of trees in the park. Again children laughing caught her attention, and her gaze followed the sounds to the park's small-tot lot. Young mothers stood together talking while keeping a watchful eye on their offspring. Others guided toddlers down sliding boards or stood behind swings, gently pushing each time the seat arced back. Bemused, Tara watched the happy, worry-free youngsters play. She had always loved children, been happy and eager to help her mother when first George and then Karl were born.

A gentle smile tugged at her lips; a tiny ache tugged at her heart. Would she ever meet a man whose children she would not only be willing to raise but wanted to bear with a deep and passionate longing? Had she set her sights too high, made her requirements too rigid? Apparently not, for she had met more than one young man who'd not only met her requirements but had other extra added attractions as well. Yet they had all left her cold, with no desire to continue the relationship, let alone deepen it.

Was she destined to spend the rest of her life alone, searching for some illusive thing that could set a spark to her emotions? Was she never to know the joy evident on the faces of the young mothers she now observed? Did they realize, she wondered, how precious the time was that they held in their hands as their babies grew? Did anyone ever?

Giving herself a mental shake. Tara breathed in deeply, filling her lungs with the sweet, smoky taste of autumn. She had become pensive and moody and, with a determined effort, she drew her eyes away from the children, turned, and began retracing her steps to the office.

A long, low wolf-whistle, issued from the window of a passing car, brought a smile to Tara's lips, a spring to her step. Her long, silvery hair bounced on her shoulders and against her back in rhythm with her stride. The soft breeze played havoc with the feather-cut hair that curved down, then flipped back on either side of her center part.

Her walk—*or stalk,* Tara thought wryly—had restored her equilibrium. For all of fifteen minutes, back there at the park, she hadn't given one thought to the head honcho. But now he was back to torment her thoughts. She had walked off the sharpest edge of her anger, but the core was still there, burning low but steadily.

What games was this man playing at? And how in the world would she explain her behavior this morning to David? Her worry on that score proved groundless, for she had no sooner returned to her office when David came out of his. Alone.

"I'm going out to lunch with Alek, Tara. He's waiting in the car now. I probably won't be back for the rest of the day. You'll have to handle anything that comes up." David's voice was completely normal, yet Tara felt herself grow warm at the speculative glance he passed over her.

"David, about this morning. I don't know how to explain, except—" She paused, searching for words, and David cut in gently. "Don't worry about it, Tara. You should know by now I'm broad-minded and anyway, Alek explained everything, even though it wasn't necessary. It's really none of my business. Now I've got to go, as we're meeting the contractor. See you tomorrow."

More confused than ever, Tara sat stunned. What in the name of sanity was going on? What explanation could Alek have given for his outrageous actions? And why wasn't it any of David's business? You would think a madman running around loose would be everybody's business.

The more she thought about it, the more convinced she became that Alek Rykovsky was playing some sort of cat-and-mouse game. But to what purpose? More than likely, she thought, his pride had been injured and he wanted to make her uncomfortable. Well! he was certainly succeeding there. But why involve David?

By the time the rose arrived Friday morning, she hardly gave the identity of its sender a second thought. After the events of the day before, it didn't seem to matter much. Besides, she had slept badly and was tired, not at all looking forward to round three with the Mad Russian. She was at a total loss as to what he hoped to gain, and so completely missed the clues.

It was a quiet weekend. Too quiet. Tara was not in the habit of running out several nights a week, but she usually went out at least one night during the weekend. Sometimes with a man, but more often with a group of young friends, which included David and Sallie, for dinner or stay-at-home evenings of cards and conversation. This was the second weekend in a row she had not received a call or invitation from one of her friends, not even Sallie.

The only unusual thing that happened was on Saturday and Sunday morning when she went to the door to answer the bell only to find the hall empty except for the now familiar florist box containing a single white rose.

By Sunday night Tara decided the whole thing was very weird. She liked her quiet, but this was too much. Beginning to feel vaguely like the last person on earth, she reached for the phone with the intention of calling Sallie when its sudden jangling ring startled her so badly, she actually jumped.

"I didn't interrupt anything, did I, Tara?" Betsy's voice was as much of a surprise as her words, as Betsy seldom called and then usually only when she wanted something, as it seemed she did now.

"Interrupt anything? For heaven's sake, Betsy, it's after ten thirty. Tomorrow's a working day. I'll soon be going to bed." What kind of a wild existence did her sister think she lived, anyway?

"Well, Sis, you're such a close-mouthed thing, one never knows. Except of course, what one may read in the papers or"—she paused—"hear through the grapevine."

There was a definite insinuation on Betsy's last four words and Tara felt her skin prickle.

"What?"

"Doesn't matter. Look, Tara, the reason I called was, if you decide to give up your apartment, will you let Ken and me know? Maybe even talk to your landlord for us?"

Give up her apartment? What in the world? Her tone was an equal mixture of exasperation and puzzlement. "Betsy, I don't know what you've heard or think, but—"

"Oh! I had no intentions of prying," Betsy interrupted, her words coming in a rush, tripping over each other. "I've told you how small Ken's place is and I thought I'd get my bid in if you were considering it. You know, I'm a big girl now and I'm hip to the ways of the world and I do understand. I mean, he's such a magnificent . . . fantastic hunk of man."

Skinny Kenny? Magnificent? Fantastic? Tara knew her sister was inclined to exaggerate, but this was too much. Puzzlement won out over exasperation. "Bets, I think some explanation is necessary," Tara began, only to have Betsy interrupt again.

"No, really, just keep us in mind. Okay? Bye." She hung up and Tara stared at the receiver in her hand as if she had never seen one before. Sighing deeply, she wondered if everyone around her was slipping over the edge, or if it was she who was going bananas.

A single white rose continued to arrive daily at the office, and by midweek Tara simply sniffed it appreciatively, stuck it in the vase, and went about her work. She was grateful for one thing: Aleksei Rykovsky hadn't shown up at the office at all and David treated her as if nothing had ever happened.

It was almost noon on Friday when Sallie dashed into the office. "Hi, Tara. Is David terribly busy? I have something I want to check with him and I'm in an awful rush."

"David's never too busy to see you, Sallie." Tara laughed. "Go on in and surprise him."

In less than ten minutes Sallie was back, standing in front of her desk, pulling soft tan pigskin gloves over her hand.

"I wanted to check with him about the wine for tomorrow night. I was going to call him from home, but then Mother came to look after Tina, and I didn't think of it again until after I'd left the house." Sallie spoke quickly, glancing at the clock. "I'll miss you tomorrow night, Tara, but David explained everything and I do understand. At least I think I do." Sallie's expression held concern; she seemed almost hurt. "Oh, Lord! I have to run. I'm meeting Dave's mother for lunch and I'm going to be late." She grimaced, threw Tara a half-smile, and dashed out again.

Tara experienced the same prickling sensation in her skin she'd had the previous Sunday while talking to her sister, and with it a mild sense of alarm. What was this all about? It was beginning to seem that everyone understood everything but her. She was tempted to confront David but she could hardly go in and blurt out, "Why haven't you invited me to your party?"

She worried about Sallie's words and attitude the rest of the day and finally decided the only cause she could think of was Aleksei Rykovsky's extraordinary behavior the week before and her own unwilling involvement in it. But good Lord, she had been unwilling; surely they realized that. Then pride kept her from going in to question David.

As she left the office that afternoon, she hesitated with a sudden aversion to spending the entire evening alone, confined within those few small rooms. Then with a quick, decisive step she walked to the car. Her mother's birthday was the following week and, as she had a sweet tooth that was rarely indulged, Tara decided to take a run to her favorite candy shop and buy her mother a large box of chocolates.

She turned onto Route 222 heading south and was past the consistory building before the beauty of the late October afternoon struck her. When she glanced at the grounds of Cedar Crest College to her right, her breath caught in her throat. The long fingers of the westering sun bathed the fall foliage in a golden glow, setting the russet leaves alight. The glory of the Pennsylvania autumn had always affected her with soul-wrenching intensity and today, caught so suddenly, the beauty of it all cut into her deeply. Hurt, confused by the events of the last few weeks, she was doubly vulnerable to the heart-twistingly beautiful power of nature.

She felt the hot sting of tears behind her eyes and shook her head impatiently. *This is ridiculous,* she thought moodily. The last few weeks she had spent most of her time either in her apartment or at the office. She needed a break, a diversion. She'd visit the gift shop on the floor above the candy shop, make herself a present of some small object. Hadn't she always heard that spending money on something not really needed could always lift a woman's spirits?

In the candy shop she gave her order to the clerk for the special assortment her mother loved, then slipped up the narrow stairway to the floor above. The gift shop was well stocked, the merchandise displayed on tables and shelves along the walls and down the center of the room, leaving a narrow aisle to walk around. Tara moved slowly, her eyes darting around, trying to see everything. Then her eyes stopped and focused on a painting on the wall. Studying the brilliant fall scene intently, she gave a sudden, startled "Oh" when a body jolted into her from behind.

"I'm terribly sorry," a pleasant male voice said close to her ear. "I'm afraid I wasn't watching where I was going."

She turned, mouth opened to reply but the words were never uttered for he exclaimed. "Tara! I don't know if you remember me. Craig Hartman, we met at David's six months ago."

Recognition brought a quick smile to her face. "Of course I remember. You're the young man who was getting ready to go to South America for your company."

"Right. I just got back on Tuesday. As a matter of fact I was going to call you as soon as I'd finished my report to the firm."

"Really?" she laughed. "Why?"

"To ask you to have dinner with me some evening." He grinned boyishly, and Tara remembered she'd liked this young man when first meeting him. "This is incredible seeing you here, of all places. What are you doing here?"

"Just browsing while I wait for a candy order to be packaged. And you?"

Again the boyish smile spread over his face. "I remembered late this afternoon that my sister's first wedding anniversary is tomorrow and dashed over here, after I left the office, for a gift. I was looking at the paintings and not watching where I was going when I bumped into you."

Tara grinned back. "And I was looking at one and didn't see you coming." She glanced back at the fall scene and his eyes followed hers. "That *is* nice," he murmured. "Are you going to buy it?"

"No," she laughed softly. "I'm afraid my budget wouldn't allow it."

"Then I think I will. Pat has a spot in her living room where it will go perfectly." He motioned to the sales clerk and asked her to wrap it up, then turned back to Tara. "Have dinner with me this evening," he said abruptly. "We can go from here. I know it's early, but we can have a drink or two first, get to know each other a little."

"But I haven't been home," she said, laughing in surprise. "I'm still in my work clothes."

His eyes went over her slowly, appreciatively, before he stated warmly: "You look lovely. Besides which, I've just come from work myself. What difference does it make? I'm sure they won't refuse to serve us."

They didn't, and over dinner she studied him unobtrusively. He wasn't much taller then she and, though slender, was compactly built. Fair, closely clipped curly hair complemented light blue eyes, and she thought that although he didn't possess the devastating handsomeness of one Aleksei Rykovsky, he was certainly a very attractive man. Then she slid her eyes away with a flash of irritation at herself. What in the world had made her think of that miserable man, let alone make a comparison between him and Craig?

"Hey, there."

Tara looked up, startled and wide-eyed, at Craig's laughing voice. "I thought you'd dozed off for a minute. Not very good for my ego at all."

Tara laughed with him, firmly pushing the thought of the Mad Russian from her mind.

It was a pleasant evening. They laughed and talked for hours, discovering they had a few mutual friends besides David and Sallie.

When finally they said good night at the door of her apartment, Craig having followed her car in his own, she felt happier and more relaxed than she had in weeks.

Her lightened mood lasted through the weekend, even though the white rose appeared exactly as before, and the phone remained strangely silent.

She was walking to the filing cabinet early Monday afternoon when the phone rang and she stopped beside her desk to answer it. It was her mother, and she asked Tara, in an oddly strained voice, if they could have lunch together one day that week.

"Of course, Mama," she answered, a small wrinkle forming between her eyes at the strange tone of her mother's voice. "I'll tell you what. I was planning to take you shopping for your birthday present on Saturday. Why don't we wait, and I'll buy you lunch at Hess's?"

Her mother hesitated then agreed dully, and Tara felt a flicker of alarm. Was she not feeling well? Her mother loved the rare treat of having lunch at the large department store, famous for its sumptuous food, the large, luscious desserts, and her apparent disinterest now worried Tara.

"All right, Mama, I'll pick you up at nine thirty Saturday morning. Okay?" Her mother agreed in the same strained tone, then said good-bye and hung up.

Her frown deepening, Tara lowered the receiver slowly as the office door opened behind her. A small shiver slithered up her spine, and the instrument clattered onto its cradle from nerveless fingers. She knew, somehow, who had come into the office and felt goose bumps tickle her upper arms moments before she felt his hand lift her hair and his lips touch her neck. She parted her lips but words wouldn't come. Shock, outrage, and something she didn't want to examine seemed to have frozen her mind and body.

His voice was a barely discernible murmur at her ear. "Have a good time Friday night, pansy eyes?"

She made a small, inarticulate sound in her throat, and he laughed softly, deeply before adding in a much stronger tone, "I've tried to stay away from this office, telling myself the nights should be enough, but it seems I've grown greedy and my self doesn't listen."

A shudder tore through her body at the caressing, loverlike tone, and she closed her eyes, willing him to go away. She felt David walk past them and go into his office, closing the door with a soft click, and her moan was a painful thing in her throat: "Oh, God!"

"Don't worry, darling," the fiend with the lover's voice whispered. "You'll understand everything very soon now, I'm afraid." Then he caught her rigid chin with his long fingers, turned her head, and brushed her mouth against his in a soft, tantalizing kiss before quickly releasing her and following David.

She was completely bewildered, feeling shattered and vaguely tearful.

The feeling remained throughout the week, and she hardly noticed the white morning roses. One thing she did notice was the strange, speculative looks aimed at her from her co-workers in the front office. And that made her even more edgy and nervous.

3

By Saturday morning Tara had managed to pull herself together yet she still had to force a cheerful smile to her lips when she picked up her mother. The smile faded quickly at her first glimpse of her mother's face. Lines of strain pulled at the corners of her mouth, and she avoided Tara's eyes as she seated herself in the car.

As she drove downtown, Tara made a few vain attempts at conversation but finally gave up as the only responses she received were mumbled monosyllables.

They shopped a few hours, Tara becoming ever more concerned at her mother's lack of interest at everything they looked at. Finally, at eleven thirty, Tara gave up, saying gently, "Let's go have lunch now, Mama. Maybe we'll feel more like it after we've eaten."

She studied her mother during lunch, growing more uneasy by the minute. Her mother barely touched her food, and when they'd finished and were sipping their coffee, Tara asked anxiously, "Mama what's wrong? Aren't you feeling well?"

The eyes that Marlene Schmitt turned to Tara sent a shaft of pain to her heart, so reproachful and hurt was their expression.

"I'm sick at heart, Tara," her mother finally answered sadly. "So much so, I feel physically ill. After the way you talked to Betsy just three weeks ago, I can't believe you're doing this. And Tara, I can't bear it."

Tara's eyes widened at the pain in her mother's voice. What had she done to cause her mother this anguish?

"But Mama, what have I done?" Tara asked anxiously, watching with alarm her mother's eyes fill with tears.

"Oh, Tara, don't. I know I'm a little old-fashioned and naive, but I'm no fool."

"Mama, please—"

"No. I would listen to you, take your side, in most things. But not this." She paused, a sob catching in her throat, then went on, cutting off the defensive words on Tara's lips. "Your father asked—no, told—me to bring you back to the house. I must warn you, he is beside himself with anger."

The last word was no sooner out of her mother's mouth when Tara rushed into urgent speech.

"Mama, if you'll just ex—"

"Tara, please," her mother said softly, glancing around the crowded room. "I can't discuss this here. I won't talk here. I want to go home."

Tara sighed in frustration. "All right. Let's go and get it over with."

They drove home in silence, Marlene Schmitt quietly wiping the tears from her cheeks with a sodden tissue.

Tara bit her lip in vexation, frantically casting about in her mind for some transgression she may have committed to cause her mother such unhappiness.

She followed her mother into the house, her steps faltering as she entered the living room. They were all there. Her father, his face flushed a dark, angry red; Betsy; George; and even the fourteen-year-old Karl. Anger stirred, replacing some of her anxiety. *What in the world is this anyway?* she wondered. The words *kangaroo court* flashed into her mind, and she pushed the thought away. Good Lord! This was her family, not a band of enemies. Yet the atmosphere of censure was so thick, it touched her skin chillingly.

Ever defiant, the light of battle gleamed in Tara's eyes. She had no idea what this was all about but she'd be damned if she'd stand before those condemning eyes meekly. Her father's first words took the wind from her sails.

"Well, Tara. I'm surprised you have the nerve to face any of us after your big talk three weeks ago."

"Dad," Tara began patiently, "I haven't the vaguest idea what—"

"Haven't you?" Her father nearly choked on the words. "Haven't you just?" His eyes went around the room, touching every face, then settled again on Tara. "Look at her. Proud as a damned peacock. Anyone else would have the sense to be ashamed, but not our Tara. Oh, no. Rules were made for everyone else. Tara makes hers up as she goes along. You make me sick, girl."

"Herman—" his wife pleaded.

"Don't 'Herman' me. I've listened to you since she was a teen-ager. 'Tara's intelligent,' you said. 'She has good sense,' you said. 'She'll make us proud.' *Ha!* What she's doing is intelligent? Makes good sense? It's degrading, disgusting. I should have beat the rebellion out of her years ago."

The defiance in Tara's eyes had slowly changed to bewilderment. Never had she seen her father quite so angry. This was serious. Really serious. And she didn't have a clue as to what he was talking about.

"Dad, please. If you'll just explain—"

It seemed she was not to be allowed to speak, for he interrupted with a shouted, "Me explain? You think we're dumb Dutchmen, don't you? You think we're so stupid, we don't understand. You think your mother doesn't understand the gossip of her friends? You think your sister and brothers don't understand the behind-the-hand snickers of their friends? You think I don't understand the dirty remarks made by the men I work with?"

Tara wet her suddenly dry lips. Her father's dark, mottled color frightened her, but his words frightened her more. This was more than serious; this was ugly. When she didn't reply at once, her father shouted, "Do you think we haven't heard of this man's reputation with women?"

Tara's head snapped up. *What man?* The silent question was answered loudly.

"Do you think we haven't heard how this rich Russian uses them and then kicks them aside? Oh, sure," he added, his voice dripping sarcasm. "He gives them anything they want. Anything, that is, except his name."

"You're wrong," Tara whispered, horrified.

"Of course." His sarcasm grew yet stronger. "That can't happen to you. You're too good for that." His eyes bored into her with hatred. "You've always thought yourself too good. Too good for us or this house. Too good for the nice, hardworking young men who were interested in you. But not too good, apparently, to crawl into bed with that swine Rykovsky."

"Herman, don't." Tara heard her mother scream, but she couldn't help her.

She could hardly breathe. Her father's words had hit her like a punch in the ribs, and she stood, white and trembling, staring at his face. Then she spun on her heel and ran, her mother's sobs beating on her ears.

Hours later, as she closed her apartment door behind her, she had no recollection of getting to her car. Or, for that matter, of driving up into the mountains. She had been brought to her senses by the long, blaring sound of the horn of the car she nearly ran head into. Shaken, sick to her stomach, face wet with tears she didn't even remember shedding, she slowed down the car then pulled in and stopped at the first observation parking area she came to. She hadn't left the car, as there were many tourists walking around, admiring the splendor of the panoramic view of the mountains, overlapping each other as if trying to push themselves forward in a proud display of their brilliant fall finery.

Tara sat still, hands gripping the steering wheel. Suddenly everything made sense. At least almost everything. Now she understood her sister's strange phone call two weeks ago. Now she understood David and Sallie's reserved attitude. And now she understood the sly looks of everyone in the office, the odd silence of her friends. They all thought she and Aleksei Rykovsky were—her mind shied from the word momentarily—*lovers*. The word pushed its way forward. They all thought he was her lover. Vivid pictures followed the word into her mind and she gasped aloud. Seemingly of its own volition, her arm lifted her hand to her face and drew the back of it across her mouth then quickly turned to press cold fingers to slightly parted lips. She could actually feel his mouth against hers. Could feel again that confusing mixture of excitement and fear his lips had aroused. Her fingertips tingled and, lifting her hand, she stared at her fingers as if hypnotized. "Oh, God, no," she whispered.

Now she pushed herself away from the apartment door against which she'd slumped and stumbled across her living room and into the bedroom. Dropping her handbag and jacket onto the floor, she fell across the bed fully clothed, exhausted, her mind numbed into blankness. She had no idea how long she lay staring into space when the shrill ringing of the phone roused her. Dragging her body from the bed, she walked slowly to the living room, legs still shaking. Dropping heavily onto the chair by the phone, she picked up the receiver and said, dully, "Hello."

A pause, then Craig Hartman's voice came over the wire, hesitant, uncertain. "Tara?"

"Yes . . . Craig?"

"I thought I had the wrong number," he laughed softly. "It didn't sound like you. Did you just get in?"

"Yes," she answered blankly. "But how did you know?"

"I rang your phone a couple of times this afternoon."

"Why?"

"To ask you to have dinner with me, silly. It's not too late. Will you come out with me?"

"Oh, Craig," she answered wearily. "Not tonight. I'm not feeling well."

He was instant concern. "I'm sorry. What's wrong?"

"Nothing serious. I have a blinding headache and I'm going to take some aspirin and go to bed."

"Sounds best. Hope you feel better tomorrow. May I call you one night next week?"

"Yes, any night. Thank you for inviting me."

"You bet! Take care of yourself. I'll call. Good night."

"Good night, Craig."

Tara replaced the receiver then sat staring at the white Princess phone, her brow knit in concentration. The numbness that had gripped her mind at the memory of Aleksei Rykovsky's kiss had been swept away, and her brain was asking questions.

What was his reputation with women? Tara had no idea. She seldom listened to that sort of gossip simply because she could not care less how other people conducted their private lives. What had her father said? Something about how he used women then tossed them aside. *Very probably true,* Tara thought, her lips curling slightly. The word *womanizer* seemed to fit in perfectly with *tyrant*—arrogant and bossy.

Aleksei Rykovsky's emerging character was an unsavory one. Yet not completely so, Tara admitted to herself grudgingly. His reputation concerning his work was excellent; this Tara knew. Not only from things David had said but also from what she'd observed herself.

According to David, whom Tara wouldn't dream of doubting, Alek was the most ethical businessman he'd ever met. The signing of a contract with Rykovsky, David had told her, was a mere formality. For, once given, his word was as binding as his signature. He managed his plant with a combination of rigid discipline and humane understanding. The finished product, before it left his plant, had to be of the highest quality. And his patience, when dealing either with other businessmen or his employees, was legend.

This last Tara had found a little hard to believe. She remembered vividly one afternoon in late August at the new plant site. She had gone with David to take notes as he conferred with Alek and the construction boss. It had been hot, the humidity hanging in the seventies. Tara had felt sticky and slightly headachy; the condition was not helped by the fact that Alek had been late, and they'd stood in the hot sun waiting for him. When he had finally arrived with a brief word of apology, Tara had felt her headache grow stronger at the sheer impact of his appearance.

Tara's eyes had run over him swiftly as he approached them. He had left his jacket in the car and Tara wet dry lips, watching the lithe movement of his body as he strode forward. Dark brown slacks hugged his slim hips and muscular thighs and his shirt clung damply to an alarmingly broad expanse of chest and shoulders. Deeply tanned arms contrasted strikingly with the creamy color of his short-sleeved shirt and the slim gold watch on his wrist. He still wore his tie but, in concession to the heat, he had pulled the knot loose and opened the two top buttons of his shirt. Frowning, Tara had shifted her eyes away with a flash of irritation at the blatantly sensual look of him. Not once, either then or since, had Tara considered the incongruity of her irritation: She had been on the site some twenty-five minutes and had not been annoyed by, or really even noticed, the fact that most of the workers were either bare-chested or had their shirts opened to the waist.

Other than a nod in her direction on arrival, Alek had seemed unaware of her existence while she stood beside David, pencil flying over her notepad. When the context of the discussion changed to that of not requiring note taking, Tara moved back and away a few feet to give the men privacy.

Flipping the pages as she checked over her notes, Tara had been only surfacely aware of the large, burly workman walking in her direction. As he moved to pass by, not much more than a foot in front of her, he stumbled and Tara glanced up with a startled "Oh!" Arms flailing the air as if to regain his balance, his one hand arced past her face and the next instant she went rigid as his large, grimy fingers clutched her right breast.

The subsequent action had the element of a film viewed from a speeded-up projector; and yet every movement remained clear in Tara's memory. Stepping back and away from those clutching fingers, Tara glanced in dismay at the soil mark on her otherwise pristine white sleeveless scooped-neck top. At the same time, from the moment the man had stumbled, Tara had peripherally seen Alek's head jerk up then had seen him moving, crossing the few feet of sun-baked yellow-brown earth in two long-legged strides. He reached the man at the same instant Tara stepped back, and her surprise changed to alarm as she saw his arm flash up then down, the edge of his hand striking a blow to the man's shoulder that drove him to his knees. Long hard fingers strategically placed at the back of the man's neck kept him there.

"Are you trying to find out what it would be like to be paralyzed for the rest of your life?"

The tone of Alek's voice had sent a shuddering chill through Tara's body. Icy, deadly, his words hung like a pall on the suddenly still, hot air. Tara became aware of the work stoppage of the men in their vicinity, the intent look of attention on the men's faces, including David and the construction boss.

The burly workman at Alek's feet gave a strangled sound in the negative, and Alek's hand moved from the back of his neck.

"If you, or any other member of this work crew, ever make an advance on Mr. Jennings's secretary again, you'll find out pretty damned quickly, so pass the word. Now get the hell away from here and get back to work."

For such a large man, the worker was on his feet and moving away at what Tara was sure was a record pace.

She had very little time to observe the man's retreat, for Alek's eyes, blazing with blue fury, were turned on her. Swiftly they raked the upper part of her body then returned to bore into hers. His voice a harsh whisper, he snapped, "As for you, Miss Schmitt, may I suggest that in the future you dress with a little more decorum when you're on the site. Unless, of course, you enjoy this kind of attention."

With that he turned and walked back to David. Shocked, Tara stood open-mouthed, staring at his back. Shock was at once replaced by humiliation and anger at what she considered his unwarranted attack on both herself and the hapless workman. That his last whispered words had obviously reached no other ears but her own was little consolation.

Turning, cheeks red with embarrassment, Tara spun around and stalked to David's car, slamming the door after sliding onto the front seat. *That arrogant, obnoxious brute,* she raged silently. Where did he get off speaking to her like that? Dress with more decorum indeed! Her clothes were perfectly decent. Moreover, they were in perfectly good taste.

Honest in his business dealings, he may be, Tara thought. *Fanatical in his demand for quality work, perhaps. But patient? Hardly.*

Now, still sitting next to the phone, Tara wondered about his supposed reputation with women. With a manner as abrasive as his, how in the world had he acquired it? No woman playing with all fifty-two of her cards would care to get within shouting distance, let alone close enough to be used then tossed aside. . . .

Her stomach gave a protestingly empty growl, startling her out of her thoughts. She had overslept this morning and had gulped a half glass of orange juice for breakfast. Tara had barely picked at her lunch and now at—she glanced at her watch—eight fifteen her body was sending out a cry for nourishment.

Like an automaton she stood up and walked into the kitchen; she started a pot of coffee, put an egg in the poacher, and dropped two pieces of bread in the toaster. A few minutes later, as she munched her egg and toast thoughtfully, her mind went back to the question: *Who had perpetrated a rumor of this kind? Why would someone want to? And equally baffling, how?* She had seen the man only four times in three weeks. Three times in the office, and then only briefly, and that one time here at her own apartment. Surely not even the most imaginative person could make anything of a twenty-minute visit. And no one had witnessed those incidents in the office except David. David? Tara shook her head firmly. David would have told no one but Sallie, and Sallie, Tara was positive, would not repeat it. But then who? and why? and dammit, how?

Tara got up, walked to the counter, and refilled her coffee cup. As she turned back to the table, she became still with an altogether new thought. *Her* name and reputation were not the only ones involved here. Had word of this reached Aleksei Rykovsky's ears? She somehow felt certain that it had. He was not the man to miss anything. Whatever must he be thinking?

The phone's ringing broke her thoughts, and she went to answer it, carrying her coffee with her.

"Hello."

"Tara, it's me, Betsy." *As if I wouldn't know,* Tara thought wryly. "Look, Sis, I just wanted you to know I don't feel the same as Dad does."

"About what?" Tara asked, tiredly.

"Oh, you know," her sister snorted impatiently. "About you and him. I think you would have been dumb not to grab him, he's so handsome and rich."

Tara was quiet so long digesting the greedy sound and intent of her sister's words that Betsy said sharply, "Tara?"

"Good-bye, Betsy." Tara pressed her finger on the disconnect button on the inside of the receiver then carefully placed it on the table next to the cradle. She certainly didn't need any more calls or opinions like that tonight.

Sipping at her still hot coffee, she turned to go back to the kitchen when the door chime rang. *Oh, now what?* she thought balefully. Staring at the door, she considered not answering, when it chimed again.

Sighing deeply, she walked across the pale beige carpet, unlocked the door, pulled it open, and froze. Cool and relaxed, Alek Rykovsky stood in the hall, his hands jammed in the pockets of his black raincoat. *Was it raining?* Tara wondered irrelevantly. *Must be,* she decided, noting the damp spots on his wide shoulders. His coat hung open and he looked trim and muscular in the close-fitting, black brushed-denim jeans and a white turtleneck bulky knit sweater. *He was one unnerving sight,* Tara admitted ruefully to herself. If someone had to smear her name in connection with a man, at least whoever it was had chosen a handsome devil.

"May I come in?" he asked pointedly. "Or are you going to just stand there looking daggers at me?"

She jerked her eyes away, feeling her face go hot. Embarrassment put a sharp edge to her tongue.

"Come in if you must," she said cuttingly, pulling the door wider. Perfectly shaped lips twitching, he strolled past her, and in agitation she slammed the door shut. Lifting her cup to her lips, she took a long, calming sip.

"I'd like some of that." He nodded at her cup.

Turning abruptly, she marched into the kitchen with Alek right on her heels. She went to the counter, snatched a mug from its peg on the mug tree, filled it to the brim, then turned and gave an exclaimed "Oh," not having realized he was still close behind her. Some of the hot liquid splashed over the side of the cup and onto her hand, and he snatched the cup away from her with a growled "What the hell are you trying to do? Scald yourself?"

"I—I—didn't know you were so close," she stammered.

The fires that had momentarily lit his eyes were banked into a bright glitter. "Do I frighten you, Tara?" he chided.

"No, of course not," she snapped. "You startled me, that's all." She turned to refill her own cup, trying in vain to control her shaking hands.

"Hmmm," he murmured judiciously, shrugging out of his raincoat. He draped the coat over the back of a kitchen chair, picked up his cup and drank from it, then, one dark brow arched questioningly, said, "You seem upset about something. Anything wrong?"

Something about his too casual tone annoyed her and, her voice oversweet, she purred, "Have you heard the latest gossip?"

"About us?" he replied, his tone equally sweet.

Anger flared fiercely, and her usually soft brown eyes flashed. "No, the Prince of Wales," she spat. "Of course about us."

He nodded, watching her mounting anger solemnly.

"Who would do something like this," she burst out angrily.

"Don't you know?"

She jerked her head up to stare at him, suspecting some sort of condemnation. His face was expressionless, his eyes coolly calculating. "No, I don't know! I can't believe for a minute that any of my friends would spread such a vicious story."

"The idea of you and me together is vicious?"

Tara eyed him stormily, hating the theatrically affronted tone of his voice. "You may be amused, Mr. Rykovsky. This kind of thing enhances a man's aura. But my reputation is ruined."

"Is that so very important today?" he asked dryly.

"Of course it is," she cried.

"Well, you may have a point," he murmured. "Come to think of it, you're right."

"What do you mean?"

He drained his cup, walked to the sink, rinsed it, and placed it in the draining rack. Then he turned, took her cup from her hand, and did the same to it before asking, "Wouldn't we be more comfortable in the living room?" Not waiting for an answer, he scooped up his coat and strode out of the kitchen.

Gritting her teeth, Tara followed him, entering the living room in time to see him drop into a chair and stretch his long legs out comfortably.

"If you're sure you're comfortable, Mr. Rykovsky, perhaps you'd explain what you said before."

"What was that?" he asked innocently, then smiled sardonically. "Oh, yes, about your being right. Well, you see, Tara, for all our big talk of equal rights, I'm afraid a great many of us men are still dreadfully chauvinistic. Most will jump happily into bed with any 'liberated' woman who'll have him. But, and it's a very big *but,* these very same men, when they finally decide they are ready to get married, will look around for a relatively untouched woman. I say relatively untouched because even the most naive of us are aware that today there are not really that many virginal women over the age of twenty. So you see, it's the old double standard. While he wants to bed as many as possible, he wants to marry an untouched one. Deplorable perhaps, but nonetheless true. It's the nature of the beast."

As he spoke, Tara felt her anger grow apace with her embarrassment. Now, pink-cheeked, eyes snapping, she jumped up out of her chair.

"Beast is right. How grossly unjust that attitude is."

"That goes without saying. But then, who ever said that life was just?"

He stood up slowly, lazily uncoiling like a large, dark cat. Tara walked across the room to the window facing the street, suddenly, unaccountably, nervous.

"I don't know what to do about this," she almost whispered. "My family's upset. My friends have made themselves scarce. Incredibly, in this day and age, I feel ostracized."

"You have one option that would stop the talk at once." He spoke quietly, his eyes keen on her face as she turned to look questioningly at him.

"Accept my proposal. Marry me." He walked slowly to her and she felt her heart begin to thud frantically, her legs tremble.

Hoping to stop his determined movement toward her, she sneered. "You mean you're unlike other men? You're willing to saddle yourself with a—what is the word—*tainted* woman?"

He laughed low in his throat, the sound slipping down her spine on tiny, icy feet.

"As I'm supposed to be the man who 'tainted' you, I can't see that it makes any difference."

He stopped in front of her, reaching up to touch her silvery hair, gleaming in the soft glow of the table lamp beside her.

"Such fantastic hair," he murmured. "I want to see it fanned out on a pillow under me, Tara." He pinched a few strands between thumb and forefinger and drew his hand down its long length. "I want to bind myself in it like a silken net." Tara felt the serpent of excitement uncoil in her midriff as he brought the strands to his lips. "I want to draw it across your beautiful mouth and kiss you breathless through it." In unwilling fascination she watched his eyes darken, narrow with desire; felt his hand slide to her nape; felt long fingers curl into the soft thickness and draw her face to his. His mouth a breath away from hers, he whispered hoarsely, "Marry me, Tara." Then he covered her trembling lips with his hard, firm ones in an urgent, demanding kiss.

Tara stiffened, fighting the insidious languor that invaded her body as if fighting for her life. She had been kissed many times but never had she felt like this. Her veins seemed to be flowing with liquid fire that burned and seared and ate up her resistance. His hands moved down her spine, then gripped convulsively, flattening her against the long, hard length of his body. She felt dizzy, light-headed, barely able to hear the small voice of reason that cried, *Step back,* when all she wanted was to get closer, closer. His hand moved up and under her knit top, and she shivered deliciously at the feel of his fingers on her bare skin. The voice of reason broke through when his hand moved over her breast possessively. Using her last remaining dregs of will, she tore her mouth from his and spun out and away from his arms, sobbing, "No. No. No."

He didn't come after her but stood studying her pale, frightened face intently, breathing deeply to regain control.

"You're a fool, Tara," he finally said, his voice calm, devoid of inflection. "I could give you everything you ever wanted. And you are not indifferent to me. I've just proven that."

Tara stood rigid, forcing herself to meet the hard, blue glitter of his eyes. Hands clenched into fists to keep from trembling, she wondered, in a vague panic, why she'd felt chilled to the bone since spinning out of his arms. Then fatigue struck; suddenly her shoulders drooped, and she felt sick to tears, the events of this horribly long day pressing down on her. She turned from him to stare sightlessly through the window and said, wearily, "Go away."

She didn't see the swift flash of concern in his eyes and when she turned back to him, it was gone.

"The offer will stay open, Tara, if you change your mind." His eyes raked her, noting her pallor, the blue smudges of tiredness under her eyes. He took one step toward her, and she cried out, "Will you please go and leave me alone. Mr. Rykovsky, please."

"Since we're supposedly sleeping together, don't you think you could call me Alek," he chided gently.

Her head dropped and her voice was a tired, ragged whisper. "Alek, please, please go."

Her chin was lifted by one long finger and she found herself gazing into surprisingly gentle blue eyes. His mouth brushed hers lightly. "You're exhausted, pansy eyes. Stay in bed tomorrow and think about me. Lock up after me." Again his lips brushed hers, then he whispered, "Good night, lover, for whether you think so now or not, I am going to be your lover."

Then he moved swiftly across the room, snatching up his raincoat without pausing, and went through the door, closing it softly.

Tara stared after him, tears running down her face, feeling unaccountably abandoned. Too tired to probe her emotions or even think, she walked across the room and locked the door as commanded. And it had been a command. Then she turned off the lights and went to her bedroom, leaving the phone off the hook.

4

Sunday was a short day, as Tara slept past noon. She woke with a dull headache and equally dull senses and moved about the apartment like a pale, uninterested wraith. What could she do to combat the rumors being spread connecting her name with Alek's? What could she do when she didn't even know the source of those rumors? And could she really do anything if she did know the source? A charge of slander has to be proved, and even if she could prove it, did she want that kind of publicity? The questions tormented her all day and by early evening had turned her dull headache into a piercing throb. At nine thirty, feeling half sick to her stomach, she gave it up and went to bed.

Nine hours of deep, uninterrupted sleep did wonders for her. Rested and refreshed, her headache gone, she faced Monday morning unflinchingly. She dressed extra carefully in a white long-sleeved silk shirt; black, gray, and white plaid skirt; black vest, the front panels embroidered in white-silk thread; and three-inch narrow-heeled gray suede boots to the knee. Topping the outfit off with a belted, black suede jacket that made her silver-blond hair look almost white, she slung her gray shoulder bag over her arm and swung out of the apartment fighting fit.

The long, careful look and silent whistle of appreciation she received from David when he entered the office boosted her morale even more. The smile she bestowed on him was breathtaking and the most natural David had seen in over a week. He stared bemusedly at her then grinned back and headed for his own office, pausing in the doorway to say, "Ask Terry Connors to come to my office, please."

Tara nodded, lifted the phone, punched the interoffice button, and waited for Connie Delp, the front-office typist, to answer.

A few minutes later Terry sauntered into her office for all the world like he owned the building. "Morning, beautiful, how's tricks?"

The words themselves were innocuous but the suggestive twist to his lips lent them a meaning that sent a cold stab of fear through her midsection. She had no time to question him, however. as he went straight through to David's office.

She sat pondering his words a few seconds, then gave herself a mental shake. She was getting hyper over all this, for heaven's sake; if she wasn't careful, she'd soon be reading double meanings into everything anyone said to her. In annoyance she turned back to her work, soon forgetting the incident.

An hour and a half later Terry left David's office and stopped at her desk. Glancing up questioningly, Tara caught the same twisted smile on his face before he sobered and said softly, "How about having dinner with me some time?"

Tara felt her scalp tingle in premonition, but she managed to keep her voice level. "I told you before that I won't go out with you, Terry."

"Yeah, but that was then and now is now." His smile was an insinuation that made her skin crawl.

"Nothing has happened to change my mind," she said evenly.

"Oh, I don't expect you to two-time him. Not many women have that kind of guts. But when he's through with you—and with his track record it won't be too long—maybe you'll be glad of an invitation out."

While he was speaking, Tara felt her nerves tighten, her fingers grip the edge of her typewriter. With effort she kept her voice cool. "I don't know what you're talking about."

"Come off it, sweetheart," he jeered. "Everyone knows."

He grinned at her crookedly, his head tilted to one side, then he gave a short, nasty laugh. "You're cool as well as beautiful, baby, and I can see what he wants with you, but you can stow the innocent act. Hell, he may as well have taken an ad in the paper." He waved his hand at the bud vase on the corner of her desk. "The roses, the few—how should I say it?—'polite' inquiries he made about you months ago. His car parked in front of your apartment all night— every night—only confirmed everyone's suspicions." Again he gave that nasty laugh. "He even spoke to me one morning as I was on my way to work, after he'd left your apartment."

He stood a moment studying her stricken, wide-eyed face, then snorted, "I told you to can the act, kid. You may think we're a bunch of idiots, but even us peasants can add one and one and come up with two. You must have something special, seeing as how he comes to you rather than move you into his building, the way he usually does with his mistresses."

Tara had been staring in unseeing disbelief, but at his last words her vision cleared and focused on his leering face.

"Get out of my office," she said through clenched teeth, "before I call David and tell him you're annoying me."

"You win, sweetheart," Terry sneered. "But just remember who your friends are after he's through with you." He walked to the door then paused with his hand on the knob and shot over his shoulder, "I mean when the lesser males start calling, more than happy to sample the big man's leavings." On the last word he stepped through the doorway and closed the door with a sharp click.

White-faced, trembling, an odd buzzing sound in her head, Tara stared at the door, devoid, for the moment, of all feeling.

"Aleksei Rykovsky!"

The two words, murmured in a harsh whisper, sounded more like a bitter curse than a man's name. Following the words, which caused actual physical pain, white-hot anger tore through her mind; cleansing anger, motivating anger that unlocked the frozen state she'd been in and set her mind in action. She still had no idea why but now she knew how and, most importantly, who.

With careful, deliberate movement Tara pressed the intercom button and said coolly, "David, I'm sorry but I must leave the office for a short time. I have an appointment."

David, his tone indicating he was deeply immersed in his work, answered unconcernedly, "Okay, Tara, have Connie pick up on any incoming calls and take as long as you like."

"Thank you."

Tara relayed the instruction to Connie, then, her every movement still careful and deliberate, she covered her typewriter, slipped her arms into her jacket, removed her handbag from her bottom desk drawer, plucked the white rose from the bud vase and dropped it into her wastebasket, and left the office. She was going scalp-hunting.

It was less than a twenty-minute drive from David's office to Alek's large, antiquated machine shop. Tara used those minutes to put together the pieces of this bizarre puzzle. His words of Saturday night came as clearly as if he were sitting next to her in the car and had just spoken them.

"Don't you know?"

She had thought, then, that he was in some way accusing her of keeping information from him. Now she realized he had been probing to ascertain if she had any suspicions of him.

She went over and over the whole sordid mess and decided, not for the first time, that this man was not quite on-center; something was twisted inside. If it hadn't been for the anger that had resolved itself into a cold, hard fury, she might have been afraid of what she was about to do.

Alek's offices were located on the second floor of the sprawling old building. As Tara mounted the narrow staircase, she stiffened her spine in preparation to do battle. Steps evenly paced, firm, she walked along the long narrow hallway, glancing at closed doors marked PERSONNEL, SALES, and ACCOUNTING until finally reaching what she knew was her destination, the very last door, marked PRIVATE.

Gripping the knob, she drew a deep breath and walked in. The woman sitting at a desk some five feet inside the door was about thirty with a calm, withdrawn face and cool, intelligent eyes.

"May I help you?"

The impersonal smile and well modulated tones were the epitome of the superefficient secretary. No slouch in that department herself, Tara matched exactly her tone and manner.

"Yes, I would like to see Mr. Rykovsky, please. If it's convenient."

The cool eyes flickered with a degree of respect. "You have an appointment?"

Tara's lips twitched in wry amusement. This paragon knew damned well she had no appointment.

"No I haven't, but if he is not too busy, I'd appreciate a few minutes. It is rather important."

"I see," judiciously. "If you'll have a seat, I'll inquire, Miss . . . ?"

"Schmitt. Tara Schmitt."

She was left to cool her heels some fifteen minutes before that impersonal voice said, "Mr. Rykovsky will see you now, Miss Schmitt."

Tara's heels may have cooled, but her emotions were still at flash point, although this was not revealed as she rose gracefully to her feet, her outward appearance under rigid control.

"Thank you." Her voice a quiet murmur, she stepped past the secretary, who held open the door, and into the large room, seemingly dwarfed by the over-whelmingly masculine presence of its owner.

"Good morning, Tara." His low, silky voice slid over her, setting her teeth on edge. "You're looking exceptionally beautiful this morning."

And he is looking exceptionally handsome, she thought bitterly. Dressed in an obviously expensive, perfectly tailored charcoal-gray vested suit, complemented by a pearl-gray silk shirt and oyster-white tie, the effect of him on the senses was devastating. *How could it be,* Tara wondered, *that someone could appear so shatteringly good on the outside and be so thoroughly rotten on the inside?*

She watched his eyes grow sharp when, without speaking, she stood studying him, even though the voice remained smooth.

"Sit down, Tara."

"I prefer to stand, Mr. Rykovsky."

"Mr. Rykovsky? Saturday night it was Alek." The voice was still smooth but beginning to show awareness of things being not quite right.

"Saturday night I was still an ignorant, innocent fool," she stated coldly.

One dark eyebrow arched fleetingly; the voice matched the eyes in sharpness. "You're upset. What's happened?"

"Upset?" she cried. "Upset? You set out with a deliberate intent to ruin my reputation then dare to stand there calmly and say I'm upset? No, *Mister* Rykovsky, I am not upset. I am red-hot furious."

His face went suddenly expressionless; his narrowed eyes went wary as he watched the pink flares of angry color tinge her cheeks, her soft brown eyes flash.

"All right," he said evenly. "You know. Now sit down and calm yourself, and we'll discuss it."

Eyes wide in astonishment, she nearly choked. "Calm myself? I don't want to calm myself. And I don't want to discuss it. What I want is an explanation for what you've done and—" The sound of her voice, beginning to rise sharply, made her check her words. Breathing deeply, trying to regain control, she glared at him across the few feet of deep-pile carpeting that separated them.

"Tara"—his gentle voice tried to soothe—"if you'll calm—"

She didn't let him finish. Fighting to regain control, nails gouging into her palms, she ground out: "Were you bored? Was this your perverted idea of a joke? A way to break up a dull time in your life? Well, I don't think you're funny. I think you're sick. You need your head ex—"

"Tara." The silky voice had taken on a decidedly serrated edge, then smoothed out again. "That's enough. Now be quiet and listen a minute. If you let yourself think, you'll know why I did it. I told you twice. It was no joke, and I was not trying to be funny. Also I'm not sick. I simply know what I want and I am not afraid to go after it."

"No matter what method you use," she gasped. "Or who gets hurt?"

"I admit, in this instance, my methods were a bit unorthodox, but really, Tara, you're not all that injured. Good grief, woman, do you really think, today, that anyone gives a damn who is sleeping with who?"

He had remained so imperturbable, so unaffected through this incredible interview, that Tara was gripped with the urge to scream at him.

"My family gives a damn. *You* don't have to watch my mother cry or face my father's anger."

"That's right, I don't," he stated firmly. "But I will if you give the word. Say you'll marry me, and I'll be at your parents' door within the hour to pacify them."

Tara was beginning to feel as if she'd stepped into some sort of unreal world, a fantasy land. *Things like this just don't happen,* she thought. Shaking her head as if to clear her mind, she said, haltingly, "I don't understand. I'm sure there must be any number of eager females ready and willing to comply with your slightest whim. Why have you singled me out to torment?"

His face hardened and a muscle rippled at the corner of his tautened jawline. "You're right. There are a number of females ready and willing." His eyes, searing like twin blue flames, raked her body boldly, heightening her color still more with embarrassment. "But, for some reason, my body demands the possession of yours. It is as simple as that. I want you. I intend having you."

Eyes wide in disbelief, she stared at him several seconds. The self-assurance, the powerful drive, the pure, unadulterated arrogance of this man was beyond her comprehension. Throat dry, she whispered, "My father was right. You are a swine."

"No name-calling, Tara." The tone gave a soft warning.

Beyond the point of heeding any warning, soft or firm, she laughed cynically. "Name-calling? I couldn't force past my lips the names I'd like to call you." Tears of anger, frustration, bitterness, blurred her eyes. Grimly she added, "You, in your exalted position of the male, may think that today no one really gives a damn. But then you didn't have to stand and listen to your father, in so many words, call you a wh-whore." Her throat had closed, and she barely managed to get the last word out. Gulping air quickly, she stifled a sob, saying, "You don't have to listen to the snickering innuendos of the people in your office or the dirty suggestions of Terry Conners."

"Tara!"

Alek had remained standing behind his desk from the time she'd entered his office almost an hour ago. Now, moving with the lithe swiftness of a large mountain cat, he was around the desk and in front of her, his long-fingered hands grasping her shoulders painfully.

"I'll kill him," he snarled.

"And my father?" she cried wildly. "And every other man who'll think I'm fair game from now on?"

"Stop it," he commanded harshly, giving her a hard shake.

It was the last straw. All the fight went out of her and the tears that had been threatening for the last five minutes overflowed and ran down her flushed cheeks. Emotionally strung out, she suddenly felt too tired to care anymore and she stood, dimly studying the faintly embossed pattern on his tie. The pattern swirled and swam and she closed her eyes. She heard him sigh deeply, felt his hands loosen their hold on her shoulders, slide around her back. She felt the muscles and sinews in his arms tighten as he gathered her close. A strange feeling of being safe, protected, blanketed her numbed mind. Wearily, she rested her forehead against the hard wall that was his chest and, crying freely, released the misery that gripped her throat.

"Tara . . . don't."

The harsh tone of a moment ago had been replaced by a soft entreaty. He lowered his head over hers in yet another strangely protective gesture, and she felt his lips move against her hair. His head lowered again and now, his lips close to her ear, his words penetrated the mistiness.

"*Dusha moya*, Tara, *ya te lyoob-lyoo.*"

He'd said those same strange words once before, yet it wouldn't be till much later that she'd wonder about their meaning. For now the words had a somehow soothing effect, and she shivered as a momentary peace enveloped her.

Vaguely she became aware of a tiny, nagging voice that told her that she should not be inside the warm, protective circle of his arms. But it felt so right, as if she belonged there more than anywhere else in the world. In the effort to silence that tiny, insistent voice, she turned her head and felt her slightly parted lips make contact with his taut, rough jaw. In bemusement she heard his sharply indrawn breath.

"Don't cry, pansy eyes. Nothing on this earth is worth your tears."

His tone, more than his words, was a gentle seducement. Warm, liquid gold flowed over and through her, seeming to enclose the two of them in a soft, golden world of their own. Without conscious thought her hands slid inside his jacket and she felt vague resentment against the material of his vest and shirt that denied her fingers the feel of his skin.

At her touch he went still, then his one hand moved up and under her hair, fingers spreading, to cradle her head. Slowly he turned her face to his, his lips brushing her cheek lightly, his breath tickling her eyelashes. Time seemed suspended inside that golden circle, and with a soft sigh Tara relaxed, allowing her arms to slide around his waist.

"I shouldn't be here," she murmured, forgetting and not caring, for the moment, why.

"You shouldn't be anywhere else. You belong exactly where you are." *Soft, his tone is so soft,* she thought. It was an inducement that drew her farther into that magic circle.

"Tara."

A hoarsely whispered groan, and then his mouth covered hers, gently, sweetly silencing that tiny nagging voice of reason.

His kiss was a tender exploration of her mouth, making no demands, asking nothing of her. At first she lay passive in his arms, her bruised emotions soothed by the glow of contentment stealing through her. But ever receptive to gentleness, tenderness, she was soon responding, her lips making an exploration of their own.

The kiss seemed to go on forever and ended much too soon. She murmured a soft protest when his mouth left hers and buried her face in the curve of his shoulder. Light as snowflakes, his lips touched her closed eyelids then moved to rest against her temple. Strong fingers gently massaged the back of her neck and for a few seconds Tara drifted in a gold-hued void that knew no thought or pain.

His words broke the golden spell, allowing the tiny voice to become a shout. "You're getting yourself upset over this, Tara, when it could be settled so simply by marrying me."

What do you think you're doing? the now shrill voice of her conscience demanded. *What happened to that sense of outrage that filled you on hearing Terry Conners's words? What about the fine, bright flame of fury that propelled you to this confrontation?* A feeling of intense self-betrayal shot through her and she shuddered in self-disgust.

Alek misinterpreted her shudder as a sign of surrender, and he murmured, "Well, Tara?"

Tara drew a deep breath, took one step back, and pushed her hands hard against his chest. Unprepared for her action, his hold broke, and she was free of the reason-destroying circle of his arms.

Turning quickly, she ran for the door, her hand groping for the knob. Flinging the door open, shame and guilt strangling her throat, she whispered "No" to his commanded, "Tara, wait."

Blindly, she ran past his wide-eyed, incredulous secretary, along the hall, down the narrow stairway, and out the entrance door as if a pack of wild dogs were snapping at her ankles.

Trembling almost uncontrollably, she drove straight to her apartment with one thought pounding in her head. *Get home, be safe. Get home, be safe.*

Still running, she dashed up the steps and along the short hall to her apartment. Gasping for breath, she unlocked the door; dashed inside, slammed it shut, double-locked it, and leaned back against it.

On shaky legs she stumbled across the room and dropped onto the sofa. What in the sweet world was the matter with her? Never had she experienced this cloying, panicky feeling. She felt her throat close; then her eyes filled and with a murmured "Oh, Lord," her body fell sideways onto the cushions and she was crying, sobbing like a child, hurt, alone, lost.

For over an hour Tara lay in a crumbled heap, the wracking sobs and tears slowly dwindling to sniffles and an occasional hiccup. Gradually awareness crept back and with a sigh she pushed herself upright. She had to call David.

David's voice was a reassuringly normal sound in a world gone suddenly very abnormal.

"I'm sorry, David," she sniffed, "but I won't be back today, I'm not feeling well."

Instant concern colored David's warm voice. "What's wrong, Tara?" A short pause, then: "Honey, have you been crying?"

"No, no," she reassured hastily. "I think I've had a sudden allergic reaction to something. I've been sneezing like mad and my eyes have been watering and I look a mess." *Well,* she thought, grimacing, *the last part's true.*

"Are you sure?" He sounded skeptical. "What could have brought this on?"

Tara cast about frantically and grabbed at the first thing that came to mind. "I'm not sure, but I think it must be the roses I've had on my desk the last few weeks." *Would he buy it?* she wondered. He did.

"More than likely. Have you seen a doctor?"

"No. I—I don't think that's necessary. I'll take an allergy capsule."

"Well, if it doesn't help you get better by tomorrow morning, get yourself to a doctor. Don't worry about the office but call me and let me know how you feel."

"All right, David, I will. And thank you."

"For what?" he snorted, then warned. "Now take care, Tara, I mean it."

"Yes, sir," came the meek reply. "Oh, and David, would you do something for me?"

"Anything I can."

"Would you call and stop delivery on the roses? The name of the florist is on the box in my wastebasket."

"Sure thing, honey. Be good and get well."

He hung up. Tara smiled gently as she replaced the receiver. David hated saying good-bye and so he never did.

Speaking with David had restored her equilibrium somewhat, and with a firmer tread she went to the kitchen and brewed a pot of coffee. While the coffee perked away happily, she made herself half a sandwich and ate it in grim determination. When the electric pot shut itself off, she placed the pot, a small jug of milk, and a mug on a tray and returned to the living room.

Sitting with the mug of the steaming brew cradled in her hands, she turned her mind to her recent encounter and the events that led to it. She still found it incredible, if not completely unbelievable, that anyone would go to such lengths to amuse himself. In her book, that constituted a pretty weird sense of humor.

"It was no joke, and I was not trying to be funny."

His words slithered through her mind, and she shivered violently.

"Garbage." She said the word aloud and then repeated it silently. *Garbage.* Everything he'd said was exactly that. So much garbage. How she longed to make him pay for what he'd done to her. But how? Reluctantly she admitted to herself that chances of her hurting him in some way were practically nil.

As were her chances of repairing the damage he'd done. How did one combat nebulous hints? Innuendo? Veiled sugestions? She could go to her family and her closest friends and explain exactly what had happened, but would they believe it? Would she if she heard a story like that from someone? Not likely. Oh, yes, he'd been clever. Very clever. So what could she do? Move away? Where? And was it worth it? As he'd suggested, speculation, talk, couldn't cause her any lasting pain. *But he could,* an insidious voice whispered deep in her mind.

In sudden renewed fear, almost panic, she argued with the errant thought. How could he hurt her anymore? She didn't care what he said or did. Wouldn't care if he dropped dead tonight. The sudden twist of pain that clutched at her heart shocked her.

Frantically she moved about, refilling her coffee cup, walking to the TV to switch it on, anything to still those silly thoughts and emotions.

She watched a few minutes of the news then, much calmer, she decided her only course of action was to put on a bright face and brazen it out. In time the talk would die down, become a ninety-day wonder, and in due time she'd be able to forget it—and him.

But will you? that small, perverse voice demanded.

5

The following two days went fairly well. She breezed into the office as usual, gave Terry a frosty smile as usual, talked a few minutes with Jeannie at coffee-break time, and breathed a heartfelt sigh of relief that the roses had stopped being delivered. Chalk one up for her.

On Tuesday evening she'd crept outside and scanned the street for his car. There it was, bold as brass, and it left a somewhat brassy taste in her mouth. Where the devil did the miserable man go after he parked it there? Back in her apartment she pondered on what, if anything, she could do about its presence. Should she call the police and report it as abandoned? And if they checked the license number and found out who it belonged to, then what? Alek Rykovsky was a respected businessman. If asked why his car was parked there, he could say he'd been visiting friends or had lent it to a friend in the neighborhood and he'd be believed without further question. And where would that leave her? Looking pretty damned silly. With reluctance she told herself: *Ignore the car.*

Wednesday moved along as Tuesday had, and she was beginning to think she'd get through this mess with some degree of composure. She even had an added bonus discovering Alek's car among the missing. Then the bottom fell out. Craig called. His first words jarred her out of her complacency.

"Look, Tara, I know you're alone because I happen to know Rykovsky's at a testimonial dinner tonight."

"Craig, I—"

"No, don't bother to explain. I understand. The only thing that makes me mad is that you didn't tell me the night we had dinner together. He sure as hell isn't trying to keep it a secret. If you'd told me, I wouldn't have built up any hopes. And I had."

"Craig, please, let me explain."

"Not necessary. You owe me nothing. But look, Tara, if anything happens, I mean, if you split or anything and need a shoulder to cry on, call me, will you?"

Why bother? Why even bother to explain to people who just wouldn't listen, or wouldn't believe it if they did?

"Yes, Craig," she answered softly, a wealth of defeat in her voice.

She went to bed depressed and woke the same way, but plastered a determined smile on her face anyway.

The morning went by without a hitch, and her spirits lifted. In an attempt to keep them up Tara decided to leave the office at lunchtime and treat herself to a fattening lunch of lasagna at her favorite Italian restaurant. She returned to the office a few minutes late but replete in body and restored in well-being.

The low hum of several voices came from David's office, and she checked her appointment book to see if she'd failed to write down a meeting. The space was blank so she decided, with a shrug, this was probably an impromptu thing that David had called during the lunch hour.

She tackled the filing pile from the morning's work and was busy at it when David's door opened. Before she could close the file drawer, a hand slid around the back of her neck and long fingers pressed against her jawline, turning her face around and up. Eyes wide with surprise, she saw Alek's blue eyes glitter with intent, and then his mouth claimed hers. In the few seconds her mouth was held captive she registered the expressions on the faces of the two men who had followed Alek out of David's office: David's face was a picture of uncertain concern, Terry Connors's of positive envy.

The two men stood watching as if frozen, then moved quickly toward opposite doors as Alek lifted his head. But not quickly enough to miss hearing Alek's words.

"I'm sorry about last night, darling, but the dinner lasted much later than I thought it would, and I didn't want to disturb you."

The doors facing them closed simultaneously. David's very gently, the other with a sharp snap.

Tara could have wept in pure frustration. Of course that sneaky Terry would have noticed the absence of Alek's car last night. That accounted for the speculative look he'd run over her this morning. And Alek? He was covering his tracks.

Seething with instant anger, she ignored the tingle in her fingers and lashed out, "You diabolical—!" She got no further, for Alek cut in with a silky warning.

"Careful, sweetheart. I told you before, no name-calling."

"Go to hell," she whispered angrily.

With a swift jerk he turned her fully around and she had to force herself to meet the blue flame of anger in his eyes.

"You're walking on very thin ice, my sweet. Take care you don't break through and find yourself in over your head." His voice was soft but chilling. "Why don't you give it up? Turn over your sword, hilt first, and we'll go on from there."

"I have no intention on going on to anything with you." For some reason Tara couldn't raise her voice above a whisper; she wet her lips, then went on. "So why don't you give it up? Leave me alone. Stop this madness."

"Madness? Hardly that." He laughed softly and planted a tiny kiss at the corner of her mouth. "Just a matter of chemistry. To be blunt, beautiful, you turn me on something fierce. I'd give you proof, but I don't think this is quite the time or the place."

Struck by the blatant audacity of the fiend, all she could find to say was, "Get out of here before I start screaming rape."

He laughed again, an easy, relaxed laugh that caused a vague sort of longing deep inside her; then, thank goodness, he walked to the door.

"Okay, kid, I'll let you get back to work. But I'm not nearly through with you yet."

After he'd gone, Tara turned back to the file cabinet, then paused with her hand on the drawer handle as an odd thought struck her. *Beautiful, sweetheart, kid.* The same words Terry had used on Monday morning. Alek had even thrown in *darling* and *my sweet.* Coming from Terry's mouth, the endearments had been offensive, an insult. Why then did they sound so exciting, somehow natural, from the lips of that hateful devil? The thought made Tara uncomfortable, and she pushed it away.

The remainder of the afternoon was a shambles. Try as she would, Tara could not seem to pull herself together, to still her trembling fingers. She made numerous typing errors, kept dropping things, and in the space of a few hours, almost wiped out her beautifully kept filing cabinets.

By the time she left the office, she was on the verge of tears. She ached, literally hurt all over, as if she'd been pulled through a hedge backward. While her teeth were punishing her lower lip as she walked to her car, her mind cried fiercely, *Why does he keep on with this?* Surely he knew by now how much she disliked, disapproved of him.

Sliding into the car, she slammed the door, jabbed the key into the ignition. She had thought, after that fiasco in his office on Monday . . . her hand paused on the key; hot pink color swept her cheeks. She could not, would not, let herself think about that.

Her fingers flipped the key, the engine fired into life, and with unthinking recklessness Tara drove off the lot and into the flow of traffic, ignoring the angry horn blasts from several irate drivers.

Where to go? What to do? she asked herself. She just couldn't face that apartment alone tonight. She was becoming positively claustrophobic in those small rooms. *Sallie?* Tara shook her head. *Explanations would have to be made. Who in the world would believe something like this?* Tara was having trouble believing it herself. Besides, Tara felt she had no right to endanger the working relationship between David and Alek.

Tara drove aimlessly for some time. Up one street, down another. Glancing around uninterestedly as she sat at a corner waiting for the light to change, Tara's eyes passed then came back to rest on a small tavern on the opposite corner. She had been in that tavern several times with friends. The food served was plain but good, the prices fair.

The light changed to green, and with sudden decision Tara hunted up a parking space, parked, and locked the car. A woman did not have to be afraid to enter this tavern alone. It was family owned and run. The wife did the cooking and serving, the husband tended the bar, and their son worked in both places, wherever he was most needed. They allowed, as they put it, no "funny business" in their place and they had posted a large sign to that effect. Both the owner and his son were big enough to back it up.

Though she rarely had a drink, Tara had suddenly decided she needed one. Hell! At this minute she felt she needed a dozen. Leaving the car, she skirted around the front entrance that led into the bar and entered the side door that opened into the dining room.

The room was half full of what Tara judged were neighborhood regulars. Moving toward the front of the building, Tara stopped at a small table, just inside the large open archway, that gave full view of the barroom. Young Jake Klinger, Jr., was working the end of the bar near the entrance to the dining room, and as Tara sat down he glanced up, grinned, and waved.

"Hi, Tara, howzit?"

Somehow she managed to return the grin convincingly.

"Fine, Jake, how are things with you?"

"Fair to middlin'," he replied laconically, then turned to serve his customer with the glass of beer he'd just tapped. That done, he sauntered around the end of the bar and to her table.

"What can I get you, gorgeous?"

Tara smiled, her eyes on the menu written in chalk on a blackboard hanging on the wall. After the lunch she'd eaten and the afternoon she'd put in, she didn't feel at all hungry. But she knew that if she drank and didn't eat, she'd be out for the count, or sick, in no time.

"I think I'll have a ham-and-cheese on dark rye and a Seven and Seven, please."

"You got it, baby."

Tara smiled again as Jake walked through the swing door into the kitchen, to give his mother the sandwich order. He was well named, truly a junior, for he looked remarkably like his father. Both Jakes were not very tall, but broad, built strong as bulls; they both had open, pleasant faces and gentle, compassionate brown eyes.

He paused on his way back, long enough to slide her sandwich plate in front of her, then went on into the bar to mix her drink. When Jake set the glass on the table, he said quietly, "This one's on me, sweet lips." Then he winked broadly, pursed his lips in a silent kiss, and went back behind the bar.

Tara laughed softly as she bit into her sandwich. Eating her sandwich without really tasting it, she pondered the different reactions male and female had to each other.

Jake's teasing familiarity amused her, whereas Terry's use of endearments on Monday had made her feel cheap. As to the way she reacted to the same brand of teasing from Alek, well . . . she did not even care to think about that. Was it, as Alek had suggested, simple body chemistry?

By the time she pushed her empty plate to the center of the table, Tara was working on her third drink and telling herself to go home. Hearing a vaguely familiar voice say, "It's all right, I know the lady," Tara glanced into the barroom as a young man detached himself from the bar, a drink in each hand, and headed toward her.

As Tara watched him approach. her mind nibbled at recognition. Her memory clicked, and she put half a name to his face. Barry something-or-other, an architectural engineer she'd met last summer at a clambake she'd attended with friends. At the time, he'd appeared easygoing and well-mannered and Tara had agreed to go out with him the following week. It was a mistake for, although the evening had been a pleasant one, he had no sooner parked his car in front of her apartment when he was all over her like a bad rash. She had had literally to fight her way out of his car. And there was the reason she could not remember his last name. After she'd safely reached her apartment, she had dubbed him Barry Octopus. And now Mr. Octopus had come to stop at her table.

"Hiya, Tara, all alone?"

His grin was engaging (very probably practiced), revealing stunning white teeth (very probably capped). He had obviously taken to the style of permanents for men, for his previously straight, light-brown hair was now a mass of tiny curls on his well-shaped head. In tight, faded blue jeans and snuggly fitting knit shirt, he was very attractive and knew it.

"Yes, Barry, I'm alone."

Placing one of the drinks in front of her, he said quietly, "May I join you for a few minutes?"

Tara didn't want the drink. She didn't want his company either, but shrugging lightly, she murmured, "For a few minutes only. I'm leaving soon."

"Why? The night's young."

And you're so beautiful, Tara added, finishing his line wryly, somehow managing to keep a straight face.

"I've got a date later, that's why," she lied.

"Ah, yes, I've heard about your latest . . . date. Really moving up in the world, aren't you?"

Tara's voice was as cold as the glass her fingers clenched.

"If you're going to be offensive, Barry, you can go back to the bar, and take your drink with you."

He eyed her steadily a moment then he laughed easily.

"Truth hurt? Never mind. Hell, I wasn't trying to be offensive or then again maybe I was. After the cold shoulder I'd received, the pure-as-the-driven-snow act you'd put on, well, I'll admit when I first heard about it, I was shocked. He has a rather overwhelming reputation with women. But then he has a rather overwhelming bankroll also."

"Good-bye, Barry."

Tara was hanging on to her temper as tightly as she was hanging on to her glass.

Reaching across the table, his hand caught hers.

"Aw, come on, Tara," he coaxed. "With all the dames he's got on the string, surely he wouldn't object to you and I having a little fun together."

Eyes flashing with contempt, Tara snatched her hand away.

"Maybe *he* wouldn't, but I would," she said through clenched teeth. "Now go away and leave me alone."

Grasping for her hand again, he began urgently, "Don't get mad—"

"You having trouble, Miss Schmitt?"

With an audible sigh of relief, Tara looked up to see Jake senior leaning across the end of the bar, looking broad as a tank and just as menacing, eyeing Barry dispassionately.

"He was just leaving and so am I, Jake. Could I have my check please?"

"Sure thing," he nodded, then added, "Why don't you come back to the bar, Barry? I'll buy you a drink."

Barry hesitated then gave in gracefully.

"Okay, Jake, you're on. Sorry if I was out of line, Tara."

Ignoring Barry, Tara paid her check and left, feeling even worse than when she entered. The sight of Alek's car parked directly in front of her apartment plunged her spirits even lower.

Filled with rage, frustration, and humiliation, she paced the apartment for hours. First Terry, now Barry. How many others believed he was paying her rent, keeping her? Tears of weariness and defeat blinding her, she finally fell into bed. Teeth clenched, she whispered aloud, "Damn you, Aleksei Rykovsky."

Friday was a drag. Tara had never been so glad to see quitting time before in her life. As she left the office, she massaged her temple distractedly; she had a headache. Her eyes felt puffy and irritated from the hours she'd spent crying the night before. Lord, it seemed she'd had a headache and done nothing but cry for the last month. Was there no end to it?

Feeling too uninterested and dispirited to prepare a meal, she ate dinner at a small lunchroom close to her apartment then went home. Home? The lonely hours spent in solitude in those few small rooms were beginning to make what was once a haven into a cage. She felt trapped. Trapped by the unbridled passion of a man too used to getting what he wanted.

The tears were flowing again before she reached the door of her apartment, and the pain in her head had intensified into sharp, stabbing blows. Tara dropped her jacket and handbag on the nearest chair and went to the bathroom, groping blindly inside the medicine cabinet for the aspirin bottle. She swallowed the two white pills then stood regarding her reflection in the cabinet-door mirror. Watery, haunted eyes stared back at her, black-smudged mascara adding a clownish touch. What a pale, pitiful sight she was, she thought abstractedly. At nine thirty, head still pounding, she swallowed two more aspirin and went to bed, positive she wouldn't sleep.

She was wrong. She slept deeply and well and woke Saturday morning with at least some of her usual vigor restored. As she consumed a light breakfast of juice, toast, and coffee, her eyes roamed around the small kitchen. *What you need, friend,* she told herself bracingly, *is some physical activity. Today you clean the kitchen.*

Within minutes she'd thrown herself into the job at hand, saving the most hated chore, the kitchen stove, till last.

Tara had the rangetop in a half dozen assorted pieces, scrubbing the drip pan under the burners, when the door chimes pealed.

"Oh, hell," she muttered, tugging the rubber gloves off her hands and dropping them in the sink. Walking to the door, she wondered if she should slide the chain into place, then shrugged and opened the door.

"May I come in, Tara? Or are you still mad at me?" Betsy eyed her uncertainly on the other side of the threshold.

"I'm not mad at you, Bets," Tara denied. "A little disappointed, maybe, but not mad. Come in."

Betsy stepped inside, slipped out of her long knit coat, and tossed it over a chair, all the while glancing around unobtrusively.

Tara watched her cynically, sighing softly with the knowledge her sister was looking for occupancy of a man.

"I'm cleaning the kitchen and was about ready to take a break," Tara said quietly. "Would you like a cup of coffee?"

"Yes, thanks," Betsy answered. "It's cold out there this morning. A hot drink will taste good."

Tara didn't miss the strained edge to her sister's voice, but she made no comment as she poured the coffee then placed the mugs, sugar bowl, and a small jug of milk on the table.

Betsy eyed her warily as she lit a cigarette then offered the pack to her, murmuring when Tara shook her head, "You quit?"

"I'm trying to," Tara answered. "I don't even have them around anymore." She hesitated, then said, "On second thought, I think I will have one, thank you." And added silently as she lit it, *I somehow think I'm going to need it.*

They sipped their coffee in an uncomfortable silence a few minutes, then Betsy blurted, "Tara, I think you should call Mama."

"Why? She hasn't bothered to call me." Tara was surprised at the bitterness of her own voice.

"I know," her sister said placatingly. "But I still think you should. I'm worried about her, Tara. You're the only one she ever opened up to at all. She won't talk to me. I've tried."

"Is she sick?" Tara asked in alarm.

"Not sick exactly," Betsy replied. "But she's not eating or sleeping well and she's been crying a lot."

Welcome to the club, Mama, Tara thought wearily, then forced her attention back to her sister as she continued.

"Do you think Mama could be going through the change of life?"

"I don't know. I suppose so, even though she is only forty-five. I've heard of women much younger going into it. And for that matter, much older, so I guess she could be." But for herself Tara was convinced her mother's trouble stemmed directly from the controversy surrounding her oldest child. "All right, Bets," Tara promised. "I'll call her later today and see if I can find out anything. Will you stay for lunch?"

"No. Thanks anyway. I've been skipping lunch." Then she added at Tara's raised eyebrows, "I've gained a few pounds and with the holidays coming up, I thought I'd better be careful or come January first, I'm liable to find I can't get into my clothes."

Tara smiled and relaxed at the more normal tone Betsy's voice had acquired. Not much later Betsy left, saying she had some shopping to do, and Tara went back to the stove.

After a hurried sandwich-and-coffee lunch, Tara went to the phone, drew a deep breath, and quickly dialed her mother's number. Her heart sank on hearing her father's gruff hello.

"Hello, Dad. Is Mother there?"

There was a noticeable pause before her father replied. "Yes, she's here. But she doesn't want to talk to you, Tara, and neither do I." And with that he slammed down the receiver.

Tara stood still, a look of hurt disbelief on her face, before slowly replacing her own receiver with trembling fingers. Feeling her eyes beginning to mist over, she shook her head in swift anger. No, she would not cry anymore; she was going to fight. *I don't know how I'll fight him,* she thought fiercely, *but I'll find a way. I have to. I can't take much more of this.*

To keep depression at bay she sprang into frenzied activity, giving the rest of the apartment its weekly cleaning, running to the basement laundry-room with a basket of wash, shampooing her hair, and manicuring her nails.

Sunday she walked for hours, coming back to the apartment cold and tired and nowhere near a way to get at Alek. A little after ten she sat moodily trying to concentrate, without much success, on a play on TV. Though Tara was unsure exactly what the play was about other than a philandering husband, one scene, near the end, caught then held her attention. The wronged wife was speaking to a friend in a harshly bitter tone. "He's offered me a large settlement if I'll give him a divorce." She laughed hollowly before continuing. "He should live so long, the sneaky rat. Oh! I'll get that money. That and a lot more. He'll pay through the nose. I'll make his life a living hell. By the time I'm through with him, he'll wish he'd never looked at a woman."

Tara sat nibbling her lip, a germ of an idea beginning to wriggle to life. Her breath caught painfully in her throat. Could she do it? Did she want to?

She set off to work Monday morning, her step firm and determined. No definite plan presented itself. She'd have to play it by ear, wing it, as it were. The morning passed slowly and although Tara became exceedingly more nervous, her resolve strengthened and set. All it needed now was the opportunity.

That arrived shortly after lunch when David came into the office, followed by a deceptively lazy-looking Alek. Before either man could speak, Tara said haltingly, "I—I'd like to speak to you, David. It's important."

David's voice mirrored the surprise on his face.

"All right, Tara." Then, turning to Alek, he murmured, "If you'll excuse us a few minutes."

Alek began, "Of course—" when Tara interrupted, "No! Please David, as this involves Alek too, I'd like him present."

Alek's eyes turned sharp, watchful, while David's expression changed from surprise to confusion.

"Whatever you say. Come into my office, both of you."

David waved his hand at the leather chair in front of his desk as he seated himself in his swivel chair opposite. Alek indicated he was quite comfortable where he was, perched indolently on the side of the large desk, which suited Tara, as she had an excellent view of both men's faces.

She let the silence hang a few seconds before stating quietly, "David, I want to give notice. I'm leaving."

"Give notice!" David exclaimed. "Leaving? But why?"

Tara's eyes sliced to Alek, then quickly away. In that brief glance she could swear he was holding his breath. She gulped in air, then said boldly, "I'm getting married and, even though we haven't discussed it, I don't think he wants me to work afterward." She swung her gaze directly to Alek's hooded blue one and added, "Do you—darling?" then held her breath.

He was a cool one, she had to give him that. For, other than a slight tightening along the jaw, he betrayed no reaction. One dark eyebrow arching slowly, he drawled, "While I would enjoy you giving your undivided attention to me, if you want to continue working, that is entirely up to you—my love." As he finished, the corner of his mouth twitched with amusement.

Tara gritted her teeth. *The fiend. I call his bluff and he has the gall to be amused.* She was beginning to wonder just who had called whose bluff.

David looked and sounded stunned. "Getting married? When?"

Tara hesitated only a moment. "The second Saturday in December."

"The second Saturday," he echoed, his eyes flying to his desk calendar. "But that's less than a month away. Why didn't you tell me sooner?" He turned to Alek, his voice sharp. "Or you? My God, man, we see each other nearly every day, and I've made no secret of how Sallie and I feel about Tara. Couldn't you have said something?"

Alek's smile was totally disarming. "I've been waiting, impatiently I might add, for the lady to set a date. This is as much of a surprise to me as it is to you." Glittering blue eyes were turned on Tara. "I didn't realize you had such a flair for the dramatic, my sweet."

"I think you'll find, my liege"—Tara's smile was pure saccharine—"I'm full of little surprises."

"I'll just bet." He laughed softly.

Throughout this exchange David's head swiveled from one to the other, a frown of consternation on his face. Catching the expression, Alek's laugh deepened. "Don't worry, David, you're not going to lose her, either as a friend or, apparently, as a secretary. That is, of course, if you're agreeable to her taking two weeks for a honeymoon, and the rest of the day."

Neither of the men seemed to notice Tara's gasp, as David was too busy shaking Alek's hand while acquiescing to his demands, and Alek was too busy grinning fatuously while accepting his congratulations.

Before Tara had time to gather her wits, Alek was grasping her arm and propelling her from both David's and her own office, pausing only long enough to snatch up her handbag and jacket. Flinging the latter around her shoulders, he led her out of the building and into his car.

"My car!" she squeaked.

"We'll get it later" came the brusque reply.

He drove without speaking for some time, leaving the city behind as he turned onto a country road nearly devoid of traffic. At the first roadside rest area, he pulled off the road and stopped. After turning off the ignition, he sat staring out the windshield, his silence somewhat ominous. When, after countless minutes, he finally spoke, she jumped, startled.

"You're committed now, you know. There will be no backing out." The hard edge to his tone softened somewhat as he asked, "Has something happened to effect this sudden change in your attitude?"

"It was brought home to me that I had very little choice," she replied softly, suddenly having to fight to keep tears from spilling over. "You have made a farce of all my hopes and plans. I'm afraid you're in for a shock if you're expecting an experienced woman. I'm one of the unmodern ones. I . . . I had thought to save my virginity for my husband, give it to him as a g-gift." Her last word was spoken on a strangled sob, and she turned her head away.

Tara heard his indrawn breath, felt him move a moment before his fingers, gently grasping her chin, turned her face back to him. His face was close, his voice very low. "And so you shall."

His mouth covered hers in a kiss both reticent and possessive; possession won. He drew her as closely to him as the console between the bucket seats would allow. Suddenly he released her and was moving away, cursing softly. Before she knew what he was about, he was out and around the car, yanking open the door next to her. In one unbroken movement he leaned inside, grasped her shoulders, pulled her out and into his arms. Shifting his weight to balance hers, he stood with his feet planted firmly a foot apart, crushing her body against the long, hard length of his.

He groaned softly and muttered, "God, Tara, I want you." Then his mouth began plundering hers hungrily, drawing from her a response she had had no idea she was capable of. His hands moved urgently over her body, arching her to him, giving her shocking proof of his words.

First the ground rocked, then the world spun, and she was drowning in a sea of intense, electrifying pleasure. Fire whipped through her veins, igniting pulse points and nerve ends in its wake. Arms tightening convulsively around his neck, teetering on the very edge of total surrender, she moaned a soft protest when his mouth left hers. Opening her eyes, she saw him glance around before murmuring huskily, "Where the hell can we go?"

His words brought a measure of unwanted sanity and with a choking sob she wrenched away from him to stumble sharply into the side of the car. She cried out in pain, but the pain brought further sanity, enabling her to plead, "No, Alek, stop," when he reached for her.

"No?" he rasped. "Stop? What are you trying to do, drive me mad?"

She was sobbing openly now, frightened badly, as much by her own body's astonishingly urgent need as his. Shaking her head, she sobbed wildly, "I'm frightened. You as much as promised me, not fifteen minutes ago, that you'd wait. I can't go on. Not here, not like this. Alek, please."

His face went hard, a muscle kicking in his taut jaw. His hands clenched into hard, white-knuckled fists, and he drew deep, long breaths. "All right, Tara." He groaned through clenched teeth. "We'll do it your way. But you can be grateful you set the day as closely as you did, for I'm damned if I'll wait one day longer.''

His words chilled Tara, promising difficulties for her nebulous plans. It was not until later, on the way back to town, that she admitted ruefully to herself that he had gained control much more quickly than she. For while he was cool and withdrawn, handling the car with smooth expertise, she was still a humming bundle filled with awareness of him. And she knew that if he touched her now, she'd melt as quickly as a snowflake in August.

As they entered the city, Alek glanced at the expensive, slim gold watch on his wrist and said, ''We have a few things to do before dinner. First I want to stop to make a phone call, and then we'll go shopping for your engagement ring.''

His words jerked Tara away from her confusing emotions. ''I don't want an engagement ring,'' she said flatly.

''Don't want . . . ?'' he began, giving her a startled glance. Then his eyes hardened, grew icy. ''Don't try playing games with me, Tara. You'll wear my ring.'' He finished grimly: ''You said you'll marry me, and marry me you will.''

''I'm not playing games,'' she replied coolly. ''I have no intention of backing out of the marriage. But if you buy an engagement ring, I won't wear it. The only ring of yours I'll wear is my wedding ring.''

His beautifully chiseled mouth flattened into a thin line.

''Why?''

''I simply do not want one.''

Tara could feel his anger crackling outward, touching her, and she shivered.

He pulled up and parked at the first phone booth he came to, snapping, ''I'll be back in a minute,'' and stepped out of the car, slamming the door behind him. He returned shortly, again slamming the door, turned, and gave her a smile that didn't quite make it to those glinting blue eyes.

''I phoned my mother. Told her I was bringing her future daughter-in-law to meet her and my father. We've been invited to dinner. I'm sure you'll want to bathe and change, as I do.'' His smile changed, becoming cruelly sardonic. ''But first we'll stop at your parents' home. I'm sure your family, especially your father, will be delighted with our announcement.''

Tara felt her blood turn to ice water and she shivered again. This was a ruthless man she was dealing with. Did she really have the courage to carry out her idea?

6

The closer they drew to her parents' home, the more tense and withdrawn Tara became. How would her parents react to Alek? Especially her father? He might fly into a rage. Hadn't he referred to Alek as ''that Russian''? *''That swine Rykovsky''?* On the other hand he might be so relieved to know Alek was going to make an honest woman of her, he might accept his future son-in-law gracefully. *Too many* mights, she told herself nervously; *I might just be sick.*

Alek said nothing, but Tara caught the several eagle-eyed glances he threw at her. As they turned into the street her parents lived on, Tara noted the long fingers of golden afternoon sun. *Oh, great!* she thought. Not only would her father be home from work but by now Betsy would be too. One was never sure of her brothers, but this close to suppertime, they probably would be too. Her mother, of course, was nearly always home. Tara grimaced inside. A regular family conclave.

Alek parked at the curb in front of her parents' small frame home and said quietly, "Stay put," as her hand jerked to the door handle. Almost lazily, he left the car and moved around to open her door, helping her out as a lover would. Leaning close to her, he teased, "Someone may be watching from the window."

At any other time Tara would have walked, unannounced, into her father's house but now, after his crushing words to her on Saturday, she hesitated. Ignoring Alek's questioningly raised eyebrows, she placed a none-too-steady finger on the doorbell.

The door was opened a few inches by Karl, who gave her a disgusted look and complained, "What did ya ring the bell for, for cripes' sake?" He turned back into the hall at once, yelling, "Mom, Tara's here," not having seen Alek at all.

As she moved a few steps into the small hallway, Alek close behind her, she heard her father curse, then the rustle of a newspaper being flung to the floor.

Her father reached the doorway to the living room, George at his heels, just as her mother came hurrying along the short hall from the kitchen and Betsy came clattering down the stairs to stop abruptly in back of Karl, who had started up but had stopped and turned at their father's curse. All five began speaking at once.

"Tara, I told you on Saturday—"

"Oh, Tara, I'm so glad to see—"

"Tara, I thought you were going to call—"

"Gee, Tara, did you come in that car out—"

"Tara, what's going on any—"

"Be quiet, all of you."

The barrage ceased, Alek had not raised his voice, but the tone sliced through the babble like a rapier through butter. The tone of a man used to giving orders and having them obeyed without question: there were none.

The same tone broke the stunned silence as, eyes hard as the stone they matched, Alek addressed her father. "Mr. Schmitt, I'd like to speak to you in private a few minutes."

Eyes softening, he turned to her mother. "Perhaps you could give Tara a cup of coffee in the kitchen?"

"Yes, of course," her mother fluttered. "Come along, Tara. I just made a fresh pot for supper."

Tara hesitated, watching her father's angry red face, until he mumbled, grudgingly, to Alek. "All right, come into the living room." Then: "Make yourselves scarce, boys."

George threw a curious glance at Alek, then went up the stairs after Karl, and Tara followed her mother into the kitchen, Betsy right behind her.

Marlene poured coffee into two cups, placed them in front of Tara and Betsy, then asked, tremulously, "Who is that man, Tara? Why does he want to talk to your father alone?"

Before Tara could draw her attention from her mother's tired, unhappy face,

Betsy answered excitedly, "That's none other than Mr. Aleksei Rykovsky, Mama." Turning wide eyes to Tara, she went on. "Why does he want to talk to Dad?"

Tara had been asking herself that same question. Surely it would have been easier to tell them all while they'd been gathered in the hall.

She contemplated what to answer as she sipped her coffee.

"Well, I'm not quite sure—"

"Marlene," her father's voice cut her off. "Come in here and bring Tara with you."

Biting her lip, her mother turned apprehensive eyes to Tara. Forcing a light laugh, Tara quipped, "I guess we'd better go and face the music." Swinging out of the kitchen, she answered, "May as well," to Betsy's "Can I come too?"

The two men stood facing each other across the room. Alek in front of the worn sofa, her father in front of his favorite chair. Tara took one step inside the room and stopped, her mother on one side, Betsy on the other. Apprehensively she glanced at Alek, then her father, then back to Alek again, unable to read anything in the face of either man.

"Come here, Tara."

Alek's voice was low, his tone gentle, and without question Tara went to him, her eyes trying to read his impassive face, the small smile playing at his mouth.

Her mother and Betsy followed her into the room and out of the corner of her eye she saw her brothers slip inside the doorway. Deliberately, it seemed to Tara, Alek had kept his eyes on her face until they were all in the room, then he turned that brilliant blue gaze on her mother and said quietly, "Mrs. Schmitt, your husband has just given me his permission to marry your daughter. I sincerely hope you will give yours also."

He had asked for permission! Alek Rykovsky! Incredible, Tara thought. Tara felt her breath catch, heard Betsy's small "oh," saw her mother go pink, glance at her husband then back at Alek before stuttering, "I-I—if Herman says—"

"He does," Herman interrupted. Then, as if suddenly becoming aware that they were all standing, he said, "Won't you sit down, sir?"

Too much! Tara thought. She stared at her father. The only other men she'd ever heard her father speak to in that deferential manner were their priest and doctor. And not always their doctor.

Alek murmured "Thank you," lowered himself to the sofa then held his hand out, palm up, and said softly, "Tara."

Bemused, Tara sat down next to him, placed her hand in his large, well shaped one, and felt it squeezed as he said to her mother, "Tara and I would like to be married on the second Saturday in December. I hope there will be enough time to make the necessary arrangements."

Her mother's eyes flew to her, and Tara answered hurriedly, "Yes, of course there'll be enough time. A small wedding really doesn't take much arrange—"

"You'll naturally want to be married in your own church," he cut in smoothly. "But I hope you'll have no objections to my own priest presiding."

Tara turned astonished eyes to him. "You're Catholic, Alek?"

"Yes, my love, I am." Again that small smile played around his mouth. She watched it in fascination, then his actual words struck her.

"In church?" she choked. "But that's not necessary. I thought a quiet wedding, no fuss."

She heard her father snort, her mother exclaim, "But Tara!" But Alek again commanded the floor.

"We will have a full Catholic wedding, darling. Including mass. We're only going to do this once; we may as well do it right. You may have as few or as many attendants as you wish." The devil danced in his eyes as he added, "Just don't exhaust yourself with the preparations."

Tara felt her cheeks flush at his meaning: He didn't want an overtired bride on his wedding night. She felt his arm slide around her waist, draw her closer to him. *What's he playing at now,* she wondered fretfully. Then was surprised at the explanation that leaped into her mind. The endearments, the touching, the tone of voice were all calculated to assure her father, all of them, that she was loved, cared for, protected. *But why would he bother to do that?* she argued with herself. *He had what he wanted. At least he* thought *he did.* Nevertheless the feeling persisted that he was deliberately acting the role of a man very much in love simply to reassure her parents.

The action of Alek glancing at his watch forced Tara's attention back to the conversation. He was speaking to her father, and his words jolted her alert.

"And, as I just said, the number of the wedding party, the type of wedding, is entirely up to Tara, but if you have no objections, I will arrange the reception." He held up one hand as both her father and mother started to protest. "Let me finish, please. I'm afraid it will be, by necessity, both rather large and expensive. I have quite a few friends and business associates. I would not want to have any one of them feel slighted because they were not invited. Many of them will be coming from a distance. Not only from out of town, but out of state as well. Arrangements must be made for their accommodations." Until this point his voice had been smooth, almost soft. Now it took on a thin, hard edge. "I insist on paying for it, as the majority of the names on the guest list will come from me." He glanced at her mother, and again the tone grew gentle. "I would appreciate it if you could have your guest list completed within a few days. We have less than a month, and I'd like the invitations in the mail by the end of this week."

"The end of this week!"

"But Alek, that's impossible."

Tara and her mother spoke in unison. Tara was too surprised to say anymore, but her mother continued. "That's not nearly enough time. Not only do we have to make up the guest list but we have to see the printers, pick out the invitations—"

"That won't be necessary," he interrupted. "Just make up your list as quickly as possible. My staff will take care of the rest. The invitations will be handwritten. Believe me, you will be satisfied with the result."

"Well, if you say so," her mother murmured.

Tara was beginning to feel very uneasy. When had she lost control of this farce? She was actually not being consulted at all, for all his talk of the size of the wedding being up to her. Feeling that she had to make some sort of stand she said, firmly, "Alek, I really do not want a large wedding. I had thought a small, quiet affair with just the families and maybe a few close friends."

The wicked gleam in his eyes alerted her, yet his words shocked her, causing a momentary hush in the room. "My sweet love, would you deprive the rest of our friends, everyone, the pleasure of witnessing the culmination of the union about which there has been so much speculation?"

Tara felt tears sting her eyes. "Alek." It was a low cry of protest, almost instantly covered by the hurried speech of nearly everyone in the room.

"It is settled." Alek's tone indicated he would listen to no arguments.

"Well then, Tara," Marlene said briskly. "You and I had better get working on a list."

"Not this evening," Alek stated. "Tara and I have a dinner engagement with my parents." He paused a moment then went on. "Darling, as it appears you are going to have to be spending a lot of time here anyway, why don't you pack what you'll need and move in here until the wedding. We can empty your apartment at our leisure later."

Tara stared at him in stunned amazement, unable, for a minute, to speak. *Too fast,* she told herself. *Everything was happening much too fast.* Why had she told David the second Saturday in December? She was beginning to feel rushed, stifled. And who did he think he was? *We? Our?* And she definitely did not want to move back here. She opened her mouth to say no, but not fast enough.

"Tara, that's a wonderful idea." Her mother's eyes were bright with excitement and enthusiasm. "It would save you all that running back and forth. Oh, honey, please, it will be such fun."

The word *no* trembling on her soft mouth, Tara sighed in defeat, unable to utter the word that would extinguish the light in her mother's eyes, cast a shadow on the happy face. But Alek would hear more about this later.

"All right, Mama," Tara answered tiredly. "I'll bring my things one night this week."

"I'll bring her and her things," Alek inserted. "Tomorrow night. If that's convenient." He didn't look at Tara's angrily flushed face, but kept his polite gaze on her mother, acknowledging her nod with a smile.

"I have my own car," Tara said through gritted teeth.

"Yes, darling, I know that." His words came slowly, evenly measured, as if he were speaking to a child who was not too bright. "Nevertheless, I will bring you tomorrow night. Now I think we really must go, as Mother is expecting us in an hour and a half."

His hand firmly grasping hers, he stood up and strode across the room, hand outstretched to her father. "A pleasure to meet you, sir. I assume we'll be seeing quite a bit of each other during the next few weeks?"

"Yes, yes, of course," Herman hastened to assure him, "and a pleasure to finally meet you, Mr. Rykovsky."

"Alek. I insist." His tone was so silky-smooth, Tara felt her teeth clench. He wished her mother a gentle good night, then started to move out of the room. He paused to raise an eyebrow at Betsy and murmur, "I'm depending on you to help Tara with all the arrangements. Will you do that?"

"Are you kidding?" Betsy laughed. "I'd like to see someone stop me."

He grinned, then moved on only to stop again at George.

"You're in your last year of high school?" he asked abruptly.

George nodded, eyes guarded.

"You're going to college?"

"If I can get a scholarship. Why?"

Alek studied him a second, then, as if reaching a swift decision, gave a brief nod and said, "If you want a job after school, come to see me. And if the scholarship doesn't materialize, we'll have a talk. Good night." He turned his head to include Karl, then made for the hall and their coats, tugging Tara behind him.

He held her coat for her, then shrugged into his own, bid them all a collective good night and, his hand at her back, propelled her out of the house. By the time he had seated her in the car, the dazed, steamrollered feeling had passed and Tara was doing a slow burn.

"How dare you," she seethed the instant he slid behind the wheel.

"How dare I what?"

Her hands clenched at his innocent tone. "Damn you, you know what," she snapped. "I do not want a large wedding and I certainly do not want to move back home and I damn well will not have you arranging my life."

"Don't swear at me again, Tara." His voice, while soft, had a warning edge of steel in it.

"All right," she sighed, "I'm sorry. But I mean it, Alek. Don't think for one minute that just because I agreed to marry you, I have any intention of playing the meek little hausfrau, blindly obeying your every dictate. I won't."

"Whatever you say, sweetheart. Now please stop nagging at me as if we were already married and look at that lovely moon. Not quite full but beautiful anyway."

The sound of his soft laughter seemed to wrap itself around her heart, and Tara had to remind herself sharply who he was and what he'd done.

"I don't want to look at the moon," she said irritably. "And I don't really want to have dinner with your parents, although I suppose we owe them a courtesy visit. And don't call me 'sweetheart.' Save your breath, and the endearments, for your next audience."

She heard his sharply indrawn breath, saw his hands tighten on the steering wheel before he growled, "I will call you anything I wish, when I wish. I'm sorry if the prospect of meeting my parents is repellent to you, but you may be in for a surprise. I'd be willing to bet you'll like them. They are very nice people."

In this he was proved correct. They *were* very nice people, and she did like them. He had dropped her at the apartment with a terse, "I'll be back in a half hour. Can you be ready by then?" At her nod he said, "Good," sharply. The moment she was out of the car, he shot away from the curb, still obviously very angry.

The drive to his parents' home was completed in tense silence, which Tara herself broke unconsciously when he drove along the driveway and parked in front of the sprawling redwood-and-glass ranch house.

"Oh, it's beautiful!" she breathed softly. Tara had expected something large and formal and this lovely rambling house was a delightful surprise.

"Yes, it is," Alek replied softly. "And so are the people who live in it."

Tara had known she'd angered him with her waspish words about not wanting to meet his parents, but now something about the tone of his voice told her he had also been hurt. *Impossible,* she said to herself, pushing the thought away. Nothing she could say to this unfeeling man could hurt him.

On entering, Tara was delighted to find the inside as lovely as the outside. It was decorated beautifully in soft, muted tones, the overall effect one of warmth, welcome. The warmth and welcome were reflected on the face of the woman who came to meet them, hands outstretched.

"Darling, you're right on time." The low, musical voice of Alek's mother's was not a surprise, coming from such an exquisitely beautiful woman. Small, splendidly proportioned, she had the most perfect bone structure Tara had ever seen. *So this is where he came by his devastating good looks,* she thought.

Before Alek could murmur more than, "Good evening, Mother," she was speaking again, taking Tara's hands in her own. "And this is Tara. Such a lovely name, and what a lovely thing you are too. No wonder Alek is in such a rush to get you to the altar. But come in, please, we have just enough time for a drink before dinner. And here's Peter, right on time to mix them."

Tara was forced to change her opinion of a few moments ago. For coming toward her was the original mold from which Alek had been made. One glance and Tara knew exactly what Alek would look like in twenty-five years. After the introductions were made, Peter Rykovsky tilted one dark brow at his son and said quite seriously, "Well, son, I didn't think it possible, but you have found yourself a woman whose beauty matches your mother's. My deep and sincere congratulations."

"Thank you, sir."

Pink-cheeked, Tara glanced at Alek in astonishment for the tone of respect he'd conveyed in those three short words.

As they sipped their drinks, Alek filled his parents in on the wedding plans they had made earlier. Peter and Alene's reaction to Tara's idea of a small, intimate wedding was the same as her own family's had been.

"Oh, no, my dear," Alene reproved gently. "I'm sure that would be a mistake. Every girl should be able to remember her wedding day as being as perfect as possible. By all means keep the wedding party small, if that's what you prefer. A wedding doesn't have to be large to be beautiful. But I do think Alek is right in his insistence on a church ceremony." Her soft laughter gave proof of the happiness bubbling inside as she added, "I must admit to a degree of selfishness in my considerations. I have waited so long for this day. When Alek celebrated his thirty-fourth birthday last spring, I decided, perhaps I had better resign myself to the idea of his remaining a bachelor and never giving me the grandchild I so long to hold."

Tara started, paling visibly, although her reaction went unnoticed. Alek and his father wore identical expressions of deep love and tenderness as they gazed on the misty-eyed, wistful, but adoring face of Alene. Tara felt terrible. Motivated by anger and frustration, she had acted without thought, now the ramifications of that act were piling up around her like so many stones, imprisoning her inside a cell of her own making. Panic gripped her throat, and she gulped the remains of drink in an effort to dislodge it.

A grandchild! Not once had she considered that possibility. Why hadn't she? It was the natural order of things. First the wedding, then . . . A shiver rippled through her body. Her own parents had not said anything but they, too, would be looking forward to their first grandchild—after a decent interval. *Oh, Lord!* Tara's mind clung to her last thought. *A decent interval!* Everyone thought she and Alek were already lovers. Now suddenly they were being married within a few weeks. How many of her friends would be counting the months? Watching for signs? *But I've done nothing, nothing,* her mind cried silently, envisioning the different type of speculative glances she would probably now be receiving. A feeling of intense dislike—almost hatred—for Alek burned through her and she closed her eyes.

Locked in a pain-filled world of her own, Tara was startled by Peter's voice, heavily laced with concern, alerting her to where she was.

"Tara, child, are you ill? You've gone positively white."

She saw Alek's gaze swivel from his mother's face to her own an instant before he was moving to her side. His eyes, his face, puzzled her, for he looked almost frightened. Alek frightened? His softly murmured words chased all contemplation of his expression from her mind.

"What's wrong, darling. Are you ill?"

The endearment set her teeth on edge and she had to fight to keep from screaming at him, *You fraud, you are what is wrong. You and the scheming and plotting you've done.* Using every ounce of willpower she possessed, she brought her emotions under control. "I'm afraid the drink has hit rock bottom," she lied shakily. "I've eaten very little all day, and my empty stomach doesn't seem to want to tolerate the alcohol."

Long, unbelievably gentle fingers brushed her cheek, felt the moisture that had gathered at her temple.

"Would you like to go home?"

Jerkily she leaned back, away from his caressing voice, his disturbingly light touch. *Yes,* she pleaded silently, *I want to go home. I want to hide myself away until everything that has happened the last week is long forgotten.*

"Would you like to lie down, my dear?" Peter asked anxiously.

Before Tara's confused mind could formulate an answer to either man, Alene was helping her to her feet, stating practically, "What this child needs is some food. Come along, Tara," she coaxed. "Something solid inside your stomach will banish this queasy feeling in no time." Leading Tara into the dining room, she shook her head in mock dismay, chiding, "Men are so helpless in situations like this. For some reason the strongest of them, and these two must be close to the top of the list, fall apart when someone they love is unwell."

A bubble of hysterical laughter became trapped in Tara's chest. If Alek was close to the top of the list of the strongest, he had to be even higher on the list of best actors if he could convince his mother with his performance.

Alene's diagnosis proved correct, for by the time they were halfway through the meal, Tara, her color restored, was laughing at Peter's obvious attempts to amuse her.

Tara was totally captivated by Alek's parents and under any other circumstances would have loved having them as in-laws. Strange, she mused, Peter and Alek were so much alike, yet she failed to detect any sign of the tyrant in Peter. His treatment of his wife was the type great love stories were written about; after nearly forty years of marriage his eyes touched her with an expression that Tara could only describe as adoration. Tara quickly learned where Alek had acquired the art of using endearments with such ease of manner. Peter seldom spoke to Alene without some form of endearment. That his feelings were returned in full was evident: Alene made no attempt to hide the fact that her world revolved around her husband and son.

As Tara basked in the warmth Alene and Peter generated, the evening slipped away from her. The only thing that marred her enjoyment was the caressing, possessive tone Alek used whenever he spoke to her.

When he drove her home, he pulled up in front of her building and said, "It's late, I won't come up with you." Tara breathed a sigh of relief then tensed as his hands cupped her face and drew her close. He kissed her slowly, lingeringly, and Tara felt the tenseness seep out of her, tiny little sparks igniting all over her.

When he lifted his head, he again whispered those same Russian words then said, "As your car is still on the office parking lot, I'll drive you to work tomorrow. Is seven thirty all right?"

"Y-Yes, that will be fine," Tara stammered. "I—I must go in. Good night."

There was no conversation exchanged between them the next morning other than a polite "Good morning, Tara," and an equally polite "Good morning, Alek," until he drew up at the office. Placing a hand on her arm as she moved to get out of the car, he said, "I'll come by at seven thirty to help you with your things."

Impotent anger surged through Tara and, pulling her arm away from his hand, she snapped, "All right," then thrust open the door and slammed it shut, his laughter following her as she hurried into the building.

"Tara, you really know how to keep a secret. Why didn't you tell us?" Jeannie's words hit her as she came through the door, but she was saved from confusion by the newspaper Jeannie shoved in front of her. In a lower corner of the front page was a picture of Alek with the caption LOCAL INDUSTRIALIST TO WED. Tara skimmed the small column that ran the length of the picture then pasted a smile on her face as she looked up at Jeannie. "If I'd told you, it wouldn't have been a secret. Besides, we wanted to discuss it with our parents first."

When had he done this, she thought furiously. Somehow she managed to maintain the smile as she glanced around the room murmuring thank-yous to the good wishes being called out. Her eyes brushed Terry then came back. The only words to describe the expression on his face were utter disbelief. His eyes seemed to ask, How did you do it when all the others failed?

With a forced note of happiness she asked Jeannie if she could borrow the paper then, still smiling, she went into her own office, dropped into her chair, and read the article more thoroughly.

Mr. Aleksei Rykovsky, son of Mr. and Mrs. Peter Rykovsky, owner-manager of the Fine Edge Machine Company, has announced his forthcoming marriage to Miss Tara Schmitt, daughter of Mr. and Mrs. Herman Schmitt. A December wedding is being planned. Miss Schmitt is the confidential secretary of Mr. David

Jennings, one of the city's up-and-coming architects
and the designer of the new plant Mr. Rykovsky is
having built.

David came in the office, paper under his arm, as Tara was finishing the
article. "I brought you the paper, but I see you already have one."

"Yes," she replied sweetly, lifting the sheet. "Plugs for everyone. Isn't that
nice?"

David gave her an odd look then shrugged and headed for his office. "Oh,
yes. I almost forgot. Sallie asked me to give you her very best wishes."

Sallie! Oh, Lord, Tara groaned inwardly, *I should have called her. But when?*
She reached for the phone and dialed David's home number. Sallie answered
on the third ring.

"Hi, Sallie. It's Tara."

"Tara! Oh, I'm so glad you called. Did David give you my message?"

"Yes, thank you." Somehow she managed to instill the lilt of happiness into
her voice. "Sallie, I know it's short notice, and we'll be rushed like mad, but
please say you'll be my matron of honor."

Sallie's light laughter danced along the wire. "Of course I will, I'd have been
crushed if you hadn't asked me. When can we get together?"

"Could you get away for a few hours tomorrow night? Come over to my
mother's?"

"Yes, certainly. Your mother's?"

Tara knew she'd have to make an explanation that was convincing. Sallie
knew all too well how she felt about living at home.

"Yes, I'm going to move back home until the wedding. With so much to do
in so little time, I'm hoping to save wear and tear on my nervous system."

"Probably the best idea," Sallie replied, musingly. Tara exhaled very slowly
with relief as Sallie added, "I'll come over right after dinner, okay?"

"Fine, I'll see you then. Now I'd better get to work before the boss catches
me goofing off. Bye, Sal."

Tara hung up, Sallie's happy laughter ringing in her ears. She felt a growing
sense of panic, as if she were caught in a net and someone was drawing it tighter
and tighter. What had she started?

7

That evening Tara stood in her bedroom, suitcases open on the bed, clothes
scattered around them, when the doorbell rang at exactly seven thirty.

"Oh, rats," she muttered under her breath then stormed out of the bedroom
to the door. Turning the lock, she flipped the door open, spun on her heel, and
stalked back into the bedroom without even glancing into the hall.

Staring in disgust at the cases and clothes a few minutes later, Alek's voice,
low, menacing, touched her like a cold breeze. "Don't ever do that again,
Tara."

Surprise turned to shock when she swung her head to stare at him. He was standing just inside the bedroom doorway, and his stance, everything about the hard look of him, was more chilling, menacing than his voice had been.

"Do what?" Tara wet her dry lips, suddenly frightened. "What did I do?"

His tone was harsh, the words clipped. "Don't ever unlock your door and turn away without looking to see who it is again. Are you looking to get robbed, or mugged, or worse?"

"But I knew it was you." Tara made her voice hard in an effort to hide the fear curling in her chest.

"You thought it was me," he rapped. "Not quite the same thing."

Unable to face that brittle blue stare, she turned her head to gaze unseeingly at the bed. Shock was added to shock at his lightning change of mood. His tone was now light and teasing, he sauntered across the room to her, eyes flicking over the cluttered bed.

"I thought you'd be almost finished packing by this time."

Anger replaced the fear inside and, without pausing to think, Tara flashed, "I don't know what to take and what to leave. I don't want to go to my mother's. I want to stay here in my own place. I'm used to my freedom. Do you realize that not only will I lose my privacy, I'll have to share a bedroom with Betsy?"

"Get you used to the idea of sharing a room," he teased laughingly.

In exasperation she turned glaring eyes to him. "Damn you, Alek, it's not funny."

Before the last word was out, she knew she'd gone too far. His face went hard, and his hands shot up to grip her upper arms, his long fingers digging in painfully. "I told you not to swear at me again," he growled dangerously.

She opened her mouth to apologize but not quickly enough. He pulled her against his hard chest, and his mouth crushed hers punishingly, brutally. Her hands, flat against his chest, pushed futilely at him, and she tried vainly to pull away from him. His one hand released her and, with a low, swinging arc, his arm swept the cases from the bed. His hand regripped her arm and he turned her, pushing her back and down. Her back hit the bed, his full weight on top of her, and she felt her breath explode inside her chest. The fear she had experienced earlier was nothing compared to the blind panic that now clutched at her throat.

Like a wild thing she struggled against him, hands pushing, legs kicking. Twisting her head frantically, she finally succeeded in tearing her mouth away from his cruel, bruising lips. Gasping for air, she choked, "You're nothing but an unprincipled savage. You're hurting me."

His darkened eyes glittered into hers, and he rasped, "Sometimes I'd like to do more than hurt you. At times I'd like to break your stiff neck." His mouth sought hers again, and Tara jerked her head away, feeling his lips slide roughly across her cheek. He was still a moment, then his hand moved from her arm, sliding slowly to the beginning swell of her breast. Lips close to her ear, he groaned, "Tara, in a few weeks I'll be your husband. Surely a few weeks can't make all that much difference." His hand slid caressingly over her breast and, his voice a harsh whisper, he urged, "Tara, let me. Let me."

Tara had to fight a different kind of fear now. The fear of the betraying, yielding softness invading her body.

"No," she cried. "Alek, you promised me."

His cool breath caressed her cheek as he sighed, then lifted his hand and pushed himself up and away from her. He stood tense, staring at her broodingly for a long minute before snapping, "All right, let's gather this stuff together and get the hell out of here before I change my mind." The thought flashed into Tara's mind that this was the reason for his insistence she stay with her parents. Was he afraid that the inevitable would happen if they were alone here? She shook her head in negation. *No, not Alek. Too out of character.* His reason was obvious. While she was surrounded by her family, there was less chance she'd change her mind, call the whole thing off.

By nine o'clock Tara was settled into her sister's room. Betsy had emptied some drawers and made room in the closet for her things, then stayed to help her unpack.

After the scene in her apartment bedroom, they had made fast work of the packing. Alek had carried the heavier things down the stairs and stowed them in his trunk. Then he had followed her car in his own to her father's house, where her brothers had taken over, lugging the cases up to Betsy's room.

Tara and Betsy were stowing the cases under the twin beds when their mother called, "I've made coffee, girls. Come have a cup while it's hot."

The sisters grinned at each other at the term *girls* then, side by side, went down the stairs and into the living room to join Alek and their parents.

"Well, Tara, come sit down. You look so tired, you're pale." Her father's changed attitude toward her was a secret source of amusement to Tara, and she had to work at controlling the twitch on her lips—a job made almost impossible when she encountered the wickedly laughing gleam in Alek's eyes.

"Yes, darling, come sit next to me and have some coffee. It will help you relax."

Although she did as he asked, Tara was convinced that if she was to relax, the last place in the world for her to sit was next to Alek.

As they drank their coffee, they discussed their plans for the next few days. Tara told her mother about having Sallie for her matron of honor, and that Sallie would be coming over tomorrow night. Then, glancing at her hopeful-faced sister, she grinned and said teasingly, "I hope you'll agree to be my maid of honor, as I'm planning on it."

"Oh, Tara." Betsy laughed shakily. "I was beginning to be afraid you weren't going to ask me."

"Not ask you? You nit, do you think I'd get married without you?"

Tara's voice was a little shaky, and she was glad when her mother turned the conversation to Alek.

"Have you decided on a best man yet, Alek?"

"Yes, I have. As a matter of fact I spoke to him today. My cousin Theo assured me he'd be delighted to prop me up, so to speak."

"Your cousin lives here in Allentown?" her father asked.

"No, Theo lives in Athens." At her parents' startled expression he explained briefly: "My mother's sister married a Greek. The Zenopopoulos family is a very old, respected one. Their firstborn son, Theo, runs the family shipping line now that my uncle Dimitri has retired."

"You have something of an international family, it appears," Tara said quietly.

His eyes came back to hers; his smile was pure charm.

"Yes, my sweet, I suppose I have. But only on my mother's side. She was born in Great Britain and her mother, now widowed, still lives in London, as does her brother, my uncle Edward. Her eldest brother, William, married a girl from Scotland. They live in Edinburgh. My father is second-generation American. He and I are the only ones left, as his parents are both dead, and he was an only child. As I am."

"I see," Tara replied, not quite sure she understood the underlying inflection he'd placed on his last words.

"Do you, my love? I wonder."

Confused, feeling as if she'd missed an important point, Tara changed the subject. "I think we'd better work on the guest list tonight," she said to her mother. "Have you had a chance to work on it at all today?"

"I've finished it." Marlene slanted a quick glance at her husband before adding, "Your father and I worked on it last night after you left."

Will wonders never cease? Tara asked herself wryly, somehow managing to keep the surprise she felt from showing. Her father's complete change of face since Alek had spoken to him the night before was both a source of amusement and irritation. It was as if he felt that now he had to handle her with kid gloves so as not to damage the merchandise Alek had claimed as his own. Tara couldn't decide if she wanted to laugh out loud or scream at him. What she had suspected weeks ago had been proved correct. Her father, recognizing in Alek the top dog of arrogant tyrants, had capitulated completely. Mentally tossing her head at the funny little games men played, Tara offered, "I'll go over the list later and add my own to it. It will be ready tomorrow, Alek."

He left soon after that, drawing her with him when he stepped out the door. Her hand firmly on the doorknob to prevent the door from closing entirely, she shook her head when he asked, "I won't be seeing you at all tomorrow night?" His eyebrows went up in question when she replied, "Or Thursday." At his expression she added hurriedly, "I want to go shopping. The gowns must be selected as soon as possible."

He frowned but murmured, "All right, but don't make any plans for Friday. We're having dinner together. I'll come for you at seven."

She had no time to answer, for, bending his head, his lips caught hers in a light kiss that proceeded swiftly to one that was hard and demanding. She stood passive, her lips cool under his, for a few seconds. Then, frightened by the warmth spreading through her body, she pushed her arm against the door and stepped back into the comparative safety of the brightly lit hallway. His eyes flashed with irritation, and she whispered breathlessly, "I must go in, Alek, I'm cold."

"I could have warmed you," he murmured harshly as he turned abruptly and walked to his car.

I no longer doubt it, Tara admitted to herself somewhat fearfully.

Sallie stopped by, as planned, the following evening and after a few hours of haggling with everyone in the house, Tara had her own way. They all protested, but Tara was determined to keep the wedding party small. Betsy and Sallie would be her only attendants.

Right after dinner Thursday evening, Tara, her mother, Betsy, and Sallie set out for the most exclusive bridal shop in town. Tara had no preconceived idea of what she wanted but she chose the second gown she looked at, paling slightly when the salesclerk told her the price. The other three women took much longer in selecting their gowns, enjoying themselves immensely, trying on gown after gown, while Tara sat, shifting restlessly in her chair, smoking one cigarette after another. Glancing at the growing number of cigarette butts, she grimaced in self-disgust. *I'm hooked again,* she thought sourly. *Another thing I have to thank Alek Rykovsky for.*

She and Alek did not go out for dinner on Friday evening after all. As Sallie was preparing to go home after they'd returned from shopping, having gone from the bridal shop to a shoe store, she said gayly, "Tara, David and I have planned an engagement party for tomorrow night. Just a small gathering, casual dress, so I'll see you then."

Tara felt suddenly panicky at the prospect of facing the rest of her friends for the first time since the wedding announcement and she stammered, "But, Sallie, I—I don't know, I mean, I don't think Alek—"

"Don't be silly," Sallie interrupted. "David spoke to Alek about it this afternoon and he said Alek was delighted. Now I've got to run. See you tomorrow night. Bye."

The party was an ordeal for Tara. She dressed casually but carefully in a peacock-blue evening pantsuit in crepe de chine, which moved and flowed with and around her body as she walked. After a light application of makeup, she stepped back from the mirror to observe the overall effect and smiled with satisfaction. Alek's expression, as he ran his eyes slowly over her, was an added boost to her confidence. But it was short-lived, slipping away to be replaced by growing nervousness and tension, as she fought to maintain the picture of the happy bride in front of her friends.

The evening seemed to drag on forever, Alek's possessive attitude and endearments making her alternatively angry and more nervous. When it was finally over and they were back in Alek's car on their way home, she let her head fall back against the seat and sighed with exhaustion. There would be more parties of this type, and she knew it and prayed for the strength to get through them with at least some degree of aplomb.

Her mind was drifting aimlessly when he brought the car to a stop in front of her parents' house, and her body jerked in alarm when his hands cupped her face, and he touched her mouth with his own. Turning her face, sliding her mouth from his, she whispered, "Alek, please, I'm so tired. All I want to do is go to bed."

Her action had placed her ear close to his lips and he replied, urgently, "Not nearly as badly as I do."

The words, his tone, sent a shaft of such intense longing through Tara, she was shocked, suddenly frightened. She didn't understand these feelings he could so easily arouse, and in sheer self-defense, she whipped up her anger. Her hand gripped the door handle and pushed the door open as she moved away from him. "I'm going in," she snapped. Then she turned to look directly at him and observe, "It seems to me that the only things men think about are sex and money."

"And that's bad?" He laughed softly.

"Don't laugh at me, Alek," she warned.

"All right, I won't," came the indulgent reply.

"And don't patronize me either," she cried, turning to jump from the car. His hand grasped her arm, forced her around to face him. "Whoa, take it easy." His eyes glittered, his voice held a touch of concern. "You *are* tired. You sound like you're ready to fly into fourteen different directions at once. Sleep in tomorrow. I told you, I didn't want you wearing yourself out."

His last statement brought color to her pale cheeks, a flash to her tired eyes. Who the hell was he to tell her anything?

"Let me go, Alek." She spoke through gritted teeth to keep from screaming at him. "I'm going inside."

Slamming the door as she got out of the car, Tara ran up the walk and had the key in the door lock when Alek caught up with her. His arms slid around her waist, pulling her back against him, crushing the velvet of the long evening cape she'd thrown over her shoulders.

"Tara, I know this evening wasn't easy for you, but don't you think you're overreacting a little?" His breath was a soft caress against her hair, and in a weak moment Tara let her head rest on his hard chest. "If you allow yourself to get this uptight every time we're in the company of our friends, you'll be a total wreck in no time. Relax. Enjoy the attention you're receiving as the bride-to-be. The decision to marry was yours, you know."

Renewed anger banished weariness temporarily and, twisting away from his arm violently, she said bitterly, "Oh, yes, I know, the final decision was mine. But I was left with little choice and I didn't want, nor can I enjoy, the attention of my friends." Sarcasm overlaid the bitterness as she added, "Now, if I have your permission, I'd like to go in."

"Tara!"

"Good night, Alek."

With that she turned the key, pushed the door open, stepped inside, and shut the door firmly on his face.

The following two weeks rushed by hectically, Tara constantly fighting down the growing feeling of panic. What had she started? Would she go through with it? Was there any way she could stop it now? She knew the answer to that. Her mother's happy face, as she sat carefully numbering the increasing flow of wedding gifts and arranging them on a long folding table her father had set up in the living room, gave it to her. There was a sparkle in her eyes as she smoothed work-reddened hands over the white tablecloth and touched, again and again, the obviously expensive gifts. She looked years younger and laughed often, and Tara felt trapped, afraid to go ahead, unable to step back. Betsy and Sallie were enjoying the preparations almost as much as her mother and through it all Tara plastered a smile on her face.

She could find no escape, even in the office, and the smile grew brittle. Suddenly all the friends who'd been silent for weeks became very vocal and Tara had to fight down a mushrooming cynicism. God! She had never been so popular in her life. Totally unimpressed, she moved through the days, giving all the proper answers, laughing at all the proper times, and withdrew into her own hiding place inside herself. Denied even the solace of a room of her own, she cried inside, bitter, resentful tears that never touched her cheeks but lent a sparkle to her eyes that was mistaken for happiness, excitement. She drove herself in the office, rearranging files that were already in perfect order, cleaning desk drawers that had always been neat. She knew David attributed her industry to a desire to have her office in order for her replacement while she was on her honeymoon.

The very word *honeymoon,* which she was beginning to hear more and more frequently in teasing tones, was enough to send a tiny flutter—of what? Fear—up her spine. And she was tired. Lord, was she tired.

Tara looked forward to Thanksgiving as to an oasis in the desert. Although she would be spending most of the day with Alek, she hoped that, surrounded by family, she would be able to rest, relax, be herself. *It seems,* she told herself at the end of the day, *that fools never learn.*

The arrangements were for her and Alek to have the traditional Thanksgiving dinner at one o'clock with her family then, in early evening, go on to his parents' for a cold buffet. Alene and Peter had invited a few close friends to join them, Sallie and David included.

Tara was blissfully alone in the kitchen Thanksgiving morning, humming to herself as she prepared vegetables for a salad, when Alek's soft voice stalked across the room to her from the kitchen doorway.

"Good morning, my love. Happy Thanksgiving."

As Tara jerked around from the sink with a startled "Oh," the paring knife she'd been using slipped from her fingers and bounced around on the floor tiles, dangerously close to her ankles.

"Careful!"

Alek was across the room in three long strides, his hand outstretched to grasp her arm and pull her away.

"Are you hurt? Did it hurt you? Why the hell did you let go of it?"

The sharp, staccato questions struck her like blows and, feeling attacked, she answered defensively, "I—I . . . you startled me."

He bent, retrieved the knife with his free hand, dropped it into the sink, then turned her into his arms, holding her loosely.

"That is the second time you nearly injured yourself because, as you say, I startled you. Tara," he said probing gently, "what is it about me that unnerves you so? Are you afraid of me?"

How could she answer him? She didn't know the answers anymore. She felt confused, uncertain. Oh, why had she started this? She was afraid of him. But why? And did he really think she'd ever admit it?

Shaking her head in negation, she said, lying, "Don't be silly. I was deep in thought and—"

"You won't let me near you, will you?" he sighed. "You're hiding behind that invisible fortress you've built around yourself. Tara, don't you realize that while you're locking me out, you're also locking yourself in?"

She didn't want to listen to any more. Making a move to turn out of his arms, she snapped, "I don't know what you're talking about. Now go away so I can finish the salad."

His arms tightened, refusing to let her go. Bending his head, he whispered, "You didn't return my greeting."

"I—"

"But that's all right, I prefer a silent one anyway."

His mouth caught hers, locking on firmly. Tara steeled herself to remain passive then felt a jolt in the pit of her stomach as his lips forced hers apart, demanding a response. Panic crawled through her when she felt the tip of his tongue, and her hands pushed against his chest. He reacted by dropping his hands to her hips, pulling her roughly against him. The hard muscles of his thighs pressed against her urgently.

Her resistance weakened, and as her mouth grew softer, his became harder, bolder. She felt floaty, light-headed, and, her breath quickening in unison with his, her arms snaked up around his neck and clung.

Tightening his arms, he drew her even closer, his hands moving gently along her spine, pressing her softness against the long, hard length of his body. Thought disappeared and was replaced by sensations. The golden curtain dropped around them, and she felt a strange contentment seep through her. For the first time in weeks she felt safe, secure. Sighing softly, she allowed her lips to be parted yet farther, wanting to drown in the firm sweetness of his mouth.

The slamming of the front door reverberated through her like shock waves, setting off an alarm in her mind. Her father's voice, chastising Karl for letting it slam, brought both shame and reason. What did she think she was doing? Was her mind slipping? Was a soldier ever so weary, he sought rest in the camp of his enemy?

With a small cry of self-disgust she backed away from him, eyes closed in pain, her hand covering her quivering lips.

"Tara?"

Shaking her head wildly, she turned away. "Don't say anything."

"Tara, this is ridiculous. If you'd—"

"No! You make me sick. I make myself sick." She spun around to face him, eyes wide, frightened, refusing to see the almost desperate expression in his eyes, to hear the almost pleading note in his voice. "You can go to—you can go to the living room. Keep my father company while I make the salad."

She had been speaking softly, tremulously. Now her tone went hard: "Go away, Alek."

He started toward her then stopped as the kitchen door was pushed open. Marlene's voice preceded her into the room.

"You should have come to church with us, Tara—" On seeing Alek she paused, hands behind her back as she tied an apron around her still slim waist. "Oh! Good morning, Alek. Happy Thanksgiving. I swear, if it wasn't for the mouth-watering smell of that turkey in the oven, I wouldn't believe it was Thanksgiving, it is so mild outside. Why—" She stopped, eyes swinging from Tara to Alek then back to Tara, suddenly feeling the tension that danced between the two. "Is"—she paused, wet her lips—"is anything wrong?"

At the look of anxiety that had replaced the happy glow on her mother's face, Tara caught herself up sharply. Marshaling her rioting emotions, she managed a shaky laugh.

"Of course not, Mama. I was just trying to chase Alek into the living room to Dad, so I can get on with the salad."

Tara saw, but refused to let register, the small sigh Alek expelled before he turned a composed, warm face to her mother.

"Hello, Marlene. Happy Thanksgiving." He had been using her parents' Christian names, at their request, for several days now, yet each time he addressed one of them, Tara felt an uncomfortable twinge. He did it so easily, so effortlessly, as if he'd known and liked them for years.

"I suppose," he went on teasingly, "that if I want to taste said bird in the oven, I had better retreat to the living room, and Herman, as graciously as possible. And you were right. The aroma is mouth-watering. If you've taught Tara all your little kitchen secrets, I'm afraid I'll have to watch my waistline very carefully after we're married."

Tara's fingers curled into her palms, the nails digging into her flesh as she watched her mother's expression change from worry to flushed pleasure. He had completely captivated her mother. Had in fact captivated every member of her family. Betsy became all flustered and pink-cheeked whenever he favored her with one of his teasing, devastatingly gentle smiles. Her brothers trailed around behind him as if in the wake of some vaulted, invincible hero, their expressions bordering on awe. And her father! That was the kicker. Her father walked around with his chest expanded, eyes bright with pride, whenever Alek slipped and called him *sir* instead of *Herman*.

Their attitude, the whole situation, filled Tara with disgust. *They acted as if he were one of the lords of the earth,* she had thought scathingly several times, rather than the devious, arrogant, tyrannical boss he in fact was. Not once did she question her own deeply ingrained opinion of him. He was the enemy. Period.

Tara spent the rest of the day in cold resentment; he had ruined the holiday for her. By the time they reached his parents' home, her resentment had changed to simmering anger. His possessive attitude, his endearments, had her fighting the urge to hit him.

Alene had planned a casual evening and, after the cold buffet supper had been cleared away, they gathered in the living room. As there were more people than chairs, Tara sat on the floor between Alek's and Peter's chairs. The conversation ran the gamut from fashion to politics, becoming more lively when Women's Lib was mentioned.

Tara was just beginning to relax and enjoy herself when Alek's hand dropped onto her shoulder and his cool voice drawled, "I wonder if most women really know what they want?" His eyes rested briefly on his mother's face, then he added, "The most contented women I know are the ones who realize their happiness stems from being well cared for and cherished by the men they belong to."

The overbearing beast! Red flares exploded inside Tara's head. Trembling in anger, she turned her head to stare pointedly at his hand before lifting her head to give him the full blast of fury in her eyes. To keep from shouting Tara had to push her words through her teeth.

"If a slave is your secret desire, Alek, count me out. I will be a slave for no man."

Alek's face paled and, in soothing tones, he murmured, "Tara, I didn't mean—"

"I have reason to know," Tara interrupted bitingly, "you mean exactly what you say. *Belonging to* means ownership and ownership of a human being means slavery. I am, and intend to remain, my own person. With or without your approval. And will you please remove your hand.''

Tara's last words were spoken so cuttingly, Alek snatched his hand away as if he'd been burned. A tide of red crawled across his cheeks, and his eyes held an unfamiliar look of humiliation.

A deathly silence covered the room for some minutes, then Peter's quiet voice eased the tension.

"You deserved that, son," he said easily. "Strangely enough, your mother put me in my place much the same way forty years ago."

"And hard as it may be to believe, Tara," Alene chimed in laughingly, "Peter was even more cocky than Alek."

Her teasing gibe relieved the strain in the room, and everyone began talking at once. Even so, Alek did not touch her for the remainder of the evening.

By the Saturday before the wedding Tara was bewildered and near tears. She couldn't or wouldn't understand her own emotions any longer, and she felt depressed and somehow scared. That afternoon she sat doing her nails, nibbling at her lower lip. There was to be yet another—the last of many—party that night at the home of a lawyer friend of Alek's. From what she had gleaned from Sallie, it was to be a large one, some forty or so guests. This was to be the first really formal party for them, and Tara had shopped for hours till she found the right dress. The fact that her beautiful future mother-in-law would be there was an added spur to her choice. Alene had exquisite taste and always looked as if she had just stepped out of the pages of a haute couture magazine. Also Alek had told her she'd be meeting his cousin Theo at this party, as he was arriving Saturday morning.

The gown was of flame-colored chiffon in the caftan style, free-flowing and sensuous, molding the lines of her figure as she moved, revealing one moment, concealing the next. It was edged in silver braid that in the light reflected onto her hair, giving it a silvery sheen.

As she walked into the living room that evening, she was glad she'd taken more care than usual with her appearance. Alek, in black evening wear, was a devastating threat to any female's senses, and Tara felt her heartbeat quicken. The glittering, sapphire gaze he slowly ran over her didn't help her breathing any, and she drew a deep, calming breath when he murmured, "We had better be going," and turned his eyes away from her to say good night to her parents.

In the car Tara was quiet, her mouth and throat felt dry as bone, and she admitted to herself that she was scared. Tonight, for the first time, she would be meeting Alek's more important friends, and she was naturally anxious.

As he turned the car into the private drive leading to his friends' home, Alek slanted her a sharp glance, then, as if he had been monitoring her thoughts, said gently, "They're only people, you know. Very little different from other people. Some may have more money, some more intelligence, and most, more ambition and drive. But people, just the same. I doubt there'll be a woman there more lovely or poised than you. I wonder sometimes if you fully realize how beautiful and desirable you are." He parked the car in the midst of dozens of others, then turned to face her fully. "Chin up, my sweet. Let's have one of those heart-stopping smiles of yours," he teased.

Feeling a soothing warmth flow through her, Tara did smile, if a little tremulously. Bending his head, he brushed his mouth across hers and whispered, "Now go in there and knock their socks off."

The house was very large, very imposing, and more than a little daunting. As they entered the large, impressive hall, Tara unconsciously straightened her shoulders and lifted her head, completely unaware, as she walked into the room full of people, that she had the graceful bearing of a young queen.

Her first impressions were of lights and sounds and colors. The room was brightly lit, the light reflecting even more light as it struck fiery, rainbow-colored sparks off the jewelry that adorned the throats, wrists, fingers, and earlobes of the brilliantly gowned women. The sound was a blend of laughing voices and muted background music coming from several speakers positioned at different spots in the room.

She was vaguely aware of Alek introducing her to her host and hostess, John and Adele Freeland, and they in turn were introducing her to the people standing closest to them. In amazement Tara heard herself responding in a tone of cool self-assurance. Then the press of people separated her from Alek, and what little confidence Tara had, left her completely. She was beginning to feel panic rise when, on a sigh of sheer relief, she saw Alek's father making his way to her through the crowd.

"Good evening, my dear." Peter Rykovsky's voice was a warm caress to badly fraying nerves. Without so much as a by-your-leave he took her cold fingers in his warm hand and said imperiously, "I've been ordered by my lady to bring this delectable young thing to her, and, as you know, Alene's wish is my command."

Warm laughter followed them as he led her adroitly through the milling people, not stopping until Tara stood directly in front of Alene. "Ah, there you are, darling," Alene's lovely voice greeted her. "Come meet my nephew Theo."

Tara turned and felt the breath catch in her throat. Standing next to Alene was a young man who could easily have posed for at least a half dozen Greek statues. His face and form were classically beautiful; his dark, curly hair appeared sculpted to his head; and his eyes were clear and blue as a summer sky. Even, white teeth flashed as he smiled at her and in a voice that held only a hint of an accent he said, "All my life I've secretly thought that Alek was not only the shrewdest but also the luckiest devil alive. Now my beliefs are confirmed. I think I've fallen in love on sight. I don't suppose, beautiful creature, you'd care to run away with me this minute and leave old Alek at the altar, would you?"

In speechless confusion Tara heard Alene's laughing comment and Peter's dry retort. *This young man was almost as outrageous as Alek,* Tara thought. What surprises would the rest of the family have for her?

She was saved from answering him as Sallie joined their small circle, and once again she was being led away. They had taken only a few steps when she had to stop short, her path being barred by an exotically lovely woman whose black eyes glittered maliciously at her. In a tone of barely controlled fury, she purred icily, "I haven't yet met the bride-to-be, Sallie."

A flicker of alarm touched Tara's spine at the hostility underlying the woman's tone, and she looked at her sharply. She was of average height, voluptuously built, with full breasts, a small waist, and full hips that tapered to long, slender legs. Her skin was olive-toned, and right now a dusky pink tinged her cheeks. Hair as shiny black as sealskin lay smooth and sleek against her head in a short cap-cut. Beautifully arched black brows set off snapping black eyes, which were surrounded by long black lashes. The almond shape of her eyes added to the exotic look of her. The feeling of alarm grew stronger at Sallie's obvious reluctance to introduce them. After what seemed like a long pause Sallie said hurriedly, "Tara Schmitt—Kitty Davenport."

Kitty! *More like the jungle cat,* Tara thought as she acknowledged the introduction. Her thought was proved correct with the woman's next words: "I hope you're enjoying yourself now," she purred. "It won't be long before the novelty of innocence wears off for Alek, and then your nights will be very cold and long."

"Kitty!" Sallie's voice held shocked reproof, even though she'd managed to keep it at a normal tone. Grasping Tara's arm, she drew her away from the nasty laugh that broke from Kitty's dark-red lips. When they were a few feet away from her, Tara whispered, "What was that all about?"

Sallie began to shake her head, then paused and finally said, "I may as well tell you. You'll find out sooner or later anyway." Still grasping her arm, she drew her into a relatively quiet corner, glanced around, then said softly, "Until a few months ago Kitty was Alek's—uh—girl friend. She has been vocally bitter about their breakup. I can't imagine why she was invited to this party."

The searing stab of pain that tore through Tara at Sallie's words stunned her, and she turned her head to hide her pain-filled eyes. She was jealous! Fiercely, hotly jealous, and the knowledge of it frightened and confused her. As if looking for a lifeline, she glanced around the room frantically, and her glance was caught, held by a glittering blue one. Even across the width of the large room Tara saw Alek's eyes grow sharp, questioning. As her eyes stared into that sapphire blaze, a small voice cried out inside, *Dear God, no. No, no, no. I can't, I won't be in love with him. . . . But you are* came a silent taunt.

Remember how he's hurt you, what he is, she told that silent voice, then she deliberately turned back to Sallie and said coldly, "Girl friend? You mean *mistress,* don't you? Did he pay for an apartment for her in his building or did she just share his?" It was a futile effort to reject her emotions. The pain and humiliation grew to the dimensions of torture, and she was only vaguely aware of the concern in Sallie's voice. "Oh, Tara, does it really matter? It was over months ago."

Yes, Tara thought. *But for how long?* How long would it be before Alek, once having acquired the one thing he'd been denied, became bored and began looking around for a diversion? And Kitty would be there in his sight; of that Tara felt quite sure.

8

Tara opened her eyes the morning of her wedding and closed them again quickly, tightly. The weather matched her emotional condition. The sky was weeping hard, and although Tara's eyes were now dry, inside her heart the tears fell as swiftly as the raindrops. The days she lived through since the party—a week ago tonight—had been pure hell.

Vainly and painfully she had fought against the realization of her love for Alek. She had spent as little time with him as possible, telling him she had too much to do. His skeptical eyes questioned her, although he didn't voice his doubts. She went to her apartment several evenings, ostensibly to pack her things for removal to Alek's apartment, only to pace from room to room crying bitter tears. She didn't want to love him. She didn't even want to like him.

What was she to do? The desire to make him pay for what he'd done to her had been cauterized by that searing knife of jealousy on Saturday night. She hurt badly yet she knew, somehow, that the pain she now knew was nothing to what would come later. Twice she had left the apartment to go back to her parents, firmly determined to tell them she could not go through with the wedding. Both times the words died on her lips at the sight of her mother's face.

The rehearsal last night had been an ordeal that was not helped by Theo's light banter. When it had finally been over, Alek had led Tara outside to his car, brushing aside her protested "Alek, my car," with a curt "I'll bring you back for it."

He had not driven far, parking the car again on a dimly lighted street. Resting an arm on the steering wheel, he slanted a long look at her before asking tightly, "Last-minute jitters, Tara? You've been withdrawn and jumpy all week. Is something wrong? Aren't you feeling well?"

"I feel fine," she murmured, twisting her hands in her lap. "I'm a little tired, that's all."

He turned to face her fully, his one long hand covering hers stilled their agitated movement. Head bent, Tara studied his slim-fingered hand, felt its warmth seep into her cold skin. A small shiver rippled along her spine as his hand moved, slid up her arm to grasp her shoulder. "Look at me, Tara."

When she didn't comply at once, he released her shoulder and caught her chin in his fingers, lifting her head and turning her face to his descending mouth. She forced herself to remain passive, silently fighting down the tingling in her fingers, the warmth spreading through her body. Feeling somehow that if she didn't break contact with his persuading mouth, she'd be lost forever, she pulled her lips away from his with a small sob.

"Alek, please take me home. I'm very tired, and isn't Theo having a bachelor party for you tonight?"

"Yes he is, but there's no hurry." His fingers caressed her cheek, brushed lightly at the few strands of silky hair that had fallen across her face, His mouth followed the progress of his hand and, as his fingers slid into the deep waves of her hair, his lips, close to her ear, whispered, "Only one more day, pansy eyes, and this mad rushing around will be over. You can rest then, and I'll help you. The medicine I've got for you works better than any tranquilizer ever made." Then his mouth found hers again, hard, demanding a response from her. Trembling, breathless, she could feel her resistance slipping away, and in desperation she brought her hands up to his head and pushed him away. "Alek, don't."

He flung himself back behind the steering wheel, breathing hard, smoldering, darkened eyes roaming her face.

"You're right," he rasped. "I'd better take you home before I decide the hell with the party and take you to my place." He paused then added roughly, "I want you badly, Tara. Tomorrow can't come soon enough."

Now, lying in her bed, Tara groaned aloud at the memory and turned her face into the pillow. Why hadn't she backed out of this days ago, as soon as she'd felt that soul-destroying stab of jealousy? She wanted to run away and hide, and it was too late. Within a few hours she would be his wife. His words, like a scratched record, kept repeating in her head. *"I want you badly." I want you. Want. Want. Want.*

The rain still poured from leaden skies when Tara, pale, ethereal, and unknowingly beautiful, was dressed and ready to leave for the church. A bubble of hysterical laughter caught then lodged in her throat at the incongruity of tugging clear plastic boots over her white satin slippers and carefully catching her long, full skirt around her knees, under the protective rain cape her father placed around her shoulders. From house to car, from car to church, George held a large golf umbrella over her.

The feeling of unreality that had gripped Tara from the minute she'd begun dressing mushroomed and grew until now, poised, ready to follow Betsy down the aisle, she felt cold, numb. The signaling organ chord was struck, her father's shoulder nudged hers, and she moved in measured step beside him, unaware of the several small gasps or open stares of admiration that greeted her appearance.

The gown Tara had chosen was of white satin, starkly beautiful in its simplicity. It fit snugly from the high collar that encircled her throat to the nipped-in waist, and from her shoulders to where the sleeves ended in a V point on the back of her hands at the middle fingers. From the waist the skirt belled out full and voluminous, ending in a short train in back. It was completely without adornment of either fabric or jewelry.

In a strangely withdrawn state Tara walked slowly down the long aisle, drawing ever nearer to the two cousins, both handsome in different ways. They watched her progress with different expressions: Theo's smile was soft, his eyes warmly appreciating her beauty. Alek's unsmiling countenance was held in, taut, expressionless. His eyes blazed with a fierce possessiveness, and something Tara couldn't define.

The withdrawn, cold state lasted throughout most of the ceremony, and not until the blessing was being given did Tara feel the first pangs of guilt. She had agreed to marry this man for a very unholy reason. Revenge. In any way that presented itself, she had decided to make him pay for what he'd done to her. The fact that his reason—lust—was equally sinful didn't matter. The fact that she now loved him didn't excuse her either. She was in the house of God and she was committing a reprehensible act; she felt, if possible, more miserable than before.

Finally it was all over. Not just the ceremony, but the picture-taking as well. And now the hand that tugged the plastic boots over her slippers felt weighted from the heavy, wide gold band Alek had slid onto her finger. And the car that whisked them to the Hotel Traylor for the reception was shared by her husband.

She was thankful for the numbed coldness that had enveloped her again during the long period of picture-taking, and it carried her through the reception. A smile cramping her neck and jaw muscles, she went through the motions of the leadoff dance, the cake-cutting, and the tossing of the bouquet, all the while blinking at the incessant flash of light from the hired photographer. On the point of thinking it would go on forever, Tara felt the firm clasp of Alek's hand and walked beside him as he made a determined move to the door.

The plan had been for them to change clothes at Alek's—now their—apartment, then go on to New York for a week. It had grown colder, and the rain still slashed against the windshield. After Alek had maneuvered the car into the steady stream of late-afternoon traffic, he said abruptly, "I wouldn't be a bit surprised if this rain turns to snow in a little while. We're not driving to New York in this tonight, we'll wait and leave in the morning."

At the sound of finality in his tone, Tara gulped back the protest forming on her lips, her panic at the prospect of being alone with him that much sooner closing her throat to speech.

His apartment, in a fairly new modern complex, was large and luxurious. Tara had been in it once before, on Thursday night, when they had transported her clothes from her father's house. She had been given the grand tour of: Alek's large bedroom and a smaller one, both with their own baths; a roomy, well-equipped kitchen and cozy dining area; and a huge living room, part of which had been sectioned off as a bar area. The furnishings were Scandinavian modern, the lines straight and clean, yet overall the impression was one of the kind of comfort that comes only with money.

Alek turned the key in the lock, pushed the door open, reached inside to flick on the light switch, then ushered Tara in, saying dryly, "I think I'll save the over-the-threshold tradition until we move into a home of our own, if you don't mind."

Tara shook her head and walked into the room, only to stop and glance around irresolutely. The sound of the door being closed softly, the click of the lock springing into place, set her in motion, and she hurried toward the bedroom, her voice breathless. "I—I think I'll change. The bottom of my gown got wet and it's heavy and uncomfortable."

She dashed into the bedroom, closed the door behind her, and leaned weakly against it, gasping for air. Dear Lord, what was she going to do? She didn't think she could face him again, yet she was trapped inside this apartment with him. Moving away from the door, she walked around the room nervously, her eyes not registering the light-wood tone of the double dresser, the chest of drawers, the desk, the big overstuffed chair covered in pale green tweed, the deep rich green of carpeting and draperies or pristine white of walls, ceiling, and woodwork. But mostly her eyes avoided the wide double bed with its coverlet in a bold, dark-green-and-white geometric design.

Without thinking, her trembling fingers slid open the zippers on the inside of her sleeves, moved to tug at the long one that ran from the back of her neck to her waist. She managed to get it halfway down, then no amount of stretching or reaching would move it an inch farther. In agitated frustration, Tara tugged on her sleeves, hoping to slip the gown off her shoulders, enabling her to twist the zip around to the front. She was on the verge of tears when the bedroom door opened and Alek asked softly, "Need any help?"

"I can't get the damned zipper down," she cried irritably and heard his low laugh as he came across the room to her. She felt his fingers at her back, then the zip was sliding easily to its base. A pause, then his hands parted the material, slid inside and around her waist, scorching her skin through the thin fabric of her slip. As if his fingers actually burned her, she jerked away from him.

"Alek, I'd like to take a shower." Trembling, she turned to face him, a plea in her eyes. "Please."

His eyes glowed darkly as they roved over her body then came back to study her face. "That is a strikingly beautiful gown." His voice was a blatant caress, rippling over her skin like warm satin. "It almost does you justice. All right, my sweet, have your shower. I'll use the other bathroom and take one too." Then his voice sounded a mild warning note. "You have exactly one half hour." With that he calmly walked to the closet, yanked out a long dark-brown hooded robe, and sauntered out of the room.

Tara released her tensely held breath on a long sigh then quickly removed her gown and underthings, tossing the lot onto the overstuffed chair. Plunging her hand into the closet, she grabbed the long white satin robe she'd hung there Thursday night and ran into the chocolate-brown-and-white-tiled bathroom. Impatiently she twisted and pinned up her almost waist-long hair, shrugging at the short, curly neck hairs that escaped the shower cap she pulled onto her head. Standing under the hot, stinging spray, she longed for a few extra minutes to stand and let the fingerlike jets work the tenseness out of her body. But she didn't have a few extra minutes, for she had made up her mind to dress and leave the apartment before Alek finished his shower.

In fumbling haste she dried her body, slipped into her robe, and scrubbed her teeth. Her hair a silver-blond mass of waves rioting over her shoulders and down her back, she pulled open the bathroom door, stepped through it, and stopped cold at the sound of Alek's sharply indrawn breath.

He was standing just inside the bedroom door as if he'd just that minute entered. The robe hung to the top of his bare feet, the belt looped tightly around his lean waist, the hood lay loosely on his back.

Tara stood motionless, as if mesmerized. His softly spoken words, as he moved toward her, startled her into awareness. "God, Tara, you're beautiful."

Cautiously she moved away from him, toward the far-window wall, her voice sounding hoarse and strained to her ears. "This is a mistake. I can't stay here, Alek. I'd like you to leave the room so I can dress. I'm going home."

He paused, then continued to her, stopping a foot in front of her. In growing alarm she watched his face harden, his eyes change from confusion to wariness to anger.

"Like hell I'll leave this room." She flinched at the whip-flick cutting sting of his voice. "If there's been a mistake, you made it and you'll live with it, and me. You're not going anywhere. You *are* home."

Shrinking inside at the coldness of his tone, Tara drew a deep breath and, moving quickly, she circled around him and made for the door. Her hair was her undoing, for as she swung away from him, it fanned out and around her head. With lightning swiftness his arm shot out, and he caught a handful, making her cry out with the pain that stung her scalp. He gave a tug to turn her around to him and she lost her balance and crashed to the floor on her knees in front of him. Giving another sharp tug he jerked her head back, turned her face up to the cold, hard planes of his. Through tightly clenched teeth he growled,

"You're my wife, Tara, and you'll stay my wife. I've waited long enough; I'll wait no longer."

Defiance blazed out of her eyes and in an attempt to inflict pain on him, as he was on her, she flashed, "You're a savage. Underneath that thin veneer of civilization you're as wild and unruly as a marauding cossack. A savage, do you hear?"

His glittering blue eyes never leaving hers, he dropped onto his knees in front of her. "I hear," he rasped. "And this evening, my love, you are going to find out what it feels like to be made love to by a savage."

His mouth crushed hers, then his head jerked back, and she watched in horrified fascination as a drop of blood formed and grew at the wound in his lip her biting teeth had inflicted. His tongue flicked out, removed the blood, which was replaced at once with another drop. Alek lowered his head slowly to her again and, his lips almost touching hers, he whispered, "And you call me a savage?" Then with cool deliberation he caught her lip between his teeth and bit hard. His mouth covering hers smothered her outcry and she tasted the salty flavor of his blood. Or was it hers?

With all her concentration centered on remaining passive, unaffected by the disturbing pressure of his mouth, Tara was only vaguely aware of his fingers relaxing, sliding away from her hair. His other arm was around her tightly, pinning both of hers to her side. Slowly he began to move, sideways and down, drawing her with him. His free hand braced on the floor, he lowered them both to the soft pile carpeting, his lips still locked on hers.

Turning her at the last moment, her back hit the floor with a dull thud at the same time his hard chest struck hers, knocking the wind out of her. Feeling suffocated, Tara managed to turn her head away from him, gasping for air. Not once breaking contact, his lips slid across her soft cheek to her ear, and she uttered a tiny gasp when his teeth nibbled at her lobe.

"Tara, I don't want to force you." Tara shivered at the impassioned whisper. "But this marriage will be consummated tonight. I *will* make you mine. Never have I wanted to own a woman the way I want to own you. Don't fight me, love, or, in different ways, you'll hurt us both."

Fleetingly she wondered at the meaning of his words, then all thought fled, for his lips were sending small tongues of flame into every vein in her body. With tiny, devastating kisses his lips moved from her ear to the corner of her mouth where, along with the tip of his tongue, he teased and tantalized until every one of her senses cried out with the need to feel those lips, that tongue, against her own.

"Alek."

His name broke from her throat with a small sob as she moved her head the fraction of an inch needed to slide her mouth under his. She heard the breath catch in his throat, as if in disbelief, then his mouth crushed hers more savagely than before, in an excitingly desperate kind of way, plundering, seeking every ounce of sweetness there.

It seemed the whole world was on fire, and she was the very center of the blaze. Filled with a sudden, urgent need to touch him, her hands broke free of his imprisoning hold and, parting the lapels of his robe, she slid her hands across his chest, exhilaration singing through her when she felt him shudder at her touch.

With a groan his mouth left hers and he buried his face in the curve of her neck, his hand brushing her robe aside roughly. She felt his warm breath tickle her skin, heard again the same incomprehensible Russian words he'd spoken before. Moving quickly, he lifted her and removed her robe, then shed his own, his eyes scorching her body as they roved slowly over her.

Having him away from her, even that short distance, brought a measure of sanity. What was she doing? She had to stop this. But she loved him so. Needed him so. Two tears escaped over the edge of her lower lids and rolled slowly across her cheeks into her hair. Instantly he was beside her, his hands cupping her face.

"Tara, darling, don't be frightened."

Frightened? Yes, she was frightened of her own response, of the overwhelming longing to be close to him, belong to him.

Dropping tiny, fiery kisses, his lips surveyed her face while his hands caressed and aroused her body. His softly murmured words added fuel to the rapidly spreading flames inside her.

Moaning softly, she curled her arms tightly around his neck, gave up her mouth in total surrender. Somewhere in the deep recess of her mind she knew she'd have to pay for it for the rest of her life. Yesterday was over. Tomorrow was far away. The only thing that held any meaning for her was here, and now, and him. The apartment, the city, the world dissolved, and it was as if they were alone on a tiny island, soaring through time and space.

His hard body moved over hers, and his lips close to her ear whispered, "I must hurt you, love, but I promise you the pain will not last long, and it will set you free. Free to give me as much or as little as you wish. Free to accept everything I have to offer."

On his last words pain ripped through the lower part of her body and, stiffening with outrage and shock, she arched away from him, the cry of rejection that tore from her lips drowning inside his mouth. With infinite patience and surprising restraint he kissed, caressed, soothed her tension-contracted body until the pain receded and was replaced by a fierce urgency inside her to know a oneness with him.

The gentle appeaser was gone with her first renewed stirrings, replaced by a hard, demanding lover, intent on fulfillment. When he exploded off the edge of their tiny island in space, he took her with him. Shuddering, gasping for breath, for one small moment she seemed to face the pure white light of the sun, then she went spiraling through the darkness of space, held softly, securely, within the steellike coils of his arms. If someone had told Tara one week, one day ago, that surrendering herself completely to Alek would fill her with such ecstasy, she would never have believed it, as much as she loved him. This beauty and contentment that engulfed every part of her being were part of the make-believe used in romantic literature and films. The idea that all the passion that ever poured out of the pen of poets or lyricists had to be based in some fact had never occurred to her.

Slowly the awareness of time and place crept back to her. She felt the soft carpet against her skin, the night-cooled air in the room lightly cooling her flesh.

She felt Alek's thumping heart return to a normal beat, heard his ragged breathing grow more even. Still held tightly against his hard body, she felt his breath stir her hair as he whispered in an almost awed tone, "Never in all my wildest fantasizing have I dreamed that anything could be so perfect." His arms tightened possessively and his mouth covered hers in a deep consuming kiss. When he lifted his head, his voice was firm, though still soft. "The marriage has been consummated in three ways, Tara. With the mingling of our blood, the joining of our bodies, and the coupling of our souls. If what we've just experienced is savagery, then I give up all claims to civilization."

Tara slept, then was jarred awake again when Alek lifted her from the floor and carried her to the bed. It seemed very late and she was shivering; goose bumps covered her arms and shoulders. He left her a moment and the room was plunged into darkness. Then he was back, sliding onto the bed next to her, drawing the covers up and around them before pulling her into his arms hard against him.

"I'm so cold." The words trembled from her lips shakily.

"I know. I'm sorry. I fell asleep. I haven't slept that deeply since I was a child."

His murmured words were revealing something of importance to her, but the deeper meaning of them was lost to her sleep-hazy mind.

Slowly, as warmth returned to her body, heat returned to his, and within minutes he was whispering her name between fierce, demanding kisses, his hands possessive, his body pressing hers into the mattress urgently.

If she'd have thought, she would have believed it impossible to experience that same oneness as before. Yet if anything, their wild, explosive flight through space this time ended in a more perfect unity. More slowly, languorously, she drifted back to an awareness of Alek's mouth lazily branding small kisses over her face, her throat, her shoulders, and lingeringly, her breasts. Sighing in deep contentment, she was beyond wondering at the strangely fervent tone of his voice, or the meaning of the oft repeated Russian words. Almost purring, she curled against him like a well-petted kitten, her fingers idly stroking his muscle-ridged back. One minute she felt more vibrantly alive than ever before in her life, and in the next, sensuously drowsy, she slipped into a deep, relaxed sleep.

The early-morning rays of sun touching Tara's face wakened her. Closing her eyes again quickly, she moved to roll onto her side and grew still, suddenly aware of a weight on her chest. Turning her head slowly, she opened her eyes and stared at Alek sprawled beside her, one arm flung across her breasts.

Memory returned in a flash, and she felt the hot string of tears behind her lids. Afraid to move, barely breathing, her eyes roved over him lovingly. The covers were twisted about his slim waist, leaving his broad shoulders and chest exposed to the chill air in the room. Slowly she curled her fingers into her palm, fighting down the urge to touch, to slide her fingers over his smooth skin, to feel the curly spring of dark hair tickle her palm.

Eyes moving slowly, missing nothing, trailed up to the strong column of his throat and rested a moment on the steady pulsebeat there. Her throat closing with emotion, she lifted her eyes to his head. Silky black waves were tousled, one swath lying endearingly across his forehead, and Tara felt a pang remembering it was her fingers that had caused the disorder. Long, thick, inky lashes threw shadows onto his high cheekbones, the lines of which, along with his firm jaw, were somewhat softened in sleep. Her eyes rested on his beautifully chiseled mouth; her lips ached with the need to kiss him.

Her lashes glistened with tears; consumed with the desire to wake him, to beg him to hold her close, she tore her eyes away and stared at the ceiling. Her mind working furiously, Tara tried to find an alternative to what she knew she must do. Finally her lids closed in defeat. It was no good. It would never be any good. And she knew it. Her heart cried at the realization, but she knew she couldn't stay with him. Gone were the vaguely formed plans to make him pay for what he'd done to her. Before, she'd been angry, hurt. Now she was terrified.

Why did the night have to end? she thought bitterly. Why had she slept and wasted so much of it? He had been so gentle, then so demanding, his hands and mouth awaking a sleeping tiger of passion she had never dreamed she possessed. She shivered with remembrances, then her eyes flew open. What must he think of her now? She didn't even want to think about that, so she pushed the thought aside, then felt a shaft of blinding pain as a new consideration slithered its way into her mind. His love-making had been so completely mind-shattering. It had affected her two ways, physically and mentally, striking to the very core of her being. She had known she was in love with him for some days; now she belonged to him. What would it be like to be actually loved by him?

The thought drove the pain deeper, and she stirred restlessly. There was the cause of her misery, the reason she could not stay with him. For he did not love her. What had his words been? She had no need to ask herself the question, for she could hear his voice as if it had been yesterday: *"If the only way I can have you is through marriage, I'll marry you."*

Just in time Tara caught back the sob that rose in her throat. If she stayed with him now, slept with him, he'd crush her spirit and independence. Loving him so deeply, she'd be like clay in his hands. His nearness made her ache; his touch set her on fire. Her dependence on him would grow, and within a short amount of time he could make a near-slave of her. And being the epitome of dominance, he would relish the enslavement. She would end hating herself and probably him also.

No, no, no, she told herself. She would not, she could not, let that happen. She must end it, now, this morning.

As if it were a sign, he moved in his sleep, lifting his arm from her and flinging it back over his head. She was free and with a shiver she slid her naked body off the bed. Their robes lay in a heap where he had tossed them last night and, scooping hers up, she slipped into it and wrapped it around her slim form, tying the belt securely.

Like a sleepwalker she moved to stand at the windows, staring down at the Sunday morning street empty of traffic, her arms wrapped around her trembling body.

"Good morning, pansy eyes. Come back to bed." Alek's sleepy soft voice reached out across the room to envelop her like a caress. "There's something I want to tell you. Something I forgot in the—uh—heat of the moment last night."

Tara shook her head, her fingers biting deeply into her upper arms in an effort to still her increased trembling.

"Tara," he crooned, "this bed is getting colder by the second. It's early yet. Come back here and we'll warm it together."

"No." It sounded like a frog's croak and Tara cleared her throat nervously. "No, Alek, I'm not coming back to bed with you. Not now. Not ever again."

The silence that blanketed the room had the cold stillness of death. Tara's nails dug unmercifully into her flesh. Why didn't he speak? Swear at her? Anything but this silence that seemed to stretch forever and tear her nerves apart. When he finally did speak, the sound of his voice was as chilling as the silence had been.

"When you speak to me, Tara, please have the courtesy to look at me."

The insolent tone of his words had the same effect on Tara as if he'd smacked her with a cold, wet towel. She spun around, head up, eyes blazing with defiance. The sight of him stole the stinging retort from her lips. He had pushed himself back and up against the pillows, more in a reclining than a sitting position. His long torso, exposed to at least two inches below the navel, had a golden, toast-brown hue in the morning sun. He didn't move or say anything, and yet the invitation was as clear as if he'd held out his arms and whispered, "Come to me."

And she wanted to. With every fiber and particle of her being, she wanted to. She had lain in this man's arms all night. He had opened doors, shown her beauty she had never dreamed existed. For one sharp instant she felt not only willing to be his slave, but longed for it. She actually took one step toward him when her eyes touched his face, and she was stopped cold, pinned to the spot by two rapier-sharp points of glinting blue.

"That's better," he said coolly. "Now what the hell is this all about?"

Tara drew a deep calm breath. Somehow she had to match his coolness. "Exactly what I said, Alek. I won't sleep with you again." Lord, was that detached voice hers?

"You can say that to me after last night?" Anger ruffled the coolness now. Anger and a touch of disbelief. "Do you have any idea how rare an experience like that is?"

Without realizing it, she was shaking her head. She didn't know, not really, but she was beginning to. So many things that she'd never quite understood began to make sense. "The world well lost for love"—that had always baffled her. The idea that anyone could turn his back on the world, or his own small corner of it, had been beyond her comprehension. Yet now, if he loved her, just a little, she would happily do just that. But he didn't, and the knowledge was tearing her to shreds.

Catching back the urge to put her pain into words, to cry out, "Alek, please love me," she replied hoarsely, "It doesn't matter."

"It doesn't matter?" His words were barely whispered, and yet the astonishment in them had the impact of a shout. His eyes closed briefly, and Tara told herself she misread the emotion she'd glimpsed in them. She knew she did not have the power to hurt him. The truth of this hit her forcefully when he lifted his lids, for his eyes were hard and cold and filled with contempt for her. He moved abruptly to get up and, startled, Tara stepped back, catching a glimpse of his long, muscular thigh before her lids veiled her eyes.

"You can open your eyes now," Alek murmured sardonically a few moments later, then his voice went flat. "Would you care to tell me what you intend to do?"

He had put on his robe, and as Tara opened her eyes, he drew a pack of cigarettes from the pocket. Without asking, he lit one, handed it to her then lit one for himself, squinting at her through the gray smoke. Tara drew deeply on the cigarette, then exhaled slowly before answering equally flatly, "Go back to my apartment. Go back to work. Get a divorce."

"Of course. This is the way you get your revenge. Right?"

His voice was dangerously soft and his eyes watched sharply, through narrowed lids, for her response.

She didn't disappoint him. Swallowing with difficulty she gasped, "You— you knew?"

He sighed almost wearily. "Credit me with at least a little intelligence, Tara. You ran up the white flag too abruptly. Did an about-face too quickly to be believable. I knew at once you were up to something. It took me all of about ninety seconds to come up with the word *revenge*. You had decided to make me pay. My mistake was in thinking you were planning to make me pay through the wallet. I have to admit, you threw me when you refused an engagement ring. But then I decided you were waiting until everything was legal to put the bite on me."

Tara flinched and whispered, "You don't have a very high opinion of me, do you?"

"I pushed you pretty hard," he said quietly. "You were hurt and angry and wanted to retaliate." Shrugging carelessly, he added, "I wanted you and I was willing to pay the price."

His words stung, brought a flush of color to her cheeks, and she said angrily, "Pay the price? Like I was a common—"

"Don't say it, Tara," he cut in warningly. "That's not true, so don't ever say it." He was quiet a moment, then he asked softly, "Last night wasn't part of the plan, was it?"

Tara wet her lips nervously and slid her eyes away from his, unable to maintain that hard blue contact. "There—there was no actual plan. I just felt I had to make you pay, somehow."

"And now you're going to walk out of this room and out of my life?" She should have been warned by the silky sound of his voice but, in trying to hang on to her own composure, she missed it and answered calmly, "Yes."

"Think again." Startled eyes flew back to his at the finality of his tone. Before she could protest, he went on blandly. "Have you thought what you are going to tell people? Sallie and David? The rest of your friends? The people you work with?" He paused, then underlined: "Your parents. Yesterday you were the picture of a gloriously happy bride. What can you give as a reason for leaving me? That you suddenly fell out of love? Hardly. That I beat you? Where are the marks? That I'm a terrible lover? Well, as everyone was convinced we anticipated our vows anyway, I don't think that will do. So what can you tell them? Can you imagine what your father is going to say?" He paused again before adding ruthlessly, "Or your mother's face?"

Her mother! A low strangled moan escaped Tara's lips. *Dear Lord.* She hadn't thought. Had been too full of thoughts of him to spare any for anything or anyone else. A picture of her mother's face the day before, serenely happy, looking almost young again, formed in front of Tara's eyes. In pain she closed her lids against the image.

Insensitive to her distress, words hard, measured, as if underlined darkly, Alek drove on ruthlessly. "Which, do you think, will be harder for her to take? The *idea* of her daughter sleeping with a man without benefit of clergy or the *fact* of her daughter leaving her husband the day after a full Catholic wedding?"

As he spoke, he walked slowly to her, coming to a stop so close, she could feel his breath on her hair. She kept her eyes tightly closed, vainly trying to control the shudder that ripped through her body at his nearness.

"Look at me, Tara."

It was a command. One, his hard tone warned her, she dared not disobey. Slowly, she lifted her head and her eyelids, then swallowed with difficulty. His eyes were as cold and hard as the stone they matched.

"As I said, you'd better think again. For if you go through with this, I won't make it easy for you. In fact I'll make it very hard. I'll fight you publicly. Make an unholy field day for the newspapers." His voice dropped to a menacing growl. "In short, Tara, I'll tear you apart."

"But why?" Eyes wide with confusion and more than a little fear, Tara's cry was one of despair.

"The Rykovskys do not divorce." Flat, final, the words struck her like blows. "You seem to forget, I also have parents. Who, by the way, love you already. I will not have them hurt."

His hands came up to cradle her face; long brown fingers, unbelievably gentle after his harsh words, brushed at the tears that had escaped her lids and rolled down her morning-shiny cheeks. His voice was now low, husky, yet still firmly determined. "No, Tara. You've made your bed and now we'll lie in it. Together."

"No!" In desperation she jerked away from him. Away from his warm, caressing fingers. Those hard, compelling eyes. That hypnotic, druglike voice that was sapping the resistance from her body. She put the width of the room between them before she turned to face him again, eyes blazing. "I'll stay with you. Play the role of the adoring wife. But I want nothing from you, either material or physical. I will not share your bed." She paused to draw a deep, calming breath, then added quietly, "And if you try and force me, I'll go, and to hell with the consequences."

"Don't do this, Tara." His quiet voice seemed to float on the angry silence left by her bitter words. "We could have a good life together if you'd—"

Weakening, and frightened of it, Tara cut in scathingly, "If only I'd agree to every one of your dictates. Thank you, but no thank you. I've given you my terms, Alek. It's the only way I'll stay."

His face a mask, he studied her a moment, then turned away with a shrug so unconcerned, so indifferent, it sent a shaft of hot pain into Tara's heart.

"Now, if you don't mind, I think we'd better dress." His detached tone deepened Tara's pain. "I'm hungry, and I'd planned to stop for breakfast on the way to New York."

"You still want to go?" she gasped.

He turned back swiftly, eyes hard and cold. "My dear wife, do we have a choice? The reservations are made. Everyone thinks we're there now. Our only other option is to pen ourselves in this apartment for a week. Would you prefer that?''

"No!" Tara answered quickly, then more slowly, "No, of course not. I— I'll be ready in half an hour." As she turned to escape his unyielding stare, his taunting voice stopped her on the threshold. "One more thing, Tara. I'm a normal male, with all the natural drives. I was fully prepared to live up to the vows I made yesterday, as regards fidelity. Your attitude changes that. Do you understand?''

Tara froze, unable to force herself to look back at him, a picture of the smirking Kitty locked in her mind. Fingers like ice, she pulled the door wide and stepped into the hall.

"Do you?" Alek insisted.

"Yes."

It was a hoarse whisper hanging in the air. Tara had fled.

9

The following Sunday afternoon Tara sat in a state of bemusement listening to her husband's smooth, quiet voice as it blended with the low hum of the T-bird's engine as they neared home.

It had been a surprisingly relaxing week. Alek had revealed a facet of his character unseen by Tara up till now. He had been courteous and considerate, easygoing and almost light-hearted, as he squired her around New York.

They had walked the city until she thought her legs would drop off, and she doubted there were any elaborate Christmas decorations anywhere that they had not admired. Secretly her favorites were the angels and the enormous tree in Rockefeller Center. They had started early every morning and had gone full tilt until after midnight every night. They had dined at a variety of restaurants, from Lüchow's and Tavern-on-the-Green to Mama Leone's, the Top of the Six's, and even Windows on the World.

One night he took her to a famous disco, surprising her even more on the dance floor with his perfectly executed, somewhat sensuous step. And Tara had to admit to more than a twinge of pride and jealousy at the blatantly admiring female glances cast over his long, slim form clothed in snugly fitting pale gray slacks and sweater over a pin-striped black-and-white shirt.

As they were having breakfast Wednesday morning Tara said suddenly, "Alek, if you don't mind, I'd like to do some shopping today. I haven't finished my Christmas shopping and I think it'd be fun, especially for Mama and Betsy, to receive gifts from New York.''

"Why should I mind?" he asked blandly, then added sardonically, "It's your honeymoon too, you know. I'm sure I can amuse myself for a few hours. Where would you like to go? Bloomingdale's? Saks?''

"I don't know. The few times I've been in New York have been on day tours. Just time enough to see a show, squeeze in some sight-seeing. I've never done any shopping here.''

"Bloomingdale's," he stated firmly. "If you've never been there, it'll blow your mind.''

It did. Tara was fascinated with the store. When she had the time and money, she loved to shop. This morning she had both. When Alek had deposited her at the entrance, he had stuffed a wad of bills into her bag, told her he'd be outside the same entrance at three o'clock, and added dryly, "Have fun."

Three o'clock? she had thought. What in the world was she to do for five hours? Time slipped away easily. At first Tara was content to stroll around aimlessly, delighted with the unusual and varied selection of merchandise. When she finally did get down to serious shopping, she spent long minutes on her choice of gifts for her mother, Betsy, and Sallie, feeling a pang of guilt as the money Alek had given her quickly dwindled.

With her father and brothers in mind, Tara wandered into the men's department, growing suddenly taut with an intense longing. It seemed every third article her eyes touched screamed Alek's name at her. Alek was always well groomed, and though Tara knew he had a huge closet full of beautifully tailored clothes, she wanted to buy him everything.

For a few moments, a small smile on her lips, she allowed her thoughts to run riot, picturing low-slung expensive sports cars, sparkling white yachts, sleek-lined Thoroughbreds. Pulling her thoughts up short with a mental shake, she lovingly touched fine-knit cashmere sweaters, beautifully made raw-silk shirts.

On the point of walking away, she stopped. Well, why not? It was Christmastime, wasn't it? The time for buying gifts. Also the excuse she needed. With a determined step she turned back, a happy gleam in her eyes, and promptly lost all sense of time. She bought discriminately but lavishly, this time extracting bills from her own wallet, not caring about the rate of speed with which they disappeared.

Tara could have gone on for hours, but a glimpse of her watch brought her shopping spree to an abrupt halt with a disbelieving gasp. It was a few minutes after three. She was keeping Alek waiting.

Alek's eyebrows rose in amusement when she finally staggered out of the store under the weight of her packages.

"When the lady says she's going to shop, she's going to shop," he teased. "Did you enjoy yourself?"

"Oh, Alek," she replied happily, unaware that for the first time since they'd met, she had responded to him warmly, spontaneously. "I've had a wonderful time and I'm starving."

She missed the quick narrowing of his eyes, his brief hesitation, for they were gone in a flash, and he was chiding her gently. "Didn't you take time to have lunch?"

"Lunch?" she laughed happily. "I never even thought of food."

Relieving her of the bulk of her burden, he helped her into the cab he had managed to hail and smiled dryly. "In that case I think we can find you a crust of bread and a glass of water somewhere."

After dropping her purchases in their room, Alek led Tara to a small table in the hotel's bar. When he gave the waiter an order of a sandwich and coffee for her and only a drink for himself, she turned questioning eyes to him.

Smiling easily, he murmured, "I didn't forget to eat lunch."

Happy with her day and for the first time in weeks at peace in her own mind, Tara returned his smile with a brilliant one of her own. The waiter appeared at their table at the same moment, and Tara missed the low sound of breath catching in Alek's throat, the fleeting expression of longing, of hunger in his eyes.

At no time during the week had Alek made a move of a physical nature toward her. Other than taking her elbow while crossing streets and occasionally sliding his arm around her waist in extracrowded places, he did not touch her. Every night had been the same. He'd see her to their hotel room then go to the bar for thirty or so minutes to give her time to get into her nightgown and into one of the two double beds in the room.

Now, not more than forty-five minutes from home, the atmosphere in the car was the exact opposite of that of a week ago. Tara sat back comfortably, her bemusement stemming from Alek's homebound conversation. Some stray remark had touched at a memory, and he had been relating anecdotes from his boyhood. It was the first time he'd opened up to her and, at her hesitant query about his ancestors, he'd gone quiet and she was afraid he'd withdrawn again when he resumed his smooth, quiet tone.

"The Rykovskys go back a long way and were, at one time, entertained by the czars. My great-grandparents were uneasy under the rule of Alexander the Third and possibly read the handwriting on the wall. At any rate, they transferred as much of their property as possible into cash and left Russia around 1883, when my grandfather was still quite small. They landed and stayed in Philadelphia for a while, and then a merchant my great-grandfather had met and made friends with invited them to come and visit him in his neck of the woods. That, of course, was the Allentown area. They came, liked what they saw, and settled. My great-grandfather was an intelligent, well-educated man who liked to tinker with machines and tools. After he was settled, he built a small shop and put his hobby to work. Although my grandfather and then my father added to it, the original shop is still there."

"And now you're building a new one," Tara said softly.

"Yes, we've outgrown the old."

Again he was quiet a few moments, then he slanted a glance at her and smiled. "You said once that I have an international family, and in a sense you're right. While doing the grand tour, my grandfather met and eventually married the shy, youngest daughter of a wealthy French wine-producing family. I still have some relatives somewhere in the Loire district. My father met and married my mother when he was stationed in Great Britain during World War Two. So, to that extent, there is a European flavor to the family, but it stops with me. I'm a straight-down-the-line American. My cousins delight in referring to me as 'the Yankee capitalist,' and they're right—I am. I've been all over Europe at one time or another and although I've always enjoyed it, the best part was coming home. I'm afraid what you see here is a true-blue patriot. I love my country."

The devil danced in the eyes that slanted her another quick look, before he added teasingly, "I'm also hung up on American women. I've known, since the time I was old enough to notice girls, that I'd marry an American woman. I've met and, quite frankly, made love to some stunning women all over the world, and yet I wouldn't exchange what I have sitting next to me now for any one of them."

At once pleased and flustered, Tara sought vainly for something to say. When she didn't reply, he went on, "I've inadvertently broken a few Rykovsky family traditions, but there was one I was very happily looking forward to breaking—deliberately.''

"What was that?'' she murmured, an uneasy premonition snaking up her spine.

"For six generations the Rykovsky brides have been blessed with only one child. A male.'' Alek paused, and with growing unease Tara watched his jawline tighten, his knuckles whiten as he gripped the steering wheel. "I wanted a son, of course,'' he went on tersely. "Maybe two. But I also wanted a daughter, possibly more.''

Tara found it impossible for a moment to speak around the lump in her throat. When she did finally get the words out they came jerkily. "I—If you'd agree to a divorce, you could get on with finding a proper mother for your children.'' She could barely push the last word past the pain in her throat at the sudden vision of a dark-haired little boy with devilish blue eyes. Suddenly her arms ached with painful longing to hold that child close to her breast.

"A proper mother.'' His low, bitter tone was like a slap across her face, and Tara averted her head to hide the tears that stung her eyes.

He cursed savagely under his breath, then ground out, "I told you the Rykovskys do not divorce. I have no intention of blazing a new trail in that direction.'' The grim determination in his voice sent a shudder through her. He meant it. He had no intention of giving her her freedom. She felt caught in the trap she'd set herself. They were close to home, and the remaining miles were covered in the hostile silence; the companionable atmosphere of before had been shattered.

Tara lived through the week until Christmas with a growing feeling of unreality. In the short periods of time she and Alek were alone together, they maintained a sort of armed truce. When they were in the company of their respective families or friends, they played the blissfully happy newlyweds.

Tara filled her days by emptying her apartment, disposing of the furniture she didn't want, arranging in Alek's apartment the things she did. And moving her clothes and personal things into the spare bedroom. Alek went back to his office, snapping, "If I remember correctly, your stated wish was that you want nothing from me. I assume that includes my help, so go to it.''

Alek rarely came home for dinner and in fact was seldom home by the time she went to bed. It didn't take much speculation on her part to come up with an answer to where he was spending his nights. She spent her own nights alternately hating him, and curled up in bed, arms clutching her midsection, trying to fight down the aching need to feel his arms closing around her, his mouth seeking hers. *God!* she thought. She loved him. And if she had thought she had cried a lot before, she knew now, those tears had been just for openers.

Saturday morning Tara was making her bed when she heard the door to the apartment open, a strange rustling sound, then the door close again. Intrigued, she left the bedroom, walked along the short hall to the living room and stopped, staring in wonder at the live tree Alek had dragged into the room.

Standing the tree straight, he asked blandly, "Do you like it?''

"Yes, of course. I love live Christmas trees, but why?''

"Because it's Christmas,'' he snapped. "And because, although we won't be doing much entertaining, I'm sure the families will stop over sometime during the holidays. And I don't feel up to lengthy explanations as to why there is none. So,'' he gestured disinterestedly, "the tree." He then proceeded to surprise her even more by removing a large carton of tree decorations from the storage closet.

Tara tried to show little enthusiasm as she helped him trim the tree. It wasn't easy. She really did love live Christmas trees and had always enjoyed fussing with the decorations, thinking it one of the best rituals of the holiday. She was also glad she now had a place to set her gifts. Even if she was a little apprehensive about Alek's reaction to his. As soon as the tree was finished, Alek showered, dressed, and left the apartment, telling her he didn't know what time he'd be back.

On the morning of Christmas Eve Tara stood in the kitchen dully watching the coffee perk. It was late, almost eleven, and although she had just awakened, she did not feel rested. She had lain awake, tense and stiff, until after three in the morning.

The apartment was so still and quiet that Tara was sure she was alone and so turned with a start when Alek walked into the kitchen. He looked terrible, pale and weary with lines of strain around his eyes and mouth. Tara was torn between deep compassion and vindictive satisfaction at his obvious exhaustion.

Without a word he walked across the room to her, then tossed a small, gaily wrapped gift onto the counter in front of her.

"Your Christmas present," he said shortly. "I'm giving it to you now because I'd like you to wear it to my parents' party tonight."

Tara eyed the small package with trepidation, then removed the wrapping with shaking fingers. With growing alarm she lifted the lid of the tiny, black-velvet-covered box then gasped aloud at the ring nestled in its bed of white satin. The single sapphire was large and square-cut and reflected exactly the color of Alek's eyes.

"Alek, I told you—" she began in a tremulous voice when he interrupted with a low snarl, "I know what you told me. But you will wear this, at least in the presence of my parents. They expect it. The Rykovsky men have always adorned their brides with jewels. So you'll do me the favor of wearing it. Not for me, for them. Other than that, I don't care what you do with it. Toss it to the back of a drawer, where it won't offend your eyes."

Tara winced at his harshly bitter tone and, fighting back tears, whispered, "All right, I'll wear it tonight. It—it is beautiful and—"

"Don't strain yourself, Tara, and don't look so frightened, I'm not going to demand payment in return."

Tara had no doubt as to what *payment* he meant, and she turned sharply back to the counter to hide her pain-filled eyes. "Alek, that's not fair." Try as she would, she could not keep the hurt from her voice.

"Not fair?" he snapped. "Lord, I don't believe you said that." Then his tone changed to one of utter weariness. "Oh, the hell with it. I don't want to argue, I have a headache that won't quit and I'm dying of thirst. Isn't that coffee finished yet?"

By the time they left for his parents' party, his bad humor seemed to have vanished along with his headache, and he was his usual controlled, urbane self. Tara wore his ring and tried not to see the cynicism in his eyes as she replied properly to the exclamations of admiration from the other guests.

Christmas morning, still wearing his ring, Tara slipped out of the kitchen as Alek read the paper while drinking his coffee. Gnawing nervously on her lip, she placed his gifts in a neat pile, returned to the kitchen, and set them on the table in front of him. The paper was lowered slowly. Face hard, free of expression, he stared for long moments at the presents before lifting questioning eyes to hers.

"You tell me you'll accept no gifts from me. Then you turn around and buy some *for* me. Why?" Alek's tone confused her, made her feel as if he were asking far more than the actual words stated. For a moment she was tempted to blurt out the truth. That because she loved so deeply she had not been able to resist the urge; she had in fact wanted to buy him the earth.

His eyes, so guarded, so unreadable, stopped her. Swallowing around the dryness in her throat, she managed a careless shrug and answered, "As you said yesterday, it is expected."

The packages were opened silently, his eyes piercing hers each time another lid was lifted. When finally the last one was opened, he stood and came to her, kissed her mouth gently and murmured, "Thank you, Tara. I'm sure our families will be as pleased with your taste and choices as I am."

For a moment he seemed far away, as if caught up in a memory, then he added quietly, "I don't understand you at all, Tara. There are times when I'm sure I have you all figured out, then you say or do something that completely baffles me, and I wonder if I'll ever understand you."

Slowly, over the next few days, as they attended numerous holiday parties and gatherings, she noticed a subtle change in him. It started on Christmas Day, when they made a quick stop at David and Sallie's to deliver their gifts. After unwrapping the exquisite doll they had bought her, the three-year-old Tina had run to Alek, her chubby arms outstretched and laughing, and he had scooped her up into his arms. Tina's small head hid Alek's face from all but Tara, and she felt a hard contraction around her heart at the expression that passed across his face fleetingly as he hugged the child to him. Deep, painful longing had been revealed in that instant, and Tara felt overwhelmed with guilt at her unwillingness to give him the child she now knew he wanted desperately.

From that moment on he seemed to withdraw from her. No longer did she receive his tender glances or softly spoken endearments when in the company of others, and he left her side often and for longer periods of time. By New Year's Eve it became apparent that their friends were aware of his attitude also.

They were attending a rather large party at a private club some distance outside of town and, from the covert glances she was getting, Tara knew her friends were asking themselves if the honeymoon was over. Alek disappeared several times for very long periods, and the fact that Kitty was also conspicuously absent at the same time filled Tara with both jealous fear and embarrassed fury.

Fury conquered fear when midnight came, and then passed, and Tara stood alone in a room full of celebrants kissing and toasting in the new year. Head held high, her step determined, Tara made her way out of the room, ignoring the speculative looks turned her way. She was almost to the cloakroom when she heard a familiar voice call to her to wait and with a sigh she turned and watched Craig Hartman walk up to her. Both his expression and voice held concern.

"Are you leaving?"

She nodded, and when he asked how she was going to get home, she answered briefly, "Taxi."

"No you're not," he stated firmly. "I'll take you."

"But—"

He didn't wait to hear her protest but walked into the cloakroom, emerging seconds later shrugging into his coat and carrying hers.

He helped her into her coat then said softly, "Come along," and Tara moved with him out the door, unaware of the alarmed expression that had replaced the usually placid one in David's eyes as he watched them leave.

They drove in silence for about five minutes, then Craig stopped the car on the gravel-covered shoulder of the dark country road. Tara turned in her seat in surprise. "Craig, what—"

"It's not working, is it, Tara?" he interrupted gently.

"Craig, really, I don't want to talk—"

"No, I can understand that," he interrupted again. Then his tone changed, became angry. "But how he could prefer that overblown, destructive bitch over you, I'll never—"

This time it was Tara who interrupted. "Craig, you don't know—"

"No, you're right," he cut in. "But I know her, and she's not worth one minute of your unhappiness."

Before she could think of a reply, Craig added earnestly, "Tara, I told you once that if you ever needed a shoulder to cry on, mine was available. It may not be as broad as his but—"

That was as far as he got, for the door next to Tara was yanked open, her arm was grasped in a grip of steel and she was jerked unceremoniously from her seat. Her outcry was drowned by the low, menacing growl of Alek's voice. "Get the hell out of there and go wait for me in my car."

"Now look here, Rykovsky—" Craig began, only to be cut off by Alek's snarled, "No, *you* look, Hartman." That was all Tara heard before she fled to the T-bird and slid onto the front seat.

10

The drive home was completed in ominous quiet, and as soon as she stepped into the apartment, Tara dashed for her bedroom, locking the door behind her. She dropped her coat onto her small rocker then spun around, breath catching in her throat, when she heard Alek call her name and saw the doorknob twist sharply. The next instant her eyes flew wide with disbelief as she heard Alek's foot smash against the door, saw the wood splinter around the lock, and on the second blow from his foot the door slammed back against the wall. Alek's advance on her was reminiscent of the stalk of a predator, and he had the same wild, savage look.

Badly frightened, Tara raised her hands in a defensive movement. With one careless swing of his arm Alek knocked them down then, grasping her upper arms, dragged her roughly against him.

"What is this man to you?" he spat.

"A—a friend," she stuttered.

"He looked *very* friendly," he snarled. His hands moved up and over her shoulders then curled around her throat. "Has he made love to you? The truth, Tara." His fingers tightened and his eyes blazed furiously into hers.

"No! Alek, please," Tara choked.

As if he hadn't heard her, past all reason in his anger, his fingers tightened still more, and Tara groaned softly in pain and fear.

"I'll be damned," he rasped, "if I'll let another man have what's legally mine yet denied me. I could strangle you, Tara, for the hell you've put me through these last weeks."

"Alek, don't," Tara could barely whisper. "I give you my word, I—"

"Damn your doe-soft eyes," he groaned, then his mouth was crushing hers punishingly, bruisingly, as his hand released her throat, slid urgently down her back, molding her body against his.

"Did you really think a locked door would keep me out?" he sneered, when finally his mouth left hers. "Have you been locking your door all this time?"

Shattered, unable to speak, Tara shook her head dumbly.

"Then why tonight?" he asked silkily. "Is there some reason you tried to hide away tonight?"

Tara strove for control, for a measure of calmness in her voice.

"You were so angry. You frightened me, Alek."

"You have every reason to be frightened, my sweet." His soft laugh was not a pretty sound, and his use of the present tense had not escaped her.

"Alek," she breathed desperately, "you can't really believe that I—"

"Can't I?" he cut her off harshly. "Why not? You forget, I held you in my arms all night, felt your response, your need. Whether you admit it to yourself or not, you wanted me as badly as I wanted you. Those needs cannot be turned off like a faucet. I know because right now my body is screaming for possession of yours, and I no longer intend to deny myself that satisfaction."

Tara struggled against him frantically, but it was a losing battle, for in truth she was fighting two opponents, Alek and her own rising desire for him.

Later, lying beside him, replete and spent, she closed her eyes in pain at her own deflections. His possession of her had been as wild and savage as his appearance had been and she had gloried in it, soaking in his lovemaking as thirstily as a drunk slaking his thirst after a long abstinence.

Seconds later a small shiver rippled through her as Alek's lips moved slowly across her cheek then stopped at her own, teasing, tormenting around the outer edge of her mouth, until with a soft moan, she reached up and grasped his head and brought his mouth to her own. When finally he lifted his head, he whispered harshly, "Damn you, Tara, there's no end to my wanting you."

The words, his tone, cut into her like a knife and in self-defense she said fiercely, "I hate you, Aleksei Rykovsky."

He went still for a breathless moment, then his fingers dug painfully into her hair and, his lips close to hers, he groaned, "Well, I guess that's better than indifference. Hate me some more, Tara Rykovsky."

It was late in the morning when Tara woke, wondering why she ached all over. Memory returned in a rush and, turning her head, she gave a long sigh of relief on seeing she was alone. She felt unrested, not very well, and worst of all, used—badly, unjustly used. The thought made her wince, and with a dry sob she covered her face with her hands. Silent tears of conviction running down her face, Tara knew she had to pack and leave, today, before she found herself blabbering her love to Alek like some demented, love-starved idiot, and cringing under his amused triumph.

Giving herself a mental shake, Tara left the bed tiredly, her eyes avoiding the rumpled sheets and covers. Feeling drained, she went to the kitchen and made a pot of coffee, watching it perk dully while she sipped her orange juice. Where was Alek? The answer that presented itself brought pain, and she rejected it with a sharp shake of her head. She didn't know why, but somehow she knew positively that Alek would not leave her bed and go to another woman.

Impatient with the coffeepot, she left the kitchen, stopped at the closet in the short hall, removed her suitcase, and went back to her bedroom. With swift, jerky movements she straightened the bed covers then opened the case on the bed.

For some reason the mild exertion had brought a light film of perspiration to her face and hands and she turned from the case to go to the bathroom. As she stood under the hot, stinging spray in the shower a shudder tore through Tara's body. What was she going to do? For the first time in many years she was uncertain about the direction of her life. Her mind gnawed away at that thought as she dried herself, dressed quickly in jeans and a white rib-knit pullover, and slid her feet into wine-red clogs.

Since her early teens she had set goals for herself and one by one had achieved them. And now all of them seemed unimportant. The thought shook her, and she stopped in the act of placing underwear in her case, her arm motionless in midair. Suddenly she felt very, very old, while at the same time very, very young and she was consumed with the need to talk to someone. Someone older, with more experience of life.

The filmy underthings dropped into the case from numb fingers at the face that flashed into Tara's mind. Her mother? She hadn't sought her mother's counsel since her thirteenth year and yet she had an overriding urge to go to her now.

Before she could change her mind, she hurried into the kitchen to the wall phone there and dialed her mother's number. While the connection was being made and then her mother's phone rang. she poured herself a cup of coffee, only to set it onto the counter with shaking hands when her mother's voice said hello.

"Mama. It's Tara," she said breathlessly, then went on in a rush: "Are you busy? I—I need someone to talk to and I wondered . . . oh, Mama, can I come talk to you? Please?"

There was a short pause, then her mother's voice, strangely calm, came over the wire quietly. "Yes, of course, Tara. Come right away. I'll be waiting for you."

Hands still shaking badly, Tara replaced the receiver; she dashed into the bedroom, shrugged into a Navy pea jacket, scooped up her handbag, and left the apartment. The untouched coffee sat cooling on the counter; the half filled suitcase lay open on her bed; the dresser drawers remained ajar.

On entering her father's house, Tara stood inside the door, glancing around in question at the unusual quiet.

"I'm in the kitchen, Tara," her mother called. "Come have a cup of coffee."

Marlene Schmitt stood at the sink, pouring coffee into two heavy earthenware mugs and, as Tara seated herself at the table, she turned and said, "We can talk here. Betsy is spending the day with Kenny and his parents, and your father took the boys out to give us some privacy."

"Mother!" Tara exclaimed. "You didn't say anything to Dad, did you?"

Marlene's eyebrows went up as she sat down opposite Tara. Then, her tone slightly chiding, she murmured, "There wasn't much I could tell him, other than that you seemed upset and were coming over to talk. He didn't ask questions, simply gathered up the boys and left."

Tara eyed her mother wonderingly as she sipped her coffee. Never before could she remember hearing quite that calm, unruffled tone and for the moment she was left speechless. Her next words left her stunned.

"Your father is not the unfeeling brute you think he is, Tara." And when Tara tried to speak out in protest, her mother held up her hand and added, "Nor am I quite the blind fool. No, don't interrupt. Please, let me finish. Failure to do all you'd like to for your family can do strange things to some men, and that is what has happened to your father. I've watched it happening for a long time. But he is a good man, Tara. I love him. I always have."

Tara stared at her mother as if at a stranger. Had she been wrong all these years? Misread the situation? She had thought her mother stayed with her father because of her and her sister and brothers, and out of a sense of duty. But now?

Marlene's soft voice brought her attention back to the present and her own situation.

"There's a problem with Alek, isn't there?"

Looking at her mother through different eyes, Tara felt her throat close and she whispered, "Yes."

"I thought so. I have for some time now. For all your bright smiles and happy chatter, I knew you were unhappy. And so is Alek."

"Mama, you don't understand," Tara cried. And her mother came back, "Possibly not, but I understand this. Alek is a bright, ambitious, very attractive man. And he is a man, Tara. The kind of man who needs a mature woman beside him. One who is willing to give, as well as take."

Tara felt tears sting her eyelids. Was that the type of woman that, in her single-mindedness, she had projected? One who was not willing to give? Before she could form an argument, her mother said, "Less than a month ago you made a commitment to that man. Have you lived up to it?"

Vision blurred by tears, unable to speak, Tara shook her head.

"Honey, do you love him?"

Tears now unashamedly running down her cheeks, Tara sobbed, "Yes. Oh, Mama, yes. But he doesn't love me." She paused, then added bitterly, "He says he wants me, and that's not the same, is it?"

"No, it isn't," Marlene answered very softly, her fingers brushing gently at the tears. "But that's something, and as long as there's something, some emotion, there's reason to work at it. It probably won't be easy, Tara. But then nothing worth having ever does come easy."

As Tara drove back to the apartment, her mind went over what her mother said. There had been more, much more, but in essence, what it had amounted to was this: Tara had worked hard for everything she had wanted; surely the one thing she wanted most in the world was worth twice the work.

Tara was still unsure of what she'd do or say to Alek, if anything, when she got home. But she was grateful for one thing: This new and deeper understanding between her mother and herself. She had been on her own for some time; now, for the first time, she felt really grown-up.

Suddenly Tara knew she was not yet ready to go home. She had to think this through, make a decision one way or the other. Eyes steady on the road, she drove into the mountains. All the splendor of fall was gone now, but even denuded of their summer finery, the Poconos were a balm to her mind.

Time slipped by unnoticed as did the large and small billboards advertising the lodges, motels, and many points of interest and activities offered.

Her mind drove on in rhythm with the car's engine, paging back over the last few months, going over everything, step by step. And over and over, threading through her thoughts, her mother's voice asked softly, *"Honey, do you love him?"*

What should she do? The events leading up to this day, many of which were caused by Alek, no longer held any importance. The question driving her on now was: *Did* he still want her? Her throat still hurt from the pressure of his fingers last night. Every muscle in her body felt sore. She felt sure he had not set out to make love to her, but to punish her. He had been rough with her, as if deliberately acting out the role of savage she'd cast him in. His stated intention had been to own her. Now that he did, had he lost interest?

He had become so cool, so withdrawn over the last week. A shudder rippled through her as she remembered the previous Thursday. She had left the office to find a mist-shrouded fairyland of ice, glittering and treacherous. She had driven home at a mere crawl, holding her breath each time she felt the tires lose their grip and begin to slide. By the time she had shut off the engine inside the apartment building's covered parking area, her palms and forehead were damp with sweat, and she had felt totally exhausted.

As she'd thrust her key into the apartment door, she'd had one thought in mind: to soak in a hot tub and forget that world of ice outside. She took one step through the doorway when Alek's voice rapped, "Where the hell have you been?"

He was standing at the bar, phone at his ear, his one palm covering the mouthpiece. Before she could answer, his hand slid away and he said shortly, "Yes, it's her."

Just as she was about to close the door, Tara had stopped, frozen by his next words.

"Yes, Kitty, I know, but I don't know what else to tell you. Perhaps in a week, maybe less."

What had possessed her? Even now Tara didn't know. At the time she had not stopped to think, to ask for an explanation. She had run out of the apartment to her car and back to that ice-covered world that had nothing on her heart.

How long she'd slithered around aimlessly, she had no idea, but when finally she had turned back to the apartment, it was raining hard, the ice fast disappearing. There was no sign of Alek when she got back, and as she soaked in the tub, Tara wondered dully if he was with Kitty. The searing pain of jealousy she'd felt on the night she'd first realized she was in love with him was nothing compared to the agony she'd gone through while sliding around on the glassy streets. And now, tired to the bone, she was almost beyond feeling.

She was lying on the bed, staring at the ceiling, her bedside lamp still on, when she heard the front door slam moments before Alek was standing in her doorway, face cold, eyes blazing.

"How long have you been here?"

"A—a half hour or so."

"While I've been running around nearly killing myself looking for you." His voice had been ugly, not much more than a snarl. "Would that have made your revenge complete, I wonder?"

"Alek, please, I'm sorry—"

But it had been too late; he was gone, slamming out of the apartment as violently as he'd entered.

Tara's hands gripped the wheel as she shivered again. Vaguely she registered the road sign indicating the number of miles to Camelback. Then last night, she wondered, had his neglect, indifference, been his way of showing her he no longer cared if she left him? got a divorce? But then why had he been so angry about Craig? His pride? Of course. She could hear him now. *"Has he made love to you?"* That fierce Rykovsky pride would not be able to bear the thought of someone else having what he still called his own. The thoughts swirled and whirled, leading nowhere.

Camelback!! Good grief, she had to turn this car around, go home. And there was her answer, clear as a perfect spring day. She had to go home, and Alek was all the home she ever wanted. Silently she answered her mother's question. *Yes, Mama, I love him. More than I ever thought it possible to love any one person. I'm afraid, Mama, so afraid. For if he no longer wants me, I no longer want to live.*

Alek's car was parked in the apartment lot and with trembling fingers, Tara let herself into the apartment. She stood listening to the silence in the empty living room a moment then, slipping off her jacket, she went to her bedroom to stand staring at the open case on her bed. Alek's voice, from the doorway, went through her like an electric shock.

"Where have you been?"

"Alek, I—"

"No. Never mind. As long as you're all right. The way you left the apartment, I thought something had happened." His voice was so cool, so withdrawn, Tara shivered. His eyes left her face, rested long moments on the suitcase, then came back to hers. "Before you leave, I have something to say to you. If you'll come into the living room, please?"

He turned and walked away, and Tara was left staring at the empty doorway, fingers of real fear digging at her stomach. She didn't know what he had to say, but she was almost positive she didn't want to hear it and she actually had to force herself to follow him.

He was standing gazing out of the window when she entered the room, and the sight of him clutched at her heart. Why, of all the men she had known, did it have to be this one who could rob the strength from her knees, make her ache in anticipation? He was everything she had avowed she had not wanted in a man, yet he was the only man she wanted.

He was standing very straight, almost stiff, and as he turned from the window, Tara felt the breath catch in her throat. His face had an austere, lifeless cast and the usually glittering blue eyes looked flat, empty. His eyes went over her slowly as if studying every detail, and when he finally spoke, it was in that same cool, withdrawn tone.

"I'm a proud man, Tara, as you know. This is possibly the hardest thing I'll ever have to say, and I'll only say it one time. Don't leave me." He paused and his tone became softer. "I beg you, stay with me. I give you my word I'll do everything in my power to make it a good life for both of us."

Eyes wide with astonishment, Tara stared at him, unable to move for a full fifteen seconds. Then, with a small incoherent cry, she was across the room, flinging herself against his chest.

"Oh, Alek," she whispered. "And here I was, about to beg you to let me stay."

"Let you stay?" he repeated incredulously, his arms hard and tight around her. "I never wanted you to go. You know that. I've been berating myself all day for what happened last night. For giving you what I thought was the perfect excuse for leaving me."

Her hand slid underneath his pullover, then up and over his warm skin, with an urgency in her to touch him. She felt a shudder ripple through his body as he buried his face in her hair and groaned, "Oh, God, Tara, I love you. I swear if I ever walk in again and find your suitcase open, I *will* strangle you. These few weeks have been pure hell, wanting to hold you like this all the time I tried to work during the day, lying alone in that damn bed at night."

"Which reminds me," Tara stepped back and looked up into eyes now alive and glowing with love and tenderness. "Where have you been every night? You didn't spend very many hours alone in that bed."

"Are you jealous, Tara?" he laughed down at her.

"Yes, damn you. And what were you and Kitty up to last night?"

He laughed again, kissed her fast and hard, then said softly, "Simmer down, hellion, and don't swear at me. Kitty wants to open her own boutique and needed some backing. I've looked over her plans and decided to invest. And that's all."

"On New Year's Eve?" she cried in disbelief.

"Well, I may have been trying to punish you a little. Damn it, Tara, you've been driving me crazy for months. I thought, after that unbelievable wedding night, that you'd realize what you meant to me. What you have meant to me since not long after I met you. In the last week I've felt at the end of my wits and patience. It was either stay away from you or drag you off to the nearest bed. It seems I did both."

He stopped long enough to give her another hard kiss, then a little shake. "As for Kitty. There is nothing between us but business. Anything else was over some time ago. And she never lived in this apartment or slept in our bed." His arms loosened and his hands came up to cup her face, long fingers sliding into her hair. Lips close to hers, he rasped, "Tara, if you don't soon tell me you love me, I won't be responsible for my actions."

Soft brown eyes gazed into anxious blue ones then, quietly, but very clearly, Tara said, "I love you, Alek."

"Dear God," he moaned. "I was beginning to think I'd never hear you say it." Then his mouth was crushing hers, his hands moving down her back, molding the softness of her body to the hard strength of his. Tara's mind whirled, then the room spun as he scooped her into his arms and strode into the bedroom. Their bedroom.

As he lowered her gently onto the bed, Tara whispered, "Since right after you met me, Alek?"

"Yes, pansy eyes."

"But, I don't understand."

"Oh, Tara. You were so cold. You seemed to take such an aversion to me. I guess, at first, my vanity was stung. I made up my mind to find out more about you."

Kicking off his shoes, he slid onto the bed beside her, then proceeded to drive her slightly mad with tiny, fervent kisses, until she caught at his head and pulled it back with a pleaded, "Alek?"

"All right," he sighed. One long finger tracing the contours of her face, he went on. "It didn't take long to find out you went out only with men who had—ah—shall we say, good prospects? But somehow that didn't seem to quite fit you. So I dug a little deeper, observed a little harder, and came up with the answer. You were scared to death of strong-willed men. By then I was so damn in love, I knew I had to have you, by whatever methods. But how to get close to you, get under the fence you'd built around yourself? You avoided me whenever possible, cut me dead whenever I spoke to you. That's when I put my plan into motion. I didn't want to hurt you, for when you hurt, I hurt. But I did want you."

"And in all this time, until today, that's all you've said. 'I want you.'"

"Not true, pansy eyes. I've been telling you I loved you since the first night I came to your apartment. I knew you were not yet ready to hear it, so I said it in Russian. If you remember the morning after our wedding I said I had something to tell you when I asked you to come back to bed. I was fully prepared to lay my heart and my life at your feet. In English."

"Those Russian words!" Tara exclaimed. "But how could I know?"

Then, her arms snaking around his neck, she whispered, "Translate at once—please."

Alek's breath was a cool caress against her mouth as he murmured the Russian words, then whispered, "Roughly translated, it's 'My darling, Tara, I love you.'"

Too Close for Comfort

by Lori Herter

1

Puzzled gray eyes spotted the handwritten note lying on the table.

> Jo—
> Heard the fishing's great in La Paz! Leaving today, December 22. Made reservations for us at the Hotel La Playa. Left a map and guidebook so you can follow.
> Baja's civilized nowadays—the new road is paved all the way. Should be a nice drive. Hope we see you by Christmas!
>
> Dad

Joey exhaled a long sigh through soft, well-formed lips. "Well, that explains why nobody's here," Joey Scott muttered to herself as she glanced about the empty, tidied-up trailer home.

She had left Los Angeles early that morning—Christmas morning—to drive the two hundred miles to Estero Beach, just outside Ensenada, to spend the holidays with her parents. For the past several years they had kept a mobile home in a permanent rental space at a large trailer park there, driving down often for long weekends and holidays.

Joey had intended to leave for Mexico with them five days before, but as often happened, a problem had cropped up at work which forced her to delay her departure. She had promised her parents she would drive down as soon as she could, and now that she had finally arrived, *they* were gone.

Disappointment showed on her lovely young face as her eyes moved down the sheet of paper to another note, this one written in a finer hand.

> Dear Joey,
> We tried to phone you, but for some reason the lines wouldn't go through to L.A. I'm sorry about this change in our plans, but you know your father. Someone who just visited La Paz told him a fish story and he can't wait to get there.

"That sounds typical," Joey mumbled, breathing out another long sigh.

> I tried to tell him you shouldn't drive down there all alone to meet us, but he wouldn't pay any heed.

You're so capable of looking after yourself, I think sometimes he forgets you're a girl.

Some people we met here told me that parts of Highway 1 aren't in good condition and the service stations are often out of gas, so please, dear, be careful. And don't drive at night—they say it's very dangerous. There are supposed to be some good hotels along the way, but I still don't like the idea of your traveling such a long distance over barren desert alone in that little car.

Joey, if you'd rather not come, I will understand perfectly. You can notify us at the hotel if you decide against it. Please take care of yourself. Merry Christmas.

Love,
Mother

"And a Merry Christmas to you," Joey said a bit sardonically as she let the piece of paper drop back onto the table. Yes, this was just like something her father would do. He usually pleased himself first without giving a thought to anyone else. It apparently didn't occur to him that his wife and daughter might like to do something other than what he had in mind.

"It's partly Mother's fault," Joey mused as she pulled out a chair to sit down at the small table. "She's let him get away with it all these years. If he had been *my* husband . . ."

She quickly dropped the absurd thought. She would never marry anyone like her father; she had decided that long ago. It wasn't that there was a lack of affection between father and daughter. He was an engaging, energetic man, a person who could get along well with almost anyone. Joey would have been the first to acknowledge that he had provided well for her mother and had loved her all his life.

But it seemed to Joey that her mother had paid a high price for the security she enjoyed, for she had very little influence on her husband's decisions.

Still, Joey could understand her mother's acquiescence to such a dependent role throughout her twenty-five years of marriage, knowing that her mother was from a more conservative generation and was a quiet, unassertive woman as well.

Though her mother might be content with such a marriage, Josepha Scott had decided she never could. If she married at all—and in her mind that was quite a big "if"—it would have to be to a man who was ready and willing to accept a wife on a strictly equal footing. Based on her observations of her parents' marriage and her experience dealing with men in the working world, she had come to the conclusion that such a man might not exist. More to the point, she cherished the freedom she now enjoyed as a single woman living alone and felt threatened by anything or anyone she thought might curb her independence.

Breaking into her own thoughts to remind herself that she had a decision to make, she picked up the map left for her on the table. As she unfolded the paper to its fullest dimensions and scanned the long strip of land depicted on it, she was amazed, not having realized before how far Baja California extended south into the Pacific. A second glance told her that she had only been looking at the upper portion of the peninsula. Turning the long sheet of paper over, she discovered a map covering the peninsula's lower half printed on the other side. Looking toward the bottom, she noted that the location of La Paz was less than 150 miles from Cabo San Lucas, the resort town located at the very tip of the peninsula.

She began to grow uneasy about the idea of making such a long drive over an area that was notorious for its rough, and for the most part uninhabited, terrain. Scrutinizing the map more carefully, she noted that most of the larger towns were very far apart. There were a number of small villages scattered in between, but she guessed these would have few facilities for the traveler. In some areas it was a long way even between the smaller villages.

She picked up the paperback guidebook. After leafing through it for a few minutes, she grew more reassured. The book was very thorough in its descriptions of what one would find along Highway 1, the road which ran the length of the peninsula and was just recently completed by the Mexican government. Gas stations, hotels, restaurants, markets, and scenic spots were all pinpointed and described. Mention was also made of the Green Angels, a fleet of small trucks manned by bilingual mechanics whose sole purpose was to patrol the highway and aid any motoring tourists in distress.

Checking the distance table on the map, she determined it was 854 miles from Ensenada to La Paz. She estimated that if she left that afternoon, she probably could make it to her destination two days later. Glancing through the accommodations listed, she noted, as her mother had written, that there was a string of government-financed hotels along the way, built to attract tourists to the area and said to be comparable to better hotels in the United States.

Though she could anticipate many miles of dry, inhospitable desert to cross on her own, the more she read the guidebook, the less forbidding the drive to La Paz seemed. Since her only alternative was to spend her two weeks of vacation, including New Year's, alone, Joey decided there was really no reason at all why she shouldn't make the trip. "It will be good experience for me," she told herself.

Joey was at heart a cautious person and not prone to being adventurous. She continually nurtured and took pride in her growing self-reliance, however, and sought to develop an ability to cope with difficult circumstances. She wanted very much to be a woman who could stand on her own, particularly since she often felt convinced there would never be a permanent man in her life.

The drive alone down the Baja California peninsula was beginning to take on the form of a challenge—a test of her strength to deal with the unknown. She had become comfortable with, indeed had almost overcome, the problems that faced a young career woman in the business world. She decided it was time she had some new test of her ability to handle unexpected and unfamiliar situations, so that her evolving independence would have the opportunity for further development and growth.

Now she smiled at her mother's hints of danger and her thinly veiled suggestion that Joey would be better off not making the trip. It would take more than some rough road and rugged desert to scare her. And certainly, if her middle-aged father could handle the drive, there was no reason at all why she couldn't.

2

After stocking her tiny champagne-colored hatchback with a few cans of tuna, a box of crackers, and two one-gallon bottles of purified water taken from her parents' supplies, Joey drove down the palm-lined road leading out of the well-kept trailer park.

She decided to make a quick run into Ensenada to fill her gas tank before heading south on the long journey to La Paz. Turning into a modern service station she often used when staying with her parents at Estero Beach, she pulled to a stop in front of a pump supplying unleaded gas. *"Llene el tanque, por favor,"* she told the dark-eyed Mexican attendant, using one of the few Spanish phrases she knew.

The large station was busy with several other cars filling up. Near the next island of pumps, a small group of men were standing alongside a blue van with a high, domelike top, chatting in quick, softly spoken Spanish. Casually she noted that one of the men was unusually tall for a Mexican. She also noted, with distaste, that his conversation did not hinder him from freely eyeing a shapely American redhead who was getting into her car near one of the other pumps. Apparently leering males were not limited to one nationality, Joey concluded with sardonic resignation.

She got out of her car to make a fast check of her tires. As she stepped toward the back wheel, a low gust of wind made her long, tawny-blond hair flutter softly. It fell like a thick, shiny web of gossamer over her shoulders and back, the silken strands clinging to the long-sleeved black velour top she wore over rust-colored pants.

Her tall slender form moved lithely with athletic grace, this owing to her formidable weekly schedule of tennis and racketball. Her beautiful face conveyed in its natural features an impish quality, with rosy cheeks and a full, rounded mouth shaped as though it were designed for a pout. A small, upturned nose completed the mischievously angelic look. But her cool, gray eyes, with their direct and appraising gaze, gave glimpse to the keenly competent individual housed within the doll-like face and body.

The gray eyes paused in their inspection of the tires to meet the eagerly flirtatious gaze of the station attendant, who was haphazardly washing her car windows, his mind not on his work. From long experience with such situations, Joey had learned not to drop her eyes in confusion as some women might. She met his eyes directly, issuing back to him a look that was coldly polite, and unquestionably discouraging. It was the young attendant who lowered his eyes and made a more industrious effort at the windows.

The nuance of superiority in her gaze was there because the man was clearly looking upon her as an object of desire instead of as a person. To Joey, such men operated on a lower mental level than her own, and she had little patience with them. Unfortunately it often seemed to her that such men comprised the majority of the male population, a fact which never ceased to surprise and irritate her.

Joey was a certified public accountant for a small accounting firm, and in her work had to deal with many male clients on a professional basis. Almost invariably in each new office to which she was sent as a consultant there were at least one or two men who seemed more taken with her physical than her mental attributes. This was evidenced by the way they lingered about her desk, keeping her from her work with meaningless small talk and playful *double-entendres*. Inevitably there had been a few along the way who had wanted to be more than just playful.

Necessity had forced Joey, during her two years of experience in the working world, to develop a way of handling such men. The practised look in her eyes meant to convey to them that she regarded herself as a professional in her field, their equal, and that she had no tolerance or time for anyone who would not deal with her as such.

She was walking back toward the driver's side of her car, after ascertaining that her tires were in good shape, when she realized she was under the surveillance of another pair of admiring male eyes. These belonged to the tall man she had noticed a few minutes before, only he was alone now and leaning nonchalantly against the bright blue van.

The eyes perusing her were a warm coffee color, lustrous against his smooth brown skin and straight black hair. His rugged, angular features reflected a proud Mexican heritage, while his general bearing seemed to indicate an even disposition and easy self-confidence.

His all-encompassing gaze lingered over the sleek feminine lines of her figure, dwelling on the thick long blond locks that had fallen softly over her well-defined bosom. She colored under the uninhibited gaze that seemed to strip her of her attire, and her blush drew his candid eyes to her face.

She quickly pulled herself together and looked directly back at him, giving him one of her most intimidating stares. The brown eyes seemed momentarily surprised, then fairly twinkled as the dark skin creased at their outer corners. His mouth formed a grin, baring strong white teeth which contrasted sharply with his dark coloring.

Joey's cool gray eyes were brought to life in a flash of anger. She gave him a scathing glare, wishing her eyes were lasers that could burn a hole through him and stop his insolent eyes. But his grin merely diminished a bit, while his gaze became more sensual, more intense. She realized with a shock that his penetrating eyes were silently issuing her an open invitation for intimacy!

Joey's expression was resolute as she quickly turned away, but her hands trembled when she pulled open her car door and darted into the driver's seat. She had slammed the door shut and started the engine when the station attendant appeared at her window asking for her payment. With unsteady fingers she extracted from her purse the right amount of brightly colored paper currency and handed it to him.

With her right hand nervously working the stickshift, her car began to jerk violently in response to the unsteady pressure of her foot on the clutch as she began to pull out of the station. After a few moments she had the car smoothly under control, and she glanced up to her rearview mirror. In the reflection she saw the tall Mexican still standing there, hands on hips, looking after her with a grin of amusement on his face and a glint sparkling in his eyes.

Within a quarter of an hour she was well out of Ensenada and driving south on Highway 1 past farmland and distant rugged hills. But Joey's mind wasn't on the scenery.

"Why did you have to get so rattled?" she asked herself aloud in the privacy

of her car. "You really looked like a fool, you know that?" She stretched up
to give herself an upbraiding glare in the rearview mirror, then instinctively
checked the road behind her, as though afraid someone were watching. The road
in back was empty.

"You've run into men like him before." She continued her self-inflicted
tongue lashing. "He's just like the others. Maybe more brazen, more . . . more . . .
well, go ahead and say it . . . more virile. But so what? You should have been
able to handle that without falling all over yourself!"

The event deeply disturbed her. She had thought she had learned to be capable
of dealing calmly with all types of people. It was essential to her work that she
be able to do so, as she often was required to obtain information necessary for
her accounting procedures from individuals who were uncooperative, inefficient,
or not as intelligent as she. She had learned to handle these situations well and
had become so adept at discouraging would-be ladies' men that she no longer
regarded them as a hindrance—merely a nuisance.

But what if one day one of her clients should turn out to be a man like him?
The thought almost made her quake. How had he been able, without so much
as one word exchanged between them, to break through her defenses so quickly,
leaving her feeling shaken and vulnerable? Her mind continued to wrestle with
that question for a long while.

She passed through the small agricultural community of Maneadero, where
Highway 1 narrowed from a four-lane road to two lanes. As there were no
shoulders provided along the pavement, the road seemed very narrow indeed.
A short distance later she came to a small sign with ALTO, Spanish for stop,
printed in large letters. To the right, she noticed a small, modern, brick building
with windows along the front. She immediately was reminded of the instructions
in her guidebook regarding the Mexican government's requirement that visitors
stop at the check station near Maneadero before proceeding south. Carefully she
turned off the road onto the dirt and parked in front of the building.

She walked up to the Mexican official sitting behind an open window and
handed him the tourist card she had obtained at the Mexican consulate in Los
Angeles. She knew it was necessary that the official validate her card here, as
it had not been checked earlier when she had crossed the border.

The middle-aged man in uniform carefully inspected her papers. He looked
up and said something to her in Spanish which she could not understand. *"No
hablo español,"* she told him.

"Birth certificate," he said in heavily accented English.

"Birth certificate?"

"Sí."

"I don't understand—*no comprendo.*"

"You must show me birth certificate."

"But I took it with me to the Mexican consulate to get the tourist card. I
didn't think I'd need it here. I've never been asked for it at the border."

"Buenas tardes," a low voice interrupted. Joey turned in irritation, then froze
on her feet. It was the same tall Mexican; his blue van was pulled up behind
her car. He continued speaking in Spanish to the official behind the window.
When they had exchanged a few words the man in uniform addressed her again.

"Do you have a passport?"

"Yes, but I didn't bring it."

A large masculine hand deftly reached into one of the little-used pockets of her dangling shoulder bag, which she had failed to rezip, and removed a small book. He placed it in her hands, amusement dancing in his brown eyes.

She blinked as she looked at her passport. How stupid of her! She had taken a four-day show tour to London a couple of months before and had forgotten to take it out of her bag when she returned.

"Oh, yes, I do have my passport," she said in her best business voice as she handed it to the official. After looking it over, he stamped her tourist card and returned both documents to her. She thanked him and then turned to the tall man standing next to her. *"Muchas gracias,"* she said with determined politeness.

"De nada," he softly responded, a bemused gleam in his eye that made Joey rage within. Twice in one day she had succeeded in making a complete idiot of herself in front of a man she didn't know and didn't want to know. The fact that he was so obviously enjoying her frustration revolted her.

He extended his right hand toward her, eyes shining, and raised his dark brows in a tentative expression. Joey wet her lips with her tongue; she would have to shake hands with him to be polite. He *had* been of assistance to her. How unsettling to have to be beholden to a man like him! Stoically she put her small hand in his. His long fingers closed securely around it, holding it captive.

He had a strong, well-formed hand, she noted. Lean and muscular, like the rest of him. It was uncalloused and the nails were trimmed and clean. He apparently did not earn his living by manual labor. Her eyes traveled along his arm, sheathed in an expensive-looking brown leather jacket, and then up to his face. He was looking at her, a curious expression in his eyes. She gently pulled her hand away.

"Adiós," she said quietly, dropping her eyes from his and turning to walk toward her car.

"Hasta luego," he called out in a nonchalant tone when she had covered the short distance to her vehicle.

She started the ignition and drove off, this time taking care to do it much more smoothly than before. *"Hasta luego . . . hasta luego . . .* what does that mean?" she mumbled under her breath when she was well away from the check station. Suddenly it came to her: See you later.

"Good Lord, I hope not," she groaned. But since he apparently was also driving along Highway 1, it seemed more than possible she could run into him again, as that road was the main thoroughfare through Baja California. "He is Mexican, though," she reminded herself. "Maybe he lives or has business in one of the towns along the way. It's unlikely he'd be driving the whole distance to La Paz. At least, I hope it's unlikely," she muttered ruefully.

Her expression suddenly changed as a new thought entered her mind. Unconsciously, her hands tightened their grip on the wheel. "If he's Mexican," she said slowly, "why was he at the check station? It's only foreign visitors that need to stop." She paled a bit. "What if . . . what if he's following me? Why else would he have stopped?" Her breathing quickened as she recalled the sensual way he had looked at her at the gas station. Did he want to make good that unspoken invitation?

"Now calm down!" she instructed herself as she pushed back into her seat.

"You're getting carried away. There are many logical possibilities why he could have stopped. Maybe he knew the man behind the window. Maybe he works for the Mexican government himself and oversees the check station. And as for that look he gave you, he probably doles that out to every woman he sees," she decided, thinking of the redhead she had caught him observing. "He'd be the type who thinks he's God's gift to the female gender," she said with scorn. But her conscience silently reminded her that, judging by his appearance, the assessment might not be far from wrong. "I hate men like that!" she declared aloud, stifling the small voice within.

Glancing at her rearview mirror, she checked the empty road behind her. "You see, not a car in sight. Now concentrate on the scenery instead of that man! No doubt he thinks women are a dime a dozen, so he's not going to go out of his way to chase you!" she chided, irritated with her own obstinate tendency to overreact. It was an occasional but troublesome character flaw that she was intent on improving.

She did as she had instructed herself and began to look at the countryside. The road was winding through vineyards as she was coming into a wide, lush valley, lying peacefully between rugged, low hills.

She continued to drive through farmland interspersed with occasional small villages for almost three hours. She had gotten a late start, and it was nearing five o'clock when she came into San Quintin.

It was quite a large town strung haphazardly along the road for several miles, with many different shops and stores, cafés, banks, and mechanic's shops. It was often difficult to distinguish one business from another, for the small individual buildings of varying design did little to advertise what services were provided within. They were set rather far back from the road by American standards, and in between was barren dirt instead of sidewalks. She speculated that it must have rained quite recently, and very heavily too, for large puddles of standing water covered much of the flat land on either side of the road.

Following the instructions in her guidebook, she made her way through the town and took a right turn onto a road which led her to the hotel near the beach at which she had wanted to stay. The sun was fading quickly and it was beginning to turn chilly, so she welcomed the warmth of the lobby as she entered the modern building. She walked to the long desk and asked for a room.

"You are lucky, we do have a room left," the woman behind the desk told her in English that was not too difficult to decipher. "The road is better now and the cars can go through, so we are no longer so crowded."

"What was the problem?" Joey asked with concern.

"The heavy rains two days ago wash out the road, but today the water has gone down enough so the cars can pass," she explained.

"I see," Joey responded slowly, wondering if she had been wise to try to drive to La Paz after all. She took the key the woman gave her and, following her directions, found her room.

It was a large, beautifully furnished room with a private bath. "Not bad," she thought with a smile. She went back to the car to bring in her suitcase.

After relaxing for a while, she changed into a beige skirt and bright, multicolored blouse and walked to the hotel's small dining room. Shortly she was seated at a table near one corner of the pleasant room. It was about half full of people and several waiters strolled about. It took a while before she was presented with a menu, and she was busy perusing it when a loud, distinctly American voice distracted her.

"Hey, Mark! Over here! Well, how do you like that—small world, eh?" a man, apparently at the table behind hers, was saying boisterously.

"Hello, Ted! I didn't know you would be down here," another male American voice answered in quieter tones. Judging by the direction of the voice, he seemed to be approaching the other man's table. "Come to fish?"

"Yeah. We've been at Mulegé for a week, but coming back has been rough with these darn washouts. It wasn't bad going down."

"Where's your wife?"

"Oh, she's got a touch of Montezuma's revenge, so she's skipping dinner. She'll be okay, though. Where are you headed, Mark?"

"Cabo San Lucas."

"To pick up your old lady?"

"That's right."

Old lady! Joey cringed at the term. That any man could refer to someone's wife as his old lady seemed to her the height of disrespect.

"She's a lively little thing, isn't she?" Ted, who sounded older than the other man, commented.

"That she is," the younger, quieter voice answered with a nuance of pride.

"With her to take care of you, Mark, I can see why you haven't bothered getting married."

This was becoming more intriguing by the second. Apparently the woman in question wasn't even the younger man's wife!

"I live by myself, Ted," she heard the quiet voice respond with a chuckle.

"She must be just a part-time old lady," thought Joey sarcastically. Curiosity was getting the better of her. She had to see what sort of men would talk over such personal matters so openly in a restaurant. Cautiously she turned around.

"Buenas tardes," the tall, black-haired man said, his lustrous brown eyes already on her. Dressed in a shirt, white pullover sweater, and tan pants, he was standing by the table behind hers where a middle-aged man was seated.

Joey was stunned. It was the same Mexican she had met on the road. But he was an American! He must have thought it a joke at the check station when he had let her believe he was a local. She gave him a very abbreviated nod of recognition and stiffly turned back to face her table again, anger making her stomach churn.

"Well, Mark, I was just about to get up and leave," the older man said with more enthusiasm than the statement required. "Great to see you again." Then he added in a lower, conspiratorial tone, "Good luck *fishing*." This was immediately followed by a throaty, between-us-boys laugh.

"Okay, Ted," the tall man answered calmly. "See you later."

After a moment Joey heard a few footsteps coming toward her. "Mind if I sit down?" Mark asked, resting a hand on the high back of her chair.

"Yes," she said, turning her face upward to meet his gaze.

The dark eyes widened and a slow smile crossed his face. "Mind if I ask why?"

"I prefer to eat alone," she responded coolly, facing forward again.

Casually he moved to the chair opposite hers on the other side of the table and, stooping slightly, leaned with folded arms over the chair's back. "Here we are," he said with a poetic gesture of his hand, "two Americans meeting by chance in a foreign land, and you don't even want to talk to me?"

"This hotel seems to be full of Americans. Besides, I thought you were Mexican," she replied, an insinuating tone in her voice.

"I am—Mexican descent. And because I speak fluent Spanish, you assumed I was born south of the border. If you had checked, you would have seen my California license plate."

Joey realized she had been too busy looking at the man to pay much attention to his vehicle. "You knew *I* was American. You could have spoken to me in English at the check station," she countered.

"That would have been too easy," he responded with a grin.

"Do you enjoy amusing yourself at the expense of others?" she asked querulously.

"Sure—especially when they get huffy about it. Now, I might remind you that if I hadn't intervened, you might not be sitting here right now. And since this dining room is beginning to get crowded, I suggest it would be polite if you asked me to join you."

Joey swallowed and lowered her eyes from his expectant gaze. "Go ahead and sit down," she murmured grudgingly. She might have known he would take advantage of the favor he had done her.

"So kind of you to ask me," he joked, taking the seat opposite her. He leaned back in the chair and tilted his head to one side. "Tell me, why do you dislike me so much? We don't even know each other."

The directness of his question took her unexpectedly. "I . . . I just don't like your type, that's all."

"I'm a type?" he asked with surprise. "What type am I?"

"A womanizer—a man with no respect or sensitivity toward women," she said nervously, hoping to discourage his pursuit by bluntly telling him what she thought of him.

"Really! And how have you come to that conclusion?"

She hesitated. The conversation she had just overheard would have proven her point, but she didn't want to appear an eavesdropper. "The way you looked me over in Ensenada," she replied, trying not to appear embarrassed, though she felt the color rising in her cheeks.

"A man admiring a beautiful woman. Is there something wrong with that?" he said calmly, staring at her.

Joey was beginning to feel skittish under his eyes, but she went on boldly. "You were admiring a face and body. It wouldn't have interested you to find out what kind of person I was."

"Since I had never met you, what else was I supposed to admire? And I'm trying very hard now to figure out what kind of a person you are."

Did he have to be so adept at sparring with her? She longed to confront him with that blatantly sensual invitation he had silently given her, but she found herself incapable of expressing it aloud—at least to him. Even now there was a certain look in his eyes as he softly added, "You seem to have assumed a lot about me in the few brief moments we've been together."

Been together. For some reason, the words made Joey's heart beat faster. Why did everything he did and say seem so suggestive?

"I just don't like being treated like a . . . sex object," she said defensively. It was with great difficulty she uttered the last words to him, but she managed, regaining some pride in having at least made clear her point of view.

It appeared he would have answered her, but before he could, a waiter arrived at their table to take their orders. Joey quickly named the first thing listed on the menu. She hadn't had an opportunity to make up her mind, but wanted to appear as though she were in total control of herself.

Mark gave his order and asked for a bottle of wine for them to share. She looked up at him abruptly; she had no wish to make an occasion of this meal. But he merely met her eyes with a steady, affable gaze, quelling her unspoken objection.

"What's your name?" he asked in a friendly tone when the waiter had gone. He apparently wanted to drop their previous topic and start anew.

"Josepha Scott."

"Josepha . . ." he pondered. "I would have guessed your name to be Cindy or Sally . . . or Barbie."

"I'm not a doll," she stated matter-of-factly.

"You look like one," he countered with a smile. "Don't you have a nickname or something?"

"My father and some of my co-workers call me Jo. Others call me Joey."

His smile broadened. "Joey . . . that's adorable. It suits you. But how did your parents come to name you Josepha?"

"I was their first and only child. My father had wanted a boy, but unfortunately he couldn't control nature and had to make do with a daughter. They had planned to name me Joseph, after a relative, so they made it Josepha instead."

"I may be mistaken, but it sounds like you aren't too fond of your father."

She smiled slightly. "Oh, I am. He's a well-meaning person. It's just that he has a tendency to think women are around to cater to his wishes. One has to be a man to gain his true respect."

"I see. Another insensitive male?"

"I suppose you might say that."

"You seem to get more than your share of them."

"It often strikes me that way," she readily agreed.

The conversation died of its own accord for a few moments.

"You haven't asked what *my* name is," he said, breaking the stiff silence.

"No, I haven't," Joey replied smoothly, implying the neglect was intentional.

He smiled. "I'm Mark Chavira." As there was no comment, he added, "I live in Orange County. I'm in real estate development." There was still no response from the beautiful mannequinlike creature sitting across from him. "What do *you* do?" he finally asked.

"I work for the Layton and Brook Accountancy Corporation in Los Angeles. I'm a certified public accountant," she told him, quietly anticipating the response she often received from men upon hearing this revelation. She was not disappointed; the dark brown eyes widened. True to form, she assumed, he was surprised that an attractive young woman could also be a competent businessperson. But an instant later he startled her by smiling cordially while his eyes became infused with admiration.

"I have great regard for those in your profession." The tone of his voice reflected his sincerity. "Without accountants to assist me in my work, my records would be a shambles and investors wouldn't have much faith in me."

This statement left Joey at a loss. In her experience men often preferred to ignore her business status or they gave her a tolerant respect. The generosity of this man's statement threw her. Suddenly feeling strangely shy, she dropped her eyes to the wineglass that had been placed in front of her.

"My expertise lies in finding good tracts of land and putting the right buildings on them," he continued. "I back away when it comes to the details involved in keeping records in order and accounts balanced. I'm one of those who can see the forest clearly, but the trees are blurred," he said with a chuckle.

This artless confession confused Joey more. She was not used to hearing a man so readily point out his weaknesses, especially to a woman. In fact, she herself would not be willing to openly admit her shortcomings. She had always thought it advantageous to appear proficient in all things.

Her curiosity aroused, she drew him out over dinner in what unexpectedly turned into a pleasant conversation. From what he told her about his work, she deduced that he must be quite successful. Though he did not boast, the passing mention of shopping centers and office buildings that his organization had developed indicated his was no small-time operation.

Joey was eager to learn more, but as their empty plates were removed, he said amiably, "Enough of this business talk. Tell me about yourself. How is it you're driving alone through Baja California on Christmas Day?"

"I'm going down to join my parents. We were to spend the holidays at Estero Beach, but my father changed his mind. They left a note saying I should meet them in La Paz."

Mark looked concerned. "Your father wanted you to drive all that way alone? Has he ever driven to La Paz himself?"

"No, I don't think so. Why?"

He shook his head. "It's a long, lonely trip through an empty, isolate desert. The terrain is rough and the road is full of potholes. Your father must not have realized what the area is like, because I don't think any man would want his daughter to make the trip alone."

"Well, my father often does minimize obstacles, but if others drive down there, there's no reason I shouldn't," she said, holding her chin a bit higher. "You're driving alone, aren't you?"

"Yes," he agreed, "but I know the area from many previous trips, and I'm self-contained in my van. If I can't get a hotel room, as I couldn't tonight, or I'm not near a restaurant, I always have food and shelter with me. Besides . . . a young woman traveling alone . . ." He left off, shaking his head.

Joey's confidence was undermined a bit by these remarks, but she would not allow herself to be set back. She decided to attack his weakest point.

"I don't see what difference it should make that I'm female. Besides, I stocked some provisions and I could sleep in my car if I had to."

The concern came back into his eyes. "I have to admire your g . . . intestinal fortitude, but your courage may be foolhardy. Baja California is no place for a woman alone. One runs into all sorts of people along Highway 1, not all of them trustworthy. If you should get stranded, you could find yourself in quite a predicament. And the problem would be compounded by the fact that you don't know much Spanish. Not many of the local people in this area speak English.''

"I still don't see what my being a woman has to do with it," she retorted stubbornly, blithely overlooking his other arguments.

He grinned. "I take it you're very equality-minded. I appreciate your feelings, but I'm afraid I'll have to maintain my point of view. While women can and do function just as well as men in a modern metropolis, it's a different story when it comes to surviving in a rugged, unimproved area. I think you must agree that women are physically weaker than men. That's probably why women in less civilized times were willing to accept male protection. You must remember, Joey, that traveling through Baja California, with the exception of its few larger cities, is somewhat like going back in time a hundred years or more. Everything may be fine as long as you don't run into any problems, but I don't like to think what might happen to you if you lost what little protection your automobile provides.''

Joey swallowed hard, as if physically trying to keep her fears from rising up and overwhelming her. She allowed resentment to take over. "My first impression of you was correct. You seem to think of a woman as merely a helpless, cute little toy. You probably can't even fathom the notion that we are intelligent and resourceful individuals. Not every obstacle is overcome by muscle power. We may cope with a tough situation differently than a man would, but we still cope!''

He took his napkin and casually threw it next to his empty coffee cup. "I didn't intend to start an argument with you, Joey, and I do admire your courage. Just be careful on the road, okay?" he said with a conciliatory smile.

She nodded her head slightly in agreement, dropping her eyes to the table, for she was already beginning to feel dissatisfied with herself about sounding so obstinate. Even if she didn't like him or his attitudes, there was no reason to let herself become antagonized, she reasoned. Why should his opinions be of any consequence to her?

The waiter brought the check and handed it to Chavira. Joey saw Mark begin to reach for his wallet and hurried to say, "I'll pay for my own," as she reached to the floor for her shoulderbag.

"Pay for your own! No, no, I'll get it," he said with a smile.

"No, really, I insist. I always pay my own way," she said, taking out her own wallet.

"Now, I can't believe that. As a CPA, you must allow your clients to take you out to lunch.''

"Of course, just as I often take them to lunch at our company's expense. But you aren't one of my clients. In nonbusiness matters, I prefer separate checks. It keeps things simpler.'' Besides, she added to herself, I don't want to owe you any more favors.

He kept an amused and thoughtful silence for a moment. "I don't see that anything's so complicated. Why not let me pay for this, and you can pick up the tab next time? It would all work out evenly in the end and save us the chore of dividing the bill.''

Joey tried to keep her patience. "Next time? I don't foresee any next time, Mr. Chavira. And as for dividing the check, it's no chore for me. I'll be happy to do the arithmetic."

He leaned back in his chair, still holding the wallet in his hand, and studied her with interest. "I don't think I've ever met a woman quite so determined as you are to have her way," he said, a hint of admiration in his eyes.

"Now you have," she stated a little smugly. She reached over and turned the bill toward her so that she could read it. "Let's see . . ." she muttered as she began to figure her portion of the total.

Suddenly it was snatched up from under her eyes. "I'm afraid I can be equally determined, Miss Scott. I'm paying the check," he said as he rose from his chair.

Quickly she got up to intercept him. "Why won't you honor my wishes in this?" she demanded.

He put his hands on his hips and looked down into her unyielding, upturned face, taking a step closer. Humor played in his eyes as he said, "Why, Joey? Let's say because I'm bigger than you, so I can do as I please. Do you think you can stop me?" He raised his brows and waited for her answer.

Anger sparked in her eyes and a few choice retorts rose to her lips. She kept herself from uttering them. He was obviously baiting her; why give him the satisfaction of seeing that he had managed to rouse her temper? Abruptly she turned away from him and coolly stalked out of his presence, walking between tables toward the door.

Once out in the lobby of the hotel she quickened her stride and headed toward the hallway down which her room was located. Of all the domineering, pigheaded, overbearing men! she fumed, angrily jerking her key out of her bag.

She heard quick footsteps coming up behind her. "Joey, wait!" Mark was beside her now, looking down at her tight-lipped profile. "I'm sorry if I've offended you, but you were so stubborn I couldn't resist giving you a little setdown. After your claims that you can cope with anything, I thought for your own good you should be made aware that you're not quite invincible."

"So you've proved your point," she said icily, looking straight ahead and continuing her fast pace. "Would you please leave me alone now?"

He bowed his head for a moment, but kept up with her. "Look, I . . . was wrong. I shouldn't have made you angry like this. I'm sorry. But I do think you were making a mountain out of a molehill about paying the check," he persisted.

Immediately she stopped in the middle of the long, narrow hallway and faced him. "I feel I have every right to choose who I keep company with and who I'll allow to take me to dinner! I have no respect for skirt chasers who foist their unwelcome attentions on me."

"Womanizer! Skirt chaser!" he exclaimed, continuing beside her as she resumed her pace. "How do you know I'm those things?"

She suddenly stopped again, realizing she had passed her room. She turned and retraced a few steps until she came to her door.

"It's not really very hard," she said, holding the key poised by the doorknob as he came up to her. "I remember the way you leered at me in Ensenada, only minutes after you had finished similarly eyeing a redhead who was at the same gas station. Why else would you have insisted on joining me for dinner? It doesn't take much insight to see that you're after me."

"The redhead," he murmured thoughtfully, leaning casually against the door-frame. "You're very observant. I would never have remembered." He smiled a little. "So you think the reason I bought you dinner was to try to make time with you."

"Why else?" she asked flatly, looking up at him. At last she felt she was gaining the upper hand. In another moment or two she would be rid of him.

"Indeed—why else?" he replied. An unsettling light entered his eye as he looked over her face. He drew himself away from the wall in an easy movement and stood erect in front of her. "Well . . . I certainly wouldn't want to spoil your image of me," he said in a soft, smooth, voice. He moved closer and very calmly placed his hands at her waist. "Particularly when you're so sure you're right." He pulled her closer and his eyes settled sensually on her soft mouth. Panic showed clearly on Joey's face as she pressed her hands against his chest, vainly trying to push herself out of his grasp. "Relax, Joey, this will be over in a minute."

He pulled her up against him and pressed his lips to hers. She could feel his warm breath against her cheek as his arms enclosed her. Locked in his strong embrace, it seemed to Joey that he took every last second of his minute before he finally let her go.

After taking a moment to recapture her breath and her wits, she cried with wrath, "You are the rudest man I have ever met!"

He put his hands on his hips and quietly laughed. "That's quite a distinction! Since I'll have such an important place in your memory, I'll have to give you another chance to savor my revolting personality." He took the key from her hand and turned to unlock her door. "I'll pick you up for breakfast at seven thirty tomorrow," he said as he dangled the key in front of her.

She snatched it out of his long fingers. "I don't want to see you at breakfast, or ever again!"

He smiled broadly, bemusement making his eyes sparkle. Leaning toward her he said, "Good night, Joey. Merry Christmas!" then turned and took a few steps down the hall. He stopped briefly to call back to her, "Remember—seven thirty!"

Joey hurried into her room, slamming the door behind her. "What a horrible man!" she rasped as she threw down her shoulderbag and key onto the dresser. "Rude, domineering, presumptuous . . . strong." Suddenly the sensation of being locked in his arms swept over her again. She stood as if in a trance in the middle of the room, her arms crossed tightly over her chest and her long hair cascading over her slender shoulders, while a multitude of contradictory thoughts and feelings rushed through her. In the course of a day he had made her suspect, fear, and dislike him. But his kiss had been curiously gentle as he had kept her pressed firmly against him. The memory of it warmed and comforted her until suddenly she realized she was on the verge of tears.

Shaking her head sharply, she tried to rid herself of the lump in her throat. "I'm not afraid, I'm not lonely, and I don't need a man to make me happy!" she recited through clenched teeth. "Particularly not *that* man!"

Her expression became resolute. "Sorry to spoil your plans for breakfast, Mr.

Chavira, but I won't be here at seven thirty tomorrow morning," she said as she began undressing with a vengeance, throwing her clothes onto the bed. She raced into the bathroom, took a shower, brushed her teeth, and put on her nightgown.

Realizing she had not brought along her travel alarm, she searched about the room for the telephone. There was none. "I can't even get a wake-up call!" she muttered in frustration. "Well, there's no need," she assured herself. "I always wake up when I want to anyway. And tomorrow," she told herself with a smug smile, "I'm getting up at six thirty and I'll be on the road by seven!" She fell asleep to the pleasant image of Mark Chavira knocking at the door of her empty room.

3

Joey awakened suddenly, opening startled eyes as she lifted her head from the pillow. A loud rapping sound quickly brought her to a sitting position.

"Joey, it's seven thirty! You up?" she heard Mark Chavira's voice from the outer hall.

"Oh, no," she groaned. Realizing her plans were ruined, she quickly put her mind in gear. "If I don't answer, maybe he'll think I've left," she silently reasoned, stiffening her body to ensure no sound would give her presence away.

"Your car is still outside, Joey, so I know you're in there," came his teasing voice.

Stifling an oath, she threw aside the covers and grabbed her long navy blue robe, tying the belt as she hurried to the door.

"Well, good morning!" Chavira crowed with disgusting good cheer when she had opened the door. Noting her peevish expression, he asked in solicitous tones, "Did I wake you up?" while a mocking smile betrayed his amusement at her sleepy eyes and rumpled hair.

"I don't have my travel alarm and there's no phone in the room," she explained impatiently.

"You might have slept til noon, if you didn't have me around. Aren't you grateful?" he asked, eyes twinkling.

"Eternally. It will take me a while to get dressed, so why don't you just go ahead and have breakfast . . . ."

"You should know by now you can't get rid of me that easily. I'll wait for you in the lobby," he said good-naturedly.

He made no move to go, however. His attention was drawn to her attire, particularly the ruffles of her white flannel nightgown, accented by small, decorative ribbons, which peeked out from under her robe at her throat, wrists, and over her bare toes.

"Something wrong?" she asked, pulling the robe closer about her.

He leaned lazily against the doorframe. "I just happened to be wondering late last night what a modern, independent young woman like yourself wears to bed."

"I'm surprised you don't already know," she answered, affecting a tone of impatient indifference.

"It was quite an interesting problem," he continued, unperturbed. "I decided that either she would wear pajamas like a man, to symbolize her equality, or she would put on a flimsy black negligee to prove herself unfettered by the old restrictive moral code. But here you are, Joey, covered from neck to toe in pure white flannel and little pink bows, the image of Victorian innocence."

Joey cast her eyes downward in uneasy silence.

"It isn't that I disapprove," he continued in a soft voice. "I think you look charming. In fact, it's what I would have expected after that kiss last night."

Her apprehensive gray eyes flicked up to his momentarily before lowering again to the floor. Clasping the knob unsteadily, she began to close the door, murmuring, "I'll be ready in a few minutes."

She heard him softly reply, "I'll be waiting," before she shut him out. A trembling hand went to her forehead, as if to remove him from her mind as well. His incisive comments were unnerving, as if he possessed some secret magnifying glass with which he could see through the thick armor of protective self-reliance she worked so hard to keep in place. His uncanny intuition shook her deeply.

She had regained a tenuous control over her nerves by the time she had left her room to meet him in the lobby. She was dressed in casual green pants and a matching sweater, her hair hurriedly but neatly brushed into place. It was chilly and she shivered a bit as she approached him.

"You'd better wear a jacket when you go out; it's pretty cold this morning," he admonished her.

Joey nodded in response. They walked into the dining room and sat down at a table. Before long their orders were taken and they were left together in uneasy silence.

"Where did you stay last night?" she ventured, finding the silence too nerve-racking.

"There's a trailer park near here, so I pulled in and slept in my van. The place had nice facilities, but the hot water wasn't working. Taking a cold shower in these temperatures isn't much fun."

"I didn't have any hot water either, but at least the room was heated," she said with a smile.

"That's some consolation. How far are you planning to drive today?"

"Guerrero Negro or San Ignacio."

"That's pretty ambitious for the shape the road is in. They've had some washouts south of here, you know."

"I didn't get as far as I had hoped to yesterday. Even if I make it to San Ignacio, I'll still be behind schedule."

"Your parents are expecting you by a certain time?"

"No, but they may begin to wonder where I am. And the sooner I get there, the more time I'll have to spend with them," she explained.

"I understand, but you'll make it to Guerrero Negro today only if you're very lucky. Don't be tempted to drive at night. It's very dangerous, did you know that?"

"I remember reading that in my guidebook. Something about cattle on the road?"

"Yes, they often wander onto the asphalt at night for warmth. Many are black or brown, so they're hard to see in the dark. If you ran into one, both your car and the cow could be demolished.''

"I'll try to avoid night driving then."

"Don't even consider it!" he corrected firmly.

There's no need to be so domineering about it, she silently grumbled. Their breakfast plates were brought, and as they dug into scrambled eggs and bacon, Mark abruptly changed the subject.

"How long have you been working for Layton and Brook?"

Surprised that he had remembered the name of her company, she replied, "For two years—since I graduated from college."

"That makes you about twenty-four, then?"

"Yes," she answered, a little piqued that he had asked the question merely to ascertain her age. "How old are you?"

"Thirty-three. I suppose you passed your CPA exam on the first try."

"Yes," she replied, caught off guard again.

"You're such a determined young woman, I thought that would be the case. Was it a surprise to any of the male students in your class?"

"I don't know. Since I always got better grades than most of them, they didn't hang around me much," she said with some asperity.

"Well, it could be a blow to some young men to be outdone by a cute little chick—you'll pardon the expression," he said, smiling with the apology. "You must have had a boyfriend though."

Joey's expression became guarded. "Yes," she said, staring at her plate.

Her reaction seemed to kindle Mark's interest. "Was it serious?" he asked quietly.

Joey's lips formed a brittle smile. "I thought it was. Apparently he didn't."

"What happened—did he walk out on you?"

"He wasn't honest enough to do anything as straightforward as that," she said, a tenseness hardening her eyes. "I discovered him with my roommate one day. They were . . . in a rather compromising pose. Even then he tried to cover it over with lame excuses. So I walked out on *him*." Her voice unintentionally revealed her bitterness.

"Poor Joey," Mark said, his attention focused on the hurt in her eyes that her tautly composed expression could not conceal. "No wonder you have a low opinion of men."

"My opinion of men is based on more than just that," Joey retorted defensively. "I don't like . . ."

"Hey, Mark! Thought I might run into you this morning." It was Ted, the gray-haired man with baggy eyes that Mark had spoken with the night before. Joey had been too distracted even to notice him approach.

"Hello, Ted," Mark said, rising up a bit to shake hands.

"Well, I see you did have some luck . . ." the older man quipped, with a long glance toward Joey, ". . . fishing, that is." He directed a sly look to Mark.

"Ted, this is Joey Scott," Mark hurried to say. "She's a CPA for a firm in Los Angeles."

"Oh, you don't say." Ted responded, somewhat discomfited. Recovering, he threw in, "Prettiest little CPA *I* ever saw!"

"This is Ted Morley," Mark plunged on with the introductions. "He's one of my investors."

Joey nodded briefly.

"I didn't realize you two were . . . ah . . . business associates. Traveling together to Cabo San Lucas to work on your investment project?" Ted asked Mark, all innocence.

"No, no," Mark made haste to reply, directing an uneasy glance at Joey. "We happened to become acquainted on the road and then ran into each other again last night at dinner. I invited Joey to meet me for breakfast this morning," he explained. "Is your wife still sick?" he asked as if trying to deflect the other man's train of thought.

"No, she seems to be all right. I just came on ahead to get a table. You know how women are—always fussing with their hair and one thing or another. I got tired of waiting. Besides, the scenery's better here," he said, giving Joey a sidelong look. "Now if my wife would come out looking like this little lady, I wouldn't mind waiting around." He lifted his eyes toward the doorway. "Oh, here she is now. I'd better get back before she finds something to complain about. See you around, Mark. Nice to meet you, Miss . . . ah . . ."

"Scott," Joey supplied.

"So long, Ted," Mark said, showing a touch of relief.

"One of your friends?" Joey asked glacially.

"I'm sure you have to deal with all types of people in your job, just as I do," he said without apology. "Ted has money, but not much tact. He's a good businessman, though—owns a small chain of drugstores."

Their waiter came by and, after clearing away their empty plates, placed the check on the table. Joey eyed the slip of paper, but made no move to pick it up. She raised her gaze to Mark, who was looking at her expectantly. "I don't suppose you'd let me pay for my own," she said tersely.

He grinned. "Just to prove how gallant I can be, I'll let you pay the whole thing, if you'd like."

Somehow she had to smile. "Thank you," she said with humorous sarcasm as she reached to pick up the bill.

In a few minutes they were walking down the hall to her room, engaged in an innocuous conversation about the weather. When they reached her door, Mark drew up in front of her in his languid way and said, "Thank you for breakfast, Miss Scott. Please allow me to repay your kindness." In an instant his arms had closed about her and he lowered his slightly smiling mouth toward hers.

"No!" she whispered, her lips brushing his as she twisted her head away. His kiss landed on her cheek.

"What's the matter, Joey?" came his gentle, low voice in her ear as he continued to hold her close. "Did you enjoy it too much last night? I know I did." The firm hands at her back pressed her tighter against his chest.

"I didn't like it in the least!" she stormed, wriggling out of his grasp. "You are the most conceited, loathsome . . ."

"I'm flattered you find me such a colorful character," he exclaimed with provoking good humor.

Snatching her key from her bag with an angry hand, she said harshly, "I hope I never have to set eyes on you again!"

"Since we're both traveling in the same direction, it's very likely we *will* see each other again," he said with an assured smile.

"Then I hope you'll find the decency to leave me alone!" she told him vehemently before entering her room and slamming the door in his face.

Within half an hour Joey was back on the road, driving past cultivated green fields interspersed by areas of natural desert growth. The sky was overcast, and as the road followed the coastline the gray Pacific Ocean was barely in sight to the west. Occasionally she would pass a few small homes scattered haphazardly a little distance from the highway, some made of gray cement, some of stucco and brightly painted, while others were precariously constructed of wood scraps and left bare. Clotheslines of colorful wash radiated from the houses, while dogs roamed about aimlessly or lay dozing nearby on the ground.

Joey's mind was too preoccupied to pay more than intermittent attention to the passing countryside, however. Again Mark Chavira had somehow managed to come close to her vulnerable core, leaving her nervous system unbalanced. Now he had probed into her past, discovering there the lingering hurt she had hoped she'd forgotten. Though she hadn't thought of it for many months, she realized the wrenching memory of her shattered romance was with her still.

But what was Mark Chavira about that he seemed so intent on dissecting her personality? Why should he care whether she liked her father, what had happened to break up an old romance, or that she wore an old-fashioned nightgown to bed? His prying was too close for comfort.

Her complete attention was drawn back to the highway suddenly, when she realized she was approaching a standing pool of muddy water which completely covered a portion of the road just ahead. The water was contained in a low spot on the road, but its expanse was greater than the length of her car. It was difficult to estimate how deep it was. She drove almost to the water's edge and stopped. There were no other cars in sight.

Pondering the situation for a moment, she decided there was nothing to do but forge ahead. Slowly she moved her car forward. Beneath the water the pavement felt secure, if a little bumpy, and she saw that the pool was not so deep after all. Soon she was through it and back on dry road again. Pleased with herself, she breathed a relaxed sigh and pushed her foot on the accelerator to regain her previous speed.

She passed through two more small washouts before coming into a town next to a wide river valley. Noting her gas tank was little more than half full, she pulled into a service station. The attendant began filling her tank with unleaded gas as she requested, but in a few minutes he came back to her car window and told her in mixed Spanish and English that the pump had run out of gas. She had gotten only about two gallons. She paid the attendant and drove out of the town, making a mental note to stop at the next station she saw.

The road turned east and inland outside of town, and Joey drove on past scrubby vegetation and low, eroded hills in the distance. Soon she noticed a number of cars, campers, and trucks, most of them American, had pulled off the pavement, and ahead was a bottleneck of vehicles in the road. Beyond that she caught a glimpse of another expanse of water and mud. She pulled off of the road and parked her car in the sandy dirt.

After getting out and locking up her car, she walked alongside the road toward the washout to get a better look at the situation. When she got closer, she was struck by the immense size of the washout, but then saw what the real problem was. A yellow van coming from the other direction, muddy water lapping over its California license plate, was sitting almost at right angles across the inundated road. Pulling behind it, a huge mobile home had become stuck at a precarious angle in soft mud alongside the pavement.

She guessed the driver had thought it better to go off the road to avoid the submerged stretch of pavement, not realizing his heavy trailer would quickly sink into the sandy mire. He apparently had tried to turn back onto the pavement again, but his sinking trailer had held him fast. Thus the road was virtually blocked until the van and its trailer could be moved.

Joey was wondering how long a delay was in store when she felt a hand at her back and heard a low voice say, "I told you we'd meet again."

"Oh, no," Joey sighed inwardly. She turned toward Mark briefly, saying, "So we have," then abruptly hastened back toward her car. She was conscious of quick, solid footsteps gaining on her.

"Where are you off to in such a hurry?" he was asking an instant later when he had caught up with her.

"Back to my car."

"Planning on going somewhere?"

At once she realized how silly she looked. The only place she could go was back where she came from. She slowed her pace, trying to cover her frustration at her inability to deal with Mark in any sort of poised manner. "Do you suppose it will be a long delay?" she asked in an even voice.

"I expect it will," he replied. "It looks to me like they'll have to bring in special equipment to pull that heavy trailer out of the mud. No telling how long that'll take."

Joey was dismayed. "I wanted to make it to Guerrero Negro by tonight," she said in a worried tone.

"Don't count on it." They walked on in silence for a few paces. "Since we'll be stuck here for a while, why don't we go back to my van? We could play cards—have some sandwiches."

To be alone with Mark Chavira in a van was about the last thing Joey would choose to do. "No, thanks," she said sharply.

By this time they had reached her car. As she unlocked her door, he said, "You'd rather sit here by yourself?"

"Yes," she replied in a challenging undertone.

His dark eyes turned cool as he regarded her intently. "You still don't like me, do you?"

"No, Mr. Chavira, I don't. And I wish you would do as I asked earlier and leave me alone!"

She saw his jaw muscles tighten. "All right, Joey. Any way you want it. I wish you luck," he replied in a softly controlled voice.

She got into her car and firmly shut the door. "He doesn't take rejection very well," she gloated waspishly. But her attempted laugh caught in her throat as through the car window she watched him walk away from her, a tall paragon of masculinity, pride showing in each long, firm stride. Should a sudden earthquake shake the ground beneath him, she knew it would never jar his calm assurance.

She sensed an odd, unfamiliar feeling within, pulling her spirits down as she watched him stop to chat with a young couple standing next to the car just behind his parked van. She found herself wondering what he was saying, noting how easily he made conversation with strangers, for already the three were laughing together. She bowed her head, her eyes settling on her slender fingers idly resting on the bottom of the steering wheel. Maybe she should apologize. . . .

Sharp knocking on her side window brought her to attention. She turned to her left and saw two faces peering in at her. As she lowered the window halfway, she took the opportunity to study them more carefully.

They appeared to be young men in their twenties, unshaven, and dressed in old blue jeans and jackets. After her window was open, she detected the faint smell of liquor.

"Hey, you travelin' alone?" one of them asked, his hand wrapped around a paper cup, whose contents looked about to spill.

Joey sensed it was best not to answer that question. "Was there something you wanted?" she asked in a short tone of voice.

The young American seemed to find her answer amusing and slithered a glance to his companion. Returning his eyes to her, he said, "My friend and I have some Margarita mix and lots of good tequila. We thought maybe you'd like to join us. Our pick-up truck is just across the road . . ." He moved aside a bit to clear her view.

"No, thanks."

"Oh, come on! You'll get bored sittin' here all by yourself. Why not join us? Have some fun."

"I said no, thanks!"

"Look, you don't have to get snooty about it. My friend and I saw you sittin' here lookin' kinda lonely. We figured we'd be neighborly and invite you over. You're a foxy lookin' lady. Why don't you try bein' a little more sociable?" Suddenly he had opened her car door. "Hey, the rest of you is even better," he said, a glint forming in his eye. "Come on!" He reached in to grab her arm. "Just one friendly drink, huh?"

Joey quickly reached for her bag and pushed herself past them out of the car. She began walking in fast, determined paces up the road.

"Hey, where're you goin'?" he said as the two fell in step behind her.

Joey kept walking, her eyes on Mark, whose back was to her while he continued to talk with the young couple. As she moved toward him, he drew away from them and began to walk toward his van. She quickened her pace.

"Mark," she called just as he was about to open the door to the driver's side.

He turned, a warm smile brightening his face when he saw her coming to him. The smile faded as he noted her agitated expression. "What's wrong?" He raised his eyes to the two men following and instantly knew. His eyes became like brown flint and his mouth a grim line as he stared at them. The hardness of his expression frightened her a bit, though the hands which had reached to grasp her arms remained gentle.

"Look, man, we thought she was alone," she heard the one who had done all the talking explain. Mark pulled her toward him and continued to stare at them over the top of her head. "Hey, no harm done, huh? We'll uh . . . be on our way." Footsteps in the sandy dirt behind her indicated they were walking off toward their truck.

Joey breathed a bit easier while Mark let go of her. As he leaned up against his van and folded his arms over his chest, she became aware that his stern regard was now directed toward her. Not daring to look up, she whispered, "Go ahead and say it."

"All right. You didn't want my company, but you came running to me the minute you were in trouble. When I saw you coming, I thought perhaps you wanted to . . . be friends."

"Apologize," she corrected. "I should have come to apologize. I was thinking about it when those men came over."

"Thinking about it?" he said with a smile. "And would you have come if they hadn't bothered you?"

Joey hesitated. "I don't know," she answered sheepishly.

He softly chuckled. "Well, at least you're honest. I'm glad you came to me, whatever the reason, Joey." He reached out a hand and took her by the elbow. "How about a sandwich? No strings attached," he offered, a gleam of amusement in his eye.

"Thanks," she replied, smiling.

Mark led Joey around the van to the side facing away from the road and pulled open the large sliding door at the center of the long vehicle. Two steps up and she was standing on soft, plush, dark blue carpeting. Opposite the sliding door were dark wood cabinets and a tiny stainless steel sink with a pump faucet. Across the back of the van was a long upholstered seat which she guessed could double as a bed. In front of the small couch was a tiny table, and there were curtained windows above and to either side of it. The high dome top enabled them to stand erect inside without worry of hitting their heads.

"This is very nice," she said, sincerely admiring the spotless, compact vehicle.

"Thank you!" he replied with enthusiasm. "That's the first compliment you've ever given me. Would you like to sit in back or up front?"

"Oh, the front I think," she replied, eyeing the comfortable-looking high-back passenger seat. "That way we can keep track of any progress they make on the stuck trailer."

"So far they haven't gotten anywhere. They can't seem to disengage the trailer from the van, probably because the trailer's tilted at such an angle. It may have bent something out of shape," he explained. "Would you like a beer?"

"That sounds good," she said as she moved toward the brown leather passenger seat. "Oh, it swivels!" she said brightly, sitting down and proceeding to turn herself about, much as any five-year-old would.

"Are you sure you're old enough to have this?" he said, extending to her a filled plastic glass and half-full bottle of beer.

"Yes," she replied, a little embarrassed at her own lapse of decorum. "Oh, I couldn't drink all that. I'll just take the glass."

He smiled and sat down in the driver's seat next to her, holding the rejected bottle of beer. "You know, when you let go of your tough act, you can be really charming. Not that you aren't charming the other way, too. . . ." His voice dropped off while his eyes became fixed upon her in a gentle, trance-like gaze.

She was helpless to do anything but return his look. Catching himself, he straightened and asked, "What kind of sandwich would you like?"

"Anything would be fine," she said, her voice revealing the sudden jittery feeling which threatened to overcome her.

He got up and slipped off his jacket, then opened a long cabinet to hang it up. Light from a full-length mirror set in the narrow door flashed into her eyes as he closed it again. Bending his long legs, he half kneeled to the floor and opened another, smaller door next to the closet. From this he withdrew sandwich meats, cheese, and a jar of mayonnaise. Reaching into the cabinet above it, he grabbed a loaf of bread and a knife. He brought all these to the small table at the back. Joey rose to follow him, hoping to be of some assistance. In a few minutes they had made two well-stacked sandwiches, and after putting the remaining food back into the icebox, took their seats at the front again.

Light pouring through the window was beginning to make Joey feel warm, so she also took off her jacket and, declining his offer to hang it up, threw it on the carpeted floor near her chair. They ate in silence for a while, enjoying the sun's warmth and keeping an eye on the trailer and van that were still as they were half an hour ago.

Soon she drew her eyes away from the situation outside and discovered Mark was staring at her. "What's wrong?" she asked.

"I was just thinking that for all your bold self-assurance, you seem to have trouble handling men."

Embarrassed she replied, "I don't usually have any trouble."

"I think I know what the problem is. As far as I've been able to discover, your only encounters with men are in city office buildings where a certain amount of self-restraint and decorum have to be maintained. Here in the desert, men can behave more as they'd wish."

"I guess that tends to prove your theory that a woman can't take care of herself out here without a man around to protect her," she remarked with mild acidity.

"Well, it doesn't disprove it."

"I just wish men would leave me alone," she said sourly.

"Oh, come now. You don't mean that for a minute," he said with a laugh.

"Of course I do!"

"If you didn't want to attract men, you wouldn't keep your appearance so sleek and beautiful. You'd cut off all that lovely blond hair and wear dowdy clothes."

"I work in offices—I have to keep up my appearance," she countered.

"Perhaps, but you're not obligated to look like a knockout fashion model."

"What are you trying to say?" she asked. "That I really *want* to have men chasing me?"

"I would say the evidence points to that."

"Well, I'm afraid you're wrong. I'm perfectly happy on my own. I don't need male attention to feed my ego."

"Don't you need companionship . . . love?" he asked, his voice oddly soft and low.

She looked down at her half-consumed sandwich. "That's just a lot of romantic nonsense. Men don't really care for women that way. Women would just like to think that they do. Some of us eventually wise up," she said bitterly.

"How do you know what men feel? You aren't a man," he said in a restrained voice, as though controlling his temper. She looked up and saw the firm challenge in his dark eyes and steady gaze.

"I know how I've been treated by men," she quietly retorted.

His eyes softened. He leaned back in the seat, silent for a moment, then said, "Tell me about your old college beau. What was he like?"

"Why do you want to know about him?" she asked rather sharply, again wondering why Mark was always so eager to dig into her past.

"Just curious. Was he a football player or something?"

She had to chuckle, remembering Robin Bloomfield's tall, but very slender physique. "No, he would have been too skinny to make the team. He wasn't much interested in sports anyway. He was studying drama."

"How did you meet him?"

"At a party. He had a bright, witty personality and nice manners. He was always the center of attention at gatherings."

"And good looking, too, I suppose."

"Yes . . ." she said quietly, her mind conjuring up the image of Robin's sandy hair and blue eyes, his light coloring and adorably handsome features. ". . . yes, he was nice looking. Kind of cute and funny."

"The type of young man you thought you could trust . . . feel safe with?"

"Yes, I suppose so," she hesitated, not sure what he was getting at.

"And with all his charm and good manners, you never suspected he wasn't being true to you."

It seemed Mark had guessed the whole story. "No, I didn't," she replied slowly. "Some . . . some of my friends warned me that he was, well . . . a flirt, but I couldn't believe it," she confessed, not knowing why she should tell Mark any of this.

"Why not?" he asked in the kindest of voices.

Her lower lip trembled slightly. "Because when he was with me, he'd always . . . stop . . . when I asked him to." She made a fluttery smile. "You see, my parents raised me rather strictly, and in those days I was always careful not to go too far with a man." Joey didn't say that things really hadn't changed at all from those days, in fact she had purposely added the phrase to make herself appear more sophisticated. She glanced up at Mark, but his dark eyes and face were impassive as he quietly listened. "Anyway," she continued in a firmer voice, "since he was always a gentleman with me, I just couldn't believe he was the kind who would try to take advantage of women."

Mark smiled, as if to himself. "It never occurred to you that he might be getting his needs met elsewhere, with easier targets?"

"No," she said with chagrin.

"Were you that much in love with him?" he asked, a touch of disbelief in his tone, as if to say, You couldn't have been.

How could she answer? She couldn't begin, nor would she want to try to convey the reverent attachment she had formed for Robin. To her he had seemed the most appealing, the most wonderful person she had ever met, and she was astounded when such an engaging and popular young man had actually shown interest in her. She had been so proud to think of him as hers during the months they had dated. "I loved him," she simply stated.

"Had you thought of marrying him?"

"I had begun to hope he would ask me when . . ." she left off, feeling it was unnecessary to complete the sentence.

"When . . ." he repeated, urging her to finish.

Annoyed, she quickly rejoined, "When I came back to campus early after visiting my parents and found him in my room, in the midst of seducing my roommate. It was obvious he had almost completed his mission when I unceremoniously walked in on them." Her tone was growing sarcastic. "My foolish roommate cried and cried, while Robin made laborious explanations and apologies. Fortunately, I had the wisdom not to believe any of it."

"And since then you've never trusted any man."

"I don't see why I should," she said defensively.

"You find it safer to keep men at arms' length rather than chance falling under another romantic spell."

"Who are you, Dr. Freud?" she shot at him. "What do you care what I think about men? Why do you keep asking all these questions?" she demanded.

His dark countenance, unmoved by her outburst, continued to be impassive, except for the deep intensity with which his large eyes probed hers. "Because I find you absolutely fascinating, Joey. I have to find out what makes you the way you are." He paused, and as she said nothing, he added, "There's one more question I—"

"I don't want to hear it!" she interrupted, turning her head away.

"You told me you felt safe with this fellow—that's why you liked him," he continued. "Tell me, do you feel safe with me?" His penetrating gaze remained steady and expectant.

"I . . . I don't know what you mean," she responded, very much disturbed.

"I think you do; that's why you don't want to answer," he said calmly. "You're afraid of me, aren't you? In fact, you're actually afraid of most men . . ."

Joey rose from her seat, but she felt herself being grabbed around the waist before she could reach the door. "Let me go!" she said, wrestling against his strong arms.

"Joey, please, don't go." Mark turned her around to face him, his hands firmly clasped over her shoulders. She covered her face with both palms, hiding a fit of emotion. "It's all right," he said softly. "Don't be embarrassed about anything we've said or about what you feel. Everyone has fears." Joey didn't know what to think or feel. Meanwhile Mark's low voice continued to gently assault her sensibilities. "I just thought if we brought your feelings into the open, we could deal with them, and then perhaps you would find that you . . . could like me after all. Do you understand what I mean?"

"I don't understand anything about you," she replied, pushing out of his grasp and moving back to her seat. She sat stiffly hunched forward on the edge of the chair, her head bowed.

"I'm really not very complicated, Joey," he said, squatting in front of her. "I prefer to deal with people in a direct manner. I like you, but you don't have a very high regard for me. I just want to find out why and see if I can change your opinion."

She didn't want to look at him, but something inexorably drew her eyes to his. His voice had been calm, but his brown eyes were concerned and watchful. She had never studied him at such close range before. Her eyes moved over the smooth dark skin drawn taut over his firm jawline and high cheekbones and the straight black hair swept gently over his broad forehead. He seemed so alive and vital; she felt an unexpected desire to reach over and touch him.

The dark eyebrows drew together slightly while his eyes seemed to widen in wonder, responding to her inquisitive stare, as if he sensed that she was looking at him for the first time as a real person and had not found him unattractive.

She dropped her eyes to her lap for a moment. "I don't know why you should like me," she said shyly. "I've said some pretty nasty things to you."

He smiled with such genuine happiness, it surprised her and, curiously, made her uneasy. "That's okay," he told her. "I probably deserved it. I'll admit I sometimes deliberately provoked you just to see your reaction. But that's over with now. Now we can be more straightforward with one another, and I'm glad."

His eyes were shining with kindness and contentment, as though he had gained what he had been seeking from her. She felt strangely frightened.

He rose up, leaned forward, and peered out the front window. "Looks as though the situation outside is still the same. Would you like to play some cards?"

"Okay," she replied, glad for some distraction that would tend to hinder further conversation.

He took out a deck from one of the cabinets. "What games do you know how to play?"

"Just poker."

His shoulders shook with mild laughter. "Poker? Where did you learn that?"

"My father taught me."

"Oh, I see," he said, dealing cards onto the wooden drink holder which extended forward between the two seats. "Your father didn't have a son to teach, so he taught you instead."

Did he have to be right about everything? "I suppose so," she mumbled.

They had played several hands when their attention was drawn to the window. A sturdy truck with four-wheel drive was backing up toward the imbedded trailer. Meanwhile the van, which apparently had finally been detached from the trailer, was now moving under its own power out of the water and onto dry road. Their game slowed for the next hour or so as they watched men with shovels work about the trailer while the truck was being attached to it.

At last, after much difficulty, the truck moved slowly forward, pulling the huge trailer out of the mire. Cheering and applause broke out among the throng of delayed travelers waiting about.

"Looks like we can go now!" Joey said with delight. She was surprised that Mark seemed less than enthusiastic.

"Looks that way," he echoed quietly, pulling the cards together. "You play a good game of poker, Joey."

"Thanks," she said, laughing a bit. "It's been a while since I've played. Thanks for asking me over, Mark," she added a little nervously. "For helping me out with those two men also."

"Any time." He seemed uneasy and disappointed. Not knowing what to make of him, she reached down for her jacket and stood up to go. He rose and opened the door for her, stepping down onto the ground after her.

"Good-bye," she said, extending her hand.

His eyes grew warm and sad. "You don't have to be so quick to leave," he said softly, ignoring her outstretched hand and drawing her into his arms.

She was startled. "Mark, you said there were no strings attached when you invited me in."

"No, Joey, no strings. This is for free." He pulled her close, enveloping her in a long, slow kiss. For some reason, this time it did not occur to her to resist. His mouth clung persistently to hers and she was conscious of being pressed against him while his strong hands moved slowly over her back. She was lulled by the warm, secure feeling that permeated her entire being.

At last he took his mouth from hers, then tightened his embrace for a moment before gently releasing her. His eyes were lustrous and eager as he said, "Why don't you follow me, Joey? We're going in the same direction anyway. Why not travel together, caravan style?"

Quickly she pulled away from him. "No! No, I . . . I want to be on my own."

"But why?" he asked, clearly not understanding the wary fear he saw in her eyes.

"I don't know. I just want it that way," she said, backing away.

"Wait! Don't misunderstand," he said urgently, taking a step toward her. "I didn't mean it to be anything that . . . let's say, that your parents wouldn't approve of. I just meant that if we travel together, neither of us would be alone. It's safer that way."

"I understand, but . . . I don't want to. I'd rather be on my own, Mark. Good-bye."

She turned from him and walked quickly to her car without looking back. But imprinted in her mind were the dejected dark eyes she had sought to escape, without knowing why. All she understood was that she wanted to get out of there—away from him.

Quickly she started her car and pulled onto the road. She passed the blue van and fell into the small line of vehicles that had formed to drive slowly through the washout. After waiting anxiously for several minutes, it finally came her turn. Carefully she drove into the large pool covering the road, water spraying out from her wheels in all directions. It seemed it might become perilously deep, but she continued and soon reached the other side safely, relieved that the water and Mark Chavira were behind her.

She immediately picked up her speed and moved on. Soon she was passing cars traveling at a slower pace, wanting to put as much distance as she could between herself and the blue van. She could no longer see it in her mirror, but she pressed on nevertheless, all the while a question ringing through her mind: What does he want from me? What does he want?

4

The sun was gradually setting over the desert hills, a glowing red ball hanging amid ribbons of yellow and salmon-tinted clouds. It was growing dark and Joey was still almost eighty miles from Guerrero Negro. She had been unable to get gas all afternoon, as the service stations were invariably out of unleaded. She estimated she had little more than enough to make it to her destination and was grateful her small car made good mileage.

She had driven as fast as she dared, but constant potholes, several more small washouts, and difficulties passing slower vehicles safely on a narrow two-lane highway had slowed her progress dreadfully. Her only comfort was that she had not caught sight of the blue van since she had passed through the large washout hours ago.

Now her only goal was to make it to Guerrero Negro, which she must, as she had passed the last hotel over an hour ago, and according to her guidebook, there were none along the road to her destination. She did not mind, however, for the farther south she got, the closer she was to La Paz and the farther ahead, she hoped, of Mark Chavira. If only she had more gas in her tank, and it wasn't growing so dark. . . .

Her thoughts returned to Mark again, to rehash what she had been turning about in her mind all afternoon. Why was he so interested in her? Why had he looked at her that way? And why should his attentions worry her so? She felt as though he were drawing her to him and would hold her prisoner if she did not stay out of his reach. She meant to keep her freedom, and somehow she was sure he wanted to ensnare her—to clip her wings and tear her apart with questions and more questions until there was nothing left to hold her together.

She listened to her own thoughts and wondered if she was becoming paranoid. What had this man done to her? She had known him only two days and already she was becoming high-strung and skittish. If she could just manage to stay away from him, she would be all right.

It was completely dark now, and she brightened her headlights to better illuminate the dim road ahead. She was coming into a hilly section and as she rounded the curves of the meandering road, her lights played upon the spindly, oddly shaped cirio trees near the highway, creating an eerie appearance. She tried to maintain her speed in spite of the fact that potholes were difficult to spot in the dim light.

After slowing to maneuver some sharp curves, she saw the road straighten ahead and purposely picked up her speed. Steadily she gained velocity until all at once the car began to vibrate violently as it sped over some unforeseen potholes and she heard the sudden sharp bang of a blowout. For several terrible seconds she could not control the car. It skidded off the road, bouncing over the rough desert floor until it came to a jolting stop amid the sound of breaking glass and grinding metal.

She sat completely stunned for a moment, barely able to realize what had happened. It was the sudden thought that something might catch fire that propelled her to action. She opened the door, almost forgetting to unfasten her seat belt, and ran out and away from the vehicle.

For a long while she stood a safe distance away in the cold night air, studying the sight before her. One headlight was smashed, but the other still functioned, and by its light she could see that her car had run into a low, flat, outcropping rock, one edge of which jutted out of the ground high enough to do great damage to the front of her car. In addition to the headlight, the front bumper and grill appeared to be mangled, and the hood was buckled from the impact.

Much later, she slowly moved back toward the car, assuming it must be safe to do so by then. The only sound she could hear was her shoes scraping through the sandy soil, while all about her was total darkness, except for the low light of her remaining headlight starkly illuminating the desert in a ghostly manner. The sense of her aloneness in the middle of a barren landscape was beginning to make a devastating impact.

"Mark was right," she whispered fearfully into the chill air, painfully recalling all his warnings about traveling alone and driving at night. In spite of the fact that she had been trying to avoid him, at this moment she wished he were here. He would know what to do.

"You got yourself into this, you'll have to handle it alone," she said aloud, trying to conjure up her self-reliance. It occurred to her that the Green Angels would certainly be of assistance, but they only patrolled the road during the day. She would have to spend the entire night alone, and perhaps a good part of the next day also, before one came along. She shivered at the thought, realizing she hadn't eaten since noon and had no blankets. She would just have to make do with her cans of tuna and crackers and put on all the warm clothing she had brought. Yes, she could manage, she assured herself. But to be so isolated . . .

She heard a motor in the distance and soon saw a pair of headlights moving up the highway toward her. She started up with the hope of finding help, but then became wary, thinking it might be men like those she had met earlier that day who could try to take advantage of her in her predicament.

The vehicle slowed to a stop. She could just barely make out its form behind the brightly glowing headlights. She stood like a statue as she heard a door slam. Suddenly a strong beam of light reached her eyes and she was momentarily blinded.

"Joey! Are you all right?"

"Mark!" she cried, recognizing his voice immediately. She moved toward him and quickly found herself caught up in his arms.

It seemed he would squeeze the life out of her while his angry voice assailed her ears. "What the hell is the matter with you? I told you not to drive at night! Do you have to be so damned independent you won't even listen to common sense?"

"I know, Mark. You were right," she whispered against his leather jacket as she clung to his tall frame. "I just wanted to get away . . . to get to Guerrero Negro."

"Get away from me is what you meant to say. You little fool! You could have been killed!" He took a moment to control himself, then in a softer tone asked, "Were you hurt at all?"

"No, I don't think so," she replied in a broken voice, wiping away tears she could not hold back. "J-just my car . . ."

"So I noticed." Keeping an arm around her, he gently pulled her along as he strode toward the damaged automobile. He shone his strong flashlight over the smashed front end. "You really slammed into this rock, didn't you," he commented dryly as he surveyed the damage, holding the light at various angles to get the full picture. "Well, it may not be that bad after all," he added, rather to himself.

"You mean I may be able to drive it?" she asked, full of hope.

"No, I just mean I don't think you've totalled it," he replied sardonically. "I suspect your radiator's split open. You'll have to have it towed out of here. My God, what did you do to that tire?" He directed the flashlight toward the mangled rubber tube beneath the front end.

"I think I hit a deep pothole—it was hard to see in the dark—and the tire burst. I lost control and went off the road." Trying to keep herself from succumbing to emotion again, she put her hands over her face.

Mark drew Joey to him in a comforting embrace. "Don't worry, I'll take care of you," he quietly reassured her. "I don't mind."

Another emotion now beginning to take over, she tried to push away from him. "I'm okay," she sniffed.

"You've had a shock, Joey. It's better if you go ahead and cry," he told her, keeping her close.

"No, I'm all right now," she insisted in a firm voice, as she pulled out of his embrace to stand on her own.

He allowed his arms to fall back to his sides. "You don't have to prove to me you can take it like a man!" An impatient sigh escaped him. Looking toward her car, he said in a resigned manner, "We'd better turn off the lights and transfer your luggage to my van."

"You'll take me to Guerrero Negro to find a mechanic?"

"Sure—tomorrow."

"You're right, a mechanic wouldn't come out to tow it at this time of night," she reasoned. "Well, at least we can drive in and stay at the hotel there."

Mark shook his head. "I'm not driving anymore tonight, Joey. We'll spend the night here in my van," he said in a tone that forbad contradiction.

"W-what do you mean?"

"After this you should know how dangerous it is to drive at night. I'm not going any farther until morning."

"Then why did you drive this far?" she argued, panic settling in.

"Because I didn't see your car parked anywhere along the way and I was afraid you'd try something like this. I decided I'd better keep going—against my good judgment—to make sure nothing had happened to you."

"I didn't ask you to look after me!"

"Someone ought to. You haven't done a very good job of taking care of yourself."

Humiliation increased her anger. "Why should you bother to trouble yourself about my welfare?"

He stared down at her, but his features were barely discernible in the darkness. "I don't know. It certainly isn't for the thanks I get!" He went to her car, turned off the headlight and removed her keys from the steering wheel shaft, then closed and locked the door and went around to the back.

Joey watched him quietly, her mind in too much confusion for her to be of any assistance. As always, he had evoked a myriad of feelings which left her unable to act with anything resembling purpose and reason. For the moment, regret won out over the contending emotions of anger, humiliation, and fear. "Mark, I'm sorry," she found herself saying with heartfelt sincerity. "I didn't mean to be ungrateful. I . . . I'm glad you're here."

He said nothing as he lifted her suitcase and tote bag out of the rear compartment of her hatchback, setting them on the ground before locking the car.

"Can I help with those?" she asked in a small voice.

"Here, you can hold the flashlight." He handed it to her, and as he carried her bags to the van she walked beside him, somehow feeling like a small child who was being allowed to help Daddy.

They had reached the van and he was depositing her luggage inside when an idea occurred to her. "Mark, I could sleep in my car," she suggested. "It would give you more room in here."

He sank down onto the back seat, near which he had placed her luggage, and casually laid one arm over the small table. "I don't need any more room," he said patiently. "You'll be more comfortable and safer in here with me." Her wary expression caused him to add, "I promise you, Joey, you *will* be safe. I'm not in the mood for molesting captive women tonight."

"I didn't mean that," she hurried to say, wondering why he had chosen to use the word captive. "I'm not afraid," she asserted in a thin voice.

"No? Then you can't have any reasonable objection to sleeping in here. There won't be any tongues wagging since there's no one to see us."

Defeated by logic, Joey made no response. He got up and took a few steps to the side door, moving past her in the close quarters. She flinched as she felt his jacket brush against her breast and took a step back, bumping into the wall of the van. His hand on the door handle, he turned and looked at her. "You're not afraid of me?"

She swallowed and cast her eyes to the floor.

After sliding the door shut, he moved back to her and placed a gentle hand on her upper arm. "I would never harm you, Joey. Try to believe that." He reached down for her hand. "Come and sit in front with me. I want to find a good place to pull off the road."

She did as he asked. He drove a short distance to a pull-off and parked, then turned off the headlights and switched on the van's interior lights.

"Have you eaten anything since lunch?"

She shook her head.

"I've got some canned beef stew. How about that?"

"That would be fine, thank you," she replied, wishing her voice didn't sound like that of a well-brought-up little girl. Apparently he thought so too, for she noticed his smile as he rose from the driver's seat.

He went to a lower cabinet and withdrew what looked like a metal carrying case. He slid the door open again and took the case outside, where she watched with interest as he converted it into a tiny, two-burner stove. Following his directions, she brought out a saucepan, a tea kettle with water from the small sink, and a large can of stew.

Before long they were eating a hot meal and drinking steaming instant coffee from paper plates and cups. Afterward, she cleaned up while he repacked the portable stove.

When everything was once again in order, he closed the sliding side door and locked it. Immediately panic seized Joey's heart. She had never before been so totally alone with a man, and now she was locked in—cut off from any means of escape. She watched mutely as he took down a pillow and bedding from the upper shelf of the long closet, her heart steadily pounding in anxiety.

"I think you'll find this back seat makes a pretty comfortable bed," he told her, setting down the bedding and pulling out the small table from the hole in the floor which held its metal stem. He took the table apart and set it out of the way, then removed the seat's back pads, widening it. In a few moments he had converted it into a small, cozy-looking little bed, complete with sheets, blanket, and a pillow.

"There you are," he said, stepping back. "I guess you'll want to change into your nightgown."

"Oh, no, I can sleep in my clothes," she immediately assured him.

"Suit yourself, but I'm changing out of these," he said, indicating his own attire.

Joey's eyes widened in horror.

Mark broke into a quiet laugh, apparently unable to subdue his keen amusement over the situation. "Keep calm, Joey. I'll show you how we can manage it with the utmost propriety."

He stepped toward the driver's seat and loosened a long, heavy curtain which had been pulled together and fastened against the wall near the seat. It was held to the roof by runners, and when he pulled it across the width of the van, it completely separated the two front seats from the rest of the vehicle. "I should have enough room to change out in front and you can have the rest to yourself. How's that?"

"I guess that's okay. Wh-where will you sleep?" Her mind had already moved on to an even more formidable problem.

He smiled. "I'll put my sleeping bag down on the floor. That's how I always sleep in here. The carpeting is heavily padded and it's comfortable enough. Anything else troubling you?" The smile continued to hover at the corners of his mouth.

"No," she answered in a nettled tone, vexed that he should find it all so amusing.

"Okay. Let me get my pajamas," he said as he reached into the closet, "and then I'll leave you to yourself. Tell me when you're finished changing."

He disappeared behind the drape. Joey waited a few cautious moments, then, keeping a watchful eye on the curtain, she opened her suitcase and pulled out her long white nightgown. She changed as quickly as she could and was careful to put all her articles of clothing back into the suitcase, then closed the lid.

Joey pulled aside the covers and slid down into the surprisingly comfortable little bed, then pulled the blanket back over her. "I'm finished now," she called out rather weakly, her hands unconsciously clinging to the blanket pulled high up under her chin.

She watched as the drape was pulled aside, then promptly stopped breathing. Mark appeared wearing only brown pajama pants, his broad muscular chest completely bare. He stopped when he saw Joey's gaping expression. "I lost the top to these long ago," he explained with a nuance of embarrassment at her stare. "In fact, I usually don't wear . . . well, never mind. I didn't mean to startle you."

While she recovered, her eyes fixed on the ceiling, he brought out and unrolled a long sleeping bag down the length of the carpeted floor. After finishing that task, he took a few steps toward her. "Are you comfortable there?" he asked, looking over the small feminine form shrinking beneath the blanket.

"I'm fine," she was quick to respond, hoping he did not intend to come any closer.

A bemused grin crossed his face. "Is there anything I can get you? A glass of water? A teddy bear?"

"No."

"I'll put out the lights, then. Good night, Joey."

"'Night."

The lights went out and it was completely dark. Joey could hear Mark sliding into his sleeping bag and zipping himself in. After a short while, his gentle, rhythmic breathing told her he was asleep. Only then did she begin to relax and allow her mind to drift over the day's events.

Since early that morning she had used all her ingenuity and energy to try to elude Mark Chavira. Now here she was, locked in his van and lying only a few feet away from him, stranded somewhere in the middle of a desert, her wrecked car a few hundred yards away.

Strange that under the circumstances she should be experiencing the sense of secure serenity that now was stealing over her as she lay quietly in the dark stillness of the night.

5

"It's morning, Joey." A gentle rocking motion on her shoulder accompanied the words. Pulling herself out of a sound sleep, she opened her eyes and met smiling brown ones looking down at her.

"What time is it?" she asked, sounding very groggy.

"Six thirty. We'd better get an early start. It's a ways to Guerrero Negro and we'll have to lead the mechanic back here again to tow your car."

"Yes, you're right," she said, sitting up. She noticed his brown pullover sweater and darker brown pants. "Oh, you're already dressed," she said, feeling as though she were holding up progress.

"That's okay. I'll go out and start up the stove while you change in here. How about eggs, toast, and coffee for breakfast?"

"Sounds wonderful!" She noticed he was looking at her quizzically. "What's the matter?"

"That nightgown. Did you get it out of a museum?" he asked, eyes twinkling in amusement.

She pulled the blanket up to cover herself, replying hotly, "I bought it at an expensive shop in L.A."

Breaking into a full smile, he kissed her burning cheek and ruffled her hair. In the next minute he was gone, closing the door of the van behind him.

She remained where she was for a moment, head bowed and still blushing.

But a smile soon crept over her face and her eyes were warm and bright as she pushed the covers aside.

They left after breakfast and the entire morning was spent making arrangements for her car. Upon arriving in the city of Guerrero Negro, they found a mechanic with a tow truck and hours were spent driving back to the desolate spot where they had camped to pick up her car and tow it back.

Once back in the city, the mechanic explained to Mark in Spanish that the car would need several parts replaced, including the radiator, adding that it would take a week or two for some of the parts to be obtained.

"That long?" Joey gasped, when Mark had translated for her. "I'll never make it to La Paz, then," she said, deeply distressed.

"There may be some bus you could take . . ." Mark pointed out.

"Yes, I suppose so," she commented without enthusiasm.

". . . or you could ride with me. I'll be passing through La Paz on my way to Cabo San Lucas."

Her face brightened, then grew cautious. "I hate to impose on you any more than I have," she said slowly.

"It's no imposition; you won't be taking me out of my way."

Joey absently stared at the ground while pondering the situation. The thought of taking a bus to La Paz was not appealing, as she assumed she would be the only American on it and her Spanish was limited. She could stay at a hotel in Guerrero Negro and try to notify her parents to come and pick her up, but that would interfere with her father's beloved fishing schedule and would certainly spoil his vacation. Besides that, she hated to feel dependent on her parents for help. The remaining alternative—going with Mark—seemed the best.

Even so, nagging doubts lingered, making her hesitant to accept his offer. Though she had to admit that she was beginning to like him, and he had certainly been more than kind to her, there was yet something lurking beneath the surface of her emotions that made her uneasy, something that warned her to beware.

Still, she reasoned, if they left now, they would arrive in La Paz the next day, requiring them to be together only one more night. And, after all, hadn't he been quite the gentleman last night? Yes, under the circumstances, she decided, his offer was the best solution.

"All right, I'll go with you, Mark—and thanks," she told him.

"I'm glad," he replied, taking her arm to lead her to the van. "We'll leave your car here then, and you'll have to pick it up on the way back. With luck, it'll be ready and waiting for you. Before we leave, did you want to try to phone your parents? Finding a telephone may not be easy and I'm not sure how the connections would be, but we can try. They may be worried about you."

"Oh, I don't think so. I'm sure they've assumed by now that I didn't leave home until Christmas day. I'm always leaving at the last minute because of my job. They've probably heard about the roads, too, and will expect me to be delayed by the washouts. Luckily they came through ahead of the bad weather."

"Don't you think they'd be concerned?"

"I suppose my mother may be a little worried, but my father's probably too busy enjoying his fishing to think much about it." She chuckled as a new thought entered her head. "Besides, if I call them, no doubt they'd ask how my car is holding up and then I'd have to tell them what happened. After that I'd have to explain how I've accepted a ride in a van with a strange man I've met on the road. I think they'd be more worried *after* the phone call!''

She was surprised that Mark seemed disturbed by her lighthearted remarks. ''Yes, they probably would be,'' he replied in a serious tone. After taking a long breath, he shrugged his shoulders. ''I guess there's nothing we can do about that now. We'd better get on our way,'' he said, taking her by the hand. ''Let's stop at a restaurant for lunch first.''

They went to a small restaurant where Joey bravely ordered the Mexican combination plate that Mark recommended. As they ate the spicy but delicious food, Mark was estimating how far they could travel that day.

''I think we can easily make it to Mulegé, barring any unforeseen problems. The roads are in better shape farther south—not so many potholes. There are several nice beaches just south of Mulegé on Bahia Concepción. They have some camping facilities, though most are fairly rustic. I usually stay there a day or two and fish. In fact, maybe we can catch supper. Do you like to fish?''

''No, not much. I'm a great disappointment to my father in that respect. I take after my mother and get seasick easily, so he goes on his fishing excursions by himself. He tried to interest me in casting from a pier, but I always thought it was kind of boring. Besides, I didn't like having to watch the poor fish flopping around, dying a slow death.''

''Yes, it's a little cruel, I suppose,'' Mark agreed with a smile. ''There's nothing like fresh fish for dinner though.''

''Well, that's true,'' Joey had to admit.

They were silent for a while, concentrating on finishing their meal, but Mark soon broke the conversational lull. ''So . . .'' he said, as if thinking aloud, ''seems like your father hoped you could take the place of the son he had wanted. Does he discount you now because you're 'only a woman'?''

''No, not exactly,'' Joey responded with a perky smile. ''He always brags that I've done all right—for a girl.''

Mark chuckled along with her. ''I'm glad to see you can laugh about it.''

''My father has his shortcomings, but I have to admit that he taught me to stand on my own two feet. He made me ambitious to form a career for myself and sent me to the best college he could afford. It was because he wanted to be proud of my accomplishments as he would a son's, and I'm grateful for that. Some fathers would raise a daughter to have lower expectations for herself.''

''That's true, but it's a shame he doesn't appreciate your feminine qualities more.''

The reference to her femininity made Joey self-conscious and she was glad their waiter chose that moment to bring the check. ''Mark, you'll have to let me pay for this,'' she said, placing a finger on the slip of paper. ''You've done so much for me lately.''

He slowly grinned. ''All right, but I assure you it's been a pleasure to come to your rescue.''

In a while they were back on the road, continuing south on Highway 1, which now cut a virtually straight swath over flat, featureless desert. A few cattle could occasionally be seen amid the cactus and low shrubbery, but these were the only diversions in the landscape. The sun shone brightly through a clear sky, however, and Joey was in good spirits as she kept up a conversation with Mark.

"So, Joey, how do you feel about marriage?" The question came as a jolt after their rather academic discussion of the area's plant life.

"W-what do you mean?" she stuttered. For an instant, his words had sounded almost like a proposal.

"Well, do you want to get married eventually, or with your low opinion of men, have you vowed to remain single?"

She relaxed a bit, realizing it was just another of his probes into her psyche. "I haven't made any vow, but I imagine I'll probably stay single. I'm involved with my career, I have my own identity. It would be an intrusion to have to adjust to someone else's habits, to have to worry about pleasing a husband all the time."

"Afraid of being turned into a barefoot and pregnant housewife?"

She considered the question. "Yes, you might say that. That's what happened to my mother. She had intended to study nursing, but then she met my father and that was the end of that. She's spent the last twenty-five years cooking, cleaning, raising me, and agreeing with everything my father says. And all her years of work have gone largely unappreciated—at least by my father."

"I imagine there are many housewives who get little compensation for all the work they do, but you shouldn't assume that *all* men are like your father. How do you know you won't meet a man who doesn't mind your having a career? Someone who might encourage you and take pride in your work? Perhaps even be willing to share the housework or agreeable to the idea of hiring a cook and a maid? Are you sure such a man can't exist?"

"Do you personally know any man like that?" she queried rather smugly, giving him a steady glance.

He cautiously drummed a thumb on the steering wheel, eyes fixed on the road. "I believe I do," he said guardedly.

Something in his manner of response disturbed her. "Well, even if such a man does exist, I'm happily independent, thank you," she asserted, turning her face toward the window again.

"I understand the value of independence, Joey, but can't you be self-fulfilled and still accept the notion that a close physical and emotional relationship with someone of the opposite sex is one of life's greatest pleasures?"

Joey shifted uneasily in her seat. "If it's so great, how come you're not married?"

He was quiet for a moment and then softly answered, "Sometimes it takes a while to meet the right person."

"But . . . you mean you would really *like* to be married?"

"Sure." His self-conscious dark eyes momentarily rested upon her before he turned them back to the road.

Joey was suddenly at a loss. What was going on here? Why were they discussing marriage of all things? The feeling of panic, which was lately becoming too familiar, crept over her. Why had he brought up the subject?

Nervously she looked out her side window trying to keep herself from fidgeting. After a moment she cautiously snuck a glance at Mark. He was silent and strangely withdrawn, eyes blankly focused on the road.

She kept quiet for a few more minutes, until the leaden silence got to be unbearable. "Do you travel in Baja California a lot?" she ventured, breaking into the strained atmosphere.

Abruptly his eyes shot to hers. "Have we changed the subject?" he asked severely. After a moment he answered in a more subdued manner, "Yes, I come down here two or three times a year."

"Why is that?" she asked as brightly as she could, hoping to hide her jarred nerves.

"I have relatives on my mother's side in Cabo San Lucas. They run a restaurant there in which I've invested, so I like to go down to visit them and see how they're coming along. They've been working on a new addition for the past year or so."

"Your expertise must be of great help to them."

"Well, they do have a lot of questions for me every time I go down there," he admitted.

"Was your mother born in Mexico?"

"Yes, but she's been an American citizen for many years. Her family came up to live in the United States for a while when she was in her teens. She married at eighteen and a short time later her parents and two younger brothers moved back. It's the two brothers, my uncles, and their sons who run the restaurant."

"Was your father from Mexico too?"

"His family was of Mexican origin, but had been in California for generations. Actually he was half Scandinavian—my grandfather married a Norwegian."

"That must be why you're so tall," she said with a grin.

"Maybe," he replied, a smile at last stealing across his uncharacteristically grim countenance.

The next several minutes passed in a more comfortable silence. Something in the distance caught Joey's eye. "Are those palm trees up ahead?"

"Date palms. We're coming to San Ignacio. It's a picturesque town—kind of an oasis in the desert—and it has an old eighteenth-century mission. Would you like to stop for a little while?"

She readily agreed and before long they were driving by a lush forest of green palms. Mark parked in the town square under a huge leafy tree with spreading branches. A magnificent old mission, built of stone, was located on one side of the square. An open market was on the other and surrounding the small park at the center were low buildings of varying design and upkeep.

Mark led Joey first toward the mission, explaining that it was founded in 1728 and took fifty years to build. Before entering, they stopped to admire the huge, beautifully carved, heavy wooden doors which led inside.

The interior was small, but ornate with gold leaf and statues. Signs tacked on a wall near the entrance indicated it was still an active church.

"It's lovely," she whispered.

"Isn't it?" he agreed. "Just the right size for a small wedding," he added, looking directly at her with a playful glint in his eye.

Joey met his gaze for a moment, then turned away and headed toward the door. He followed, and when they were outside again he teased, "I detect a distinct tendency on your part to bolt at any reference to the word marriage. Would you care to explore the reasons behind your reaction with me?"

"No!" she replied, annoyed at his sudden turn for amusement.

"Afraid even to discuss it?" he prodded.

"I thought we had already discussed marriage quite thoroughly."

"But we haven't discussed why you're afraid to discuss it," he clarified.

"What? Oh, you're not even making sense anymore," she complained, not bothering to hide her irritation. They had reached his van by this time.

"We aren't ready to go just yet," he said. "I wanted to pick up a few supplies at the store over here." He pointed to a small grocery on the corner.

They spent several minutes inside buying canned goods, fresh fruit, bread, and extra bottles of purified water. They returned to the van where she quietly stood next to him, helping him put the goods into the cabinets. When they were finished, he turned her about to face him and asked with an artfully winsome look in his eye, "Are you enjoying the trip, Joey?"

After a pause she replied, "Yes," unable to resist the sympathetic brown eyes that fairly begged for a positive response.

"I want you to be happy, you know. Don't let my teasing upset you."

His eyes and voice were softly hypnotic and she nodded in vague acquiescence. Slowly his lips moved down to hers and at their touch she found herself melting in his embrace. Only half aware of her reaction, she willingly returned his kiss, but soon found herself so warm and comfortable in his arms that it began to frighten her. Trembling slightly, she pushed away, but he gently pulled her back, holding her against him and tucking her head under his chin.

"Don't be afraid of it, Joey," he whispered into her hair. "Don't be afraid of your own heart."

They held fast to one another for several warm, long moments. At last he brought his hands to her shoulders, kissed the top of her head, and said quietly, "We'd better be going."

She sat down in the passenger seat while he slid behind the wheel. After starting the motor, he looked at her again, then put out a hand to caress her lightly flushed cheek. As if of one mind, they slowly leaned toward one another to enjoy another brief kiss, then reluctantly pulled apart and Mark drove off.

Joey sat quietly, her head resting against the seat's high back, not quite in touch with her own emotions but somehow blissfully content. She felt alive and happy, basking in the warmth coursing through her and not caring if it took forever to reach La Paz.

They were back on the arid desert now, winding through low hills. The van sped past a small sign.

"It's 135 kilometers to Mulegé," she quoted to Mark. "That's—let's see— 84 miles," she quickly figured in her head.

Mark looked at her, eyes widened in surprise.

"Did you come to a different figure?" she asked, puzzled.

"No," he said with a laugh, "I didn't arrive at any figure. I left my pocket calculator at home." He shot her a shrewd glance and added, "I always said it was wise to keep a good accountant on hand."

As she laughed, he stretched out his hand to grasp hers, gently entwining his fingers into her slender ones. His long brown fingers felt strong and secure and she was reluctant to let go when at last he had to pull his hand away to negotiate a turn.

After a few moments of silence Mark rekindled their previous topic of conversation. "We never finished our discussion on your aversion to talking about marriage."

"Do we have to?" Joey said lackadaisically, quelling the uneasiness the subject automatically aroused within her.

"I'd like to get to the bottom of it."

"You mean after all this time you've spent psychoanalyzing me, you're still trying to figure me out?" she said, hoping to sidetrack him.

"I don't think I could ever hope to figure you out completely. You're too womanly and mysterious for a mere male to ever know what goes on inside your head."

She softly snickered. "Never mind all the soft soap. I've been flattered enough by you men to know most of what you say isn't true."

"Now that's an interesting statement to make," he said, glancing at her briefly before turning his eyes back to the road. "Why don't you believe men when they flatter you? Don't you think you're attractive?"

His questions made her pause. "Well, yes . . . I . . . I know I'm attractive. Otherwise men wouldn't pay so much attention to me. But some of the things they say are just too overdone to be taken seriously. They're just trying to butter me up in hopes of getting somewhere. Take your words 'womanly and mysterious.' Now be honest. That description might apply to Greta Garbo, but not me."

"Why not? You don't think you're womanly?"

To her surprise the question made her uneasy. She didn't know how to respond. "I suppose in a way I am . . . but . . . I'm certainly no love goddess like Garbo or Marilyn Monroe."

"You don't think so? Then how do you explain all these problems you seem to have keeping men away? Only yesterday you said, after we had gotten rid of those two who were bothering you, that you wished men would leave you alone."

"How men behave is their problem, not mine," she snapped.

He chuckled softly. "I didn't mean you were to blame, but it seems to me obvious that men react to you in a positive and responsive way. Why do you think that is?"

"I don't know," she replied tersely, wishing he would get off the subject.

"Do you ever have occasion to look in a mirror, Joey?"

She sighed impatiently. "Of course."

"And what do you see in the mirror?"

She shrugged. "A girl of average height and weight with long hair."

"Only a girl?"

She drew her brows together. "What?"

"You're of age, Joey. Shouldn't you describe yourself as a woman?"

She let out another long sigh, wearying of his nitpicking. "All right. I'm a *woman* of average height with long hair."

"Average height and long hair. Is that the best you can say for yourself?"

Joey did not care to respond, for she was tired of the whole conversation.

"Would you like to know what I see when I look at you?"

"I suppose you'll tell me whether I want to know or not," she answered with sarcasm.

"I see a young woman with a slender, exquisitely shaped figure—the kind that any man could hardly pass by, beautiful hair, and a face Helen of Troy might have envied. And giving life to the image is a mysteriously complicated, unpredictable, and bewitchingly feminine personality. I mean every word of that, Joey, whether you believe it or not.''

Joey's head was bowed and she was looking at her hands in her lap. It embarrassed and upset her to hear such remarks. She suspected he was exaggerating to make her feel good, yet he seemed so sincere that what he said almost took her breath away. She felt his eyes upon her now, waiting for some response. Knowing it would do no good to contradict him, she decided it would be best to try to accept the compliment graciously. ''That's kind of you to say, Mark,'' she told him softly.

'''*Kind* of me','' he repeated, shaking his head in dismay. ''Tell me, Joey, did your father ever give you compliments when you were growing up?''

''Yes. Many times. He was proud of my high grades at school. And he used to brag to his friends that I was good in sports, and about the interest I took in my hobbies.''

''What were your hobbies?''

''Oh, I built my own crystal set, had a model railroad . . .''

''Sounds like you were a tomboy!'' Mark said with a smile.

''That's what my mother always said,'' Joey agreed, smiling now herself.

''Perhaps to please your father you unconsciously tried to be the son he wanted. You told me that one has to be a man to gain his true respect.'' He glanced at her to note her reaction.

She looked at him defensively. ''I don't think, as a child, I would have been aware of his attitudes. Besides, I really liked the pastimes I had then.''

''There's nothing wrong with a girl being interested in crystal sets and trains, but I'm wondering if *you* didn't tend to choose them because you got so much approval for pursuing them. Did your father ever tell you you were pretty?''

Joey wet her lips. ''No,'' she replied softly, her eyes falling back to her lap.

''That's a shame, because I imagine you must have been very pretty. It seems he never validated your femininity very much. Maybe that's why you're uneasy with the idea of being attractive to men. Of course, being two-timed by your former boyfriend wouldn't have helped your self-image, either,'' he said with some asperity. ''That guy must have been a fool.'' He glanced at her pensive profile. Cautiously he added, ''I hope your bad experiences in the past haven't ruined your image of men forever, Joey. There may be a few of us around who are worth having, you know.''

Joey caught his glance, moved in spite of herself by his earnest dark eyes. Self-consciously she turned away and looked out her side window. She could almost believe him, she thought, as she gazed out at the passing desert landscape. The beat of her heart began to quicken. If only she *could* believe him. It might be nice . . . to be in love again. . . .

Within a few hours, after driving southeast along Highway 1, they reached the shore of the Gulf of California, the body of water which separates mainland Mexico from the Baja California peninsula. They continued south along the coast to Mulegé, passing the tropical date palms lining the river near which the sleepy town was situated. After continuing south about a dozen more miles, they reached the beautiful shores of Bahia Concepción, a large bay off the Gulf of California.

Mark pulled off the paved highway onto a steep dirt road which led several hundred yards down to and along a sandy beach, complete with picturesque thatched roof shelters constructed for campers. The clear ocean water appeared green near shore and gray-blue farther out. Across the water, small islands could be seen as well as the hilly strip of land that created the bay.

There were a number of other motor homes and tents set up along the beach. Mark pulled up next to an unused thatched shelter. Looking out the window at the bay he asked, "Do you like shrimp?"

"Yes," she replied, puzzled at the question.

"Well, then, supper may be easy tonight. See that rusty little boat anchored offshore? It's a shrimp boat. Now all I have to do is find a way to get out there. Too bad I didn't bring my rowboat this trip."

They got out of the van into the warm sea air and Joey stood by somewhat mystified as Mark took a few steps toward the water's edge and looked both ways along the beach. She watched as he walked up to the people camped next to them, apparently a family of five including three sons of varying ages.

"Shrimp boat? No kidding!" she could hear the boys' father exclaim after Mark had spoken a few words. Within minutes the boys and their father were pulling a small rowboat into the water while Mark dashed back to the van and returned with a plastic container.

"Want to come with us?" he asked Joey as he was hurrying back toward the boat.

"Where are you going?"

"We're going to row out to the shrimp boat and buy some shrimp."

"Sure, come on along," the boys' father called to her. "We can squeeze you in."

The small boat already looked full with three boys, two of whom were almost full grown, and their father. She wondered how Mark would fit in, much less herself. "No, I get seasick," she replied, finding the best excuse she could.

Mark laughed and tweaked her nose before striding the few yards to the boat. She held her breath as the boat tipped precariously when he climbed in and took the scant space allotted him on the end seat.

Feeling rather abandoned, she watched the boat grow smaller and smaller as it gradually made its way over the gentle waves to the shrimp boat. When they reached it, she could barely make Mark out standing up in the boat to negotiate with the men on the rusting old craft. She prayed he wouldn't topple into the water.

After a few more minutes they were heading back toward shore. She breathed a sigh of relief, embarrassed at the silly tears forming in her eyes. "Joey," she whispered to herself with a rueful little smile, "I think you *are* falling in love again," admitting the feeling she had been trying hard to repress. "But it's a little scary . . ." her whispered words trailed off as she stared at the rowboat drawing nearer the shore.

"Hey, Mom, we got some shrimp!" the youngest boy shouted as they were maneuvering the boat onto the beach.

Mark called his thanks to the owners of the rowboat as he strode toward Joey. "Dinner, madame," he intoned, as he presented her with the container full of shrimp.

"They look good," she said brightly, trying not to notice the smell as she took the container. "Did you have to stand up in the boat like that?" she complained, her voice growing small and high-pitched.

He smiled broadly. "I saw your worried little face as we started rowing out," he said, tweaking her nose again. "I can swim, you know. Anyway, I had to pay the men for the shrimp. Standing up was the only way."

"Oh . . ."

He put an arm around her waist and pulled her to his side. "You know, Joey, I think you're beginning to like me. Hmmm?"

"Yeah . . ." she sheepishly admitted, softly drawing out the word.

"Yeah," he imitated before kissing her on the nose. "Let's get supper going," he said, moving her along at a faster pace toward the van. "Do you cook shrimp in any particular way?"

She regarded him with some alarm. "I don't know anything about cooking shrimp!"

His free hand rose to his hip. "Look, lady, I just put the groceries on the table. Cooking is woman's work," he deadpanned.

"Huh?"

He laughed as he drew her nearer. "I'll give you a cooking lesson, Joey."

A short time later he had her mincing garlic on a paper plate while he set up the portable stove. "Do you cook much for yourself?" he asked as she was sitting on the step in the van's doorway, a large travel book on Mexico across her lap to support the thin plate.

"Just breakfast. I eat lunch out."

"What about dinner?"

"Well . . ." She hesitated to tell the truth. "I eat with my parents every night. My apartment isn't far from their house."

"No wonder you don't know how to cook! Sounds to me like you've been spoiled," he declared.

"It saves me time," she pointed out in her own defense, "and my mother feels better knowing that I'm eating well. You know how mothers are."

"Spoiled brat!" he said with mock piety. "By the way, what does your father do for a living—when he's not fishing."

She smiled. "He's a real estate broker, but he's been easing into retirement the last few years."

"Really? What's his name?"

"Ed Scott."

Mark shook his head. "I guess I haven't run across that name. But, then, my dealings are all in Orange County. He works in the L.A. area, I suppose."

"Yes, he does," she told him. Then with a sigh she asked, "I've finished the garlic. Anything else I can do?"

"Do you know how to cook rice?"

"Maybe. Are there directions on the box?"

"You're in luck," Mark said, laughing. "You'll find it in the upper cabinet."

Smiling, Joey rose and stepped up into the van. There were two upper cabinets, so she tried the one to the left first. As she pulled the door open, a paper accidentally fell out, landing near her foot. Looking into the cabinet, she surmised quickly that she had chosen the wrong one. It was filled with odds and ends:

an old pair of sneakers, a broken pair of sunglasses, a number of guidebooks, and other papers. She began to close the cabinet door, but then remembered the paper that had fallen. Bending to pick it up, she saw it was an envelope, its contents knocked halfway out.

The letter inside appeared to be written in Spanish. As she took it in her hand and stood up again, casually noting the return address on the envelope, a photograph slipped out and fell to the floor. She bent down again to retrieve it, and then wished she had never seen it.

It was a photograph of a very young woman, exceptionally pretty, with long, shining black hair, sparkling dark eyes, and a smile that was carefree and beguiling. She was pictured from the waist up wearing a sundress, and what was revealed of her slender figure and well-formed bosom was equally devastating. A sharp pang of jealousy ran through Joey as she quickly reinserted the photograph into the envelope and threw it into the cabinet, closing the door.

Well, I couldn't expect to be the first woman he's ever taken an interest in, she silently chided herself as she opened the next cabinet. She spotted the package of rice and took it out. Still, she thought, the woman in the picture seemed rather young for Mark; she appeared to be barely more than a girl, eighteen at most. Joey would have thought that Mark would be attracted to someone a little more sophisticated.

Her jealousy becoming mixed with resentment now, Joey wondered if Mark was still seeing the girl. She remembered the return address written on the envelope—Cabo San Lucas—and wondered how he managed to keep a romance going when he only visited the city two or three times a year. Of course he hadn't mentioned how long he stayed on each visit, Joey thought waspishly.

But perhaps the romance, if indeed there was one, was over. Would he be showing such interest in her if there were already someone else in his life?

Joey tried to concentrate on the directions for the rice, when another thought came to her. Didn't he say he had relatives in Cabo San Lucas? Maybe this girl was a relative. Of course! That would explain everything very easily. That must be it! Mark wasn't one to go about robbing cradles, however attractive the babe might be. It was probably just a photograph of a cousin or niece sent to him by one of his relatives, probably the girl's doting parents.

Happier now, Joey reread the directions on the box she was holding. But her questioning mind pulled her thoughts away again. Somehow it seemed illogical that a handsome bachelor would keep with him a picture of a girl so beautiful if she were only a relative.

"Oh, you're just being silly!" Joey admonished herself aloud.

"Are you having some problem with the rice?" Mark called from outside. "I hear you muttering to yourself."

"No, Mark. I . . . I think I've got it figured out," she called back, glad he couldn't see her embarrassed face.

About forty-five minutes later they were sitting on the sand under the thatched shelter enjoying rice smothered with shrimp in a beer-and-garlic sauce, and canned mixed vegetables. The sun was setting and it was growing dark and chilly. Joey buttoned up her jacket and sipped her hot coffee. "This meal was wonderful, Mark. How come you know how to cook? Most men don't take much interest in it."

"I see I have to remind you that the greatest chefs in the world are men. I've just learned a few easy ways to prepare seafood, since I camp and fish every once in a while. It's my mother who's the real expert. She can make anything taste good."

"My mother's a good cook too. I haven't been able to develop her proficiency at it."

"I know what it is: You're afraid of getting stuck behind a stove," he said with a knowing look.

"As a man, you don't have to worry about such things," she pointed out.

"I'll give you that, but let's not get into the battle of the sexes again."

"Afraid you'll lose?" she impishly countered.

"No . . ." he said, putting down his cup and empty paper plate. In an instant he was upon her, playfully wrestling her to the ground. As he pinned her down he said, looming over her, "You made some comment about losing?"

"Might doesn't make right!" she declared through her giggles.

Slowly and deliberately he lowered his face until their noses were the merest centimeter apart. "If you have might, you don't need to be right, little girl." His mouth came down on hers, pressing her head into the sand as the full weight of his chest relaxed over hers, snugly imprisoning her body beneath him. Her arms came up over his shoulders, pulling him closer as she revelled in the warmth and feel of his strong, manly body.

Her soft, full mouth eagerly responded to the insistent pressure of his lips, but as their passion grew, he suddenly stopped the kiss and came back up to a sitting position, drawing her up with him. When he had caught his breath a little, he said, as he cradled her in his arms, "I don't know if I can handle the new you, Joey. You go to my head."

She gave a little laugh and snuggled closer. "Hey, wait a minute," he said, edging away. "How about some more coffee?" He rose and picked up the pot, then poured them both some more. After turning on the light inside the van, he settled himself next to her again, but at a little distance.

The light through the van's open door shone softly over the sand in front of them and gently illuminated their faces. It was quite dark now, and stars were beginning to appear in the night sky. Gentle waves lapped softly on the shore a few feet away.

"I can see why you like to camp here," Joey said as she enjoyed the atmosphere and her proximity to the handsome man beside her.

"Baja California has a lot of nice places, but with the new road a lot of them are becoming overrun with tourists. I'm beginning to wish I had kept the beat-up old Jeep I used to have. The four-wheel drive enabled me to go out into the back country on primitive roads regular cars can't handle. Out there you're really alone with nature—of course you have to do without modern comforts, but it's worth it."

"Why didn't you keep the Jeep, then?"

"I decided to buy the van and didn't want to have both vehicles besides my two cars. My house is big, but I don't have that much garage space."

"But I still don't see why you bought a van when you liked the Jeep so much," she said, puzzled.

He forced a sigh. "Well, that's what happens when a man starts traveling with a woman. They're not much for roughing it, you know.'' He glanced at her, as though waiting for her to rise to the bait. Her face remained expressionless, however, as though she hadn't heard. After a moment he gave a light shrug and took a sip from his cup.

But Joey *had* heard: ''. . . traveling with a woman.'' The words reverberated in her mind. The image of the beautiful girl in the picture flashed before her. She sat stunned, then grew cold inside as another vivid memory overtook her: the conversation she had overheard in the restaurant between Mark and Ted Morley. Had her growing love made that odious insight into Mark's private life slip from her mind?

Mentally groping, she recalled that Ted had asked him if he was going to Cabo San Lucas to pick up a woman; yes, she could remember the whole conversation. ''That's right,'' were Mark's exact words in answer to the other man's casual query. And then it had become clear that Mark was single. In fact, Ted had joked that with this ''lively little thing'' to ''take care'' of Mark, he could understand why Mark hadn't ''bothered'' to get married.

Joey's mind went further back to the first time she saw him at the gas station in Ensenada—leering at a redhead. Joey shuddered, recalling the sensually intimate way he had then looked at her, a woman he had never even met. How could she have allowed herself to be taken in? The way he had dogged her steps, made advances, forced his company on her—it must all be a part of his technique. She was attractive enough to suit him and he was in the mood for another conquest—at loose ends with his old standby away in Cabo San Lucas. What a stroke of luck for him when her car broke down! Now he could play the gallant rescuer, take his time . . . and he probably expected her to be more than just grateful.

''Joey! You're spilling your coffee,'' Mark said as he took the cup from her hand. ''What's the matter? Are you all right?''

''Yes,'' she whispered.

''Are you sure?'' he asked insistently, brushing back the hair which had fallen forward over her face.

She leaned out of his reach. ''I'm fine—just tired, that's all.''

''It's been a long day,'' he sympathized. ''Maybe you'd like to go to bed?''

She turned on him sharply with large, wary eyes.

''Joey, what's the matter with you?'' His voice was full of concern as he moved closer and attempted to put an arm about her.

''Don't touch me!'' she warned, scrambling out of his grasp.

''What?''

''I think I know what you're up to, Mark, and I'm not going to play into your hands anymore.''

He studied her a moment. ''I don't know what on earth you're talking about.''

''No?'' she taunted. ''I had you pegged right the first time I saw you—just another woman chaser on the make. I don't know how I could have been so foolish! But then you do have an unusual strategy.''

Mark's expression grew taut. ''Would you mind stating clearly what you're getting at.''

''Certainly! I'm just here to help you pass the time until you get back to your girl friend in Cabo San Lucas, isn't that right?'' The question was more an accusation.

"What girl friend?"

"Oh, come now. I suppose you don't recall telling me a few minutes ago that you bought your van because you started traveling with a woman.''

He suddenly began to laugh. "You misunderstood what I . . .''

"Did I?'' she sharply interrupted. "Perhaps you didn't know I overheard your conversation with Ted at San Quintin. He asked if you were going down to pick up your woman, and you told him you were. I assume that's the woman you travel with—unless, of course, there are others.''

He was staring at her grimly. "You sure have a creative mind.''

"My mind didn't invent that conversation!'' she said, glaring back. "And then there were all of Ted's tactless innuendos. He obviously knew you were going after me. Apparently he's familiar with your habits!''

He took a long breath and dropped his eyes to the ground. "Ted has a creative mind, too.'' He lifted his eyes back to her face. Staring levelly into her eyes, he said quietly, "Joey, I have no other woman.''

"Do you expect me to believe that? After words I've heard from your own mouth?'' She would have told him of the picture she had seen, but did not want it to appear that she had been snooping in his personal belongings.

"It's possible there could be a perfectly innocent explanation . . .''

"I'm sure! If anyone could come up with one, you certainly could!''

He took a handful of sand and threw it to the side. His dark eyes pierced through the night air in fiery glimmers. "I thought that you and I had established a trust in one another. I thought that we were . . . close friends, at least. But a friend wouldn't jump to conclusions on the basis of a casual statement, or on an overheard and partially understood conversation. A friend would be patient and trusting—''

"Oh, don't start psyching me out again!'' she interrupted. "I must say you do have an ingenious technique—attacking a woman's vulnerabilities until you've got her so confused she thinks she's falling in love with you. I must have caught on to your scheme just as you were going to move in for the kill!''

As if this were too much, he suddenly rose to his feet and walked toward the van. He stopped by the open door and turned around. His penetrating eyes studied her softly lit face for a moment before he strode back, coming down on one knee directly in front of where she was sitting. Placing both hands on the sand for balance, he leaned forward until his face was only inches from hers. In a husky voice, he said, "A few minutes ago we were kissing. I could have easily let it escalate into more than that, but I didn't. If I were trying to seduce you, don't you think I would have done it then?''

She leaned away from his intimidating stare, but her voice remained adamant. "That's no doubt just part of your method for developing trust. You probably con a woman into believing that making love with you is *her* idea!''

He pushed himself up again and stood before her, looking down at her implacable, upturned face. "You're so afraid of a close relationship, you'll jump at straws and cling to them just to save yourself from one! You're still frightened of me and you'd do anything to sabotage your feelings about me because they scare you, too. Opening up to another person—trusting a man—is just too frightening, isn't it? You're so much safer in your own little neuter world!''

She stood up and brusquely walked past him. ''You can continue with this monologue if it'll help you save face. I'm going to sleep.''

He caught her arm and turned her around again. ''Aren't you afraid I'll try to take advantage of you?'' he taunted, a dark light flickering through his eyes.

''Under the circumstances, I think it would be best if you took your sleeping bag and slept outside tonight,'' she told him disdainfully.

She began to move away, but he pulled her back, keeping a tight grip on her arm. ''I think you've forgotten what the circumstances are. *You're* traveling with *me*. I won't be turned out of my own van!''

She stood perfectly still, her pulse quickening, while the grip on her arm tightened even more. ''*I'll* sleep outside then.''

''No, you won't. It's too cold at night for greenhorns like you. Besides,''— his voice grew sly and harsh—''what makes you think you'd be any safer out here?''

She swallowed as the blood drained from her face and her gray eyes grew large. ''You said last night you would never harm me,'' she said in a small voice.

''But you've decided not to believe anything I say. Why should I care what I do?'' His voice was quiet and his eyes piercing.

Her breathing grew shallow. Suddenly she felt very helpless.

''Go inside and change,'' he ordered in a low voice while he released his vicelike grip on her arm.

Her eyes widened in fear. ''Mark . . .'' she whispered through trembling lips.

''Well, go on!'' he said in a stronger tone, giving her a small shove toward the van. She obeyed and went inside. He slid the door closed behind her.

With shaking hands she took off her clothes and put on her long white nightgown, then slipped her navy robe over it. Hands clenched, she sat down on the back couch to try and think what to do. Would he really try to . . . ?

Abruptly the door slid open and Mark stepped up into the van, shutting the door behind him, locking them in. He looked in her direction. ''All ready, I see,'' he muttered. He walked over and lifted out the small removable table, placing it against the wall. With a tired sigh he said, ''Here, I'll make up your bed.'' After he had taken down the linens from the closet, he looked at her again. ''Well, you'll have to get up,'' he told her in a short tone of voice.

She quickly rose and moved out of the way to stand with weakening knees near the door. In a few more minutes, her little bed was all prepared. He turned toward her and she took a step backward, her gray eyes frozen in fear.

''For heaven's sake, Joey, I'm not going to touch you!'' he said with impatient anger. ''Get under the covers and go to sleep. Maybe it'll help clear out some of the tangled weeds in your brain!''

6

"Rise and shine, Joey." The words cut through the webs of sleep to the accompaniment of splashing water. "Come on, it's eight o'clock. I've let you sleep as long as I could."

Clumsily Joey rolled over and opened her swollen, red-rimmed eyes. She saw Mark standing at the small sink, wiping his face with a towel. She guessed he had been shaving. He was dressed in a light shirt and pants and his hair was wet.

"Maybe I should give you a dunk in the ocean," he said, throwing her a glance. "The water's nice and cold—it'd wake you up in a hurry."

"Is that what you did?" she asked in a scratchy voice. "Your hair is wet."

"Since there aren't any shower facilities here, it was a viable alternative. I'll let you change in here while I start breakfast," he said, moving toward the door. He closed it behind him and she was alone.

She heaved a deep sigh and rubbed her eyes. Life seemed so miserable. Even the sky was overcast and the ocean looked leaden, she noted, as she pushed aside the thin window curtain over her bed. She wished she could have slept better. It was only a few hours ago that she finally had drifted into a deep sleep. Maybe a dip in the ocean was a good idea; she felt grubby since there had been no chance to bathe the day before.

With another sigh she threw aside the covers and got up. In a few minutes she had found and changed into her green bikini, tied her hair atop her head, and was looking in her tote bag for the extra towel she had brought.

When Joey appeared outside, the towel draped over her shoulders, Mark did a double take. "You're really going in?" he said, much surprised. "Don't stay too long—you'll get pneumonia!" he told her sternly.

Joey walked the few feet to the water's edge, shivering a bit in the sharp breeze. The weather had done a turnaround from the soft sunny day they had enjoyed yesterday. She dropped her towel to the sand, inhaled deeply, and took a running plunge.

The temperature of the water was a sudden shock, making Joey gasp, while the sharp edges of seashells hurt her feet. Calling up all her stamina, she managed to endure a few minutes in the frigid water until she heard Mark admonish her to come back.

She moved toward shore where he was waiting, holding her towel. Quickly he put it around her shivering body and walked with her to the van. He reached in and grabbed his own towel and helped to dry her gooseflesh.

"N-not s-so rough," she complained.

"We have to get back the circulation," he said, rubbing her slender arms. "Look, your fingernails are blue. At least you didn't get your hair wet."

He reached to wipe away a stray drop trickling down her neck, while his eyes scanned her face. "You didn't sleep well last night, did you?" he asked softly. "Neither did I. You kept me awake with your sniffling and stifled sobs." His eyes peered into hers. "Were you crying because you were still frightened, or because you were sad about the rift between us?"

She bowed her head and he draped his towel over her shoulders. Casually he

455

brought his hands down to her bare waist and firmly pressed them against her soft flesh. The intense warmth of his hands sent new shivers through her.

"Joey," his voice caressed her ears, "let's stop all this nonsense. You know there's something between us—something wonderful. Don't let it die."

He raised one hand to her chin and tilted her face upward. His mouth felt warm on her cold lips; she clung for an instant, then turned her head to one side. "No. Stop it!"

"You liked it yesterday," he murmured, pressing his lips against her delicate throat.

"Before I was reminded what a womanizer you are!" she cried, pushing both hands against his chest to get out of his clutches. "There's nothing between us. There couldn't be!"

"You know that's not true!" he said, grasping her roughly by the shoulders. "You care for me as much as I care for you!"

"You only care about one thing!" she said through clenched teeth. "I don't want you or any other man! You're all the same underneath!" She brushed past him and locked herself in the van.

A while later she reappeared, fully dressed, in blue slacks and a white T-shirt under her jacket. Mark had been preparing breakfast. He silently handed her a paper plate of eggs and toast and poured her a cup of hot coffee.

An atmosphere of offended gloom prevailed over their breakfast, accompanied only by the sound of the increasingly large waves washing up on shore and the distant laughter of other campers' children at play. The sky grew more overcast, blocking out the sun, with rain threatening.

"What time do you suppose we'll arrive in La Paz this afternoon?" Joey asked coolly, breaking a long silence.

"What makes you think we'll get to La Paz today?" he responded with equal frigidity.

"It's only about three hundred miles. We should be able to make that," she said with alarm.

"Not if we stop at Loreto to fish."

"Why should we do that?" she asked, incredulous.

"Because that's what I always do when I pass this way."

"But . . ."

"Must I remind you again that you are along only out of the kindness of my heart? *I'm* in no hurry to get to La Paz, and if I choose to spend the day fishing, that's my privilege."

"But, Mark, my parents are waiting."

"You didn't have much concern for them yesterday," he reminded her.

"Because I thought I'd be with them today!"

"That's just too bad, Joey," he said, beginning to pack up the portable stove. "If you had listened to my advice in the first place and not driven at night, you wouldn't be in this fix."

"You're doing this on purpose, aren't you? Out of spite!"

"An insensitive male like me? Why would I bother?" he said lightly. "Maybe I just enjoy fishing—like your dad."

Deeply incensed, she threw her half-filled cup of coffee at him, but the strong wind caused it to miss its target. "I hate you, Mark!" she raged. "Of all the rotten men I've had the misfortune to meet, you are the worst!"

His eyes flared in anger and for a moment he seemed ready to lunge at her. She stopped breathing and unconsciously braced herself. But in another instant, his temper was under control. He went back to his work on the stove and muttered unsympathetically, "You have your troubles, don't you, Joey?" She turned away to hide her frustrated tears.

After two long, silent hours on the road, they reached the town of Loreto on the Gulf of California and Mark parked the van at the beach near where a long pier extended into the water. The rain that had threatened never came and the clouds had now broken up, allowing bright sunshine to prevail. But the air was still crisp and strong winds caused frothy waves to wash up on shore.

Mark pulled out his fishing gear, then made himself a sandwich, After taking a bottle of beer from the ice box, he turned to Joey. "I'll be out on the pier. You can join me if you like—I have another rod."

"No, thanks!"

"Okay, stay here and mope then. Don't forget to eat lunch," he called in an offhanded tone as he stepped out of the van.

Her chin quivering, Joey watched through the window as his long, easy strides took him across the beach and down to the end of the pier. *How could he be so rude and unfeeling! This trip would have turned out fine if only I hadn't run into him!*

Restlessly Joey got up and paced the short length of the van. How to pass the afternoon? She could eat, but she wasn't hungry. It was too cold to sunbathe.

"I know," she said to herself as she reached to the floor for her shoulderbag. "I've been meaning to do this anyway." She took out a pencil and a piece of paper from a note pad she always carried. Sitting down at the small table in the back, she began to estimate and then list her share of all the expenses they had accrued since traveling together.

She guessed at the monetary value of the food she had eaten from his ice box and the shrimp from the night before. Her accountant's mind had carefully noted and mentally stored the exact amounts he had paid each time they had stopped for gasoline, which fortunately had been in plentiful supply since Guerrero Negro. She listed half of each gas payment along with the food expenses.

After some time the listing was complete up to and including that morning's breakfast. She would add on all further expenses until they reached La Paz, where she intended to repay him down to the last centavo. Receiving only money in return for his assistance might be a disappointment for him, but it would put her conscience at ease regarding any debts she owed him, she reasoned.

That task accomplished, she was again at a loss for something to do. She bristled at the thought that this was the way her mother usually spent the larger part of her vacations—sitting around waiting for her father to come back from fishing. She was certainly not going to follow that example! There was no reason at all why she needed to stay in the van. Why not walk the short distance to town and do some exploring on her own?

She grabbed her bag and jacket and did just that. It was a small town with low buildings of various sizes and ages strung closely together along its narrow streets. The most impressive feature was a graceful stone mission with a bell tower that dominated the town.

She found herself among other American visitors as she walked down the sidewalk toward the mission. A family with lively, joking youngsters entered with her and she was amused by their banter.

Next to the mission was a small museum. She paid the admission fee of a few pesos and walked about studying the collection of displays and artifacts. It was warm inside and she was unzipping her jacket when two young men came in. They were rather clean cut types, one blond and the other a redhead with freckles. They nodded and gave her a brief hello, obviously having ascertained that she was a fellow American.

As they walked about for a while, Joey noted that the redheaded young man frequently tried to catch her eye with a kind of shy smile. "Have you been in this town long?" he asked at last.

"No, I just got here today," she replied, returning his smile.

"Oh, I thought maybe you were staying here with your family or something. By the way, my name is Ray and this is Keith."

"I'm Joey. Nice to meet you. Are you from California?"

"Yeah, Los Angeles. We're students at U.C.L.A. We came down here on the winter break."

"I'm from L.A. too. What are you studying at the university?" she asked with interest.

"Business administration," they droned in unison.

She chuckled at their unenthusiastic response. "I know how you feel. I majored in accounting and it does get pretty tiresome cracking the books day after day."

"Are you traveling down here on your own?" Ray asked, puzzled.

"No . . . well . . . yes, actually I am on my own," Joey began, flustered at the question. "I started out alone, but then my car broke down. A man I happened to meet offered me a ride to La Paz, where I'm to join my parents. I was hoping to get there today, but he decided he wanted to do some fishing here," she summarized, not quite able to keep the bitterness out of her voice.

They were finished with the museum in a short time and were walking back out onto the street. Ray, the redhead, whispered something to his friend. Keith nodded and said to Joey, "We're leaving now for La Paz. You can ride with us if you like."

The offer took her by surprise. "Oh, no, I couldn't . . ."

"We have plenty of room," Ray said. "You could be with your parents this evening. Besides, don't you feel kind of uneasy about staying alone overnight with this guy you just met on the road? Did you know him before?"

"No," Joey said, coloring a bit. "I don't know you, either," she pointed out good-naturedly.

"You've got a point there," Ray said with a chuckle. "But like I said, La Paz is only a few hours away and you could be there tonight if you come with us. It's up to you."

What a dilemma, thought Joey. On one hand nothing would make her happier than to be safe and sound with her parents. The image of Mark coming back from his fishing to an empty van was also tempting. On the other hand, she didn't know these two any better than she knew him, though they seemed sincere and respectable enough.

"Joey, what are you doing here?" a familiar, quiet voice from behind interrupted her thoughts.

She started at the sound. "Just . . . just looking around the town," she said, glancing quickly at Ray and Keith.

Mark moved to her side and put an arm about her waist. "How about coming back to the beach now?" he asked in a pleasant enough tone, but she could detect an underlying hint of implacability.

Joey's heart was pounding, as though she were an escaped prisoner, caught by her jailer, seeing her one chance at freedom fading quickly. She felt the arm of steel pulling at her waist. "Okay," she whispered, bowing her head.

"Are you going to be all right?" Ray asked, putting out a hand to detain her.

"She'll be perfectly all right," Mark assured them and continued escorting her away from the mission in the direction of the beach.

When they were about a block away, he said, "Would you have gone with them?"

Joey's heart sank as she realized he had overheard their plotting. Recovering, she said with rancor, "Why not? They could have taken me to La Paz tonight."

For a moment his eyes took on a stricken look, then reverted to a masklike appearance. "How can you be sure that's all they would have done?"

"They seemed very nice!" she retorted. "They were concerned about me."

"Just good Samaritans? You don't think your long blond curls and form-fitting T-shirt had anything to do with it?" he said, looking her over.

Startled, she looked down at her open jacket and quickly rezipped it. "Not all men are like *you*. I didn't notice *them* ogling me."

"You're being inconsistent, you know. This morning you claimed men were all alike. Just because they didn't openly stare at your shapely bosom doesn't mean they didn't notice."

"Do you have to be so crude?" she said with disgust.

"You're the one who chose your attire this morning. Are you going to blame a man for looking? I suppose I wasn't supposed to have noticed your skimpy bikini, either. Why dress like a woman if you don't want to be one?"

"What is that supposed to mean?"

"For a girl who claims she doesn't want or need masculine attention, your manner of dress today seems heavily geared to attract it. Maybe you'd better spend some time trying to figure out what it is you really *do* want," he said as they reached the van.

Joey's voice was hushed with anger. "I suppose in your conceited way of looking at things, you think that what I want is you!"

He stared at her steadily. "You said it, Joey, not me."

"My heavens, you're intolerable!" she choked out. "You are the most vain, loathsome creature that . . ."

"Save it. We've been over that ground before," he told her impatiently. "I'll be out on the pier." He turned to go, then stopped and faced her again, a severe, parental look in his eye. "Stay here by the beach, will you? I don't want you going back into town."

"So you can keep an eye on me?" she said with spiteful sarcasm.

"You have a propensity for getting into trouble."

"And you've elected yourself my warden. What if I get bored?" she taunted.

"Then come and tell me, and I'll go for a walk with you. Otherwise, stay here. I don't want my girl"—astonished gray eyes checked his words—"I don't want you walking around by yourself, collecting followers eager to help an enticing damsel in distress!" On that angry note, he turned and walked in the direction of the pier.

His girl! By what right did he call her that? Joey steamed. Talk about collectors! Wasn't he the one who, by all indications, had a harem of women scattered about, waiting on him? Well, one anyway, in Cabo San Lucas; and he obviously was trying to add herself to his menagerie. His girl! She stormed into the van and slid the door shut with a strong shove.

It was warm inside and she restlessly shrugged off her jacket, revealing her much maligned T-shirt. "I didn't know it had shrunk," she muttered to herself. "Why should I wear my good clothes just to sit around in a van all day!" she peeved.

Her eyes came across the ice box and she was reminded that she hadn't yet eaten lunch. With a sigh she opened the small compartment, took out some sandwich meats and bread, and the last cold bottle of beer. She found some unrefrigerated bottles stored in a corner and put two in the ice box before reclosing it.

After making her sandwich, she found the bottle opener and, placing the bottle on the waist-high sink top, set about uncapping it. She always had a hard time with bottles—the caps seemed tough and the openers were never shaped to grab hold easily. This one proved no exception. After a few false starts, the opener finally latched onto the cap, but in giving it her most powerful—and frustrated—grip, she managed to tip the bottle over just as the cap was coming off. In an instant her T-shirt was soaked in cold, foamy beer.

"Oh, great!" she fumed, setting the half full bottle upright and grabbing her towel, which was drying over the back of the driver's seat. She mopped up herself, the sink, and what had spilled on the carpet.

"I guess I'll have to change this top," she mumbled, uncomfortable with the sticky feel of the wet material and the smell of the beer. She noted ruefully that the wetness had made the T-shirt transparent and the outlines of her bra could be clearly discerned. "God forbid he should see me like this!"

She drew the curtain behind the driver's seat to prevent anyone from seeing through the front windows and made sure the van's back window curtains were in place. Thus secured, she took off her T-shirt and bra. After a quick washup at the sink, she knelt down by her suitcase on the floor and pulled out a long-sleeved yellow print blouse which buttoned down the front. Putting it aside for the moment, she searched through the pockets of her suitcase for a clean brassiere.

The sound of footsteps coming near the van made her stop suddenly. She paused a second to make sure her ears hadn't deceived her. The footsteps on the pavement were very close now. In a panic she grabbed her blouse and had just gotten her arms through the sleeves when the sliding door suddenly began to move. She was pulling the front sides of the garment together to cover her when Mark stepped up into the van.

"My line broke . . ." he began, then stopped as his eyes took in her state of semi-undress.

"I s-spilled beer on my T-shirt," she said, trying to steady her voice as she clutched more tightly to the front opening of the blouse. "Would you wait outside until I'm finished changing, please?"

His eyes honed in on her in a dark, set stare, an odd light giving them increased lustre. He shook his head just slightly, but his eyes did not move as he said, "That glimpse of you was too tantalizing." He took a step back, slid the door shut, and moved toward her. His voice was smooth and low as he knelt in front of where she was sitting huddled on the floor. "You looked so sweet and soft just now, Joey, like the warm, responsive woman I know you can be. Let's see if we can find the real you."

Her heart almost stopping with panic, she said in a small voice as she tried to edge backwards, "Leave me alone, Mark."

"That isn't what you want, is it?" he said, shrugging off his leather jacket and tossing it aside.

Her eyes widening as she watched him, she strove to regain her wits. Assuming a brazen look of outrage to hide her deep fright, she taunted, "You think any woman will eagerly melt in your arms, don't you? Well, you're wasting your time with me. This is one woman who's immune . . ."

"Are you?" He leaned forward and pulled her into his arms.

"Leave me alone!" she cried, trying to squirm out of his grasp and deeply conscious of the warm lips pressing against her neck, making her skin quiver.

"Never," he breathed. "You'll be mine, whatever it takes." She sensed his passion was growing out of control as he covered her face and throat with hard, tender kisses and his arms held her captive. She was helpless to do anything against such masculine strength and felt herself succumbing to his unyielding persistence.

A small moan escaped her lips when his warm, somewhat rough hand slipped beneath her unbuttoned blouse to firmly caress the softness beneath. His mouth came down on hers and she was lost in sensual oblivion, unconsciously pulling him closer with her arms, answering with her lips, and wanting nothing but him.

"I knew it could be like this between us," he whispered against her cheek some long moments later. He held her away from him a bit and gently stroked her hair, his hand coming to rest over her ear. "You're so beautiful," he murmured, his eyes a soft, yearning brown. "Look at you now—no trace of fear, just warm and eager and loving."

Carefully holding her against him, he leaned forward and pulled open the long closet door just behind her. The full length mirror shone its reflected soft light as the narrow door swung aside. He lifted her up slightly and carefully turned her about until she was facing her own image in the lower part of the long, silvery glass.

"Look at yourself," he gently urged, his hands clasped about her rib cage, as he peered at her reflection from over her shoulder. "See how womanly you are now, your hair falling over your breasts, your mouth soft and yielding, and your eyes—look at your eyes—so tender and longing." He gave her a little shake. "Do you see yourself?"

Lost in the mesmerizing flow of his low voice and his physical nearness, she strained to bring herself together, to focus her shining, softened eyes on her own reflection. How curious she looked, she thought as she regarded herself—like a little waif with her hair tossled about, her eyes needy and vulnerable, and her mouth pink and rounded from his kisses.

"Do you still deny that you need a man's love, Joey? Can you still say that you don't want me?"

She saw his intent eyes upon her in the mirror and gave herself a mental shake. She looked again at her own reflection, this time in conscious reality, and she became appalled. Like some woman of loose morals, her bosom was half uncovered, her hair unkempt, and her expression wanton. She stiffened and pulled her blouse together, bowing her head to hide her face in shame.

"Joey, what's wrong?" Mark asked, his voice troubled.

She turned on him, her eyes full of the recognition that he had nearly achieved the ultimate this time in stripping her defenses and using her vulnerabilities. "I despise you," she said in a hissed whisper full of fury and hate.

He seemed stunned with disbelief, then his eyes narrowed in intense rage. With a swift, infuriated movement, he snatched up his jacket and in an instant was gone, shoving the door closed behind him with such force that the van shook with his vengeance.

In a moment all was quiet as his footsteps faded away. With fingers that trembled, Joey went about the belated task of buttoning her blouse. That finished, she drew up her knees and folded her arms about her legs. Resting her forehead on her knees, she tried to gain hold of herself, constricting her eyelids to hold back the tears. But soon she was overcome by wrenching sobs, deploring her abandoned behavior with a man only too eager to take advantage of her weaknesses, and grieving for the ache deep within that knew no solace.

7

It was growing warm in the van with the bright sun beating in, and Joey lowered her window a bit to invite in more air. They had been driving nonstop for almost four hours now, and she was growing restless with anxiety. It seemed that they had been traveling forever across a dry region of endless chalk-colored hills and buttes. Certainly La Paz couldn't be too far off now, she thought wearily.

She glanced at the stony profile to her left. Mark seemed to be tiring, too, judging by the listless tedium conveyed in his pose. He was leaning to one side, his left arm carelessly draped over his opened window and his right hand casually hooked over the top of the steering wheel. His eyes were set on the road in a dour expression and he appeared engrossed in his own thoughts. She had no need to wonder what those thoughts must be.

He had said hardly a word and had been belligerent in manner ever since their terrible encounter of the day before. After storming out, he had returned to the van a few hours later and wordlessly drove them to a nearby trailer park where they had camped for the night.

He had prepared a fine dinner of the roosterfish he had caught, but neither of them appeared to be hungry enough to do it justice. After dinner he had lugged out his sleeping bag and spread it on the ground next to the van, leaving her the complete privacy of the vehicle. Then came the only time he had spoken to her the whole evening: As they were about to retire he ordered her to lock the door of the van from the inside. Even now she wondered at this unexpected admonition. But what difference did it make what his reasons were? They would soon be rid of each other.

She leaned her head against the high-backed seat and closed her eyes. After only a few moments, however, she found herself looking at Mark again from the corner of her eye. His smooth black hair and dark skin contrasted sharply with his white, navy-trimmed knit sport shirt. It emphasized his broad shoulders and clung to his muscular physique.

Yes, she had to admit he was handsome, as her eyes took in his well-defined profile, the firm jaw, and the thick straight hair that ruffled over the back of his collar. She sensed the quiet strength in the rhythmic rise and fall of his chest with each slow breath he took. Her lips parted slightly now, as her eyes traveled over his bared muscular forearms and strong, well-formed hands. Had those arms really held her . . . those hands caressed her body?

She winced and turned her head away to gaze blurry-eyed out the side window. It was suddenly too painful to study him. It hurt too much to be reminded of the wild emotions he had aroused in her—and to remember that he had only been trying to use her, that he was on his way to Cabo San Lucas and his mistress.

"What hotel are your parents staying at?"

The question, uttered in a monotone, cut through her consciousness. "What? Oh . . . the Hotel La Playa," she told him.

He gave a nod of recognition and continued to keep his eyes fixed on the winding road.

"Will . . . will we be in La Paz soon?" she asked, straightening up. She was not eager to speak to him, but was pressured by the anxiety of not knowing when this torturous ride would be over.

"You can see it ahead there," he told her, pointing briefly out the window. They had come to a high bluff which looked over a sweeping panorama of the Gulf of California and Bahia de La Paz. A cluster of tiny white buildings could be discerned on the far side of the bay where Mark had directed her attention. At last, La Paz was in sight! She breathed a silent, but long sigh of relief as the road led them on a sharp descent toward the coastal plain.

It was after a drive of another twenty miles or so along the bay when at last they came upon the city. Mark turned down a long entrance road leading to the hotel, which now loomed ahead. It was a tall, modern building of about a dozen stories, constructed of gray stone and situated on the beach of Bahia de La Paz.

Shortly they were in the hotel's parking lot, and as Mark looked for a space, Joey found her nerves incredibly on edge. Her fingers twisting about one another in anxiety, she silently wondered what the good-bye would be like. What would they say to one another? How would it finally end?

He parked, then went to the back of the van, took out her luggage and put it outside on the pavement. Heart beating rapidly, Joey went to pick up the bags.

"I'll take them for you," he said as he was locking up the vehicle. "The reception desk is upstairs."

She waited quietly and then they walked up a number of gray stone steps until they came to the modern, attractive lobby, which was only semi-enclosed and open to the warm, tropical air. He set her bags down by the reception desk.

"Are a Mr. and Mrs. Ed Scott registered here?" he asked the girl behind the desk.

She checked her records. "Yes, they are—room four sixteen."

Mark nodded and turned to Joey, his eyes hard and his face grim. "I guess that's it then."

"Yes . . ." she replied in a barely audible voice, trying desperately to think of something to say.

"Good-bye." He had spoken the word before she quite realized it and all at once was walking away from her and back down the steps.

Suddenly remembering, she called out, "Mark, wait!" and ran down the few steps it took to reach him. He stopped and waited for her, his face expressionless, but his eyes strangely bright and expectant.

"I wanted to repay you," she said, reaching into her shoulderbag. She withdrew some Mexican currency and a sheet of notepaper, which she extended to him. "I made a list and added up my share of the expenses. I think you'll find it's all in order—and here's what I owe you."

He made no move to take the money she held out to him, but stared at her, his eyes reddening and his facial muscles tensing. "Haven't we come any further than the day we first met?" he said in a voice that was strained and harsh. "Are we still strangers to one another?"

"If you mean you expected to be repaid in some other way, I'm afraid you'll have to make do with the money," she said snappishly.

He drew his brows together as if in pain. "You don't owe me anything! Is doing something for someone else out of kindness a foreign concept to you? Don't you think it's possible I may have helped you just because I wanted to— because the reward was in the doing and not because I expected something in return?" He studied her blank expression. "No, you don't understand that. You can't trust anyone enough not to question their motives. It's easier for you to deal with human emotion in business terms, so you quantify everything, reducing life to a list of debits and credits."

He stopped speaking and regarded her through taut, glassy eyes. "I feel sorry for you, Joey," he added in a quieter voice. "Unless you learn to trust people— including men—you're going to wind up a very lonely woman." He pushed aside her outstretched hand. "Keep your damn money. There's only one thing I'd ever accept from you, and you're not capable of giving it!" He turned and hurried down the steps without looking back. In a moment he was out of view, gone from her life.

Joey looked at the money still clutched in her tremorous hand, then down the steps to the spot where she last saw him. She opened her mouth as if to cry out, but found no words for her tongue to pronounce. Emptiness overcame her and she seemed at one with the cold stone steps on which she stood—dead inside.

"Jo? Jo—is that you?"

She heard a man's footsteps behind her and turned to face a gray-headed, middle-aged man of medium height and somewhat portly build. "Dad!" she cried, reawakening to her surroundings.

"Oh, thank God you got here all right! We've been so worried!" He gave her a strong embrace. "Jo, your mother has been so upset," he said, putting an arm about her and leading her slowly up the steps. "I haven't been out fishing since we got here! We heard about those heavy storms and the washouts, people stranded and whatnot—well, she's just been beside herself! I've had to stay close by and try to comfort her. I told her you had a good head on your shoulders and you'd make it through all right. I didn't let on, but I was worried, too."

They turned into the lobby and she pointed out her luggage, not wanting to interrupt. He picked up her bags and continued as they walked toward the elevator. "I didn't know what the road was like and about the trouble getting gas in some areas—I thought those were just stories. And then the storms! The weather was clear when we went through. I couldn't imagine driving through washouts; the potholes were bad enough. And we didn't know where you were—if you were stuck in the thick of the storms or had left later than we expected."

He paused a moment as they entered the elevator together. "Well, it's all my fault," he went on. "I should have waited for you at Estero Beach so you could have gone with us. I never thought it would be like this."

"That's okay, Dad. It wasn't so bad. I . . . I made it all right," she said, putting on a smile and hoping to ease his mind. She in fact was rather astounded. She had never seen her father in such a dither.

The elevator opened onto the fourth floor. "The room's this way," he said, quickening his pace as they walked along a flower-trimmed balcony overlooking the open air restaurant and the shimmering pool beyond. Farther out was the broad sandy beach and blue waters of the bay.

Joey wasn't sure, but it seemed to her that her father's hand shook a bit as he turned the key in the door to their room. "Milly!" he called as he opened the door and set the luggage down inside. "Milly, look who I found!" He brought Joey into the large, beautifully furnished room and pushed her forward, as if presenting her to his wife.

Her mother, still dressed in her robe though it was noontime, looked up from a book she was reading by the window. Her reddened eyes opened wide and in a moment she was on her feet with her arms flung about her daughter. "Oh, thank heaven!" she gasped through her tears.

"I'm okay, Mother," Joey said softly, trying to soothe the slightly plump little woman who was clinging to her.

"We've been waiting so many days," her mother said, sniffing back her sobs. "I was afraid you drowned in one of those washouts!"

Joey smiled. "I didn't leave until Christmas Day and the storms were over when I went through. There was only one large washout where I was delayed for a few hours because a trailer got stuck."

Her father's expression was puzzled. "Then you should have made it here by yesterday, if not sooner," he said.

"Yes, well . . . I had a few other delays," Joey hedged.

"I'm sure it must have been very trying for you, dear," Joey's mother said with sympathy. "I should never have allowed this to happen. It's my fault—I should have insisted we wait for you at Estero Beach."

"No, no, Milly. It's my fault and I admit it. Don't blame yourself," Ed Scott told his wife.

"If I want to blame myself, I will!" the small woman quietly retorted as Joey's eyes widened. Mrs. Scott turned back to her daughter. "Now, tell me more about your trip, dear," she said, motioning for Joey to sit down on the edge of one of the room's two double beds. Milly took a place beside her, while Mr. Scott quietly took a chair by the window. "How did your little car hold up?"

Joey took a deep, slow breath. She would have to tell them sooner or later. "I'm afraid I got into an accident . . ."

"Oh, no!"

"Well, I wasn't hurt, Mother," she hurried to explain, "but my car is in Guerrero Negro being repaired."

"How did you get here?" her father asked with surprise.

She took another breath. "I . . . happened to meet someone on the road—another American—and got a ride."

"Oh, that was nice! Who was it? A family on vacation?" her mother asked.

"No . . . uh . . . it was a man, traveling on his own in a van," she said, deciding to tell the whole story at once and get it over with.

"What?" her father reentered the conversation. "Oh, you mean it was some elderly man?"

"No, Dad, he was in his early thirties—and not married." She looked down at the carpet as she waited for the thunder to follow her lightning bolt.

"You took a ride in a van from some stranger!"

"What else was she to do in her predicament?" Milly Scott asked her husband crossly. "I'm sure she must have analyzed the situation first."

"But, Milly, she left her car in Guerrero Negro. A person can't make it from there to here in one day very easily." He turned his eyes back to Joey. "Didn't you have to spend the night somewhere?"

"Well, of course she would have stayed at a hotel—in her own room!" her mother explained with impatience.

"No, Mother, I spent the night with him in his van. In fact, I spent three nights camping with him." An icy silence followed her quiet statement.

"How dare you tell me that!" her father suddenly raged. "I didn't raise my daughter to go sleeping around with strangers!"

"Now just a minute," Mrs. Scott put in, her voice not quite so firm as before. "She didn't say she . . . was intimate with him. Besides that, she's of age—she doesn't owe us any explanations."

"The hell she doesn't. . . ."

"Mother's right. I don't owe you an explanation," she told her father sternly. "But I'll give you one, if you choose to believe it. Nothing happened between . . . between this man and me that you wouldn't approve of. He didn't touch me," she assured them, blanching the truth a bit. Since Mark was out of her life, it wouldn't matter anyway.

"I believe you, Joey," her mother assured her.

"Okay, Jo," her father said quietly. "You've never lied before; there's no reason to doubt you now. But it's hard to imagine—morals being what they are these days—that a young bachelor wouldn't try to take advantage of you. You are a beautiful girl, after all."

Joey lifted her eyes to her father's face. He had never before made any comment on her comely appearance. Her conscience suddenly bothering her, she said, "Well, he did seem to be attracted to me, but I didn't let him get very far."

"Good for you, Jo! I always said you could take care of yourself," her father vocally applauded. "Who was this guy anyway?"

Joey was quiet for a moment. "His name was Mark Chavira. He was from Orange County . . ."

"Chavira?" her father interrupted. "He wasn't a real estate developer, was he?"

"Yes, he . . ."

"You traveled with Mark Chavira?" he said with astonishment. "Are you sure? He's one of the most successful men in California—and becoming one of the richest! You must have seen him mentioned in the newspapers—the business and real estate sections?"

"I usually just have time to read the front page . . ." she weakly replied, stunned by her father's information.

"Well, he made the front page of *The Wall Street Journal* a few months ago. It was an article telling how he made his development company the most prominent in Orange County before he was even thirty—and you know all the building that's been going on in that area. That man has such an instinct for buying property, it's uncanny. Boy, if I had had his ability . . ."

Joey's mind drifted from her father's voice to her own thoughts. No wonder Mark had always seemed so assured, so secure within himself that he could laugh at his own shortcomings. He was already so successful, he didn't need to impress anyone.

"Maybe you should have gone after him, Jo." The sound of her nickname broke her line of thought. "If you had snagged him for a husband, you could have been set for life."

"I don't want to be set for life," she told her father. "I'd rather rely on myself."

"Well, he's probably got more women after him than he knows what to do with, anyway," her father quipped, attempting to lightheartedly dismiss his previous comment.

"I imagine he does," Joey agreed sullenly.

"It doesn't matter how successful a man is," her mother put in unexpectedly. "It's what he's like to live with day in and day out that's most important!"

"Yeah . . . well . . ." her father said, clearing his throat and shifting about in his seat. "What do you say we three go to lunch downstairs. How about it?" he said brightly, as though trying to work up some enthusiasm for the idea.

"I suppose I *should* eat something," Joey said, not feeling very hungry.

"I'm not dressed yet. I've been so upset. Why don't you go with your father and I'll stay here and order a little something from room service."

"We'll wait for you, Milly," Ed Scott said eagerly.

"Of course, Mother," Joey agreed.

"No, I'd rather stay here, dear," she told Joey. "You go ahead."

Joey said no more to try to persuade her. It was clear something had changed between her parents and for the moment she thought it best to let matters alone.

She said good-bye to her mother and followed her father to the restaurant downstairs. Here they were quickly seated at a small table.

They were silent for a few minutes after they ordered their sandwiches. Her father's enthusiasm had disappeared on the way downstairs and he now appeared depressed and worried. After absently pushing his glass and utensils about on his place mat, he at last said, "Well, I guess you've noticed I don't rate too highly with your mother lately."

"Yes, I . . ."

"I haven't seen her carry on this way in all the years we've been married," he continued. "She says I'm inconsiderate . . . that I always have my own way. Well, maybe she's right. I realize I did the wrong thing in asking you to drive here alone, and I admit it. By the way, I owe you an apology for that, Jo."

"That's okay, Dad."

"I've apologized to your mother, too, over and over. I never expected her to be so unforgiving."

"Maybe it's just because she was so worried. She'll probably be more herself now."

Ed Scott shook his head. "I don't know. She's hardly been speaking to me and refuses to eat with me. You can see that hasn't changed, even though you're back, safe and sound. And then last night,"—he grew visibly troubled and spoke more hesitantly—"she said something about . . . leaving me."

Joey felt herself growing pale. She never dreamed things could be this bad.

"I really don't know what to do, Jo. I can't see myself without her. I've been so contented all these years. She's always been there."

"Have you ever wondered if she was content?" Joey asked as gently as she could.

"She never said she wasn't," he replied, shrugging his shoulders.

"Well, I don't think she's ever thought much about herself. She was too busy taking care of us. Have you ever told her how much you appreciate her always being there for you?"

"Well . . ."

"Have you ever asked her what she would like to do for fun? Do you think she likes to sit around and amuse herself while you go off on your fishing trips?"

"But, Jo, she never complained," her father pointed out.

"Dad, I think she thought it was her duty as a wife to please you, so she went along with whatever you wanted." Joey desperately tried to think of some other way to get through to him. "Look, do you think Mother is an attractive woman?"

"Of course!" he readily answered. "She's certainly a lot prettier than other women her age. She was always beautiful."

"Yes, she is. Now don't you think it's possible other men have noticed her? If you don't appreciate her and spend some time seeing to it that she's happy, someone else might come along who's only too willing to give her the attention she needs."

"Oh, but your mother wouldn't—"

"Let me tell you something," Joey interrupted. "I tried to tell you this once before, but you were all up in the air over the whopper you had just caught. Last time we were at Estero Beach, when you were out fishing, a very polite and handsome middle-aged man—a widower, he said—spent the afternoon talking to Mother. He seemed very disappointed when she mentioned we were leaving the next day. And I think it was the most enjoyable day Mother had on that whole vacation.''

"Is that true?" her father said, deeply shocked. "I never realized . . . I guess you're right, I'd better do something.''

"You've already made a good beginning—giving up your fishing to be with her when she needed comfort,'' Joey pointed out optimistically. "Why don't you continue to spend more time with her and do things she would like to do. Take her shopping, sightseeing. Entertain her like you did when you were courting.''

"But she won't even have lunch with me. I'll have to get out of the doghouse first.''

Joey paused to think, as his point was well taken. "Maybe if I have a talk with her. I'll tell you what—why don't you go out and buy her something you think she'd like, some nice gift. Meanwhile I'll see if I can plead your case.''

"I suppose it's worth a try,'' her father said with a long sigh.

Joey could tell how upset he was by the tone of his voice and his inability to finish his sandwich; his stocky figure attested to his usual appetite. Her eyes glazed over and she was touched. Perhaps men weren't so insensitive after all— some men, at any rate.

When Joey returned to the hotel room, she was relieved to see that her mother appeared to be more herself. She was dressed in pink slacks and a matching top; her short hair, softly frosted to hide the gray, was combed into its usual neatly attractive style. She was a lovely woman, Joey thought, a sweet face to match her usual temperament, a kindly smile, and though she carried a few extra pounds, they seemed to have distributed themselves to the right places. A light coat of makeup brightened the unusually pale complexion that Joey had noticed earlier.

"You look much better, Mother,'' she said brightly.

"Yes, I had a bite to eat and I feel better now that I know you're all right. How was your lunch?''

"Fine . . .'' Joey hesitated, not knowing how to bring up the touchy subject. "I had a little talk with Dad. He was concerned that you've been so upset. He blamed himself.''

"It *was* his fault,'' Mrs. Scott interrupted. "But it's mine, too. I . . . I should have said something more forceful than I did to make him wait for you at Estero Beach.''

"Now, Mother, what could you have said? We both know how Dad is when he's set on something.''

"Well, it's true he never listens much to my opinions, but this time I should have *made* him listen . . . somehow. There's no excuse for me not to take more responsibility than I do in our family,'' Milly said with newfound conviction. "I blamed him at first because he's always been inconsiderate when he's bent on following his own plans, but I'm beginning to see that it may be partly my fault that he's like that. I've always given in to please him. I thought I was being nice, but I see now that so much compliance can sometimes lead to trouble, even danger. I wouldn't have cared for myself, but my giving in to his wishes put you in danger. I should never have allowed that to happen," she finished, shaking her head in disapproval.

"Please don't blame yourself. It's nobody's fault. It just happened. Dad didn't realize the roads were that bad and no one could have predicted the rainstorms and floods. He's really sorry about it all. Why, he didn't eat even half of his lunch, he felt so bad."

"Good. He needs to lose weight," her mother commented tersely.

Joey was reluctant to press the subject further, but she felt constrained to do so. "Dad said something that . . . well . . . that you had thought of leaving him." She found her voice failing her.

Milly Scott raised her eyes to her daughter's worried ones, then looked down. A little smile formed on her lips. "Yes, I guess I did. I was very upset last night. I was sure I'd never see you again. In my grief and anger I decided I didn't want to live with him anymore. I even made plans," she said, chuckling a bit. "I was going to move out, get my own apartment, like you have, and get a job. I was going to go back to school and study nursing in the evenings. You've always told me how you like being independent and unattached. Somehow I thought that was the thing that I should do."

"Are you?" Joey asked, holding her breath.

Mrs. Scott smiled again. "No, Joey. I've been married too long to change my life around. And in spite of your father's shortcomings, I guess I still love him. Besides, his life would fall apart without me, whether he realizes it or not," she added ruefully.

"I think he does," Joey said, relaxing now. "Being independent has its drawbacks anyway. I don't think you would have liked it."

Milly Scott's eyes widened a bit at Joey's words. "I'm surprised to hear you say that. You've never mentioned any drawbacks before."

"Well, *any* life-style will have some aspects that are less than perfect. Of course, *I* would certainly still prefer being single to being married," Joey said, sounding more like she was trying to convince herself than her mother of the firmness of her conviction, "but I have to admit that sometimes it does get a little . . . well . . . lonely. I don't think it would have suited someone like you, who's been living with a husband for so long."

"Sometimes you feel lonely?" Mrs. Scott asked with gentle concern. "When, for example?"

Joey hesitated before speaking and moved toward the window to look out onto the bay. "Oh, I remember one Saturday last spring. It was the first weekend I managed to have off from work after the tax season. It was a warm day and I guess I just got a case of spring fever."

"I thought you had gotten over those fits in your teens, when you used to be depressed because the young men you liked still looked upon you as a tomboy," her mother said with a kindly chuckle. "Tell me about it."

"Well, it was just a . . . a feeling. I was sort of restless and melancholy for no reason. There was a warm breeze that day and it was sunny—flowers all over. I went out and took a walk by myself. I saw pairs of lovers walking hand in hand, looking so happy. I felt . . . it was silly, but I felt lonely and romantic. I wished I had someone."

Joey was suddenly embarrassed, realizing her eyes were brimming with unshed tears. Quickly she blotted her eyes. "My goodness," she said with a self-conscious little laugh, "I guess the warm breezes here have afflicted me again."

Mrs. Scott studied her daughter, her expression a combination of wisdom and wonder. For a moment she looked as though she wanted to ask something, but then thought better of it and dropped her gaze thoughtfully to the floor.

"Anyway, Mother, I'm glad you're not really going to leave Dad. He may have his flaws, but he really loves you, you know."

Her mother raised her eyes to Joey's again and smiled. "I know."

"You'll have dinner with him tonight?" Joey asked hesitantly. "He said you had been refusing to eat with him."

"Of course. I'll have dinner with you both, I hope! I think my emotional outbursts are over with now," Mrs. Scott said, laughing a little at herself.

Joey smiled and gazed out again at the beautiful blue of the bay, glad she no longer had to worry about the preservation of her parents' marriage.

After a few moments of silence, her mother suddenly asked, "Joey, do you think I'm too old to go back to studying nursing?"

"Too old! Why, of course not."

"Well, maybe I ought to go back to school and try it then. I've been thinking, perhaps I ought to do something that gets me out of the house a little more. I've had a lot of free time in these years since you left home."

Joey's eyes brightened immediately. "That's a wonderful idea! I think it would do you good to have some outside interest." She paused to think a moment and her gleeful expression faded. "I don't know how Dad would feel about it, though."

Mrs. Scott was very pensive for quite a while. At last she lifted her head and said, "I don't think it matters that much how he feels about it. Since I'll be the one with all the homework, it seems to me it's *my* decision to make."

A widening smile of surprise and satisfaction came over Joey's face. "You're absolutely right, Mother! It *is* your decision."

8

It was a kind of dull, listless day during the first week of the New Year. The morning sky was overcast and though the temperature was comfortable it was not quite warm enough to make swimming pleasurable. Joey took her usual lounge chair by one corner of the pool, the place she had occupied hour after hour every day since she had arrived.

Her parents—the love birds as she referred to them in her private thoughts—were off sightseeing again. Her mother had decided she wanted to see Land's End, the rocky southern tip of the Baja California peninsula at Cabo San Lucas, and Mr. Scott had eagerly complied with his wife's wishes, as he had ever since Joey had rejoined them.

As usual they had tried to coax Joey into coming with them, but she preferred to spend the day by herself again—to allow her parents time alone together, she rationalized. The fact was she had lost interest in seeing any more of Mexico and had shuddered at the suggestion she accompany them to Cabo San Lucas. She would be content never to see the popular resort in her life.

So, when her parents had left early that morning to make the more than three-hour drive to the tip of the peninsula, Joey had again donned her bikini, picked up her sun hat, beach robe, suntan lotion, and a few magazines and walked down to sit beside the pool. The previous days spent this way had been sunny, or at least partially sunny, and she had acquired a healthy-looking tan, having been careful to make use of her long beach robe and hat to cover herself when she felt she might be overdoing her exposure.

But though her stunning figure and glowing complexion made her look the picture of health, her eyes, hidden behind sunglasses, remained red-rimmed and forlorn.

She picked up a fashion magazine she had recently purchased and absently leafed through the pages, but as was usually the case, she soon found her mind was not on the latest modes from Paris or the newest beauty tips. Her thoughts, as always, traveled unerringly to Mark, to their final conversation, to the image of his tall figure as he stood before her predicting that she would become a lonely woman—a woman to whom life was nothing more than a list of debits and credits.

It couldn't be true, she told herself. She could feel; she had emotions, hadn't she? She was capable of love—she had loved! Only she had chosen badly.

Mark had said she needed to learn trust. But how could she trust men who had obviously tried to deceive her? First Robin and now Mark. Both had tried to make her believe that they had had no other women but her.

Of course she could have been wrong about Mark; she had no hard evidence against him. She hadn't actually caught him with another woman, as she had Robin. And Mark had seemed so sincere when he told her he had no one else, even appearing injured and insulted when she didn't believe him.

Now she regretted not having allowed him to explain. Maybe she had misunderstood the conversation she had overheard. And perhaps the beautiful girl in the photograph was a relative of his. She had lately recalled that Ted Morley used the term old lady when he referred to the woman in Cabo San Lucas that Mark was to pick up. Wasn't it possible he could have meant a woman who actually was of an older age—perhaps a mother or grandmother? Maybe she had been mistaken in assuming he was using the slang meaning of wife or mistress.

Still, she could not forget the sensually predatory way Mark had looked her over in Ensenada and Ted's careless remarks which indicated that he, at least, looked upon Mark as a womanizer on the prowl. After pursuing her so relentlessly, would Mark have left her as abruptly as he had if he really cared for her? Would a man with his self-confidence give up so easily if a woman were really special to him? No, she decided, tears forming in her eyes, if he had really cared he would have . . .

"Joey?" Her dolorous thoughts were interrupted by a hesitant male voice.

"Yes?" she said with a sniff, blinking to clear the tears from her eyes. "Oh, hello, Ray . . . Keith," she said, looking up to the two young men gazing down at her. Surreptitiously she wiped away a tear and put on a smile. "Nice to see you again."

"I'm glad to see you got here all right," Ray, the redheaded one who seemed to be more talkative, replied. "Is something wrong?" he asked solicitously, noticing a tear streaming down her other cheek from beneath her sunglasses.

"Oh, no," she assured him. "Just something in my eye. Have you been in La Paz all this time?"

"We spent a couple of days here and then went down to Cabo San Lucas. We're starting to head home now—just stopped here for lunch. Have you been staying at this hotel?"

"Yes."

"Must be nice," Keith put in with an envious smile. "We're getting a little tired of trailer parks."

"I know how you have to pinch pennies when you're a student," Joey sympathized. "How . . . how did you like Cabo San Lucas?"

"Oh, it was great!" Ray exclaimed, a broad smile breaking across his freckled face. "There are some guys on the beach there with big motorized rowboats. They take people out to see the offshore arches and rock formations at Land's End. We went out on one of the boats—saw pelicans and seals sunning themselves out there on the rocks. The arches were spectacular. It was really a neat place! Then we walked through the lobbies and grounds of some of the big resort hotels."

"That's all we could afford to do is walk through," Keith added with a laugh.

"Yeah," agreed Ray. "Maybe someday we'll be rich enough to stay at one of those places. Well, we'd better get going. We just came out here by the pool to take a look at the beach and happened to see you. I'm really glad we ran into you again. I was a little worried when we left you in Loreto. That guy you were with looked like he could be pretty tough if he wanted to be. And you didn't sound like you were too happy traveling with him."

"Oh, he was all right. He . . . he got me here safely," she said, struggling for words.

"That's good. I won't have that on my conscience anymore. Well, good luck! Enjoy the rest of your vacation!" Ray said, turning to go.

"Good-bye," Keith added with a wave.

She waved and watched them walk back toward the building until they disappeared into the lobby area. "I wish I could meet more fellows like them," she muttered. "Only a little older," she added ruefully. A man with a conscience! That was something unusual.

She wondered how much of a conscience Mark had. True, he had seen to it that she was safely deposited at her hotel, even though he was angry with her. And he wouldn't accept her money . . .

Her thoughts stopped as she recalled his parting words: "There's only one thing I'd ever accept from you, and you're not capable of giving it." What had he meant? What wasn't she capable of giving? Friendship? Love? Or was it just physical satisfaction he was looking for?

Oh, why think about it anymore? She'd go crazy if she did! With a restless movement she tossed her magazine and sunglasses aside and got up off of the chair. Turning about, she looked out from the raised pool area to the beach and bay below. Thinking some exercise might help straighten out her circular thought patterns, she put on her long white beach cover-up made of a thin gauzelike material and walked over to the flight of steps that led down to the broad, sand beach.

She walked all the way out to the water's edge and strolled alongside it, the waves gently lapping over her bare feet from time to time. Like a lost soul, her long hair and white garment blowing about her slender body in the breeze, she looked bleakly out to the far horizon, scanning the indistinct line that separated sky and sea. Even the elements, like her thoughts, were confused and ran together.

She looked up and noted that the cloud layer above was breaking, allowing scattered sunshine to come through. Perversely, she was disappointed. She preferred the gray dullness the morning sky had brought; it suited her clouded spirit. Sunshine had a way of making her feel lonely.

She walked to a point parallel to the hotel's edge and then turned around and began to stroll back the other way. She recalled her discussion with her mother about the way she had felt so lonely that warm, sunny Saturday a number of months ago. For the first time she had admitted aloud that being single, independent, and living alone were not keeping her as happy and carefree as she would have liked to believe.

During the first year she had her own apartment, when she started working after graduation from college, she had thought she could be happy with that mode of living forever. But the second year alone had not pleased her quite so much, and she found she was glad to be able to go to her old home to have her evening meals with her parents rather than to have to eat alone.

And now? If she were totally truthful with herself, she had to admit that she wasn't really happy at all. Her life consisted of work, sleep, meals with her parents, tennis, and occasional outings with the few girl friends she had left who were also still single. She was successful in her nascent career, but that was the only aspect of her life that brought her a sense of well-being.

She stopped and looked out to the horizon again as the sun broke through the clouds above her, suddenly bathing her in warmth and light. Her eyes became moist and her lips trembled. "It's true, I do . . . want . . . to be married," she whispered to herself, her tongue having difficulty in actually verbalizing the admission.

But after she had pronounced the words, a kind of peace stole over her, a release of tension quieting her quickened heartbeat, as though her troubled spirit had at last resolved its unbearable conflict.

She walked on a few more paces. After several minutes, however, she sensed her brief euphoria gradually slipping away from her like the waves on the sand. She found that the idea of actually being married to a man was terribly frightening. Would it mean giving up her career? Would she lose all her autonomy? Would her own identity be completely absorbed into her husband's, never to be found again? Suddenly she was feeling she would rather go back to the idea of staying single.

"No, I don't want to do that," she told herself softly. "I can't stay like this. Oh, what's the matter with me? I'm afraid of being lonely and afraid of being married. I might as well be afraid of life!"

Angry with herself now, she walked on a few agitated paces, then stopped and looked up at the brightening sky. "I'll manage it somehow," she assured herself in a firm whisper, lowering her gaze to her own footsteps in the sand. "It'll take me a while to get used to the idea of marriage, to rethink my old attitudes, to find a man with whom I can share a mutual respect—a man I can trust and love." She watched as a wave flowed over her feet, then slipped away, carrying with it the very footprints she had been contemplating. She took a shallow, shuddering breath. "Oh, Mark, Mark," she moaned, her voice barely audible, "why couldn't it have been you? Why . . . ?"

"Do you always go about whispering things to yourself?"

The low, sardonic voice went through her like a shock wave. She swung around to face a very real Mark Chavira staring down at her, the ephemeral image she had been carrying suddenly turned into flesh and blood. Her mouth parted slightly as her eyes, huge with wonder, looked wistfully over his handsome features. His black hair mussed from the strong breeze, his skin tone deepened by recent exposure to the sun, he studied her face through dark eyes that burned with hard, anxious questions.

As she returned his gaze, she was unaware of the large wave that rolled over her feet, suddenly undermining the sand beneath her. He reached out and put his hands on her upper arms to steady her balance, then pulled her farther back onto the beach. When they had stepped back onto dry sand, he stopped, but she continued to move forward until she was against him, slipping her arms about his waist and resting her head below his shoulder.

He seemed momentarily stunned but soon encircled her in his arms and drew her even closer. "Well!" he exclaimed somewhat breathlessly. "To what do I owe this honor?" She looked up at him with tears flowing down her cheeks, her throat so tight with emotion she could not speak. His expression softened and lights danced in his eyes. "Don't tell me you actually missed me!"

"Yes," she whispered, taking in an uneven breath.

"Did you? You mean it? That's more than I'd even hoped for," he said softly, drawing her close against him once more.

He's back! He came back for me! her heart chimed. Then, suddenly anxious to be reassured, she asked, "What brings you to La Paz? Are you on your way home?" the thought coming to mind that he might just be passing through as Ray and Keith had been.

"No, I'm returning to Cabo San Lucas tomorrow. I came here today to . . . to tell you that I'll let you pay me back after all."

"Oh," she said, her heart beginning to sink.

"You can buy me a drink at the hotel's disco tonight," he told her with a smile.

Her mouth forced a faint answering smile. "Okay," she replied, as she felt herself tumbling back to earth.

They began to walk along the shore together as Mark studied her downcast demeanor. "What's wrong?" he asked, brushing back the long windblown hair from one side of her face. "Don't you like discos?"

"They're all right, I guess," she replied. She hesitated, then decided to ask the question that troubled her mind. She stopped walking and turned to face him. "Mark, what did you mean when you said there was only one thing you'd ever accept from me? I . . . I didn't think you meant my buying you a drink," she said with a nervous smile.

His expression became grave. "No, I didn't." He grew quiet and began walking again with slow strides, his eyes on the sand in front of him.

She followed. "What did you mean then?" she asked with jittery persistence.

He stopped and looked down at her. His eyes seemed at once determined and apprehensive. "Joey, I'm in love with you. What I wanted—what I still want— is your love." He lowered his eyes to the sand, ". . . that is if you think you *can* love me."

Joey was speechless for a moment, afraid to believe her ears. Then she gushed, "Oh, Mark, I can and I do love you!" as she was throwing her arms about his neck, her heart joyously pounding with complete happiness. "I do love you!" she repeated, her cheek against his tanned neck, left bare by his open shirt collar. She pressed her lips against the warm skin and felt his strong arms constricting about her waist. "Mark," she gasped, raising her lips to invite his kiss. He took her mouth ardently with his own, pressing her tightly against him.

After a long while they breathlessly loosened their holds, smiling, even laughing a bit at themselves. Putting an arm about one another they began to walk slowly along the water's edge, dodging the waves and playfully pulling each other off balance. They were behaving just like all the pairs of lovers Joey had observed walking along the beach, she thought, as she nuzzled against Mark's shoulder.

"Why didn't you tell me you loved me before?" she asked.

"With you calling me every name in the book at any opportunity? I think I told you that I cared, but you were always so suspicious."

"I know, Mark. I'm sorry. I shouldn't have doubted you," she told him earnestly. "I know now that you were sincere."

"Are you sure?" he said with a smile, his eyes pinning her down. "I thought you had me down as a roguish skirt chaser. What about my other woman in Cabo San Lucas?"

"Oh, please don't talk about it," she begged, deeply ashamed. "I guess I just have a vivid imagination, blowing mistaken impressions all out of proportion. I've been leery of men for so long, it's probably distorted my thinking. I hope I'm cured now."

"With the bad experiences you've had, it's understandable," he said, giving her a comforting hug. "If there's anything you'd like me to explain . . ."

"No," she said firmly, her hand making a horizontal motion in the air. "I don't want you to explain anything. You've come back for me and that's all I need to know. You wouldn't have bothered if you'd had all those other women I was imagining."

"Good God, how many did you think I had?" he asked, much amused.

"Oh, hundreds!" she exclaimed, laughing at herself.

"I didn't know I had such a macho image," he said, raising his brows, while his eyes momentarily held a worldly, dissipated look.

"Oh, yes," she breathed, edging close to him. "That's why I was so afraid of you. I sensed you were more than I could handle. I was right!"

He chuckled silently. "Because I tracked you down and kept you prisoner in my van?"

"No," she said, laughing. "I thought I could be happy without a man, and you proved I was wrong."

"Taming an independent woman—I suppose that is sort of a macho-style accomplishment, at that," he said, looking rather satisfied with himself. He turned and looked into her eyes. "But Joey, I want you to realize that I'm really pretty soft-hearted underneath. I don't want you to think that I fit the image of an unbending, unemotional male. You said I was insensitive and . . ."

"And I was wrong. I know now you aren't." She glanced up at him and smiled. "You forgot to say you're also patient and forgiving. You must be to put up with me!"

"That's true," he agreed with mock conceit, then his eyes grew tender. "But you're worth it!"

They exchanged an affectionate kiss and, arms about one another, began to walk slowly back toward the hotel. "By the way," Joey said as they were climbing the steps to the pool area, "how come you didn't tell me you were rich and famous?"

"I'm rich and famous?" he responded with raised brows.

"My father knew you by name, said that you've been written up in all the papers, and that you're one of the most prominent businessmen in California."

Mark took a breath. "My company has been doing well, it's true . . ." he understated.

"Tell me how you accomplished it," she said eagerly, taking him by the arm. They had reached the top of the steps and she led him past the pool to some comfortable seats by the open-air bar. "Don't be modest. I want to know everything!"

"There's not that much to tell. I went to college, studied business and real estate, then went out and applied myself," he said, matter-of-factly.

"Just like that, huh?" she said, snapping her fingers.

"Well, it took a little time," he granted.

"And a little genius! Don't be so evasive. I understand business matters, or have you forgotten?"

His mouth formed a little smile while his eyes traveled knowingly from her childlike face with its small, turned-up nose and adorably pouting mouth to the brief but well-filled bikini discernible beneath her thin cover-up. "I do tend to forget that from time to time," he admitted.

She lowered her eyes and smiled, having thoroughly enjoyed his perusal. "So tell me about your career," she resumed her prodding. "I've been remiss in reading the newspapers regularly, so you'll have to fill me in on everything from your very first project to all your latest developments."

"That'll take all afternoon!"

"You have something better to do?" she sassed with a charming pout.

Mark made a wry face. "I see now how you get production from your difficult clients!"

They spent the next few hours talking leisurely over drinks and a late lunch at the outdoor restaurant while Mark outlined the history of the notoriously successful company he had founded. Joey asked many pertinent questions which he seemed only too happy to answer, his eyes taking on a certain pride as each of her queries reflected her keen business mind.

They were sitting by the pool late in the afternoon when Ed and Milly Scott returned from their day-long excursion. They approached the young couple and introductions were made and a cordial conversation ensued, accented by a profusion of thank-yous from Joey's parents for her safe deliverance and Mark's engaging efforts to secure their goodwill in return. In fact, the three were so predisposed to like one another, it almost made Joey uneasy.

"He's such a fine young man. So handsome, too," her mother was saying when Joey and her parents were back in their room. They were changing to have dinner with Mark at another hotel in the heart of La Paz.

"Oh, Mark's a great guy," her father agreed, as he was tying his tie before the mirror. "Any time you want to walk down the aisle with him is fine with me, Jo."

"What?" Joey gasped.

"Now, Ed, don't rush her. They haven't known each other long," her mother gently chided.

"If you ask me," Mr. Scott said omnisciently, "he's got his mind made up already!"

"But maybe Joey doesn't," his wife pointed out.

He turned away from the mirror and looked directly at his daughter. "Now, Jo, you don't want to pass him up." He broke into a smile. "I know, you women like to play hard to get. But it's obvious you two are crazy about each other, so there's no use being coy."

"I'm not, Dad," Joey objected, her thoughts suddenly confused. She loved Mark and only that morning had decided she wanted to be married, so why was she feeling panicky listening to this conversation?

"Sometimes these things take time, Ed. There's no need to force the issue. It's a matter to be handled between them alone, and I'm sure everything will fall into place in due course. Let's not embarrass Joey with any more conjecturing. And I don't want to hear any broad hints over dinner!" Milly Scott told her husband firmly.

Joey relaxed a bit at her mother's soothing words. Things were just happening a little too fast, that was all. There was a long step between deciding in theory to marry and actually marrying one man in particular. She realized her old fears were still lingering and she would need some time to exorcise them. Besides, Mark would be there to help her make all the adjustments, she thought, as a smile crept over her face.

Her mood suddenly carefree, she walked over to the mirror her father had just vacated to apply some makeup. Her complexion was so radiant, she found she needed very little. She combed her hair and checked her dress, a stylish, rose-colored garment with bouffant sleeves gathered at the wrists. It buttoned up the front to a high collar and its full skirt accentuated her small waist.

They met Mark in the lobby and drove together into town to a stately old hotel on a busy street which edged the waterfront. In the hotel's restaurant, they were seated at a heavy wooden table set beside a large window overlooking the bay. Joey found that conversation was easily maintained by her parents and Mark as they enjoyed their delicious fresh fish dinners.

"You mentioned this afternoon that you visited Cabo San Lucas," Mark was saying to the Scotts. "How did you like it?"

"Great place!" her father exclaimed. "And Milly liked it so much she was even willing to get into a boat to see Land's End!"

"Really?" said Joey with surprise, knowing her mother's fear of water and her tendency toward seasickness.

"Oh, your father did some of his fast talking to get me into one of those rowboats—that's all they were, you know. So off we went, farther and farther away from the beach, to see the huge rock formations. I was petrified, of course, but once we got back on shore, I was glad I went. It was very beautiful and majestic."

"I wish I had seen it, now," Joey said, recalling similar glowing reports from Ray and Keith.

"Would you like to?" Mark asked eagerly. "Actually, I was going to invite you all to come to Cabo tomorrow to meet some of my relatives who own a restaurant there. But you may not feel like making the long trip again so soon . . ." he said, now addressing himself mainly to the elder Scotts.

Milly Scott's face brightened. "I wouldn't mind. Oh, I forgot, I promised Ed he could spend the day fishing," she said, turning to her husband. "He's been so good about taking me around," she explained, "I decided to let him get in some of the fishing he was so anxious to do. He signed up to go out tomorrow morning."

"Oh, I guess I could skip it," Mr. Scott said a trifle reluctantly.

"No, I've heard how much you enjoy fishing. I do too," Mark sympathized jovially. "As long as you're here I wouldn't want you to miss it; La Paz is an ideal fishing area. Perhaps you wouldn't mind if your wife and daughter came out on their own?"

"Now that's a good idea!" Ed Scott said with enthusiasm. "You and Jo could take our car," he said to his wife. "It was a nice drive and the road wasn't bad. What do you think?"

"I'd love to if Joey is willing," Mrs. Scott responded, looking toward her daughter.

"Oh, sure," Joey replied, bewildered by the sudden turn of events. The idea of meeting Mark's relatives took her by surprise. "Should . . . should we follow you when you leave tomorrow?" she asked the handsome man sitting next to her.

"Well, you can if you want to get up at the crack of dawn. I promised my uncles I would be back bright and early to help them out. You see, they've been putting on an addition to the restaurant and they're running a little behind schedule. There's going to be a wedding in the family in a few days and the place was supposed to be ready for a party afterward. I've been helping out with painting and putting the place in order. There's a lot to do even though the basic construction work is finished," Mark explained.

"After today I don't think I'd be able to get up that early," Mrs. Scott said with a smile. "I think it would be best if we left later in the morning, don't you, Joey?"

Her daughter readily agreed, not wanting to be in a position to spend the entire day with his relatives—a possibility which made her uneasy. She wondered what they would make of Mark's bringing her and her mother around to meet them. They might be as quick to jump to conclusions as her parents were. She told Mark they would arrive at about one or two o'clock in the afternoon.

After dinner they took a stroll down the palm-lined walk along the water's edge. It was a beautiful, clear evening and the air was warm and calm. Streetlights gave the city a soft glow as cars and pedestrians moved about, and offshore a few boats and ships of varying sizes were silently moored.

"Say, Mark, am I mistaken, or was there a write-up about your home in one of the local California magazines some time ago?" Mr. Scott turned to ask, as they walked in pairs, the Scotts taking the lead.

"Yes, there was. It was right after I had had it built and the interior designers were finished with their work," Mark told him.

"Looked like a beautiful home," Mr. Scott commented with the air of the experienced realtor that he was. "How many rooms?"

"Oh, let's see: six bedrooms, four bathrooms, two living rooms, dining room, breakfast room, office, den, game room, library, and . . . oh, yes, the kitchen. Of course there's a pool, and also a specially constructed outdoor barbecue. I've been thinking of adding a tennis court."

As Joey's head spun with this lengthy enumeration, her mother quipped, "Don't you get lost in all that space?"

"It has been a great deal more house than I need," Mark admitted, "but I built it with an eye toward selling it someday, unless, of course, things change," he added, turning his eyes on his lovely companion.

Joey glanced up at his intent, dark eyes and quickly looked away. The thought of being put in charge of running such a house was more than she could handle at the moment. She felt Mark take her hand and sensed his eyes were seeking hers again, but she dared not look up at him. A claustrophobic feeling began to overcome her and she fought the urge to escape.

Mark put an arm around her shoulders and gave her a little shake. With his free hand, he turned her head to look at him. His eyes were filled with amusement and understanding, as though he had read her mind and was silently chiding her for making a mountain out of a molehill. She smiled back, realizing that was exactly what she was doing, embarrassed now at her habit of escalating fears all out of proportion to reality. Suddenly she felt exuberant and lovingly slipped an arm about Mark's waist, under his sport coat. He was so good for her, she thought, marveling at his sensitivity to her emotional needs.

When they all had had enough walking, they drove back to the La Playa. Joey's parents graciously excused themselves to retire, saying it was already later than they usually stayed up, and encouraged the younger couple to go to the disco as they had planned.

"Do you think your parents like me?" Mark asked, as they were walking past the outdoor lobby to the entrance of the disco.

"Like you! They've practically been falling all over you," Joey exclaimed with a touch of asperity.

"I thought they seemed to like me, but with the questionable circumstances of our meeting and traveling together, I wouldn't blame them if they were a little dubious."

"They were when I first told them the story, but I explained that it was all perfectly innocent. And when my father found out who you were, you were completely exonerated."

"So they take me to be a proper gentleman?"

"Yes. Well, you are . . . more or less," she said with a sly grin.

He regarded her expression with amusement. "I'll have you know it wasn't easy, young lady. Why do you think I slept outside that last night? After our encounter earlier in the day, I couldn't trust myself anymore.''

"So that was why you told me to lock the door. I thought maybe it was to prevent you from wringing my neck.''

"That was my second reason,'' he sallied, trying to maintain a straight face.

As they neared the entrance to the disco, Joey looked out to the pool area, curious to see if it was being used. There was one lone swimmer in the water.

"It's kind of late to be swimming,'' she commented, looking back to Mark.

It seemed he hadn't heard her, his attention being completely engrossed in the attire of a young woman entering the disco with her escort. The attractive girl was wearing a clinging dress which uncovered more than covered her smashing figure. Joey and Mark watched together as she disappeared behind the door.

"Wow!'' she heard Mark gasp under his breath before he turned to Joey with, "Did you say something?''

"Oh, it wasn't very important,'' she said in an airy but clearly injured tone of voice.

"Did you expect me not to notice her?'' he said, correctly interpreting her reaction.

"Well, you didn't have to gawk. She's obviously just trying to attract attention to herself.''

"Now, Joey, you know how men are. There'd be something wrong with me if I didn't look. It doesn't mean anything.''

"How come you don't stare at me then? My figure's just as good as hers,'' she said in a slightly provocative manner.

There was a comfortable look in his eye as he replied, "Your figure is better. But at the moment it's not so much on display.''

"And you're forced to look for the ones that are,'' she finished.

"Joey . . .'' His voice was edged with exasperation.

"We'd better go in,'' she said, smiling to herself as she opened the door to the disco. She was glad she had managed to unsettle his calm attitude over the matter. Though her former misgivings about men were softening, she still felt men should be made to pay for their errant ways.

They entered the dimly lit room and found a small table just vacated near the crowded dance floor. Joey's spirits drooped a little as she picked out a few other well-proportioned young women in stylishly skimpy attire jiggling about on the dance floor. She looked at Mark and was both amused and miffed to see his surreptitious glances in their direction. She began to feel dowdy and schoolmarmish in her high-buttoned dress.

"Would you excuse me for a moment?'' she asked Mark quietly before running off to the ladies' room.

When Joey returned a few minutes later to take her seat next to Mark, her appearance was somewhat altered. The buttons down the front of her dress from her collar almost to her waist were all undone, subtly revealing the smooth skin and shadowy, well-formed curves beneath.

Mark's startled expression instantly turned grim. "What have you done!''

Surprised at his reaction, she replied, "This is the way models wear their clothes in fashion magazines. Besides, I have to compete with all these other women for your attention.''

"Will you sit up straight!" he ordered, glancing about at other men nearby. "You don't have to compete with anyone."

She complied by straightening her posture. "Come on now, you haven't missed one woman here in a low-cut dress. What's wrong with my wanting you to notice me, too?"

"Joey, I don't want all the men in here leering at you."

"You mean it's all right for you to ogle other women, but no one is supposed to look at me?"

"Right!" he said obstinately. "Now, will you button yourself up?"

"No!"

"Joey . . ."

"No!" she repeated, her expression as mulish as his.

"All right, young lady!" he said as he grabbed her tightly by the wrist, forcing her to rise from her seat. He pulled her by the arm relentlessly, passing curious onlookers, until they were through the door and outside again.

"How dare you!" she cried as she rubbed the bruised wrist he had at last released.

"No wife of mine is going to appear that way in public!" he stormed.

"I'm not your wife!" she retorted with a quivering lip.

Her statement made him pause. His dark eyes studied her for a moment, then slowly lowered to the ground. "You know I want you to be," he said quietly.

She swallowed convulsively. "W-why would I want to marry anyone who orders me around?" she asked in a small voice that seemed to cut through the night air.

His expression became troubled. "I'm sorry," he said, taking her hands in his. "I shouldn't have been so boorish, but I just couldn't tolerate the thought of other men eyeing what belongs to me, as if you were still on the market."

"You have no right to speak of me as if I were a piece of property you owned!"

"I didn't mean it to sound like that," he amended hastily. "I—" Mark was interrupted by a large group of people leaving the disco, who were forced to dodge them as they stood by the door. Mark pulled her away. "Why don't we go up to the top floor and see if there's a view," he suggested. "Maybe we can be alone there."

She nodded her acquiescence and they proceeded to take the elevator up to the top of the building. They walked out onto the empty balcony, past a number of hotel rooms, until they reached the end. "I guess it's too dark to see much," he said, looking out over the bay, "but at least we shouldn't be bothered." He took her hands again and looked down at her face. "Look, maybe I am possessive about you," he said, resuming their previous topic, "but that's the way a man behaves when he's in love and unsure of the woman he cares about. I like to think of you as mine."

"But . . . but I'm not. I don't belong to anyone," she asserted, suddenly finding her independence very precious.

His brows drew together. "You don't realize how much it hurts me to hear you say that. Don't I mean anything to you?"

The question threw her into confusion. "Yes, of course you do," she whispered.

"Do you still love me?"

"Yes."

He smiled, as if it were all so simple. "Then you belong to me, just as I belong to you—don't you see?"

She was deeply troubled and could not form a response. He enfolded her in warm, comforting arms. "Joey, is it making a commitment that frightens you so?" he asked softly. "Or are you afraid I'll take away your freedom and police your life, even tell you what you can and can't wear?"

"Yes!" she whispered.

"You're afraid I'll be one of those domineering men, like your father, perhaps, who'll only allow you to say yes, sir?"

She nodded her head.

"Well, I won't," he said, giving her a shake by the shoulders. "As long as you stay away from wearing plunging necklines in public, I'd want you to feel free to wear and do whatever you'd like. And your father didn't seem so high-handed as you described him. Is he really that bad?"

Feeling somewhat reassured, Joey made a little smile. "My mother's beginning to bring him under control."

"Good for her! Now, if your mother can do it, do you really have doubts about your ability to keep *me* in line?"

"Maybe you're right. She's managed to turn him to jelly lately," she replied, laughing a bit now as her fears began to ebb.

"It's not so hard," Mark said without joining in her amusement. "I feel like I've been losing my grip ever since I met you. You're the most unmanageable, unpredictable woman I ever saw. It's like trying to capture a butterfly—you always flit off in some unexpected direction. Don't run away from me anymore, Joey," he whispered, pressing her closer and lowering his mouth to hers.

She willingly succumbed to his hard embrace, putting her arms around his neck and eagerly returning his kiss. His hands moved restively over her back, tangling in her long, silky hair.

"Say you'll be mine, Joey. Say you'll marry me," he prodded in a soft, urgent voice. "Will you?" His dark eyes riveted on hers through the dim light, expectant and impatient.

She stared back at him wide-eyed and unblinking for a long, suspended moment, knowing how much her future weighed upon her answer, but somehow unable to feel it. All the intuitive senses and emotions she usually relied upon suddenly had left her and her mind seemed strangely dulled. The dark eyes fixed upon her were growing more bleak with each fraction of a second she hesitated. All she knew now was that she couldn't bear to make him unhappy. "Yes," she responded in a tiny whisper.

His eyes became liquid and shimmering. "Joey," Mark said in an uneven voice, "I'll try to make you happy. You won't regret it." His arms tightened around her. She felt numb, as if her head and body were made of cotton, like a stuffed doll. But as he kissed her again, her vital, human force returned with increased strength, making her doubly sensitive to the feel of his hands and lips. She soon became lost in the warmth and darkness of his arms, wishing never to be found.

She felt Mark pulling away before she wanted to end the kiss. Rising up on tiptoes, she sought his lips again, but he restrained her. "There are some people coming," he told her quietly and then she became aware of the footsteps and soft conversation behind her. Feeling a little foolish, she drew away from him to a more decorous distance.

In another minute she heard a door close. "They're gone now," Mark told her with a smile. He took a step toward her and put his hands at her waist. "Where were we?"

Her small hands rose to the back of his neck and pulled him toward her. This time their kiss was immediately intense, as though a fiery electric current were passing between them. His hands moved roughly over her, soon finding the loose front opening of her dress, while his lips grew more demanding. The sensation of his long fingers moving caressingly over her soft, sensitive skin created an aching, a frightfully urgent desire within. Her breathing growing unsteady and her heart pounding, she clung to him, wanting more . . . more. . . .

Joey had barely heard the first distant burst of laughter. It came again, closer now, accompanied by the unwelcome sound of more footsteps at the other end of the balcony. Mark reluctantly took his mouth from hers, but they did not pull apart this time; it would have been too painful. He dropped his hands to her waist and inclined his head toward hers until the noisy couple approaching had found their room and gone in, shutting the door behind them.

Mark lifted his eyes to hers and they looked at one another with sadness and longing. "Busy place," he remarked, making an effort to smile.

"Mark, couldn't we go to your room? We could be alone," she said, her voice fading as she saw the pain in his eyes.

He slowly shook his head. "Do you know what you're asking? If you came with me to my room, you wouldn't leave until morning. I wouldn't have enough will power to let you go. I barely have enough now. Do you want to have to explain to your parents where you were all night? With the upbringing they've given you, would you feel right about it yourself?"

Joey bowed her head. "No," she admitted through quivering lips, tears forming in her eyes.

"Besides, you've had doubts about me, unfounded doubts, but apparently very real. I don't want to give you any reason to question the sincerity of my intentions toward you. You might willingly let yourself be carried away tonight and then feel tomorrow, in the cold light of day, that you had been used. I would rather wait until you're my wife and can come to me with complete trust than take any chances of reawakening your doubts."

She put her arms around his waist and buried her face in his chest. "Oh, Mark, I trust you. I don't know how I could have ever doubted you. But you're right," she said, pulling away, "it would be better not to . . . be alone with you. I didn't realize what I was saying."

"No, I don't think you did," he said, smiling down as he dried her eyes. "It's probably a good thing you've kept your distance from men all this time. I think you could be seduced very easily."

"Only by you," she amended with a pout.

"Good. I'll take you to your room now. I have to get up early anyway," he said, putting an arm about her and leading her back toward the elevator. "And you'd better button up that dress in case your parents are still awake."

"Okay," she softly replied as she dutifully started the chore. She smiled and a warmth stole over her. Mark was too good for her, she decided, happily noting that this was a statement she had always doubted she could make about any man.

9

It was a bright sunny morning as Joey and Milly Scott drove along Highway 1 toward Cabo San Lucas, passing through a dry, hilly landscape with the now-familiar desert vegetation. Joey blinked her eyes hard, feeling tired from not having slept well the night before. They had left much earlier than expected. Her mother, who apparently hadn't needed as much sleep as she had anticipated, had awakened early and hurried Joey along, anxious to be off.

"It will be nice to meet Mark's relatives, won't it, dear?"

"Oh, sure," Joey replied, gripping the steering wheel more tightly and wishing she hadn't been reminded of their reason for making the trip.

"What an advantage to have relations to visit in Cabo San Lucas! Just think, if you married Mark. Oh, I'm sorry. I didn't mean to sound pushy," Milly said, noticing her daughter's edgy reaction to the mention of marriage. "It's just that Mark is such a fine person and he seems so taken with you. In fact I thought I heard him drop a hint or two. I think you should begin to prepare yourself for a proposal, Joey."

"He . . . he did propose, Mother."

"He did!"

"Last night."

"What did you say?" her mother asked, breathless.

"I said yes. At least I think that's what I said. I'm sure that's what I said."

"You don't remember?" Mrs. Scott asked incredulously.

Joey briefly raised a tremulous hand to her forehead. "Well, it happened so fast . . . my mind was in a whirl. I felt pretty good about the whole idea when I came in and went to bed, but I woke up a few hours later in a panic. It was dark, and I felt, well, jittery and . . . and trapped. I kept going over what he and I said to each other, turning the words about in my mind, until after a while, I wasn't sure anymore what I told him. I suppose I was hoping I had really said, 'Let me think about it.' Things are clearer this morning, and I feel a little more secure again. I love Mark, but getting married is scary!"

"It is a big change in one's life," her mother agreed, a little troubled over her daughter's misgivings. "He probably just took you too much by storm. I'm sure you'll feel better about it soon."

"You know that I had always thought I would stay single. I never saw any advantage to being married," Joey explained. "Although I was lonely being unattached . . ." she admitted, reminding herself of that troublesome fact. "Now, within two weeks of meeting Mark, I'm engaged!"

Milly smiled sympathetically. "That isn't much time. He's obviously in a hurry, but maybe you could talk him into a period of engagement—perhaps a few months. That would give you some time to get used to the idea before actually taking the plunge."

"That may be a good idea! I hadn't thought of that," Joey exclaimed, her spirits suddenly lifting. "I could use the busy season as an excuse. In fact, I don't see how I could make any wedding plans until the tax season is over in the spring. I'll have to begin working overtime as soon as I get back. That would give me a few months to adjust," she said, mentally contemplating how well everything could fall into place. "If I still wasn't sure by that time, I could drag out making the wedding plans. . . ."

"Joey, it's his wedding, too. He might want to dash you off to Las Vegas, in which case there wouldn't be any plans to take your time with," her mother pointed out, bursting Joey's comfortable bubble of procrastination.

"Then I . . . I'd just refuse to go," she said, her apprehensions returning.

"I'm sure he wouldn't do anything that would make you unhappy," her mother reassured her. "I imagine he'd be willing to wait for a reasonable time since you haven't known each other long, but I don't think he'd let you get away with continually putting the date off. You'll have to face it sometime, Joey, or you may lose him. All changes in life are a little frightening, but if you don't go through them, you don't progress. I've been learning that myself."

"Yes, I suppose you're right," Joey agreed reluctantly.

"I know you're very much in love with him—you were miserable until he came back yesterday. Do you want to risk having that empty feeling for the rest of your life, just because you were afraid to give marriage a chance?"

"No," Joey replied in a forlorn voice. "But, Mother, what if I'm not happy being married. I know you're different from me, but I don't think I'd be content with the domestic life-style you've had."

"Well, I don't know that I've been entirely content with it myself," her mother admitted. "But you have a different temperament than I, so your marriage would probably be different as well. Also, Mark seems a little more perceptive than your father is about some matters. I don't see why you and Mark shouldn't be able to work things out together to suit yourselves."

"I hope so," Joey said with a worried sigh.

Soon they were entering the growing resort town of Cabo San Lucas, fronting a small harbor at the southernmost tip of Baja California. It was smaller than La Paz and not so well developed; more a sleepy village when compared to the urban center that was La Paz. But in the distance could be seen modern, elegant resort hotels, overlooking huge sandy beaches and the sea, which accommodated hundreds of tourists from many parts of the world.

Following the directions Mark had given them at dinner, Joey drove up to a pleasant looking, well-kept, low building marked RESTAURANTE. There were tables outside as well as inside, but there were no customers and the place did not appear to be open for business. Off to the side there was evidence of recent construction with lumber and building equipment lying around. It was about 10:30 in the morning as Joey parked the car in front of the building.

"I guess this is the place," Joey said, trepidation showing in her voice. "I'll bet it's not open yet. We're awfully early."

"Maybe they're inside. Why don't you go in and see?" her mother urged.

Joey was hesitant. "I feel kind of funny about this. I mean, Mark wasn't expecting us until this afternoon."

"Joey, we drove all this way to see him. I'm sure he won't mind if we're early. What makes you so diffident all of a sudden?"

"Meeting his relatives, I guess," she answered truthfully. "I tend to look at it as bringing me that much closer to the altar."

Her mother laughed. "Simply meeting his uncles and cousins doesn't seal your future. Just take things one step at a time. Meanwhile, you have the love of a man a lot of women would give their eye teeth for, so try to be happy about it!"

"All right, Mother. Thanks," Joey said with a little smile, somewhat reassured by her calm good sense. She got out of the car and walked across the small street toward the restaurant. As she approached, she could see through a window that there were a few people inside the building, apparently putting the place in order. They appeared to be older—a woman and two men. Joey guessed the two men would be Mark's uncles. Suddenly she felt very uneasy. She hated to go and knock on the door asking for Mark, and thus cause them to speculate about her identity and reason for calling. She quickly decided it would be much better if she could simply locate him on her own without bothering his relatives. Besides, she rationalized, they may not speak English anyway.

Joey turned from her path toward the front entrance and followed the building around to the side, toward what appeared to be the newly constructed addition. Carefully stepping over some pieces of lumber lying on the sandy ground, she at last came to an open doorway and, stepping up to it, peered in.

She was not at all prepared for the scene that met her eyes. There, a short way inside, was Mark standing with his arms about a very beautiful, black-haired young girl. The girl in the picture! He was hugging her tightly and smiling down at her, while she, in turn, was raising her arms to encircle his neck and stretching up to kiss him.

Joey's heart seemed to stop. For a moment she turned to stone, her stunned eyes taking in the embracing couple—the lovely young Mexican girl, her slender body leaning against Mark's as she affectionately kissed him, and Mark's whole-hearted, adoring response. All her old suspicions had been true. He did have another woman.

Joey backed away from the door without a sound, fearing her presence would be discovered. When she was out of their view, she turned and hurried back to her car, darted behind the wheel and closed the door.

"What happened?" her mother urgently asked, watching her daughter's quick, but unsteady movements in starting the car and putting it in gear.

Joey waited until she had driven well away from the restaurant and had better control of her emotions before answering. "I saw him with someone else. He was kissing her!" she told her mother in a choked voice. "I guess I won't be marrying him after all!" she added with a hollow, contemptuous sarcasm. "He's just like all the others. Why should a woman trust any man?"

"Now try to be calm, Joey. Tell me again what happened," her mother begged.

Joey's chin quivered. "I went around to the addition and found the entrance. When I looked in, I saw him with a young girl in his arms. She looked like she was used to his attentions—she was hanging all over him. And Mark was encouraging her!" Joey's voice broke and she blinked hard to clear her vision. Tears ran down her cheeks as she finished. "I got away as fast as I could and came back to the car."

"Did he see you?"

"No."

"Then he never had a chance to explain . . ."

Joey looked at her mother as if she had lost her reason. "Explain! Why would I want to hear any explanation? What possible excuse could he have for his behavior? The day after asking me to marry him, I find him in the arms of another woman—or rather, girl," she corrected herself with disdain. "She couldn't be much more than half his age. In fact, I found a picture of her in his van when I was traveling with him. I wondered then . . ."

"But, Joey, I just can't believe this of him," Mrs. Scott said with sincerity. "Isn't it possible this girl could be one of his relatives? People are often affectionate with their relatives."

"A kissing cousin?" Joey said with derisive sarcasm. "No, Mother, this girl was far too beautiful and far too eager to be merely a relative."

"What will you do?"

"Do? Nothing! Never see him again."

"Oh, Joey," her mother said sadly. "Shouldn't you give him a chance to explain himself? I can't believe he would do this to you."

"Mother, this isn't the first time I've been led to doubt him. He's been nothing but a woman chaser from the beginning. If you knew the way he leered at me the first time I saw him! Why, even last night, when he was out with me, he was looking over every other attractive woman in sight."

"Then why did you agree to marry him? You must have sensed something good in him, as your father and I did," her mother asked in a common-sense manner.

Joey was in the midst of turning back onto Highway 1 to return to La Paz and conveniently used the diversion to pretend she was distracted, for she did not know how to answer her mother.

"He . . . he has a way about him," she replied after a few moments. "That's why he's so successful with women. He knows how to delude them, mesmerize them until they don't know if they're coming or going."

Mrs. Scott silently shook her head. "I thought he was so open and straightforward. Are you sure you didn't read more into what you saw than was there?"

"No, Mother," Joey answered in exasperation. "Remember, I've been through this before. Once you find a man who claims to love you in the arms of another woman, it leaves little doubt in your mind."

"Oh, yes—Robin. I had forgotten him," her mother sympathized. "But, you know, I never really liked Robin. The few times I met him I always sensed there was something secretive underneath his engaging manner. I never felt that way about Mark. I thought he was exactly the way he appeared to be—honest and reliable."

The car drew to a halt at the side of the road. Her face crumpling into tears, Joey leaned forward and pressed her forehead against the backs of her hands as they gripped the top of the steering wheel. Her mother leaned over to comfort her.

"For a while, I thought he was, too," Joey cried brokenly, between sobs. "I really believed he was."

10

Joey stood before her bathroom mirror hurriedly pinning her long hair into a plain chignon at the base of her neck. She didn't bother with makeup, not caring that she looked pale and drawn, with dark circles under her eyes from insufficient sleep. She took a quick glance at her watch, tucked her blouse more securely beneath her skirt's waistband, which lately seemed to have increased in circumference, and walked into her small living room.

Her apartment was in disorder, as was usual during the busy season. She had no time to spare for housecleaning, but as she was the only one who saw the mess, she rationalized that it didn't really matter much. Having decided to skip breakfast again, she grabbed her jacket, picked up her heavy, oversized briefcase filled with papers she had brought home the night before, and walked out the door.

In the small apartment building's parking lot, she put the briefcase into the back of her subcompact, which had been restored to working order by the mechanics in Guerrero Negro. It had been ready when she and her parents returned there on their way home from La Paz early in January.

It had been a hasty return. Joey had persuaded her parents to begin their journey home the very next day after the ill-fated trip to Cabo San Lucas. She suspected Mark would come back to La Paz to look for her and took the precaution of leaving the La Playa and staying at a different hotel that last night. Her parents reluctantly came with her to the new hotel, and in that way she erased any possibility of Mark's contacting her by phone or coming that evening in person to find out why she had not shown up. It would have seemed to him that she had simply disappeared.

Since then, Joey learned that he had come looking for her. In fact, Mark had not ceased trying to contact her during the two months she had been back in California. The first phone call came at her office about a week after she had returned. As soon as he had identified himself, she hung the phone up. Then, coming home late that evening after work, she had found her telephone ringing when she walked in and had hurried to pick it up.

"Hello?"

"Joey?"

"Yes . . ." she reluctantly replied, suspicious of the low, male voice. It sounded like Mark, but how could he have obtained her unlisted number?

"Joey, what's going on? And don't hang up! Why didn't you see me at the restaurant?" He waited for an answer, but received none. "I drove all the way back to La Paz that evening and then I found you had checked out of your hotel. What on earth made you leave so fast? Couldn't you have left me word somehow?" There was a long silence over the wire after his barrage of questions. "Joey?"

"How did you get my number?" Joey asked in a strained but cold voice.

A pause before answering indicated his distress at her response. "I found a listing for your father's real estate office and then got his home phone. I called your parents and talked to your mother. She . . . she seemed to indicate you were upset about something, but wouldn't give me any details. She just gave me your number so I could talk to you myself, which is what I intend to do. Now, tell me what's wrong. What's going on?"

489

Cold as steel, Joey replied, "I don't want to talk to you. Don't call me again."

Quickly she had replaced the receiver, silencing the argumentative low voice protesting her words. How could she discuss her hurt and humiliation with him? How could she bear to hear his inevitable excuses and lies when she told him what she had seen? She still carried the memory of another such confrontation with Robin and couldn't endure the thought of living through a repetition of that scene to have another wretched remembrance to torment her for months and years to come. Her faith in Mark, whom she had loved much more than she had Robin, had been broken. There was no need to make the wound even larger than it already was.

That was the last time she had spoken to Mark, though he had called many more times. On each occasion she had speedily hung up the very instant she recognized his voice. The method seemed to work, for he had ceased trying to call her about a month ago.

However, it was only a short time later that he had attempted to see her. She was working on an audit one Sunday afternoon at the desk in her bedroom. Something made her glance out her second-story window, which overlooked her building's parking lot, and she caught a glimpse of a tall, dark-haired man, looking very much like Mark Chavira, moving just out of sight toward the building. In another moment her doorbell was ringing. Nervously she paced back and forth while she listened to it ring a dozen or more times. After several minutes she saw him walking back to his car with what seemed to be angry strides. With widened, watchful eyes she observed him, a mixture of feelings churning in her heart—fear, anger, and a hurt sort of wistfulness. If he loved her so little as to be untrue to her, why couldn't he leave her alone?

For the past three weeks, however, it seemed her desperate wish had come true. There were no more phone calls or attempted visits. Even her parents, whom she had stopped seeing at dinner because they continually made unwelcome suggestions that she was being unfair to Mark, seemed to have finally given up trying.

When Joey had stopped coming by for supper, Mrs. Scott had taken to calling her almost every evening. In spite of the fact that her daughter was still angry with her for giving Mark her phone number, Mrs. Scott continued to take his part, urging Joey to at least allow him to explain, even to give him another chance. Joey began to suspect that Mark was keeping contact with her parents, particularly her mother, and was managing to bend her already softened heart in his direction. On one occasion Mrs. Scott had tried valiantly to coax Joey to come to dinner on a particular night, arguing that they hadn't seen enough of her lately. Joey had steadfastly declined, claiming her heavy workload as an excuse, for she feared if she went to her parents' house that evening she would find the table set for four instead of three.

But finally it seemed even her mother had lost hope for remedying the situation, and for the past two weeks or so Joey had enjoyed a semblance of peace. At last she could concentrate more fully on her work and meeting her deadlines. If only she could sleep better at night, she would be fine, she had lately told herself. If only she didn't dream of Mark so often, think of him, remember his arms about her . . . only to remember those same arms embracing someone else.

Never again would she let her heart be captured by a man, she had decided with certainty and determination. She would forever remain her own woman—independent, unattached, self-sufficient.

She got into her small car, its marred front end having been cosmetically improved at a body shop, and drove about fifteen minutes to the two-story office building in Los Angeles which housed Layton and Brook Accountancy Corporation, along with several other small businesses.

After greeting the receptionist and one of her co-workers, she walked to her cubbyhole office and laid her heavy briefcase on the gray carpet, already cluttered with files, reference books, and papers. She threw her suit jacket onto one of the wooden chairs placed in the small room and sat down behind her well-used, but serviceable, wooden desk. She turned the desk calendar to the current day, March 16.

"Hi, Jo! How's it going?" asked Thomas Brook, the firm's junior partner, who popped in to see her. He was a tall man, overweight, with red-blond hair now beginning to turn gray as he entered his late forties.

"Hello, Tom. Pretty good," Joey replied, always glad to chat with Tom Brook. He was invariably pleasant and easygoing, unlike the firm's senior partner and founder, Harlan Layton—or Mr. Layton as he preferred to be called.

"How's the Springfield Foods account coming?"

"I finished it last night," she replied, bending over to drag her briefcase next to her chair so she could reach the file he had asked about.

"Great! I'll look it over then. Good work, Jo! Looks like we can make our deadline for that after all. You must have been up most of the night," he said, taking the thick pile of papers from her hands.

"Until about two thirty, but I don't mind. I'm glad to get it out of the way."

"Just because it's the busy season doesn't mean you have to kill yourself, you know. You've been looking awfully dragged out since you got back from Mexico."

"She's gotten skinnier, too," said Chris Langley, the firm's newest accountant, who suddenly appeared at her door. He was a young man, just out of college, with moderate good looks and a cocky, irreverent disposition. "She used to be pretty foxy looking, but the last couple of months she's just gone down the drain."

"Thanks, Chris," Joey replied, unperturbed. It was of no consequence to her what he or any other man thought of her appearance.

"She's just tired from working so hard—a feeling which you've probably never experienced," Tom remarked half-seriously to Chris.

"You're right about that," Chris quipped light-heartedly before breezing off down the hall.

"I don't know about that kid," Tom said, shaking his head. "I thought he would have settled down by now. Well, take it easy, okay, Jo?"

"Sure," she said with a smile as he left her office.

Take it easy! She didn't want to take it easy. It was better to bury herself in work than to think or feel or remember. Someday, when enough time had passed, she would be cured. But until then, the only answer was work.

Her determined thoughts were broken into by the sound of her name being called excitedly from down the hall.

"Jo! Jo! You here?" Suddenly Mr. Layton appeared at her door. He was a short man, very thin, with iron-gray hair, whose normally pale complexion was now brightened with agitation. "Come into my office, Jo," he said, motioning quickly.

Immediately she rose and followed him to his large office at the end of the short hall, wondering all the while what on earth was causing such a commotion. He directed her to sit in the leather chair opposite his desk as he closed the door behind them.

"Great news, Jo!" he said, almost out of breath. "I just got a call from Sunrise Development Company. They want us to take over their account—immediately! I guess they're not satisfied with their old accounting firm, didn't say just why. Anyway, they specifically insisted that you be in charge of it."

"Why?" she asked, totally at a loss.

"I don't know," he said, spreading his hands in the air. "You had one account last year in Orange County. Maybe they heard of you by word of mouth."

"Orange County . . ." Joey said, her voice dropping as the company's name suddenly began to ring an ominous bell in her head.

"Yes!" he said impatiently. "Haven't you heard of Sunrise Development Company? It's the biggest and most prosperous one in that whole county, maybe even the state! What a windfall! I've been waiting for twenty-five years for a well-known company to hire us. Just think of the prestige it'll bring, being able to mention their name as one of our clients. We'll probably be able to raise our rates, expand. Think of the new business we can attract!"

Joey's heart was beginning to pound, but she tried to remain calm. "Who was it that called you?"

"Mark Chavira himself!" Mr. Layton replied triumphantly.

Feeling the blood draining from her face, she suddenly felt faint and grasped the arms of her chair.

"You all right?" Layton asked gruffly. "Tom keeps telling me you're working too hard. Here, take a sip of this coffee," he said, pushing a half-full Styrofoam cup across the desk.

Weakly she leaned forward and took it, fighting hard to regain her composure. She had to get herself out of this somehow.

"Since it's such an important client, wouldn't it be better to put someone more experienced on the job?" she asked, trying to keep her voice steady.

"Ordinarily I would—I'd take it myself—but Chavira insisted it should be you. In fact, he said it had to be you, or we didn't get the account. You must have made a good impression somewhere along the way for people to recommend you so highly. Not that I'm surprised. You've been doing a fine job for us, Jo. I wouldn't worry about not being able to handle it. If you have any problems, just ask me. Oh, and don't think you won't be rewarded for this. I'm seeing to it that you get an immediate raise."

"W-what about my other clients?" she asked, clinging with hope to the only remaining objection she could think of. "I don't think I have time for a new account."

"Oh, listen, don't worry about that," he said with a sweep of his hand. "I'll reassign some of your work. You can spend all the time you need on Sunrise. I don't want anything to interfere with your work on *that* account . . ."

His phone rang, and she was glad to have some time to ponder while he was involved in conversation. Why wouldn't Mark leave her alone? He had his other woman. Why should he continue to pursue her? It must be clear to him by now that she no longer wanted his attentions. Oh, what difference did it make what his motivation was? Now he almost had her cornered! It was unthinkable to have to see Mark again, much less to have to work for him. Her heart could not stand to confront him with his fickleness, to reveal her own humiliation, and to listen to his inevitable false explanations. She must keep her dignity this time. She must not fall into his trap. Besides, if she saw Mark again, if she allowed him the opportunity to talk to her, to make advances . . . she feared she might believe his lies.

She must find a way out now, and quickly! She could tell Mr. Layton what had happened between her and Mark, embarrassing though it would be. But thinking that over for a moment, she decided that Layton would probably not be very sympathetic. Sympathy was not in his nature, but greed was. He coveted that account and wouldn't let a young woman's romantic problems stand in the way. If she refused to take the job, she would very likely get fired.

She could quit and try to get a position elsewhere, but what would be the use of resorting to such an extreme measure if Mark was willing to go to these lengths to reach her? It was certainly not for business reasons that he had recruited a small, little-known L.A. accounting firm, in the middle of the tax season, to take over his company's work. Well acquainted with his tenacity, she knew he would catch up with her sooner or later. Meanwhile she would be in the position of a fugitive, always on edge and never knowing when she would be found and pursued again. Maybe it *was* best to face him now and have it out with him, so that he would never again come after her. Was there any easier solution?

Mr. Layton was finishing up his conversation. Thinking quickly, Joey asked as he put down the receiver, "Do you think I could have someone working with me on the Sunrise account? Maybe Chris, or one of the others?"

It would be an advantage not to be alone, she reasoned. Another person around would necessarily buffer any exchanges between her and Mark. Also, if she were lucky, she could ask the person working under her direction to take over the brunt of the work, thereby making it unnecessary for her to go to Mark's office very often, that is, if Mark still wanted her company's services after their initial meeting. But, judging by past experience, he probably would; he was not one to give up in a day. He would probably hold her to her work obligations so he could have several weeks to deal with her.

"Maybe," Layton replied thoughtfully. "Chris would be the only one I could send—the others are just too busy. Even he has the Friedenburger account that he's got to finish by the end of the week. If he makes good progress on that, I suppose I could arrange for him to work with you. Would that make you feel better?"

"Yes," she breathed, relaxing a bit. "When do I have to go out to Sunrise?"

"I said you'd be there the day after tomorrow."

"I see," she whispered, taken aback by how soon she'd have to see Mark again.

"He asked for that day specifically, because he'll have some time in the afternoon to go over the books with you. Apparently he's got a tight schedule."

"I'll be there then," she said, managing to smile. Layton's last statement gave her some cause for relief. If Mark was away from his office a great deal, it made it even less likely that she would see him often, especially if she could have Chris to take over the work. In fact, if she were fortunate, she might have to see him only once, at the first meeting. Perhaps she could muster enough stamina to steel herself for one confrontation.

The remainder of that day and the next passed much more quickly than Joey would have liked. When the day came that she had to go out to the Sunrise Development Company, she still felt mentally unprepared to see Mark again. She had hoped that somehow she could have pulled herself together, so that she could meet him with cool self-possession. Instead she had become increasingly nervous, eating very little and sleeping less.

She came to work that morning wearing a tailored, but unadorned, tan suit and a cream-colored blouse with an open collar. Her hair was severely pinned back in the style she had lately been wearing.

"You look terrible today, Jo. Are you feeling all right?" Tom asked with concern when he came into her office shortly after she arrived.

"Oh, I'm okay," she said, trying to hide her jitters.

"You look awfully pale and your hands are trembling. Have you taken your temperature? Maybe you're coming down with the flu."

"No, I don't think I'm sick," she assured him. "I just had a little trouble sleeping last night."

"Nervous about going out to that big new account?" he asked with a smile.

" Well . . . yes."

"Don't worry, you'll do a fine job. Don't let their prestige scare you. It's just another company."

"Okay," she replied with a gentle grin, knowing he was not aware of the true reason for her state of nerves. "Is Chris in yet? Mr. Layton told him to try to finish the Friedenburger account so he could go out to Sunrise with me this afternoon."

"No, not yet. He's not noted for his punctuality, you know."

"I just hope he finished. I . . . I'd like to have some moral support when I go out to Sunrise," she said, forcing a smile.

"From Chris? I hope you're not *that* desperate!"

"Did I hear my name being bandied about?"

Joey looked up to see Chris poking his head into her office. Relief immediately began to replace the tension showing in her face.

"Speak of the devil!" said Tom. "On time again today. That's three days in a row—a new record!"

"Chris . . ." Joey began, but was beaten to the punch by the young man she was addressing.

"Did you see the big basketball game last night on TV?" he asked Tom with great enthusiasm.

"I just turned it on for the last few minutes. I was too busy to watch any more than that," Tom replied.

"Oh, you missed all the best plays, then," Chris told him with a dismissive wave of his hand. "What a game! I never saw anything like it," he continued, enraptured, and drew Tom out of Joey's office toward the coffee machine in the hall.

Almost dying of nervous impatience, she sat at her desk and listened as Chris gave Tom a lengthy play-by-play account outside her door. When he finally finished, a full ten minutes later, the two men parted and went to their separate offices. Releasing a sigh of pent-up emotion, Joey quickly got up and walked to Chris's office, a tiny room similar to hers.

"Chris," she said, almost holding her breath, "did you finish the Friedenburger account?"

For a second he looked at her blankly. Then, as light dawned in his eyes, he said offhandedly, "No, still working on it, Jo."

The floor seemed to give way beneath her. "But Mr. Layton asked you to have it done by today so you could go with me to Sunrise."

"He said to try to have it done. I didn't get the impression he was particularly concerned. Why do you need me on that job anyway?"

"So you didn't even try?" she asked in an angry panic, ignoring his question.

"Jo, the big game was on last night," he explained calmly. "I wouldn't miss that come hell or high water."

"How much more work do you have to do on the account?" she asked, hoping she wasn't reaching for straws. "Could you finish it this morning?"

"No way. I have to see another client in half an hour."

"Couldn't you postpone your appointment to finish it? Wouldn't you like to have the experience of working on a prestigious client like Sunrise?" she asked.

"And have to drive all the way to Orange County day after day? No thanks! Now that we have that one, we'll be drawing other big accounts. I'll wait for one that's closer," he said complacently.

"You may not be around that long!" she silently retorted, furious at his careless attitude. Saying no more, she turned and rushed back to her own office, shutting the door behind her. Leaning against the doorframe, she pressed the palms of her hands to her face and let the tears of nervous frustration flow. Her last bastion of protection was taken away. Now she would have to see Mark alone.

In a moment, she tore her hands from her face. "Oh, what difference does it make?" she asked herself, suddenly angry over the whole situation. Mark was just another man, wasn't he? She had managed to deal with him before on her own. Surely she was capable of handling this. She shouldn't allow herself to be turned into a sliver of quivering gelatin by any man!

Her newly regained determination managed to hold through the morning and into the noon hour, when she was on the freeway driving southward to Newport Beach in Orange County. But as she approached a tall, sparkling new office building near a fashionable and elegant-looking shopping mall, her nerve began to fail again.

Jitters returning, she left her car in the parking area and walked into the lobby of the building. A coldness came over her when she saw Sunrise Development Company listed on the lobby directory, and her stomach was feeling queasy even before she got into the elevator.

She stepped out onto the designated floor and walked down the hall, her heart pounding with the thought that she might run into Mark at any moment, until she came to the door of the Sunrise Development Company's office suite. Below the stylishly lettered name was a modern design representing a sunrise. It seemed like a prophetic symbol, only to Joey's mind it looked more like a sunset. Almost sick with apprehension, but knowing there was no other choice, she opened the door with an icy hand and walked in.

"Hello, may I help you?" asked a pleasant young woman of about Joey's age sitting at a desk directly inside.

"I'm Josepha Scott from Layton and Brook Accountancy."

"Oh, yes!" she replied with an instant smile. "We've been expecting you. Come this way, please." She rose to her feet and walked toward a closed door.

Joey stood as if frozen in the middle of the room.

"Mr. Chavira will be in later, but he asked me to have you use his office for today," the secretary explained, casually turning toward Joey as she reached the door.

The information that Mark would not be behind the closed door was the only thing that enabled Joey to move to catch up with the young woman. The unmarked door opened into a large office dominated by a huge desk of beautifully finished hardwood. There were floor-to-ceiling windows behind long, loose-weave drapes on two sides of the rectangular room, allowing bright sunlight to permeate the spacious office. In one corner was a scale model of a shopping center enclosed in glass. On the walls, which were covered in textured beige cloth to harmonize with the plush, burnt-orange carpeting, were a number of artist's renderings of various new buildings and shopping centers. A comfortable couch and two easy chairs were arranged around a low coffee table.

The secretary pulled up an orange-brown leather chair to the front of the large, tablelike desk. "He suggested you could work here. I'll go and tell Mrs. Tolliver, our comptroller, that you've arrived."

The young woman left, silently closing the door behind her. The polite smile on Joey's face quickly faded. She sat alone in the handsomely furnished room, almost feeling Mark's presence. Her eyes drifted to the high back leather chair on the opposite side of the desk. How long before Mark would be sitting there, staring back at her with his dark, probing eyes, asking why she had left La Paz so suddenly?

All at once the door opened and she jumped. Her frantic eyes turned toward whoever was entering.

"Hello, I'm Hilda Tolliver," said a brown-haired, well-dressed woman of about forty-five who came into the room carrying a pile of papers. "You're from Layton and Brook?"

"Yes, Josepha Scott," she replied, nervously rising and extending her hand.

"It's very nice to meet you," the poised, friendly woman said, briefly shaking Joey's hand after she had set the papers on the desk. "I've brought in our general ledger, the construction ledger, and our last financial statement and tax return for you to look over. If you'll have a seat, I'll start briefing you on our company and our current construction projects," she said, pulling up a second chair to the desk. "Would you like some coffee?"

The next hour or so was spent covering all financial aspects of the firm's business. "Is there anything I haven't mentioned that you have a question about?" Mrs. Tolliver asked when their conversation was about to conclude.

"Yes," Joey said hesitantly, her heart beginning to beat faster. "Was there any particular reason why your company switched accounting firms? So far I haven't had any indication that the previous firm mishandled your books."

Mrs. Tolliver smiled. "That's a good question! I thought they had been doing an adequate job. I guess Mark had had a few minor disagreements with them, but nothing serious. It seemed very odd to change at this time of year, too, when all the CPA firms are so swamped with work. But Mark came in one morning a few days ago, said we were going to change accountants, and that was that. He looked so determined, I wasn't about to argue with him."

She glanced at Joey as if conscious that she may have sounded disloyal. "Don't get me wrong, Mark Chavira is a wonderful boss, but lately . . . well, he's been a little edgy. He went down to Baja California over Christmas to pick up his mother, and ever since he got back he's been rather morose. None of us on the staff knows why as yet. We're afraid perhaps his mother is ill or something. I thought I'd mention it in case he seems strangely out of humor for such a successful young man. It's only a temporary thing, I hope."

"His mother was in Baja?" Joey asked breathlessly, forgetting herself in the shock of this new revelation.

"Yes, I believe she has relatives there. He drives her down to stay with them for several weeks at a time about twice a year. She's a widow now, and likes to keep in touch with her remaining family. Well, I'll leave you to look over the books. Mark should be back in a while. He's out at a ground-breaking ceremony. Let me know if you have any questions."

"Thank you," Joey said absently as the other woman left the room. So, perhaps the old lady Ted had referred to actually was Mark's mother. Maybe she had been wrong in assuming that the woman he traveled with was the young, dark-haired girl in the photograph. Confused, Joey leaned forward to rest her elbows on the desk and buried her face in her hands. Had she been wrong about everything?

A moment passed, then she took her hands from her face and sat back in the chair, attempting to calmly put everything into perspective. No, she couldn't have been that wrong about his character. She may have been mistaken about the identity of the woman with whom she traveled in his van, but she had caught him embracing the young girl. He probably renewed his romance with her during each visit he made to his relatives accompanying his mother. No, this new piece of information changed nothing. He was still the womanizer who had chased after her through Baja California, and nothing altered the fact that he had lied when he told her he had no other woman. He was still a man she did not want in her life.

Her mind settled once again about that question, she straightened up and began shuffling through the papers on the desk in front of her. She might as well get to work, ridiculous though this situation was. She wondered how long it would take before she was angrily dismissed. If he was still pursuing her, that was inevitably what would happen, for she would certainly reject him again after listening to his lame excuses.

But perhaps he would make her stay on to punish her with abusive words and torment her with his armchair psychology. How would she endure it? How hateful he was to put her through this! Somehow she must find the resources within herself to fight him.

The minutes passed slowly as she leafed through the papers with clammy hands and icy fingertips. It was impossible to concentrate and her eyes did not want to focus on the columns of figures laid out in front of her. Three o'clock came and went, then three thirty, and still he had not come. She began to hope that he would not come at all.

It was nearing four o'clock when her ears picked up the sound of a male voice outside the door.

"Is the accountant here?" was his sharp question.

"Yes, she's in your office," was the secretary's barely audible reply.

Joey instantly grew petrified. There was a short silence and then the door swung open. All at once she saw Mark Chavira's dark eyes staring down at her, his expression grim and watchful. Quaking within, her mouth dry as cotton, she nevertheless found her eyes being drawn magnetically to his.

The long weeks of separation seemed to slip away in the few fleeting moments they gazed at one another, and now it was as if she had left La Paz only yesterday. Time had done little to alter the deep emotions that lay between them.

The door closed. Saying nothing, he strode over to his desk and sat down across from her in the big leather chair. Leaning back, he continued to study her, his eyes hard and clear—almost omniscient.

Joey's mind grew foggy as she searched the familiar face which continually haunted her thoughts, waking and sleeping. It was more gaunt now. He seemed tired, no longer quite the carefree, self-possessed man she had known. But his gray three-piece suit and necktie did nothing to subdue his rugged appearance, his compelling masculinity.

His eyes still on her, he took in a slow, deep breath and exhaled it softly. "You're hard won, Joey," he told her in a quiet voice.

She dropped her eyes, taking in his words with a shudder.

"I almost wouldn't have recognized you," he went on. "Have you been ill?"

She shook her head negatively, unable now to meet his eyes.

"It can't be that you've been pining away for me," he said, a hint of sarcasm to his tone.

"No," she replied, finding her voice. "Why have you brought me here?" she asked, wanting to get the issue over with quickly.

"Why have you come?" he countered.

"I had to or lose my job!"

"Yes, I thought it would be that way," he said, smiling to himself.

"Why did you go through all this trouble to get me here?" she asked, her voice cold, but cracking with tenseness and anxiety.

He regarded her intently. "Obviously because I had to see you again. We're getting married, remember? I want to know why you left La Paz without a word and why you've been avoiding me ever since. I had to devise some way to keep you near me for a while, so I'd have a chance to get you to explain yourself. This was the only way, short of kidnapping you."

She kept her eyes lowered, studying her tightly clenched hands in her lap. "I'm not marrying you."

"Why not?" he calmly asked.

Her lips trembled but her voice was now firm. "Because I did come to see you that day at Cabo San Lucas. Only I got there early—hours before you were expecting me—and I found you kissing some young girl. You lied to me," she accused, raising her reddened eyes to his. "You told me there was no one else. I should have known that wasn't true. I found a picture of her by accident in your van."

Mark stoically nodded his head. "Yes, that's what your mother said you believed."

"My mother! I thought you had managed to get her on your side," she said bitterly.

"I was desperate, Joey. I had to get information from somewhere. Don't be angry with her. She thought she was doing it for your own good."

"You've probably mesmerized her into believing you're innocent the way you do every other woman," she said with scorn.

"Maybe I am innocent, Joey. Did that ever occur to you? Or are you so afraid of marriage, you'll believe anything to avoid it?"

"I saw her in your arms, Mark! What else can I believe?"

Chavira gave a short sigh and reached into his coat pocket. He withdrew an envelope, opened it, and took out a small pile of color snapshots. Rising from his chair, he walked around the desk and sat down in the chair Mrs. Tolliver had used. "I'd like you to look at these," he said, handing her the pictures.

Reluctantly she took them, taking particular care not to touch his hand in doing so. Looking through the snapshots, she saw they were pictures taken at a wedding and reception. Mark was in some of them.

"Do you recognize the bride?" he asked.

She looked closely at a couple of the pictures. The bride was a lovely young girl, slender, with long black hair. "It's the girl I saw you with," she said very softly, feelings of both relief and agitation welling up within.

"Yes. She's Carmelita, one of my cousins. I've known her since she was born. That letter with the picture you apparently came across was one she had written telling of her wedding plans and inviting my mother and me to come. The picture had been taken at her engagement. My mother wanted to help with the preparations, so I drove her down there late in November. I went down again myself around Christmas, as you know, to stay for the wedding and take my mother home again."

Joey was suddenly beginning to feel foolish, but she asked stubbornly, "Why were you kissing her?"

He sighed and smiled. "Mexican people are very affectionate. You could find that out for yourself if you'd relax a little," he said with an amused glint in his eye. "Your mother told me you arrived about ten thirty. I think that was probably about the time I was telling Carmelita that I would give her and her new husband a honeymoon trip to California as a wedding present. She was very happy about that."

"You've had a lot of time to think up that excuse," Joey weakly protested.

"Joey, if you like we can drive down to Cabo this weekend and you can ask her and her husband about it yourself," he said convincingly. "I'm sure she'd be happy to assure you that she is in fact my cousin and that there never was anything out of the ordinary about our relationship. In fact I imagine she'd find it all rather amusing, your thinking that she was in love with me. She's very young, just turned eighteen, and she's always seemed to regard me as a confirmed old bachelor. Every time I see her she needles me about not being married yet, and now she ribs me that she's beaten me to the altar.''

He paused and studied Joey's downcast expression. "Well, would you like to go down to Cabo and question her this weekend?''

Joey's reply was barely a whisper. "No.''

"You believe me then?''

Reluctantly she nodded her head.

He made a light chuckle. "How come you're so depressed? Because this means you'll have to marry me after all? You thought you had found a means of escape and now you're caught again! Is that it?''

She shifted uneasily. "No . . .'' she answered lamely.

"No? Why did you just run away without at least asking me for an explanation about what you saw?''

"Because I . . . I didn't think you could possibly have any. I was hurt. I just wanted to get away.''

"Get away. That's what you've been trying to do ever since I met you. Your mother told me you were very nervous that morning about having accepted my marriage proposal. You've been eager to believe the worst about me all along.''

"I had good reason," Joey protested.

"Good reason!'' Mark objected with amused outrage. "What good reason?''

"Many reasons. For example that conversation I overheard between you and Ted in the restaurant. I realize now that the old lady he was so tactlessly referring to was your mother, but at the time I somehow had the impression that he was talking about some young woman you were having an affair with. Since Ted seemed to look upon you—even admire you—as a womanizer, that was naturally what I assumed. Besides, he thought you were after me.''

"Well, I was after you. He was right about that. But you see, because I'm a bachelor Ted likes to think that I have all kinds of fun that he thinks he's missing. And if you ever spend any time talking to him, I'm sure you'd soon realize he isn't enough in touch with the younger generation to know their interpretation of the term old lady. Does that clear up your doubts?''

"Well, I suppose it settles that question, but there were other things. Like . . . like the first time I saw you in Ensenada. The way you looked me over, and right after I had seen you eyeing that redhead. Why shouldn't I have concluded that you were a skirt chaser?''

"You mean at the gas station? How did I look at you?''

"Exactly the same way you looked at the redhead.''

He sighed patiently. "I don't even remember a redhead, Joey. How did I look at you? What did you find so intolerable about my behavior?''

Joey was incensed. "Why, you . . . you leered at me! Like you wanted to seduce me!''

Mark was thoughtful for a moment and a nostalgic smile slowly came over his face. "Yes, I remember now. You practically stripped your gears trying to get out of there. Underneath that bold, indignant stance was just a scared little girl. I thought you were so adorable, I memorized your license number as you were driving away. I would have found you again one way or another even if we hadn't met on the road.''

Joey swallowed hard, feeling her destiny being sealed. "But answer my question. Why did you look at me like that?" she asked earnestly. "That's why I had a bad opinion of you from the very beginning."

He narrowed his eyes at her. "It seems I remember now your trying to pin me down on this once before."

She nodded. "At dinner in San Quintin."

"And my answer wasn't satisfactory?"

"No. You just said there was nothing wrong with a man admiring a beautiful woman."

"Well, is there?"

"You men don't understand what it's like to be treated like a sex object! It's degrading,'' she said, some of her old fire returning.

"Now hold on a minute," he said, reaching to close his fingers about her wrist. "Let's analyze this calmly, shall we? I was standing there at the gas station and I noticed you checking your tires . . .''

"And you were leering at me," she interjected, conscious of the warmth of his fingers on her skin, but not attempting to extricate herself from their grasp.

He pondered a moment. "I was admiring you, but I don't think I was leering—not yet."

"You seemed more intrigued with my anatomy than anything else," she pointed out.

He let go of her wrist, and she found she was disappointed at the loss of physical contact. She began to sense where her heart would lead her, whatever his explanation, and, surprisingly, she felt a warm relaxation stealing over her.

Mark leaned back in his chair, casually crossing his arms over his vest. "Well," he answered, "you do have a beautiful figure, you know. As a man, was I expected not to notice? Maybe I just happened to be looking at the wrong place when you turned around. I assure you I had noted your lovely face—those intelligent, innocent eyes, the turned-up nose, the flawless complexion."

Joey pretended to be dubious. "Okay, let's say you were admiring me. Then I gave you an indignant look."

"Imperious might be a better word, like I was trespassing on hallowed ground. It just served as bait. I had to see what such a fascinating creature would do under stronger provocation, so I gave you a genuine leer. Your expression turned even more venomous. It became an amusing challenge, then, so I tried the old come-on look I used on girls when I was sixteen. It never worked then either, now that I think of it. Anyway, you panicked and drove off.'' He looked at her with sadness and amusement. "And you've been afraid of me ever since."

Joey gazed down at her lap and said nothing.

"Any other complaints?" he asked, after a few moments.

"Yes. The underhanded way you got me here," she replied with a slightly provocative pout.

"Well, Joey, you hung up on me every time I tried to call you. And you wouldn't see me. You were home that Sunday I came over; I saw your car in the parking lot. You just didn't answer the doorbell, did you?"

Joey silently acknowledged the truth of his statement.

"I thought so. What was I to do? I had to devise some way to get you in a situation where you couldn't escape me. One time when I was talking with your mother over the phone, I asked her what your boss was like. When she described him from things you had told her, I suspected he was just the type to help me, unwittingly, to set up a trap. I suppose it was a little deceitful to hire your firm just to get you here, but I do intend to keep your company's services. Besides, you've been pretty tricky yourself, with all these maneuvers to escape me."

Joey veiled her eyes with her lashes, not knowing what to say. Mark was right, of course, but she was reluctant to admit it. In a moment she realized she was under the scrutiny of his studious gaze.

"What is this ridiculous hair style?" he said, his narrowed, displeased eyes moving over her plain coiffure. He rose from his seat and squatted beside her, as if to get a closer look. "I'm surprised you didn't put one of those thick black hairnets over the whole thing," he muttered.

An involuntary smile crept over Joey's lips. All at once she felt his hands attacking the mound of hair at the base of her head. "Mark, what are you doing?" she asked, raising her hands protectively towards her head.

"Getting rid of this monstrosity," he replied, unexpertly pulling out hairpins and throwing them onto the desk. Soon her long silky hair came loose and fell softly about her shoulders. "There. That's more like the Joey I used to know," he said, looking over his work.

Kneeling beside her chair, he leaned forward and gently kissed her lips. If she had hoped she would be impervious to his touch, she wasn't. She began to feel jittery again, but it was a pleasant nervousness. When he kissed her a second time, she found herself responding, returning the pressure of his lips. She could feel a rosy warmth filling the cold void in her body, bringing her alive again. When he drew away, he looked into a lovely face, no longer pale with strain and fatigue, but radiant and glowing with love.

"Joey, you missed me, didn't you? Say you missed me," he ardently whispered.

"I missed you," she admitted in a tiny voice, her hands entwined at the back of his neck.

"You told me once you'd marry me. Tell me again—now," he urged.

"Oh, Mark," she murmured, turning her face away, "please don't rush me."

"I have to, or we'll never see our wedding day." He shifted himself in front of her so he could look into her troubled eyes. "Still afraid you don't know what you'd be getting into?"

She nodded her head.

"Come on, then," he said, taking her gently by the hand and rising to his feet. "Let's sit back here on the couch and talk about it." With hesitance she got up and followed him to the comfortable sofa at the other side of the room. When they were settled next to each other on the soft cushions, he said, "Now let's see if I can paint a picture of what our married life would be like." He thought a moment. "First of all you'd come and live at my house . . ."

"And I'd have to take care of all the bedrooms, bathrooms, living rooms . . ."

"Joey," he interrupted, "how do you think they get taken care of now? I have a cleaning woman, a gardener, and a part-time cook. There's no reason for me to dismiss them just because you move in. You won't have to do any housework, if you don't want to."

"Really?" she said, not quite believing him.

"Well, I don't like to brag, but if it'll help my cause, I am a fairly wealthy man, you know."

"Maybe I wouldn't fit into your social circles," she said, seizing onto a new objection she hadn't thought of before.

"My social circles include people like Ted, so I don't think you need to worry about being outclassed. That was a silly comment," he said, reaching up to tweak her nose. "Okay, so you'd live at my house. I know you like your career, so you can continue working if you like, though you'd probably have to change firms after we're married—conflict of interest, you know. Maybe you'd want one closer to home anyway. Or, if you don't want to work at an outside job, you can work with me."

He leaned toward her and placed a hand on her shoulder. "That's the beautiful part of this relationship, Joey. My work takes up most of my life. But you understand business and can share my interests, even give me advice. Do you know when I first was positive you were the girl for me?"

She shook her head.

"When we were on the road and you mentally converted kilometers into miles without batting an eyelash. I said to myself, 'I need this beautiful human calculator around when my investors come up with questions about their future profits.' You could be such an asset to me . . ."

"You just want me for my business expertise?" she whined, pretending to be offended.

"Only during the day," he assured her, breaking into a grin. "At night I'll need you for other things."

"Like what?" she innocently asked.

He gave her a knowing look, almost repeating the leer she had so despised when she first saw him. She didn't mind it this time, however. In fact, it made her heart beat faster. It seemed he sensed her quickening pulse and he gathered her into his arms, pressing her strongly against him. Eagerly she accepted and returned his warm, ardent kisses. Now she knew how foolish she had been to run away from his love all these weeks. In his arms was where she belonged.

"Don't you see how wonderful it could be?" he said softly, some long moments later as he leaned back, still holding her close. "We'd make a perfect team—in the office and in the bedroom."

His low voice crept into her ear along with his steady heartbeat as she rested her head against his chest, feeling secure in the strong arms about her. It seemed all her fears and misgivings had finally vanished.

"How about it, then. Will you marry me?" he asked.

"I will, Mark. I'd be a fool if I didn't," she replied, blinking back tears of joy. "I've been too much of a fool already," she added, nestling her cheek against his vest.

As if still uncertain, he asked, "Is there anything else that worries you? Anything more you want?"

She lifted her head and looked up into his handsome face. "Yes, this," she whispered, reaching up to pull his head down toward hers. Pressing herself against him, she kissed him wholeheartedly, then urgently.

"All right, young lady," he said, pulling his lips from hers and holding her away from him slightly. He looked with amusement into her disappointed eyes. "You'll just have to wait until we're married for more." He smiled at her dumbfounded expression. "You know the old saying, Joey. 'A farmer won't buy the cow if he can get the milk for free.'"

She looked at him, puzzled. "That's what mothers used to tell their daughters."

"With women so independent these days, it might be a wise adage for men to follow. I'm afraid you still may become skittish and start putting me off about setting the date. So, until the wedding band is safely on your finger, you can't have anything more than a brief good-night kiss."

She looked at him with dejected eyes. "How soon can we get married?"

"I was hoping you'd ask! How about the second Saturday next month?"

Her eyes grew suspicious. "Why did you pick that date?"

"I happened to have called a few churches in the area, and that was the earliest opening I could get."

"That's only three or four weeks from now!"

"You won't have to exist on good-night kisses for long," he pointed out. "We can use one of the new restaurants I've built for the reception. One of my tenants in the last shopping center I developed runs a bridal shop, and she said she could arrange for a gown for you on short notice. All we have to do is get the blood tests and marriage license."

"You must have been awfully sure of yourself to have planned all this!"

"One of us has to think positively," he said with innocence.

She grew distressed. "In La Paz you said you wouldn't be a domineering husband. Now you're making plans without . . ."

"I won't be domineering, I promise. You'd never let me get away with it, even if I tried," he said, giving a lock of her hair a gentle tug. "But you haven't been around lately, so I took advantage of what was probably my last opportunity to have a free hand. I have to get you to the altar somehow. I looked a long time before I found you. I'm not going to let you escape now. We've already had too many close calls. So let's just set the date for next month and get it over with. Once that hurdle is behind you, I think you'll find yourself a very happy Mrs. Chavira. Okay?"

She took a deep breath. "Okay," she acquiesced, sensing he was right, as always. It was time to trust her heart, and Mark.

Apparently forgetting his words about farmers and free milk, he rewarded her for her correct answer with a very long, very lingering kiss.